Musical Functionalism

The Musical Thoughts of
Arnold Schoenberg and Paul Hindemith

Musical Functionalism

The Musical Thoughts of Arnold Schoenberg and Paul Hindemith

by
Magnar Breivik

MUSIC IN INTERDISCIPLINARY DIALOGUE No. 8
Siglind Bruhn, General Editor

PENDRAGON PRESS
Hillsdale, NY

Other Titles in the INTERPLAY Series

No. 1 *Masqued Mysteries Unmasked:*
       Pythagoreanism and Early Modern North European Music Theater
       by Kristin Rygg (2000)
No. 2 *Musical Ekphrasis: Composers Responding to Poetry and Painting*
       by Siglind Bruhn (2000)
No. 3 *Voicing the Ineffable: Musical Representation of Religious Experience*
       Eleven essays edited by Siglind Bruhn (2001)
No. 4 *The Musical Order of the World: Kepler, Hesse, Hindemith*
       by Siglind Bruhn (2004)
No. 5 *Neo-Mythologism in Music:*
       From Scriabin and Schoenberg to Schnittke and Crumb
       by Victoria Adamenko (2007)
No. 6 *Sonic Transformations of Literary Texts:*
       From Program Music to Musical Ekphrasis
       Nine essays edited by Siglind Bruhn (2008)
No. 7 *The Orpheus Myth and the Powers of Music*
       by Vladimir L. Marchenkov (2009)

Cover design by Stuart Ross based on photo collage *MW 20100804* by Meinolf Wewel (http://home.fotocommunity.de/meinolf.wewel)

Library of Congress Cataloging-in-Publication Data

Breivik, Magnar.
  Musical functionalism : the musical thoughts of Arnold Schoenberg and Paul Hindemith / by Magnar Breivik.
    p. cm. -- (Interplay : music in interdisciplinary dialogue ; no. 8)
  Includes bibliographical references and index.
  ISBN 978-1-57647-170-8 (alk. paper)
  1. Schoenberg, Arnold, 1874-1951 -- Criticism and interpretation. 2. Hindemith, Paul, 1895-1963 -- Criticism and interpretation. 3. Music -- Philosophy and aesthetics. 4. Music and architecture. I. Title.
  ML3845.B647 2011
  781.092'2--dc22

2011003125

Copyright 2011 by Magnar Breivik

Table of Contents

Preface	ix
Introduction	xi
Musical Functionalism: Perspectives in Early 20th-Century Art	1
The Concept of Functionalism	1
On the Material's Own Will	12
Craft and Creation	22
The Organic Form as Construction	32
Form and Norm	42
"Sachlichkeit" and "Neue Sachlichkeit"	58
The Concept of Musical Functionalism	65
The Musical Material	73
The Crisis of Tonality	73
Adorno and the Material of Music	82
Schoenberg: The Motive as Musical Material	94
Focus	94
A Group Portrait of 1895	97
Materialgerechtigkeit	99
Tonal or Atonal?	100
Musical Prose	107
"Der musikalische Gedanke"	110
Musical Logic	112
The Musical Motive	116
The Musical Motive and Material Consistency:	
No. 1 from Schoenberg's *Sechs kleine Klavierstücke*	118
"Komposition mit zwölf nur aufeinander bezogenen Tönen"	135
Summary	139

Hindemith: The Interval as Musical Material	141
Hindemith and Schoenberg	141
Materialgerechtigkeit	147
"Zahl und Schönheit, Mathematik und Kunst"	152
The Interval, Series I *and* Series II	155
The Interval and the Chord	163
Harmonic Fluctuation	167
Chord Connection, Degree-Progression, and Tonality	168
Non-Chord Tones	170
Theory of Melody	171
Tonal or Atonal?	172
The Interval as a Factor of Material Consistency:	
Hindemith's Interludium 9 from *Ludus Tonalis*	175
Summary	188
Musical Form	193
Aspects of Musical Form	193
Schoenberg: From *Gedanke* to Form	200
Introduction	200
"Formgefühl"	202
Conception and Wholeness, Logic and Form	204
Form, Comprehensibility, and Coherence	215
Elements of Form	227
Twelve-tone Method, Basic Form, and Comprehensibility	234
Construction and Norm:	
Schoenberg's Gavotte from *Suite for Piano*	239
Summary	258
Hindemith: From Vision to Form	260
Introduction	260
Form and Nature	262
"Vision, Einfall und Handwerk"	266
In Time and Space	271
"Rhythmus ist Form"	273
Mental Parallel Construction, Form, and Tradition	278
Form and Norm:	
Hindemith's Shimmy from *1922. Suite for Piano*	284
Summary	306

Table of Contents vii

Musical Function 309
  Functional Objectivity 309
  Functional Music and Musical Functionalism 318
  Schoenberg: Active Listening and Musical Recognition 330
    Introduction 330
    Gebrauchsmusik and l'art pour l'art 332
    The Public Educator 334
    "Der Verein für musikalische Privataufführungen" 341
    Summary 348
  Hindemith: Active Performance and Musical Recognition 349
    Introduction 349
    "Gemeinschaft für Musik" 350
    "Die Verbindung von Volk und Kunst" 353
    "Vorspielen und Selbstspielen" 356
    "Musik nach Maß" 362
    "Forderungen an den Laien" 371
    "Die musikalische Gemeinschaft" 376
    From "Hören" to "Machen" 377
    Musica instrumentalis 380
    "A Singing and Playing Community" 384
    Summary 388

Coda: Schoenberg and Hindemith in the Context of Functionalism 389

Bibliography 399
List of Illustrations 411
Index of Names 413
About the Author 417

Preface and Acknowledgments

This study on the musical thoughts of Arnold Schoenberg and Paul Hindemith builds on the awareness that basic connections exist between music and architecture. Such an approach does not imply that these two manifestations of human creativity are considered immediately comparable; neither are they looked upon as representing two sides of the same coin. Rather, connections are drawn on an epistemological plane, focusing on questions about artistic material, form, and function. Reflections on such issues are central to Schoenberg and Hindemith in a way that invokes the term *musical functionalism* as a useful tool for an exploration of their thoughts on music. Before commencing the discussion on these two composers' views on the basics of their work and vocation, this book touches upon fundamental problems that are encountered when categorizing stylistic terms. Particularly in their traditional use, many terms have a tendency to demarcate the territory of works of art too rigidly. The reception histories of Schoenberg and Hindemith respectively have been influenced by this kind of demarcation. Hence, in addition to the value of an in-depth examination of these individual composers' musical thoughts in a broader perspective of 20th-century art, the concept of musical functionalism may also contribute to a wider view on Schoenberg and Hindemith as contemporary giants in the history of music.

It is impossible to mention everyone whose encouragement and interest have sustained this project. I can express my profound gratitude only to those most immediately involved. Ståle Wikshåland, University of Oslo, proved to be a most valuable interlocutor during the first stages of this book. The Faculty of Humanities at the Norwegian University of Science and Technology (NTNU) provided generous support in connection with research visits, archival studies, and translation issues. Translations were also funded by The Research Council of Norway; I am particularly grateful to John Anthony for his keen assistance in the last stages of the English elaboration. I am also indebted to Heidi M. Breivik for her technical assistance on some of the music examples. Most of my thanks should, however, go to the editor of this book, Siglind Bruhn. Without her kind encouragement, never-failing patience, and fruitful suggestions, this publication would never have seen the light of day. Last but not least, as this book has evolved over time, I have been thoroughly dependent on the continuous support from people who are near and dear to me on a daily basis. My gratitude to all of them is beyond words.

Introduction

In his 1766 book *Laokoon, oder, über die Grenzen der Malerei und Poesie*, Gotthold Ephraim Lessing refers to the Greek writer Simonides of Ceos (556-468 B.C.E.), famous for his saying that painting is mute poetry and poetry a speaking picture.[1] In *The New Laokoon: An Essay on the Confusion of the Arts*, written some 150 years later, the American literary critic Irving Babbitt reminds his readers of this simile, asserting that in modern times—which, for him, is the 19th century—another opinion seems to hold almost equal status, namely that of architecture as *frozen music*.[2] Babbitt interprets these words, which he attributes to Friedrich Schlegel,[3] as an expression signaling that emotion has conquered form to such a degree that it has even come to influence architecture, the most form-bound of all the arts. Architecture, he concludes with a note of irony, must apparently be understood as benumbed or congealed emotion. Such a notion may result, Babbitt believes, from the Germans giving such a high status to music, the art least bound by form. Yet he fears that this inversion of Lessing's dictum may lead to the understanding that other forms of art can only approach perfection by absorbing something of the essence of music. For Babbitt, such a perspective represents not only a questionable mix of the arts' expressive character, but also a danger of slipping towards artistic flattening.

Positing connections between architecture and music has a long tradition. In the 1st century B.C.E. Vitruvius included elements of Greek music theory in his writings on architecture. Medieval thinkers held that architectonic proportions were based on cosmological dimensions; and the early motet is often compared with the Gothic cathedral. Goethe proposed an analogy between architecture and music that closely resembles the one Babbitt found in Schlegel, although for Goethe it is architecture's *ambience* that comes closest to music's effect.[4]

---

[1] See G.E. Lessing, *Laocoön: An Essay on the Limits of Painting and Poetry*, E.A. McCormick, trans. (Baltimore/London: The Johns Hopkins University Press, 1984), 4.

[2] I. Babbitt, *The New Laokoon: An Essay on the Confusion of the Arts* (Boston: Houghton Mifflin, 1910), 61.

[3] This view is also known from F.W.J. Schelling's writings.

[4] See J.W. Goethe, *Maximen und Reflexionen* (Leipzig, Insel-Verlag, 1988), 221, and J.P. Eckermann's *Gespräche mit Goethe in den Letzten Jahren seines Lebens* (Berlin: Aufbau-Verlag, 1982), entry for 23 March 1829.

Arthur Schopenhauer, similarly concerned with how architecture relates to music, refers to Goethe's "witticism" on architecture as congealed music.[5] Schopenhauer grants that he, too, can accept a certain analogy between musical rhythm and architectonic symmetry, but claims that this in no way touches the essence of the two art forms: "Indeed, it would be ridiculous to try to put the most limited and feeble of all the arts [architecture] on an equal footing in essential respects with the most extensive and effective [music]."[6] Stravinsky in his *Chroniques de ma vie*[7] concurs with Goethe's understanding of architecture as petrified music; but the analogy seems relevant for opposite reasons. Stravinsky is fascinated by the order and structure revealed in the play of architectonic forms, since such forms are inherent in all musical impression. The composer Ernst Toch, not content with half measures, also refers to architecture as frozen music but concludes that music should then be called sounding architecture. "Perfect *form* crowns the masterpiece of architecture as well as the masterpiece of music," he says.[8]

In all their brevity, these aphorisms from Schlegel to Toch express an epistemological development. One of the patterns visible in the 150-year period they span is the movement from a view of architecture as striving toward the essence of music to the thought of music striving towards the formal structure of architecture.

The functionalist concept presupposes considerations that crucially affect the philosophical basis of several artistic forms of expression, including music. In choosing *musical functionalism* as an approach for the present investigation, the aim has been to give the particular equivalency stated above a substance that lifts it beyond the more general notions of a presumed *Zeitgeist*. Hence, the most vital purpose of using the concept of musical functionalism is the attempt to come to terms with the foundation of important traits in the development of 20th-century music. This foundation underlies what may otherwise be regarded as the stylistic surface. Nevertheless, focusing attention on this foundation also challenges established views of certain stylistic terms.

The problem of style is in itself complex, and many an aesthetician has attempted to solve its inconsistencies. Stylistic categories and divisions into

---

[5] See A. Schopenhauer, *The World as Will and Representation* II, E.F.J. Payne, trans. (New York: Dover Publications, 1966 [1958]), 454.

[6] *The World as Will and Representation* II, 454.

[7] For the English translation see Igor Stravinsky, *An Autobiography* (London: Calder & Boyars, 1975 [1936]), 54.

[8] E. Toch, *The Shaping Forces in Music: An Inquiry into the Nature of Harmony, Melody, Counterpoint, Form* (New York: Dover Publications, 1977), 155.

Introduction xiii

epochs were originally adopted from art history, along lines proposed in the writings of Guido Adler (1855-1941). Robert Haas's 1934 study of music during the Baroque era established an understanding of music history as a history of style.[9] Toward the end of the 1970s, the focus shifted again, with emphasis now on the problems of *delimiting* music history to considerations of style. Carl Dahlhaus was an important representative of this view, as documented in his 1977 *Grundlagen der Musikgeschichte*.[10] Not many historians today would regard music history as tantamount to the history of musical style; today's research into music history uses a number of different approaches. Nevertheless, stylistic terms, however hollow they may be, form an important part of musicology's common inventory. In themselves, these terms seldom cover all levels of style as a phenomenon; it is always supposed that a term refers to a more comprehensive concept. The question what a specific stylistic denomination really captures can give rise to many a discussion, as is certainly the case with the concept of style itself.

A closer look at some 20th-century terms will help in sketching the stylistic picture to which the concept of musical functionalism relates. With regard to the architectural metaphor, it may seem that far too many terms pretend to say something about the entire building by referring only to a part. While terms such as constructivism, dodecaphony, and serialism are adequate to a certain degree since they refer to central aspects of the craftsman-like prerequisites of music's construction, terminological references to music's technical aspects have a tendency to appear reductionist. Associations can easily go in the direction of what is artificially and pretentiously esoteric, to works that lead their own life without any apparent concern with the potential of human experience. It is opportune to forget that such terms originate in the prevailing view that musical material is guided by rationality and regularity, a thought recognized already by Pythagoras. However, these terms characteristically shape the recognition of the consequences that follow from this view on musical material, including the belief that composers can ascribe to their materials the potential for a constructive logic. Phrased in the language of craftsmanship: the composer is granted the ability to make his or her own mix or alloy, which then acquires its own unalterable characteristics. In music, it is the sounding piece that realizes the art's material. In a terminological emphasis on music's material it can easily be forgotten that a work's value as an aesthetic object depends, in the final instance, on its composer's artistic ability to enter into fruitful dialog with his or her material. Presenting

---

[9]*Die Musik des Barocks* [E. Bücken, ed., *Handbuch der Musikwissenschaft* 1 (Potsdam: Athenaion, 1934).

[10]English as *Foundations of Music History*, trans. J.B. Robinson (Cambridge, New York: Cambridge University Press, 1983).

the material is not enough; it must always be formed or arranged. The important question is not whether stylistic terms are correct or incorrect from a philological point of view, but whether they run the risk, in many contexts already on the terminological level, of emphasizing technical aspects in such a way that the intended musical experience comes out of focus. Music teachers and other mediators may reflect such attitudes towards style in good faith. Analysis of a twelve-tone work turns into a hunt for the series, despite Schoenberg's famous self-definition as not a *twelve-tone* composer but a twelve-tone *composer*. Technical terms are problematic largely because, having originated as designators of compositional method, they are upgraded to signifiers of style, a task for which they are ill equipped. What began as a procedure, usually in refreshing opposition to yesterday's conventions, becomes a style. This lack of terminological precision opens the doors to all manners of category errors, to procedure being confused with style in a way that misinterprets Schoenberg's twelve-tone method as his musical style.

Not always are the consequences of this misapplication quite so dramatic. The term Expressionism is primarily associated with literature and painting. Schoenberg wrote his monodrama *Erwartung* (1909)—the work that is commonly considered the heart and core of musical expressionism—almost a decade before the composer and author Heinz Tiessen first used the term in connection with music in a broader sense.[11] Schoenberg himself, however, never characterized any of his works as "expressionist." How, after all, is one to define musical Expressionism? From a musical point of view, the first of Hindemith's so-called expressionist one-act operas, *Mörder, Hoffnung der Frauen* (1919), cannot be compared with the restless exaltations in *Erwartung*. But Hindemith chose as his libretto Kokoschkas's 1907 play, which literary historians consider the first expressionist drama, and when music from the first part of the 20th century sets expressionist texts, it tends to be caught up in that stylistic term. So how is one to deal with absolute music, i.e., music not setting a text? Expressionism points both to effusions of a deeply rooted psychological need for expression and to a liberation from music's traditional formal schemata. Music described as expressionistic is often marked by a skillfully crafted polyphonic web and characterized by impetuous gestures and waves. Tiessen uses the term Expressionism with regard to music in a very deliberate way. "If *impressionism* had destroyed melody, then *expressionism* destroyed *harmony*," he writes, in a brave attempt at systematizing tendencies in his recent past.[12]

---

[11] In a lecture at the Goethebund, Koenigsberg, 21 June 1918.

[12] Transl. from H. Tiessen, *Zur Geschichte der jüngsten Musik (1913-1928): Probleme und Entwicklungen* (Mainz: Melosverlag/B. Schotts Söhne, 1928), 49.

Introduction

A closer look at the development of so-called musical Expressionism reveals that such music is often distinguished by particularly strict control, rigid consistency, and motivic economy. The problem with the term seems to be the opposite of what afflicts serialism and dodecaphony. Since Expressionism focuses on music's boundless potential as an expressive art, it tends to draw attention away from the solidity of the material and the technical substance. A stylistic term that says something about musical expression may well be worth our consideration, but not to the extent that it is taken to point to all that is important about the style. In the music-historical perspective, the question whether Expressionism represented the culmination of Romantic subjectivity is of capital interest. An alternative view would describe it as rather awakening a new understanding of the possibilities and characteristics of music material, in a time when the stimulus was liberation from the traditional tonality system. Both views are important, not least because they both contribute to the recognition of musical modernity, albeit in different ways.

Similar observations may be made in connection with other terms relevant to the first three decades of the 20th century. The designations Neo-Classicism, linked to music from the early years of the century, and *Neue Sachlichkeit* (New Objectivity) describing music of the 1920s, seem to suggest a basic need for artistic objectivity to substitute for subjectivity. From the very beginning, anti-Romantic attitudes helped to influence these terms. Music connected to them is usually regarded as a symptom of a reaction to the Romantic or expressionist past, representing a supposedly clarifying and cleansing break with what has gone before. Conversely, the two terms can also be understood as representing a continuation of the understanding of material that develops within musical Expressionism, but now within a narrower framework. In his book *Expressionism Reassessed,* Christopher Hailey discusses this point:

> In music, identifying Expressionism with stylistic categories such as dissonance and atonality has obscured critical appreciation of profound ties between composers as diverse as Stephan, Schreker, Reger and the Second Viennese School. What is more, neo-classicism and Neue Sachlichkeit, as well as the music phenomenology of the twenties, are not so much reactions to as extensions and natural consequences of Expressionism, suggesting parallels with the eighteenth century, when neo-classicism and Sturm und Drang co-existed, indeed, fed from the same sources in the works of Haydn and Mozart, Gluck and C.P.E. Bach, Goethe and Schiller. Like the Sturm und Drang movement, Expressionism was in a sense not so much revolutionary as profoundly reactionary, a kind

of taking stock, a critical reassessment as in Lessing's Laokoön, a search for purification and necessary prelude to an aesthetic of classical balance.[13]

The question of Neo-Classicism's position in music history involves a difficulty caused both by the diversity of the term's applications and its retrospective prefix "neo". Neo-Classicism has come to be understood as more conservative than innovative, a fact strengthened not least by the position assigned to parts of Stravinsky's work in 20th-century music history. Theodor Wiesengrund Adorno was among those who contributed to connecting both Stravinsky and the concept of Neo-Classicism with a restorative and reactionary mode of expression.[14] The need inherent in Neo-Classicism for an innovation that advocates clarity, purity, and transparency is easily lost in the conservative associations prompted by this term. Moreover, with the addition of Neo-Baroque features and the predilection of its proponents for texts and myths from antiquity, the term really becomes a pluralist concept. Neo-Classicism, then, has become a collective term with highly diversified contents.

For music historians, a particular difficulty with *Neue Sachlichkeit* is that it presents a stylistic term drawing on a word that was widely fashionable at the time. Fashionable words can quickly become slogans and have a tendency to lose touch with their origins the more they are used. The question is whether *Neue Sachlichkeit* can be understood as a stylistic term at all, whether it has not absorbed contemporary trends in a wider perspective.

Neue Sachlichkeit originated in painting, although even here it has such a comprehensive range that it is difficult to consider it a stylistic signifier. Rather, it stands for a basic artistic attitude that, through various stylistic means—everything from photographic representation to grotesque caricature —aims to tie the painting closer to so-called objective and tangible reality. A widespread misunderstanding is that the adherents to *Neue Sachlichkeit* seek to present art as cold and without expression. The exact opposite is often the case: the objective manner of depiction aims at a self-impression of intense reality. In music influenced by basic artistic attitudes of the time, *Neue Sachlichkeit* is considered to represent a new objectivity in expression, medium, and compositional structure, hence a move towards artistic economy. Consequently, there is a distinct overlap with musical Neo-Classicism.

---

[13]Christopher Hailey, "Musical Expressionism," *Expressionism Reassessed*, S. Behr, D. Fanning, and D. Jarman, eds. (Manchester: Manchester University Press, 1993), 110.

[14]See Th.W. Adorno, "Stravinsky and Restoration," *Philosophy of Modern Music*, Anne G. Mitchell and Wesley V. Blomster, trans. (New York: Continuum, 1985), 135-217.

Introduction

However, *Neue Sachlichkeit* is also associated with other musical phenomena, as for instance the approach toward musical performance characteristic for the 1920s. Here, the term does not describe the composer's style but the musician's attitude. The ideal was that the work should speak for itself, hampered as little as possible by the performer's subjectivity. For this way of thinking, music is objective in the sense that it has the widest possible appeal when no negatively subjective elements hinder communication with listeners. These ideals are one with the time's great interest for renaissance and baroque music and with the search for the performance practices of earlier epochs; they also govern the performance of *new* music, where the composer's voice is intended to be heard without any superfluous prompting.

For many, both *Sachlichkeit* and *Neue Sachlichkeit* are inextricably bound up with the term *Gebrauchsmusik*—the demand that music should satisfy a utilitarian function. Music is *eine Sache* (a thing, hence an object) that must lend itself to certain purposes, those of the professionals, the amateurs, or the listeners. From this description it may seem that there is but a small step to the musically nondescript and soulless, concerned only with everyday trivialities. The term itself is partly to blame for this negative slant, yet one must also bear in mind that objectivity in compositional process and musical structure is understood as restoring the craft of music to honor and dignity. It is at this point that the dual nature of the concept becomes fully visible: it refers both to the work's inner constitution and to its relationships in an outer context. So wide is the spectrum of views that converge in *Neue Sachlichkeit* that as a stylistic term in music it requires closer definition.

In the stylistic picture that materializes in the first decades of the 20th century, one can discern the formation of other more profound demarcations. The concept of modernity begins to take shape already before the turn of the century. The consciousness of modernity is made manifest in what one may call modernist self-identification; men and women look upon themselves as *modern* and upon the times as *new*. In the 1920s, *new music* becomes a current term, particularly in the German-speaking world. This term presupposes a distinction between what is old and what is new. But what exactly is new music at this time? According to writers such as Hans Mersmann and Heinrich Strobel, it is Neo-Classicism, with Stravinsky as its distinguished pioneer, and *Neue Sachlichkeit,* led by Hindemith. What is regarded as particularly promising is this music's ability to consolidate the diverse stylistic picture of the time and its all-including objectivity. The Schoenbergian, supposedly subjective, exclusivity is posited as its counterpart. However, the 1920s view of music is more contradictory than this binary opposition suggests. Adorno defends the opposite viewpoint: that it is the Second Viennese School with Schoenberg at its head that represents new music. Schoenberg and his followers took the consequences of music's historical development seriously, he argues, while *Gebrauchsmusik* and *Neue Sachlichkeit,* marked by stabilization and consolidation, could only lead contemporary music into a regressive impasse.

These opposing views represent something far more serious than just different opinions of the same problem. What is being expressed are two essential features that came to characterize the whole century: One is the term new music, used positively to justify certain schools of thought in contemporary music and, by implication, negatively to reject different musical phenomena of the day. The other is the support of the persistent view that there are two diverging paths in the century's music history, defined by the concepts of tonality and atonality respectively. Subsequently, tonality and atonality are regarded as fundamentally irreconcilable. In this terrain, too, compositional and ideological attitudes appear sharply opposed to one another—there are both trenches and barricades. Schoenberg describes the prevailing situation thus:

> Because of the many attempts to connect the past with the future one might be inclined to call this an Apollonian period. But the fury with which addicts of various schools fight for their theories presents rather a Dionysian aspect.[15]

The concept of functionalism attributes a decisive role to thoughts adapted from architecture, design, and the pictorial arts. In the following chapters, this concept will serve as a lens through which the music and thoughts of Arnold Schoenberg and Paul Hindemith can be examined. The dual focus on functionalism on the one hand and the two seminal composers of the early 20th century on the other hand bears witness to a dual ambition: to present musical functionalism in itself as well as significant aspects of Schoenberg's and Hindemith's thoughts, both in relation to the aesthetics implied in the term and for their own sake. We have now entered a new millennium, and these two giant composers have gone down in history as classics of the previous era. If this study can contribute to the understanding and appreciation of such central figures in the musical life of the 20th century, a worthy aim will have been achieved.

---

[15] A. Schoenberg, *Structural Functions of Harmony*, L. Stein, ed. (New York etc.: Norton, 1969), 193.

Musical Functionalism: Perspectives in Early 20th-Century Art

The Concept of Functionalism

The application of the term *functionalism* to 20th-century design and architecture does not denote any uniform, unequivocal style. This is probably why the designation is often found as a synonymous term for *modernism*, *international style*, *new objectivity*, etc. It may thus be useful to begin with a closer look at these alternative terms.

The rise of *modernism* in architecture began s often dated to 1910—the year in which Adolf Loos (1870-1933) expounded his views in his article "Architektur"—and is considered to have lasted throughout most of the 20th century. Loos's even more pioneering essay "Ornament und verbrechen" [*sic*] (Ornament and crime) had been published a few years earlier, in 1908. Also at about the same time, the Deutscher Werkbund, an organization for industry and design, was founded, while Peter Behrens (1868-1940) and Walter Gropius (1883-1969) began raising their architecturally epoch-making factory buildings. Retrospectively, Gropius came to regard the years around 1910 as the starting-point of the ideas that led to the establishment of the Bauhaus a decade later.[1] In music history, these years were equally significant for modernist developments: Schoenberg's break with the principles of traditional tonality is usually dated to 1908.

The term *international style* is commonly attributed to Henry Russel-Hitchcock and Philip Johnson's characterization of new tendencies in European architecture evolving in the early 1930s. The adjective draws attention to the international element that came to be so closely connected to functionalism as a modernist form of expression. From the mid-1920s onward, Gropius had employed the terminologically related wording *internationale Architektur*. The *international style* emphasized the combination of artistic expression, function, and technology, and is considered to have led to the development of the modern skyscraper.

---

[1]See W. Gropius, *Die neue Architektur und das Bauhaus: Grundzüge und Entwicklung einer Konzeption* (Mainz etc.: Florian Kupferberg, 1965), 20.

New objectivity is linked to the 1920s *Neue Sachlichkeit*, a term that gained substantial currency in several areas of art and culture. This term will be discussed more fully at a later point in this book.

Even though the term functionalism is not used in any consistent or incontestable way, there have been attempts to clarify its boundaries. In his book on 20th-century styles in Norwegian architecture and design, Kaare Stang defines functionalism as a term embracing stylistic tenets born and elaborated during the years 1930 to 1950. "Form must follow function" was the motto of the time:

> For the functionalists, simple beauty lay in the object's function and user-friendliness. There was to be no unnecessary decoration. The visual language of primary forms was often built on simple geometric forms: squares, circles, and semi-circles. Functionalism's aesthetic demands were guided by strict rationality of purpose.[2]

Stang particularly stresses functionalism's social beginnings in building policies. Aspects of use and rationality of purpose played a crucial role, together with an emphasis on anti-ornamental simplicity and a predilection for primary forms. In her book on functionalism in modern architecture, the Norwegian art historian Wenche Findal declares the two World Wars as the temporal frame for the style and *aesthetics* as its vital dimension:

> Functionalism was primarily a term to describe aesthetic values and is often used to characterize architecture with a simplified formal order, built according to certain modernist principles, generally dated to the inter-war period.[3]

This chapter is not intended as a contribution to a terminological debate; neither will the concept of functionalism be given any universally valid definition. Rather, the aim is to point out features that contribute to the concept's diversity, and then assemble these in a more delimited focus. This will in turn pave the way for the discussion of *musical functionalism*. An examination of the basic concept, combined with insights into art and culture that further illuminate its context, may be helpful to establish a common reference for considering the thoughts of Schoenberg and Hindemith in the functionalist perspective.

The term functionalism accents the recognition that a work's function must always determine its form. This does not mean that function and form should be regarded as identical. (It may appear, for instance, that an object

---

[2]Translated from K. Stang, *Moderne tider: 1900-tallets stilarter i norsk arkitektur, kunstindustri og design* (Oslo: Cappelen, 1996), 57.

[3]Translated from W. Findal, *Norsk modernistisk arkitektur: Om funksjonalismen* (Oslo: Cappelen, 1996), 9.

assumes a function different from the one originally intended.) Rather, the term guards against the misconception that a work could result solely from its creator's free will and his or her subjective plan, prioritizing instead the structural aspects involved in the creative act, as expressed in a claim made by Le Corbusier (1887-1965), that "the exterior is the result of an interior."[4] Consequently, the concept of functionalism starts out as equivocal, partly extending *beyond* the work, partly *into* the work itself. Albrecht Wellmer emphasizes this view in his book *Zur Dialektik von Moderne und Postmoderne: Vernunftkritik nach Adorno* (On the dialectis of modernism and postmodernism: a critique of reason after Adorno):

> I will be using the term 'functionalism' in a wider sense here, so that it includes the demands for justice to the material and transparency of construction along with the postulate 'form follows function'.[5]

The fact that functionalism has more sides to it may seem to weaken its unequivocality. On the positive side, however, the scope of the term draws attention to the nuances comprised in the concept, allowing it to assess and weigh the various aspects within the nature of the functionalist object, and permitting the concept to cover a whole range of characteristic features in 20th-century art and culture.

The historical origin of the term functionalism has not been definitively determined. The American sculptor and writer Horatio Greenough (1805-1852) is often put forward as its creator. Yet since the pithy 1890s dictum "form follows function," coined by Louis Henry Sullivan (1856-1924), has remained the dominant motto of functionalism, some people may consider this catchword to be the real origin of the term—despite the fact that it did not come into general use until the 1920s.

One immediate association often connected with the term functionalism is the assumed re-evaluation of the time-honored dichotomy between art object and object of utility. In art history, this distinction is known already from the writings of Karl Philipp Moritz (1757-1793), in particular his essay "Attempt at uniting all the fine arts and sciences under the concept of what is accomplished in itself."[6] The idea that a work, product, or object should have a function for the individual—that it should satisfy one or several human functional needs, and preferably have an inherent social or societal

---

[4] Le Corbusier, *Towards a New Architecture,* trans. Frederick Etchells (London: The Architectural Press/New York: Frederick A. Praeger, 1963), 11.

[5] Translated from A. Wellmer, *Zur Dialektik von Moderne und Postmoderne: Vernunftkritik nach Adorno* (Frankfurt a. M.: Suhrkamp, 1993), 119.

[6] See K.Ph. Moritz, "Versuch einer Vereinigung aller schönen Künste und Wissenschaften unter dem Begriff des in sich selbst Vollendeten," *Berlinische Monatsschrift 5* (1785), 225-230.

justification—is crucial for the development of the functionalist concept. Architects and designers have never really lost sight of functionality, strongly emphasized already in Vitruvius's *De Architectura*. Even the most bizarre architecture and design, both from ancient and modern times, accord to purpose of function in one way or another. Functionalism in the 20th century originated in the desire for a special weighting of exactly this aspect. As the concept developed, essential components of 19th-century architecture were criticized as toning down the consciousness of functionality through what critical voices characterized as hollow historicism and an eclectic jumble of styles. This critique presupposed that architecture and design are able to exploit non-contemporary elements of style, and that the object through its design can conceal its own use, potentialities declared as making a work *untruthful*. This view had been developing since the end of the 19th century, and it was within such an understanding that the foundation was laid for the *truthful* alternative in 20th-century functionalism.

Functionalism is a compound phenomenon. Sullivan's deceivingly unpretentious motto "form follows function," about which more will be said later, seems simplistic, dissembling the truth it seeks to reveal. It says nothing about what the terms "form" and "function" really mean or how the two categories are causally related to one another. The phrase seems to suggest that its two components are each unequivocal, which is not the case. Sullivan himself would hardly have been at ease with the narrow, utilitarian understanding that posterity appropriated from his words. The architectural historian Peter Blake may be right in asserting that Sullivan's motto has become "one of the most widely misunderstood statements of aesthetic principle of all time."[7] A concept like *multifunctionality* contributes further to relativize the meaning of Sullivan's statement. To borrow an example from the architectural theoretician William J. Mitchell: A window's function can be both that of providing light from without and preventing loss of warmth from within. These functions can easily be to each other's cost. In relation to the situation, climatic conditions, and nature of the house, there are a number of design possibilities that are dependent on wise calculations, conscientious selections, and accurate evaluations.[8] Any evaluation of the balance between functionality and design will always include subjective elements. Aesthetic considerations are pertinent. The question is which elements will finally decide the concrete result.

---

[7] P. Blake, *Frank Lloyd Wright: Architecture and Space* (Harmondsworth, UK: Penguin Books, 1963), 27.

[8] See J.W. Mitchell, *The Logic of Architecture: Design, Computation, and Cognition* (Cambridge, MA: MIT Press, 1994), 225-226.

Another understanding of the concept of multifunctionality is that a whole building may house several functions, also allowing changes and adaptations of use. The Norwegian architectural historian Signe Horn Fuglesang diagnoses a uniform aesthetics that goes beyond functional specialization as one of functionalism's most important characteristics:

> Functionalism was the futuristic, the international, the new social-democratic building style of civic spirit. More than anything else it is a *symbolic* style—as we know, the buildings are not particularly practical. In the course of a decade, functionalism swept away not only the historical attempts but also even the principles of a monumental building's iconography and modality. A uniform aesthetics decided proportions, materials, and details of form, no matter whether the building was a factory, university or department store.[9]

Th.W. Adorno allies himself with the understanding of the concept's relativity by stressing the historical preconditions necessarily connected to it. "What was functional yesterday may become the opposite; Loos very much preserved this historical dynamism in the concept of ornaments," he writes in his essay "Funktionalismus heute."[10] In his opinion, purpose cannot be considered in isolation from historical development: "In crafted objects, the purposeless and the purposeful can therefore not be separated from each other in any absolute way since they are historically interwoven."[11] Adorno lifts functionalism out of its historical context while at the same time seeking to correct the general view of the style as constricting or utilitarian. He asserts that the most important impulse of the concept lies in a thorough mediation between *material, form,* and *purpose*. Albrecht Wellmer corroborates this perspective.[12] The same interaction between material, form, and purpose is what underlies the concept of musical functionalism.

As already suggested, the idea of the functionalist work also takes into account the fundamental importance of aesthetic dimensions. From a historical viewpoint, functionalism may be regarded as founded on "anti-aesthetic aesthetics," in the sense that it is based on strong reservations against the traditional concept of aesthetics. The concept's supposedly negative charge is due, for example, to Alexander G. Baumgarten's notion of aesthetics as the theory of *the beautiful*; it does not take into account that aesthetics includes

---

[9]Translated from S.H. Fuglesang, "Regionalitet i historisk perspektiv," W. Findal, ed., *Nordisk funksjonalisme: Det internasjonale og det nasjonale* (Oslo: Gyldendal, 1995), 21.

[10]Translated from Th.W. Adorno, "Funktionalismus heute," *Ohne Leitbild, Kulturkritik und Gesellschaft I* [*Gesammelte Schriften* 10/1] (Frankfurt am Main: Suhrkamp, 1977), 376.

[11]Translated from "Funktionalismus heute," 378.

[12]See A. Wellmer, *Zur Dialektik von Moderne und Postmoderne,* 122-123.

something more. This somewhat limited idea nurtures the Romanticist view of art. "Hence the house should have nothing to do with art, and architecture not be counted among the arts? It is so," writes Adolf Loos in 1910.[13] Loos's point is not to claim that art in itself is objectionable or contemptible, but that its domains are found outside the everyday reality in which people must function. For Loos, it is imperative to give humans an architecture that can satisfy their true and realistic everyday needs. Referring to the foundation of the Bauhaus, Gropius states that "each one from within his area longed to bridge the irreparable divide between reality and spirit."[14] In Loos' view there is not sufficient anchorage for any bridgehead between architecture and art. Rather, architecture must be freed from art or, more to the point, from the concept of art prevailing at the time. "A work of art is brought into the world without there being any prior need for it. A house meets a need. A work of art is responsible to no one, a house to everyone,"[15] asserts Loos in his characteristic mode of expression. All architecture serving a concrete purpose—with the exception of gravestones and monuments—is excluded from the realm of art, he says.

The divide between art and architecture is an important part of Loos's wish to draw attention away from the *beautiful* to the *truthful*. To understand this thought, it is important to realize that the concept of beauty prevailing around the turn of the century was subject to opinions that had little to do with Romanticism's deep-felt sincerity. In authoritative circles, particularly in Vienna's radical milieu, it was believed that "beautiful," superficial decoration tended toward concealing the artwork's essential truth. This observation is an important starting-point for Loos's essay "Ornament und verbrechen." Moral and ethical aspects are of great importance for the development of the functionalist concept. Loos believes the new, unadorned style to reflect civilization's progressive development.

Yet beauty and truth are not conceptual opposites. On the contrary, the true, the good, and the beautiful are recognized as absolutes springing from a common root that reaches back to antiquity. The question is whether a narrow understanding of the concept of beauty encompasses the recognition of what is *functionally truthful* as being also *aesthetically superior*. Sullivan rejects the idea that the functional is beautiful no matter what. In a dialogue between "master" and "student" contained in one of his *Kindergarten Chats*, he writes:

---

[13] Translated from A. Loos, "Architektur," *Trotzdem. Sämtliche Schriften in zwei Bänden* I (Vienna etc: Herold, 1962), 315.

[14] Translated from *Die neue Architektur und das Bauhaus*, 20.

[15] Translated from "Architektur," 315.

> That is why I am endeavouring, ever more fervently, to impress upon you the simple truth—immeasurable in power of expansion—of the subjective possibilities of objective things. In short, to clarify for you the origin and power of BEAUTY: to let you see that it is resident in function and form.
> So is ugliness, isn't it?
> To be sure.
> Is there anything that does not reside in function and form?
> Not that I have been able to discover.[16]

According to Sullivan, the correspondence between form and function may very well lead to what is not beautiful, even to something repulsive or ugly, a factor surely to be reckoned with when considering functionalism. The criterion of aesthetic evaluation must remain valid—both Loos and Le Corbusier emphasize the aesthetic aspects of the simple and unadorned object of utility.

However, the common notion that strictly utilitarian form should compensate for demands of a traditionally aesthetic and artistic nature seems to be strongly connected to the concept of functionalism. Public housing, built from the late 1920s onward and infamous for its gray tenements ("container architecture" and "housing machine" are popular epithets applied to this style), has helped draw attention in the direction of this mathematico-scientific modernism, pioneered by the Swiss architect Hannes Meyer, one of the last directors of the Bauhaus.[17] Wellmer and others deplore the resultant architectonic constructions as *vulgar functionalism*.[18] They capture what is problematic in functionalism's dual role as concept and style: such housing constructions can be regarded pessimistically as representative of the functionalist style and therein confirm the worst prejudices held by the detractors of functionalism; or they can be perceived optimistically as light and airy, appealing with their flat roofs, geometric forms, and the play of glass against concrete.

The term functionalism thus relates to intermingling ideas of function and style. Yet the interactions are always easy to define, as Adorno pointed out. At the beginning, functionalist ideas were revolutionary in their aspirations toward the formative and the fundamental. Proclaiming functionalist features as *style* invites a strict standardization that may be regarded as

---

[16] L.H. Sullivan, "The Elements of Architecture: Objective and Subjective (2). The Arch," *Kindergarden Chats* (Revised 1918) *and other writings* (New York: George Wittenborn, 1968), 124.

[17] See Christian Norberg-Schulz, "En ny begynnelse," in *Nordisk funksjonalisme*, 153.

[18] See A. Wellmer, *Zur Dialektik von Moderne und Postmoderne*, 120.

difficult to accept. In the course of the century, the enthusiastic notion of a new age with a new architecture gave way to the depressing reality of mechanization and rationalization, standardization and urbanization. Wellmer is not the only critic referring to "vulgar functionalism." A pioneer like Gropius, however, could not agree with his contemporaries' negative views of the standardization process. He asserts that standard forms are based on profound criteria of quality, as they represent the best of what culture can create:

> A standard always represents a cultural zenith, the best of the best, the segregation of the essential and meta-personal from the personal and arbitrary. Even today the opinion is maintained that the "tyranny of typification" rapes the individual. This fable was disproved long ago. In all great historical epochs the existence of standard forms, consciously recognized as typical, has been a sign of a well-ordered, civilized society.[19]

The concept of functionalism also seeks to absorb what are commonly described as spiritual dimensions, not least in the indirect way inherent in the ambition to relieve everyday life in order to liberate its spiritual potential. Ludwig Grote, one of the Bauhaus advocates, emphasizes the humanistic aspect. That the necessary utilitarian function should be sufficient is a view he regards as a misunderstanding, and he endorses Gropius's opinions when he states:

> It has become common coinage to describe the new building movement from the beginning of the 1920s as functionalism, and to see the Bauhaus as the orthodox defender of a design developed only from function. [...] Gropius frequently and unequivocally rejected the charge of equating function and form. [...] Already at that time Gropius defended himself against the accusation that the Bauhaus represented, as it were, an apotheosis of rationalism. He sought rather to ascertain the shared premises and limits for the areas of design and technology. Each thing is determined by its essence. In order to design it in such a way that it functions correctly, its essence must be investigated, for it is to serve its purpose perfectly, i.e. fill its functions in a practical way, be durable, cheap and "beautiful."[20]

Grote firmly believes that in due time one will be able to speak just as much of *abstract* architecture as of *functionalist* architecture, since the functionalist aspect is considered rather a means than an end in an overall aesthetics project:

[19] Translated from *Die neue Architektur und das Bauhaus*, 13-14.

[20] Translated from L. Grote, "Das Bauhaus und der Funktionalismus," in E. Neumann, ed., *Bauhaus und Bauhäusler: Erinnerungen und Bekenntnisse* (Cologne: DuMont, 1985), 280-281.

> The integration of modern art and technology has given rise to New Building, in which function is not an end in itself but a means to realize the new aesthetics. Consequently, the functionalist concept in no way does justice to the phenomenon. It would be far more appropriate to speak of abstract architecture.[21]

Le Corbusier, one of the epoch-making representatives for the view that the practical, use-related need is far from sufficient, insists that it is crucial to reunite architecture with art. While Loos's resolute catharsis is typical for the budding functionalist concept that dominates during the years before World War I, Le Corbusier's view reveals a development within the concept. This progress is born out of the spontaneous optimism that characterized substantial parts of postwar culture. "ARCHITECTURE is a thing of art, a phenomenon of the emotions, lying outside questions of construction and beyond them," proposes Le Corbusier.[22] This remark is sharply opposed to Loos's understanding of the disparity between art and architecture. Uncluttered facades and primary forms are not only a result of a search for truth, manifested through the elimination of historicizing ornamentation: they are ends in themselves. And these ends, Le Corbusier believes, are certainly not directed by utilitarianism. Primary forms address universal principles with which humans identify themselves by virtue of their nature. For Le Corbusier, *primary* forms are also *beautiful* forms. The formal objective is directed by human beings' spiritual health, not only by their bodily well-being. The Neo-Platonist roots in which this understanding of art resides identify Le Corbusier as a purist. His concept of art is connected more to universality and classical harmony than to the 19th-century concept of beauty. The relationship between this approach and the philosophy of *De Stijl*, which will be discussed later, is obvious. Le Corbusier is concerned with contemporary technical advances, where engineers are the exemplary aesthetes since they construct the purposive product according to universal measurements and principles. This combination between realistic purpose and timeless, universal dimensions is crucial for the development of the functionalist concept; it is considered to embody a natural truth which—in the new century's faith in the future of machines and the optimism for what they can bring about—is deserving of modern man. Therefore, the consideration of functional use is connected to what could be described as *functional form*. Transcending use and focusing on aesthetics, functional form becomes tantamount to form easily grasped, to the *basic form*; a form that does not submit to the restricted function of use.

---

[21]Translated from "Das Bauhaus und der Funktionalismus," 282.

[22]*Towards a New Architecture,* 23

As already suggested, another main component of functionalism is the reference to forces played out in the object itself, in the functional construction or in the inherent organic-functional principles. Every work of art is based on construction of one kind or another. If this basic truism is emphasized with regard to architecture, design, and the 20th-century concept of functionalism, it is because construction here is something not only illustrated but also actively *revealed*. The 19th century suppressed the significance of "construction" for forms of art. The 20th century rejects such suppression; construction principles find a natural place within the functionalist concept of truth. Such principles are given a positive charge, which decisively influences the understanding of art in the 20th century. The inner functional interplay, whether of static construction or dynamic organism, is recognized on the basis of the underlying Aristotelian principles: both as the condition for and the aim of the object's composition. First, form and material are perceived as engaged with one another. Second, the object realizes itself, or its motivation, through an organic-constructive process of development. The construction thus also becomes the mediator of aesthetic dimensions.

Gustave Eiffel's famous 1889 tower is not only an interesting example of daring construction; it is also a symbol of its time, a stately landmark for its city, a magnificent monument, and today a major tourist attraction. Le Corbusier describes its destiny as follows:

> The Eiffel Tower has been accepted as architecture.
> In 1889, it was seen as the aggressive expression of mathematical calculation.
> In 1900, the aesthetes wanted to demolish it.
> In 1925, it dominated the Exhibition of Modern Decorative Arts.
> Above the plaster palaces writhing with decoration, it stood out pure as crystal.[23]

Constructivism is used as an artistic term, not least thanks to prominent pioneers such as the Russian El Lissitzky (1890-1941) and the Hungarian László Moholy-Nagy (1895-1946). The latter was of great importance for the development of the Bauhaus. Positively charged constructivism became an essential component of the functionalist concept: Structure, no longer considered merely a necessary skeleton to be concealed, gained honorable status as a positive component of the artefact as an aesthetic object. Construction became an important precondition for an artist's realization of his or her thought, idea or vision.

---

[23] Le Corbusier, *The Decorative Art of Today,* trans. and intro. James I. Dunnett (London: The Architectural Press, 1987), XXV.

The chosen material is decisive for the realization of the intended work of art. A heightened awareness of this fact is one of the most important premises of functionalism. Le Corbusier regards it as important to stress that the new materials of his time are more suitable for construction than for decoration. What emerges here is the fundamental view of material having its *own will*. The following quotation from Ludwig Mies van der Rohe (1886-1969), the last director of the Bauhaus, is typical for the functionalist recognition of material as based on rationality and logic:

> We can also learn from a brick. How sensible is this small handy shape, so useful for every purpose! What logic in its bonding, pattern and texture! What richness in the simplest surface! But what discipline this material imposes! Thus each material has its specific characteristics which we must understand if we want to use it.[24]

The notion of any material having its own will with which the human will to create must cooperate, is in no way limited to *new* types of material. The term *Materialgerechtigkeit* emerges already at the beginning of the 20th century. Its emphasis on justice and faithfulness to the distinct qualities of specific materials blends naturally with the stated wish for artistic truthfulness. In line with the thought of the innate will pertaining to any material is the view that each kind of substance has a true nature that should be exploited, not concealed. Each material must appear as it *is*. The functionalist concept carries within itself the notion of a functional handling of the materials used for construction. The fundamental point is the conviction that the human spirit does not have complete mastery over material. This applies not only to machine-driven mass production, but at least as strongly to the concepts of construction and craftsmanship. It emphasizes the positive nature of construction and reinstates craftsmanship as one of the most important preconditions of artistic creation. Thus the early century's art-pedagogic reforms, in the Bauhaus project and elsewhere, tend toward replacing Romanticist ideas with attitudes that lead back to the *ars*-concept of earlier times.

The ideas of functionalism's various streams converge in the thought that an object's material, form, and function must be decided by a far-reaching principle of functionality, where concepts like artistic truthfulness, construction, and craftsmanship play important parts. Furthermore, the concept of functionalism can be considered a trinity of

---

[24]L. Mies van der Rohe, "Inaugural address as Director of Architecture at Armour Institute of Technology," in Ph.C. Johnson, *Mies van der Rohe* (New York: The Museum of Modern Art, 1947), 193.

1) functional treatment of the chosen material
2) functional design
3) focus on the work's intended function

The following discussions address the contextual conditions that lead to, constitute, and support the functionalist understanding. The emphasis is on aspects of the three main components, *material, form,* and *function,* as they emerge and change through 20th-century art and cultural history. As regards material, focus is directed first to the thought of the material's own will, then to the craftsmanship aspect. As regards form, particular emphasis is placed on the process from organic form to primary form—from individual form to norm. As regards function, attention will focus on the ambiguity that in a given era manifests itself in concepts like *function* and *functionality,* besides its connection to terms such as *Sachlichkeit* and *Neue Sachlichkeit.*

On the Material's Own Will

Awareness of the material from which a work of art is to be created has always been among creative artists' main concerns. Any artistic material is defined by certain possibilities and limitations, a fact that has led to speculations that materials may have an inherent "will" unique to each substance, with which an artist's will has to co-operate. Such views resound in Aristotelian teleology, where matter is seen as striving toward the realization of its form. For Aristotle, matter is potential, *dynamis,* and form its actualization, *energeia.* Once creative artists recognize this, they also face the challenge of realizing the chosen material's inherent potentials. To achieve this realization, artists would need to treat their material in a *functional* way. In music, Schoenberg's thoughts on the compositional process express very similar principles.

Understanding the supposedly innate will of any material also includes recognizing its limitations, as a specific material can be stretched only within given boundaries. A central functionalist thought is that the material's capacity and inherent nature must never be neglected, views Hindemith represents similarly with regard to music.

While according to Aristotelian views, a given material can never surpass its own determinative nature, artists have always attempted to exercise control. Throughout the ages and within different cultural horizons, creative artists have approached this task from different angles. A concern that characterizes aesthetic considerations in the latter part of the 19th century is the idea of "doing justice to the material." Already in 1834, the architect Gottfried Semper wrote:

> Let the material speak for itself and come forward, undisguised, to the fore and in those relations that through experience and science have shown themselves to be most expedient. Let brick be brick, wood be wood, iron be iron, each according to its static, inherent orderliness. It is to this simple truth that one, with one's entire predilection for the innocent embroidery of decoration, must be devoted.[25]

Materialgerechtigkeit, the claim for justice to the material, gained increasing influence among designers and architects from the turn of the century onwards. The concept of *Materialgerechtigkeit* implied that any material can be subjected to a rational definition that gives its possibilities and limitations a tinge of universal validity. To use materials in a functional way thus came to imply far more than leaving its manipulation to the artists' visions and whims.

The demand for *Materialgerechtigkeit* grounded in a general interest in new materials and the use of traditional materials in new ways. The development of art at the time underwent a transition from craftsmanship to mass-production. The 1851 World Exhibition in London, "The Great Exhibition of All Nations," with Joseph Paxton's remarkable *Crystal Palace*, has gone down in history as a spectacular opening event for modern industry and design. Containing as many as fifteen thousand exhibitors, the Crystal Place showed how far one could go with constructions of iron and glass. The later Eiffel Tower, built for the 1889 World Exhibition in Paris, was to have even greater significance for future construction aesthetics and engineering art.

Industrial mass-production began developing at a brisk pace and soon made new claims not only on products' forms, but also on the particular qualities of the material used. Craftsmen demanded increased access to raw materials that would lend themselves to rational and expedient manipulations by machines. The English Arts and Crafts movement emerged in this context, founded by designer William Morris (1834-1896)—whom Gropius presented as one of the most important precursors of the Bauhaus concept—and author John Ruskin (1819-1900). A number of talented artists contributed to the breadth and influence of the movement's ideas. The Arts and Crafts movement became highly important, not least as a waystation in the foundation of the upcoming century's "modern" design. The movement's representatives regarded themselves as offering a counterweight to machine production and all that went with it. The relationship between artistic subjectivity and machine-generated standardization would be ardently debated through most of the following century. Fundamental to Arts and Crafts was the idea of

---

[25]Translated from G. Semper, "Vorläufige Bemerkungen," in H.M. Wingler, ed., *Wissenschaft Industrie und Kunst, und andere Schriften über Architektur, Kunsthandwerk und Kunstunterricht* [*Neue Bauhausbücher*] (Mainz/Berlin: Florian Kupferberg, 1966), 17.

creating in a mechanized age according to what was considered rural naturalness. Aspects of what was regarded as natural, organic decoration played an important role. The specific qualities of any given material—whether it was wood, metal, or textiles—were considered very seriously. Despite the allowance of organic decoration, there was to be no unnecessary effort to camouflage either material or basic structure.

The ideas proposed by the Arts and Crafts movement came to be influential both on the European continent and in America. It is hard to imagine the later *Deutscher Werkbund* without the English model, even though the profiles of these two organizations were quite different. One of the main points for early functionalist discussion was the idea that forming a given material should be inspired by nature and natural growth; another point centered on the question whether the aim should be to hide the material or to emphasize its substantive nature. The focus on the material's own will became the expression of an era that regarded artificiality and dishonesty as the most serious obstacles for a positive artistic and cultural development. Such questions were of vital importance to the quest for artistic truth and honesty, and thus contributed vastly to the shift from the Romantic ideal of artistic beauty to the 20th century's emphasis on artistic truthfulness.

The quest for truthfulness came to mark the attitude toward materials in architecture, design, and all the art forms, including music. In the functionalist concept, truthfulness is the crucial correlation with regard to the artistic material's possibilities and limitations:

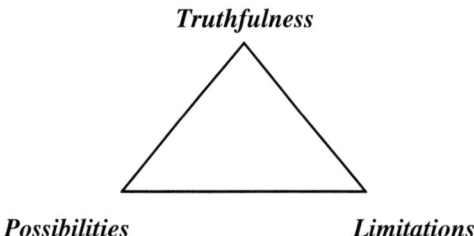

The concept of truthfulness is never easy to define. Despite the attention given to the particular material, the English Arts and Crafts was also committed to ornamental principles. The German *Jugendstil,* the Austrian *Sezessionsstil*, the English *Decorative Style,* and the French *Art Nouveau*—all of them independent but nevertheless quite similar styles that contributed to the development toward functionalism—are characterized by their efforts at simplifying ornament and relating it more closely to the art object. By extension, this specific use of ornamentation strives to create unity between space, object, and human being. As the art historian Gert Selle puts it:

> In this [*Jugendstil*] the casing, the things and the people become themselves ornament. In a different way than in historicism, where decor is applied industrially to the end-product, designs now bring new, surprising, individual expressions organically out of the form [...].[26]

The general tendency in this stylistic development is that ornaments move from surface to structure, connecting organically with the form. In this way, the ornamental principle becomes important for the work's or product's fundamental design. Ornaments are no longer regarded as belonging to the exterior, but considered organic constituents of a larger entity. A creeper's rambling stems, a lily's elegant petals, a tree's numerous branches and luxuriant foliage become an inspiration for this type of organic, ornamental unfolding.

FIGURE 1: Koloman Moser, cover page of the periodical *Ver Sacrum* (vol. II/4, 1899)

Spontaneity is sought in the laws of nature, based on the conviction that nature is the truthful and eternally solid ground in an age when mechanization and urbanization are seen as leading to human alienation. One way of creating with artistic authenticity thus relies on using organic ornaments consciously and in a profoundly structural way. Louis Henry Sullivan, one of the exponents of this viewpoint, explains in his book *A System of Architectural Ornament: According with a Philosophy of Man's Powers,* how decorative elements develop, plant-like, from the germ through opulent leaves to the complex ornamental shape (see FIGURE 3, page 40 below). Thoughts like these influenced the attitude toward materials at the time, in the sense that any material was now believed to have qualities that allow for an organic, "truthful" form. Materials can be developed in a positively recognizable and supposedly logical way. In music, Schoenberg's thoughts about musical

---

[26]Translated from G. Selle, *Design-Geschichte in Deutschland, Produktkultur als Entwurf und Erfahrung* (Cologne: DuMont, 1990), 87.

material and form, especially his views on the musical motive,[27] develop within the same framework. For him, and for many of his contemporaries, materials are more than just substances provided in the natural environment. Moved to a higher level of refinement, material and form attain the kinds of reciprocal relationship advocated by Aristotle.

Although the construction principles that materials will admit can readily be gleaned from processes observed in nature, they are also related to culture. In his 1893 book *Stilfragen*, the art historian Alois Riegel discusses the various attitudes to ornamentation as a result of a historical development taking place within different cultures.[28] Loos's statement that "the evolution of culture is synonymous with the removal of ornamentation from objects of everyday use,"[29] implies a historical-cultural point of view, in which the artistic material's own will is also seen in relation to its time. Contemporary artistic expression combines the Aristotelian understanding of material with the Hegelian view of the spirit. Yet artists must relate to the Hegelian notion of *Geist* in a *truthful* way. This assumes fundamental importance for the Second Viennese School and for Adorno's understanding of material. Musical material is regarded as containing a fundamental will for realization; at the same time, its actual historical position determines its basic characteristics. In an authentic work, the given material is realized through the dialectical interaction between substance and history. As a consequence, the presumably endurable elements of a tradition are played out against what may be regarded as negatively loaded conventions.

The critique of aspects of ornamentation is characteristic for the search for truthfulness that marks the understanding of art at the turn of the 20th century. The shift of focus toward the material's own will also finds expression in the general notion of ornamentation. "The old love of ornament must be replaced by pleasure in the material itself," says Loos.[30]

---

[27] I am aware that *motive* and *motif* are distinguished in contemporary American English, with the former used for the "reasons for acting" and the latter preferred for "musical entity." However, as both Schoenberg and Hindemith spell *motive* in their English texts, and their translators from originally German texts follow this lead, I have decided to do likewise here.

[28] An English translation of this work by E. Kain has been published as A. Riegl, *Problems of Style: Foundations for a history of ornament* (Princeton, N.J.: Princeton University 1992).

[29] A. Loos, "Ornament and Crime," *Ornament and Crime: Selected Essays,* intro. Adolf Opel, trans. Michael Mitchell (Riverside, CA: Ariadne Press, 1998), 167.

[30] The original text has the title "Von der Sparsamkeit," based on B. Markalous's collection of Loos's statements reproduced in *Wohnungskultur* 2/3 (1924). The quotation used here was translated by F.R. Jones and reproduced in A. Loos, "Regarding economy," M. Risselda, ed., *Raumplan versus Plan Libre: Adolf Loos and Le Corbusier, 1919-1930* (New York: Rizzoli, 1988), 139.

There are several reasons why Vienna, the city of Loos and Schoenberg, has such a central place in this picture. Carl E. Schorske, the author of *Fin-de-siècle Vienna: Politics and Culture*, refers to the late, but quickly developing, attention on modernism, and how lacking boundaries between intellectual disciplines stimulated concerted efforts.[31] The political situation in the German-speaking as well as in the Slavonic areas was in abeyance. For Austria, whose focus was both toward the north and the southeast, political issues were particularly connected to cultural identity. This was a time of transition, with a concept of modernism growing out of the ruins of a bygone era. Emperor Franz Joseph towered as a pompous figurehead of the old days. Art and architecture as well as the average middle-class home all strove to absorb impulses not only from vanished times but also from exotic lands. Critics claimed that narrow moral codes, social conventions, and sexual double standards laid a clammy hand over the individual, its family, and the community. The negative aspects of such artistic and cultural quagmires were shown for what they were when Viennese artists and intellectuals asserted themselves in attempts at initiating change. This does not mean that the progressive Vienna milieu was of a uniform structure throughout.

The conductor and writer Leon Botstein refers to two main groups, one around the painter Gustav Klimt (1862-1918) and the author Arthur Schnitzler (1862-1931), the other, more radical, around the literary and cultural critic Karl Kraus (1874-1936) and the architect Adolf Loos. Schoenberg would identify with the latter. The most influential personality in Vienna at the time, Sigmund Freud (1856-1939), did not identify with either.[32]

The ardent Zionist Theodor Herzl (1860-1904) played a principal role with his *Neue Freie Presse*, important not only for the Jews, but also for Vienna's cultural life as a whole. Karl Kraus, whom Stefan Zweig characterized as "the Thersites of Viennese literature—master of the poisonous mockery,"[33] represented a powerful force on the radical scene, particularly owing to his journal, *Die Fackel*, which from 1899 to 1936 appeared in 992 issues. Up to 1911, Kraus included articles from a number of contributors, among them Loos and Schoenberg; after 1911 Kraus was the sole author.[34]

---

[31]See C.E. Schorske, *Fin-de-siècle Vienna: Politics and Culture* (New York: Vintage Books/Random House, 1981), XXVI-XXVII.

[32]See L. Botstein, "Music and the Critique of Culture: Arnold Schoenberg, Heinrich Schenker and the Emergence of Modernism in Fin de Siècle Vienna," in J. Brand and Chr. Hailey, eds., *Constructive Dissonance: Arnold Schoenberg and the Transformations of Twentieth-Century Culture* (Berkeley/Los Angeles/London: University of California Press, 1997), 12.

[33]Translated from S. Zweig, *Die Welt von gestern. Erinnerungen eines Europäers* (Frankfurt a. M.: S. Fischer 1992), 127.

[34]The exception is one single essay by August Strindberg in May 1912 (no. 349/350).

In addition to his writing and acting talents Kraus was a brilliant speaker and lecturer. He carried on the tradition established by J.N.E.A. Nestroy (1801-1862), and his captivating verbal versatility secured him a solid position in the public mind.

Karl Kraus contributed to the overall aims of functionalism when he criticized not only contemporary cultural phenomena, but also, both directly and indirectly, the lenient use of language—the material of verbal creation. It is a common experience that language, like the materials used in the plastic arts, has its possibilities and limitations. The distinctive awareness of this dual condition characterizes the view developing among language critics in Vienna at the time. Their criticism is grounded in a firm belief in the potential of language as a mediator of truth.

When considering Kraus's cultural criticism, one must use a concept of culture that embraces all aspects of community life—from art via the individual's social conditions to major political issues. Kraus's efforts are not limited to one area, although his criticism of the exploitation of the weak and unfortunate members of society was vociferous. Adolf Loos once said of him: "With his head in the heavens, his feet on the ground, with heart-rending anguish for the misery of man he strides. And shouts."[35] Kraus was particularly critical of the social falseness and double standard that victimized the individual. His book *Sittlichkeit und Kriminalität*, published in 1908, is an example of these ardent efforts. The title of his most famous publication, *Die letzten Tage der Menschheit*,[36] invokes an ironic reference to the last days of the Austrian-Hungarian empire.

The sharp edge of Kraus's criticism was directed in particular at that favorite of newspaper readers: the *feuilleton*. Allan Janik, one of the authors of *Wittgenstein's Vienna*, gives the following description:

> The whole society was completely imbued with hyprocisy; and, as a result, it was the aesthetic side of the press which Kraus found most offensive of all. The cultural essay, or feuilleton, was for many the most important section of the whole paper. If the class standpoint of the paper resulted in a general distortion of the news, it was specifically distorted in the free mingling of fact and opinion, rational objectivity and subjective reaction, that was the deliberate aim of the feuilleton.[37]

---

[35]Translated from A. Loos, "Karl Kraus," *Trotzdem,* 328.

[36]This work was first published in the form of pamphlets; cf. the 1918-1922 issues of *Die Fackel.* For an abridged English version see Frederick Ungar, trans./ed., *The Last Days of ankind; a tragedy in five acts* by Karl Kraus (New York: F. Ungar Pub. Co., 1974).

[37]A. Janik and S. Toulmin, *Wittgenstein's Vienna* (New York etc.: Simon & Schuster, 1973), 79.

In this genre, fact and fiction, objective knowledge and subjective assertion are mixed in a way that often makes them difficult to distinguish. The feuilleton camouflages what is true as well as what is untrue; falsities can appear as truths and vice versa. The peculiar use of language in the feuilleton became the basis for a certain stylistic way of expression:

> [...] the feuilleton called for a species of vignette, in which a situation was described with all the color the author could muster; it was a subjective response to an objective state of affairs, intended to be conveyed in language which was laded with adverbs and especially adjectives; so much so that the objective situation was lost in the shuffle. Objective facts were thus viewed through the prism-like emotions of the writer.[38]

As already suggested, Kraus considered it imperative that the material of language be used in a truthful way, that its possibilities and limitations be employed to good purpose in the service of truth. The *phrase*, the trite cliché or pompous rhetoric, was an affliction he fervently wished to cure, and he despised empty linguistic ornaments. Kraus's own writings are rich but concise, very much to the point, and eloquent in a way so idiosyncratically German that they are considered difficult to translate.

The work of Ludwig Wittgenstein (1889-1951) should be understood, or so his biographers Allan Janik and Stephan Toulmin feel, in light of Kraus's kind of language criticism. In their study *Wittgenstein's Vienna,* the authors interpret features from Viennese culture as the significant motivating forces for Wittgenstein's concern with the relation of language to reality. While Janik and Toulmin wish to recognize Wittgenstein's 1921 *Tractatus Logico-Philosophicus* as a contribution both to 20th-century mathematical logic and to British analytical philosophy, they draw attention to the fact that in Austria, this work is predominantly considered an *ethical* dissertation:

> Those Austrians who were closest to Wittgenstein insist that whenever he concerned himself with anything, it was from the ethical point of view [...] The *Tractatus* was more than merely a book of ethics in the eyes of his family and friends; it was an ethical *deed*, which showed the nature of ethics.[39]

When reading Wittgenstein in the light of the first beams of functionalism, three distinct aspects of his views emerge: the *logical*, the *analytical*, and the *ethical*. These three elements merge in the most famous of Wittgensteinian quotations: "what can be said at all can be said clearly, and what

---

[38] *Wittgenstein's Vienna*, 79.

[39] *Wittgenstein's Vienna*, 24.

we cannot talk about we must pass over in silence."[40] Focus is once more on the ultimate consequences of the potentials and limitations of language as the material of verbal expression. The ideal of clarity included in this statement raises associations to the affinity between truthfulness and clarity that is characteristic of functionalist thought. At the same time, Wittgenstein points out that there are dimensions in life of which one must literally be silent. These are spheres that cannot be reached by human language—the domains of language cannot, then, be defined as encompassing the *total* reality of man. The distinction is essential to Wittgenstein's critique of language, and in stark contrast to Romanticism's urge to express the ineffable.

It is characteristic for the functionalist approach to material versus form that there are limits to what any given material can be used to express or represent in a concrete and unequivocal sense. Functionalist thought does not thereby strive to devalue or exclude everything that lies beyond tangible human reality. Indeed, the purism and Neo-Platonism of Le Corbusier and others who played such a large part in the development of functionalist thinking implies a deep respect for exactly such dimensions that constitute the fundamental premise for supposedly universal values.

Truthfulness, made manifest through the combination of ethics and logic in language's relation to reality, is the distinctive mark of Kraus and Wittgenstein, albeit in different ways. Both are concerned with purging language of empty, hollow trivialities, and the concept of truth in the linguistic material becomes something far more than an avoidance of false claims. As a motto for his *Tractatus*, Wittgenstein chose Kürnberger's statement: "and whatever a man knows, whatever is not mere rumbling and roaring that he has heard, can be said in three words."[41] This declaration may also suggest associations to the conciseness and precision characteristic of functionalism.

The adherence to true, ethical, logical, and purposive exploitation of the material's characteristics is also found in Adolf Loos's work. "Ornament und verbrechen" may be seen as a counterpart to Karl Kraus's fight against linguistic ornament. In 1909 Kraus wrote:

> The disfiguring of practical life through ornament, as Adolf Loos has shown, corresponds to journalism's penetration of spiritual things that leads to disastrous confusion. The phrase is the ornament of the spirit [*Geist*][...][42]

---

[40]L. Wittgenstein, *Tractatus Logico-Philosophicus*, D.F. Pears and B.F. McGuinness, trans. (London etc.: Routledge & Kegan/The Humanity Press, 1988), 3.

[41]*Tractatus Logico-Philosophicus*, title page.

[42]Translated from Karl Kraus as quoted in B. Rukschicio/R. Schahel, *Adolf Loos, Leben und Werk* (Salzburg etc.: Residenz , 1982), 121.

In "Ornament und verbrechen," economical use of material is one of the arguments against the wasteful principles of ornamentation.[43] Loos is the opponent *par excellence* of ornamentation; he is strictly against any traditionally decorative elements on utility objects. Through the products of the *Wiener Werkstätte* and the early *Deutscher Werkbund*, he also attacks the efforts, so characteristic of the *Sezessionsstil* and *Jugendstil*, to combine art with utility.[44] Loos's comments on something as prosaic as the characteristics and position of mortar are quite illustrative:

> And then we have mortar. One looks from top to bottom, and begins in a materialistic age to be ashamed on its behalf. There the good old Viennese mortar is being abused and prostituted, no longer able to say who or what it is, and it is being used to imitate stone [...]. For God and for artists, all materials are the same and just as valuable; and I am all for people looking at the world through the eyes of God and artists. Mortar is a skin [a shell]. Stone is constructive. Despite their similar chemical composition, there is the greatest difference in use between the two [...]. If the mortar has an honest function as a casing for brickwork, it needs to be ashamed just as little of its simple origin as the Tyrolean needs to be ashamed of his leather breeches in the emperor's castle.[45]

This statement, like so many others from the time, highlights the combination of logic and ethics as characteristic of the attitude toward building materials. Loos also stresses the need for clarity and constant simplification. As he sees it, the cultural development toward modernism represents a gradual liberation from ornament. "One thing I knew; to keep abreast of development I had to become still much simpler," he writes in connection with his at once famous and infamous house on the Michaelerplatz in Vienna.[46]

Truthfulness, clarity, and simplicity are terms also found throughout the writings of Le Corbusier. James Dunnett believes that the young architect came to know Loos's essays through the journal *Der Sturm* in 1912.[47] Characteristic of Le Corbusier's architecture is the anti-ornamental and presumably economical use of material. Furthermore, he is among the time's

---

[43] See A. Loos, "Ornament and Crime," *Ornament and Crime: Selected Essays,* 167-175.

[44] See, for example, the essay "Kulturentartung," *Trotzdem,* 271-275.

[45] Translated from A. Loos, "Zwei aufsätze und eine zuschrift über das haus auf dem Michaelerplatz," *Trotzdem,* 298-299.

[46] Translated from "Architektur," *Trotzdem,* 312.

[47] See James I. Dunnett's introduction to his translation of Le Corbusier, *The Decorative Art of Today,* VIII.

optimistic defenders of the aesthetics of engineering and machines, an attitude that influences his overall understanding of building materials. Le Corbusier is particularly concerned with materials of a presumably strong will, like steel, glass,[48] and concrete, since he feels that these are more suitable for construction than decoration. He also is fascinated by new materials, invented by and adapted to a time of *un esprit nouveau*—a new spirit, attitude, or mentality. To his mind, one of the Industrial Revolution's most important results was the replacement of natural with artificial materials.[49]

An optimistic stance toward creating new building materials is characteristic of most of the progressive architects in the 1920s. Ludwig Mies van der Rohe is definitely one of these:

> Industrialization of the process of construction is a question of materials. Our first consideration, therefore, must be to find a new building material. Our technologists must and will succeed in inventing a material which will be weatherproof, soundproof and insulating.[50]

This paragraph gives expression to the belief that the spirit of the time is reflected not only in the artists' attitude toward his or her material, but in the material itself. Schoenberg's understanding of the will and qualities of musical material develops within the same context, and Hindemith's thoughts have their roots in the same soil. In order to understand these two composers' backdrop, it is worth looking more closely at some of the consequences their contemporaries' thoughts on material had for the understanding of artistic creativity.

Craft and Creation

To co-operate successfully with any material's inherent will requires mastery of creative craft. Recognition of how important solid craftsmanship is to the process of artistic creation grew steadily during the decades leading up to the 20th century.

The name "Arts and Crafts movement" testifies to the wish to reconcile art with craft and vice versa. The concepts art and craft are often considered opposites, with *handicraft* becoming a productive alliance between them.

---

[48] That is to say: when used in larger surfaces.

[49] See Le Corbusier, *Vers une Architecture*, 192.

[50] L. Mies van der Rohe, "The industrialization of building methods," Ph.C. Johnson, *Mies van der Rohe* (New York: The Museum of Modern Art, 1947), 184-185.

Craft and Creation 23

When speaking of Arts and Craft it is important to emphasize that the organization's identity lies in its status as a counterweight to machine-generated mass production. The real opposites are craftsmanship and machine production. Only individual craftsmanship can create art, or at least aesthetically superior products; the proponents of machine-generated artifacts are bound to admit defeat.

Machines were regarded as the very symbols of an approaching new age. The use of machines in developing industries promised to make life easier for all. Machines were associated with optimism and belief in the future, while at the same time inducing fear—not least the fear of spiritual degeneracy, of presenting a threat both to art and to modern man's aesthetic sense. Machine-made mass production seemed to threaten individuality, and in its wake emerged an ideal of precision far above the possibilities of human hands.

For the social critic John Ruskin, the medieval craftsman—if ever so imperfect—stood as the magnificent creator:

> Let him [the medieval craftsman] but begin to imagine, to think, to try to do anything worth doing; and the engine turned precision is lost at once. Out come all his roughness, all his dullness, all his incapability; shame upon shame, failure upon failure, pause after pause; but out comes the whole majesty of him also.[51]

An idealization of the culture of medieval craftsmanship is also found at the Bauhaus. The Bauhaus movement placed great importance on the craftsmanship aspect in art education, and syllabi were based on the master-apprentice relationship. It was also in the Bauhaus spirit to reconcile craftsmanship with machine production; artists were aware that craftsmanship had changed in the age of machines: "The new age has created a new unity of craft and machine work," Gropius said.[52]

Focusing on craftsmanship was thus not just a question of looking back to bygone ages in dark suspicion of the machine's advance and conquest; it was also a matter of seeing the value of craftsmanship in a contemporary frame where both art and industry had a place. The motto for the establishment of the Deutscher Werkbund in 1907 was "refinement of industrial work in interaction with art, industry and craft through education, propaganda, and united commitment."[53] Art was presented as part of a large, contemporary concept of production, interacting with craft and machine-based industry.

---

[51] S. Adams, *The Arts & Crafts Movement* (London: Tiger Books International, 1992), 19.

[52] Translated from *Die neue Architektur und das Bauhaus*, 12.

[53] Translated from G. Selle, *Design-Geschichte in Deutschland*, 123.

With respect to the industrial development, the *Werkbund* became considerably more progressive than Arts and Crafts. Its chief founder, the architect Hermann Muthesius (1861-1927), had a positive attitude toward mass production and the formal norms laid down by industry. Coinciding with the organization's founding, another prominent *Werkbund* member, Peter Behrens, became the influential and trend-setting product designer for AEG.[54] During the years leading up to World War I, acceptance of the advantages and possibilities of machine production grew steadily, albeit not without harrowing debates.

A common denominator for art, craft, and machine-dominated production is *construction*, a term that also appears frequently both in Schoenberg's writings and in analyses of his music. As mentioned above, exposing the structural element is a characteristic feature of the functionalist work, and Sullivan, in his book *A System of Architectural Ornament,* builds his argument on the basis of the biological seed as the germ for artificial ornament.

The emphasis on nature as the model for art has its roots in Romanticism, both in the idea that nature's completeness is reflected in the work of art and in the thought that the creation of a work of art can be compared to nature's organic growth. This idea goes back to Karl Phillipp Moritz, but it is unclear whether Sullivan was familiar with Moritz's writings. Sullivan has a strong belief in man's ability to create, in the sense that the individual can create as nature does, an approach that reflects August Wilhelm Schlegel's view of the creative talent. Sullivan turns away from the romantic stance and toward the attitudes of a new century: he believes in man's unlimited abilities as an artistic yet rational constructor. Human beings have the ability to manipulate what is inorganic, Sullivan says. He illustrates his view on the basis of geometry, starting not from nature's seed but from the circle divided into four sections. This design is then further developed with different polygons, finally culminating in what Sullivan describes as "foliate and efflorescent forms."[55] (See FIGURE 4, page 41 below).

Sullivan's presentation of the creative principles of construction does not imply that artists can construct superior art only from their isolated intellect and from the mathematical skills they may have achieved. What he describes as *man's powers* is a far more complex phenomenon. Man's creative abilities can be divided into five main categories:

---

[54] AEG: Allgemeine Electrizitäts-Gesellschaft (General Electric Company), founded in Berlin in 1883.

[55] L.H. Sullivan, *A System of Architectural Ornament, According with a Philosophy of Man's Powers* (New York: The Eakins Press, 1967), Plates 3-4, n.p.

1. *"The physical powers* are well known," Sullivan says. They represent, among others, "the power to do things, to effect changes, to create situations."
2. *"The intellectual group* starts in the power of *curiosity* and ends in highly sophisticated manipulation." Observation, memory, reflection, and reasoning are the keywords.
3. *"The emotional group* embraces every impulse, every power of feeling; an enormous volcanic complex—the basis of action [...]. It is of *instinct*. It is this ability to break bounds that drives people—even if they do their best to deny it; "even as they exalt Intellect to the rank of fetish."
4. *"The moral group*: the great stabilizing power!" The stabilizing core of this force is man's free will, asserts Sullivan. This is the axis in man's existence. "Hence is *choice* the most potent of his moral powers. The deepest moral truth is this: that the power of choice resides in all men."
5. *"The spiritual group* functions as a super-quality in clarity of vision. It sees as in a dream; it feels as in the depths of instinct," says Sullivan. Limitless dimensions connect to this concept. "The *spirit* acknowledges," that "life is a dream within a greater dream, and man himself a dreamer within the dream of life." [...] "Especially does spirit contemplate its own powers, for it is the veritable *ego*." And besides contemplating itself, the spirit focuses its vision both on humanity and man with his physical, intellectual, emotional, moral, and spiritual abilities.[56]

Sullivan thus proposes what can be described as a Hegelian concept of *Geist* combined with a Nietzschean belief in human powers. Considering the spectrum of human abilities as they are presented in these five groups, Sullivan characterizes the thoroughly healthy "reality-man" as *the master craftsman*. He then links this characterization to the development of modern art:

> Thus dawns the modern light upon the art of the world. It reveals that all men in their native powers are craftsmen, whose destiny it is to create, courageously, wisely and worthily, a fit abiding place; a sane and beautiful world.[57]

The word "craftsman" may bring to mind a broader spectrum of associations than "artisan" or "handicraftsman," although one often sees these nouns used synonymously. At the time, when used in connection with artistic creation, the term "craftsman" suggested several different qualities involved in

---

[56]From Sullivan, "The Inorganic and the Organic," Introduction to *A System of Architectural Ornament*.

[57]"The Inorganic and the Organic."

the complex process that finally leads to a work of art. Refusing to limit the term to the mechanical use of the brush over canvas or to the drawing of dots and dashes in a musical score, Sullivan presents a whole slate of components he considers crucial for the process of artistic creation, all realized through craft. He focuses on the process in a way that seems demystifying, while emphasizing individuals' genuine abilities within a wider understanding of the concept of creativity. This combination of demystification and respect becomes central for the positive reevaluation of craft in the 20th century.

Le Corbusier's praise of engineers as the true aesthetes of a new age, as the brilliant ideals of modern architects, must be seen in the same context:

> Our Engineers produce architecture, for they employ a mathematical calculation which derives from natural law, and their works give us the feeling of HARMONY. The engineer therefore has his own aesthetic, for he must, in making his calculations, qualify some of the terms of his equation; and it is here that taste intervenes. [...] Art, according to Larousse, is the application of knowledge to the realization of a conception. Now, to-day, it is the engineer who *knows*, who knows the best way to construct, to heat, to ventilate, to light. Is it not true?[58]

Le Corbusier is fascinated by the precision of machines. Yet it is not naïve optimism with regard to machines that prompts him to present engineers in such a light. According to Le Corbusier, an engineer's construction procedures touch upon the laws of nature; not on the organic principles as they did for Sullivan, but on those of universal harmony, in a way that brings to mind the *harmonia* of the ancient Greeks. To Le Corbusier, the purist and Neo-Platonist, engineers appear to him as 20th-century equivalents of the *demiurge*. Sullivan and Le Corbusier, placed side by side in this field, represent Aristotelian and Platonic thoughts respectively. This juxtaposition also illustrates an important general tendency in the development of functionalism: in the time after World War I, Le Corbusier's thoughts gain ever more ground, causing a fundamental shift in views on artistic creation from the Aristotelian to the Platonic.

The craftsmanship aspect of art draws attention to what is logical and ordered, a focus that concerns the understanding of each material's own will. Any material, be it newly invented or thoroughly traditional, has qualities that must be understood and worked with skill and dexterity. These insights cause Heinz Tiessen to connect *funktionelle Sachlichkeit* to "der gemeinsame Geist des *Handwerklichen*" (the shared spirit of craftsmanship).[59] The

---

[58]*Towards a New Architecture*, 19-20.

[59]*Zur Geschichte der jüngsten Musik (1913-1918)*, 58f.

creative process is lifted out of the shadowy, purple night of Romanticism into the daylight of the 20th century. Artistic activity thus remains legitimate even in a modern age of electricity and technology.

The concept that defines the relationship between craft and creation is that of truth—the crucial notion for honest approaches to artistic materials at the time. Hence truthfulness became the guiding principle for artists' stance in the creative process.

According to Schoenberg, technique and creative ability cannot be separated from each other.[60] As he says in the opening chapter to his *Theory of Harmony* (*Harmonielehre*): "If I should succeed in teaching the pupil the handicraft of our art as completely as a carpenter can teach his, then I shall be satisfied."[61] While this statement is not sensational—most people would agree that every form of art has important craftsmanship aspects—it leads Schoenberg to an interesting follow-up: "And I would be proud if, to adapt a familiar saying, I could say: 'I have *taken* from composition pupils a bad *aesthetics* and have *given* them in return a good *course in handicraft*.'" Much can be said about the state of aesthetics in the early 1900s, at the time when Schoenberg wrote these words. Aesthetics was usually associated with the faded beauty and empty aestheticism of yesteryear, with conventional and conservative views of the concept of art. The nucleus of Schoenberg's views is that traditional aesthetics absorbs "the thoughtlessness of the thought." A manuscript written in June 1934, *Der musikalische Gedanke*, contains the following caustic observation:

> The idea that a musician might show logic or even a brain terrifies those aestheticians who thrive not only on someone else's mindlessness but even more on their own.[62]

When Schoenberg suggests to replace aesthetics with a theory of the craft that is the particular art form's *raison d'être*, he is thus moving toward a concept of aesthetics that is new compared to the common views of his time. Aesthetics should not only embrace the beautiful, but also what in Schoenberg's understanding is truthful. Before the publication of his *Harmonielehre* (*Theory of Harmony*) in 1911, Schoenberg presented his plans for several textbooks to his publisher Emil Hertzka at Universal Edition. These

---

[60] See A. Schoenberg, "Problems in Teaching Art," *Style and Idea: Selected Writings of Arnold Schoenberg,* Leonard Stein, ed.; Leo Black, trans. (Berkeley, CA etc.: University of California Press, 1984), 365-369.

[61] A. Schoenberg, *Theory of Harmony,* Roy E. Carter, trans., (Berkeley, CA : University of California Press, 1983), 12.

[62] A. Schoenberg, *The Musical Idea and the Logic, Technique, and Art of Its Presentation*, P. Carpenter and S. Neff, eds. and trans. (New York: Columbia University Press, 1995), 150.

books, Schoenberg said, were components of what would become a comprehensive *aesthetics of music*.[63] The craft concept as Schoenberg presents it in the introduction to his *Theory of Harmony* must not be understood as a radical rejection of aesthetics, but rather as a pointer to the importance of giving this concept a stronger content of truthfulness.

Schoenberg holds that craftsmanship is fundamentally necessary if one wants to create. When Carl Dahlhaus emphasizes that Schoenberg is above all true to his roots in the 19th century's cult of inspiration and genius,[64] he seems to tone down Schoenberg's conviction that the way from the genius's visionary inspiration to what finally becomes a perfected work of art is long and wearisome:

> Alas, human creators, if they be granted a vision, must travel the long path between vision and accomplishment; a hard road where, driven out of Paradise, even geniuses must reap their harvest in the sweat of their brows.[65]

Such is the painstaking process entailed in compositional craftsmanship, although Schoenberg seldom uses the term but usually speaks of *construction*. His keyword is *Gedanke* (thought), which he employs in a way that embraces impulse, idea, plan, etc. Thought thus apprehended is realized through the process of musical construction, and Schoenberg frequently refers to the thoughts and the intellectual aspects of the compositional procedure. "Composing is: *thinking in tones and rhythms*," he says.[66] (Schoenberg's concept of thought will be explored in greater detail in later chapters.) Schoenberg had a profound wish to share his thoughts on music and the craft of his art. The greater part of his life was dedicated to teaching composition and theory.

The title of Hindemith's textbook, *Unterweisung im Tonsatz* I (English: *The Craft of Musical Composition*),[67] similarly reflects the notion that what composers customarily do is put tones together. To a much greater degree

---

[63] A. Schoenberg, *Coherence, Counterpoint, Instrumentation, Instruction in Form / ZKIF: Zusammenhang, Kontrapunkt, Instrumentation, Formenlehre*, C. Cross and S. Neff, eds, and trans. (Lincoln, NE etc.: University of Nebraska Press, 1994), XXIII.

[64] See C. Dahlhaus, "Musikalischer Funktionalismus," *Schönberg und andere. Gesammelte Aufsätze zur Neuen Musik* (Mainz: Schott, 1978), 61.

[65] A. Schoenberg "Composition with Twelve Tones (1)," *Style and Idea: Selected Writings of Arnold Schoenberg*, L. Stein and L. Black, eds. and trans. (Berkeley, CA etc.: University of California Press, 1975), 215.

[66] A. Schoenberg, *The Musical Idea*, 370.

[67] P. Hindemith, *Unterweisung im Tonsatz* I: *Theoretischer Teil* (Mainz: Schott, 1937); English: *The Craft of Musical Composition* I, *Theory*, Arthur Mendel, trans. (London: Schott, 1942).

Craft and Creation than Schoenberg, Hindemith ties the terminology of craftsmanship to the creative process. A humorous example can be seen in the statement:

> When one goes to the tailor, one doesn't want his picture or photograph taken but a well-tailored suit. If anyone wants to involve himself with me, he should look at my works.[68]

When he compares the composer to a tailor in a way that resembles Schoenberg's reference to composition as carpentry, Hindemith's simile seems even more down to earth than that of his Austrian counterpart. There is undoubtedly an essential difference between Schoenberg and Hindemith, one that goes beyond conceptual nuances: in Hindemith's writings, the anti-romantic attitudes of the 1920s are dominant. And yet, it would not be correct to say that it is a romantic versus anti-romantic attitude that causes their views to differ. Rather, the difference lies in the dichotomy of construction and craftsmanship. Construction, in the sense introduced by Sullivan, represents a transition from the romantic view toward the 20th century, while craftsmanship, fully realized in 20th-century recognition, describes the objective alternative to the genius cult of the past. Schoenberg and Hindemith meet on a deeper level, where both regard an understanding of the importance of musical craftsmanship in its widest sense as fundamental for the realization of a genuine work of art.

Hindemith is intensively engaged in the vast field of musical craftsmanship. *The Craft of Musical Composition* demonstrates an assumed need to equip the reader with satisfactory proficiency and a reliable technique. "Technical skill can never be great enough. No one is too able or too accomplished to learn more then he knows," he states in the introductory chapter.[69] Hindemith's book is laid out as a presentation of his understanding of musical material. This material's true characteristics must be treated with the necessary skill, a request reminiscent of the functionalist approach. Hindemith does not consider craftsmanship as sufficient in itself; it is not here that the seminal creative force lies. Mastering the craft is rather regarded as the technical foundation for any musical creation, and the advantage of this element of the composition process is that it can in fact be taught and learned.[70] Hindemith finds his exemplars in the medieval attitudes to craftsmanship:

---

[68]Translated from A. Briner, *Paul Hindemith* (Zurich/Mainz: Atlantis/Schott, 1971), 9.

[69]*The Craft of Musical Composition* I, 11.

[70]See P. Hindemith, "Komposition und Kompositionsunterricht," *Aufsätze, Vorträge, Reden*, G. Schubert, ed. (Zürich/Mainz: Atlantis, 1994), 53.

> In this attitude toward the technical side of composition I am in agreement with views which were held long before the classic masters. We find such views in early antiquity, and far-sighted composers of the Middle Ages and of modern times hold firmly to them and pass them on.[71]

This brings Hindemith's view of craftsmanship into the perspective drawn by John Ruskin in the 19th century and the Bauhaus artists in the 20th, all of whom looked upon the ideals of the Middle Ages as patterns applicable to the technological age. There is nothing in Hindemith's thoughts that indicates that he would want to stress craftsmanship at the cost of the aesthetic element. Generally, the focus on craft at this time is on the recognizable aspects of the creative process. As will also be seen later, such focus does not exclude the fundamental importance of inspiration at the expense of more or less prosaic technical procedures. Artistic inspiration is not, however, seen as being given in the form of ingenious individuals' constant enthusiasm, but rather as a clarifying ray of light. Owing to its roots in Romanticism, the new century's concept of inspiration is above all one of *light*—not the constant brightness of rational enlightenment but rather the unexpected and fleeting glint. Gropius says as much in his Bauhaus manifesto, formulated on the occasion of the school's opening in 1919:

> *Artists are intensified craftsmen.* In rare moments of light that are beyond their volition and awareness, heavenly grace allows art to bloom from their hands' work.[72]

Artists must be able to seize these precious moments of light and let their craft and skill form a work. For Schoenberg, such a flash of inspiration is like an unfolding in extended temporal dimensions: "Inspiration is a lightening-like appearance of extraordinary duration, which dissipates slowly and ends only a long time after it has fulfilled its purpose."[73]

The concept of inspiration often leads to that of *vision*. Sullivan considered man's greatest talent or strength, the spiritual, represented in what he called "a super-quality of vision." Schoenberg also uses the word "vision," as does Hindemith, who declares vision the privilege of the genius and ties it to inspiration. The similarity between this description and Schoenberg's definition is obvious:

---

[71]P. Hindemith, *The Craft of Musical Composition,* 12.

[72]Translated from a facsimile in M. Droste, *Bauhaus 1919-1933* (Cologne: Benedikt Taschen, 1993), 18.

[73]A. Schoenberg, *The Musical Idea,* 375.

> What is a musical vision? We all know the impression of a very heavy flash of lightening in the night. Within a second's time we see a broad landscape, not only in its general outlines but with every detail. Although we could never describe each single component of the picture, we feel that not even the smallest leaf of grass escapes our attention. We experience a view, immensely comprehensive and at the same time immensely detailed, that we never could have under normal daylight conditions, and perhaps not during the night either, if our senses and nerves were not strained by the extraordinary suddenness of the event. Compositions must be conceived the same way. If we cannot, in the flash of a single moment, see a composition in its absolute entirety, with every pertinent detail in its proper place, we are not genuine creators.[74]

It may seem as if Hindemith were denying his profound belief in craftsmanship, considering instead only those creators genuine who are able immediately to realize their visions. Were composers truly the equivalents to a *demiurge*, visions could certainly materialize without wearisome preambles. Yet composers are of earthly origin and therefore must wander the thorny path toward the work's realization, supported only by the skills they have acquired. Consequently, they cannot ever bypass craftsmanship.

In a similar vein, Schoenberg expresses what he regards as separating the divine creator's sphere from that of terrestrials:

> A creator has a vision of something which has not existed before this vision. And a creator has the power to bring his vision to life, the power to realize it. In fact, the concept of creator and creation should be formed in harmony with the Divine Model; inspiration and perfection, wish and fulfilment, will and accomplishment coincide spontaneously and simultaneously. In Divine Creation there were no details to be carried out later; 'There was Light' at once and in its ultimate perfection.[75]

For both Hindemith and Schoenberg the creative artist is thus indebted to the divine model. It is characteristic of Hindemith that he visualizes the *demiurge*, as does Le Corbusier, while Schoenberg takes his cues from the *Genesis* of the Old Testament. Crucially in these images, the earthbound creator has quite a different path to wander, and it is this path that Schoenberg and Hindemith endeavor to make plain. The common denominator for

---

[74] P. Hindemith, *A Composer's World: Horizons and Limitations* (Harvard: Harvard University Press, 1952), 71.
[75] "Composition with Twelve Tones (1)," *Style and Idea,* 215.

the work of the hand and that of the spirit lies in the road that leads from artistic vision to the specific work of art. Even with earthly working procedures, the creative process is not deprived of its deep-seated spiritual dimensions.

Hindemith ends his book *A Composer's World: Horizons and Limitations,* with reflections on musicians' humility. His concluding words give both his own and many of his contemporaries' understanding of the compositional craft its relevant dimensions. Schoenberg would have been ready to endorse such sentiments:

> The ultimate reason for this humility will be the musician's conviction that beyond all the rational knowledge he has amassed and all his dexterity as a craftsman there is a region of visionary irrationality in which the veiled secrets of art dwell, sensed but not understood, implored but not commanded, imparting but not yielding. He cannot enter this region, he can only pray to be elected one of its messengers. If his prayers are granted and he, armed with wisdom and gifted with reverence for the unknowable, is the man whom heaven has blessed with the genius of creation, we may see in him the donor of the precious present we all long for: the great music of our time.[76]

The Organic Form as Construction

The rejection of ornamentation is decisive for the development of functionalist form. As the 19th century turned into the 20th, surface ornamentation was increasingly considered as a camouflage for a truthful expression of art and culture. When all external decoration is banned and consequently removed, even the understanding of form and material is fundamentally affected. In *Jugendstil*—by contrast—ornamentation was regarded as representing a structuring and form-constituting factor where the ideal of artistic truth manifests in supposedly truthful, natural growth, often in asymmetric undulating movements played out against a symmetric framework. Since another inspiration for *Jugendstil* came from the geometric forms of Japanese art, which enjoyed great popularity during the late 19th century, both the *arabesque* and the *kaleidoscope* have their place in this picture, anticipating some of the metaphors used by the Viennese music critic and musicologist Eduard Hanslick.

---

[76]*A Composer's World*, 257.

FIGURE 2: Side table, ca. 1903-05, attributed to Josef Hoffmann

Sullivan, too, holds that ornamentation can be considered genuinely organic, and does not consider this view as constituting a conflict with his position as one of the fathers of modern architecture. As seen above, Sullivan praised "the master craftsman" as the purest representative of man's inherent creative potential. In his *Kindergarten Chats*, a collection of short texts first published in 1901, he shows a tendency to revelatory and unctuous wording similar to that used by Loos and Le Corbusier, usually with a fine touch of humor and irony. Toward the end of the 1920s, Sullivan's dictum "form follows function" was often cited in support of the view that the mass-producible result of the object's external purpose should determine its form— if necessary, at the cost of artistic and aesthetic considerations. Even today, such views continue to have currency. Yet as already pointed out, this application misrepresents Sullivan's thought. One reason why his assertion can easily be misunderstood is that the word "function" invites reduction to "functional use." For Sullivan, function indicates above all the *character* of a given phenomenon, or its authentic *purpose*—the attributes that make it what it *is*. For this reason, there must be an indissoluble connection between the object's function and form: "outward appearances resemble inner purposes," as Sullivan puts it.[75] These aspects of the object are interrelated, and this interrelation has different levels and virtually limitless dimensions. He gives a number of examples of the connection between form and function, for instance:

---

[75] L.H. Sullivan, "Function and Form (1)," *Kindergarten Chats,* 43.

> [...] the form, oak-tree, resembles and expresses the purpose or function, oak; [...] the form, horse, resembles and is the logical output of the function, horse; [...] the form, wave, looks like the function, wave; [...] the form, full-blown rose, recites the poem, full-blown rose. And so does the form, man, stand for the function, man: the form, John Doe, means the function, John Doe; the form, smile, makes us aware of the function, smile; so, when I say: a man named John Doe smiles, – we have a little series of functions and forms which are inseparably related, and yet they seem very casual to us.[76]

Behind every form there is something we do not see, and it is exactly *this* which realizes itself in a form. Function is the form's cause, says Sullivan. Were one to relate Sullivan's thought to Aristotelian views, one could say that the object's function is identical with its determination: the object realizes its determination through its form. The same kind of Aristotelian thought also manifests when Sullivan regards the unfolding of creative processes in nature. The work must be an organism that can be described as

> possessed of a life of its own; an individual life that functions in all its parts; and which finds its variations in expression in the variations of its main function, and in the consequent, continuous, systematic variations in form, as the organic complexity of expression unfolds [...].[77]

As will be explored in more detail in later chapters of this book, Schoenberg is a spokesman for corresponding views in the field of music, stressing the relationship between a work as a whole and its constitutional components. Sullivan asserts that organism, structure, function, growth, development, and form are all essential dimensions of the organic principle. They are brought into being by "the initiating pressure of a living force." Function represents the impetus that drives the object forward toward realization: "The pressure, we call Function: the resultant, Form. Hence the law of function and form is discernible throughout nature."[78]

"All is function," says Sullivan.[79] His concept of function is all-embracing, and so, too, is his concept of form: "Form is everything and anything, everywhere and at every instant."[80] Since functions can be so very disparate, the basic nature of form must also vary, because

---

[76]"Function and Form (1)," 43.

[77]L.H. Sullivan, "On Poetry," *Kindergarten Chats,* 158.

[78]L.H. Sullivan, "Growth and Decay," *Kindergarten Chats,* 48.

[79]"Function and Form (1)," 45.

[80]Ibid.

The Organic Form as Construction

> [...] some forms are definite, some indefinite; some are nebulous, others concrete and sharp; some symmetrical, others purely rhythmical. Some are abstract, others material. Some appeal to the eye, some to the ear, some to the touch, some to the sense of smell, some to any one or all or any combination of these.[81]

Consequently, *musical* form—the artistic form appealing to the ear—also finds its place within Sullivan's "form follows function." All forms have a recognizable common denominator representing the relationship between what is immaterial and what is material, what is subjective and what is objective—as he says, the relation between "the Infinite Spirit and the finite mind."[82] Form is at the same time concrete and abstract. The empiricist Sullivan considers all human recognition as being dependent on the senses. Imagination, intuition, and reason are all elevated levels of a physical ability to perceive, and it is within these limits that the experience of form exists.

In Sullivan's opinion, empty words and phrases have diverted the attention from real awareness of function and form, not least in the domains of architecture: "Finally phrase-making has come to be an accepted substitute for architecture-making," he complains.[83] When Sullivan addresses his own metier, his question is: what is the fundamental function of architecture? The construction of buildings, like the creation of other artistic objects, manifests in function and form. This should appear in full clarity:

> Now, as we together are seeking the sense of *things*, as we are searching out *realities*, let us pronounce now, once and for all, that the architecture we seek is to be a reality in function and form and that that reality shall unfold within the progressing clarity of our view.[84]

That architecture has an utilitarian function is self-evident, and this fact must never be concealed. "The true work of the architect is to organize, integrate and glorify UTILITY. Then and then only is he truly a MASTER-WORKER," Sullivan writes, with abundant use of capital letters.[85] A restricted relationship to the serviceable function still does not necessarily result in "good" architecture. A building must have an organic quality based on organic thought, a prerequisite that is in no way identical with *logical* quality. Tight logic, knowledge, and so-called taste are certainly not enough. Such

---

[81]"Function and Form (1)," 45.

[82]Ibid.

[83]"Growth and Decay," 49.

[84]Ibid.

[85]L.H. Sullivan, "What is an Architect?" *Kindergarten Chats*, 141.

driving forces can easily give a dry, cold, or meaningless result. The real architect to Sullivan's mind is characterized by three main qualities:

> First of all poetic imagination; second a broad sympathy, humane character, common sense and a thoroughly disciplined mind; third, a perfected technique; and, finally, an abundant and gracious gift of expression.[86]

Even within architecture serving obvious utilitarian ends, poetic aspects and expression thus play a considerable role in Sullivan's request concerning form and function. This perspective was by and large forgotten in the alienating, standardizing tendencies that characterized architecture between the wars—tendencies for which Sullivan is wrongfully held responsible.

The ideas Sullivan expresses in *A System of Architectural Ornament* are similarly based on the premise that "form follows function." The organic principle, considered crucially important, can be realized through mathematical construction. For musical construction, as will be shown later, it is this fundamental idea that is essential—not Sullivan's thoughts on ornamentation as such.

Another important aspect in this context is Sullivan's approach to ornamentation used as a decorative phenomenon. Two features are typical for his own minute ornaments: they seem to spring directly from the surface or segment they are meant to embellish, and they are usually geometric in their basic construction—and, as the architectural historian Kenneth Frampton puts it, "there is always something decidedly Islamic about Sullivan's disposition of decoration."[87] In Frampton's opinion, the Islamic flavor has its roots in Sullivan's studies of Owen Jones's *Grammar of Ornament*,[88] where well over half of the examples are of non-European origin. Geometric severity is the hallmark of Sullivan's architecture. It may seem strange that he who, together with the engineer Dankmar Adler, is usually considered the real pioneer of the skyscraper,[89] should be favorably disposed to ornamentation. Frampton interprets the decorative element in the works of both Sullivan and his apprentice and later co-worker Frank Lloyd Wright (1867-1959) as an attempt to find a style suitable to represent the New World.[90]

---

[86]"Function and Form (2)," 48.

[87]K. Frampton, *Modern Architecture: A Critical History* (London etc.: Thames and Hudson, 1992) 54.

[88]O. Jones, *The Grammar of Ornament* (London: Bernard Quaritch, 1868).

[89]This honor, however, is mostly attributed to William Le Baron Jenny for his *Home Insurance Company Building* in Chicago (1884). See also J. Carlsen, "Skyskraperens tyranni," *Byggekunst no. 3* (Oslo 1990), 162-165.

[90]*Modern Architecture,* 57.

The Organic Form as Construction

In asserting that ornament is not an indispensable element of architecture, Sullivan proves himself very much a man of the 20th century. He begins his essay "Ornament in Architecture"[91] by pointing out that a building devoid of ornament can give a feeling of nobility and sublimity through the mere force of its mass and proportions. It is by no means certain that ornaments are able to enhance these fundamental qualities. On the contrary, it would develop our aesthetic sense to refrain totally from the use of ornamentation for some years. Then our feeling of form would be strengthened; we would discover how effective it is to think in a natural, vigorous, and healthy way.[92] After such a period of deliberate restraint, we would look upon ornamentation as a mental luxury, not as a necessity, since we would have realized both the limitations and the great values of unadorned buildings. Sullivan, a child of the 19th century, cannot ignore the fact that we all are bearers of romantic attitudes and have the urge to give them proper expression. He knows that the poetic aspect, which he considers so important for architectonic expression, is particularly manifest in ornamentation, and that even with our supposedly renewed consciousness of form we still have a need for poetry:

> We feel intuitively that our strong, athletic and simple forms will carry with natural ease the raiment of which we dream, and that our buildings thus clad in a garment of poetic imagery, half hid as it were in choice products of loom and mine, will appeal with redoubled power, like a sonorous melody overlaid with harmonious voices.[93]

Crucial for the way in which Sullivan understands ornamentation is his emphasis on the symbiotic relationship between structure and decoration—a relationship mirrored in music's interdependence of melody and harmony. Ornaments must grow out of the material's substance; they will only convince if they do not look as though they were pasted onto the surface:

> It must be manifest that an ornamental design will be more beautiful if it seems a part of the surface or substance that receives it than if it looks 'stuck on', so to speak. A little observation will lead one to see that in the former case there exists a peculiar sympathy between the ornament and the structure, which is absent in the latter. Both structure and ornament obviously benefit by this

---

[91]"Ornament and Architecture" was first published in *The Engineering Magazine*, August 1892. It is also included in *Kindergarten Chats,* 187-190, the source that is used here.
[92]"Ornament and Architecture," 187.
[93]Ibid.

sympathy; each enhancing the value of the other. And this, I take it, is the preparatory basis of what may be called an organic system of ornamentation.[94]

The germ is recognized as the real thing, the seat of identity. In an art-historical perspective, Sullivan's affinity to ideas of the Arts and Crafts movement as well as *Jugendstil* is obvious. Two tenets make him interesting for approaches to musical functionalism. The first regards his view of form as the realization of function. Function can be concerned with use or utility, but only when this is considered the essential determination of the resulting object: A teapot must serve to pour tea, in the same way as decoration must be beautifying. Judged on the basis of Sullivan's views, Hindemith's contributions to *Gebrauchsmusik* and *Sing- und Spielmusik* would not be regarded as any more functional than Schoenberg's *Pierrot Lunaire*. The other interesting tenet, referring again to the relationship between form and function, is Sullivan's view of ornamentation as *organic*. Humans have the ability to construct according to what Sullivan describes as natural principles. The seed, he says, contains the nutrition that makes development possible; yet it is the *germ* that represents the seat of power. Herein lie both the true identity and the will to develop:

> Within this delicate mechanism lies the will to power: the function which is to seek and eventually to find its full expression in form.[95]

Schoenberg attributes a similar status to the musical motive, although he would have reservations about taking the biological analogies too far. Yet a metaphor quite common in the Second Viennese School is *Urzelle*. This term was originally used by Viennese architects, among them Otto Wagner, who is often described as the father of Viennese modernism.

The continuum in the transition from seed to shoot also manifests visually; Sullivan refers to "manipulating the organic." In *A System of Architectural Ornament,* he shows how the simple leaf structure can be expanded into more complex forms. Such complex leaf structures are *technically* derivations of the simple form, but *organically* expressions of different identities of the seed. With the help of these manipulative principles inspired by nature, Sullivan demonstrates the construction of a perfected, artificial ornament (see FIGURE 3 on the facing page).

---

[94]"Ornament and Architecture," 189.

[95]L.H. Sullivan, *A System of Architectural Ornament* (n. p.)

The Organic Form as Construction

FIGURE 3: L.H. Sullivan, "Manipulation of the organic," *A System of Architectural Ornament,* from "plate 2"

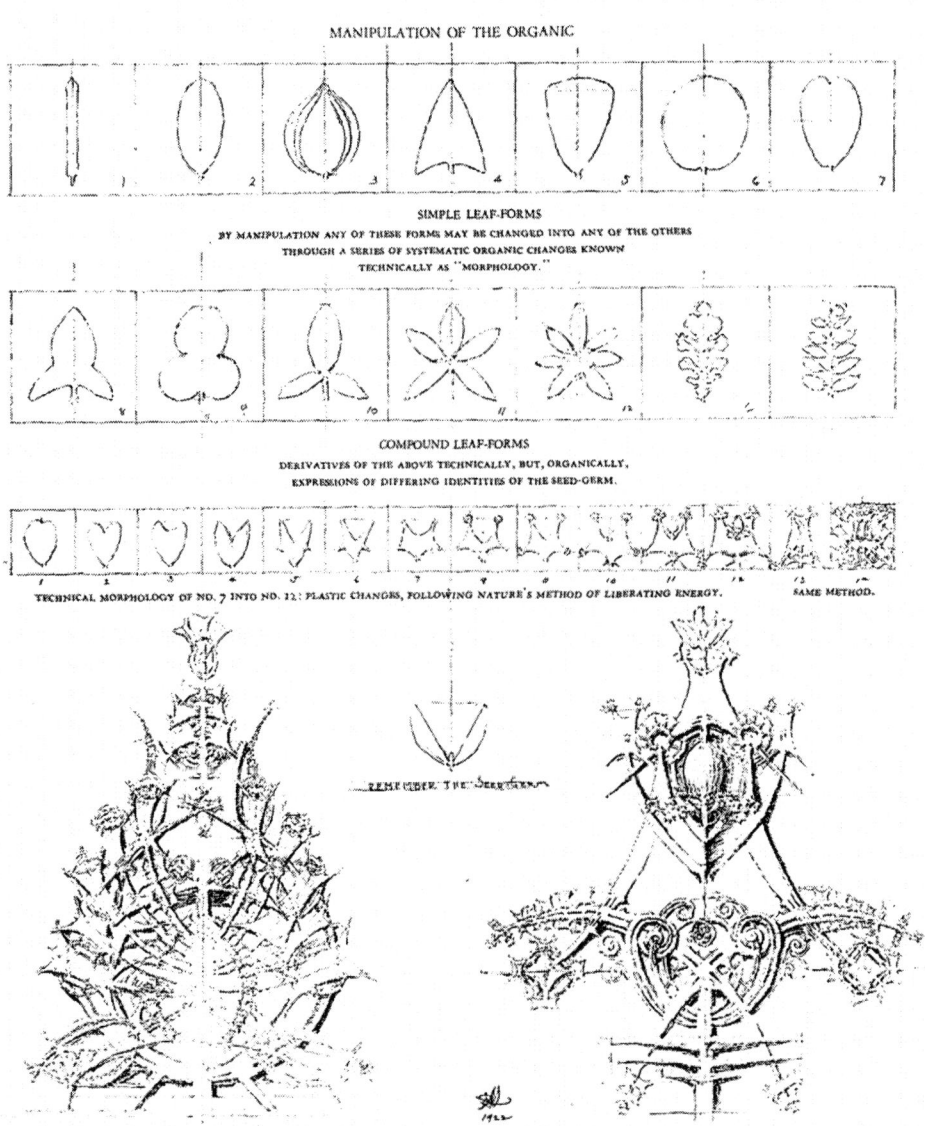

Sullivan had an almost limitless belief in the human ability to create. A creative individual must not let anything remain in its inorganic status:

> His spiritual power masters the inorganic and causes it to live in forms which his imagination brings forth from the lifeless, the amorphous. He thus transmutes into the image of his passion that which itself has no such power. Thus man in his power brings forth that which hitherto was non-existent."[96]

This would seem to be yet another expression of Schlegel's definition of man's creative ability. Sullivan takes what is rationally based and mathematically constructive as his point of departure. The fundamental forms of mathematical geometry are examples of inorganic phenomena, he says. In antiquity, esoteric meanings and occult forces were associated with them as an expression of the human need to control destiny and hold the destructive power of natural forces at bay. In Sullivan's own time, however, as the elevated and free human individual can manipulate the basic forms in accordance with the principles of nature, a new faith has arisen: a faith in *man*.[97]

When Sullivan manipulates artistic forms in plane geometry, he starts with a circle divided into four sectors. Drawing a triangle into the radius, then a square, a pentagon, etc., he creates a design of ever-increasing complexity. Working on these principles, Sullivan then constructs an ornament that will stand as an expression of his very personal style (see FIGURE 4 on the facing page).

In order to grasp this fusion between the organic and the inorganic, which is represented in one impulse—itself an expression of the human will —it is important to understand that geometric forms are bearers of energy, Sullivan says:

> [....] the rigid geometric form is considered as a container of energy upon which a germinal, liberating will is imposed by man's free choice, intelligence and skill. The plant organism derives its impulse from the seed-germ, and in its growth develops sub-centres of further growth. The seed-germ may thus be considered also as a container of energy, forming of its own will sub-centres of energy in the course of its functioning development toward the finality of its characteristic form—the expression of its identity."[98]

---

[96] *A System of Architectural Ornament.*

[97] *A System of Architectural Ornament,* text accompanying Plate 3.

[98] *A System of Architectural Ornament*, text accompanying Plate 4.

The Organic Form as Construction

FIGURE 4: L.H. Sullivan, "The Inorganic. Manipulation of forms in plane-geometry," *A System of Architectural Ornament,* "plate 3"

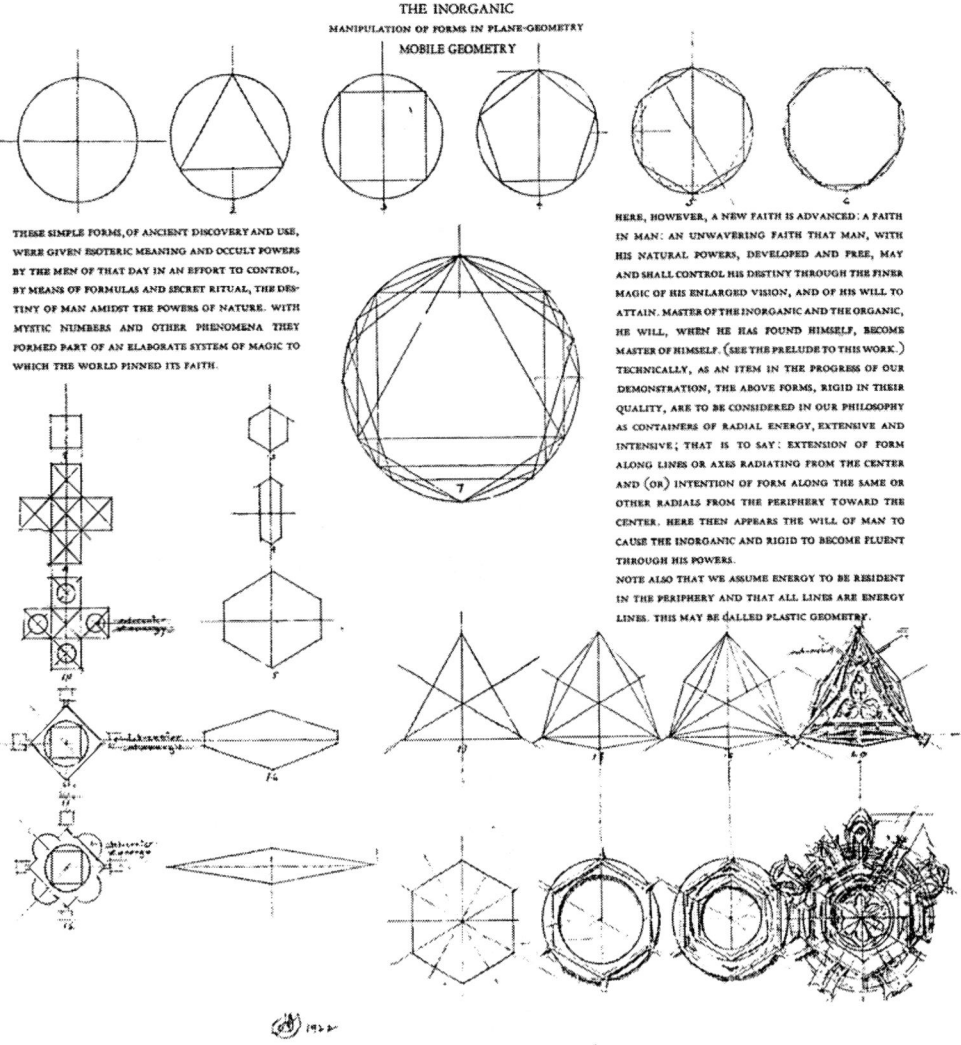

Sullivan believed that construction both channels and expresses genuine creative power. In the context of musical thought, this notion is of great importance for the positive attitude toward the idea of construction that is so fundamental to theories in the 20th century. The general emphasis on construction, in turn, paves the way for an increased focus on basic shapes and, subsequently, for the predilection for standard forms, a tendency also found in music.

Form and Norm

In the 1890s, during a three-year sojourn in the United States, Adolf Loos became familiar with the new trends in American architecture. He was particularly impressed with the thoughts of Louis Sullivan, whose "Ornament in Architecture" evidently inspired Loos's famous "Ornament und verbrechen."

"Ornament und verbrechen" became a beacon in the development of functionalism. Loos's biographers Rukschcio and Schachel believe that his entire architectural theory is compacted into this brief essay.[99] The idea to collocate ornament with crime was probably inspired by Karl Kraus, and the unusual pairing may have contributed to the frequent misquotation as "Ornament *ist* Verbrechen"—ornament is crime. This "variant," which turns a thought-provoking juxtaposition into something akin to a slogan, expresses a lack of understanding for the nuances in Loos's message. Loos has no bias against ornamentation as an artistic or socio-cultural occurrence; his view is rather that ornament has outlived itself and is no longer adequate: "As there is no longer any organic connection between ornament and our culture, ornament is no longer an expression of our culture."[100] Human development constantly aspires to higher levels, says Loos, in words that ring with associations to Hegelian and Darwinian thought:

> Ornament can no longer be reproduced by someone living on the cultural level of today. It is different for individuals and people who have not reached that level.[101]

Loos's comment on ornamentation contains a cultural criticism reminiscent of those uttered by Schoenberg and, even more distinctly, by Kraus. Loos's ideal was England and the cultivated Englishman, and he considered it one of his primary tasks to raise his countrymen to a corresponding level, as had Gottfried Semper many years before him. Loos's journal *Das Andere* (The Other), a short-lived project of the year 1903, had the apt subtitle *Ein Blatt zur Einfuehrung abendlaendischer Kultur in Oesterreich* (A magazine for the introduction of occidental culture to Austria). One of Loos's most frequently quoted statements can be understood in this educational perspective:

> I made the following discovery, which I passed on to the world: *the evolution of culture is synonymous with the removal of ornamentation from the objects of everyday use.*[102]

---

[99] See B. Rukschcio and R. Schachel, *Adolf Loos. Leben und Werk,* 118.

[100] A. Loos, "Ornament and Crime," *Ornament and Crime: Selected Essays,* 171.

[101] "Ornament and Crime," 173.

[102] "Ornament and Crime," 167.

Form and Norm

Ornaments belong to an earlier stage of development, and Loos connects them to crime. To get a sense of the many ingenious ways in which he makes that surprising connection, here are a few examples: It is, he says, no crime for a Papuan to kill his enemy and then eat him. But if a so-called modern person does the same, it is considered a felony, a degenerate act. Papuans tattoo practically everything they come across without therefore being regarded as criminals. "The modern person who tattoos himself," however, "is either a criminal or a degenerate."[103] Most significant in an artistic and cultural-historical perspective is Loos's view that the supposedly criminal act of ornamentation leads to a waste of manpower, material, and ultimately, of capital. Loos goes so far as to use the term violated material. "And as for decorating fine materials, perfect in themselves, with ornamentation? 'Improving' fine mahogany with purple stain? These are crimes."[104] This statement certainly contains a socio-economic aspect; at the same time, it harkens back to the principle of *Materialgerechtigkeit*, according to which the task of a material is to provide the essential substance, not to support what is superfluous and a mere waste. In this way the *material itself* is realized in the form:

> I want the material itself, suitably finished. A ring is a hoop-shaped piece of good gold. A cigarette case means two flat trays of good silver, perfectly smooth. The beautiful smoothness of polished silver, so fine to the touch, is the best ornamentation.[105]

Loos's views are grounded in his refined aesthetic sense, which perceives greatness in what is unornamented, simple and clearly defined. In his 1908 article "Kulturentartung," he emphasizes this aspect:

> Are these things beautiful? I'm not asking. They are in the spirit of our time and therefore rightful. [...] But I will go further and not mince words: I think my smooth, slightly curved, precisely formed cigarette case is beautiful, and that gives me a deep aesthetic joy [...].[106]

The goal is a pure, material-based form that has burned itself through its disfiguring veneer, achieving an ideal shape based on what is fundamental, presumably truthful, and unambiguous. In "Ornament und verbrechen," Loos proclaims—in his characteristic style that is full of both pathos and irony:

---

[103]"Ornament and Crime," 167.

[104]The original text, "Von der Sparsamkeit," is based on B. Markalous's collection of Loos statements in *Wohnungskultur* 2/3, 1924. The above quotation is from F.R. Jones, translated as "Regarding economy" in M. Risselda, ed., *Raumplan versus Plan Libre*, 139.

[105]M. Risselda, ed., *Raumplan versus Plan Libre*, 138.

[106]Translated from A. Loos, "Kulturentartung," *Trotzdem*, 273.

Do not weep. Do you not see the greatness of our age resides in our very inability to create new ornament? We have gone beyond ornament, we have achieved plain, undecorated simplicity. Behold, the time is at hand, fulfillment awaits us. Soon the streets of the cities will shine like white walls! Like Zion, the Holy City, Heaven's capital. The fulfillment will be ours.[107]

When architecture is cleared of superfluous ornamentation, attention is involuntarily drawn to its fundamental forms. Consequently, basic forms came to be the strongest bearers of modernist architectural expression. The same applied in design, painting, and, to a certain degree, even in music. Simplicity thus became an essential feature in the development in 20th-century formal language—especially in functionalism: hence the term *functional form*. In this picture, standardization gained decisive importance.

At the beginning of the century, *form and norm* received increased attention in the field of design and architecture. During the years preceding World War I, the discussion of these concepts grew out of the Deutscher Werkbund. In the 1920s, it was even more strongly associated with the growth of the Bauhaus. While the form-and-norm debate was typical of its time, it is also timeless, since it fundamentally concerns the basic preconditions of art. It has been significant for the development of characteristic formal features in the larger part of the 20th century.

What is really meant by "form and norm" in this discourse? The short answer is: standardization of the language of form, in a desire to combine sustainable economic production with a modern, unified style. At closer inspection, the collocation of form and norm reflects the very ideas of artistic creativity. It highlights a dual aim, where *form* as the individual artist's design of a unique work is wedded to *norm*, implying models, types, patterns, or other principles of collectivity. From this basis it is not far to an attitude that would look upon form as expressing individuality and upon norm as representing the universal in the widest sense. A characteristic feature of the development of form in the early 1900s is an initial combination of and subsequent shift from form to norm, from what is individual to what is universal. This shift manifests as a dimension of the move from organic form to basic form.

The Deutscher Werkbund had been founded as an organization that united industrial leaders, workshop owners, artists, writers, politicians, and educators. Its initiator Hermann Muthesius had studied the Arts and Crafts movement and brought a number of important impulses back from his stay in England. Although the association's stated objective was the collaboration with art, industry, and craft, the Werkbund came to embrace industrial

---

[107] A. Loos, "Ornament and Crime," 168.

Form and Norm

production far more than did Arts and Crafts, worried by the recognition that German industry had swiftly developed from strict, technically functional criteria at the cost of aesthetically satisfying design. Consequently, its leaders' primary wish was to cultivate and humanize the growing industrialization while at the same time educating the proverbial man in the street with regard to taste of beauty and quality. The Werkbund, then, came to focus on both the manufacturer and the consumer. Loos, although in other regards no supporter of the Werkbund, was motivated by similar didactic aims, as were Schoenberg and Hindemith.

Right from the start, the Werkbund attracted representatives of various interest groups. In 1909, Peter Behrens built AEG's large turbine factory in Berlin and became responsible for even the smallest of the company's design needs.

FIGURE 5: Peter Behrens, *AEG turbine factory*, Berlin, 1909

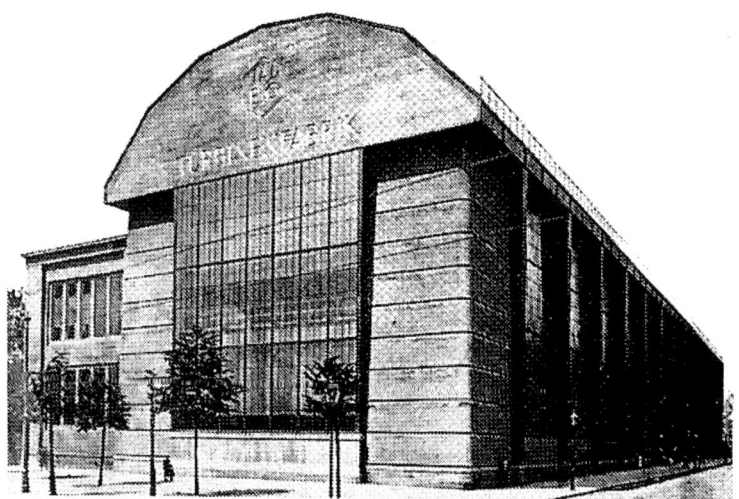

A conscious merging of form and functionality became characteristic for AEG's products: modern, simple houses or casings were adapted to the technical innovations developed by the electronic engineers. Thanks to Behrens, this success launched a tradition of industrial objectivity, a *Sachlichkeit* that focused both on the product as an object and on objective, sober forms. The fruitful link between design and mass-production, and the fortuitous personal relationship between architects Walter Gropius, Ludwig Mies van der Rohe, and Le Corbusier—who all began their careers as fellow designers in Peter Behrens's studios—explains some of the significance Behrens was to have for the understanding of form not only in the 1920s, but throughout the entire 20th century.

FIGURE 6: Peter Behrens, cover illustration, 1908

Another prominent member of the Deutscher Werkbund was Henry van de Velde (1863-1957), the most notable spokesman for *Jugendstil* and interior decoration as a *Gesamtkunstwerk*. Muthesius and van de Velde came to occupy opposing positions in the norm-versus-form debate. Muthesius advocated typification and standardization as an important aspect of restoring a taste that would be universally valid and secure.[108] He believed that standardization would lay the ground for modern methods of manufacture, mass production, and export. Van de Velde championed form, artistic freedom, and an artist's right to individual design. He abhorred the idea of adaptation to mass production and of export as the objective of art. As long as the Werkbund consisted of artists, he claimed, they would protest the typifications imposed on them; standardizing could only occur as a result of genuine *Kunstwollen* (artistic volition).[109] The most agonizing discussion on this issue took place during the Werkbund's 1914 general assembly. At this time, van de Velde's view received solid support from significant leaders such as Behrens and Gropius.

In the long run, it was Hermann Muthesius's vision that had the greater importance for the further development of industrial design. The 1920s became the heyday of standardization. At this time, industrial rationalization ensured Germany's restoration as a nation and the country's position in the world market. In many areas, the United States served as the role model, and two Americans in particular stood out as exemplars in the development of industrial and commodity-based techniques: Henry Ford (1863-1947) with his theories on economics and mass production, and Frederick Winslow Taylor (1865-1915), who initiated the painstaking research on the optimal

---

[108] See G. Selle, *Design-Geschichte in Deutschland*, 127.

[109] The concept of *Kunstwollen* is attributed to the art historian Alois Riegl.

Form and Norm

use of time, elimination of inactivity, analysis of spatial needs, and functional human adaptation to the production process. Both men left their mark on language: Ford with the name of the company newspaper of the Opel factory in Rüsselheim, *Am laufenden Band*—a title that literally translates as "at the moving conveyor belt" but has entered the German vernacular as simply meaning "without interruption"—and Taylor in giving his name to Taylorism, which led to the so-called psychotechniques: psychological and physiological tests of workers' qualification for various tasks. Taylorism soon found application outside the realm of industrial design and thus reached the majority of the people in the Weimar Republic, particularly in two areas. The extensive production of artificial limbs in the aftermath of the War, which were adapted at the same time to the inpacitated worker and the machine, contributed greatly to the optimistic attitude toward machines. Concurrently, the idea of subsistence housing and Margarete Schütte-Lihotzky's trend-setting "Frankfurter Küche"—a kitchen of extraordinary compactness—introduced Taylorism into the lives of average families and housewives.

Americanization, the belief in a vibrant and modern society, and an overall confidence in machinery's rhythm and dynamics caused an avalanche of standardization and rationalization. In 1930 Max Rössiger wrote:

> Rationalization, mechanization, the slogans of the new age. The economy no longer rocks in waltz time, neither does it stride anymore in march tempo, its music is of breathless power full of mind-distracting dissonance.[110]

The Bauhaus had its halcyon days owing not only to the increasing demand for standardization that accompanied mass production, but also to its more exclusive and presumably timeless, universal design. The keyword "universality" in turn leads back to developmental processes within the functionalist understanding of form.

When ornamentation is removed, one approaches the basic form, the fundamental, strictly necessary *gestalt*. From this point it is not far until the basic form becomes an end in itself. The Suprematist works of the Russian painter and designer Kasimir Malewitsch (1878-1935) may serve as an illustration. In the years 1914-15, Malewitsch painted his well-known Black square on a white background, which he described as his age's "naked, unframed icon."[111] His *Black Rectangle* of 1933 pertains to the same idea:

---

[110]Translated from M. Rössiger, *Die Angestellte um 1930*, Berlin, p. 80, quoted in *Tanz auf dem Vulkan, Normierung I* (Mannheim: Landesmuseum für Technik und Arbeit, 1994), 11.

[111]Translated from R.W. Gassen, "Wege der Abstraktion. Auf der Suche nach einer neuen Wirklichkeit," *Die Neue Wirklichkeit. Abstraktion als Weltentwurf*, R.W. Gassen and Bernhard Holeczek, eds. (Ludwigshafen: Wilhelm-Hack-Museum, 1994), 18.

FIGURE 7: Kasimir Malewitsch, *Black Rectangle*, 1933

Malewitsch formulated his objective as "liberating art from the world of objects."[112] By freeing the object through uncompromising abstraction, guided by the idea that basic forms are rooted in cosmological order, he felt he could claim what he called "the supremacy of pure feeling."[113] The artistic liberation from representations chained to the world of objects was thus brought about through a change of direction toward geometric forms and figures, toward basic forms. These constituted a new pictorial language, which on the one hand was considered to rest in itself and, on the other, to reach beyond itself. For Malewitsch, the painted square or rectangle was more than geometry; it constituted a sign of dynamic movement in limitless space. The joy of the universe could be perceived in these paintings, he said.[114] In this way, basic forms came to represent what was regarded as universal, in the widest sense of the word. The language of form developed completely away from what was individual to become fully absorbed by universal dimensions of existence, but there arose a synthesis of the *individual* and *universal*. An important catalyst in this process was *De Stijl*, a movement established in 1917 and directed by the painter Theo van Doesburg (1883-1931) in collaboration with the painter Piet Mondrian (1872-1944) and the architect Gerrit Rietveld (1888-1964). Its name, *The Style*, is descriptive of how fundamental and comprehensive were the principles upheld by the movement, of its determination to present an unequivocal, modern style. In 1918, the artists of *De Stijl* published a manifesto, which opens with the following six declarations:

[112]"Wege der Abstraktion...," 18.
[113]Ibid.
[114]"Wege der Abstraktion...," 20.

Form and Norm

1. There is an old and a new consciousness of the age. The old one is directed toward the individual. The new one is directed toward the universal. The conflict of the individual and the universal is reflected in the World War as well as in art today.
2. The war is destroying the old world with all that it contains: the pre-eminence of the individual in every field.
3. The new art has revealed the substance of the new consciousness of the age: an equal balance between the universal and the individual.
4. The new consciousness is ready to be realized in everything, including the everyday things of life.
5. Traditions, dogmas and the pre-eminence of the individual (the natural) stand in the way of this realization.
6. Therefore, the founders of Neo-Plasticism call on all those who believe in the reform of art and culture to destroy those things which prevent further development, just as in the new plastic art, by removing the restriction of natural forms, they have eliminated what stands in the way of the expression of pure art, the extreme consequence of every concept of art.[115]

According to *De Stijl*, art should express nothing less than the great polar forces of life: nature and spirit, the principles of femininity and masculinity, the negative and the positive, the static and the dynamic, the horizontal and the vertical. The right angle along with the three basic colors red, blue, and yellow, extended with the non-colors from white to black, were considered the elementary means of expression. The creative elements of art were fixed in a way regarded as capable of breaking with the so-called hegemony of the individual for the benefit of more collective solutions.[116] Yet there was no desire to crush the individual artistic will in favor of collectivist art. The first two declarations in the manifesto, which define the War as a reflection of the final bankruptcy of the subjective perspective, are characteristic of the radical understanding of art and culture at that time. In the third declaration, which mediates between the universal and individual, a need for synthesis appears. The objective expressed here is to combine norm with form, in other words: to abolish the differences in the form-norm debate as carried on in the *Deutscher Werkbund* a couple of years earlier. This new balance came to characterize the understanding of form in the 1920s. Undoubtedly, the trend was very much due to the considerable influence that Theo van Doesburg acquired at the Bauhaus. In 1923, the Bauhaus launched the motto "art and technique: a new entity." Attention to basic forms and colors became a characteristic of how the combination of art and

---

[115] K. Frampton, *Modern Architecture*, 142.
[116] See M. Droste, *Bauhaus 1919-1933*. 54

technique was expressed. Even Malewitsch, who was committed to liberate form from the world of objects, designed utility objects from basic forms.

FIGURE 8: Kasimir Malewitsch, teacup, 1923

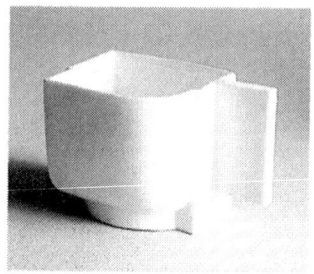

Not only Malewitsch and Russian Suprematists, but also advocates of *De Stijl*, constructivists, and artists with different backgrounds made their efforts felt in both design and architecture. Basic forms, which at the time around World War I were used in the process of liberation from the object, in the 1920s return to the object and become normative for a modern understanding of form.

Fundamental forms were considered especially well suited both to machine-fabricated, standardized elements and to profitable mass production. The way in which form was viewed within the framework of functionalism has been considerably influenced by industrialization. The frequent use in architecture and design of constructions developed from basic forms has given the impression that these forms are more functionally useful than those that are complex and asymmetric. Consequently, the use of basic forms has become the distinctive feature of the functionalist language of form.

1923, the year of "art and technique" at the Bauhaus, was a memorable year. It heralded regular broadcasting in Germany, and the film and gramophone industries were in breathtaking progress. The launching of Schoenberg's twelve-tone method is usually dated to 1923, and Hindemith's Neo-Baroque work *Das Marienleben*, opus 27, was completed in the same year. Also in 1923, Le Corbusier compiled his book *Vers une Architecture* (later translated as *Towards a New Architecture*) from publications in the journal *L'Esprit Nouveau*, which he had issued in collaboration with the painter Amédée Ozenfant and the poet Paul Dermée. At the point of intersection between machinery, the individual, and the universal, Le Corbusier stands forth as one of the dominant personalities. *Vers une Architecture* belongs to those works that have been highly significant for 20th-century architecture. Le Corbusier was strongly influenced by Adolf Loos's writings and, as the architectural scholar James Dunnett points out, by the debate between Henry van de Velde and Hermann Muthesius in the Deutscher Werkbund.[117] Yet although he spent the winter of 1907-08 in Vienna, Le Corbusier (or Charles-Édouard Jeanneret-Gris, as was still his name at the time) was not aware of "Ornament und verbrechen" until 1913.[118] Art historian Stanislaus von Moos recognizes the first traces of Loos's ideas in Le Corbusier's article "Le renouveau dans l'architecture," from the following year. He quotes from this piece: "Have we thus become savages once again after twenty centuries of civilisation? Have we readopted the mania for tattooing?"[119] The associations with "Ornament und verbrechen" are evident. The same article also contains a long, unaccredited quotation from Loos's 1910 essay "Architektur." In 1920, a French version of "Ornament und verbrechen," called *Ornement et crime*," was published in *L'Esprit Nouveau*.

Le Corbusier was a complex personality, who in the course of a long career showed many faces. It should be emphasized that the present discussion of his thoughts is based on his key writings from the 1920s. At this time in his life, the concept of truthfulness holds a central position. "A question of morality; lack of truth is intolerable, we perish in untruth," he writes.[120] In the same vein, he speaks of the *esprit de vérité*—the spirit of truth, the attitude or mentality of truthfulness or veracity that must be the foundation of a person's judgement:

> An active being carries with him the sense of truth, which is his power of judgement. It is an imperative which is at the same time his force and lucidity. The sense of truth is the strength of a man.[121]

This does not mean that every truth should be considered unalterable and eternal. Objects may certainly have a truth-value that is limited to their time, and some of these values must be rejected by posterity. Only objects that are useful because of a constant truth-value are valid, he says:

> I notice that a whole mass of objects which once bore the sense of truth have lost their content and are now no more than carcasses: I throw them out. I will throw everything out from the past except that which is still of service to me. Some things are always of service: art.[122]

---

[117] See J.I. Dunnett, "Introduction," Le Corbusier, *The Decorative Art of Today*, X.

[118] S. von Moos, "Le Corbusier and Loos," in *Raumplan versus Plan Libre*, 20.

[119] S. von Moos, "Le Corbusier and Loos," 20. The English translation of Le Corbusier's words is by I. Boyd Whyte.

[120] *Towards a New Architecture*, 17.

[121] *The Decorative Art of Today*, XXV.

[122] *The Decorative Art of Today*, XXV.

Interesting in Le Corbusier is that he—the machine optimist—regards a perfect object as "a living organism, animated by the sense of truth."[123] These are thoughts that connect to Sullivan's "form follows function."

In words whose prophetic tone resembles both that of Loos and the oracular *De Stijl* manifesto, Le Corbusier proclaims: "A great epoch has begun. There exists a new spirit."[124] "The history of Architecture," he says, "unfolds itself slowly across the centuries as a modification of structure and ornament, but in the last fifty years steel and concrete have brought new conquests, which are the index of a greater capacity for construction, and of an architecture in which the old codes have been overturned."[125] There has been a revolution, people have been given a style for their time.

Le Corbusier regarded the machine as the prime representative of the new age. Had he discussed Loos's beloved, smooth, and famously unornamented cigarette case, he would probably have said that only the machine was able to shape this object with true perfection, because

> [t]he machine brings before us shining disks, spheres, and cylinders of polished steel, shaped with a theoretical precision and exactitude which can never be seen in nature itself.[126]

Characteristics of modernity like typification, standardization, and thinking in modules are related to the machine, says Le Corbusier. Furthermore, human needs lie in human functions: "To search for human scale, for human function, is to define human needs. These needs are 'type'."[127] In an age when the demand for efficiency and economics is the driving force, the machine becomes crucial both as a generating principle and as a metaphor: Le Corbusier speaks of a house as a "tool" and as a "machine for living in."[128] He uses such terms with definitely positive connotations: the modern architect's objective is to provide his contemporaries with a living environment that functions optimally and supports human development and well-being. While Fritz Lang's motion picture *Metropolis* projected vivid visions of machine-generated horror as early as 1927, by and large the pessimistic attitude to machines was to appear later.

Nothing, Le Corbusier said, captures the nature of machines as convincingly as does geometry, which has the ability to fascinate and enchant us.

---

[123] *Ibid.*, XXVI.
[124] *Towards a New Architecture*, 9.
[125] *Ibid.*, 13.
[126] *The Decorative Art of Today*, XXIV.
[127] *Ibid.*, XXIII.
[128] *Towards a New Architecture*, 17 and 10.

Form and Norm

In this regard the machine, owing to its potential for precision, has a tremendous advantage over what Sullivan described as "man's powers." Modern machines are created according to unique laws, without historical models. And yet, these perfect products of the new age have been developed by *man*. Consequently, Le Corbusier recognizes engineers, particularly mechanical engineers, as the era's true aesthetes. Through calculation and construction, engineers are in tune with universal laws in a way that produces *harmony*. As already suggested, Le Corbusier's prototypical engineer appears as a worldly version of the *demiurge* in Plato's *Timaeus*. In contrast to Sullivan, for whom the hermetic aspects of geometry and mathematics belong to the past, Le Corbusier values these disciplines for their timeless, cosmological dimensions.

As shown in the discussion of the concept of functionalism, Le Corbusier considered architecture not a craft with the aim to generate mechanically calculated constructions, but a result of the combination of art and human emotion:

> Architectural emotion exists when the work rings within us in tune with a universe whose laws we obey, recognize and respect. When certain harmonies have been attained, the work captures us. Architecture is a matter of "harmonies," it is "a pure creation of the spirit."[129]

Le Corbusier envisages a synthesis between engineering aesthetics and architecture. Architects have much to learn from engineers, not least since the engineers' activity is ultimately and directly connected to art. Primary forms are keywords here. At this time Le Corbusier is particularly concerned with classic purity: Basic forms, rooted in universal laws, have a clarity that is technically and visually recognizable. This is what renders these forms *beautiful*: they become carriers of a beauty that can be experienced by every human being irrespective of intellectual level or culture:

> Our eyes are made to see forms in light; light and shade reveal these forms; cubes, cones, spheres, cylinders or pyramids are the great primary forms which light reveals to advantage; the image of these is distinct and tangible within us and without ambiguity. It is for that reason that these are *beautiful forms, the most beautiful forms*. Everybody is agreed as to that, the child, the savage and the metaphysician.[130]

The formal principle of purity that Le Corbusier represents in the 1920s is firmly connected to functionalist architecture and design. Once again, similar tendencies arise in various areas of musical production at this time:

---

[129] Le Corbusier, *Towards a New Architecture*, 23.

[130] *Towards a New Architecture*, 31.

The transparency of chamber music and the use of well-established formal types become the ideal contrast to the overburdened orchestral score and the stylistic abundance of expressionist-organic, undulating lines. A rejection of bewildering ambiguities in music is connected to functional aspects. In his article "Neue Gemeinschaftmusik," the music educator Karl Gofferje writes:

> Forms should not be too complicated; also in other aspects of musical composition one should strive for clear, simple structure and easily comprehensible relationships.[131]

The conviction that music with an easily recognizable form and structure is especially suited for education is found in German music pedagogy throughout most of the 20th century. In *Handbuch der Musikerziehung* (1954), Walter Rein highlights the importance of what he calls the necessary clarity of form, and continues:

> Experience has shown that the rendering of a work will be the better the more the singer or instrumentalist comprehends it, i.e., the less he loses himself in romantically obscure and vague stirrings of emotion, the more he moves in the clear certainty of the relationships that string the work of art together.[132]

Way beyond the field of music education, the ideal of structural clarity spread across the entire field of musical production. Both Schoenberg and Hindemith were guided by this goal.

The utilitarian aspect of functionalism concerns both the individual and the collective—the human being both as an individual and as a member of a community. The main thesis is that the individual is in the widest sense an *acting* being, who in one way or another participates in an active dialogue with the object. In other words, the individual can never be imagined in separation from the functionalist context. At the same time, functionalism extends beyond the utilitarian dimension. As a collective term, it subsumes various aspects of the aesthetic theories devised in the early 20th century to define the relationship between materials and the forms built from them. Consequently, the focus on the work's function, earlier introduced as the third level under the heading "The Concept of Functionalism," is given a wider perspective; the functionalist product becomes not only *Zeug* but also *Ding*, to use Heideggerian terminology.

---

[131] Translated from K. Gofferje, "Das deutsche Volksspiel V/14," in D. Kolland, *Die Jugendmusikbewegung. 'Gemeinschaftsmusik,' Theorie und Praxis* (Stuttgart: Metzler, 1979), 150.

[132] W. Rein, "Musikalische Laienbildung," in H. Fischer, ed., *Handbuch der Musikerziehung* (Berlin: Rembrandt, 1954), 127.

Form and Norm

The art historian Wolfgang Schepers identifies three concepts that put their stamp on product design between the wars: *abstraction, function*, and *production*.[133] Abstraction is strongly linked to the utility object, and thus reconnects the object-negating belief in the supremacy of pure feelings to the object. True to the Latin etymology of the word (*abstractus* = extract), artistic abstraction has a dual nature: it can denote art liberated from reference, but it can also stand for art that focuses on formal aspects such as lines, colors, geometric shapes, or standardized forms. Both meanings are born out in functionalism; at the Bauhaus, Ludwig Grote even proposed replacing the designation "functionalist architecture" with "abstract architecture."[134] The tendency toward abstraction in utility design of the time was part and parcel of the anti-ornamental aesthetics associated with Adolf Loos's polemic writings, the idea being that when the superfluous ornamentation is removed (or "abstracted") from the object, what emerges is *abstraction itself*. This train of thought led to the birth of the functionalist language of form: abstraction emphasized basic architectonic forms, regardless of whether or not they proved particularly utilitarian.

A *chair* can be taken as an example of an object that connects individual use to sculptural expression in a more universal sense. The pioneers of functionalism—Le Corbusier, Marcel Breuer (1902-1981), Ludwig Mies van der Rohe, and Alvar Aalto (1898-1976)—focused on this piece of furniture both as an artistic expression and an object for use. One of the well-known pieces of steel-tubing furniture from the 1920s is Breuer's *Stahlclubsessel*, an armchair that is still in production but better known today as the *Wassily Chair*. It was publicly exhibited for the first time in connection with the 1926 opening of the new Bauhaus building in Dessau, and listed in the institution's catalogue as *der abstrakte Stuhl* (the abstract chair):

FIGURE 9:
Marcel Breuer,
Wassily Chair,
1925-26

---

[133]See W. Schepers, "Abstraktion–Funktion–Produktion. Aspekte des Produktdesign 1918-1933," in Gassen and Holeczek, eds., *Die neue Wirklichkeit*, 323-328.

[134]See L. Grote, "Das Bauhaus und der Funktionalismus," *Bauhaus und Bauhäusler*, 282.

Schepers points out that this description is representative of the era's way of connecting modern use of material with modern art: "It [the titling] shows that the use and design of modern industrial materials (steel tubing) were already at that time described with the same terms as applied to the corresponding 'era-typical' art."[135] Chairs must satisfy both the practical needs for comfort, usefulness, movability, etc. and the aesthetic, specifically functionalist requirements with regard to material and formal design. In connection with his *Lattenstuhl* (picket-back chair), a simple wooden chair he designed and produced already in 1922, Breuer explains: "The starting-point was the problem of comfortable sitting combined with the simplest construction."[136]

FIGURE 10: Marcel Breuer, *Picket-back Chair*, 1923

A functionalist product must be *good* in the widest sense of the word—as regards both construction and use. This is not to say that a simple construction automatically leads to the most immediate application. Gerrit Thomas Rietveld, the advocate of *De Stijl*, is also the creator of the famous *Rot-blauer Stuhl* (Red-blue chair) of 1918:

FIGURE 11: Gerrit Thomas Rietveld, *Red-blue Chair*, 1918-1923

This varnished wooden chair is conceived and constructed along the lines of what the aestheticians of the era considered universal principles. However, it is fair to say that the chair probably stands more for a spiritual position than for qualities affording comfortable sitting. This points to one of the dilemmas that were to bedevil functionalism: the relationship between the ideal understanding of material and form and the function of use. Gert

---

[135]"Abstraktion–Funktion–Produktion.....," 325.

[136]Breuer quoted in, "Abstraktion–Funktion–Produktion…," 325.

Form and Norm

Selle points to the abstractionist tendency that characterized chair production in the 1920s, deploring a process that threatened to abandon functionality of use in favor of a uniquely visual rationality:

> In the end, the thing looks like something to sit in rather than being something especially good to sit in [....]. The armchair has been reduced to an industry-generated, functionalized skeleton for sitting; the sensual act of sitting is as if pared down to its meager kernel, to the idea of the functions of sitting or what in the advanced production history is still considered proper for the sitting body of industrial human beings.[137]

In this process, attention turns away from the object's utilitarian function toward its objective autonomy.

Das Neue Frankfurt, a building project that, in the space of a mere five years (1925-1930), provided eleven percent of the city's population with new housing, exemplifies this fundamental conflict. Intended to improve housing conditions for working-class people, the project is characteristic of functionalism's close relationship with social efforts. Awkwardness arose when it became obvious that average workers, much as they needed accommodation in a time that trapped them between inflation and mass unemployment, did not relate to what Selle calls "form without ornament." In other words, workers did not identify with objective, functionalist expression. As a result, officials and civil servants moved into the New Frankfurt housing areas, but hardly any workers. This conflict between the utility aspect of functionalism and its aesthetic ideas encouraged sophisticated customers to buy functionalist products—so as to be associated with modern expression more than from a sincere desire for useful commodities in everyday life. Despite all the idealism and community spirit that went into their production, the Bauhaus's most trend-setting objects never became common property but were reserved for the few. This unwanted exclusivity was not only due to production costs but also to the basic language of style.

The view of functionalist products thus oscillates between an understanding of their status as aesthetic objects and their down-to-earth usefulness. Aesthetics and utility aspects inevitably become intertwined, since they invariably contain elements of both perspectives. Although one might say that this applies to every object at any time, this duality is especially consequential in functionalist thought since it so crucially touches upon the basic preconditions of any genuine work of art.

---

[137] *Design-Geschichte in Deutschland*, 177.

"Sachlichkeit" and "Neue Sachlichkeit"

The development of functionalism is closely associated with the general tendencies of *Sachlichkeit*, objectivity, matter-of-factness, and sobriety that were influential during the 1920s. As the application of the term shows, functionalism was even occasionally equated with *Neue Sachlichkeit*. Given this proximity of the two concepts, a closer look at *Neue Sachlichkeit* may serve to deepen the understanding of functionalism's third level: the focus on the work's function. The usage of terms like *Sachlichkeit* and *Neue Sachlichkeit* also shows the dual way in which art objects' autonomy was understood at the time.

Originally a term used in painting, *Neue Sachlichkeit* was adopted as a recurrent slogan in the cultural and social life of the Weimar Republic, influencing painting and architecture, music and literature, film and photography, and more. This broad application does not indicate that objectivity was regarded as having only one face; quite to the contrary. In a lecture in 1936, the art historian Fritz Schmalenbach warned that applying the term *Neue Sachlichkeit* also to painting and architecture was problematic, one of the reasons being that the respective understanding of *form* was so different.[138]

"Es liegt in der Luft eine Sachlichkeit" (The air is filled with an objectivity), the title of a Schiffer/Spoliansky musical revue in 1928, aptly captures contemporary excitement in a manner suitable to this branch of entertainment. The fact that *Sachlichkeit* became a popular catchword is undoubtedly due to the term's identification with a common attitude rather than with a delimited concept. This ambiguity makes the term even more difficult to handle, particularly in contexts where precise definitions are called for.

The central question is: to what exactly does the term *Sachlichkeit* refer? In his book *The New Sobriety: Art and Politics in the Weimar Period 1917-33*, the art historian J. Willet states that "we have to be careful not to let the looseness of the term [*Neue Sachlichkeit*] lead us to use it in contexts where the Germans would not have used it themselves."[139] To understand how this term is used in German, a look at the following definitions translated from a German *Duden* may prove helpful:

> **Sach-lich** <Adj.>: **1.** Not decided by feelings or prejudices [sober and] without personal expression; only based on the factual context at hand; objective [...] **2.** Grounded in fact, as indicated by fact [...] **3.** Without ornaments or flourishes; characterized by purpose and

---

[138] See F. Schmalenbach, "Jugendstil und Neue Sachlichkeit," *Das Werk* 5 (1937), 129-134.

[139] S. Hinton, "Neue Sachlichkeit," in H.H. Eggebrecht, ed., *Terminologie der Musik im 20. Jahrhundert* [*HMT-Sonderband* 1] (Stuttgart: Frank Steiner, 1995), 320.

lack of adornment; sober [...] **Sach-lich-keit**, fem. The attitude of being objective (1) cool s. **2.** The state of being objective (3) Neue Sachlichkeit [New Objectivity] (*a school in painting, then also in literature in the 1920s, whose characteristic concern was an objective rendering of reality).*[140]

Comparing these definitions with their counterparts in an English dictionary, one finds correspondences with the adjective *objective*:

Objective *adj.* **1a** of an object of action or feeling **b** constituting object: e g **b(1)** existing independently of the mind **b(2)** belonging to the external world and observable or verifiable esp by scientific methods [...] **c** concerned with or expressing the nature of external reality rather than personal feelings or beliefs **d(1)** dealing with facts without distortion by personal feelings or prejudices **d(2)** of or being methods that eliminate or are intended to eliminate the subjective by limiting choices to fixed alternatives requiring a minimum of creative interpretation [...] **objectively** adv. **objectiveness** n. **objectivity** n.[141]

Here, the noun *objectivity* does not appear to correspond to the German term *Sachlichkeit*. For a close equivalence, one must rather look further down the page to *objectivism*.

Objectivism *n* **1** a theory stressing objective reality, esp as distinguished from subjective experience or appearance **2** an ethical theory that moral values are objectively real or possess universal validity **3** the theory or practice of objective art or literature— **objectivist** n, **objectivistic** adj.[142]

Based on this comparison, the English term "objectivity" does not seem to point directly at what is unadorned and purposeful. This explains Willett's problem in finding an English equivalent. Its absence, however, does not mean that *Sachlichkeit* was a uniquely German phenomenon, although it was in Germany, as the art historian Alfred H. Barr, Jr., ascertains, "where

---

[140]"**sach|lich** <Adj.>: **1.** *nicht von Gefühlen od. Vorurteilen bestimmt; [nüchtern u.] ohne Gefühlsbeteiligung; nur auf den in Frage stehenden Sachzusammenhang bezogen; objektiv* [...] **2.** *in der Sache begründet; von der Sache her* [...] **3.** *ohne Verzierungen oder Schnörkel; durch Zweckgebundenheit u. Schmucklosigkeit gekennzeichnet; nüchtern.* [...] **Sach|lich|keit**, die; –: *das Sachlichsein* (1) : kühle S. **2.** das Sachlichsein (3): Neue Sachlichkeit (Richtung der Malerei, dann auch der Literatur der 20er Jahre, für die eine objektive Wiedergabe der Realität charakteristisches Anliegen war." *Duden. Deutsches Universalwörterbuch* (Mannheim etc.: Dudenverlag, 1989), 1280-1281.

[141]*Longman Webster English College Dictionary* (New York: Merriam-Webster, 1984), 1010.

[142]Ibid.

the *neue Sachlichkeit* first became self-conscious."[143] *Objectivity*, the usual English translation,[144] focuses too strongly on the object as concrete substance, Willett feels; its application in this context is therefore only partly correct.[145] He uses the noun *sobriety* in his book title, but this word, too, has its own particular connotations. When Fritz Schmalenbach uses *objectivity*, he is referring to what Germans would call *Gegenständlichkeit*.[146] The crucial terminological question concerns the relationship between *Sachlichkeit* and *Sache*—between objectivity and object, or between what is supposedly objective and the object itself. It is exactly here that the concept of *Sachlichkeit* is constructively ambiguous.

Kenneth Frampton considers Hermann Muthesius the first to have used the term *Sachlichkeit* in architectural circles, as substantiated in a number of articles written between 1897 and 1903 for the journal *Dekorative Kunst*. Muthesius connects *Sachlichkeit* specifically with the English Arts and Crafts movement. He attributes to the concept a simple, functional, and sober content, where *Sachlichkeit* denotes an "objective, functionalist and eminently yeoman attitude to the design of objects, tending toward the reform of industrial society itself."[147] The art historian Gerd Presler connects the use of *Sachlichkeit* with Adolf Loos and Alfred Lichtwark, the director of the Hamburger Kunsthalle during the years 1886-1914. Peter Behrens's sweeping reforms for AEG also influenced the connotations of the term; Behrens was considered the pioneer in industrial *Sachlichkeit*. From an artistic point of view, an important aspect of Behrens's commitment is his advocacy of a sober, economical, and clearly defined language of form, based on expedient and profitable materials. As a result of this emphasis, attention focuses on the object itself, *die Sache*: the sober, unadorned, and clearly defined form highlights the identity and function of the object. The keyword is functional design. *Sachlichkeit*, as a concept within functionalism, gains a dual connotation, referring both to stylistic expression and to an approach to the object as a self-contained phenomenon.

This duality is not as obvious as one might expect. Frampton stresses that the art historian Heinrich Wölfflin, e.g., held a view that differed from Muthesius's. In the first chapter of his 1915 book *Kunstgeschichtliche Grundbegriffe*, Wölfflin introduces the *linear* and the *pictorial* as his main concepts:

---

[143] A.H. Barr, Jr., "Otto Dix," *The Arts*, 17/4 (1931), 237.

[144] *Neue Sachlichkeit* is usually translated by *New Objectivity*.

[145] Cf. "Neue Sachlichkeit," 320.

[146] See F. Schmalenbach, "The term *Neue Sachlichkeit*," *The Art Bulletin* 22/3 (1940), 162.

[147] *Modern Architecture*, 130.

"Sachlichkeit" and "Neue Sachlichkeit" 61

"Drawing styles perceive [things] in lines, painting styles, in masses. To see in a linear way means, therefore, that the purpose and beauty of things are first sought in their contours."[148] In the context of *Sachlichkeit*, this definition is interesting insofar as it refers to the renewal of styles around 1800 as "eine neue 'lineare' Art" (a new, "linear" way), and that one of Wölfflin's conclusions is

> The new line arrives in the service of a new objectivity [...]. Nature's truth and beauty depends on what is tangible and measurable.[149]

Wölfflin is referring to the clear contours and the artistic endeavors toward tangible reality that are characteristic of *Sachlichkeit*. Objective expression is supposed to be part and parcel of a representation of nature that shows purity of line and is as exact as possible; the pictorial composition is related to the artist's object in a representational way. The objective rendering is one with what is being rendered, in a manner that the depicted object can be taken hold of and measured, and the essence of it all is *die Wahrheit*, the truth. This applies particularly to the objects of figurative art. For Muthesius and Behrens, this level of *Sachlichkeit* points inwards, to the object itself, while also pointing beyond it. Accordingly, the two men's views do not diverge as much as Frampton suggests in his presentation; the differences result from the differences in artistic media.

Although Wölfflin uses the term *eine neue Sachlichkeit* as early as 1915, the term *Neue Sachlichkeit* in art is usually attributed to Gustav Friedrich Hartlaub (1884-1963), then director of the Mannheim Kunsthalle. Alfred H. Barr, Jr. confirms this ascription when he writes (in 1931):

> The phrase *die neue Sachlichkeit* was invented several years ago by Dr. G.F. Hartlaub [...] as a category for a number of European painters who seemed to be turning their backs upon the devious subjective quicksands of expressionism and the arid plateaux of abstract design in order to walk again upon the firm and lucid paths of the objective world.[150]

In 1923 Hartlaub took the first decisive step toward the exhibition that would establish the term *Neue Sachlichkeit* and cause it to spread like wildfire in the Weimar Republic. In a pamphlet published on 18 May that year, he stated his intentions:

---

[148] Translated from H. Wölfflin, *Kunstgeschichtliche Grundbegriffe. Das Problem der Stilentwicklung in der neueren Kunst* (Basel etc.: Schwabe & Co., 1970) 33.

[149] Translated from *Kunstgeschichtliche Grundbegriffe...*, 271.

[150] "Otto Dix," 236-237.

> This fall I wish to organize a moderately large exhibition of paintings and graphics, which may be entitled 'Die neue Sachlichkeit.' I see it as my concern to reconcile representative works of those artists who during the last 10 years have been neither impressionistically dispersed [or vague] nor expressionistically abstract, neither purely sensual and extrovert nor purely constructive and introvert. I wish to exhibit artists who with a confessional touch have remained, or have become again, true to positive, tangible reality.[151]

Among those who discuss *Neue Sachlichkeit* in a historical perspective, Fritz Schmalenbach has good credentials since he refers to conversations with and information from Hartlaub himself. Schmalenbach addresses an obvious but nevertheless interesting question: Is this "new" objectivity intended to relate back to an earlier understanding of the concept? According to Schmalenbach, Hartlaub launched the term with the aim of describing an artistic position that arises as "new" from the ruins of the past, and contrasted it with much earlier, "realistic" styles:

> We are told that the contrast to an "inartistic," bourgeois, and banal nineteenth-century realism, such as was observed for instance in the work of the Düsseldorf School or in that of Richard Müller of Dresden, was intended when the term was devised.[152]

For Hartlaub, the term *Neue Sachlichkeit* applies primarily to paintings that depict tangible, everyday reality—in distinct contrast to the utopian imagery of expressionism. The Mannheim exhibition was ultimately entitled *Ausstellung "Neue Sachlichkeit"—Deutsche Malerei seit dem Expressionismus* (Exhibition "Neue Sachlichkeit"—German Painting after [literally: since] Expressionism). The collection showed in Mannheim for three months (14 June to 13 September 1925) and then went on tour. The reach of the itinerant exhibit helped greatly to give the new term a wide currency.

As regards the final settling of accounts with expressionism, it appears that Hartlaub still had reservations to the view that the exhibition should represent a decisive dissociation with the immediate artistic past. The introduction in the catalogue opens with the following statement:

> On the threshold of this exhibition of recent German paintings, it is important to avert a dangerous error. In bearing witness to artistic endeavors that have made themselves felt *after* Expressionism, and—in a certain sense—appear to represent a backlash against it, this exhibition in no way takes a stand *against* Expressionism and

---

[151] Translated from F. Schmalenbach, "The term *Neue Sachlichkeit*," *The Art Bulletin* 22/3: 161.

[152] "The term *Neue Sachlichkeit*," 163. Schmalenbach stresses that he had strong reservations about Hartlaub's negative assessment of this so-called realism of the 1800s.

"Sachlichkeit" and "Neue Sachlichkeit" 63

> the generation of artists belonging to it. It is very doubtful whether or not Expressionism is dead; the continuing development of its best representatives especially in recent years gives one pause.[153]

The roster of luminaries represented in this first *Neue Sachlichkeit* exposition illustrates the breadth of the event: it included Max Beckmann, Otto Dix, Georg Grosz, Alexander Kanoldt, Georg Schrimpf, and Karl Hubbuch among others. The variety of stylistic expressions was so wide-ranging that it would have been misleading to speak of a unified style in a traditional sense. Rather, the exhibition demonstrated a shared position or mutual attitude where a common denominator was the relationship to tangible reality through *Gegenständlichkeit* and objectivity.

Hartlaub suggested two wings in the exhibition: a veristic wing (also called "left wing") concerned with contemporary, everyday material, and a classicist wing focusing on artistic principles of a timeless quality. Political connotations are implicit in the term "left wing." In his official presentation of the event, Hartlaub wisely does not refer to the other as a right wing:

> A casual assessment allows to distinguish two groups: One of them —one feels tempted to call it a "left wing"—tears what is objective out of the world of actual facts and jolts the experience out at its own tempo, at its own heat. The other seeks the *timelessly* valid object, then to actualize the eternal, existential regularities of the domain of art. The ones have been called "verists," the others might almost be called classicists. Both terms are only *partly* correct, define the collection only vaguely and could easily lead to a renewed domination of the artistic *concept* over the actual wealth of phenomena.[154]

Hartlaub's categories are interesting also when transposed to the field of music, where similar tendencies appeared in the 1920s. In the one wing, Hanns Eisler as well as the famous collaborators Kurt Weill and Bertolt Brecht wrote music intended to express explicit social criticism, while in the other wing, Schoenberg and Hindemith created music in a "timeless," Neo-Classical and Neo-Baroque style. As Hartlaub suggests, it is difficult to make clear distinctions; the opposing wings are better described as different faces of objectivity. Hindemith's music, even when restricted to a sample from this relatively short time period, can hardly be assigned to any wing. The same is true for Schoenberg, whose *Suite für Klavier*, op. 25 is far removed from the ideas of contemporary actuality that inform, for example, his opera *Von heute auf morgen*.

---

[153]Translated from the facsimile reproduced in M. Fath, *Neue Sachlichkeit* [*Mannheimer Museumshefte* 1] (Speyer: Hermann G. Klein, 1994), 4.

[154]Translated from M. Fath, *Neue Sachlichkeit...*, 6

A number of additional terms used in the context of *Neue Sachlichkeit* need to be briefly introduced. Wieland Schmied draws the following map, tracing connections to the Italian *Pittura Metafisica*:

> The concept "magic realism" ["Magischer Realismus"] still had at least the advantage that it embraced more than the term "new objectivity" ["Neue Sachlichkeit"]; it suggested an affinity to the magical experience of the alienated and incomprehensible things prepared by the Pittura Metafisica, defined by the newly arising veristic Surrealism in Paris, and given expression in Giorgio de Chiricos's townscapes and Max Ernst's early collages.

Schmied also provides a very helpful overview of the desiderata associated with *Neue Sachlichkeit* in painting. The points he lists emphasize a sharp and sober view, a focus on the mundane, a predilection for static features in the pictorial composition, an obliteration of the traces of brush-work, and a general concern with objects of worldly reality:

1. sobriety and clarity of gaze, and a perception that is unsentimental and largely free of emotion;
2. focus of the gaze on what is quotidian and banal, on insignificant and unassuming themes, with no fear anything "hideous";
3. pictorial compositions that are static and solid, suggesting virtually airless, glassy space, along with general preference for the static over the dynamic;
4. obliteration of any traces of the painting process, so that the painting may be kept free all gestures of hand-writing; and
5. finally, a new spiritual engagement with the object world.[155]

In his presentation of the Mannheim exhibition, Hartlaub implicitly broadens the term objectivity to include other forms of pictorial expression. He stresses that *abstract constructivism* strives for *Sachlichkeit* in precisely the same way as does his own object-related exhibition, despite the fact that the art is subsumed under another heading:

> The exhibition does not intend to show a *cross-section* of all post-expressionists' artistic endeavors. It leaves aside the art created within the abstract, "constructivist" schools. These experiments, in which the new will to objectivity [*Sachlichkeit*] expresses itself in quite a different way, will be reserved for a separate exhibition.[156]

Hartlaub thus subsumes two essentially different positions under one single concept, implying that figurative and abstract art are united on this

---

[155] Translated from W. Schmied, *Neue Sachlichkeit und Magischer Realismus...*, 26.

[156] Translated from M. Fath, *Neue Sachlichkeit...*, 6.

level of objectivity. Consequently, *Sachlichkeit* is not to be considered a surface phenomenon, but a concept that evades divisions and penetrates the core of more fundamental positions. For pictorial art, the result is that artists as diverse as Kasimir Malewitsch, László Moholy-Nagy, Lyonel Feininger, and Piet Mondrian are thought to pursue objectivity in fundamentally the same way as Grosz and Dix.

Sachlichkeit thus has a dual nature. Where pictorial representation is figurative, it refers to an object outside itself; where the aim is abstract constructivism, it points back at itself as an autonomous object. This links it to architecture and design, where functionalism, characterized by a similar conceptual ambiguity, equally looks not only inwards but also beyond itself. This dual perspective is of vital importance when discussing musical phenomena at this time. The objective-functionalist attitude is not only expressed in music written for extra-musical utility purposes: *function* is also part of understanding the musical work as an autonomous object of art.

The Concept of Musical Functionalism

"Artworks aim at jostling people out of their indolence (*Bequemlichkeit*); houses are intended to provide comfort (*Bequemlichkeit*)," writes Adolf Loos a few years before World War I, playing on the dual meaning of the German word.[157] "The comfortable singability of the choral score ought to be the choral composer's first law," says Paul Hindemith in a lecture in the latter half of the 1920s.[158] The two statements are connected in that both regard artworks in relation to aspects of human functionality. Both reveal a particular concern for human needs, potentials, and limitations, and thus reflect one of the most characteristic features of functionalist thought.

A central tenet of modernist understanding is the belief that the new ideals regarding material and form pervasively reflect a modern lifestyle. Walter Gropius's stance toward the art of building, as it contributed to inspiring the foundation of the Bauhaus, is an example of the need to see several components—both decorative items and utility objects—as parts of a larger architectonic whole. The opening statement of the Bauhaus manifesto posits structure as the *raison d'être* of all plastic art.[159] The notion that the creative activity of painters, sculptors, and architects should aspire to, and culminate in, *building* is of the greatest importance for the institution's

---

[157]Translated from "Architektur," *Trotzdem*, 315.

[158]Translated from P. Hindemith, "Wie soll der ideale Chorsatz der Gegenwart oder besser der nächsten Zukunft beschaffen sein?" *Aufsätze, Vorträge, Reden*, 26.

[159]Translated from *Bauhaus 1919-1933*, 18.

earliest development. Since striving for functionality was the most characteristic feature, its different activities necessarily resulted in a stylistically varied production. Already at its beginning, and significantly through the work at the Bauhaus, functionalism thus absorbed several areas of creative activity. One central question of this study is how music situates itself in this functionalist perspective.

Musical functionalism did not exist as a term until Carl Dahlhaus coined it in an essay entitled "Musikalischer Funktionalismus." Features that encourage this designation are not, however, sufficiently general to warrant a common stylistic denominator. Moreover, there is music whose stylistic features seem to camouflage what is in fact a common functionalist foundation. Dahlhaus's own statement, "[a]s an expressionist, Schoenberg was a functionalist and as a functionalist, an expressionist," is an example of such recognition.[160] When features akin to functionalist ideas appear in the thoughts of composers like Schoenberg and Hindemith, these are not necessarily of such a nature that they would define these composers' music as expressions of a common functionalist style.

Since the Bauhaus was the soil in which functionalism flourished, it would seem natural to begin the search for a potential functionalist understanding of music in this progressive movement. The Bauhaus had the ambition of including all the arts. Nevertheless, it seems that, like literature, music did not play any decisive role at the institution. Contemporary music was discussed and music was an important part of the school's social and cultural life. There were talented musicians among the students, and many of the Bauhaus teachers, including Klee, Kandinsky, Lyonel Feininger, and Oskar Schlemmer, were known to have a keen interest in music. The rumor that Schoenberg had once been requested to join the staff is not correct.[161] It is, however, true that Erwin Ratz, one of Schoenberg's most talented students, was secretary to both Gropius and Adolf Meyer, another Bauhaus instructor. The pianist Gertrud Grunow, a music teacher who worked as an assistant to the painter Johannes Itten in the Bauhaus's first period (1919-1923), aimed at guiding her students toward what she saw as the connection between sound, color, and movement. This was not foreign to the time,[162] but in no way can it be related to any specific functionalist understanding of music.

---

[160]Translated from C. Dahlhaus, "Musikalisher Funktionalismus," *Schönberg und andere. Gesammelte Aufsätze zur Neuen Musik* (Mainz-London: Schott, 1978), 63.

[161]Kandinsky had proposed Schoenberg as the successor to Bruno Hinze-Reinhold, director of the Weimar Music Academy, and not as a music teacher at the Bauhaus. However, as the sole composer, Schoenberg was curatorium representative in the so-called "Circle of Friends of the Bauhaus."

[162]J. Hauer's *Vom Wesen des Musikalischen*, for example, was published in 1920.

The Concept of Musical Functionalism

Oskar Schlemmer's *Triadisches Ballett* was based on the subtle use of *trias*—the number three. In this scenic integration of dance, pantomime, and music, the dancers were dressed as geometric figurines. Magdalena Droste describes the work as *dancelike constructivism.* Yet once again the music, written by Hindemith,[163] does not manifest anything that might be described as a functionalist approach.[164]

Constructivist forms and formations combined with mechanically inspired movement, were favorite devices in the scenic experiments at the Bauhaus. Music's potential as an active and independent medium, however, appears to have been of secondary importance. The musicologist and composer Hans Heinz Stuckenschmidt, who gives a vivid account of his dealings with the *Bauhauswoche 1923*, was engaged to write the music for Kurt Schmidt's *Mechanisches Kabarett*. His description affords an unpretentious glimpse behind the scenes:

> After the first common meal I went with Kurt Schmidt to his studio where there were constructions of cardboard, wire, canvas, and wood the height of a man, all in primary geometric forms: circles, triangles, squares, rectangles, trapezoids, and of course all in the primary colors yellow, red, and blue. Schmidt hung a red square around his neck and fastened it with leather straps so that he disappeared behind it. Two of his co-workers did the same with a circle and a square. Then these strange geometric figures with their hidden bearers danced a ghostly round-dance. Near the wall stood an old piano. It was out of tune and had a hideous clang. I improvised a few chords and sharp rhythms. Immediately the cardboard figures began to respond, spontaneously inventing an abstract dance of square, circle, and triangle. After perhaps 15 minutes Kurt Schmidt divested himself of his square, somewhat out-of-breath but quite satisfied. Instinctively I had guessed and carried out what he had imagined and vaguely conceived: a primitive accompaniment that corresponded approximately with the primary geometric figures. Harmonically, it consisted solely of chained triads, its melody of folksong formulas, its rhythm of elements from dance and march. I treated the piano in the manner of George Antheil, with fortissimo explosions and furious glissandi all across the keyboard.[165]

Schmidt seems to consider the accompanist's abrupt improvisation an appropriate match to his geometric forms, yet the impression may have arisen in response to the performance's mechanical nature rather than from any commanding understanding of formal principles.

---

[163] A version for mechanical organ has been produced on CD (Koch/Schwann 3-1202-2).

[164] *Bauhaus 1919-1933,* 101.

[165] Translated from H.H. Stuckenschmidt, *Musik am Bauhaus* (Berlin: Bauhaus Archiv, 1978/1979), 6-7.

Students at the school formed a jazz group called *Die Bauhauskapelle*, which came to be considered one of the best in Germany. They also organized concerts featuring music by contemporary composers such as Schoenberg, Bartók, Stravinsky, and Hindemith. Despite this commendable openness and interest for the musical innovations of the time in terms of performances, there was hardly any unique recognition of the theoretical foundations of musical composition at this institution.

A valid approach to musical functionalism must, then, be attempted from another angle. The term "functionality" is not unknown in the field of musicology. An important question in this book is what connection there might be between concepts such as, for example, *functional music* and *musical functionalism*. According to Albrecht von Massow in *Terminologie der Musik im 20. Jahrhundert* (Terminology of Music in the 20th century), the term "functional music" arose in the 1940s. It covered a musico-sociological category that included music created for certain purposes, whether economic or civic. In a narrow sense, functional music came to stand for "background music, as music for work or the supermarket."[166] These forms of expression had their roots in the work song. In a wider sense, the term also denoted a classification of musical genres that were linked to social or public uses, such as dances, marches, fanfares, etc. It is likely that the latter understanding of functional music also seemed a less negatively loaded synonym for *Gebrauchsmusik*, the collective term employed during the inter-war years. Moreover, *Gebrauchsmusik* is often tied to anti-romantic attitudes and ideas of communitarian activity in a way that is not necessarily characteristic of functional music as a whole.

"Functional music" is often contrasted with "autonomous music," although these terms are not implicit logical antonyms. When evaluating these two musical categories, the criteria tend to be quite different: functional music is usually considered on socio-historical conditions, autonomous music from a viewpoint believed to be universal and aesthetic. With the stock of ideas inherited from Romanticism, a functional work is apt to be associated with what is prosaic and trivial, while its "autonomous" counterpart relates to what is poetic and spiritually elevated. Moreover, the 19th-century understanding of "autonomous form" versus "functional form" is bound up with the problem of autonomy versus functionality, where the latter term is applied to music that receives its structural features from the requirements of ballet dancing and the like.[167]

---

[166] See A.v Massow, "Funktionale Musik," *Terminologie der Musik im 20. Jahrhundert*, 157.

[167] See H. Danuser, *Die Musik des 20. Jahrhundert*s [C. Dahlhaus/H. Danuser, eds., *Neues Handbuch der Musikwissenschaft* 7] (Laaber: Laaber, 1984/1996), 73.

The Concept of Musical Functionalism

While the dichotomy between functional music and autonomous music may be fruitful as the first step toward categorization, there is still the problem of maintaining delineation. Functional music can be autonomous, autonomous music can be used functionally. Adorno's statement, "[w]hat was functional yesterday can turn into its opposite,"[168] is relevant also for functional music. If musical functionalism is understood as arising as a parallel to 20th-century architecture and design, then functional music and musical functionalism have as little, or as much, in common as do functional architecture and functionalist architecture. Consequently, musical functionalism (or functionalist music) is not identical with functional music, despite the linguistic proximity.

Functionality in connection with music can be understood in several ways, of which the most significant for the purpose of this study is that of functionality as a structuring principle. Just as in the discussion of architecture and design, functionality implies an understanding of the characteristic features of a work's inner constituent forces, so also is functional harmony, a term employed in music theory, closely allied to traditional tonality as established by Jean-Philippe Rameau and later codified by Hugo Riemann. At its heart is the view that the three primary triads in the major and minor keys have a fixed relation to each other, and that every chord that can be related to these has a particular function in a musical development. Throughout most of the 20th century, functionality on the structural level remained connected with what in everyday language is called traditional harmony.

Recognizing and dealing with functional harmony is part of the craft of musical composition. A certain amount of functionality is supposed to lie in the harmonic material itself. The music student as well as the composer must recognize this functionality in order to apply it in a constructive way. In this sense, musical functionality is connected with dexterity, knowledge, and recognition: a functional movement is one that shows craftsmanlike mastery. It is from such an understanding that Heinz Tiessen, toward the end of the 1920s, opens a presentation of what he calls *Funktionelle Sachlichkeit* with the words:

> But a greater influence [...] on music was this common attitude to the spirit of *craftsmanship* and its *restoration*; if one wanted to pinpoint the dominant attitude of the time among all that was divergent, [it would seem that] the purely *technical quality* of function became a unifying idea for the younger generation.[169]

---

[168]Translated from "Funktionalismus heute," 376.

[169]Translated from *Zur Geschichte der jüngsten Musik (1913-1928)*, 58-59.

According to this analysis, the so-called musical functions expressed in a score encompass something far more than, and often quite different from, functional harmony. Wallace Berry endorses this premise in his book *Structural Functions in Music*, in which he addresses the relationship between musical structure and its expressive effect. "Function" is established as an intermediary in a complex picture. Any occurrences on the various levels of the musical structure have their function in a work's unfolding, and cannot, Berry decides, be separated from expression: the musical object and the human subject are inextricably bound together. Attempting to clarify the forces that are being played out in a work and to reveal universal structural phenomena, Berry analyses examples taken from across the entire spectrum of Western music—from Machaut and des Prez to the Second Viennese School and Boulez. He presupposes that a work is created following a logic and rationality that relate to the basic concepts of ascending and descending motion, tension and relaxation, accelerando and ritardando, etc.

In contrast to Berry, Mark Delaere establishes his own term, *funktionelle Atonalität* (functional atonality), as an antithesis to triad-based functional tonality, with the aim both of demonstrating the functionality on which the Second Viennese School is supposedly based and of presenting strategies for analysis.[170] Delaere briefly discusses the problematic aspects of the term "atonality" and then exposes the logic that lies at the basis of the presumed atonal freedom. His aim is to prove that the parameters used in musical structures that follow the premises of so-called free atonality are rational and logical.

Both Berry and Delaere relate functionality to the logical aspects of musical structure. The organic work is based on functional principles. That Berry regards expression and interpretation as parts of this picture is of lesser importance for his analytic strategies. Focusing on a work's structure and logic may reveal significant features of what can be termed musical functionalism.

An excellent guide to a deeper understanding of musical functionalism as a concept is Adorno. In the introduction to his "Funktionalismus heute" (functionalism today), he begins by admitting his incompetence in the field of architecture, but then proceeds without apparent problems to point out fundamental connections between his education as a composer and the ideas central to the development of architectural functionalism. He feels particular kinship with the endeavors toward objectivity:

---

[170]M. Delaere, *Funktionelle Atonalität: Analytische Strategien für die frei-atonale Musik der Wiener Schule* (Wilhelmshaven: Florian Noetzel , 1993).

> If there is any idea that survived in the Werkbund movement, it is that of objective competence as opposed to unconstrained aesthetics foreign to the material. From the background of my own profession, music, I consider this request self-evident, thanks to a school that had close, personal connections with both Adolf Loos and the Bauhaus and considered itself spiritually related to the endeavors of objectivity.[171]

Adorno does not mean objectivity of expression, but rather the material objectivity expressed in the art object itself. He encourages recognizing functionalism as inherent in the musical tendencies of his time. Consequently, he focuses on fundamental, epistemological commonality as a source for the concept of musical functionalism. Schoenberg also comments on this relationship, albeit in more general terms. His book, *Stil und Gedanke* (*Style and Idea*), is dedicated to several of his counterparts in non-musical aesthetics, among them Adolf Loos and Karl Kraus,

> [...] all these people with whom I could speak in the same way as I express myself in certain parts of this book. They belonged to those with whom one need not argue about the principles of music, of art, of artistic and civic morals. There was a mutual, clear, and quiet mutual understanding of all these things, despite the fact that each of us was forever working to deepen these principles, make them more stringent, and refine them to their limits.[172]

Both Adorno and Schoenberg are expressing a profound kinship with the ideas that fostered functionalism in architecture and design.

In his article "Musikalischer Funktionalismus," Carl Dahlhaus is even more explicit about this connection:

> When, around 1910, Arnold Schoenberg was obsessed by the idea that it must be possible to express musical thoughts without ornamental padding or paraphrase, directly and plainly, one can certainly speak of musical functionalism, for this notion was of a spiritual kin to Adolf Loos's hostility to ornamentation and Karl Kraus's to [empty] phrases.[173]

Dahlhaus extends this thought to characteristic features in composers such as Stravinsky, Hindemith, Weill, and Eisler, thereby also introducing questions of musical form and music's function. Dahlhaus's aim is not to compare these composers with regard to musical expression and style, but rather to suggest a common platform for vital tendencies within this broad

---

[171]Translated from "Funktionalismus heute," 375.

[172]Translated from the dedication page of *Stil und Gedanke*.

[173]Translated from "Musikalischer Funktionalismus," 62.

spectrum of compositional variety. He believes that the term musical functionalism is an apt label to characterize some very important, basic traits. Adorno's, Schoenberg's, and Dahlhaus's references to functionalist thought reflect crucial aspects of the concept since they point to characteristic features of material, form, and function. This study aims to deepen such an understanding by emphasizing the following perspectives:

First, musical functionalism builds on an awareness of the autonomy of and the potential for truthfulness inherent in any given material, requesting that composers be respectful of both. This awareness fosters attention to aspects of structure and craftsmanship, and in turn makes it possible to speak of a functional treatment of material, as is done in the fields of architecture and design.

Second, construction is perceived as closely related to form, a point that is of central importance in the thoughts of musical functionalism. Equally significant is the normative aspect, expressed in the use of basic forms that are supposedly easily recognizable; hence the notion of "functional form."

Third, musical functionalism focuses on the capacity of music as an activating element for the individual of modern times. This recognition does not exclude the evaluation of artistic worth and music's aesthetic dimensions: Functionality rather pervades the work and at the same time transcends its activity-related purpose. Against the backdrop of these definitions, the concept of musical functionalism emerges as subject to the division discussed earlier in the context of functionalism in architecture and design:

1. Functional treatment of the chosen material
2. Functional design
3. Focus on the work's intended function

This tripartite requirement defines the concept of musical functionalism as developed in this book, and will serve as the foundation for the presentation of Schoenberg's and Hindemith's thoughts.

The Musical Material

The Crisis of Tonality

The shift in focus from artistic material as a potential to a particular material's own will is also discernable in 20th-century music. The most important distinction between music and other forms of art is that music is an auditory experience of sound. Sound in itself is thus often regarded as the basic ingredient in musical material. Music history offers several examples of the desire to explore sound *an sich*: see Webern's *Klangfarbenmelodie*, Varèse's efforts to achieve "the liberation of sound," Schaeffer's *musique concrète*, various experiments in sound within the frame of traditional music ensembles, the unconventional use of conventional instruments, and electro-acoustic as well as computer-generated music, to mention just a few. Like dissonance, sound has been emancipated, which has strengthened its identity and position as an essential component in music's basic material. Recognition of this fact has been a major catalyst in the development of present compositional diversity. Nonetheless, the views on music's fundamental material have been far from unambiguous: It has never been an easy matter to distinguish any potential in the material from an alleged will. Furthermore, different works of music described as "contemporary" in the 20th century may cover a broad and highly varied range of attitudes to sound.

In the era of Arnold Schoenberg (1874-1951) and Paul Hindemith (1895-1963), the common concept of musical material comprised a combination of what were considered the main elements of music: melody, harmony, and rhythm. In his book *The Beautiful in Music* (*Vom Musikalisch-Schönen. Ein Beitrag zur Revision der Ästhetik der Tonkunst*, 1854), Eduard Hanslick defines material in a way that represents such a view:

> The crude material which the composer has to fashion, the vast profusion of which it is impossible to estimate fully, is the entire scale of musical notes and their inherent adaptability to an endless variety of melodies, harmonies, and rhythms.[1]

---

[1] E. Hanslick, *The Beautiful in Music*, Gustav Cohen, trans. (Indianapolis etc.: Bobbs-Merrill, 1957), 47.

In Hanslick's opinion, the range of notes is a horizontal and vertical potential that may be realized in rhythm. Thus tones *and* their possibilities constitute the material of music. However, the tones must be refined to a level where their possibilities are implicit. Artistic musical material is not something that is just out there in nature:

> On examining in what sense nature provides music with its material, we find that she supplies nothing but the rough elements, from which man contrives to elicit sounds. [...] At the outset, therefore, we are furnished only with material for the production of material, that is, of sound of high or low pitch; in other words the measurable tone.[2]

Nature can deliver rudimentary raw material to music only because it gives material substance to the instruments that will produce the sound. To Hanslick, genuine musical material is already on a level where it can be considered *geistfähig*: "The act of composing is mental working on material capable of receiving the forms which the mind intends to give"[3] or, to remain closer to the German original: "Composing is a spiritual activity in a spiritually workable material." The properties of the material of music make it uniquely appropriate for further development through artistic creation.

When examining the possibilities of musical material, one must also address the question of its limitations. Putting aside purely technical-acoustic considerations and adopting Hanslick's point of view, there must always be a comprehensible correlative guiding the elaboration of the material into a work of art. This correlative will rest on a type of artistic logic that allows a work to unfold and be appreciated within a given cultural horizon. This kind of logic does not necessarily have to be founded on rigid, theory-based rules, but the material qualities of the work will always be based on compositional traditions and conventions.

In Hanslick's time, musical logic was understood according to syntactic principles based on the regularity of functional harmony. Tonality thus became a keyword in the views on musical material. The development of 20th-century music is unimaginable without this concept as a referential axis. Both Schoenberg and Hindemith's recognition of the material of their

---

[2]*The Beautiful in Music,* 101-102.

[3]*The Beautiful in Music,* 51-52. ["Komponieren ist ein Arbeiten des Geistes im geistfähigem Material."]

art was highly influenced by traditional views, although they rejected conservative notions of tonality as unsuitable for the modern age.

The contemporary views on the logic of musical material were based on the laws of functional harmony, where dissonance is regarded as a transitional stage to be resolved in stabilizing consonance. Functional harmony is, now as then, based on a hierarchical system to which also melody, rhythm, and metrics belong. This conviction determines the possibilities in musical material as defined by Hanslick.

The most decisive development in the latter half of the 19th century is that functional tonality loses its dominance. Its foundation of diatonic principles becomes increasingly open to modality and chromaticism. Violinist and theoretician Joel Lester summarizes the decline of functional tonality in five points:

1. The increasing use of chromaticism, which weakens the diatonic basis of functional tonality, the secure status of the key, and the secure status of goals within a key.
2. The increasing use of dissonance in the form of nonharmonic tones, dissonant chords, and altered chords, which weakens the consonance-dissonance distinction crucial to harmonic stability and resolution.
3. The increasing use of distant harmonic relationships between consecutive chords and key areas, which weakens the distinction between closely related and distantly related tonal areas, and blurs the status of harmonic goals.
4. The use of modal alterations and nondiatonic scales, often for exotic effects, which also weakens the clarity of harmonic and melodic goals.
5. The avoidance of direct statements of the basic functional harmonic progressions and voice leading, since in this new harmonic and tonal environment, simple progressions sounded too old-fashioned and banal[4]

From a historical perspective, modality is as much a part of the scales of ancient times as of the sophisticated pre-functional age before the major/minor principles of Baroque music. Furthermore, modal scales are characteristic of folk music in the West. Modal features give music qualities often considered colorful and exotic: colorful because they affect the harmonic standard of functionality, and exotic because they allude to bygone times and what might be found beyond the confines of traditional art music. In the German music world, modal features initially represented an expansion of

---

[4]J. Lester, *Analytic Approaches to Twentieth-Century Music* (New York etc.: Norton, 1989), 7.

functional tonality, but they also paved the ground for a development towards the concept of extended tonality.

The escalating use of chromaticism threatened functional tonality in quite a different way. The chromatic element is already present in, for instance, the seventh step of the diatonic scale—in the so-called leading-tone—which is also crucially important for traditional harmony. This step helps to establish the tonal plane or center in a short or longer portion of a musical progression. As the use of chromaticism increases, the unequivocality of functional harmony declines. This process does not necessarily undermine functional harmony itself: the works of composers like Schumann, Chopin, and Liszt comprise abundant examples of movements containing both modal features and extensive chromaticism, without any transgression of the fundamental limitations. Such expressive characteristics are based on chord progressions that relate to basic patterns of functional harmony. It is a different matter when chromaticism pervades music's basic structure, challenging functional harmony itself. Historically speaking, its *coup de grâce* is found in the prelude to *Tristan und Isolde* by Richard Wagner, completed in 1859:

EXAMPLE 1: Richard Wagner, *Tristan und Isolde*, opening of Prelude to Act 1 (piano reduction)

In this music, pervasive chromaticism continuously dominates the unfolding music in a development without any real functional-harmonic rests. Tonal planes are not established in the traditional sense, they are rather counteracted as chromatics, or other types of dissonance are added to each stage which in turn lead the development into new harmonic waves. In this piece of music the chromatics create an intensity of expression, full of spiraling tension and a repression of feelings that highlights the drama's fundamental idea and character. Nonetheless, Wagner's music relates to traditional tonality in the sense that the laws of functional harmony are present as a more or less confining framework. In the introductory measures of the *Tristan* prelude, A minor serves as the underlying tonal reference. The chord in the second measure, the famous *Tristan chord*, can be interpreted as a dominant of the dominant, with an added sixth (leading on to the seventh) and a lowered fifth in the bass. The augmented fourth, the tritone, between the lowest voices gives the music a tense tonal ambiguity. The varied use of this interval became a characteristic feature of tonal development from the 19th to the 20th century. The third is introduced chromatically, thereby giving the chord, even though dissonant, the sense of growing organically out of the unison introductory measure. The use of F, in the first and second measures respectively, reinforces this relationship. The seventh, which is introduced on the last beat, temporarily releases the tension. A chord with a higher degree of dissonance then leads towards a chord with lower dissonance. Maintaining the interpretation of this chord as the dominant of the dominant, the chord then moves on to a dominant seventh, following the conventions of functional harmony, and giving the same relative release of tension through the dissonant fourth leading to the fifth on the second beat.

The question is, then, what significance the functional framework really has for the tonal principles that Wagner appears to use. This is the point where this music acquires the status of being the perfect example of the dramatically worded "crisis of tonality." "Crisis" in this context is highly descriptive, considering the fundamental status of functional tonality in the history of Western music. "For nowhere does the order of the twelve-tone method proceed more rigorously out of historical tendencies of the material than in harmony," says Adorno, "and if schemata of twelve-tone harmony were to be worked out, the beginning of Wagner's Prelude to *Tristan* could probably be viewed more simply in this perspective than in the function of a-minor."[5]

In the *Festschrift* on the occasion of Schoenberg's 60th birthday, Paul Stefan writes that Wagner's *Tristan* did not gain favor in Vienna until after the composer's death. Schoenberg wrote his first compositions about a decade later. "It is no coincidence that in his first works Schoenberg relates to what was for Vienna the still new 'Tristan'," says Stefan. "And as 'Tristan' had been impossible to perform, Arnold Schoenberg's works soon became impossible too."[6] It is from this early phase of Schoenberg's development that Alexander Zemlinsky, his only teacher, recalls the following statement from a member of the board of the *Wiener Tonkünstlerverein* evaluating the brand new *Verklärte Nacht* (1899): "Indeed, it sounds as if

---

[5]Th.W. Adorno, *Philosophy of Modern Music,* Anne G. Mitchell and Wesley V. Blomster, trans (New York: Continuum, 2003), 81.

[6]"Nicht zufällig hat Schönberg in seinen ersten Werken gerade an den für Wien damals noch so neuen 'Tristan' angeknüpft" [...] "Und so wie der 'Tristan' unaufführbar gewesen war, so wurden es alsbald die Werke Arnold Schönbergs." Translated from P. Stefan, "Zusammenhänge," *Arnold Schönberg zum 60. Geburtstag, 13 September 1934* (Vienna: Universal Edition, 1934), 38-39.

someone had wiped over the still wet score of *Tristan*."[7] Schoenberg was perceived as continuing Wagner's use of music's basic material right from the start of his career, although not always with the accompanying goodwill of the public and critics.

Richard Strauss is another example of how the traditional view of tonality gradually lost its base. Strauss was labeled a "cacophonist" years before his opera *Elektra* (1909). His symphonic poem *Don Juan* written between 1888 and 1889, is often regarded as the musical herald of modernism. In this work it is not the avoidance of functional-harmonic quiescent points that is essential. The key issue is rather Strauss's use of harmonically ambiguous formulae to unsettle the tonic plane. The chromatic alterations rattle the very foundations of what is predictable in functional harmony:

EXAMPLE 2: Richard Strauss, *Don Juan*, op. 20 (piano reduction), mm. 29–31.

From the perspective of functional harmony, the relationship between C minor, as in m. 29, and G major, in m. 31, could hardly be closer. Yet the three chords in m. 30 threaten to break this connection. The first chord in the second measure is introduced both chromatically and as a mediant, as $A\flat^7$ becomes a dominant submediant of C minor, or an altered dominant of the dominant. However, the diminished-fifth leap between mm. 29 and 30 from C_4 to $F\sharp_3$, again a tritone, camouflages the harmonic relationship. Neither is the progression immediately followed up by G major (for instance as a fourth-sixth suspension) but rather by a new chromatic or mediant introduction of F^7. Attention is drawn to a series of chords dominated by a chromatic development towards a diminished chord on E. After this procedure, one might expect $E\flat^7$—a chord that would continue in accordance with the preceding harmonic progression, relating to G as the earlier $A\flat^7$ did to C minor. But this is not the case: Strauss allows the chromatics, combined with repeated notes in the upper voices, to take the harmonic progression further. The result is that G_5 (m. 31) is experienced as a surprising leap up to a new tonal level.

---

[7]After A. Zemlinsky, "Jugenderinnerungen," *Arnold Schönberg zum 60. Geburtstag*, 34. ["Das klingt ja, als ob man über die noch nasse Tristan-Partitur darüber gewischt hätte."]

The Crisis of Tonality

Challenging the established relationships between tonal levels is an essential feature of the breakdown of the traditional tonality founded on functional harmony. The unconventional organization of tonality in, for example, the symphonies of Gustav Mahler is also part of this picture. Schoenberg refers to a movement in Beethoven's E-minor quartet op. 59 no. 2 as an instance of such "fluctuating tonality." The movement begins with the relatively remote C major leading to E minor.[8] This tonal polarity awakens associations with Mahler's *schattenhafte* Seventh Symphony in E minor, with its C-major finale. The work is but one example of a process that undermines functional harmony as a form-constituting element. With the dissolution of traditional tonality, the unique possibility of the key establishing both contrast and coherence—not least in the construction of large, formal units—is lost. In the 1920s, Schoenberg's pupil Erwin Stein comments on the crisis of form that follows in the wake of contemporary tonal development.[9] In the same process, rhythm also tends to be freed from meter. We can speak here of "the emancipation of rhythm," which, needless to say, does not simplify the problem of musical form. However, if rhythm is dissolved in new, asymmetrical constellations, it is also used as a stabilizing mechanical link within new tonal idioms, allowing for new, or rather rediscovered, formal possibilities. The exploitation of various ostinato devices is an example of the latter.

The development of the concept of tonality, from the 1800s and into the 20th century, is a comprehensive and indeed multifaceted process. The above-mentioned examples show early signs of two main tendencies: In the Wagner example, chromatics undermines the functional-harmonic principles due to a dominance of dissonance in the harmonic progression. In the Strauss example, chromatics and the use of dissonance lay the ground for new ways of organizing tonal levels that challenge the canon of functional harmony. Both principles acquire great importance in 20th-century music, not least for Schoenberg and Hindemith.

The use of chromaticism is based on the minor second, an interval that is of great importance for deciding both harmonic and melodic direction. When there is an effort to maintain some of this interval's characteristics, while attention is at the same time drawn away from its traditionally functional qualities, there is a tendency for the interval to be inverted or transcribed to a major seventh or minor ninth. The minor-second step, frequently used in music of an expressive nature, is thereby transformed into

---

[8]See A. Schoenberg, *Theory of Harmony*, 383.

[9]See E. Stein, "Neue Formprinzipien," *Arnold Schönberg zum fünfzigsten Geburtstage, 13. September 1924* [Sonderheft der *Musikblätter des Anbruch*] (Vienna 1924), 286.

a leap, which according to traditional conventions is perceived as being even more expressive. Consequently, there is a remarkable interplay as the general changes in the musical material, especially in the German music world, also intensify the musical *espressivo* conventions. Adorno remarks on the relationship between dissonances and musical material in the following way:

> Dissonances arose as the expression of tension, contradiction, and pain. They take on fixed contours and became "material."[10]

For Adorno, the vital point is that in this way the dissonances are lifted out of the subjective sphere of expression, however, as he puts it: without denying their true origin.

In this development we see more use of both tense chromatics and leaps—often of the "forbidden" type according to the rules of functional harmony. This tendency contributes to distortions of the traditionally stepwise flow of the melody. Melody is dissolved in a way that could justify the dramatic statement of a "crisis of melody." Similar to the alleged crisis of form, such an inclination is also an inevitable consequence of the emergent understanding of musical material. From a functionalist point of view, it is the musical *Materialgerechtigkeit* that applies here. The same can be said for harmony and form, rhythm and meter.

This view of tonality and its vast perspectives are all part of the fundamental understanding of the musical material. Just when the material's basic components are being questioned, the material itself is inevitably undergoing change, losing essential features of its substance and thus at risk of falling apart. This is the main reason why the problems of tonality became such a central part of the discussion for more than a hundred years of development in Western music. The tortuous development of compositional methods, principles, and systems so characteristic of the 20th century represents a series of attempts at either revealing or imbuing material with its own will. The question is whether the musical material's will is as clearly defined as in previous centuries, or whether the concept of material in the 1900s must be perceived as an issue of a far greater complexity. From a functionalist perspective, one can recognize the coexistence of several different materials, amalgamations, or alloys, each with its own unique characteristics. The variety of musical material thus agrees with functionalism's openness to new and modern materials.

Nonetheless, there have been attempts to find a basic material logic that shows a degree of universality—at least within a foreseeable period of time. It would also appear that efforts have been made to understand the material's

---

[10]*Philosophy of Modern Music,* 86.

The Crisis of Tonality

inherent orderliness from a more unambiguous standpoint, as in earlier times, without really acknowledging its potential diversity as a valuable innovation in itself. At this point another element from functionalist understanding emerges: the quest for artistic truthfulness, which must also master the relationship to the musical material. Both Schoenberg and Hindemith find their recognition of the material's will in the interplay between the diversity of possibilities and limitations and in the demand for truthfulness. The unconditional truth is the imperative guide, and in their recognition of the musical material's will they further develop their respective artistic materials within a functionalist understanding.

"The crisis of tonality" is not just a history about loss and decline. One of its most significant consequences is that it paves the ground for new and unique possibilities for musical construction. One may well state that all music at all times contains a strong or weak element of construction. Characteristic of developments in music during the 20th century, however, is that the constructive principles tend to pervade even the micro-level of compositional structure. The principles of construction often represent the primary, basic support on which the material depends to realize its determination, to use Sullivan's words. Referring to Le Corbusier, one could say that many types of musical material in the 20th century seem to be generally more applicable to construction than to decoration. This recognition again leads to main features of the functionalist understanding of material.

Adorno is one of the prominent spokesmen for the constructive possibilities of the material of modern music. As far as a 20th-century understanding of the material of art is concerned, Adorno has generally enjoyed an important position, not least as an ardent advocate of the Second Viennese School and as an originator of fundamental premises for modernist views on music. Adorno's ideas will always be regarded as an integral part of the music philosophies of his time. From a historical perspective, there are several reasons for looking more closely into his recognition of the material of music, since Adorno is a link between the understanding of the musical material from a vanishing age and the so-called modern 20th century.

Adorno and the Material of Music

The writings of Theodor Wiesengrund Adorno are of seminal importance for the modernist understanding of music. Adorno aligned himself with the Second Viennese School and contributed more than any other to its philosophical underpinnings. In the introduction to the English version of his book *Alban Berg: Der Meister der kleinsten Übergangs*, the translators characterize Adorno's role as follows:

> As a self-styled intellectual publicist for the "Second Viennese School," Adorno could speak with authority on technical matters, while at the same time abstracting from them philosophical insights which secured for this music a place of privilege for the intellectual elite of the inter- and post-war years.[11]

In the wake of Adorno's thoughts, modernism's concept of truth, with its intellectual and often uncompromising attitude to different forms of artistic expression, has also been allowed to flourish, if not always fully in Adorno's spirit. His cultural views were both contemporarily up to date and progressive, yet also rooted in tradition. Adorno thus places himself very centrally in a history-of-ideas tradition. This combination makes it particularly interesting to study Adorno's writings from a historical perspective, putting aside what agreement or disagreement there might be with his music philosophy.

Adorno's views on the material of music are present in issues that we have already stated as essential to the general functionalist understanding of material. As mentioned above, he sees a connection between the ideas of functionalism and the compositional school to which he feels he belongs. It is a sympathetic relationship in several areas, he says, not least when it comes to opposition to the so-called *materialfremde Ästhetik*, an opposition to the kind of aesthetics that cannot be derived from the material's actual constitution.

With regard to Adorno's approach to the material of music, two sources are particularly important. One is his book *Philosophy of Modern Music* (*Philosophie der neuen Musik*, originally published in 1949); the other is the collection of his public discussions and extensive correspondence with the composer Ernst Krenek, which continued with varying intensity from the end of the 1920s well into the 1960s. Several articles also touch on the same theme.

---

[11]Th.W. Adorno, *Alban Berg: Master of the Smallest Link*, J. Brand and C. Hailey, trans. (Cambridge, UK: Cambridge University Press, 1994), XII.

Adorno's *Philosophy of Modern Music* comprises two main sections: "Schoenberg and Progress," a somewhat earlier essay, and "Stravinsky and Restoration." The following discussion will concentrate on the first, as it deals particularly with Schoenberg. Adorno's understanding of material will then be further discussed through his examination of Hindemith's music as expressed in the collection of articles entitled "Ad vocem Hindemith."

First, some general comments on *Philosophy of Modern Music*. In this book, Adorno treats Arnold Schoenberg and Igor Stravinsky as opposites on several levels—a dialectic approach that enables him to chisel his views with the greatest emphasis. Schoenberg is regarded as a representative of the allegedly true and progressive view that is also Adorno's own, while Stravinsky, with his so-called masks, is interpreted as Schoenberg's regressive opposite. Thus in several respects, *Philosophy of Modern Music* is also an important discussion on Stravinsky. While today we might consider some of Adorno's critique of Stravinsky not only dubious but also decidedly below the belt, this is due in part to his literary style: He does not hesitate to insert comments, allegories, and statements which may lead the reader's associations in different directions. Adorno was already active in the early 1920s when Schoenberg, despite his established position as a modernist, was beginning to be regarded as somewhat passé. Composers like Stravinsky and Hindemith were seen by many as representing the new post-war age and Adorno could not let this belief go uncontested. This goes a long way to explaining why he felt he could not mince his words. But many of Adorno's critics will suggest that he could have expressed himself more objectively, not least for the sake of posterity. To be fair, one should remember that Adorno's relationship with Stravinsky was not as black and white as his book suggests.

Hegelian aesthetics are an important underpinning in the way Adorno formulates his views on music. He begins *Philosophy* by quoting Hegel:

> For in human Art we are not merely dealing with playthings, however pleasant or useful they may be, but [...] with a revelation of truth.[12]

This quotation illuminates basic elements in Adorno's understanding. First, it concerns the focus on art as revealing the truth, which, when applied to music, means that one's approach must be truthful, according to the type of *Materialgerechtigkeit* that music demands. This view, recognizable from the functionalist understanding, appears in both Schoenberg and Hindemith. The second aspect is the reference to art as *play*. *Schein und Spiel* (illusion and play) are concepts often encountered in Adorno's writings. He finds a

---

[12] *Philosophy of Modern Music*, 3.

representative for a negative and polemic attitude to this dichotomy in Arnold Schoenberg.[13] "With the negation of illusion and play music tends towards recognition," Adorno says, and continues:

> What radical music perceives is the untransfigured suffering of man. His impotence has increased to the point that it no longer tolerates illusion and play.[14]

Adorno believes that there exists no all-consuming opposition but a dual relationship between music's *Wahrheitsgehalt* (truth contents), on the one hand, and *Schein und Spiel* on the other. He feels that the music of earlier times afforded more room for the completeness of this range. The phenomenology of play can therefore also reveal an artistic truth. The problem, however, is that the *ludus* aspect can quickly come to represent an empty filler: it can lead to futile *Spielerei,* a vacuous performance. Consequently, for Adorno's view on music, it is important to realize that the concepts *Spiel* and *Spielerei* do not only differ from each other: they may also represent two fundamentally different phenomena.

Adorno concurs with Hegel's understanding of history as the unfolding of *der Weltgeist*.[15] The intellect, the sense of reality, and cultural understanding are all in constant development. Humans are always part of this process, whether they like it or not. This objective *Geist*, in the Hegelian sense, has settled in the musical material, Adorno adds:

> The demands made upon the subject by the material are conditioned much more by the fact that the "material" is itself a crystallization of the creative impulse [*Geist*], an element socially predetermined through the consciousness of man.[16]

In Adorno's opinion, the material of music is thus present as an objective substance in preformed condition as a result of the progress of human consciousness. The material's development has reached a stage determined by the dialectics between nature and history. The composer must always relate to the musical material's most advanced level, for here lies its authenticity. There has been a break with tonality. Subsequently, modes of expression from functional harmony no longer have the same significance

---

[13]*Philosophy of Modern Music*, 41.

[14]Ibid.

[15]Hegel's concept of *Geist* embraces religious, philosophic, and scientific understanding, common sense, intellect, a moral and social life, etc.

[16]*Philosophy of Modern Music*, 33. ["Die Forderungen, die vom Material ans Subjekt ergehen, rühren vielmehr davon her, dass das 'Material' selber sedimentierter Geist, ein gesellschaftlich, durchs Bewusstsein von Menschen hindurch Präformiertes ist."]

as before; they cannot be grasped as they were in earlier times. Authenticity is certainly not found by going backwards into music's historical development process.

The subjective element in the creative process [the *Geist*] is found in the composer's dialogue with his material, but, because of its objective consistency, the material places certain demands on the subject. These can be described as regularities: "As a previous subjectivity—now forgetful of itself—such an objectified impulse of the material has its own kinetic laws."[17]

Adorno's focus on the musical material's possibilities and limitations is basically no different from Hanslick's. However, Adorno is more committed in his approach, and more deliberate in using a cultural-historical perspective. He is convinced that the decline of tonality, and the subsequent prominent position dissonance gains, has profound consequences for the make-up of the musical material. Dissonance is difficult for some people to penetrate only because it forces them to confront their real human condition, he maintains. The music we take to heart is not on the same wavelength as our real situation: "Exactly the opposite is the case of the all-too-familiar, which is so far removed from the dominant forces of life today that the public's own experience scarcely still communicates with that for which traditional music bore witness."[18] The material's make-up reflects not only a stage in the music-historical development; it also reflects the social conditions, the society, and the time within which it unfolds. As mentioned above, Adorno sees the sedimentation of society interacting with the individual in the musical material. His opposition to the negatively perceived traditional tendencies in the music of his time is not just an expression of a progressive understanding of culture; it is also associated with contemporary pessimism, where the clouds of the general decline are looming on the horizon. Into this picture comes Marxism with its concepts of alienation and materialism, which became very important for Adorno. The combination of Hegelianism and Marxism is thus a significant point of departure for discussions on Adorno's views on art and culture.

When Adorno places such great emphasis on truth and on the musical material expressing its own time, it is necessary to point out the importance of having a so-called correct or truthful "awareness of music"; an awareness that faces the reality of the situation and sees through any false illusion. The view that tonality is a natural phenomenon is certainly an illusion:

---

[17] *Philosophy of Modern Music*, 33. ["Als ihrer selbst vergessene, vormalige Subjektivität hat solcher objektive Geist des Materials seine eigenen Bewegungsgesetze."]

[18] *Philosophy of Modern Music*, 9.

> The critics present their arguments as though the tonal idiom of the last 350 years had been derived from nature, and that to go beyond these firmly established theoretical principles were a violation thereof; whereas these ossified principles themselves are actually the very evidence of social pressure. The idea that the tonal system is exclusively of natural origin is an illusion rooted in history.[19]

For Adorno, the concept of nature is connected to what is static, timeless, and unchanging. History, on the contrary, is seen as dynamic and volatile. Conversely, the concept of *zweite Natur* (second nature) refers to something initially unnatural which seems to have become a solid, immutable substance in the human consciousness. Adorno scholar Max Paddison perceives a connection to Georg Lukács, from whom Adorno drew much of his inspiration, and translates second nature as "reified history and society."[20] Adorno regards the traditional understanding of tonality as part of human beings' second nature, and distances himself from, for instance, Hindemith's views. Yet this is not an unequivocal position. For example, Hindemith would be able to share Adorno's experience of the horizontal forces inherent in dissonant chords,[21] and Adorno's statement: "In the domain of twelve-tone method, chords essentially employing octave doublings sound false,"[22] confirms Hindemith's theories of tonality's basic regularity being founded on the relationship of the partial-tone spectrum to the properties of the ear. Like Hanslick, Adorno sees the material of music within the framework of tones, harmonies, and rhythms. Nonetheless, the question is: what kind of regularity does the historical and sociological sedimentation really demand? As mentioned above, *Materialgerechtigkeit* has a place in Adorno's terminology. The principles of so-called free atonality, a term used for the first time in *Philosophy of Modern Music*, become compositional guidelines for Adorno's understanding of material. One can perceive glimpses here of the Hegelian understanding of human development towards an ever increasing freedom. Yet, one might add, the paradox is that the so-called free atonality is not completely free from the traditional tonality from which it supposedly has been liberated: Avoiding any trace of functional harmony is just one of many compositional challenges.

---

[19]*Philosophy of Modern Music*, 11.

[20]M. Paddison, *Adorno's Aesthetics of Music* (Cambridge, UK: Cambridge University Press, 1993), 33.

[21]See *Philosophy of Modern Music*, 59.

[22]*Philosophy of Modern Music*, 35, note 4.

Conscious construction, known from the functionalist understanding of the creation process, is a key aspect of Adorno's approach, and thus the term *Sachlichkeit,* which is closely associated with logical construction, also has a positive feel to it. Adorno emphasizes a relationship between Expressionism, construction, and objectivity:

> If the drive towards well-integrated construction is to be called objectivity, then objectivity is not simply a counter-movement to Expressionism. It is the other side of the Expressionistic coin. Expressionistic music had interpreted so literally the principle of expression contained in traditionally Romantic music that it assumed the character of a case study. In so doing, a sudden change takes place. Music, as a case study in expression, is no longer "expressive."[23]

Dahlhaus presupposes a similar view of Expressionism's objective-constructive aspects when he writes: "as an expressionist, Schoenberg was a functionalist and as a functionalist, an expressionist."

Adorno's concept of construction implies a rationally far-reaching musical organization, a type of rationality that he feels is lacking in both Stravinsky and Hindemith. What he terms compositional *Musikantentum* (music-making activity or pseudo-musicianship) represents nothing less than the direct opposite of musical construction:

> This pseudo-musicianship is a clever manipulation involving one isolated aspect of musical material in place of a constructive consequential procedure which subjects all aspects of this material to the same law.[24]

Despite his pleasure in musical rationality and organization, Adorno keeps a certain distance from twelve-tone method. For him, this technique has a material veneer of dependence. There is a connection between music's so-called mathematical techniques and Logical Positivism, he claims, and, he adds: "the inclination towards numerical games is as unique to the Viennese intellect as is the game of chess in the coffee house."[25] Something about the thoroughly systematic and mathematical determinations of the twelve-tone method conflicts with Adorno's attitude to conventional musical procedures. Nevertheless, their freedom with respect to rhythm and motivic

---

[23] *Philosophy of Modern Music,* 49. ["Nennt man den Zwang zur stimmigen Konstruktion Sachlichkeit, so ist Sachlichkeit keine bloße Gegenbewegung zum Expressionismus. Sie ist der Expressionismus in seinem Anderssein. Die expressionistische Musik hatte das Prinzip des Ausdrucks der traditionell romantischen so genau genommen, dass es Protokollcharakter annahm. Damit aber schlägt es um. Musik als Ausdrucksprotokoll ist nicht länger "ausdrucksvoll."]

[24] *Philosophy of Modern Music,* 54.

[25] *Philosophy of Modern Music,* 62, note 24.

strategy persuades him to recognize even the twelve-tone method as a result of historical necessity:

> The rules are not arbitrarily designed. They are configurations of the historical force present in the material. At the same time, these rules are formulae by which they adjust themselves to this force.[26]

Adorno obviously feels at home within free atonality where linear procedures and polyphonic principles should be predominant, or so he believes. The orderliness imposed on a composer by the musical material lies not only in all voices being a result of urgent necessity: each note must rather have a specific function in the fabric of the music, and the primary tool to achieve this is a painstaking treatment of musical motives. In a conception of the musical material that predicates each note as being determined by the work's overall structure, the difference between the accidental and essential is eliminated.

Adorno's musical material, with all its sedimentation, is thus tied to the concept of construction. This in turn is tied to the artistic totality, to the formal design of a work. It follows that the form must already lie hidden in the material's inherent orderliness. This recognition makes it difficult for Adorno to accept traditional form schemata as a point of departure. What constitutes material and form may be regarded as relative. Thinking along these lines places Adorno within the Aristotelian tradition, which is so central to functionalism's early development.

In *Philosophy of Modern Music*, Adorno presents his views in the light of Schoenberg and in contrast to Stravinsky. He opens the section "Strawinsky und die Restauration" with yet another quotation from Hegel's *Ästhetik*:

> Nor is it of any real assistance to him that he further appropriates, so to speak, with his soul and substance a view of the world that belongs to the past, in other words tries to root himself in one of such and, let us say, turns Roman Catholic, as not a few have done in recent times for Art's sake, in order to give their soul some secure foundation, and so enable the definite lines of their artistic product to become themselves some thing which shall appear to have an independently valid growth.[27]

---

[26]*Philosophy of Modern Music*, 63-64.

[27]Hegel, *Ästhetik II*, quoted from Th.W. Adorno: *Philosophy of Modern Music*, 135. ["Es hilft da weiter nichts, sich vergangene Weltanschauungen wieder, so zu sagen, substantiell aneignen, d. i.: sich in Eine dieser Anschauungsweisen festhineinmachen zu wollen, als z.B. katholisch zu werden, wie es in neueren Zeiten die Kunst wegen Viele gethan, um ihr Gemüth zu fixieren, und die bestimmte Begränzung ihrer Darstellung für sich selbst zu etwas An-und-für-sich-seyendem werden zu lassen."]

Adorno and the Material of Music

With this motto Adorno approaches Stravinsky's music, which he finds representing both a reaction and a regression, claiming that the composer does not give appropriate consideration to the musical material's vast potential for up-to-date relevancy. Instead, Stravinsky leads only into a blind alley of impassibility. Rather than lingering on his relation to Stravinsky, Adorno's conception of the musical material may be further elaborated by his approach to Paul Hindemith, the other protagonist of this study.

Adorno's attitude to Hindemith is revealed most succinctly in "Ad vocem Hindemith: Eine Dokumentation," a five-part series of texts reflecting his changing view on the composer over a period of more than forty-five years (1922-1968).[28] In the early 1920s, Hindemith was thought to be among the most promising of the post-war generation of German composers. The first part of "Ad vocem Hindemith," written in 1922, shows Adorno to be one of Hindemith's many admirers. This does not mean that he accepts everything about the composer without question, but the composer impresses him greatly even beyond the fact of his unusual versatility. It is particularly interesting to note that Adorno's early writings on Hindemith contain views on music which were to appear even more strongly in other areas of the author's later production. In connection with Hindemith's rather daring one-act opera *Das Nusch-Nuschi* op. 20 (1920), Adorno points out how the work seems to grow out of an inner, organic drive. He goes on to say:

> There is a symphonification of opera, yet different than with Wagner; the opera is conceived as a grand musical form. The psychological leitmotif disappears, with the whole construction developing instead from thematic germinal cells in the suggested compulsive manner.[29]

In Hindemith's even more provocative *Sancta Susanna* op. 21 (1921), Adorno finds that these laudable features have been developed even further:

> For here, everything that happens musically is developed from *one* theme; a theme whose emotional force direct not at an individual, not at a mood, but at the irrational fundamental plot of this opera.[30]

---

[28] "Ad vocem Hindemith" is reproduced in Th.W. Adorno, *Impromptus* [*Musikalische Schriften* IV, *Gesammelte Schriften* 17] (Frankfurt a. M.: Suhrkamp, 1982), 210-246.

[29] "Ad vocem Hindemith," 215. ["Eine Symphonisierung der Oper setzt ein, anders jedoch als die Wagnersche; die Oper wird als große musikalische Form konzipiert. Die psychologische Leitmotivik verschwindet; dafür entwickelt sich in dem angedeuteten triebmäßigen Sinn aus thematischen Urzellen der ganze Bau."]

[30] "Ad vocem ...," 215. ["Denn hier wird aus *einem* Thema alles, was musikalisch überhaupt geschieht, herauswickelt; einem Thema, dessen emotionale Kraft nicht einem Individuum, nicht einer Stimmung, sondern schlechthin dem irrationalen Grundgeschehen dieser Oper gilt."]

Central features in Adorno's understanding of the musical material are the decisive significance of the so-called germinal cell, the motive, the theme for the work's construction, development, and design. The factor that later kept him from openly accepting Hindemith's music was what he felt was a growing lack of this type of consistency.

In 1921, Adorno began compositional studies under Hindemith's former teacher Bernhard Sekles. After the 1924 performance of the *Three Orchestral Pieces* from Alban Berg's *Wozzeck* in Frankfurt, he was introduced to the composer and in the following year became Berg's student. There is every reason to believe that Berg thought highly of the young man's artistic abilities. Rudolf Stephan, mentioned in the introduction of "Ad vocem Hindemith," suggests that Adorno's problematic relationship to Hindemith began with his direct contact with the Second Viennese School:

> In consequence, the critical cause of the metamorphosed basic tone in his [Adorno's] critique is found less in Hindemith's conversion to Neo-Classicism in 1923 than in an isolating change in position on the part of Adorno, which again can be conveyed through alienation towards Hindemith.[31]

Stephan is convinced that Adorno's views on Hindemith were determined by his relations with Schoenberg. This observation seems indeed convincing, since Adorno's criticism is usually aimed at features considered alien to the Schoenberg School. This applies even more strongly in his polemic directed against Stravinsky. Thus it is necessary to read both "Ad vocem Hindemith" and *Philosophy of Modern Music* in order to really understand Adorno's relationship with Hindemith and his works.

In the second section of his Hindemith collection from 1926, Adorno points to what he considers to be the superficial and mechanical objectivity that seems to have blossomed in the so-called *Musikantentum*:

> Aesthetically, objectivism, which relies on the metrics of repetition, has been both liberated and pinned down from a cultural-political perspective. Its immanently compositional correlate has disintegrated: anti-Romanticism has become Romantic.[32]

---

[31]R. Stephan, "Adorno und Hindemith. Zum Verständnis einer schwierigen Beziehung," *Hindemith-Jahrbuch* 1978/VII (Mainz etc.: Schott, 1980), 45. ["Die entscheidende Ursache des veränderten Tenors der Kritiken [Adornos] ist demnach weniger in Hindemiths 1923 vollzogener Wendung zu einem neuem neuen Klassizismus zu suchen, als in einer abgeschlossenen Positionsänderung Adornos, die durch eine Entfremdung von Hindemith gefördert worden sein mag."]

[32]"Ad vocem ...," 219. ["Ästhetisch abgelöst, kulturpolitisch zugleich fixiert hat sich der Objektivismus, der auf die Wiederholungsmetrik sich stützt. Sein innerkompositionelles Korrelat zerfiel; die Antiromantik ist romantisch geworden."]

It is interesting to compare this statement regarding anti-Romanticism and the Romantic to the previously quoted view on Expressionism as a case study in expression. Adorno has a particular knack of articulating himself through apparently paradoxical statements. As far as *Musikantentum* is concerned, Adorno laments the absence of motivic consistency in the compositional development, the lack of which also impacts the relationship between material and form:

> Hindemith's works from his "classicist" period make their entry with the demand to play in forms and, in reality, they just play around with forms.[33]

This elegant toying with the verb "to play" (*spielen*) is typical of Adorno's literary style. It enables him to demonstrate the irresponsible emptiness he finds in parts of Hindemith's production as well as in a similar use of musical material in general. As mentioned above, this view is closely associated with Adorno's ideas of truthfulness. At the same time he reveals another trait in his ideas on music: his apparent lack of understanding of the *play* that makes music a vividly vibrant experience. There is a stern and rather hostile attitude towards so-called music-making lingering in Adorno's views. Yet one must take into account that his views developed in a time in which amateurish, fancy free, and apparently self-content music-making was all the rage. Hindemith, it should be added, was also skeptical of such aspects of contemporary music life.

In the third section of "Ad vocem Hindemith," written in 1932, Adorno objects with determination to the *Warencharakter* (commodity aspect) of *Gebrauchsmusik*. In this text, his affinity to Marxist ideals is expressed more clearly than before, suggesting that he regards music as a component in the economic and political power structure of society. At the time of writing this text, Adorno was employed at the Institute for Social Research in Frankfurt, not least thanks to its industrious leader Max Horkheimer. Adorno here uses his concept *Leerlauf* (idling) to once again criticize the restless music-making emptiness that, to his mind, pervades Hindemith's works. What is the content of this music? What is its goal? Merely a somnambulistic way to pass the day—"music to 'fill' the vacuous, fearful time?"[34]

The fourth section, from 1939, is a critique of the first edition of part 1 of Hindemith's *Unterweisung im Tonsatz*, a work that will be more closely

---

[33]"Ad vocem ...," 221. ["Die Werke aus Hindemiths klassizistischer Epoche treten mit dem Anspruch auf, in den Formen zu spielen, und spielen tatsächlich mit den Formen bloß."]

[34] "Ad vocem ...," 225. [... "die Musik soll die leer ablaufende, ängstigende Zeit 'füllen'."]

examined later in this study. A few of Adorno's concerns illustrate his views: He cannot accept Hindemith's basic tenet that tonality is grounded in natural laws or regularities founded in nature. Neither does he see any historical necessity at all in Hindemith's attempts at scientific systematizations. He also rejects the composer's claim that craft is all-important to the realization of music's material. Generally, Adorno's view on craft seems to be rather narrow, not least when regarded in the light of his own emphasis on functionality, objectivity, and construction. In his opinion, the concept of compositional craft only incorporates a doubtful rationalization and trivialization of the process of artistic creation within a false framework of security. Hindemith's attempts at systems and standardizations must be understood in the same way:

> It [*Craft*] becomes reactionary as soon as the organizing schemata are presented as norms. His prohibitions are fetters on musical creativity: by means of feeble auxiliary constructions a limited, convention-oriented compositional experience is puffed up to ontology. Nothing should come into being that was not already there [...][35]

The fifth section, from 1962, is a survey of Hindemith's œuvre in all its facets: compositions, writings, teaching etc. Adorno is apparently seeking to moderate his early youthful admiration for Hindemith even more: "It was the Viennese School that also cured me, theoretically speaking, of the ruling musical cliché; in the [earlier] Hindemith article the word *musikantisch* appears as positive,"[36] he writes. Yet he is not afraid of crediting the composer with considerable musical talent—he seems to have still far more respect for Hindemith than for Stravinsky. What he considers regrettable is that Hindemith has gone astray, and thus misused his promising potential:

> In Hindemith's best works from these years it is not difficult to point out what should have been developed in order to lay the foundation for a radical kind of music that goes beyond the Expressionist generation, instead of the academic bridges he built backward.[37]

---

[35] "Ad vocem ...," 233. ["Reaktionär wird es in dem Augenblick, in dem es die Ordnungsschemata als Normen ausgibt. Seine Verbote sind Fesseln der musikalischen Produktivkraft: durch armselige Hilfskonstruktionen wird eine an der Konvention orientierte, beschränkte Komponiererfahrung zur Ontologie aufgeplustert. Nichts soll vorkommen, was nicht schon da war."]

[36] "Ad vocem ...," 237. ["Erst die Wiener Schule hat mich auch theoretisch von den herrschenden musikalischen Clichés kuriert; in dem Hindemith Aufsatz kommt das Wort musikantisch positiv vor."]

[37] "Ad vocem ...," 239. ["Es fiele nicht schwer, in den besten Arbeiten Hindemiths jener Jahre zu zeigen, was nur hätte weiter getrieben zu werden brauchen, um eine über die expressionistische Generation hinaus radikale Musik zu stiften, anstatt der akademischen Brücken, die er nach rückwärts schlug."]

In the study of Adorno's relations with Hindemith, this statement is crucial. Indirectly, it refers both to the epistemological standpoint Hindemith was to develop and the changes in the composer's music during the 1920s. It is in this process that Adorno believes the gifted Hindemith wanders off in the wrong direction, as he turns away from the positive construction principles of his earlier works. Again, Adorno seems to find Hindemith's music lacking in the tenets of the Second Viennese School, the creeds so central to his own understanding of material. Consequently, we have come full circle to Rudolf Stephan's views on the assumed Adorno-Schoenberg-Hindemith relationship.

Both Stephan and the Hindemith scholar Dieter Rexroth point out that after World War II Adorno came to regard Hindemith's reputation as overrated and considered it his task to inform others of this view. This mission may at least partly explain his frequent polemic remarks. Rexroth believes that Adorno has had great influence on how Hindemith has been received:

> Today, Theodor W. Adorno can be considered the critic who, subsequent to World War II and after Hindemith's death in 1963, provoked the most long-lasting influence on the way Hindemith has been received.[38]

It is in fact quite likely that Adorno, at least indirectly, stimulated the negative attitudes and prejudices of which Hindemith is the victim in some modernist-music circles. The erroneous idea that Schoenberg and Hindemith were irreconcilable enemies, too, forms part of this picture. When looking at Adorno in relation to Schoenberg and Hindemith, such views may be relevant enough. What is more important in the functionalist perspective, however, is the understanding of the musical material apparent in Adorno's writings, the position he holds within a general functionalist context, and the resulting significance for the understanding of musical thought in the 20th century. This situation also invites a more detailed discussion of Schoenberg's and Hindemith's views on the material of music.

---

[38] Editorial commentary in D. Rexroth, ed., *Paul Hindemith. Briefe* (Frankfurt am Main: Fischer, 1982), 99. ["Theodor W. Adorno kann heute als der Kritiker Hindemiths angesehen werden, der nach dem Zweiten Weltkrieg und nach dem Tod Hindemiths im Jahre 1963 die nachhaltigste Wirkung die Hindemith-Rezeption auslöste."]

Schoenberg: The Motive as Musical Material

> Musik soll nicht schmücken,
> sie soll wahr sein.
>
> *Arnold Schönberg*[39]

Focus

"The genuine artist must be a slave to his artistic material," writes the conductor Hermann Scherchen in 1920: "What he feels becomes tones, colors, lines; he is Zoroaster's 'reversed cripple, *only* ear, *only* eye'—only then, compelled by *one* of the human forms of expression, will he or she— musician, painter, poet—be genuine."[40] In Scherchen's opinion, the creative artist's *Besessenheit* (obsession) with his or her material is of decisive importance for the quality of the completed work. This kind of focusing on artistic material is characteristic of positive views on contemporary music after World War I.[41] More than anything else, it was the rejection of the basic principles of functional harmony that led to discussions on *eine Neugestaltung des Tonmaterials*, on the tonal material being shaped anew. In his article, "Die Wandlung des musikalischen Materials," the composer Wolfgang Fortner recognizes the century's harmonic development as the source of the most important features in the development of the musical material.[42] During the 1920s, the musical material was usually described in words that suggest associations to both the general conception of the material of art and the special preoccupation with new materials typical of that time. The material substance of music seems to represent an independent entity and a value in itself. Heinz Tiessen uses such expressions as *absolute Materialgestaltung* and *absolute Materialdurcharbeitung*. These notions give musical material an absolute status resting on its own inherent regularity, reminiscent of the way in which instrumental music achieved its elevated status in the context of Romanticism's idea of absolute music. The musical material's will is elicited together with the quest for artistic truth.

---

[39][Music ought not to beautify, it ought to be true.]

[40]Translated from H. Scherchen, "Arnold Schoenberg," *Melos* 1 (1920): 9.

[41]The mainly positive and optimistic post-first-world-war generation naturally enough did not define themselves according to such a historical-systematic description.

[42]See W. Fortner, "Die Wandlung des musikalischen Materials," *Melos* 18/6-7 (1951): 163-167.

Schoenberg: The Motive as Musical Material

Tiessen finds these traits particularly striking in what he recognizes as anti-Romantic *Sachlichkeit*, and argues for a connection with a unique concentration of *will*. As far as technical aspects of composition are concerned, he finds it noteworthy that linear, horizontal progressions become more important as a building principle than vertical harmony:

> This was gradually being expressed through *turning away from the literary program and text*, in *the dissolution of the tonal system* and *new research into tonal material*, in diminishing the perceived atmosphere of sound by reduction to *essentials*, through replacing harmony as a building principle by a newly awakened *linear activity* and finally, at the cost of the flat and lyrical stagnation of mood and condition, through resolute brevity, which came to a head in the *shrinking of musical forms*.[43]

The emphasis on brevity and the essentials, characteristic of functionalist aesthetics, is strongly connected to manifestations of the truth concept. By drawing attention to the new material's form-reducing tendencies Tiessen also focuses on the formal problems which this newly conquered field could raise at a time when functional harmony had lost its position as a form-structuring guide.

The focus on newly achieved musical material incorporates the view that it has its own unique compulsion or will; an idea that is also decisive for Schoenberg. Terms such as genuine material and pure or absolute musical language are associated with him and several of his contemporaries.[44]

In Hermann Scherchen's introductory words on the artist and material, he continues his thoughts by focusing on Schoenberg as one of this ideal combination's most prominent representatives:

---

[43] H. Tiessen, *Zur Geschichte der jüngsten Musik (1913-1928)*, 43. ["Dies äußerte sich nach und nach in der *Abwendung vom literarischen Programm und Text*, in der *Auflösung des Tonsystems* und *Neuergründung des Tonmaterials*, im Verschmähen der sinnlichen Klangatmosphäre durch Reduzierung auf *Wesentliches*, im Ausschalten der Harmonik als Bauprinzip zugunsten einer neu erwachenden *linearen Aktivität*, und endlich im Bedürfnis nach einer – die Fläche und die lyrische Stimmungs- und Zustandsstagnation verdrängenden – resoluten Knappheit, die sich bis zum *Einschrumpfen der musikalischen Formen* zuspitzte."]

[44] See for instance, H. Jalowetz, "Schönbergs Werk in der Zeit," *Arnold Schönberg zum 60. Geburtstag, 13 September 1934*, 7.

> Few artists have been as obsessed by their artistic material as Schoenberg. The hidden compulsion drives him in such a fundamental way that his creativity leads him to one problem approach after another, each solution releasing new forces and demanding new combinations.[45]

This florid characterization of Schoenberg's creativity in relation to the forces of the musical material is descriptive both of the composer's artistic works and his literary production: the attention paid to the allegedly correct handling of the material is invaluable. When recognizing the fundamental relationship between the development of 20th-century music and questions of the musical material, it is not difficult to accept the importance of Schoenberg's position during much of the century. It should also be easy to take the next step and agree with Kurt Westphal, who recognized in Schoenberg the person who, in his time, both carried on and embraced the whole of musical development:

> *He* has removed music farthest from tradition, he has reached what are presently the farthest limits in the new popular direction; but through *him* and his pioneering works there is an obvious connection between the new music and the principles of 19th-century music. *His* works act like a comment on the new music's history; each of his works represents a point in the rapid progress of modern music.[46]

In the article containing this quotation, Westphal does not often use the term "material"; he limits its use to describing the twelve pitches as *Urmaterial,* as the basic material elements. At the same time, he is concerned with the forces that are played out in music, in which this allegedly primeval material is an essential precondition. This fundamental view is also the framework of Schoenberg's understanding of the musical material.

---

[45]H. Scherchen, "Arnold Schoenberg," 9. ["Wenige Künstler sind so von der Materie ihrer Kunst besessen gewesen wie Arnold Schönberg. In ihm wirken die verbogenen Triebkräfte so elementar, dass sein Schaffen von Problemstellung zu Problemstellung führt, dass jede Lösung neue Kräfte entbindet und neue Zusammenfassungen verlangt."]

[46]K. Westphal, "Arnold Schönbergs Weg zur Zwölftöne-Musik," *Die Musik* 21/7 (1929): 492. ["*Er* hat die Musik am weitesten von der Tradition entfernt, hat die bisher äußersten Grenzen in der neu eingeschlagenen Richtung erreicht; durch *ihn* und seine Erstlingswerke hängt aber die neue Musik zugleich auch am sichtbarlichsten mit den Prinzipen der Musik des 19. Jahrhunderts zusammen. *Sein* Schaffen wirkt wie ein Kommentar zur Geschichte der neuen Musik; jedes seiner Werke hält einen Punkt in der weiterschreitenden Bewegung der modernen Musik fest."]

A Group Portrait of 1895

Schoenberg strongly identified with the radical environment he encountered as a young man in Vienna, obviously regarding himself as music's standard-bearer in the search for cultural and artistic truth. In 1895, he first met Karl Kraus, probably at the famous *Café Griensteidl*, where Kraus had been a regular for some years. Schoenberg's preoccupation with questions of linguistic formulations undoubtedly found fresh nourishment in the company of this prominent writer. "For him [Schoenberg], the purity of the German language was the undeniable precondition for clarity of thought, for precision of the verbal expression," explains Schoenberg pupil Josef Rufer.[47] In the introductions to English editions of Schoenberg's writings one often finds comments on the problems involved in translating the German text without losing nuances of meaning and undermining the author's concise style. Bryan R. Simms writes that Schoenberg was dissatisfied with the words and phrases in the first attempts at translating his *Harmonielehre* into English.[48] Generally speaking, language and the logic of language are frequently used as reference and metaphor in Schoenberg's writings on music. His respect and admiration for Kraus is expressed in concentrated form in this retrospective comment:

> In my dedication to Karl Kraus in my Theory of Harmony I said something like "I have perhaps learnt more from you than one should learn if one would remain independent..." With that, surely not the extent but hopefully the level of my esteem has been asserted.[49]

Schoenberg's correspondence with Wassily Kandinsky is well known among art historians. Schoenberg was also in close personal contact with Adolf Loos. According to Eberhard Freitag, this was Schoenberg's only long-standing contact with artists from the Vienna circles. Freitag refers to Schoenberg's common cause with respect to ideas, and continues:

---

[47]Translated from J. Rufer, "Hommage à Schönberg" (1974), quoted in F. Pfäfflin, "Karl Kraus und Arnold Schönberg: Fragmente einer Beziehung," in H.L. Arnold, ed., *Karl Kraus*, [Sonderheft *text + kritik*] (Munich: Richard Boorberg, 1975), 127. ["Die Reinheit der deutschen Sprache war ihm unabdingbare Voraussetzung für die Klarheit des Denkens, für die Präzision des sprachlichen Ausdrucksmittels."]

[48]See B.R. Simms, "Commentary: Arnold Schoenberg, 'Theory of Harmony'," R.E. Carter, trans. (Berkeley, CA, etc.: University of California Press. 1978), *Music Theory Spectrum* 4 (1982): 155–162. Schoenberg's dissatisfaction, however, was not occasioned by Carter.

[49]P. Schick, *Karl Kraus, mit Selbstzeugnissen und Bilddokumenten* (Reinbek bei Hamburg: Rowohlt, 1989), p. 151. ["In der Widmung, mit der ich Karl Kraus meine Harmonielehre schickte, sagte ich ungefähr: 'Ich habe von Ihnen vielleicht mehr gelernt, als man lernen darf, wenn man noch selbständig bleiben will...' Damit ist gewiß nicht der Umfang, wohl aber das Niveau der Schätzung festgestellt, die ich für ihn habe."]

> For both artists [Schoenberg and Loos], criticism of ornamentation means a struggle against decayed forms of style long since bereft of their functional and symbolic meaning, where decor no longer developed from organization of the whole but instead became an appliqué to conceal the fractures through a semblance of unity.[50]

The Loos biographers Burkhard Rukschcio and Roland Schachel point at the similarities between the wording in the architect's writings and passages in Schoenberg's *Harmonielehre*. The view on a work's relation to the concept of truthfulness and morality particularly reveals Loos's influence:

> Schoenberg's postulate "music shall not decorate, it shall be true," reflects Loos's recognition that "ornamentlessness is a sign of spiritual power."[51]

The connection between these two statements lies in the rejection of exterior decoration. The opposition to ornament seems to be based on what is regarded as truth and the so-called spiritual, mental, or epistemological force. Again one is confronted with the central importance of truthfulness for the spiritual dimensions of the functionalist concept. "With truth, and let it by all means be hundreds of years old, we have more inner connections than with the lie, which is everywhere among us," proclaims Loos.[52]

A focus on Schoenberg's search for truth also pervades the *Festschrift* on the occasion of his 60th birthday in 1934. The following words from his student Hans Erich Apostel are typical in this respect:

> Schoenberg was the one who told us that truth must be the first rule of a work of art. And we can meet him with honesty, that these words were not "spoken into the void."[53]

---

[50] E. Freitag, *Arnold Schönberg, mit Selbstzeugnissen und Bilddokumenten* (Reinbeck bei Hamburg: Rowohlt, 1973), 24. ["Die Kritik des Ornaments bedeutet für beide Künstler einen Kampf gegen heruntergekommene Stilformen, die ihren funktionalen und symbolischen Sinn längst eingebüßt hatten, in denen sich das Dekor nicht länger aus der Organisation des Ganzen entwickelte, sondern appliziert wurde, um mit dem Schein von Einheitlichkeit die Brüche in der Konstruktion überdecken."]

[51] B. Rukschcio and R. Schachel, *Adolf Loos. Leben und Werk*, 101. ["Das Postulat Schönbergs 'Musik soll nicht schmücken, sie soll wahr sein' reflektiert die Erkenntnis von Loos, dass 'Ornamentlosigkeit ein Zeichen geistiger Kraft' ist."]

[52] *Ibid.*, 91. ["Mit der Wahrheit, und sei sie Hunderte von Jahren alt, haben wir mehr innere Zusammenhänge als mit der Lüge, die neben uns geht."]

[53] H.E. Apostel, untitled contribution in *Arnold Schönberg zum 60. Geburtstag*, 36. ["Schönberg war es, der uns sagte, dass Wahrhaftigkeit der Primat eines Kunstwerks sei. Und wir können ihm aufrichtig entgegnen, dass diese Worte nicht 'ins Leere gesprochen' waren."] The expression "ins Leere gesprochen" (spoken into the void) may refer to the title of a collection of Loos's articles from the period 1897-1900.

Materialgerechtigkeit

The term *Materialgerechtigkeit* is a concept also used by Schoenberg. In the 1920s, he writes:

> The material of my music is different from that of others, hence the form and everything else is different, in accordance with this material. The music of my contemporaries makes gold clocks of iron, rubber tires of wood, and suchlike. Consequently, they do not work according to the nature of the material [*materialgerecht*], and expect that the coating, the paint which the finished product gets, shall make it their own.[54]

Schoenberg speaks here about his music as coming out of a unique material different than that of many others. The musical material is thus not just regarded as an object for general *Neuergründung* or *Neuaufbau*; there is, in addition, the question of different types of material. This might lead one to the view that his contemporaries are as conscientious in *their* use of the musical material as he is with *his*. But Schoenberg's point is that many of his contemporaries do not appear to work with their musical material according to its qualities and its own will. Their respective material is not handled according to its inherent rules, and any attempt to camouflage this fact through quasi-individuality is nothing more than a thin veil. There is much evidence of the functionalist belief that outer varnish and artificial facades hide the truth of the specific material. Schoenberg's intention is to demonstrate the lack of concern many of his contemporaries show for the structural and structuralizing forces of their artistic material. He considers himself a link in a historical development: it is *he* who reconciles the musical material of his time with its proper form; he appears as a self-appointed redeemer of the musical material's development. Another interesting aspect of this statement is that Schoenberg draws attention to his own presumably timeless view that artistic material and form must always directly agree with one another—a characteristic feature of the functionalist view.

---

[54]*Nachlaß* dated 21 April 1923, translated from M. Hansen, *Arnold Schönberg: Ein Konzept der Moderne* (Kassel: Bärenreiter, 1993), 196. ["Das Material, aus dem meine Musik wird, ist anders und darum, diesem Material entsprechend, wird die Form und alles anders. Die Musik meiner Zeitgenossen aber macht aus dem Eisen goldene Uhren, aus Holz Gummireifen und dgl., sie arbeitet daher nicht materialgerecht und erwartet, dass der Überzug, der Anstrich, den das fertige Produkt bekommt, das seinige tun werde."]

Tonal or Atonal?

According to Schoenberg, the musical material has reached a certain level. "I always insisted that new music was merely a logical development of musical resources," he writes with a bitter undertone in the article "How One Becomes Lonely" (1937).[55] Schoenberg is not, however, as categorical as Adorno and Hindemith are on this point. Looking at Schoenberg's development—from a Romantic style based on functional harmony via the so-called free atonality to the twelve-tone method—one may misunderstand this apparent linear progression and believe that his conception of tonality must have developed stage-by-stage along the same lines. Works such as *Suite in G* (1935) and *Kammersymphonie Nr. 2* (1939) would have to be considered tonal retreats. However, for Schoenberg, tonality in the traditional sense of the word always represents one of several ways of organizing tones: "Tonality [...] is not a necessity for a piece of music, but rather a possibility."[56]

Schoenberg calls tonality centered on one tonal level "monotonality." "I believe in *monotonality*," he writes in a letter to Anders Twa, "that there is only *one* tonality in one piece and all that was called 'another key' is only 'a region carried out like a key'—a region of the one tonality of the piece."[57] Within this type of tonality one can find tonal functions that are *centripetal*, as they are closely related to or strive towards the tonic key. One may also find *centrifugal* progressions with the opposite tendency.[58] These notions are akin to Sullivan's ideas of the extensive or intensive radial energy of form.

A tonal center can thus be demonstrated in very different ways. Schoenberg did not share Adorno's view that composers must always find themselves at the most advanced stage of the material: much rather, the composer creates in relation to the regularity innate in the material, independently of its actual stage of development. In the introduction to *Die glückliche Hand*, written in 1928, Schoenberg relates the musical material to the goals and numerical regularities out of which the universe was created.[59] But then, as he argues in his *Theory of Harmony*, it is the creative imagination that comes into contact with the universe; there are no eternally valid regularity principles of tonality:

---

[55] A. Schoenberg, "How One Becomes Lonely," *Style and Idea*, 50.

[56] A. Schoenberg, *Coherence, Counterpoint...*, 47.

[57] Excerpt quoted in A. Schoenberg, *The Musical Idea*, 383.

[58] See *The Musical Idea*, 120.

[59] A. Schoenberg, "Die glückliche Hand," *Stil und Gedanke*, 237.

> [...] any material can be suitable for art—if it is well enough defined that one can shape it in accordance with its supposed nature, yet not so well defined that the imagination has no unexplored territory in which to roam, in which to establish a mystical connection with the universe.[60]

The material's universal regularity is rediscovered in the universe, but only in the sense that human beings are of the same nature as the cosmos, believes Schoenberg. Therefore, he cannot agree with Josef Matthias Hauer and his concept of twelve-tone music as music of the spheres, as a universal language that breaks with the dominance of the spoken language on Earth.[61] Neither does Schoenberg have much time for the kind of speculation that dwells on cosmic causes and occult parallels to music:

> Hauer looks for laws. Good. But he looks for them where he will not find them. I say that it is obvious we are as nature around us is, as the cosmos is. So that is also how our music is. But then our music must also be as we are (if two magnitudes both equal a third...). But then from our nature alone I can deduce how our music is (bolder men than I would say, "how the cosmos is!").[62]

The musical material is suitable for art, says Schoenberg, remaining close to Hanslick but not going as far as using the latter's word *geistfähig*. Major significance should not be attached to this particular use of terms, although a subtle difference is suggested in their basic conception of the musical material, a difference of the specifically artistic compared to the spiritual in the widest sense. The musical material can be organized in such a way that its make-up can be understood by the human intellect. Its aesthetic value still lies in the way in which its possibilities are exploited.

Schoenberg's use of the term "the musical material" is at times both broad and quite traditional, resembling what we have seen in Hanslick and Adorno. The way he begins his brief note on the *fugue* is typical of the more comprehensive variant of the concept:

---

[60]*Theory of Harmony*, 26.

[61]More on Hauer's ideas can be found in R. Stephan, "Zur Entstehung der Zwölftonmusik," in G. Schnitzler, ed., *Musik und Zahl: Interdisziplinäre Beiträge zum Grenzbereich zwischen Musik und Mathematik* (Bonn/Bad Godesberg: Verlag für systematische Musikwissenschaft, 1976), 164.

[62]A. Schoenberg, "Hauer's Theories," *Style and Idea*, 209-210. The original version of "Hauers Theorien," written in 1923, is not included in the German version of the book, *Stil und Gedanke*.

> A fugue is a composition with maximum self-sufficiency of content. The more such self-sufficiency is manifest in the form of unity of material, the more all the shapes stem from one basic idea—that is to say, from a single theme and the way it is treated—the more artful it is.[63]

A more concise definition of the musical material can be found in Schoenberg's statement "[the] material of music is the tone."[64] When taking a closer look at Schoenberg's philosophy one discovers that this characterization must either relate to a narrow conception of the tone as the raw material of music or to the characteristic individual tone carrying a minimum potential of musical progression.[65] The creation of musical art presupposes the connection of tone, ear, and the world of feelings. Schoenberg thus draws attention to the absolute inadequacy of the musically isolated tone. Nevertheless, when it comes to the concept of the musical motive, he points out its motivic potential that exists in even the individual tone.

In traditional tonality there is no natural regularity that extends beyond its own tonal area, Schoenberg says, disagreeing with those who maintain that the principles of tonality are universal and fixed for all time. Like Adorno, he uses the concept of second nature, and also maintains that any musical development is a result of the dialectics between nature and second nature:

> [...] our present-day ear has been educated not only by the conditions nature imposed on it, but also by those produced by the system, which has become a second nature.[66]

Bearing this in mind, Schoenberg has no reservations about exploiting works from his illustrious predecessors when he wishes to explore the musical material of his own time. The supposed regularities revealed here, he argues, are no less universal than those others might find in the overtone series.

When Schoenberg uses the designation "natural," it is usually in the sense of "natural according to human nature."[67] This particular usage does not mean that he is blind to a nature-based connection between the partial-tone series and basic features in functional harmony. This association is

---

[63] A. Schoenberg, "Fugue," *Style and Idea*, 297.

[64] *Theory of Harmony*, 15.

[65] I.e., a tone with a certain length, articulation, and dynamics.

[66] *Theory of Harmony*, 56.

[67] *Theory of Harmony*, 201.

even explained in his *Theory of Harmony*.[68] If the tone C is chosen as a point of departure, two forces will pull at it, each in its own direction: one upward toward G and the other downward toward F. This is, Schoenberg argues, a result of the relationship of fifths. The fifth is the interval following the octave in the overtone series.[69] It is this fact that propels the system of functional harmony, where the steps V, I, and IV are so central. Tones played on these levels make it possible to deduce the diatonic major scale from the whole overtone range. But even so, there is no nature-given necessity in this specific type of scale:

> The discovery of our scale was a stroke of luck in the development of our music, not only with regard to its success, but also in the sense that we could just as well have found a different scale, as did for example the Arabs, the Chinese and Japanese, or the gypsies. That their music has not evolved to such heights as ours does not necessarily follow from their imperfect scales, but can also have to do with their imperfect instruments or with some other circumstance which cannot be investigated here.[70]

Schoenberg's point is that the diatonic scale is not the only reason for the great achievements of Western music. This tonal sequence is not even a goal but merely a temporary station or stop. Schoenberg looks to the future with an open mind; he does not exclude the possibility of quite different scale divisions, as Ferruccio Busoni has also suggested.[71] The tempered tone system can quickly become a thing of the past: "Probably, whenever the ear and imagination have matured enough for such music, the scale and the instruments will all at once be available."[72] Implicitly, both the ear and the imagination must always be highly adaptable to musical processes of change.

Schoenberg operates with the concept of *extended tonality*, if only to a modest degree,[73] but he cannot accept a concept such as *atonality*. To the 1922 edition of his *Harmonielehre*, he added an extensive footnote in the chapter entitled "Quarten-Akkorde," explaining the concept of tonality as

---

[68]*Theory of Harmony*, 23ff.

[69]Schoenberg uses the term *overtone*, not *partial tone*.

[70]*Theory of Harmony*, 25.

[71]See F. Busoni, *Entwurf einer neuen Ästhetik der Tonkunst* (1907), published in an English translation by Dr. Th. Baker as "Sketch of a New Esthetic of Music" in *Three Classics in the Aesthetic of Music* (New York: Dover, 1962).

[72]*Theory of Harmony*, 25-26.

[73]See A. Schoenberg, "My Evolution," *Style and Idea*, 79-92.

inclusive and not *exclusive*. In the English version, *Theory of Harmony*, the corresponding note is found in the appendix:

> The list of those who use such resources [wide-ranging chords built by fourths] today (1921) would probably be extensive. [...] Moreover, the quantity and quality of the fellow combatants does not entirely please me. For them, there is once again a new 'Direction', naturally, and they call themselves 'atonalists'. I have to dissociate myself from that, however, for I am a musician and have nothing to do with things atonal. The word 'atonal' could only signify something entirely inconsistent with the nature of tone. Even the word 'tonal' is incorrectly used if it is intended in an exclusive rather than inclusive sense. It can be valid only in the following sense: Everything implied by a series of tones (*Tonreihe*) constitutes tonality, whether it be brought together by means of direct reference to a single fundamental or by more complicated connections. [...][74]

Sporadic uses of such terms as atonal and atonality can be traced back to the early 1900s. Wallace Berry's hierarchic classification from 1979 demonstrates that the tonality concept is not easily defined:

> "Absolute" atonality?
> Atonality as a relative tendency?
> Irrelevant tonality?
> Multitonality? Pantonality?
> Tonal flux extinguishing, or severely attenuating, tonal function?
> Tonal flux within broad, prevailing tonal unity
> Extended (expanded) tonality
> Tonality of quasi-functional manifestations
> Conventional (major-minor) tonality
> Tonality of ambivalent conventions
> Tonality of modal conventions
> Purely melodic tonality
> Primitive ("pedal") tonality[75]

The terms atonal and atonality were used more deliberately from the 1920s onward. Free atonality and the so-called fixed atonality within the twelve-tone series appeared first, as mentioned above, in 1949 in Adorno's *Philosophy of Modern Music*. In 1924, Herbert Eimert published his *Atonale Musiklehre*—according to its author, not immodestly, the first of its kind. In the preface Eimert declares: "Inspired by the writings and compositions of Joseph Matthias Hauer and through personal acquaintance with the Russian composer Jefim Golyscheff [Efim Golishev], Eimert borrowed fundamental

---

[74]*Theory of Harmony*, 432.

[75]W. Berry, *Structural Functions in Music* (New York: Dover, 1987), 172.

ideas, formulated them systematically, and expanded them into this theory of music."[76] In the 1920s, the term atonality was mostly employed as a negation of tonality, and Schoenberg should be understood accordingly when he writes:

> I find above all that the expression, 'atonal music,' is most unfortunate—it is on a par with calling flying 'the art of not falling,' or swimming 'the art of not drowning.' Only in the language of publicity is it thought adequate to emphasize in this way a negative quality of whatever is being advertised.[77]

This is most probably an oblique reference to the fact that just at this time, 'atonal music' was becoming both a fashionable term and a slogan in the musical debate. Schoenberg subjects to irony how he feels about this phenomenon in the first of his *Drei Satiren für gemischten Chor* op. 28 (1925) "Am Scheideweg" (at the crossroads):

> Tonal or atonal? Just tell me
> In which stable
> In this case
> The greater number,
> So that one can cling, can cling
> To the safe wall.
> Please, no regrets![78]

Schoenberg's categorical rejection of the term atonality is consistent with his belief in there being only differences in degree, not in essence, in the way tones relate to one another. In his book *Structural Functions of Harmony*, he describes what he calls "his school" in this way:

---

[76]H. Eimert, *Atonale Musiklehre* (Leipzig: Breitkopf & Härtel, 1924), III. ["Angeregt durch die Schriften und Kompositionen von Joseph Matthias *Hauer* und durch die persönliche Bekanntschaft mit dem russischen Komponisten Jefim *Golyscheff* hat der Verfasser den beiden Komponisten vorhandenen Grundgedanken aufgenommen, systematisch formuliert und zur vorliegenden Musiklehre ausgebaut."]

[77]"Hauer's Theories," *Style and Idea*, 210.

[78]English translation from the booklet accompanying Pierre Boulez's recording of *Schönberg. Das Chorwerk* (CD S 2K 44571). The German original is rhymed:
> Tonal oder atonal? Nun sag einmal,
> In welchem Stall
> In diesem Fall
> Die größre Zahl.
> Dass man sich halten, halten kann
> Am sichern Wall
> Nur kein Schade!

> My school, including such men as Alban Berg, Anton Webern and others, does not aim at the establishment of a tonality, yet does not exclude it entirely. The procedure is based upon my theory of "the emancipation of the dissonance." Dissonances, according to this theory, are merely more remote consonances in the series of overtones.[79]

In *Theory of Harmony* Schoenberg defines consonance as being closer and therefore in a simpler relation to the initial tone of the overtone row. Dissonance represents a more remote and more complicated relation to this tone.[80] As can be gleaned from his use of the expression "the emancipation of the dissonance," his emphasis on the value of dissonance belongs to the same overall picture.[81] He then proceeds to develop his ideas on the general understanding of the tonality concept:

> A piece of music will always be tonal, at least in so far as a relation has to exist from tone to tone by virtue of which the tones, placed next to or above one another, yield a perceptible continuity. The tonality [itself] may then perhaps be neither perceptible nor provable; these relations may be obscure and difficult to comprehend, even incomprehensible.[82]

Hence, the tonality range is always wide; Schoenberg agrees that polytonality, or pantonality, describes music that is difficult to categorize from one initial tone or a fundamental tone. But where are the limits? Schoenberg is pointing at the gradual transitions in tonality due to the all-encompassing tonal space:

> If one insists on looking for names, "polytonal" or "pantonal" could be considered. Yet, before anything else, we should determine whether it is not simply 'tonal'.[83]

Polytonality and pantonality are terms that can logically and systematically be compared with the aforementioned monotonality, as they both aptly present the breadth of Schoenberg's tonality concept. Nonetheless, Schoenberg was himself sparing in the use of such terms: he believed in the comprehensive validity of 'tonality' in a manner quite like Hindemith, as will be discussed later.

---

[79] *Structural Functions of Harmony*, 193.

[80] *Theory of Harmony*, 21.

[81] See also A. Schoenberg, "Composition with Twelve Tones (1)," *Style and Idea*, 216-217.

[82] *Theory of Harmony*, 432.

[83] Ibid.

Musical Prose

One of the most important concepts in Schoenberg's understanding of music is that of musical prose. Despite its importance, the term itself was not a key component of Schoenberg's music vocabulary. The fundamentality of the concept rather reveals itself in the constant use of the musical-prose principle throughout Schoenberg's mature production, particularly in his so-called free atonal works. The final movement of the *Fünf Orchesterstücke* op. 16 from 1909, "Das obligate Rezitativ," is often mentioned as paradigmatic in this respect.

Schoenberg was not the originator of the term. From the 1800s onward, "musical prose" appeared both in discussions of recitatives, as a synthesis of speech and song, and in connection with the freer formal progressions of instrumental music. It was also used in connection with the French practice of *non mesuré* and as the opposite of bound verse principles, as, for example, in Gregorian chants. Its use as a polemic opposition to the concept of musical poesy is found in Romanticism. The term has particular importance for Schoenberg, and as Hermann Danuser puts it: "With Schoenberg, the expression musical prose achieves the function for the first time of a positive, fundamental concept solely related to the idea, central to the Viennese School, of music's specific language character."[84]

The concept of musical prose is integrated in Schoenberg's principles of the so-called developing variation—variation that leads to constructional development and not only to new motivic-thematic variants.[85] In 1917, Schoenberg mentions the terms *prose* and *rhythmatized prose* in connection with modern music in the fragmentary collection *Zusammenhang, Kontrapunkt, Instrumentation, Formlehre* (*Coherence, Counterpoint, Instrumentation, Instruction in Form*).[86] But first and foremost it is in the essay "Brahms the Progressive," in the version written on occasion of the 50th anniversary of the composer's death (1947), that Schoenberg discusses the term musical prose in a more comprehensive way.[87] The term itself is a reminder of how

---

[84]H. Danuser, "Musikalische Prosa," in H.H. Eggebrecht, ed., *Terminologie der Musik im 20. Jahrhundert* [HMT-Sonderband 1] (Stuttgart: Franz Steiner Verlag, 1995), 253. ["Bei A. Schönberg erlangt der Ausdruck mus. Prosa erstmals die Funktion eines uneingeschränkt *positiven Grundbegriffs*, bezogen einzig auf die—für die Wiener Schule zentrale— Vorstellung einer spezifischen Sprachhaftigkeit von Musik."]

[85]See G. Strang and L. Stein, eds., *Arnold Schoenberg, Fundamentals of Musical Composition* (London: Faber, 1967), 8.

[86]See *Coherence, Counterpoint ...*, 58.

[87]A. Schoenberg, "Brahms the Progressive," *Style and Idea*, 398-441.

he understands the fundamental relationship between music and language, or linguistic presentation of music. Schoenberg recognized that Brahms was usually characterized as a classicist and academician, and the essence of his essay is to show that he was something much beyond that: a great restorer of musical language, nothing less that "a great progressive." Brahms was the innovator of harmony, argues Schoenberg, a fact usually overshadowed by the focus on Wagnerian influence. Moreover, musical prose had already been expressed in Brahms's earliest works.

Schoenberg also attaches great significance to Mozart's contribution to the development of the concept, and acknowledges his own debt to the composer:

> Analysts of my music will have to realize how much I personally owe to Mozart. People who looked unbelievingly at me, thinking I made a poor joke will now understand why I called myself a 'pupil of Mozart,' must now understand my reasons. This will not help them to appreciate my music, but to understand Mozart. And it will teach young composers what are the essentials that one has to learn from masters and the way one can apply these lessons without loss of personality.[88]

Schoenberg feels that "great art must proceed to precision and brevity." There is a relation here to previously quoted statements from Loos: "One thing I knew; to keep abreast of development I had to become still much simpler" and to Wittgenstein's motto for his *Tractatus*: "...and whatever a man knows, whatever is not mere rumbling and roaring that he has heard, can be said in three words." Hence, Schoenberg is making an ethical-aesthetic statement that reflects an essential part of functionalist thinking, revealing a conception of art that is also a key to musical prose. Schoenberg agrees that repetitions, symmetry, regular phrase lengths and so on—all that can be compared to verse principles in poetry—have contributed to consolidate musical progression in the listener's memory. And such procedures, he argues, have undoubtedly helped musical understanding. Yet, deviation from regularity and symmetry does not present any serious risk. Phraseological irregularity is a familiar aspect and in itself not a contemporary innovation, he adds. Musical phrases, with or without words, can be freely constructed, as formal regularity associates them with the concept of literary prose.

But why exactly is Schoenberg so concerned with this compositional possibility? It is here, he argues, that we find a way of liberating music from

---

[88]"Brahms the Progressive," 414.

Schoenberg: The Motive as Musical Material

unnecessary repetition, the out and out superficialities and empty fillers that symmetric structure invites. Musical prose is a means in the struggle for musical truthfulness, in the way earlier associated with Kraus's contention about the literary phrase and Loos's crusade against architectural ornaments. Schoenberg's definition of the concept is simply: "This is what musical prose should be—a direct and straightforward presentation of ideas, without any patchwork, without mere padding and empty repetitions."[89]

However straightforward and unpretentious this definition may seem, the concept has profound importance for Schoenberg's work. The prose principles do not only apply to leading upper voices: they permeate the whole of the basic structure, in metrics, rhythm, phraseology, tonal organization, and formal constructions. For music to be comprehensible, the compositional presentation has unique demands that compensate for the listener's emotional attachment to symmetry[90] and regularity. The question is whether or not the musical material has a will that can be reconciled with this idealistic treatment. Schoenberg believes that this is the case, which is what connects his musical material to the realization of musical prose.

With his consistent use of terms such as *Faßlichkeit* (comprehensibility), *Zusammenhang* (coherence), *Konstruktion* (construction), and *Logik* (logic), Schoenberg comes even closer to the functionalist understanding of material. In these concepts lies the foundation of musical creativity: "[e]very piece of music is the presentation of a musical thought [*musikalischer Gedanke*]."[91] To be able to communicate in an adequate way, musical thought must be presented in a fashion that is comprehensible to the subject. If this comprehension is to happen, the work must be based on super- and subordinate structural coherence. Different kinds of coherence are created by means of musical construction, which has musical logic as its necessary point of departure. I will return to these concepts for a closer look when discussing musical form. For the musical material, one should ask what the second of Schoenberg's basic concepts, *der musikalische Gedanke*, really implies, as this particular term seems to be closely connected to how he understands the process of creativity.

---

[89]"Brahms the Progressive," 415.

[90]The term *symmetry* is here used in its widest sense. Details of Schoenberg's understanding of musical symmetry are found in his *Fundamentals of Musical Composition*, note on p. 25.

[91]*The Musical Idea*, 370.

"Der musikalische Gedanke"

Schoenberg's use of the noun *Gedanke* (thought) is readily associated with the German version of his book *Style and Idea: Stil und Gedanke*. *Gedanke* in the Schoenbergian sense stands for the aesthetic and ideal elements, while *Stil* is more closely associated with structure and construction.[92]

The concept of *Gedanke* touches both the musical work itself and its conception on a deeper level. Consequently, it may also be approached in a discussion of Schoenberg's understanding of the musical material, despite of its being tied so strongly to his understanding of form. Compared to its relation to material, *Gedanke* is as much, or more, a part of the way Schoenberg understands a work's formal development. However, like the concept of musical prose, *Gedanke* must also be considered in relation to the musical material's potential.

When Schoenberg refers to a work of music as *Gedanke*, he is appealing to the rational side of human consciousness. Furthermore, *der Gedanke* is always to be considered a specific musical occurrence, in the sense that its primary objective is not to refer to non-musical thoughts as in, for instance, the context of program music. The musical thought has its own logic that initially is absolute. Musical prose has the ability to present this kind of thought clearly, purely, and succinctly. Nonetheless, it is difficult to give a clear and concise definition of what the musical *Gedanke* really means for Schoenberg. One explanation, from his own hand, is: "An idea [*Gedanke*] is the production of a relationship between things otherwise having no relationship to one another."[93] Consequently, *der Gedanke* rests on combining different phenomena into a more comprehensive context. The actual musical presentation's character of being an independent thought lies in the fact that these contexts did not exist before the thought itself was first thought. However, its presentation must always be undertaken in such a way that it is perceived to be logical. It is not enough to connect elements that have nothing at all to do with one another. They must have one or two basic features in common.

A particular problem arises when *Gedanke* is translated into English, either by Schoenberg himself or others. As the book title *Style and Idea* shows, "idea" is the customary Anglo-American choice. Patricia Carpenter

---

[92] Schoenberg was not the first to use the term *Gedanke* in music. Carl Philipp Emanuel Bach uses it frequently. For example his statement:"Imitations belong to those thoughts [*Gedanken*] that are usually changed in repetition." Translated from C.Ph.E. Bach, *Versuch über die wahre Art das Klavier zu spielen* [1753/1762] (Wiesbaden: Breitkopf & Härtel, 1986), 290. ["Die Nachahmungen gehören mit unter diejenigen Gedanken welche bey der Wiederholung pflegen verändert zu werden."]

[93] *The Musical Idea*, 370.

and Severine Neff in a comment to their edition of *The Musical Idea* point out that this term can cover the three German words *Idee*, *Gedanke* and *Einfall*.[94] Schoenberg himself, however, seldom used the German word *Idee* as a synonym for idea.[95]

Etymologically, *Gedanke* is derived from *denken* (to think), while *Einfall* stems from *fallen* (to fall), something that "falls in." The thinking processes these two concepts envision are therefore quite different in nature. Schoenberg understands the word *Gedanke* in music in terms of "thinking" in the traditional sense. The thought follows its own inherent regularity, he says, as music does. This is a complex process that can include ideas and feelings, space, sound, and dynamics. Consequently, Schoenberg's definition of composition as "thinking in tones and rhythms" does not quite cover the process after all:

> As one does not necessarily have to think the thought in words but can also do this in complexities, ideas, yes, even in feelings, a musical thought does not necessarily have to be thought in tones but can, on the other hand, be conceived in space—and sound—in dynamic complexities, in rhythm, yes, perhaps within other emotional contexts.[96]

The point for Schoenberg is to demonstrate that musical thought is the sum of what is presented, or of the idea of what is to be presented. First the work is conceived as a whole; then follows a process whereby it is built up "in tones and rhythms." *Gedanke* can thus stand for both the conception and the realization, but *der musikalische Gedanke* does not necessarily have to represent a whole work or a whole movement. It can be a theme or a section of a larger work; it can exist alone or within a greater whole. The whole can be divided into smaller portions, where some of these may be considered as thoughts. The problem with Schoenberg's use of the *Gedanke* concept is that it embraces both abstract and logical-concrete processes, a dichotomy that is also expressed in his view on musical content. The first part resembles Hanslick's "[f]orms in sounding motion are the sole content and

---

[94]*The Musical Idea*, 17.

[95]There is one exception, however. In *Coherence, Counterpoint* ..., 4, Schoenberg refers to the idea (*Idee*) pertaining to a piece of music's conception and representation.

[96] *The Musical Idea*, 425. ["Wie man einen Gedanken nicht unbedingt in Worten *denken* muß sondern es auch in Komplexen, Vorstellungen, ja vielleicht sogar in Gefühlen davon tun kann, so muß ein musikalischer Gedanke nicht unbedingt in Tönen gedacht werden, sondern kann in Raum – und Klang – in dynamischen Komplexen, in rythmischen [sic], ja in vielleicht sonstigen Gefühlen *konzipiert* werden."]

object of music."⁹⁷ According to Schoenberg, the content of music comprises intervals, rhythms, harmonies, etc.—what may be characterized as the material constitution of music. However, music also has a spiritual content (*ein seelischer Inhalt*), "as music is composed from the promptings of states of mind that are affected by feelings."⁹⁸ This fact allows for such concepts as expression, mood, and character. However, Schoenberg does not, like Adorno, see such characteristics as 'sedimented' in the basic material, but rather in the exploitation of its possibilities.

The epistemological dichotomy of the *Gedanke* concept is its greatest asset. It is obvious that the concept refers to the universal human experience of the complexity of thought processes. The common English translation for the German *Gedanke*, "thought" with all its connotations, comes close to Schoenberg's understanding of the concept in a musical context. He instantiates this more coherently when he deals with musical analysis. In the drafts for a Preface to *Der musikalische Gedanke und die Logik, Technik, und Kunst seiner Darstellung*, which anticipates *The Musical Idea*, he writes:

> Here it will not be shown how to present an idea but rather how an idea is presented. This is not a textbook from which the student might learn how he should do it but one from which he finds out merely how others have done it.⁹⁹

Musical Logic

Next to the concepts of musical prose and musical *Gedanke*, logic is a third fundamental concept in Schoenberg's thinking. The specific realization of *der musikalische Gedanke* is based on logic. Consequently, this concept permeates both material and form, and it is of such importance that it becomes something in the way of a universal regularity, not necessarily for ever and eternity, but for what Schoenberg considers artistically elevated music in his own Western culture. Logic is the backbone of the musical material; the will of the material is expressed in musical logic. Music is thus complemented once again with a rational dimension, characteristic of the functionalist understanding of material.

In his *Tractatus*, Wittgenstein states that

---

[97]"Tönend bewegte Formen sind einzig und allein Inhalt und Gegenstand der Musik," in E. Hanslick, *The Beautiful in Music*, 48, translated as "[t]he essence of music is sound and motion."

[98]*Coherence, Counterpoint ...*, 63.

[99]*The Musical Idea*, 89.

3.03. Thought can never be of anything illogical, since, if it were, we should have to think illogically.

3.031. It used to be said that God could create anything except what would be contrary to the laws of logic. —The truth is that we could not say what an 'illogical' world would look like.

3.032. It is as impossible to represent in language anything that 'contradicts logic' as it is in geometry to represent by its co-ordinates a figure that contradicts the laws of space, or to give the co-ordinates of a point that does not exist.[100]

From 1914 Ludwig Wittgenstein became one of Loos's closest friends. In 1918 the philosopher and the engineer tried unsuccessfully to persuade the publishers of *Die Fackel* to print his *Logisch-philosophische Abhandlung* (*Tractatus*). According to Loos's biographers Rukschcio and Schachel, Wittgenstein was very eager to hear Karl Kraus's opinion.[101] There seems to be little indication that Schoenberg had any close relationship to Wittgenstein's work; yet it is striking how much their thinking, and even more so the way in which they formulated their thoughts, reflects one another. Schoenberg and Wittgenstein were both, to a significant extent, conditioned by the same cultural milieu and the same theoretical debates, and hence subject to many of the same intellectual influences. It has been maintained that some of the seemingly most distinctive features of the *Tractatus* had been commonplace in many fields, including music theory as conveyed by Schoenberg himself, for at least a decade prior to the appearance of Wittgenstein's work in 1921.[102] Schoenberg might thus well be included in the first lines of the preface to the *Tractatus*: "Perhaps this book will be understood only by someone who has himself already had the thoughts that are expressed in it—or at least similar thoughts."[103]

Schoenberg is of the opinion that logic is decisive for human comprehension. Language in general and the logic of language in particular are among those analogies frequently presented when he discusses such phenomena as musical construction. As mentioned above, musical prose is a key element in this picture. Leon Botstein regards the dichotomy in *Style and Idea* in the light of the need of the modernist Viennese milieu to explore

---

[100]L. Wittgenstein, *Tractatus Logico-Philosophicus*, 19.

[101]See B. Rukschcio and R. Schachel, *Adolf Loos, Leben und Werk*, 224.

[102]See, e.g., A. Janik and S. Toulmin, *Wittgenstein's Vienna* (New York: Simon and Schuster, 1973), 31.

[103]*Tractatus Logico-Philosophicus*, 3.

the nature of language and its relations to thought.[104] Schoenberg asserts that logical thinking is a fundamental part of his nature, and its execution simply unavoidable:

> I cannot help but think logically and if then, as I build, those well-known symptoms of musical logic show themselves—even in places where I have not consciously put them—that should surprise nobody who has any conception of what musical logic is.[105]

One must be careful in drawing comparisons between Wittgenstein and Schoenberg too strongly at this point. In the comprehension referred to by the short extract from the *Tractatus* it is possible to claim that all human-created music is based on logic. There must always be an underlying logical thought, even in the subtlest of liberation attempts—yes, perhaps to a particularly obvious degree precisely there. But Schoenberg cannot agree with such a general view, since musical logic is specifically demonstrable from regularities fashioned in the musical tradition of which he is a part. The foundation of logic lies in the highly acquired craft of musical art, for, as he argues in the fragmentary preface of *Der musikalische Gedanke*: "Here for the first time an attempt is made to extract musical logic from the facts of the musical technique of presenting an idea [*Gedankendarstellung*]"[106] The implication is that logic can be confounded when the supposed laws are broken. In a rather disrespectful examination of measures 18-23 in the first movement of Richard Strauss's *Sinfonia Domestica*, op. 15, Schoenberg points to the lack of logical closure or conclusion, for how does the music continue?

> The entrance of the second violins (bar 4) is only an embarrassment, for the thought (quite nice, by the way) is finished even though the theme is going to be extended very, very far. That this is supposed to describe the "illogic of woman" does not help, because it describes the "illogic of the man" [the composer] who, if he were endowed with logic, would also have expressed this by means of logic.[107]

This does not mean that Schoenberg regards the logical construction of music as a sufficient guarantor for a genuine work of art:

---

[104]See L. Botstein, "Music and the Critique of Culture: Arnold Schoenberg, Heinrich Schenker, and the Emergence of Modernism in Fin de Siècle Vienna," in *Constructive Dissonance: Arnold Schoenberg and the Transformations of Twentieth-Century Culture* (Berkeley, CA, etc.: University of California Press, 1997), 10.

[105]"Constructed Music," *Style and Idea*, 107.

[106]*The Musical Idea*, 91.

[107]*The Musical Idea*, 295.

> Were the construction of a musical composition merely to follow the requirements of logic, as in science, it would simply not be art but science. [...] While science will therefore have to place every case in the clearest light, art may change the relationships of meaning and heighten their effect.[108]

For Schoenberg, science refers to the natural science, not the humanities. However, the point here is that he takes artistic freedom as a basis of creativity for granted, in the same way as in superior functionalist architecture. When approaching Schoenberg from this concept of logic it is important to understand that the perspective also includes Schoenberg's respect for the unfathomable dimensions of art. He argues that there is a connection between *physis* and *metaphysis*, and this association enables the musical *Geist* to be presented as pure reason. In a note on a manuscript entitled *Der musikalische Gedanke und seine Darstellung und Durchführung* (The musical idea and its presentation and development) he writes:

> The purpose of such a limitation is gain: Here the music's spirit [*Geist*] is to be presented purely as reason, as that which explains musical feeling and suggestion on a higher level. What the artist in the act of creation does in an unconscious and sensible way must be presented here in the way he would have done it consciously. A part of the musical logic will therefore be represented, the logic one must presuppose is at hand as long as one does not just suppose that music is nothing but a game, and not that it represents higher thought, if ever so unconsciously.[109]

If one then asks the crucial question as to what Schoenberg considers to be the point of departure for musical logic, the answer is: the creation of coherence (*Zusammenhang*). From this basic principle the work must be built up or constructed. Logic thus also has particular significance for Schoenberg's understanding of form, which will be discussed later.

---

[108] *The Musical Idea,* 115.

[109] *The Musical Idea,* 418. ["Die Absicht solcher Begrenzung ist auf einen Gewinn gerichtet: Es soll der musikalische Geist hier einmal rein als Verstand dargestellt sein, als das, als was sich musikalisches Gefühl und Ahnen auf einer höheren Ebene enthüllen. Es soll das, was der Künstler beim Schaffen unbewußt und gefühlsmäßig tut, hier so dargestellt werden, wie er es täte, wenn er sich seines Handelns bewusst würde. Es soll damit ein Teil der musikalischen Logik *wiedergegeben* werden, die man als vorhanden voraussetzen muß, sofern man nicht bloß annimmt, Musik sei nur ein Spiel und nicht dass sie ein wenn auch unbewußtes höheres Denken ist."]

The Musical Motive

Schoenberg relates the musical material to several subconcepts. In his comprehensive understanding of material, the component that really carries the material's *Treibkraft* (compulsion or will) is the musical motive. Through its fundamental, logical potential, the motive realizes the presentation of musical thoughts within a given tonal idiom, not least in the framework of Schoenberg's own musical prose. The artistic regularities lie hidden in the ways in which the motive should be used. In one of Schoenberg's definitions of motive he relates it to material in the following way:

> *Definition*: A musical motive is a sounding, rhythmicized phenomenon that, by its (possibly varied) repetitions in the course of a piece of music, is capable of creating the impression that it is the material of the piece.[110]

Schoenberg also defines the motive as *Baustoff*, building material.[111] Despite the definition quoted above, the motive cannot be regarded as a collective term for Schoenberg's concept of the musical material: it is rather the generator of the force of will that permeates the complexity of the musical material. Motion is a keyword here:

> A motive is something that gives rise to motion. A motion is that change in a state of rest which turns it into its opposite. Thus, one can compare the motive with a driving force. Such a driving force will require an object on which it acts. This driving force will have to be great enough to bring the object out of its condition of rest; and the motion it causes will depend for its size, duration, and kind on the type of driving force and on the object driven.[112]

In *Theory of Harmony*, Schoenberg describes the motive as "the Motor that drives this movement of voices"[113] Yet one can also find examples of his reluctance to compare the qualities of motive with those of a motor. The motive is not the force itself, he argues, since it has already been absorbed in the impulse of the driving force:

> *A thing is* termed a motive if it is subject to the effect of a driving force, has already received its impulse, and is on the verge of reacting to it. It is comparable to a sphere on an inclined plane at the moment before it rolls away; to a fertilized seed; to an arm raised to strike, etc.[114]

---

[110] *Coherence, Counterpoint* ..., 29.

[111] *The Musical Idea*, note on p. 150.

[112] *Coherence, Counterpoint* ..., 27.

[113] *Theory of Harmony*, 34.

[114] *Coherence, Counterpoint* ..., 27.

"The motive is a unit with one or several intervallic and rhythmic characteristics," Schoenberg states in the German edition of *Models for Beginners in Composition*.[115] Moreover:

> [...]Features are the marks of the motive. They are indeed primarily of a purely musical nature: pitches (intervals), rhythm, harmony, contrapuntal combination, stress, and possibly dynamics. But nonetheless they can also pertain to expression, character, mood, color, sonority, movement, etc., insofar as these may not be presentable through the aforementioned features.[116]

In these features lies the possibility of motion and change in the state of rest. Even the smallest of musical units can have motivic significance, says Schoenberg. There are even examples of a characteristic single tone having a motivic function. The motive is the smallest component or common denominator in a musical composition.[117] Hence, the motive is often short and concise, but does not always need to be limited in size. A musical phrase can be both shorter and longer than the motive. The motive should be recognized as "the *effective* and *acting* element in each *gestalt* (theme, phrase, *Satz,* etc.)"[118] The motive's fundamental importance for the various levels of form in a musical work makes it the main component of the musical material. A motive represents a molecular entity, the DNA material determining the make-up of the work. Hence it must be definable at each and every point in the piece. This can be done because "[t]he presence of the motive can be recognized by its repetitions."[119] This does not mean that the original shape of the motive is subjected to constant duplication. Much more frequently, motivic repetition takes place within the principles of musical prose, since the motive is subject to such a diversity of possible variations. When Schoenberg discusses the concept of motive in his *Fundamentals of Musical Composition*, this emerges as a most significant point: "A motive appears constantly throughout a piece: *it is repeated*. Repetition alone often gives rise to *monotony*. Monotony can only be overcome by *variation*."[120]

---

[115]Rudolf Stephan, ed., *Arnold Schoenberg: Modelle für Anfänger im Kompositionsunterricht: Lehrgang und Glossar* (Vienna: Universal Edition, 1972), p. 8. ["Das Motiv ist eine Einheit mit einem oder mehreren intervallischen und rhythmischen Merkmalen."]

[116]*The Musical Idea*, 171.

[117]*Coherence, Counterpoint* ..., 25.

[118]*The Musical Idea*, 387.

[119]*Coherence, Counterpoint* ..., 31.

[120]*Fundamentals of Musical Composition*, 8.

118 *The Musical Material*

There are numerous possibilities of motivic variation within a logical framework. Below, this variation aspect will be traced in a small section from Schoenberg's own oeuvre, the first of his *Sechs kleine Klavierstücke,* op. 19. The music gives an example of the inherent will of the musical motive as represented in Schoenberg's thoughts on the musical material. At the same time, the discussion may serve as an example of how crucial the motivic building block really is in his music.

The Musical Motive and Material Consistency:
No. 1 from Schoenberg's Sechs kleine Klavierstücke

Schoenberg wrote his collection *Sechs kleine Klavierstücke,* op. 19 in 1911, while completing the first edition of his *Harmonielehre*. The first five pieces were composed in a single rush of creativity on 19 February that year. The last piece was written on 17 June to commemorate the death of Gustav Mahler: "the infinitely tender sound, based on three chords, is evidence of boundless grief," Schoenberg biographer Willi Reich says.[121] Hans Heinz Stuckenschmidt calls the characteristic A–F♯–B chord in this last piece "a reflection of Mahler's late works."[122] All the pieces in op.19 are conspicuously short, comprising between 9 and 17 measures. The first is the longest and the structurally most complex. One of the legendary interpreters of this work, the pianist Eduard Steuermann, is said to have described the line drawn out through this piece as an "infinite melody."[123]

Though short, the pieces in op. 19 are also strikingly full of musical content. They are therefore often described as aphorisms. Schoenberg himself said that "formulating ideas in an aphoristic manner" was something he seemed to have learnt in exactly this period of his compositional development.[124] This aphoristic feature is also found in the works of Schoenberg's pupils Anton Webern and Alban Berg during these years.

Schoenberg's op. 19 typifies concentrated musical construction. About the works written around 1908 Schoenberg says that "the foremost characteristics of these pieces *in statu nascendi* were their extreme expressiveness and their extraordinary brevity," continuing:

---

[121] W. Reich, *Arnold Schönberg, oder der konservative Revolutionär* (Vienna etc.: XX, 1968), 78. [" ... das auf drei Akkorden basierende, äußerst zarte Klangbild zeugt von unendlicher Trauer."]

[122] H.H. Stuckenschmidt, *Schoenberg: His Life, World and Work*, H. Searle, trans. (London: John Calder, 1977), 108.

[123] H.H. Stuckenschmidt, *Schoenberg...,* 136.

[124] A. Schoenberg, "A Self-Analysis," *Style and Idea*, 78.

> Later I discovered that our sense of form was right when it forced us to counterbalance extreme emotionality with extraordinary shortness. Thus, subconsciously, consequences were drawn from an innovation which, like every innovation, destroys while it produces. New colorful harmony was offered; but much was lost.[125]

Sechs kleine Klavierstücke can thus be regarded as a sounding example of the compositional crisis in which Schoenberg found himself at this phase of his life. It was not long since he had abandoned the traditional principles of tonality and with them a crucial structuring force of a work. The crucial question was whether the material he was now using had a structurally delimiting effect. Building a larger work entirely on the basis of a motive's potential within the concept of musical prose, without some more systematic, superordinate tonal principles, is undoubtedly a demanding project. Understandably, Schoenberg was searching for an alternative compositional methodology that would enable him to build more extended musical forms. In this light it is telling that the four compositions following op.19 are all based on literary texts, which function as directives for the construction.[126] In the next piano work, *Fünf Klavierstücke* op. 23 from 1920-1923, he applies for the first time what can be called twelve-tone principles, claiming that he had solved the problem of form in a newly invented method.[127]

The miniature selected for discussion was composed at a time during which Schoenberg was interested in the motive's driving force. The very short extract from his œuvre is representative in the sense that it demonstrates the type of motivic elaboration that is characteristic of his entire production. The chosen approach concurs with the true Schoenbergian tradition: he was convinced that in the area of art, one is in the privileged position to generalize on the basis of individual cases. There are various examples of this belief in his own writings. Such a modus operandi, he claims, reveals something of the difference between the artistic and the scientific approaches. In his drafts for the preface to *Der musikalische Gedanke und die Logik, Technik, und Kunst seiner Darstellung* (*The Musical Idea*), he states that:

> [a]rt is different from science. While science requires systematically all characteristic cases, art is satisfied with a lesser number of interesting ones: as many as fantasy demands in order to produce for itself an image of the whole, in order to dream about it.[128]

---

[125] A. Schoenberg, "Composition with Twelve Tones (1)," *Style and Idea*, 217.

[126] *Herzgewächse* op. 20 (1911), *Pierrot lunaire* op. 21 (1912), *Vier Orchesterlieder* op. 22 (1913-1916), and *Die Jakobsleiter* (unfinished) (1917-1922).

[127] "Composition with Twelve Tones (1)," 218.

[128] *The Musical Idea*, 93.

EXAMPLE 3: Schoenberg, No. 1 from *Sechs kleine Klavierstücke*
© 1913 by Universal Edition, Vienna/Austria; © renewed 1940.
Reprinted with permission.

In the following analysis, the focus is on the motive as the decisive factor in the consistency of Schoenberg's musical material. He regarded it as essential that the whole be established before the work is actually realized, an opinion which will be discussed later. Before dissecting a few very short segments of the first piece in op. 19, here is a brief look at some overall features:

This piece is characteristic of Schoenberg's musical prose. There are no repetitions in the traditional sense; any metric symmetry is counterbalanced by changes in beat, variations in rhythmic formulations, and by extending the beat beyond the measure. The piece also contains phraseology where potential symmetry is counteracted by frequent use of units that extend over measure divisions. The phrases, moreover, usually consist of five or seven eight-notes. A first glance at the piece also gives the impression that there are no ornamental fillers. But even with the avoidance of obvious repetitive and symmetry-based compositional features, it is beautifully balanced and clearly drawn. There is a strikingly well formed interaction between the individual voices throughout its structure; see, for example, the euphonious equilibrium in the overall light and tender nature, which is expressed within economically retained dynamics. When studying the piece both by note and by ear, one has the impression of a logical and content-rich development taking place within a condensed lapse of time. Schoenberg considers it important that a musical occurrence should be perceived in both spatial axes, vertically and horizontally. "The elements of a musical idea are partly incorporated in the horizontal plane as successive sounds, and partly in the vertical plane as simultaneous sounds," he writes in the article "Composition with Twelve Tones (1)."[129] This idea is also expressed in the procedures of twelve-tone method. The motive's logical element makes it possible to consider it as working in different directions, Schoenberg says.[130] Erwin Stein remembers Schoenberg once holding up a hat as an example: the hat is, and will be, the same no matter from which angle it is viewed.[131]

"A motive is used by repetition. The repetition may be exact, modified or developed," Schoenberg writes in *Fundamentals of Musical Composition*. "Variation, it must be remembered, is repetition in which some features are changed and the rest preserved."[132] In *Coherence, Counterpoint,*

---

[129]"Composition with Twelve Tones (1)," 220.

[130]See, e.g., A. Schoenberg, *Structural Functions of Harmony*, p. 194 and "My Evolution," *Style and Idea*, 87.

[131]See E. Stein, "Neue Formprinzipien," *Arnold Schoenberg zum fünfzigsten Geburtstage, 13. September 1924* [Sonderheft der *Musikblätter des Anbruch*] (Vienna 1924): 291.

[132]*Fundamentals of Musical Composition*, 9.

Instrumentation, Instruction in Form) Schoenberg explains how the motive can appear through a musical work:

> The motive reproduces itself by repeating and engendering new shapes from itself.
>
> A motive can be repeated in the following ways:
> I. exactly   1   a) starting from the same tone
>   b) starting from a different tone
>   c) with identical intervals
>   d) with almost the same intervals
>   e) with changed intervals (major, minor, etc.)
>   2   a) in the same rhythm
>   b) in augmentation
>   c) in diminution
>   d) in altered rhythm (ornaments, etc.)
> II. inexactly   1 by chance
>   a) in free imitation of the intervals
>   (possibly inversion of the whole or of individual parts)
>   b) in free imitation of the rhythms
>   2   variations (formal)
>   3   developing variations[133]

In *Fundamentals of Musical Composition*, Schoenberg gives an even more systematic overview:

> The rhythm is changed:
> 1. By modifying the length of the notes [...]
> 2. By note repetitions [...]
> 3. By repetition of certain rhythms [...]
> 4. By shifting rhythms to different beats [...]
> 5. By the addition of upbeats [...]
> 6. By changing the meter—a device seldom usable within a piece [...]
>
> The intervals are changed:
> 1. By changing the original order or direction of the notes [...]
> 2. By addition or omission of intervals [...]
> 3. By filling up intervals with ancillary[134] notes [...]
> 4. By reduction through omission or condensation [...]
> 5. By repetition of features [...]
> 6. By shifting features to other beats [...]
>
> The harmony is changed:

---

[133]*Coherence, Counterpoint* ..., 37.

[134] Schoenberg's own note reads: "In order to avoid aesthetically misleading and corrupted terms, *ancillary* will be preferred in referring to the so-called 'embellishing' or 'ornamental' notes of conventional melodic formulas."

1. By the use of inversions [...]
2. By additions at the end [...]
3. By insertions in the middle [...]

The melody is adapted to these changes:
1. By transposition [...]
2. By addition of passing harmonies [...]
3. By 'semi-contrapuntal' treatment of the accompaniment [...]¹³⁵

These two overviews both overlap and complement each other. In the functionalist context, Schoenberg's note 135, explaining his avoidance of words belonging to the terminological sphere of ornaments, is of particular interest. Still more important is the fact that Schoenberg connects a rational perspective to the motive by listing in his outlines the logic or regularity that must be at the heart of any adequate treatment.

If we look at the possibilities Schoenberg allows for the interval, it is evident that it can be submitted to a number of alterations without losing its status as belonging to the basic motive. The variation potential does not, however, permit every conceivable combination; such unlimited possibilities would undermine the recognizable logical principles. For Schoenberg, such changes must never produce a motivic form too foreign to the basic motive.¹³⁶ The obliging relationship between motive and elaboration is what makes the fundamental motive in a work express the material's own will. It embodies possibilities and limitations that are to have consequences for the specific, compositional construction. Within this framework, the musical material's regularity can then unfold.

In the analysis below, one fundamental issue is the degree to which Schoenberg lets the presumed will of the material determine the melodic and harmonic forces in a musical construction. For the most part, this question will be treated without strict ties to formal aspects. In such a methodology, the focus on the rhythmic logic and coherence revealing the piece as a complete and unified work of art is inevitably lost. The analysis thus focuses primarily on the motive's degree of permeation, and on the question how far it can be considered as a decisive material feature.

The piano piece is examined measure by measure. Brief comments are added along the way, but the real presentation is given in a set-up where each note is related to a horizontal and/or vertical progression. These notes are represented by black note-heads without stems, in the correct octave, to the left in each example. Rectangular markings denote a motivic form or a motivic segment. Where there is reference to different voices in the piano

---

[135] *Fundamentals of Musical Composition*, 10.

[136] *Fundamentals of Musical Composition*, 9.

excerpt, "v1" represents the highest voice within that measure or measure area; further numbering follows vertically. To the right the intervals are "translated" in relation to the basic motive or to its characteristic segments. Here, unfilled notes without stems are oriented as far as possible towards the correct octave. The number of rectangular markings here corresponds to the number on the left. It has been necessary, however, to arrange the markings somewhat differently, usually side-by-side, as, for example, one chord can consist of differently transposed motivic segments. The use of rectangles with rounded corners suggests that in most cases there are *relations* to the motive rather then exact note-to-note identifications. For the sake of clarity, certain enharmonic transcriptions have been made in the relations to the initial motive.

The piece is based on the following motive:

EXAMPLE 4: Schoenberg, op. 19/1, the motive in the left-hand upbeat

In this motive, the minor third combined with the minor second, within the frame of a major seventh, is perceived as a basic feature shaped through an ascending musical gesture. These elements belong to the motive's *Eigenschaften* (features). The intervals endow it with distinctive melodic and harmonic features. The motive consists of the notes A_3–C_4–G_4–$G^\sharp_4$, a minor third followed by a perfect fifth leading to a minor second. Motivic diversity is already implicit: the intervals' unison, second, third, and fifth, with their alterations, inversions, and placement possibilities, carry in themselves all other intervals. Accordingly, there is no interval that could not be related to the motive. Hence, it is particularly important to see if Schoenberg uses the motive in such a way that an experienceable material consistency is maintained. If one tests the fundamental motive in op. 19/1 on the basis of Schoenberg's listing of possible variations, it will appear in any number of variants. Consequently, an analysis of the use of intervals based on motive must allow for choices.

We begin with the first two measures and the preceding upbeat:

EXAMPLE 5: Schoenberg, op. 19/1, mm. 0-2

The basic motive presented in the following way is the key to the analysis below:

EXAMPLE 5a: upbeat; v2, basic motive (horizontally and vertically)

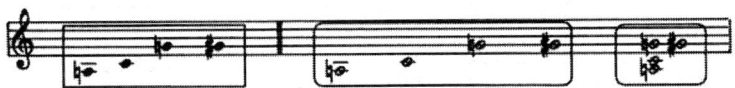

In the subsequent first measure, the upper part is based on a variant of the motive where the minor third has been altered to major. Thus already here in the first measure we find the piece's most characteristic feature in motive alteration. The falling minor seventh (actually an augmented sixth) counterbalances the rising seventh of the motive:

EXAMPLE 5b: upbeat and m. 1; v1 (horizontally)

The vertical construction in m. 1 can also be traced back to the motive, which is even represented in a combination of the horizontal and vertical. The combination of upbeat and first measure constitutes a musical *Gedanke* in which the motivic material is used in both a harmonic and a melodic way. Schoenberg is thus making use of both spatial directions. By exploiting the motive as the basic material in this way, he gives the introductory measure its characteristic sound:

EXAMPLE 5c: m. 1, eighth-notes 3 and 4 (vertically)

EXAMPLE 5d: m. 1, eighth-notes 4-6, v1+v2+v3 (horizontally and vertically)

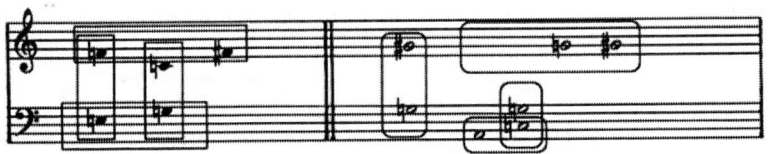

126   *The Musical Material*

The motive's final note, $G\sharp_4$, leads on to A_4 in m. 2. The motive's upward undulation also invites a counter-movement,[137] which has considerable importance for the formal development of the piece. A retrograde motion of the motive, which has now been modified by the mid-interval (the perfect fifth) being condensed to a minor third, is characteristic for m. 2. All this occurs in a descending melodic movement balanced against the mainly ascending impulses of the preceding measure and in the upbeat.

EXAMPLE 5e: m. 2, v1 (horizontally)

Rhythmically, the basic motive and its movement in four thirty-second notes is simple. In m. 2, it is complemented with a descending motion that also represents a retrograde version of the motive, containing an augmented second in place of the fifth. The motion begins with F_4, which with a minor second follows up $F\sharp_4$ in the upper voice from the preceding measure:

EXAMPLE 5f: m. 2, eighth-note 2, v2 (horizontally)

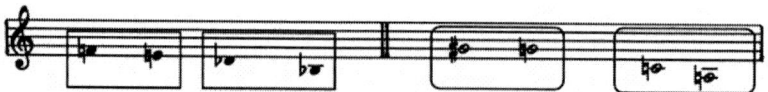

In the rest of m. 2 the motivic material is also presented in both horizontal and vertical motion:

EXAMPLE 5g: m. 2, eighth-notes 4-5 (vertically)

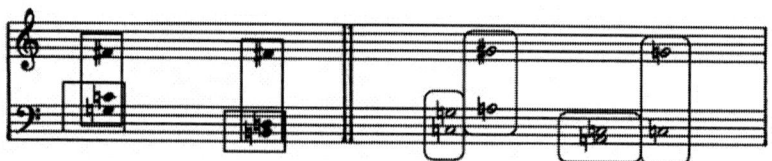

EXAMPLE 5h: m. 2, eighth-note 6 (vertically and horizontally)

---

[137]See, e.g., the relationship between the thirty-second-note motion in the upbeat and the thirty-second-note motion in m. 2.

The bass voice in m. 2 carries the development over to the more complex mm. 3-5:

EXAMPLE 6: Schoenberg, op. 19/1, mm. 3-5

The swiftly passing C_3 appoggiatura in m. 3 is in itself a good example of how determinative motive consistency applies to the smallest detail in this piece. As is shown in the following two examples, the ascending motion in the lower part can be considered as overlapping use of motivic material; a new vertical application begins before the preceding one has been completed:

EXAMPLE 6a: m. 3, eighth-notes 1-2 (horizontally)

EXAMPLE 6b: m. 3, eighth-notes 2-3 (horizontally)

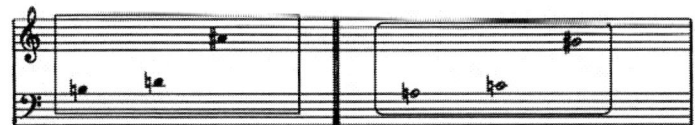

Schoenberg counteracts the possibility of rhythmic monotony that the motive may contain by adding a rubato-like, rhythmical flexibility to the linear motion. In this respect mm. 3-6 are the most important. At the same time this motion and the use of intervals are due to the possibilities afforded by the motive in retrograde and inversion. A special link is made to the motive in the augmentations: sixteenth-notes and eighth-notes in mm. 4-5 (left hand). A complex contrapuntal weaving characterizes this part of the piece. Descending and ascending motions lead on in expressive denseness, both together and against each other, on different levels of the musical structure. It is always the motive, in vertical and horizontal shape, that gives the basic material both melody and harmony:

EXAMPLE 6c: m. 3, segment of eighth-note 4 (vertically)

EXAMPLE 6d: m. 3, segment of eighth-notes 4 and 5 (vertically)

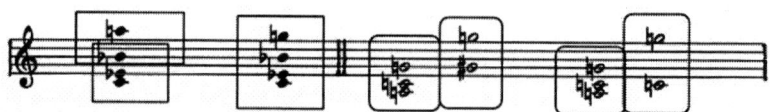

EXAMPLE 6e: m. 3, segment of eighth-notes 5-6 (vertically, v. horizontally)

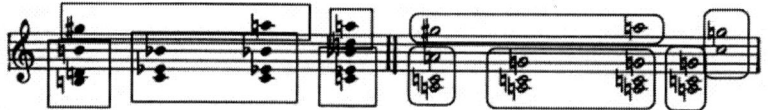

EXAMPLE 6f: m. 3, eighth-notes 4-6; v2+v3+v4 (horizontally)

EXAMPLE 6g: m. 3, eighth-notes 4-6: v. (horizontally)

EXAMPLE 6K: m. 3, eighth-note 6 and m. 4, eighth-notes 1-3: v. (horizontally)

EXAMPLE i: m. 4, eighth-note 5 (vertically)

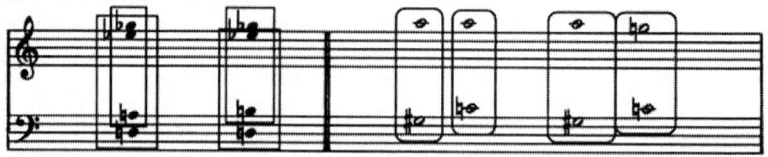

Schoenberg: The Motive as Musical Material   *129*

EXAMPLE 6K: m. 4, eighth-note 6 (vertically)

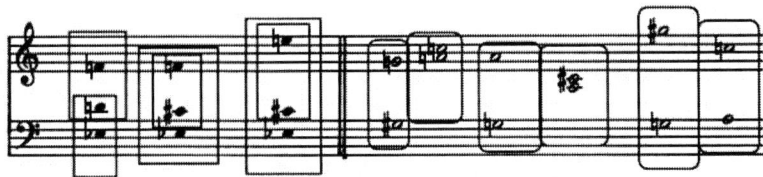

EXAMPLE 6k: m. 5, eighth-note 1 (vertically)

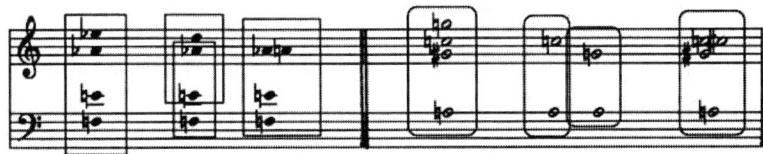

EXAMPLE 6l: m. 5, eighth-notes 2-3 (vertically)

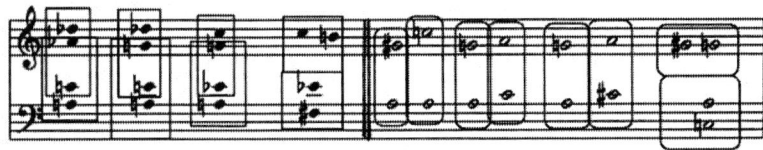

EXAMPLE 6m: m. 4, eighth-notes 5-6 and m. 5, eighth-notes 1-3: v. (horizontally)

EXAMPLE 6n: m. 4, eighth-notes 5-6 and m. 5: v. (horizontally)

EXAMPLE 6o: m. 4, eighth-notes 5-6 and m. 5, eighth-notes 1-3: v3 (horizontally)

EXAMPLE 6p: m. 4, eighth-notes 5-6 and m. 5, eighth-notes 1-3: v 4 (horizontally)

EXAMPLE 6q: m. 5, eighth-notes 5-6 (vertically)

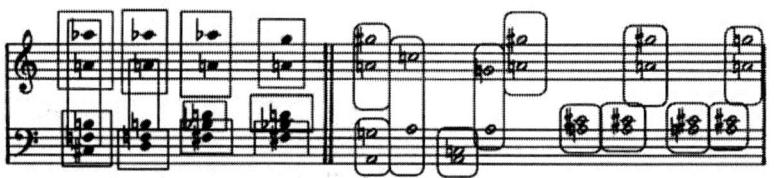

Proceeding to measures 6–8:

EXAMPLE 7: Schoenberg, op. 19/1, mm. 6-8

EXAMPLE 7a: m. 6 (vertically)

EXAMPLE 7b: m. 5, eighth-notes 5-6 and m. 6, v. (horizontally)

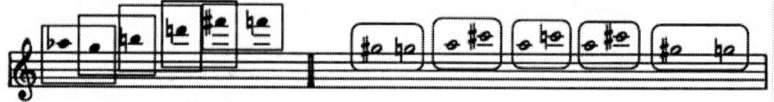

EXAMPLE 7c: m. 6, v. (horizontally)

EXAMPLE 7d: m. 6, v2+v3 (horizontally)

As a counterweight to this polyphonic section there is a homophonic, rhythmically stringent m. 7 in 2/4 time. The contrast is emphasized with pauses, staccato, and arpeggios. Yet the basic material is always the same:

EXAMPLE 7e: m. 7, subdivisions of 1st and 2nd beat (vertically)

EXAMPLE 7f: m. 7, v4 (horizontally)

In mm. 8-10 the motive returns to thirty-second notes, both through the upper part and the left-hand tremolo motion. Schoenberg uses both horizontal and vertical motive segments:

EXAMPLE 7g: m. 8, eighth-notes 1-2: v. (horizontally)

In this example the note D_4, which is sustained from m. 7, has been included as a vertical insertion in relation to $C\sharp_5$. The insertion shows how this note emphasizes the use of the major-seventh interval, the characteristic framing of the first and second thirty-second-note formation in the horizontal movement. This interval was also the frame of the basic motive. Finally, together with all the motion's tones, the sustained D_4 also relates to the motive through the intervals in their original form or their inversions.

EXAMPLE 7h: m. 8, eighth-notes 3-4: voices 1-6 (horizontally)[138]

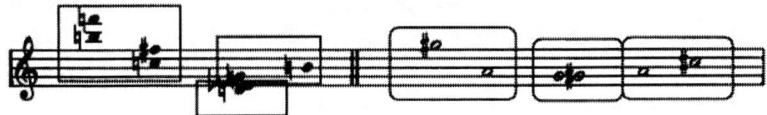

---

[138] The example can also be compressed and regarded vertically.

In mm. 9-11 Schoenberg carries out a so-called liquidation: a gradual reduction and fragmentation of the formation in m. 8.

EXAMPLE 8: Schoenberg, op. 19/1, mm. 9-12

The process of liquidation can be considered as contrary to that of the developing variation. Although not representing Schoenberg's most comprehensive example of this principle, it is still clearly demonstrable in the process leading to the final fermata. From m. 9 the substance of the material is revealed as follows:

EXAMPLE 8a: mm. 9-12, v 2 (horizontally)

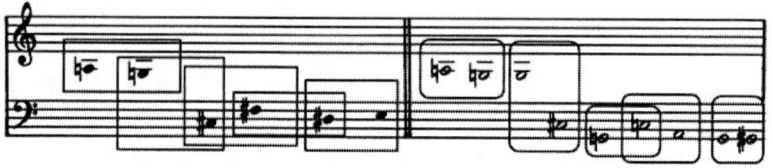

EXAMPLE 8b: mm. 10–11, v 1 (horizontally)

The liquidation process concludes with the fermata in m. 12. From m. 13 onward there follows a coda, still with the motive as the material substance.

EXAMPLE 9: Schoenberg, op. 19/1, mm. 13-17

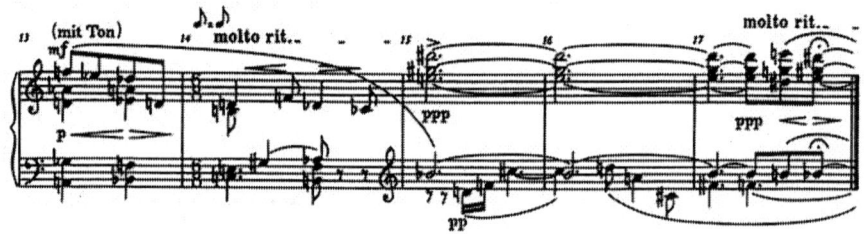

Schoenberg: The Motive as Musical Material   *133*

The musical gestures are based on different aspects of the motive, giving many associations to the first measures with the upbeat. These elements lead the piece on to its ethereal dissolution. The motive is used in the following, rather complex, way:

EXAMPLE 9a: m. 13 (vertically)

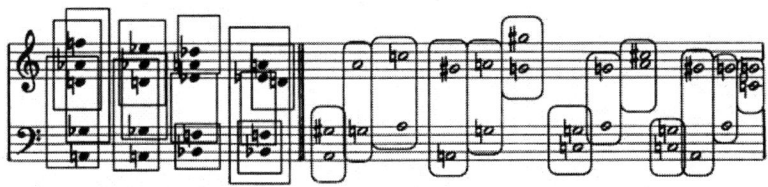

EXAMPLE 9b: m. 13, v. (horizontally)[139]

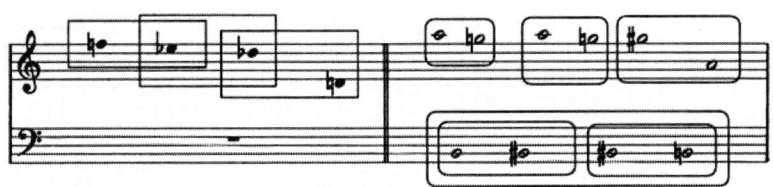

EXAMPLE 9c: m. 14, eighth-notes 1-4 (vertically)

EXAMPLE 9d: m. 14, v., which becomes v4 in mm. 15-17 (horizontally)

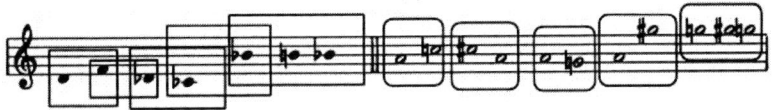

---

[139] The bass clef gives the relation between the motive and the rising/falling motion by seconds in voices 2-5 (see EXAMPLE 9a).

EXAMPLE 9e: m. 14, v. (horizontally)

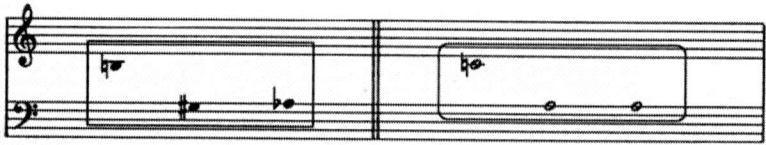

EXAMPLE 9f: m. 14, v3+v4 (horizontally)

EXAMPLE 9g: mm. 15-16, voices 1-4 and m. 17, all voices (vertically)

EXAMPLE 9h: mm. 15–17, v5 (horizontally)[140]

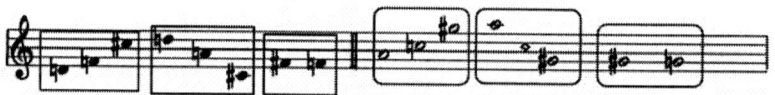

The dissecting analysis above shows that the motive is present at all times in this piece, usually in the form of one or several of its segments, thereby giving the initial melodic-harmonic shape its fundamental status. The fact that the motive proceeds through all 17 measures also gives the answer to the question of ornament: In accordance with Schoenberg's understanding of musical prose, there is no superfluous filler; everything is motive-related without repetition and symmetry. Rhythmically, the motive is presented as a tender, ascending movement. The analysis deliberately stresses the vertical and horizontal progressions; consequently, the rhythmic elements are toned down. This does not mean that rhythm is of lesser importance for the piece as a work of art. However, the intervals themselves still represent the most decisive feature of the basic motive. Playing the motive on the piano, horizontally or vertically, gives a unique, characteristic sound, which is especially created by the special combination of minor third and minor second. The tonic/dominant polarity, which one finds when considering the motive from the viewpoint of functional harmony, contributes

---

[140]The note A_4 in m. 16 is interpreted as corresponding to C_4 in the motive.

to the feeling that we are actually very close to traditional tonality. The A-minor third and the leading note G♯ are especially effective in this respect. The fifth between the third A_3-C_4 and the second G_4-$G{\sharp}_4$ is frequently altered throughout the piece, thus emphasizing the inherent dual structure of the motive.

Schoenberg's most significant alteration of the motivic intervals is the motive's minor third often becoming a major third, as it is already introduced in m. 1. Such a treatment of the third is among the most frequent interval alterations in the history of Western music. Schoenberg attaches particular importance to the third, and even more to the minor second, in the horizontal and vertical progression in this particular piece. The compositional possibilities inherent in these intervals are foremost in giving the *Klavierstück* its expressive melodic nature. The composer is subsequently sparing with the use of motive-related interval combinations as they might compete with these characteristics, thus maintaining the piece's material homogeneity both on a theoretical-analytical and an emotional level. In this way, the motive determines the material's molecular structure with utmost consistency, while Schoenberg's application simultaneously reveals the will afforded to the material by the motive. Consequently, the unique and specific material in fact determines the design of this specific composition. The material is treated in a functional manner, and thus comes forth (or appears *as itself*) both by virtue of its own intrinsic value and by virtue of its status as the decisive factor of the work's constructive consistency.

"Komposition mit zwölf nur aufeinander bezogenen Tönen"
Schoenberg's views on the concept of tonality includes the connection between two single tones. It is such relationships that are referred to in the heading above, based on his own characterization of the twelve-tone method and which he translates as a "method of composing with twelve tones which are related only with one another."[141] In this method tonal relationships are consistently liberated from the tonic principle and transferred to the outer limits of tonal space. Nevertheless, it is worth pointing out that the method still remains within what Schoenberg considers the limits of tonality.

As mentioned above, in the piano work that followed op. 19, *Fünf Klavierstücke* op. 23, Schoenberg used the twelve-tone method, which was to be so closely associated with his name, for the first time. In a letter to Nicolas Slonimsky he writes of the latter work:

---

[141]"Composition with Twelve Tones (1)," 218.

Here I arrived at a technique which I called (for myself) "composition with tones," a very vague term, but it meant something to me. Namely: In contrast to the ordinary way of using a motive, I used it already almost in the manner of a "basic set of twelve tones."[142]

Compared to op. 19, the musical material has now been infused with an innovative shaping power that provides the premises for the motive while at the same time relieving it from some of its structural obligations. In Schoenberg's approach, this particular force makes possible an extension of the formal dimensions of a musical piece.

Schoenberg began serious work on the principles of the twelve-tone method in 1921, and after a couple of years the final result was published. *Zwölfhalbtonsystem* (twelve-semitones system) was a term that was already in use at the end of the 19th century. The term is based on the well-tempered division of the octave into equal half-tone steps. At the beginning of the 20th century, when the foundations of traditional tonality were being severely challenged, the compositional use of the twelve pitches as units of equal value was considered a necessary precondition of tonality's further development. As mentioned above, Herbert Eimert attributes the first twelve-tone pieces to the Russian composer Jefim Golyscheff as early as 1914, while Josef Matthias Hauer is presented as the next composer of importance:

Twelve tone music appears for the first time in the unpublished compositions of the Russian Golyscheff in 1914. A few years later the thought of a comprehensible form of pure tonality is adopted by the Viennese theoretician and composer Hauer.[143]

That Eimert should give prominence to Golysheff and Hauer may seem strange, as posterity associates the twelve-tone method primarily with Schoenberg. From a historical perspective, however, it is important to bear in mind that around 1920, experiments in the application of various twelve-tone principles were being carried out both in Russia and Austria. At that time, Josef Matthias Hauer was the object of far more attention than is the case today. In this connection Hauer is famous for his *trope* concept: the division of the twelve pitches into six-tone groups, where the order of the

---

[142]Translated from M. Beiche, "Zwölftonmusik," *Terminologie der Musik im 20. Jahrhundert* [*HMT-Sonderband*], 444.

[143]H. Eimert, *Atonale Musiklehre*, 31. ["Zum ersten Male zwölftönige Musik findet sich 1914 in unveröffentlichten Kompositionen des Russen *Golyscheff*; einige Jahre später nimmt der Gedanke der reinen Atonalität bei dem Wiener Theoretiker und Komponisten *Hauer* greifbare Form an."]

pitches is not fixed. A hint of Schoenberg's skepticism to Hauer's views has already been mentioned. (In this brief historical overview it should also be mentioned that the term *dodecaphony*, which is applied as a matter of course today, did not come into customary use until around 1950.)

"The method of composing with twelve tones grew out of a necessity," Schoenberg says in reference to the development of tonality.[144] While Adorno can be regarded as the philosophical spokesman for this point of view, the quote shows once again that Schoenberg places himself in a historical perspective where he feels the calling not only to contribute to this progressive process but also to be its prime mover.

The main approach in Schoenberg's twelve-tone method is that the twelve chromatic pitches are placed one after another, in principle in arbitrary order, so that together they form a twelve-tone scale, row, or set. This scale is a fixed foundation, which can be traced in retrograde motion, inversion, and retrograde inversion. The mirror principle is particularly important for Schoenberg as it adds new dimensions to musical space : "The employment of these mirror forms corresponds to *the principle of the absolute and unitary perception of musical space.*"[145] This space is regarded as comparable to heaven, as described by Emanuel Swedenborg, where "there is no absolute down, no right or left, forward or backward."[146] To obtain these spatial dimensions within a twelve-tone scale, Schoenberg lets the retrograde motion begin, for example, with a transposition so that it starts with the note on which the basic set concludes. When this principle is continued through this multidimensional mirror image, the row is given in four versions. These can then be transposed again, resulting in altogether 48 transformations. In a specific composition, the row can be displayed in all its different variants, horizontally and/or vertically. As Schoenberg put it: "In twelve-tone composition the matter under discussion is in fact the succession of tones mentioned, whose comprehensibility as a musical idea is independent of whether its components are made audible one after the other or more or less simultaneously."[147]

With the twelve-tone method Schoenberg is linking his compositional principles even more tightly to a functionalist understanding of the material, where the type of rationality to which the method relates through the element of mathematical construction is particularly important. His focus on

---

[144]"Composition with Twelve Tones (1)," 216.

[145]"Composition with Twelve Tones (1)," 225.

[146]"Composition with Twelve Tones (1)," 223.

[147]"Twelve-tone Composition," *Style and Idea*, 208.

the logic of language is combined with the logic of number. At the same time, the playing of the row in retrograde motion and inversions is based on principles that have always been the characteristics of contrapuntal technique. This part of Schoenberg's procedures is thus based on ancient traditions of compositional craft that are linked to a musical logic where mathematical and numeral procedures are key elements. The traditional is combined with the universal in a way that is characteristic of the functionalist search for artistic truthfulness. Such a basic approach does not represent a denial of the expressive aspects of his art: "Use the same kind of form or expression, the same themes, melodies, sounds, rhythms as you used before," he says.[148] His most frequently quoted statement on the relationship between the twelve-tone method and musical composition is probably "my works are twelve-tone *compositions*, not *twelve-tone* compositions."[149]

The twelve-tone row represents a pre-forming of the musical material; it represents a certain tonal mix or blend. The strictly fixed tonal series must be followed consistently so that the musical material is infused with a strong will, which in itself is characteristic of the preferences functionalists attribute to artistic material.[150] According to Schoenberg, the twelve-tone row takes the place of the motive in the area of material structure:

> The basic set functions in the manner of a motive. This explains why such a basic set has to be invented anew for every piece. It has to be the first creative thought.[151]

This statement does not imply that Schoenberg has turned his back on motivic work. The point is rather that in a twelve-tone composition, the motive does not have the same status as compensation for the structuring possibilities of functional harmony, as it does in the opening piece of op. 19. The twelve-tone method as a form-structuring element will be discussed later in this study.

---

[148]"'Schoenberg's Tone-rows'." *Style and Idea*, 213.

[149]M. Hansen, *Arnold Schönberg: Ein Konzept der Moderne*, 180. ["Meine Werke sind Zwölfton-*Kompositionen* und nicht *Zwölfton*-Kompositionen."]

[150]As regards functionalist architecture, the preferred materials are glass, steel, reinforced concrete, etc.

[151]"Composition with Twelve Tone (1)," *Style and Idea*, 219.

Summary

The functionalist focus on *Materialgerechtigkeit* is of great importance to Schoenberg's attitude toward the musical material. When considering contemporary forms of musical expression, he realizes that there are different kinds of material. Nevertheless, all material must be handled in a truthful way. After "the crisis of tonality," the question of tonality or atonality becomes a general issue in contemporary musical thought. In Schoenberg's view there is no such thing as atonality in any kind of music. Tonal space is broad; it also embraces the reciprocal relationships of the twelve-tone method. By realizing the musical material through musical prose Schoenberg has found a way to purify music of superfluity and shallowness. Another fundamental concept in moving from material to form is found in Schoenberg's musical *Gedanke*, a rationally based unit that is both the initiating compulsion and the creator of unity on different structural levels. A keyword in the fulfillment of Schoenberg's material is musical logic. This type of logic has much in common with language, but the focus is on artistic logic in contrast to scientific logic.

Last but not least, the material's compulsion is manifested within the musical motive. In the motive there is a logically based potential, where the key principle is developing variation. In Schoenberg's approach, the motive represents the consistency of the musical material. His recognition and subsequent application are revealed through his own music, as seen in the piano piece from *Sechs kleine Klavierstücke*, op. 19. The twelve-tone method represents a process based on pre-formed material; Schoenberg adds to the musical composition through the combination of mathematically related construction and the compositional craft of earlier times. Consequently, he associates himself even more strongly with functionalism's positive view of rational construction, while also maintaining the artistic dimensions of his creative act.

In the unfinished opera *Moses und Aron* (1930-32) it becomes obvious that Schoenberg has realized the vast opportunities open to him through the twelve-tone method. The entire complex musical progression is based solely on one single row. The plot, describing how Moses leads his people and presents them with the Ten Commandments that are to be their salvation, can be interpreted as an allegory for the role Schoenberg felt he had in music. In his extensive musical activities he appeared to be both a leading figure in the development of music and a communicator of music's basic regularities in his culture. Schoenberg's own text in Scene 1, Act 1 may elucidate this dual meaning:

> VOICE FROM THE BURNING BUSH,
> 6 SOLO VOICES
> You've seen your kindred enslaved, the truth
> you have known,
> so you can do nothing else:
> therefore you must set your folk free!
>
> MOSES
> Who am I to combat the power
> and force of that blindness?
>
> VOICE FROM THE BURNING BUSH,
> 6 SOLO VOICES
> United with God in oneness,
> to him joined,
> from Pharaoh torn loose![152]

A few years later, in 1934, Schoenberg writes "German music will not take the path I have pointed out for it."[153] This complaint sounds like a resigned recognition of the fact that the magnificent musical exodus leading out of the old times has betrayed its chosen leader. Such a lament not only describes a strong artistic self-consciousness experiencing disappointment over the apparent lack of followers, it is also descriptive of Schoenberg's visions for the future and the profound awareness of his vocation that he had all his life. His thinking on the musical material, its nature and possibilities, must be considered in the light of this overriding perspective.

---

[152] Quoted from the leaflet for Pierre Boulez's recording (SONY CD SM2K 48 456).
[153] *The Musical Idea*, 88.

Hindemith: The Interval as Musical Material

> Seien Sie überzeugt, daß ich
> hier wie in aller Musik, die ich schreibe oder spiele,
> nicht mehr erstrebe als Klarheit und Ehrlichkeit.
>
> *Paul Hindemith*[154]

Hindemith and Schoenberg

A striking trait in Paul Hindemith's development is how the composer and theoretician appear to evolve from the musical performer. Hindemith once declared that although he had always been writing music, he did not start to believe that he had a talent for composing until he was 24.[155] There are thus important differences between Hindemith and Schoenberg's epistemological backgrounds. Hindemith's ideas about music are related to a much greater degree to personal experiences as a performing musician. In his time Hindemith was to become active in several areas of music. The combination of the need for musical expansion and profound reflection marked his musical maturity. H.H. Stuckenschmidt alleges that there is a duality to Hindemith's nature:

> [...] in Paul Hindemith's heart there always lived two souls, and quite without an agonizing or agonized "alas:" that of the playful boy, we may well say the naughty lad, and that of the thoughtful seeker for perfection and truth, strict and diligent beyond comparison.[156]

As time went by, Hindemith's thinking revealed an increasingly clearer ethical foundation, often with a slightly religious feature. This propensity is particularly expressed in *A Composer's World: Horizons and Limitations*, published in 1952, where immediately in the introduction he displays his considerations of music's epistemological dimensions:

> We must be grateful that with our art we have been placed halfway between science and religion, enjoying equally the advantages of exactitude in thinking—so far as the technical aspects in music are concerned—and the unlimited world of faith.[157]

---

[154][Be convinced that here as in all the music I write and play I strive for nothing more than clarity and honesty.]

[155]See "Komposition und Kompositionsunterricht," *Aufsätze, Vorträge, Reden*, 64-65.

[156]H.H. Stuckenschmidt, "Paul Hindemiths Aufbruch und Heimkehr," *Hindemith-Jahrbuch* 1974/IV (Mainz: Schott, 1975), 12. ["In Paul Hindemiths Brust wohnten allezeit und ganz ohne gequältes oder quälendes Ach zwei Seelen: die des verspielten Jungen, sagen wir ruhig, des Lausbuben, und die des strengen beispiellos fleißigen und nachdenklichen Suchers nach Vollendung und Wahrheit."]

[157]*A Composer's World*, IX.

In 1923, when Hindemith was 28, he published the first version of the song cycle *Das Marienleben*, op. 27. This work, based on texts by Rainer Maria Rilke, is often considered to be a sign of a shift in Hindemith's attitude as a composer. At this time, Hindemith was highly productive, with a creativity that spanned various genres. A few years previously he had written the one-act operas "Mörder, Hoffnung der Frauen" (1919), "Das Nusch-Nuschi" (1920), and *Sancta Susanna* (1921). These works, especially the latter, excited many reactions and were met with cries of dismay in the post-war opera world, not least because of their sexual over- and undertones. His *Kammermusik*, op. 24/1 (1922), and *1922 Suite für Klavier*, op. 26 were also considered both radical and audacious in form and structure. Hindemith's production during this period is a good example of what Stuckenschmidt calls the duality of his nature. Among those who found it difficult to accept Hindemith's position as an early 1920s' *Bürgerschreck* was the music historian Hans Joachim Moser:

> If in committee meetings one looked into his deep eyes, one started to doubt if the "épater le bourgeois" that he so persistently pursued in the *Suite 1922* for piano or in the three one-act operas from the years of inflation, "Mörder, Hoffnung der Frauen," "Das Nusch-Nuschi," and *Sancta Susanna*, displayed his nature at all.[158]

From the end of the 1920s onward, Hindemith's ethical stance became increasingly apparent, while at the same time his style became more balanced in expression. This changed tendency would eventually lead to revisions and new editions of earlier works, such as *Das Marienleben* (1923/1948), the cantata *Frau Musica* (1928/1943), and the operas *Cardillac* (1926/1952) and *Neues vom Tage* (1929/1953).

Regarded as a whole, the outstanding characteristic of Hindemith's musical output is its immense diversity and scope, a fact that is usually forgotten, with a more detrimental effect than in the case of Schoenberg: Adorno's stamping of Hindemith as a conservative often overshadows the fact that he represented radical progress in the 1920s and was considered the leading figure in German music right up to the 1950s. Conversely, the musical restlessness of his youthful works may receive exclusive attention at the expense of the contemplative mood that is so often prevalent in his later production.

---

[158]H.J. Moser, *Musikgeschichte in hundert Lebensbildern* (Stuttgart etc.: Reclam, 1958), 971. ["Sah man bei Senatssitzungen in seine tiefen Augen, so wurde man zweifelhaft, ob das "épater le bourgeois," das er in der *Klaviersuite 1922* oder in den drei Einaktern der Inflationsjahre "Mörder, Hoffnung der Frauen," "Das Nusch-Nuschi" und *Sancta Susanna* so arg getrieben, wirklich seine eigentliche Natur darstelle."]

Hindemith is generally considered to be a representative of a path different from the one Schoenberg followed. For this reason, Hindemith and Schoenberg have been regarded as opposites in the development of 20th-century music. On passing from the musical approaches of Schoenberg to Hindemith's thinking on music it is necessary to examine the more subtle distinctions in this relationship. David Neumeyer and Giselher Schubert are among the researchers who have been concerned with the Hindemith-Schoenberg question. The following account includes important elements from their work.[159]

It is well known that, early in his career, Hindemith was familiar with both Schoenberg and the Second Viennese School. The view that composers such as Hindemith, Weill, Prokofiev, Honegger, Milhaud, and others ignored Schoenberg's music is, according to Neumeyer and Schubert, a later fabrication. The so-called serialists in particular cultivated this conception, and Pierre Boulez has had a key role: "In his battle against Neo-Classicism Boulez claimed falsely that the music of Schoenberg and Webern was almost completely suppressed in Paris in the twenties."[160] Indeed, the Amar Quartet, with Hindemith playing the viola, premiered Anton Webern's *Bagatellen* op. 9 in Paris in December 1924. In 1959, when Webern's music was experiencing a renaissance, Hindemith said in a newspaper interview:

> My God, we played Webern—the things that today are called 'new' —we played them in the early twenties. The question of Webern's greatness was decided then. What you have now is simply a rediscovery of his music.[161]

In the 1920s Hindemith was seen as an energetic promoter of new music, both as a performer and as a member of the steering committee for the Donaueschinger Kammermusiktage.[162] His enthusiasm benefitted not least Schoenberg and Webern. In 1923, in a letter to committee member Heinrich Burkhard, Hindemith writes:

> I've heard from Hertzka [the publisher of Universal-Edition, Vienna] that Webern has a new quartet ready. Write to him at once and reserve the first performance rights for this summer. Hertzka himself didn't put it over properly, so you must arrange things with Webern

---

[159]D. Neumeyer and G. Schubert, "Arnold Schoenberg and Paul Hindemith," *Journal of the Arnold Schoenberg Institute* XIII/I, 1990, 3-46.

[160]"Arnold Schoenberg and Paul Hindemith," 3.

[161]"Arnold Schoenberg and Paul Hindemith," 4.

[162]Hindemith became a member in 1923. The other members were Heinrich Burkhard, the composer Joseph Haas and the pianist/composer Eduard Erdmann.

yourself. How is it with the Schönberg Serenade? If you don't get it, then at least try to get the new Wind Quintet. Leave no stone unturned: we must at all costs have something by him as well as by Webern. Particularly the Schönberg you must get without fail. If you have these things, Donaueschingen will be morally way above all this year's other music festivals.[163]

Schoenberg's first string quartet was one of the Amar Quartet's most frequently performed works. Hindemith was also to contribute actively to the performance of other parts of Schoenberg's work, including the *Sechs kleine Klavierstücke*, op. 19, which he arranged to be performed at concerts. Hindemith's efforts in this area peaked in 1924, when, together with Hermann Scherchen, he planned a concert of Schoenberg's works on the occasion of the composer's 50th birthday. On this event Schoenberg wrote to Scherchen:

Now I once again want to extend to you my heartfelt thanks and request that you also tell Hindemith that I am very pleased with him. With this gesture he gives a beautiful sign of the correct attitude to his elders, a sign only a person with genuine and justified self-esteem can give; only one who does not fear for his own position when another person is honored, and who justly recognizes that such an honor also honors himself, if he is committed to it. Once I said: honor can only he who himself has honor and deserves honor. Such a person knows what is due to him and therefore what is due to his peers.[164]

There is much to indicate that Schoenberg held his younger colleague in high esteem. In 1932 he still considered Hindemith's works to be close to his own: "the composers who stand closest to me (excepting my own students) are the Aryans Bartók, Hauer, Krenek and Hindemith."[165] That Schoenberg should maker such remarks three years after he had expressed himself quite vehemently on the subject of the concessions to the user in

---

[163]*Selected Letters of Paul Hindemith*, G. Skelton, ed./trans. (New Haven, CT, etc.: Yale University Press, 1995), 33-34.

[164]Erwin Stein, ed., *Arnold Schoenberg. Briefe* (Mainz: Schott, 1958), 117. ["Nun will ich Ihnen nochmals herzlichst danken und bitte Sie, auch Hindemith zu sagen, dass ich mich *außerordentlich über ihn freue*. Er gibt damit ein schönes Zeichen von richtiger Einstellung gegenüber Älteren, ein Zeichen, wie es nur ein Mensch von echtem und berechtigtem Selbstgefühl geben kann; nur einer, der nicht nötig hat, für seinen Ruhm zu fürchten, wenn ein anderer geehrt wird, und der richtig erkennt, dass eben solche Ehrung ihn ehrt, wenn er sich ihr verbündet. Ich habe einmal gesagt: ehren kann einen nur, wer selbst Ehre hat und Ehre verdient. Ein solcher weiß, was ihm gebührt, und darum auch, was seinesgleichen gebührt."]

[165]D. Neumeyer and G. Schubert, "Arnold Schoenberg and Paul Hindemith," 9.

Hindemith's and Brecht's *Lehrstück* of 1929, might seem surprising.[166] There is, however, little doubt that Schoenberg recognized the dimensions in Hindemith's talent, even if their views on music did not always concur. They obviously had far greater understanding for each other than the prevailing opinion would have it. In a humorous aside included in the *Festschrift* for his 50th birthday, Schoenberg playfully refers to his senility as he has become more tolerant: "I cannot hate anymore as I did before; and what is worse, I often even understand without holding in contempt."[167]

Volume I of Hindemith's *Unterweisung im Tonsatz*, written in 1937, at a time when he was less concerned with Schoenberg and his music—can be regarded as a more or less covert polemic against the twelve-tone method. But in no way should this be considered an attack on Schoenberg's works in general. Neumeyer and Schubert believe that Hindemith maintained his feeling of fellowship and respect for Schoenberg all his life.[168] When Hindemith discusses the twelve-tone method in various connections, it is the *twelve-tone* composition rather than the twelve-tone *composition* he is referring to.[169]

Of Hindemith's last three series of lectures, delivered at Zurich University in 1957, the first was devoted to Gesualdo, the second to Schoenberg, and the third to fundamentals of musical composition. In the first three Schoenberg lectures Hindemith discussed the quartets opp. 10, 37, and 30, respectively. Some notes and music examples from these lectures have been preserved. Neumeyer and Schubert's conclusion after examining this material reveals a significant characteristic of his Hindemith's relations with Schoenberg on the one hand and the twelve-tone method on the other:

> [...] perhaps the most significant critical point that emerges from Hindemith's work with Schoenberg's string quartets is his conviction that they represent important music, not because of, but despite the twelve-tone technique.[170]

There is little to indicate that Schoenberg undertook any thorough examination of Hindemith's work. It is also uncertain as to how much he

---

[166] See A. Schoenberg, "Glosses on the Theories of Others," *Style and Idea*, 313-315.

[167] Schoenberg's introduction to *Arnold Schönberg zum fünfzigsten Geburtstage 13. September 1924*, 270. ["Ich kann nicht so mehr hassen wie früher; und was noch ärger ist: ich kann manchmal schon verstehen, ohne zu verachten".]

[168] "Arnold Schoenberg and Paul Hindemith," 39, note 19.

[169] *A Composer's World*, 139ff.

[170] "Arnold Schoenberg and Paul Hindemith," 29.

was involved in studying *The Craft of Musical Composition*. On the other hand, Schoenberg was undoubtedly familiar with the book, at least through reports on it. He even thought that Hindemith's theory of "harmonic value" was based on considerations of the sixth chord and six-four chord in his own *Theory of Harmony*.[171] In an undated fragment he writes:

> I should perhaps consider it rather flattering that Hindemith bases so much of his theory book "Unterweisung im Tonsatz" on one little detail in my "Harmonielehre," which certainly was a discovery [...] It is my [hypothetical] attempt of explaining the difference in the tension between a sixth-chord and a four-sixth chord by the difference in the tension of the overtones. This tension is heavier in the 4-6 chord[,] accordingly [this chord] is "less" consonant than the 6-chord. This is certainly a possibility which might be applied to evaluate the degree of discordance of the chords.[172]

As late as 1947, Schoenberg specifically requested that his remarks on these chord conversions be included in the abridged American edition of the *Harmonielehre* (entitled *Structural Functions of Harmony*). The reason was explicit: "it may well be the unacknowledged source of some of Hindemith's ideas."[173] In *The Craft of Musical Composition*, Hindemith makes a harmonic analysis of a section of Schoenberg's *Klavierstück*, op. 33a based on his own methodology, concluding that the chords appear to be collected round a tonal center without his own ideals of a clear tonal organization. Schoenberg, otherwise so sensitive, noted that this critical analysis could be a starting point for an examination of Hindemith's theories.[174]

Further relationships between elements in Schoenberg and Hindemith's approaches will be discussed later. The conclusion at this point is that there was no hostility between these two composers. Neither was there any personal friendship. Their professional relationship can best be described as ambivalent: They respected the essentials of each other's work but were more critical of other aspects; it was probably no more complicated or painful than that. This conclusion may be worth bearing in mind when examining Hindemith's understanding of the musical material.

---

[171] See *Theory of Harmony*, 55-81.

[172] "Arnold Schoenberg and Paul Hindemith," 10.

[173] B.R. Simms, "Commentary: Arnold Schoenberg, "Theory of Harmony," *Music Theory Spectrum* 4 (1982), 162.

[174] "Arnold Schoenberg and Paul Hindemith," 10.

Materialgerechtigkeit

"For him, 'justice to material' [*Materialgerechtigkeit*] belongs among the basic challenges to the production of new music," writes H.J. Moser of Hindemith.[175] The need to give the musical material justice according to its nature or will was one of the main features of Hindemith's work. His German vocabulary contains such expressions as *Eigenkräfte der Töne* and *Eigenwille der Töne*, denoting the inherent force and will of the tones. Bending what he calls the tones' will with understanding and care is one of the composer's most important challenges, and "[t]o do this we need precise knowledge of the tones and of the forces that reside in them, free from aesthetic dogma [...] but leading the composer rather according to natural laws and technical experience.[176] Hindemith also expresses the view that musical material in itself could be an obstacle for a really free realization of artistic ideas. The notion that, for example, the melody should be concerned with the spiritual beyond the material's own rules is incorrect, he says, "for as soon as one has a material with certain qualities in one's hands (and tones are even quite tangible and willful material!), these qualities immediately provide measures for their treatment."[177] In Hindemith's view, the type of limits in the construction of musical material distinguishes it from other forms of art: "Beyond the specific limitations prescribed by each art's constructional material, the composer seems to be limited in a way peculiar to his craft and unknown to other creative artists."[178] The reason is that music seems to speak so directly to the listener's emotions while at the same time being dependent on them. In other forms of art, Hindemith argues, acknowledgment of the rational precedes the aesthetic in the act of perception. In music, emotion comes first. This assumed fact must also influence the treatment of material. Nevertheless, there is every indication that like Stravinsky, Hindemith saw a special challenge in the aspect of limitation:

---

[175]H.J. Moser, *Musikgeschichte in hundert Lebensbildern*, 971. ["'Materialgerechtigkeit' gehört ihm zu Grundforderungen neuer Musikproduktion".]

[176]*The Craft of Musical Composition* I (Theoretical Part), Arthur Mendel, trans. (London: Schott, 1945), 12.

[177]"Betrachtungen zur heutigen Musik," *Aufsätze, Vorträge, Reden*, 173. ["denn sobald man ein Material von bestimmten Eigenschaften in Händen hat (und die Töne sind sogar ein ziemlich handfestes und eigenwilliges Material!), ergeben sich stets aus diesen Eigenschaften Verhaltensmaßregeln für den Bearbeiter."]

[178]*A Composer's World*, 56.

> Not only perceiving the material-related limitations as a burden but, on the contrary, exploiting them to advantage as promoting creation has always been the composer's task, and is, if I can speak of my own experience, indeed one of the most attractive aspects of composing, and possibly the most interesting one, from a sporting (if one can be allowed the expression) point of view.[179]

In a lecture delivered in 1927 under the elaborate title "Wie soll der ideale Chorsatz der Gegenwart oder besser der nächsten Zukunft beschaffen sein?" (How should the ideal choral score of the present or rather of the near future be constructed?), Hindemith lays down instructions for building up the successful choral score. His sixth and last point reads as follows:

> Every choral composer should keep the easy singability of his choral setting in mind as his highest law. A choral setting of average quality but written for comfortable singing and therefore sounding tolerably is often more enjoyable that an artistic product however good, which, through inadequate knowledge of the material, is written to such a degree against the voices that the listener either does not derive any enjoyment from it at all or only a rather doubtful satisfaction, since he must all the time compare the acoustic impression with the score.[180]

The emphasis on *die bequeme Sangbarkeit* (the easy singability) as the choral setting's highest law suggests associations to Adolf Loos dictum, "Artworks aim at jostling people out of their indolence (*Bequemlichkeit*); houses are intended to provide comfort (*Bequemlichkeit*)." It is true that Loos is more crass and uncompromising than Hindemith, but there is something of the same functionalist polarization of the concept of art in them both. Hindemith lets the composer become part of the whole, where the performer or listener, i.e., the user, is allowed a definitive role in deciding how the work will "actually" be perceived. The term "art product" (*Kunstprodukt*)

---

[179]"Hören und Verstehen unbekannter Musik," *Aufsätze, Vorträge, Reden*, 302. ["Die materialbedingten Einschränkungen aber nicht nur als Last zu empfinden, sie im Gegenteil als schöpfungsfördernd vorteilhaft auszunutzen, ist von jeher die Aufgabe der Komponisten gewesen und ist, wenn ich aus meiner eigenen Erfahrung reden darf, sogar einer der reizvollsten Teile der kompositorischen Arbeit und vielleicht der (wenn der Ausdruck erlaubt ist) sportlich interessanteste."]

[180]"Wie soll der ideale Chorsatz der Gegenwart oder besser der nächsten Zukunft beschaffen sein," *Aufsätze, Vorträge, Reden*, 26. ["Als oberstes Gesetz sollte jedem Chorkomponisten die bequeme Sangbarkeit seines Chorsatzes vorschweben. Ein mittelguter, aber leicht singbar geschriebener und deshalb erträglich klingender Chor ist meistens genießbarer als ein noch so gutes Kunstprodukt, das in Unkenntnis des Materials so wider die Stimmen geschrieben ist, dass der Zuhörer entweder zu gar keinem Genuss kommt oder nur der recht zweifelhaften Befriedigung teilhaftig wird, beständig den akustischen Eindruck mit dem Notenbild vergleichen zu müssen."]

has a negative undertone that Hindemith does not associate with, for instance, the preferred term "work of art" (*Kunstwerk*). However, he finds that an art product may be more perfectly acceptable within the scope of the score than in the sounding form it eventually assumes. The functional aspect is present in both the creation and the evaluation of the work of art. Another central element in Hindemith's statement is the coupling of inadequate knowledge of the material with writing "against the voices," an observation that is certainly no general argument against new music. His point is that there are definite limits on how far a voice can be stretched and that it seldom pays to exceed these limits. One of the best examples is the singing voice, and this recognition is also an important point of departure for the later revision of *Das Marienleben*. Hindemith explains these issues in his comprehensive preface to the revision. Many difficulties can be overcome if only the performer is skilled enough. Others just cannot be overcome, no matter how diligent the practice, because they are written so much against the nature of the instruments:

> True enough, in the course of time, our ears have grown accustomed to quite a variety of sounds but our vocal chords will allow themselves to be forced into what is unnatural just as little as the trombonist will try to master his instrument with techniques for the flute.[181]

Hindemith concurs with Schoenberg when he says that the human ear has adjusted in the course of music history. Nevertheless, there are limits, not least for what practice can keep abreast of. Hindemith thus presents his recognition of a connection between the nature of musical material and the nature of human beings. This conviction must also guide the contemporary composer. It is important to realize that Hindemith uses the term "nature" in both of the above-mentioned meanings. His idea of *Materialgerechtigkeit* is closely connected to the understanding of the nature of listening and performance, to the human potential for musical function.

For Hindemith, there is no Schoenbergian concept of musical prose equivalent to Loos's rejection of ornament or to Kraus's campaign against the phrase. It is, however, quite possible to add less important elements to a harmonic progression, Hindemith says, "without letting the listener be suffocated by ornament or drowned by the inarticulate."[182] It is Hindemith's

---

[181]*Das Marienleben* (Mainz: Schott, 1948), IV. ["Unsere Ohren haben sich im Laufe der Zeit zwar an vieles gewöhnt, aber unsere Stimmbänder werden sich so wenig zwingen lassen, ihnen Unnatürliches anzutun, wie eine Posaune, der man mit einer Flötentechnik beikommen will."]

[182]"Sterbende Gewässer," *Aufsätze, Vorträge, Reden*, 325. ["ohne den Hörer im Ornament ersticken oder im Unartikulierten ertrinken zu lassen."]

focus on the concept of *sound* that parallels the views of Loos and Kraus. His broad definition of the musical material is that it consists of harmony, melody, and rhythm. "Beyond that there is nothing," he argues, "sound color, dynamics, agogics, and so on are not basic elements but merely additions, something that does not change the nature of a melody, a rhythm, a form, etc."[183] Hindemith considers sound to be an external, and hence superficial phenomenon, and an exaggerated use of such musical additive is for him, as for Loos in his field, a sign of degeneration. In his book *A Composer's World*, such thoughts become abundantly clear. Sound will always be a part of music, but this fact notwithstanding, it is very transitory: "Sound, the ever present ingredient of music, is the frailest of its qualities."[184] The seductive sound experience has been allowed to dominate at the cost of music's potential of ethical and moral powers, thus concealing a deeper level of recognition. To Hindemith, the tendencies of the time feel alarming:

> Sound and its effect on our auditory nerves apparently is the only factor considered essential. [...] Symphony orchestras have degenerated into mere distributors of superrefined sounds.[185]

Hindemith considers orchestral pieces that require congested concert podiums to be specious, self-important, and full of meaningless pomp. He feels a general antipathy towards the media of romantic performance, but he goes even further in toning down the importance of sound. It seems that he would take the complicated road from the supposedly exaggerated sound effect via sound as a substantial musical factor to what actually lies behind the sound itself. He distinguishes between music that looks good on paper and music that sounds good in practice. When it comes to Bach's *The Art of the Fugue*, written without instrument specification, Hindemith believes that the work is best enjoyed directly from the score:

> The ideal behavior is to enjoy it [*Die Kunst der Fuge*] in the same spirit of nonsounding abstraction as the composer did when he wrote it, thus executing consciously and in the highest degree the emotional and intellectual actions and reactions [...].[186]

---

[183]"Probleme eines heutigen Komponisten," *Aufsätze, Vorträge, Reden*, 203. ["Darüber hinaus gibt es nicht" [...] "Klangfarbe, Dynamik, Agogik usw. sind keine Grundelemente, sondern nur etwas Zusätzliches, wodurch aber eine Melodie, ein Rhythmus, eine Form usw. in ihrem Wesen unverändert bleiben".]

[184]*A Composer's World*, 2.

[185]*A Composer's World*, 242.

[186]*A Composer's World*, 163.

Hindemith: The Interval as Musical Material

Music contains a higher truth that is not bound by its realization in sound. To those who are of the opinion that many listeners will be excluded from experiencing music that takes its starting-point outside of sound, Hindemith poses the following question:

> Why should everyone have everything? [...] Should we not be glad to have certain pieces of music [...] kept away from the ordinary musical goings-on, if for no further reason than to give the ambitious seeker of higher musical truths an opportunity to grow?[187]

His views are extreme; they originate in his stubborn opposition to music arrangers' interference with masterpieces. Nevertheless, it is still odd that Hindemith, the arch-musician among 20th- century composers, would consider making such views public. However, his main point is that music's truth does not depend on sound. This view does not imply that musical truth cannot be realized in ringing sound.

And what does this presumed truth consist of? One important answer for Hindemith is that music's basis is both reflected in the universe and sounding in human beings. There is a connection between the nature of music and the ancient view of the harmony of the spheres:

> [t]hose harmonies so perfect that the inadequate sense organs of men could not perceive them, needing no realization in sound, since the ratios of numbers that underlie all movement and all sound are more to the reflecting spirit than the external part of music—sound—through which it becomes profaned and is brought within the sphere of man's perceptions?[188]

Hindemith's understanding of the musical material's will is found in the combination of natural regularities in the material itself, in the listening process, and in the music's actual performance. His thorough knowledge of instruments and performance obviously plays an important role. In addition, there must be a moral directive at the heart of composing: "Music has to be converted into moral power," he concludes in reference to Augustine.[189] As will be seen later in this study, this directive is particularly significant for Hindemith's view on the function of music.

---

[187] *A Composer's World*, 164.
[188] *The Craft of Musical Composition*, 53.
[189] *A Composer's World*, 6.

"Zahl und Schönheit, Mathematik und Kunst"

Like Schoenberg, Hindemith sees himself as a representative of a crucial stage in the development of music. His duty is to reintroduce order and comprehensibility into the musical material. This order cannot be based on theory alone: the listener and creator should always be of the same mind.[190] Music is, above all, communication, and this fact must always be taken into consideration. Hindemith appears as a redeemer and a guide out of a chaotic and confused phase in the history of music. The clearest expression of his sense of his vocation within the development of music appears in a lecture entitled "Sterbende Gewässer," which he gave in 1963, the year he died. There has been a remarkable expansion in the area of tonality, he says. Over time, music has gained control over all the twelve chromatic pitches in a tonal universe that has absorbed an incredible diversity of technical possibilities for composition. In this perspective one can use a term such as "tonal totality."[191] The tonal system has been developing, and the tonal system is the basic material of music.[192] But these developments are far from infinite: the point where the musical material meets its limits has already been reached. Although one may venture into the far areas of superficial sound, the basics of the musical material cannot be expanded any further:

> Unfortunately, there are limits to further progression, if one is not to slide into the worn-out element of music that avoids every form of exact control, sound. [...] the material has reached full maturity.[...]If one is to find anything new, it is certainly not in the material sphere.[193]

Hindemith thus regards the development of the musical material as an already completed process, and he is convinced that this artistic material's inherent will does not allow for it to be stretched beyond a certain point:

> If we spoke earlier [in *The Craft of Musical Composition*] of breaking the will of the tones, this must have meant that we must see to it that the force that is latent in the intervals must be prevented form simply acting freely as it chooses—not that we could by main force stamp the raw material into any shape, without regard to its natural elasticity. Under wise treatment, the tonal material can be easily bent and welded. But if too great a strain is put upon it, or if it is not handled

---

[190]See, e.g., "Komposition und Kompositionsunterricht," 54-63.

[191]"Sterbende Gewässer," 327.

[192]"Sterbende Gewässer," 315.

[193]"Sterbende Gewässer," 331. ["Leider sind diesem Weitergehen Grenzen gesetzt, wenn man nicht in das fadenscheinigste und sich jeder exakten Kontrolle entziehende Element der Musik, *das Klangliche*, abgleiten will. [...] das Material ist zu seiner vollen Reife gelangt. [...] Soll Neues gefunden werden, liegt es sicher nicht im Bereiche des Materials."]

Hindemith: The Interval as Musical Material

in accordance with the laws of its own nature, it will break like any other building material, and the music constructed from it will be useless.[194]

The musical material is subject to rules that are absolute, which prompts Hindemith to consider contemporary avant-garde experiments at innovation as futile attempts at evasion. Nature itself determines the consistency of the musical material in accordance with the overtone series, he argues. The proportions on which the series is based can be expressed through rational numbers. Consequently, the consistency of the musical material can be calculated mathematically. The essential point lies in the fact that human beings have the ability to recognize this material logic with their ears. The ear reveals the fact that numbers and beauty, mathematics and art are closely related, Hindemith believes.[195] In thinking along these lines he not only takes an active part in a historical development, but also positions himself as a representative of the Pythagorean tradition. He approaches the questions of the musical material through rationality, logic, and calculation—an artistic approach that is characteristic of the functionalists in the 1920s. This position runs parallel with Schoenberg's fundamental thoughts and attitudes at the time. Hindemith, however, takes the practical requirements of music in use much more into consideration, and this is of fundamental significance for his views.

Through his focus on compositional technique, natural laws, and ratios Hindemith connects to contemporary thoughts on universality in a way that also evokes the ideas of antiquity. He finds comprehensible references in the eras before the great classical masters, in ancient Greece and Rome, in the Middle Ages, and in the modern epoch:

> What did tonal materials mean to the ancients? Intervals spoke to them of the first days of creation of the world: mysterious as Number, of the same stuff as the basic concepts of time and space, the very dimensions of the audible as of the visible world, building stones of the universe, which, in their minds, was constructed in the same proportions as the overtone series, so that measure, music, and the cosmos inseparably merged.[196]

Where Schoenberg emphasized the importance of the overtone series for the traditional understanding of tonality and functional harmony,

---

[194]*The Craft of Musical Composition*, 86.

[195]*The Craft of Musical Composition*, 24.

[196]*The Craft of Musical Composition*, 12-13.

Hindemith argues for the unconditional validity of the regularity of overtones for all cultures at all times. He refers to the pentatonic scale as a basic system that embraces more than art music in the West:

> Its smallest tonal step is the whole tone and the minor third. Numerous remnants of this system are still found today in folk songs in many places, especially in the Celtic and Anglo-Saxon world; but it also plays an important role in the East, particularly in classical Chinese music.[197]

Hindemith does not accept music that renounces audible tonal order. If a system of musical organization can only be seen, it is alien to the genuine musical material.[198] The twelve-tone method is a typical example of such a system: "Dodecaphonic arrangements look fantastic on paper," he admits, but only on paper, since "it is impossible in a musical sense to understand the smallest of the dodecaphonic efforts by listening."[199] Hindemith is referring to the extreme consequences of the twelve-tone method, a method that consists of nothing other than "permutations of numbers from one to twelve." This play on permutations alien to the ear has subsequently given rise to serialism.[200] So-called concrete music, aleatoricism, electronic music, and music for prepared instruments feature in the same alien, superficial category of *Klangspiel* (play of sounds). Consequently, the musical material should not be worked, stretched, or bent in a way that renders its unique qualities unrecognizable to the human ear. If no logic is actually heard, the most sophisticated system offers little help however much it is anchored in mathematical rationality. Rationality must be based on an order that can be realized in a wider sense, says Hindemith, and he concludes that

> [a] true musician believes only in what he hears. No matter how ingenious a theory is, it means nothing to him until the evidence is placed before him in actual sound.[201]

---

[197]"Sterbende Gewässer," 317. ["Seine kleinsten Tonschritte sind der Ganzton und die kleine Terz. Zahlreiche Reste dieses Systems finden sich noch heute in den Volksliedern vieler Gegenden, besonders der keltischen und angelsächsischen Welt; es spielt aber auch im Osten, besonders in der klassischen chinesischen Musik, eine wichtige Rolle."]

[198]"Sterbende Gewässer," 330.

[199]"Sterbende Gewässer," 329. ["Auf dem Papier sehen die dodekaphonen Anordnungen wunderschön aus" "[...] es ist nämlich unmöglich, vom dodekaphonen Aufwand auch das Geringste im musikalischen Sinne hörend zu verstehen".]

[200]"Sterbende Gewässer," 329. ["Permutationen der Zahlen von Eins bis Zwölf."]

[201]*The Craft of Musical Composition,* 156.

The Interval, Series I *and* Series II

Hindemith's point of departure in *The Craft of Musical Composition* is the conviction that the fundamental laws of tonal relationships are founded in nature and consequently valid for all time. Three years after the book was first published in 1937, he released a new, extended edition. In his later book, *A Composer's World: Horizons and Limitations* (1952), he presents a short version of the theories from *Craft*. In the German translation of the latter publication, *Komponist in seiner Welt: Weiten und Grenzen* (1959), he adjusts his thoughts somewhat and expands on the concept of tonality.

The Craft of Musical Composition is intended primarily for teachers, writes Hindemith in the preface. He describes the universal perspectives of the book as follows:

> The teacher will find in this book basic principles of composition, derived from the natural characteristics of tones, and consequently valid for all periods.[202]

Hindemith never intended to try explaining the whole compositional process in a supposedly scientific way. In the chapter on harmony, he characterizes his book as a work "which does not aim at the complete scientific explanation of the deepest impulses that underlie musical writing, but rather seeks to be of practical use."[203] One should always bear this reservation in mind as one examines this book.

Through Hindemith's contemplations on the overtones—or partial tones, as we would call them today—one could be led to think that, like Schoenberg, he finds the overtone series to be the raw matter of musical material. In fact, Hindemith sees the raw material of music rather as the whole of the unorganized tonal spectrum, consisting of individual tones which the human ear is able to perceive. Composers are working with natural material in the sense that it is supposedly nature that decides the regularity on which the *Materialgerechtigkeit* of music is based. When it comes to the allegedly stable conditions of the musical material, Schoenberg is far more open to any future syntheses and blends. Yet for both Hindemith and Schoenberg, the aim is to treat the musical material in a presumably functional and truthful way.

Schoenberg stresses the importance of the overtone phenomenon for the diatonic scales of Western culture, for functional harmony in general, and for the position of the dissonance in particular. Conversely for Hindemith, the applications of such relationships are far from being random cultural

---

[202]*The Craft of Musical Composition,* 9.

[203]*The Craft of Musical Composition,* 110.

phenomena. He believes that certain intervals will make the same impression on every human ear—and that the octave is unique:

> When even the man of the lowest level of civilization hears the interval of an octave, he will feel that the upper note is the higher image of the lower. Accordingly, in all known tonal systems, the basic scale-patterns, with few exceptions, fill in the space between two tones an octave apart.[204]

Then comes the fifth, Hindemith says, while the thirds, sixths, seconds, and sevenths are not equally definable.
The octave and the fifth lie closest to the initial pitch in the overtone series or partial tone spectrum:

EXAMPLE 10: the partial-tone row with C as the initial pitch

Pitches numbers 1-6 constitute the major triad; consequently, the triad must play a central role, says Hindemith. This tone formation is one of the most magnificent of natural phenomena for both the layman and the professional—"simple and elemental as rain, snow, and wind"—and furthermore:

> Music, as long as it exists, will always take its departure from the major triad and return to it. The musician can not escape it any more than the painter his primary colors, or the architect his three dimensions. In composition, the triad or its direct extensions can never be avoided for more than a short time without completely confusing the listener. [...] In the world of tones, the triad corresponds to the force of gravity. It serves as our constant guiding point, our unit of measure, and our goal, even in those sections of compositions which avoid it.[205]

---

[204]*The Craft of Musical Composition*, 15.

[205]*The Craft of Musical Composition*, 22.

One of Erwin Stein's comments on Schoenberg's music, in an article entitled "Schönbergs Klang," may serve as a counterpoint to Hindemith's views on the triad. Stein considers the triads primitive compared to the more colorful dissonances.[206] Critics regard the emphasis on the triad, both as a basic feature of the musical material and as a main directive for human aural orientation, as a doubtful element in Hindemith's thinking. This is certainly a problematic point, even from his own theoretical position, since it seems to narrow down the extended harmonic possibilities he otherwise would advocate. Generally, Hindemith's thoughts on the triad are characteristic of his inconsistent probing of the relationship between "nature" and "second nature." He has a tendency to regard what (for him) is firmly integrated in human consciousness as "natural," if not determined by nature, even though it is more probably determined by culture. On several occasions he should have been tempted to make a clearer distinction on this point. However, when examining the triad, Hindemith in no way believes that a musical movement primarily based on triads is the ideal. Instead he is concerned with the general use of triads and triad-based orientation points in a musical progression. He finds that the reason for such a basic, harmonic construction is founded on the structure of the partial-tone spectrum.

When a tone is played, the vibration frequency of each tone upward in the partial tone spectrum emerges as whole-number multiplications of the fundamental's rate of vibration. In Example 10, which takes C_2 as the starting point (vibration frequency 64,) C_3 equals 128 Hertz (64+64), G_3: 192 (64+64+64), and so on. In the partial-tone series, the ordinal numbers will subsequently become cardinal numbers: the numbering expresses the basic ratios of the intervals. Consequently, the octave ratio of C_2 to C_3 is 1:2, the fifth from C_3 to G_3 is 2:3, and so forth. When these intervals are played on an instrument, the ear will be able to identify them—the more clearly, the simpler their ratios will be. All this is known from Pythagorean thought. Hindemith believes that the rare syncretism of ear (meaning the audible determination of interval qualities), nature, and mathematics is the very key to the musical material's inevitable will. The material of music has a consistency founded in nature on the basis of the interval proportions. The mathematical structure of the partial-tone series prepares the way for further calculations. Hindemith takes advantage of this fact when he deduces the twelve pitches in the scale. His calculations and thoughts, leading to what he believes to be a simple and logical system, are rather complex. Here are just a few of his key points and calculation procedures:

---

[206]See E. Stein, "Schönbergs Klang," *Arnold Schönbergs zum 60. Geburtstag*, 26.

Hindemith takes his point of departure in the tonal compass of C_2-C_3, which represents the first two partial tones with C_2 as the initial pitch. This will constitute the octave frame of a new scale or series. He could, of course, have chosen any initial pitch. He then proceeds by considering the upper note, C_3, not as the second but as the first tone in a new partial-tone range, identical, but one octave higher. An octave frame is then determined, and if one regards the pitch G_3, the third partial tone, also as the first tone, one ends up outside this frame. Considered as the second tone, however, the first tone will make up the frequency 192 divided by the ordinal number 2, which equals 96 and sounds as G_2. This tone becomes the second tone in the series. In doing this, Hindemith has laid the foundation for a procedure for which he determines this rule:

> *To arrive at each new tone of the scale, divide the vibration-number of each overtone successively by the order-numbers of the preceding tones in the series.* This formula gives us the key to all remaining calculations.[207]

Following these initial steps, Hindemith arrives at the pitches F, A, E, E♭, and A♭, which are all deduced from the first six tones of the partial-tone row. From these pitches he now deduces D, B♭, D♭, and B. The reason for the transition to what Hindemith calls a second-degree procedure is that the sixth overtone of C_2, which is the seventh partial tone (the somewhat low B♭$_4$) cannot be used. If the initial tone, in this case C_2, is termed progenitor or "father," the following seven tones, including the highest tone C_3, subsequently represent the "sons," while the next four are "grandsons," according to Hindemith. The last tone, F♯$_3$/G♭$_3$, which has a tritone relationship with the initial tone, can be deduced from either D_2 or B_2. F♯$_2$ will then form yet another generation in relation to C_2.[208]

At a first glance, Hindemith's family metaphor may seem strained, but his point is to demonstrate that the order resulting from these detailed calculations also represents certain relationships or degrees of affinity with the initial pitch. The metaphor underscores an essential point in Hindemith's understanding of tonality: The twelve tones appear in a hierarchy of relationships that reveals the essential laws of tonality. This becomes Hindemith's *Series 1 (Reihe 1)*:

---

[207] *The Craft of Musical Composition*, 34.

[208] *The Craft of Musical Composition*, 34-43.

EXAMPLE 11: Hindemith's *Series I*, based on C

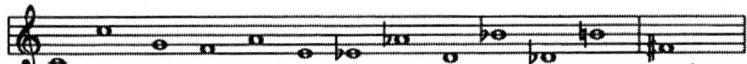

In this series—which has nothing to do with Schoenberg's twelve-tone series—the supposed relationship with the initial pitch diminishes the further one moves on. The series is thus perceived as an organic whole, which Hindemith also compares with a tonal planetary system orbiting its sun.[209] Each tone has a fixed tonal relationship with whatever initial pitch is chosen. The interval spans can be compared to the paths of the planets related to a central point.

According to Hindemith, the basic laws of tonality are recognized in the simple numerical proportions from 1 to 6. He perceives this occurrence in a universal perspective, connecting his thinking to the ideas of antiquity mediated by Boethius in the Middle Ages:

> For us there is no longer, thanks to our understanding of their common physical basis, a fundamental difference between *musica humana* and *musica instrumentalis*, and even as concerns *musica humana* and *musica mundana* we may concentrate our attention today rather on those aspects which they have in common than on those in which they differ.[210]

From 1928 to 1935 Hindemith was in contact with Hans Kayser, whose thinking laid the foundations for the later "Hans-Kayser-Institut für harmonikale Grundlagenforschung" in Vienna. *The Craft of Musical Composition* reveals many impulses going back Kayser, who believed that his influence should have been more noticeably attributed in the composer's writings.[211] The relationship between the two men was, however, ambiguous: Hindemith found many of Kayser's ideas significant and relevant to his own, but tried to keep a distance from the metaphysical aspects of Kayser's deliberations.

Whatever the sources of Hindemith's inspiration, he considered the musical interval as the main component of the musical material. "Thus the interval, formed by the connection of two tones, is the basic unit of musical construction," he says in *The Craft of Musical Composition*,[212] a key point he repeats in *A Composer's World*:

---

[209]*The Craft of Musical Composition*, 57.

[210]*The Craft of Musical Composition*, 53.

[211]See R. Haase, *Paul Hindemiths harmonikale Quellen: Sein Briefwechsel mit Hans Kayser* (Vienna: Verlag Elisabeth Lafite, 1973), 35-42.

[212]*The Craft of Musical Composition*, 57.

> No musical effect can be obtained unless the tension between at least two different single tones has been perceived. This tension may exist either between the two adjacent tones of melodic progressions or in the harmonic minimum of two tones sounded simultaneously. [...] Since this tension is demonstrated by imagined distances in space and lapses of time, that is, intervals, considered both as spatial distances and temporal stretches, we may take such intervals as the basic musical material.[213]

Hindemith does not regard the interval as a static occurrence but as a dynamic play of horizontal and vertical, temporal and spatial forces. The rhythmic potential of music lies in the horizontal plane and in its fundamental dependence on time. The interval is a naturally determined material both for the tonal system, for melody, harmony, and rhythm. Hindemith's assessment of the significance pertaining to the musical interval as a material force thus corresponds to Schoenberg's emphasis on the musical motive.

Hindemith argues that an important premise for the consistency of the musical material lies in the combination tones, which occur when two or more tones are played together.[214] To this belong both so-called residue tones and the differential tones. The latter are acoustically the most important, and on these Hindemith focuses. When, for example, C_4 (4/256) and G_4 (6/384) are played together, the differential tone C_3 (6/384÷4/256 = 2/128) will be perceived as the combination tone. Organ makers take advantage of this phenomenon, since long pipes can be spared with two shorter ones functioning at the same time. The combination tone connects with the originally played interval and so on, producing combination tones in a constantly rising order. Hindemith focuses on first and second orders; the second order is made up of the tone of the first combined with the lowest note of the interval. He discovers that combined tones "burden" or "cloud" the interval in a way that determines its character. Here the degree of incidence between the first- and second-order combination tones is crucial:

> The octave and the unison, as the most perfect intervals, are not subject to any such impurity; the fifth has only one combination tone, since those of the first and second order coincide; all other intervals carry a double burden of varying weight.[215]

---

[213] *A Composer's World*, 79.

[214] In keeping with the knowledge of the time, Hindemith considers combination tones an external phenomenon.

[215] *The Craft of Musical Composition*, 64.

Moreover, Hindemith finds that in the interval inversions, the combination tones are displaced in relation to their initial position. Fundamental positions and inversions thus organize themselves in pairs according to the combination tones. Hindemith claims these pairs acquire different sound values, and supports his postulate in the following observations:

1. In groups of tones of different pitch sounding simultaneously, the deeper tones, with the slower vibration rates, have greater weight than the higher ones (a fact based on the weight of the vibrating material—their air masses).
2. Combination tones of the first order are significantly louder than those of the second order.[216]

His argument regarding "tonal weight" is certainly debatable. The important point is, however, that Hindemith sees a possibility of determining interval roots with the help of the position of the combination tones. The claim that the intervals have differing abilities to form roots is one of his most important contributions to music theory. It is also the foundation for what Hindemith considers the concept of sound value—an aspect that Schoenberg particularly noticed in Hindemith's theories. Hindemith's ideas are especially crucial for chord determination. In connection with seconds and sevenths, however, he admits that the root analysis provides a somewhat unclear picture. Consequently, the scientific approach he strives to maintain fails him on this point: Hindemith determines the highest tone in the second and the lowest tone in the seventh as roots, in accordance with what he believes the ear perceives as common practice.[217] Again there seems to be a turn from the concept of nature to second nature in his considerations. The tritone interval does not form a root at all, Hindemith claims. It is characterized by ambiguity and always strives towards advancement to a more stable point. He characterizes the tone in this interval that takes the shortest way to the next dissolving interval root as the "root representative."[218]

Bearing these ideas in mind, Hindemith presents his *Series 2 (Reihe 2)*, an arrangement of interval values:[219]

---

[216]*The Craft of Musical Composition,* 67.

[217]*The Craft of Musical Composition,* 79-81.

[218]*The Craft of Musical Composition,* 83.

[219]This example is found in *The Craft of Musical Composition,* 87.

EXAMPLE 12: Hindemith's *Series 2* with C_4 as the starting point[220]

In his book *Paul Hindemiths harmonikale Quellen*, Rudolf Haase compares Hindemith's two series with Heinrich Husmann's later investigations of so-called sonance degrees. These degrees are based on the relation between overtones and combination tones. Hindemith's investigations do indeed approximate Husmann's results. In connection with *Series 1*, the findings are identical with the first seven intervals plus the twelfth of the Hindemith series. Sevenths and seconds in Husmann's table have opposite positions in Hindemith's system. In Husmann's system, however, these intervals are regarded as equals, so their mutual opposition has no real importance. The same concurrence applies to Hindemith's *Series 2*, with the exception of the exchange with the major sixth and major third.[221]

Musical intervals have both a harmonic and a melodic force or value, says Hindemith—but the degrees are not necessarily identical. His views are illustrated by the figures above and below the staff in EXAMPLE 12. His notion of value contains no claim as to esthetic or ethical estimations. His focal point is the degree of clarity in the formation of harmonies and melodic progressions. When it comes to harmonic force, the octave is naturally not included, while the fifth is the strongest and most unambiguous interval. The major third, however, is described as having a greater beauty, "on account of the triad formed by it with its combination tones."[222] In the arrangement of *Series 2*, the harmonic force diminishes after the major third. In isolation, the tritone interval has neither harmonic nor melodic force, says Hindemith; it must always be combined with at least one other tone for any force to be determined. The melodic force increases gradually, peaking on the major-second interval and diminishing again thereafter. A musical work is based upon a constant interaction and exchange between harmonic and melodic forces owing to the forces contained in the intervals:

---

[220] The interval roots are marked with arrows.

[221] Heinrich Husmann's investigations are presented in R. Haase, *Paul Hindemiths harmonikale Quellen*, 49.

[222] *The Craft of Musical Composition*, 88.

Harmonic force, which begins at the left, is almost helpless against the melodic strength of the seconds, whereas it is not without effect on the sevenths; on the other hand, melodic force, proceeding from the right, is helpless against the strong third, fifth, and octave. [...] In the sixths, the two forces about balance.[223]

While recognition of melodic-harmonic interaction may seem obvious, Hindemith's aim is to describe the universally determined basis for this interplay. He is indirectly disputing Schoenberg's view that one and the same *musikalische Gedanke* can be presented both horizontally and vertically: in the twelve-tone method, pitches can succeed one another in both spatial directions. In the above-mentioned analyses of Schoenberg's quartets, Hindemith points out that for Nos. 3 and 4, the technique results in stereotypical harmonic progressions, and, as a result, leads to melodic and harmonic monotony. "Thus, he [Hindemith] regarded the twelve-tone technique less as a positive compositional method guaranteeing musical coherence than as a compositional-technical obstacle that must be overcome," Neumeyer and Schubert conclude in their article on Schoenberg and Hindemith.[224]

The Interval and the Chord
Intervals—representing the consistency and compulsion of musical material—are also part of the process of building chords. Hindemith rejects the traditional view of chords as being based on thirds, believing that such a view ignores the many harmonic possibilities open to contemporary music. Furthermore, he argues that chords cannot be identified as inversions, for in a so-called inversion process their initial character is changed so that the sound is perceived as totally different. Due in part to the increasing use of chromaticism, tonal development has progressed to a stage where it is pointless to speak of major- or minor-scale alterations. That chords should supposedly be "re-definable" is also a traditional view with little relevance for sounding music. Hindemith's conclusion is that there are many possibilities for chord construction and a new way of determining the chords is needed.

From this point of departure Hindemith arrives at his understanding of chords and harmonies, which is part of the way he views the character and will of the material of music. The powers and values that are expressed through *Series 2* also affect the chords, that is: harmonies of at least three tones. Thus there are laws to be followed here as well, but these laws have little to do with functional harmony. Hindemith is focused on the degree of harmonic tension or value, which he regards as determined by nature. He

---

[223] *The Craft of Musical Composition*, 88.
[224] "Arnold Schoenberg and Paul Hindemith," 28.

gives a systematic overview of possible chords in the Table of Chord Groups, included as an appendix to *The Craft of Musical Composition*.

FIGURE 12: Hindemith's classification of chords according to their intervals

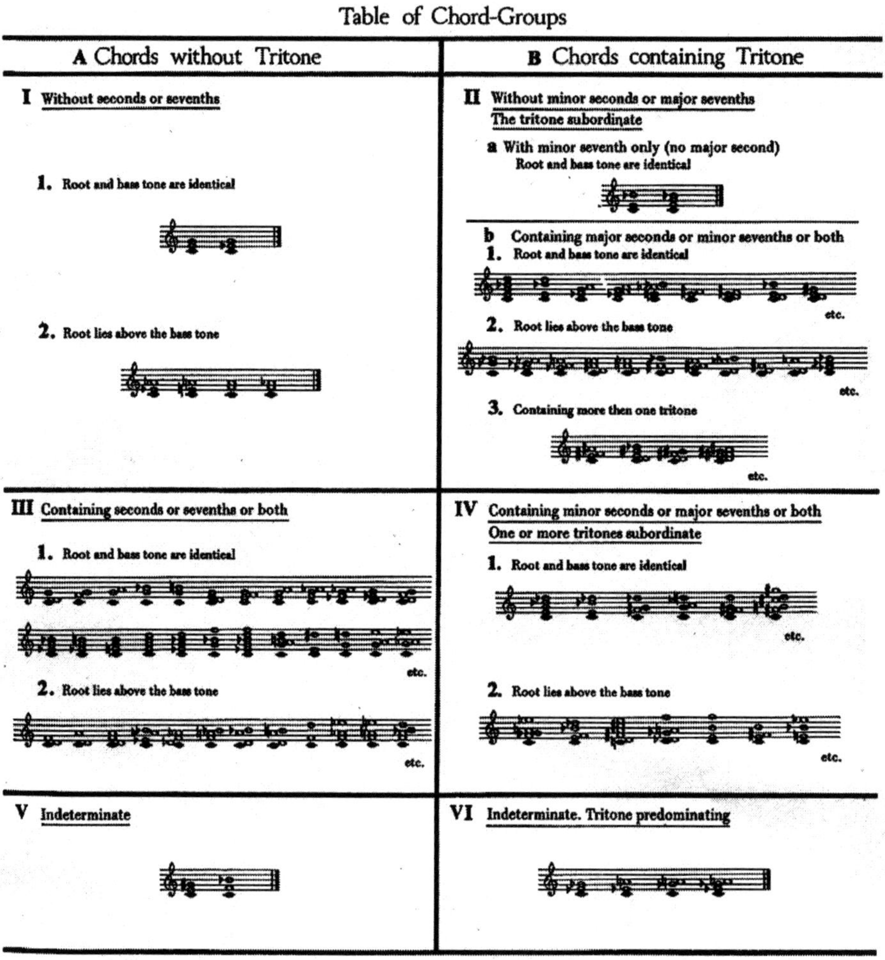

Table of Chord-Groups

A Chords without Tritone	B Chords containing Tritone
I Without seconds or sevenths	**II** Without minor seconds or major sevenths The tritone subordinate
	a With minor seventh only (no major second) Root and bass tone are identical
1. Root and bass tone are identical	
	b Containing major seconds or minor sevenths or both **1.** Root and bass tone are identical
2. Root lies above the bass tone	**2.** Root lies above the bass tone
	3. Containing more than one tritone
III Containing seconds or sevenths or both	**IV** Containing minor seconds or major sevenths or both One or more tritones subordinate
1. Root and bass tone are identical	**1.** Root and bass tone are identical
2. Root lies above the bass tone	**2.** Root lies above the bass tone
V Indeterminate	**VI** Indeterminate. Tritone predominating

A fundamental insight characterizing Hindemith's table is that the augmented fourth/diminished fifth, referred to as the tritone, is ambiguous and requires further progression like no other interval. Consequently, there must be a significant difference between chords with and without a tritone. In his table Hindemith distinguishes accordingly between two main groups, called A and B respectively. These groups consist of three sub-groups each, some with their own sub-divisions.

In group A (chords without a tritone), sub-group I consists of chords without seconds and sevenths. When the chordal roots are to be determined, Hindemith employs *Series 2*: the interval that, according to the principles of this series, has the greatest ability to form a root and thereby determines the whole chord. In debatable cases where, for example, two identical intervals are vying for hegemony, the lowest will come out ahead. In I/1, the root and bass tone coincide, "the best interval is based on the bottom tone."[225] These are the major and minor triads in root position. In the next category of this sub-group: I/2, the roots are higher up in the chord. These chords lack somewhat in harmonic value: "On account of the high position of the root they are not independent enough to form satisfying conclusions."[226] When relating the harmonies in group I to *Series I*, one finds that the intervals of which they consist represent those that have the closest relation to the initial pitch of the series.

The first sub-group of B, labeled as II,[227] includes three-part or multi-part chords where the tritone is subordinate to what Hindemith considers stronger intervals. In chords with a tritone there will always be a second and a seventh, except in the diminished triad. The "mildest" tritone chord, categorized as I/1a, has the bass as its root and contains a minor seventh. This is the category for the dominant-seventh chord of functional harmony (with or without a fifth). The degree of tension increases within group II through chords with major seconds and minor sevenths, to chords with several tritones.

Continuing to the next sub-group, labeled III, we find chords with seconds and sevenths but without tritones. These intervals represent the so-called grandsons in Hindemith's family metaphor connected to *Series 1*. "None of the chords of sub-group III are independent; all of them depend very much on the course of the melody; and they cannot be connected with all other chords,"[228] Hindemith maintains.

The following sub-group, labeled IV, contains under numbers 1 and 2 tritone chords with minor seconds and major sevenths: "All the chords that serve the most intensified expression, that make a noise, that irritate, stir the emotions, excite strong aversion—all are at home here."[229] Hindemith thus ties principles of chord construction to conventions of musical expression.

---

[225] *The Craft of Musical Composition*, 101.

[226] *The Craft of Musical Composition*, 102.

[227] Please note that Hindemith numbers consecutively across the main groups A and B.

[228] *The Craft of Musical Composition*, 103.

[229] *The Craft of Musical Composition*, 103.

The sub-groups V and VI contain chords composed of equal intervals. The augmented triad and two superimposed perfect fourths (in V) are principally indeterminate, owing to their inability to form an unambiguous root. The same pertains to the diminished triads and seventh-chord formations in B VI. Here, the indeterminate tritone, contrary to the tritone in II and IV, has a superior function. This brings Hindemith to the more distantly related sons of the grandsons in *Series 1*.

Hindemith does not consider a key, with its body of chords, to be a naturally given precondition of tonal progression. "What Nature provides is the intervals," he argues, but:

> [t]he juxtaposition of intervals, or of chords, which are the extensions of intervals, gives rise to the key. We are no longer prisoners of the key. Rather, we now have a free hand to give the tonal relations whatever aspect we deem fitting.[230]

In traditional harmony, chords receive their value from the function they have in relation to a tonal order given *a priori*. In Hindemith's system, by contrast, each chord has a fixed and constant value independent of style and epoch. The functionalist concept of clarity is well ensconced in Hindemith's evaluation hierarchy: chords in I/1 have the highest value since the sounds, according to *Series 2*, are those most clearly definable. Then the value diminishes as the ordinal numbers of the sub-groups increase, as, for example, from II/1 to II/2. Chords with tritones from group II are thus considered to have greater value than chords without tritones in group III.

This does not imply that chords are seen as isolated and individual occurrences. Three kinds of energy are active in chord structure—rhythmic, melodic, and harmonic energy—and

> [e]ach of them works in two directions. Rhythm determines the duration of the chords, and groups them by division into stressed and unstressed members of the structure. Melody in voice-leading regulates linear expansion, and in the two-voice framework sets the pitch limits. In the placing of the harmonic center of gravity and in the regulation of relationships we see harmonic energy at work.[231]

---

[230]*The Craft of Musical Composition*, 107.

[231]*The Craft of Musical Composition*, 109.

Harmonic Fluctuation

In both linear and harmonic progressions Hindemith sees harmony unfolding in a spatial frame. The bass line, whether it moves in degrees or leaps, always constitutes the foundation and is thus of particular importance for how harmonic progression is perceived.[232] Next in importance is the most prominent of the upper parts. These two voices make up what he terms the "two-voice framework," and "[i]f writing in several voices is to sound clear and intelligible, the contours of its two-voice framework must be cleanly designed and cogently organized."[233] Once again the ideal of clarity and purity underlies Hindemith's view of a well-composed work of music. If a chord in group II is followed by one in group IV, for instance, this progression causes a fall in value, while the opposite progression causes a rise: going up in the chord table increases tension. Harmonic value is thus inversely proportional to harmonic tension. "Harmonic fluctuation" describes the interaction between value and tension, a term embracing the harmonic-structural changes, courses, and undulations set in motion in a musical progression. In the example below all the chords are taken from group A:[234]

EXAMPLE 13: Hindemith's chord series demonstrating fluctuation and value

Group A:

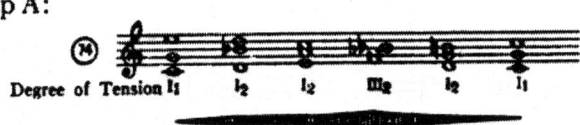

Harmonic value decreases towards III/2, while tension increases. Hindemith's reservations as to vertical and horizontal tone combinations of the twelve-tone method are summarized as follows: the principles of that method often lead to a chaos of tension-filled chords in a way that prevents a truly dynamic fluctuation. Yet planning harmonic progression from fluctuation in a rational way is still not enough:

> The composer must find for every chord and every tone the treatment that will best reconcile his artistic intention with the nature of his material.[235]

The fundamental question is always how a productive interaction between the will of the artist and the will of the material is carried out.

---

[232] In cases of pedal point Hindemith would consider the next voice above it as the most important for the actual harmonic progression.

[233] *The Craft of Musical Composition*, 114.

[234] This example is found in *The Craft of Musical Composition*, 117.

[235] *The Craft of Musical Composition*, 121.

Chord Connection, Degree-Progression, and Tonality

To examine the connection between two chords, Hindemith treats the roots as isolated from the two vertical harmonies. Once again he is left with an interval, and the interval is subjected to the regularities that are expressed through *Series 2*:

> [...] a third is a strongly harmonic interval, while the second is essentially melodic; in short, we stand once again before the whole series of interval-values. [...] A progression based on the interval of fifth between its roots naturally has a surer foundation than one based on a minor sixth: this is the strongest of all chord-progressions.[236]

Where a chord consists of several equally strong intervals, the lowest one will form the root. Hence root analysis can function as a measuring tool of the harmonic value of chord connections. Once a two-voice framework, harmonic fluctuation, and roots are ascertained, all chord connections can be evaluated and calculated.

A special problem arises with chords progressing from group B (those with tritones) to group A. The chords in groups II and IV also have roots that can be ascertained, but the crucial point is the way in which the tritone interval is carried forward. Hindemith focuses here on what he calls the "guide-tone." The guide-tone in the tritone chord is the tone in one or several tritone intervals which, measured according to *Series 2*, relates in the most harmonically favorable way to its root. There may well be chords in group B that are differently related to each other. If the dissolution of a chord of B in A shall feel satisfactory, the interval relationship must be as favorable as possible between the guide-tone of the group-B chord and the root of the group-A chord. When the root is expanded to three or more chords, temporal tonal centers can be discerned. The starting-point for Hindemith's investigation is that if one were to play the notes C-E-G in different order but with equal note value, the ear would always perceive the C-major triad, and consequently C as the tonal center:

> According to the interval-values of *Series 2*, the fifth C-G outlined by the three tones is stronger than either of the thirds C-E or E-G, and since C is the root of the fifth it dominates the entire group and becomes the center of a tonal sphere consisting of these three tones: it is their tonic.[237]

---

[236] *The Craft of Musical Composition*, 122.

[237] *The Craft of Musical Composition*, 132.

Hindemith thus returns once again to the presumably unambiguous orientation toward the major triad. A root progression is not always that simple. Aspects like metric position, rhythm, any repetitions, and so on will always play a significant role. Nonetheless, Hindemith is convinced that tonality will be quite unambiguous in cases where the roots form a triad that is found in groups I or II. If the roots form an arpeggiated chord from groups II or IV, the rhythm and harmonic fluctuation will be of greater impact. With tones more or less equal in meter and length, the root in the "best" interval (according to *Series 2*) will determine tonality. In root progressions that can be related to the indeterminate groups V and VI, one is dependent on the evaluation of rhythm and fluctuation.

Two further aspects should be mentioned here: When a chord from group A follows a chord from group B (the tritone group), the root in the last chord guides the evaluation of tonality. Generally, the final chord will always play a dominating role. It will be experienced as the goal of the harmonic progression and consequently found to be particularly significant, although it need not be the harmonically strongest.

Root calculation tells us much about the harmonic strength of a cadence. It can also be applied to more comprehensive musical progressions, where tonal relationships may be considered in relation to *Series 1*. This is where the concept of "degree-progression" comes in:

> The roots which support the burdens of larger harmonic groupings may be called degrees, and their succession in accordance with the demands of Series 1 the degree progression.[238]

In a progression consisting of four or more chords, tonal relationships dominate over single intervals. Through repetitions, for example, certain roots can attract attention as central tones. The closest relationships of the tones (still according to *Series 1*) can also contribute to strengthening the position of a central tone. By following the degree-progression of the roots, modulations and harmonic areas can also be revealed where tonalities cross each other and create a moment of aural confusion. The central tones make up their own degree-progression, which can tell us something about the tonality of the entire piece.

It should come as no surprise that Hindemith felt an affinity with Heinrich Schenker. By all accounts Hindemith was familiar with Schenker's writings from the early 1920s. In what is probably his only letter to Schenker (dated 25 October 1926), Hindemith writes:

---

[238]*The Craft of Musical Composition,* 143.

> For my part, I can tell you that I am an eager and enthusiastic reader of your books. Enthusiastic because they properly express for the first time what a good musician hears, feels and understands in his musical activities. Because they reveal the foundation for musical creativity, which, as you are correctly repeating again and again, has always had and always will have universal validity. And for music of our time it is just as important as for that of past eras.[239]

In his reply Schenker strongly disagrees with Hindemith's view that his thoughts are also valid for the new music of the time. "I myself do not concur and think," he writes, "that you, too, had better have the courage to say that today's music is completely new."[240] Nevertheless, it is quite probable that Hindemith came to see himself as carrying forth elements from Schenker's ideas, not least by accentuating aspects of the two-voice framework and degree-progression in proportion to a superior and hierarchic tonality system.

Non-Chord Tones

Hindemith claims that each new tone added to a chord structure in principle creates a new chord, although the tempo must allow the ear to perceive it. Then again, there are tones serving the chords as enrichment without thereby leading to any real change of harmony. Hindemith, like Schoenberg, often refers to traditional music theory in his own reasoning; hence he also includes so-called non-chord tones in his discussions on harmony, applying terms like returning tone, passing tone, suspension, neighboring tones, neighboring tone left by leap, neighboring tone approached by leap, anticipation, and unaccented or accented free tones.[241] His further deliberations on this will be of interest to the presumed broad readership of *The Craft of Musical Composition*. In his view, such tonal occurrences have no structural importance, however, and consequently they have no particular significance in a discussion of Hindemith's understanding of musical material.

---

[239]D. Johns, "Aimez-vous Brahms?: Ein Hindemith-Schenker-Briefwechsel," *Über Hindemith: Aufsätze zu Werk, Ästhetik und Interpretation*, S. Schaal and L. Schader, ed. (Mainz etc.: Schott, 1996), 285. ["Von mir kann ich Ihnen sagen, dass ich ein eifriger und erfreuter Leser Ihrer Bücher bin. Erfreut deshalb, weil in ihnen zum ersten Male richtig gesagt wird, was ein guter Musiker bei der Beschäftigung mit der Musik hört, fühlt und versteht. Weil in ihnen die Grundlagen des musikalischen Schaffens aufgedeckt werden, die, wie Sie so richtig immer wieder sagen, von jeher Gültigkeit hatten, und stets gültig sein werden. Und für unsere heutige Musik sind sie genau so wichtig wie für jede vergangene."]

[240]"Aimez-vous Brahms?, 289. ["Ich selbst finde das nicht u. meine [...] auch Sie sollten lieber den Mut haben zu sagen, die heutige Musik sei völlig neu."]

[241]See *The Craft of Musical Composition*, 164-174.

Theory of Melody

Hindemith's theory of melody deserves particular mention, not least since there are so few such theories in the history of music. "Melody is the element in which the personal characteristics of the composer are most clearly and most obviously revealed," he maintains.[242] Despite this admission of artistic subjectivity, Hindemith is his usual objective self when he elucidates his theory: "Melodies can, in our time, be constructed rationally."[243] Melodic motions may be seen as chains of intervals, and, therefore, a melody must also be seen as a construction that can be analyzed:

> Perhaps many people think that the forms of melody are too manifold and various to be summed up in rules. Yet they must have observed that the melodies of the masters are not built up without rhyme or reason. Anything made by man, no matter how many varieties it assumes, and how much of the superhuman it seems to contain, must reveal its secret to the close observer.[244]

Although intervals of higher and lower melodic values are played out in a melodic progression, Hindemith considers seconds as the real building material of melody,[245] but concedes that there are intervals whose harmonic value is more dominant. Consequently, degree-progressions displaying the harmonic structure of a melody may be distinguished. Ascending and descending intervals result in differences in melodic tension, a truth singers and instrumentalists can confirm from experience. Hindemith's most interesting point is the observation that the top and bottom notes in a successful melodic progression (a tonal sequence striving for a distinctly melodic character) usually have a relationship in seconds. These seconds may well be octave transposed. A truly melodic structure will thus contain overarching descending or ascending lines of seconds, and observation that leads to yet another concept in Hindemith's theory, the "step-progression":

> The primary law of melodic construction is that a smooth and convincing melodic outline is achieved only when these important points form a progression in seconds. The line that connects one high point to the next, one low point to the next, and one rhythmically prominent tone to the next, without taking into consideration the less important parts of the melody lying between these points, is called the step-progression.[246]

---

[242] *The Craft of Musical Composition*, 177.

[243] *A Composer's World*, 112.

[244] *The Craft of Musical Composition*, 176.

[245] See *The Craft of Musical Composition*, 187.

[246] *The Craft of Musical Composition*, 193-194.

Step progressions may occur simultaneously on several levels. "Every one of them may be independent of the next," and they "may be many or few, and may be fully independent or may pass from one into the other."[247] However, Hindemith guards against any rigid or forced construction that might arise as a result of such principles. He also adds that besides step-progression, organic construction is also possible by repeating tones in the same octave in the course of a melodic development.

Tonal or Atonal?
After discussing his main points on the importance of the nature-given interval for the unfolding of musical material, Hindemith provides the following summary:

> We have seen that tonal relations are founded in Nature, in the characteristics of sounding materials and of the ear, as well as in the pure relations of abstract numerical groups. We cannot escape the relationship of tones. Whenever two tones sound, either simultaneously or successively, they create a certain interval-value; whenever chords or intervals are connected they enter into a more or less close relationship. And where tonal relationships are played off one against another, tonal coherence appears. It is thus quite impossible to devise groups of tones without tonal coherence. Tonality is a natural force, like gravity.[248]

Hindemith sees no other possibilities for successful musical constructions than those that are based on tonality. As mentioned above, this conviction does not imply that he has traditional views on tonality as pertaining to a restricted style. On the contrary: he states that the main principles of tonality will always be fundamental because the musical material has a particular basic constitution valid for all time. Tonality denotes an unequivocal concept, which means that terms such as atonality and polytonality are irrelevant. The only instances where music can be called atonal are in the work of a composer

> who is motivated perhaps by a consciousness of the inadequacy of old styles to the musical needs of our day, perhaps by a search for an idiom that will express his own feelings, perhaps by sheer perversity, to invent tonal combinations which do not obey the laws of the medium and cannot be tested by the simplest means of reckoning. Such a man is not impelled by the instinct of a musician, who even in what seems his blindest groping never loses the true path entirely from view.[249]

---

[247]*The Craft of Musical Composition*, 194.

[248]*The Craft of Musical Composition*, 152.

[249]*The Craft of Musical Composition*, 153.

These straight-forward considerations demonstrate Hindemith's view of the importance of handling musical material in a functional way. It must be treated in accordance with its own laws or will; its use must allow rational testing—even by mathematical calculation. The true artistic guide, however, is the musician's instinct, the experienced and actively creating or performing user's innermost conviction.

Schoenberg would have agreed with Hindemith's skepticism over the term atonality; even more so with the further modifications Hindemith added in *Komponist in seiner Welt* (the later German edition of *A Composer's World*). Here he claims that what goes under the popular term atonality is but a tiny part of a broader tonal space: "What one maintains is atonality is inevitably only a part of tonality, only that in an 'atonal' work one moves in another of the various parts of tonal space."[250] Even a major/minor tonality is just a limited section of tonality. The term "extended tonality" has no meaning, since it presupposes a transgression based upon the acceptance of major/minor as a nucleus. "There is only one all-embracing tonality, that which is effective in the way described,"[251] Hindemith maintains. As years went by, he became even more open to including various compositional solutions, even serial techniques, in his concept of tonality. In his lecture "Hören und Verstehen unbekannter Musik," delivered at the University in Zurich in December 1955, he declares:

> Essentially it makes no difference whether I control the melodic-harmonic material with the help of church modes, of major and minor rows, of tonal main or secondary functions, or of the established order of the chromatic twelve-tone scale. The acoustically and emotionally recognizable content of music will vary, of course, according to the nature of each organizational principle, and, technically speaking, these principles do not have the same harmonic-melodic possibilities.[252]

---

[250]*Komponist in seiner Welt*, 108. ["Was man für Atonalität hält, ist unvermeidlicherweise doch wieder nur ein Teil der Tonalität" [...] "nur bewegt man sich in der 'atonalen' Arbeit in einer anderen der verschiedenen Ecken des Tonalen Raumes."]

[251]*Komponist in seiner Welt*, 107. ["Es gibt nur die eine, allumfassende Tonalität, die in der beschriebenen Weise wirksam ist."]

[252]"Hören und Verstehen unbekannter Musik," 298-299. ["Im wesentlichen besteht kein Unterschied, ob ich das melodisch-harmonische Material mit Hilfe von kirchentonartlichen Modi, von Dur- und Mollreihen, von tonalen Haupt- und Nebenfunktionen oder von festgesetzten Reihenfolgen aus der chromatischen Zwölftonleiter regiere. Der hörbare und gefühlsmäßig erfaßbare Gehalt einer Musik wird allerdings durch die Eigenart jedes einzelnen dieser Organisationsprinzipien abgewandelt, und technisch gesehen hat nicht jedes von ihnen die gleichen harmonisch-melodischen Möglichkeiten."]

These words are not to be regarded as a rejection of his former theories. The point is rather that Hindemith is willing to embrace several ways of tonal organization in his perspectives of tonality. He would have the same reservations against harmony and melody within the twelve-tone method as before, but would accept them as being a result of the tonal possibilities of that particular method. For some people the tonic following the dominant may sound like a hint of tonality's paradise, Hindemith says, while others feel comfortable only after some fixed tonal foundation is gone. The vital point is that composers should not be led by fashion and a superficial need of distraction; they should always be guided by true, artistic aspirations.

There are obvious similarities in the way in which Hindemith and Schoenberg approach the issue of tonality. In his "Opinion or Insight?" Schoenberg writes:

> [...] you neither must, may write tonally, nor must you, may you, write atonally. [...] If you can do something pure, you will be able to do it tonally or atonally; but those who think impurely—that is to say, those who do what anyone can—may go ahead and form tonal or atonal parties, and for that matter make a noise about it.[253]

Hindemith demands that the composer be highly aware of his or her chosen segment of the tonality range: "Of course, one must first be familiar with the nature and effect of the whole of tonality before selecting the part one needs."[254] This must be kept in mind if we are to understand Hindemith claiming, in *The Craft of Musical Composition*, that there are only two types of music, "good music, in which the tonal relations are handled intelligently and skilfully [sic], and bad music, which disregards them and consequently mixes them in aimless fashion."[255] In *A Composer's World*, however, he attacks his own generalization, as he considers the classifications good and bad beyond genuine artistic evaluation—as long as they are not connected to additional criteria:

> One of these criteria is, [...], the degree of resistance that the particular technical form of a composition offers to the player's or singer's technique of performance, a factor which the performer has to cope with before either the listener or the producer need be aware of it.[256]

---

[253] A. Schoenberg, *Style und Idea*, 263-264.

[254] *Komponist in seiner Welt*, 108. ["Man muß freilich zuerst das Wesen und das Wirken der Gesamttonalität kennen, ehe man die benötigten Ausschnitte auswählen kann".]

[255] *The Craft of Musical Composition*, 152.

[256] *A Composer's World*, 122-123.

Hindemith: The Interval as Musical Material

Of particular interest here is Hindemith's focus on the importance of performers and their performance for the process of musical composition, subsequently also for the actual application of the musical material. In *A Composer's World*, written about fifteen years after the first German edition of the theory volume of *Unterweisung im Tonsatz*, he even presents a short version of his theories, now with the singing voice—not the ear—as a guide. His understanding of material is tested again on the functions of human performance, in accordance with "human indolence and comfort," to go back to Loosian ideas.

The Interval as a Factor of Material Consistency:
Hindemith's Interludium 9 from *Ludus Tonalis*

Hindemith's understanding of the musical material may be illustrated by means of an interlude from his *Ludus Tonalis*. He wrote this cycle— his last work for piano solo—between August and October 1942, just a few years after the revised edition of the German original version of *The Craft of Musical Composition*. The title page shows *Series 1* in spiral issuing from C as the fundamental pitch, a drawing reminiscent of Hindemith's image of the principles of tonality as a planetary system. The archaic notation gives the impression of something fundamental and primeval:

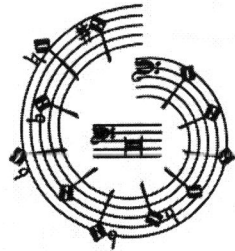

FIGURE 13: *Series 1* on the title page of Hindemith's *Ludus Tonalis*

The cycle consists of twelve fugues, which are tonally anchored in one after the other of twelve pitches of the series. Together with the eleven interludes connecting them, they are framed by a pair of Praeludium and Postludium. These two pieces are designed on a large scale, applying tonal plans from all the *Series 1* pitches. *Ludus Tonalis* allows a profound insight into Hindemith's tonal universe. The most obvious translation of the title would be "play of tones" or "play of tonalities," which should not seem enigmatic after reading *The Craft of Musical Composition*. However, David Neumeyer refers to other possible translations, such as "school" for *ludus*, as for in "piano school," and suggests that the title could also mean "school of tonal relationships." *Ludus* generally means game and play, covering a spectrum from children's games to dramatic plays on a theatrical stage. In

Neumeyer's opinion, Hindemith with his thorough knowledge of older artistic forms of expression may have appropriated the term *ludus* from titles used in medieval liturgical drama: "Thus, Ludus Tonalis, 'The Play of Tones,' would not be a game, but a drama, its tensions inherent in the relationships of tones."[257]

To the first edition, published in 1943, Hindemith added the sub-title "Studies in Counterpoint, Tonal Organization and Piano Playing," thereby connecting this work to both the prelude-and-fugue tradition established by J.S. Bach and the etude genre familiar since Chopin, Liszt, and their successors. This subtitle did not appear in later editions. The pianist and music researcher Franzpeter Goebels places Hindemith's work in a tradition of what he terms "polytonal piano works," that is: works whose individual segments are based on different tonics. As an early representative in the genre he mentions the composition *Ut Re Mi Fa Sol La* by John Bull (1562-1628).[258]

Hindemith's *Ludus Tonalis* is often referred to as a 20th-century *Well-Tempered Clavier*. The similarities with Bach's *Art of the Fugue* are even more striking, since Hindemith uses such a great degree of so-called learned counterpoint. The cycle is very complex and, as Goebels emphasizes, in many ways sums up Hindemith's entire piano production. Characteristics of earlier works are elevated to a higher plane:

> Numerus + Affectus, polyphony + homophony, expressive character piece + playful pieces, compact texture + transparent texture, structural types of Baroque and Romantic coinage. All these seemingly irreconcilable contrasts are amalgamated in remarkable classical moderation. He who follows the road of Hindemithian piano music will understand this piano opus of the master as a "testament."[259]

Ludus Tonalis may easily be associated with the image of a strict and academic Hindemith, a suspicion corrected by an experience related by the Estonian-Swedish pianist Käbi Laretei. Laretei had been asked to play the cycle in a 1952 concert at which Hindemith was to be present. As she tells it, "We thought he was far more 'intellectual' than his two contemporaries:

---

[257]D. Neumeyer, "The Genesis and Structure of Hindemith's Ludus Tonalis," *Hindemith-Jahrbuch* 1978/VII, 73.

[258]Translated from F. Goebels, "Interpretationsaspekte zum 'Ludus Tonalis'," *Hindemith-Jahrbuch* 1972/II, 140-142.

[259]"Numerus + Affectus, Polyphonie + Homophonie, Ausdruckstück + Spielstück, dichter Satz + aufgelockerter Satz, Formtypen barocker und romantischer Prägung. Alle diese scheinbar unversöhnlichen Gegensätze werden in einer bemerkenswerten klassischen Maßhaltung verschmolzen. Wer den Weg der Hindemithschen Klaviermusik verfolgt, wird dieses Klavieropus des Meisters als 'Testament' verstehen." F. Goebels, "Interpretationsaspekte zum 'Ludus Tonalis'," 150.

Bartók and Stravinsky. This was probably why I was apprehensive as to whether I understood everything in the construction, and I really read the notation carefully."[260] Yet when playing the work for the composer before the public concert, she met quite a different Hindemith:

> What made the greatest impression on me during this "séance" was that Hindemith did not say one word about the construction, mirror symmetry, theoretical analysis. On the contrary, I got to know the musician Hindemith, about whom we did not know much. [...] I had been thinking furiously about the pause after the first chord [in the Interludium after Fuga 6 in E♭], but Hindemith brushed off this notation pedantry with: "it has to sound racy, tumultuous. Think of a military march, a kettledrum. It doesn't matter if the harmonies flow into each other a little."[261]

Hindemith clearly considered the musical interpretation the central issue, a fact both performers and listeners of his work should keep in mind. Käbi Laretei would gain renown for her excellent performances of *Ludus Tonalis*.

A focus on the work's interpretation does not discount its worth as an exposition of musical construction. Single fugues as well as the Praeludium-Postludium pair have often been the object of analysis. Such is not the case with the interludes. The term denotes pieces that appear "in between" other movements, in this case between the fugues. The interludes in the *Ludus Tonalis* are principally independent pieces written within a freer formal and stylistic framework. They do not, however, stand alone in the sense that they can be changed around or cut out. Their main function is to build a bridge between consecutive fugues, first and foremost with regard to tonal orientation but also in terms of motivic and thematic construction. Within this setting the interludes are exceedingly varied in texture, form, and style. It is generally considered that they can be related to standard types of the piano piece genre. Goebels's characterizes the interlude selected for this study as an elegy, recognizing features reminiscent of Bach's E♭-minor prelude from the first volume of *The Well-Tempered Clavier*.

The interlude has not been chosen for examination because it is particularly representative of Hindemith's theories but rather because the subjective impression it imparts, in both its dimension and its character, resembles that conveyed by the Schoenberg *Klavierstück* investigated earlier—not so much stylistically as with respect to genre and expressive intensity. On a certain level, these two miniatures are comparable, although this connection should not be overinterpreted.

---

[260]Translated from K. Laretei, "Om och ikring Ludus Tonalis," *Musikrevy* 12/1 (1971), 28.
[261]Ibid.

EXAMPLE 14: Hindemith, *Ludus Tonalis*, Interludium 9.
© 1943 by Schott Music, Mainz/Germany; © renewed 1971.
Reprinted with permission.

This calm and introverted interlude forms the link between a playful Fuga 9 in B♭ and a graceful Fuga 10 in D♭. If the piece is to fulfill its function as a tonal bridge, this purpose must in some way dominate the overall tonal construction. The melodic structure is simple, characterized by a delicate expressiveness intensified by abundant ornamental figures. These melodic shapes either lead toward or surround the notes that are significant for the melody or the harmony. This characteristic is one of several features connecting the two adjacent fugues.

Another important melodic trait is the exquisite balance of steps and leaps. This is already present in the first three measures. The soloistic upper voice is supported by firmly structured, steadily progressing chords in the lower voices giving the music the character of a procession. This must be one of the features reminding Goebels of Bach's E♭-minor prelude. Another shared trait is the predominant triple meter. Yet Hindemith avoids making the metric order appear too rigid by placing melodic peaks on some of the unaccented beats, usually toward the end of the measure (for this, too, see already the first three measures). When playing the interlude for the first time one may sense a four-beat pattern at the beginning, but will probably soon understand that the music is conceived in triple time. While Hindemith lightens the stress pattern with ties, slurs, and some further alterations, he does so to a far lesser degree than Schoenberg in his piece.

Hindemith finds calculation and mastery of technical procedures quite inadequate for elevated artistic creation. A composer may come far in the compositional craft, he says, but "no one will be so stupid as to assume that what has been impossible throughout all ages is now possible: to create a work of art without creative impulse, simply by burrowing and calculating."[262]

Hindemith concludes *The Craft of Musical Composition* with a section on analysis that examines music from the Middle Ages to Schoenberg and himself. After a preliminary assurance that this should be easy to grasp for readers who have studied his book, he offers a conciliatory reservation:

> Often he [the reader] will arrive at different results from those here given. There is no harm in that. I have in each instance chosen only one of many possibilities. Moreover, the notation of a piece of music is the mere chemical precipitate of the work itself. The charm of the latter lies not in scientific exactitude, but in the fact that it arouses in the hearer not alone direct emotional enjoyment, but also a pleasure in the recognition and judgement of the impressions received. Even with the closest familiarity with the objective content of a work of art, the judgements of all observers will never completely coincide.[263]

---

[262] *The Craft of Musical Composition*, 201.

[263] *The Craft of Musical Composition*, 202.

EXAMPLE 15a: Hindemith, Interludium 9, tonal analysis

EXAMPLE 15b: Hindemith, Interludium 9, tonal analysis (continued)

This accommodating perspective on the relation between analysis and a work of art is also inherent in the following discussion. In some instances it has been necessary to select from several possibilities. The objective is to examine Hindemith's understanding of his musical material in some depth by looking at a small extract of his work, using procedures patterned on his own analytical strategies. The analytical arrangements of the examples presented in *The Craft of Musical Composition* vary somewhat according to the character and structure of the music.

On the two facing pages above, Hindemith's views on the interval as a decisive factor in music-material consistency is illustrated by considering, as he himself expresses it, "the mere chemical precipitate of the work." The analysis concentrates above all on harmonic and tonal aspects, but attention is also drawn to some elements that particularly concern the melody.

A first point on which to focus attention is the two-voice framework. There is little doubt about the upper voice, as it is made up of the melody. The lower voice consists of the bass notes in the successive chords, with a possible exception in the chords from m. 4 to the first beat in m. 5, where the bass notes may be read as a sustained note or pedal point. In such cases one should, according to Hindemith, observe the movement in the voice above. Reading the bass voice at this instance as a pedal point would easily be perceived as an unnatural break, since the use of sustained notes or tonal repetitions from chord to chord is characteristic for the whole of the harmonic progression. The almost continuous motion of the lower voice in implicit long values is an equally distinctive feature of the interlude that is easily picked up by the ear. The note D♭ in the bass of mm. 4-5 thus forms part of a stepwise, descending motion.

The elaborate melody demonstrates a number of Hindemith's non-chord tone categories. These result from the fact that the aria character of the melody includes a certain improvisational independence that often tends to liberate it from the harmonic base. There are also instances where the melodic motion itself has an important harmonic function. In such cases the chord markings of the analysis above are in parentheses, since these motions actually belong to the melody.

When evaluating the harmony and tonality of this piece, it is necessary to bear in mind that the combination of sustained notes with the more melodically than harmonically strong progressions in the lower voices contributes to a weakened perception of harmonic intelligibility. The material forces Hindemith attributes to *Series 2* are important here. The considerable use of chords from group III (containing seconds and sevenths) also seems to weaken the harmonic value. This observation leads to the issues of harmonic fluctuation.

As the chord analysis shows, sounds containing just two tones are also included. Hindemith might have disagreed with this, although he himself proceeds in a similar way in his own analyses. The reason for the inclusion here is that even these constellations are significant for establishing tonality. In mm. 4, 5, 12, 13, and 14, two chords are given on one beat, since their characteristics change in relation to the melody. A total of 29 of the 64 chords the analysis finds in the piece belong to group III. Counting chords has no significance in Hindemith's system, but it is worth noting that nearly half the chords are perceived as relatively tense but harmonically less valuable. One may recall Hindemith's own characterization of this group of chords: "These are a rough and unpolished race. [...] None of the chords of sub-group III are independent; all of them depend very much on the course of melody; and they cannot be connected with all other chords."[264] Moreover, eleven chords in the piece have even lower harmonic value according to Hindemith's own table. In this Interludium, the chordal tenseness is toned down in an espressivo manner within a limited dynamic range. Above all, the chords afford the piece a character of homogeneous sound. Hindemith thus achieves, with the help of the possibilities of distributing the intervals within the chord groups, an artistic homogeneity similar to the one Schoenberg realizes with his consistent use of the motive in op. 19/1. The chord group III is so accommodating that it absorbs various degrees of tension. The first group-III chord in m. 6, for example, sounds tenser than the chords preceding and following it, primarily because their range (in the left hand) comprises an augmented octave.

The harmonic fluctuation of the piece does not show any dramatic oscillations. However, throughout, one notices tenser chord progressions that, from a harmonic point of view, end in more unambiguous points of rest. For the most part Hindemith places the tensest chords immediately before chords in group I, that is: before the harmonically most valuable chords. The second quarter-note in m. 8, second and third quarter-notes in m. 9, third quarter-note in m. 12, and third quarter-note in m. 17 are examples of tension points which lead to relaxation and harmonic clarity. Creating harmonic waves in this manner belongs to well-known traditional principles of achieving musical balance.

The interlude includes relatively few chord combinations with tritones. The indeterminate chord groups V and VI are represented by only three instances; the most important being those on the first beat in m. 19, where the group-V chord prepares the subtle conclusion.

---

[264]*The Craft of Musical Composition,* 103.

Proceeding to the degree-progression of the piece, one must remember that not all roots are clearly perceptible to listeners' ears: a progression that seems unambiguous on paper may not be experienced as such. This is due to the complexities of the chord progression: doublings, voice leading, repetitions, sustained notes, etc. all have a role to play in determining to which tonality the ear feels led. Up to m. 10, the degree-progression is one of leaps, tonal repetitions, and sustained notes. Mm. 11-15 are dominated by steps and characterized by the melodic features of the harmonic progressions. From m. 13 the descending chromaticism is so striking that it seems to carry the whole harmonic development, as indicated in the above analysis by the notes in parentheses. From m. 16 onward, leaps and repetitions again dominate. In the last three measures, the bass line, which starts by steps, becomes decisively important for how the harmonic progression is perceived. This development is also shown in parentheses.

The stepwise progression helps to reveal the interlude's tonality. It begins with the open perfect fifth $B\flat_4$-F_5, which picks up the concluding chord F_4-D_5-$B\flat_5$ of the preceding fugue. From the beginning a $B\flat$ tonality is firmly established, underlined by the stepwise progression from $B\flat$ in m. 1 to F in m. 3. These two pitches together with $E\flat$ represent the foundation of a *Series 1* based on $B\flat$. But the root C_4 supports a cadence towards F. Consequently, the steps F, C, and $B\flat$ also represent the first three pitches in a *Series 1* with F as the progenitor. While the direction is now clear, the F level is still not so unequivocally established that one could speak of a modulation. The bass progression, which can be read as the beginning of a melodic $B\flat$-minor scale in descending motion, supports the $B\flat$ tonality. But there is a characteristic drive in this bass progression: it supports a motion away from the first perfect-fifth interval.

From F and $E\flat$ the music leads stepwise to $D\flat$ in m. 4. According to Hindemith's views on the clarity of the triad, the roots $D\flat_4$-$G\flat_4$-$B\flat\flat_4$ should support $G\flat$ as a temporary tonality. However, such a tonality is camouflaged by the repeated note $D\flat_4$, by the movement in the other voices, and by the chord constructions related to group III. Instead, a predominant $D\flat$ tonality appears, bolstered by the interchanges between steps $D\flat$, $A\flat$, and $G\flat$ and the first three pitches in a *Series 1* on $D\flat$. On the second beat in m. 6, however, the harmonic motion results in a sequential progress towards $G\flat$. According to Hindemith, such a progression is weaker than the progression towards the level of F in m. 3. The stepwise motion in the two lower voices is actually stronger melodically than harmonically.

In m. 7, whole-tone steps leading from $D\flat$ to F reach a clearly established F in the first chord of m. 8. In isolation, the interchange between steps F and $B\flat$ suggests $B\flat$ as the root in relation to *Series 2*. But the focus on F in the initial and final chords, the emphasis on this note in the melody as well as in the perfect fourth C_4-F_4 in the middle voices, give the F tonality an undisputed priority that compensates for the four preceding measures.

In m. 11 the theme is heard in A♭, moving towards E♭ on the first beat of m. 12. The melodic movement in the upper voice with the sixteenth-notes in m. 12 is important for leading to B in m. 13. The step B is enharmonic with C♭; the progression from A♭ to B (C♭) thus corresponds to that from B♭ to D♭ at the beginning of the piece. One could now assume that a B tonality would be maintained from m. 13 to 15. This does not occur, however, since Hindemith starts a new motion in the bass range from the second beat in m. 13, with an octave on G♯ and its minor third B. The stepwise progression in the bass from G♯ in m. 13 to D♯ in m. 15, with B as a sustained note, frames the chord G♯-B-D♯ (equivalent to A♭-C♭-E♭). This event turns out to be of greater importance for the perception of tonality than the degree-progressions extracted from the chords. The A♭/G♯ tonality is maintained in this way from m. 11 to 15. However, the stepwise motions in the bass undermine any univocal harmonic clarity. Again, the melodic forces in the intervallic material are the more dominant.

From the G♯/A♭-tonality the music moves up a step to B♭ in m. 16. The following three measures correspond to the earlier mm. 8-10, hence there is no need for repeated comments. Measure 19 begins with an indeterminate, augmented chord from group V. With regard to their harmony, these measures are, and remain, ambivalent throughout the remainder of the piece. G♭ and D♭ contend for hegemony. The roots present the sequence G♭-A♭-B♭♭-G♭, which points to G♭. But A♭ and G♭ are also the second and third pitch in a *Series 1* on D♭, and the perfect fifth $D♭_2$-$A♭_3$ in the bass voice is quite overriding. The final chord, however, is a minor triad on G♭, camouflaged by the notes $A♭_6$-$D♭_6$ in the melody, suggesting that the D♭ tonality also is in play. The frame for the bass progression in mm. 19-20/21 consists of the notes B♭-G♭, with D♭ as the penultimate. Consequently, the triad G♭-B♭-D♭ attracts listeners' attention, and the D♭-G♭ progression represents the first two pitches in a *Series 1* on G♭. While all this suggests a G♭ tonality, it must be added that this tonality is far from unambiguous. One has the feeling that other harmonic elements are at play that do not lead to a culmination in a G♭ triad but rather prepare for a further progression to D♭. This tonality, however, so often announced by now, still does not become manifest—until the following Fuga 10. The interlude has thus fulfilled its role as a harmonic bridge.

As the above analysis has shown, Interludium 9 rests on the tonal levels of B♭-D♭-F-A♭-B♭-G♭, all of which also support the formal structure. In light of the overall focus of this study, Hindemith's use of what he considers the consistency of musical material, one can recognize the tonal levels in this one great sounding entity as representing a chord from his group III, since the minor triad on B♭ as well as major triads on D♭ and G♭ are included. There are also other familiar formations, such as sevenths and sixths. Were one to point out a single overriding tonality plane, it would probably be B♭, since this pitch is the most obvious, being both repeated and supported by the F level.

The function of this interlude as a tonal bridge has already been stated. The tonal disposition of the entire piece can be presented as follows:

EXAMPLE 16: Interludium 9, tonal disposition

In keeping with the overall construction of the *Ludus Tonalis*, the interlude should move tonally from B♭ to D♭—a minor third. As seen above, this rising minor third does indeed characterize the tonal disposition of the piece: first from B♭ to D♭, and then from F to A♭. It was further shown that the progress from A♭ to B (C♭) was also present in connection with stepwise progression, but was not strong enough over time to form a separate tonal level. The transition to Fuga 10 is thus from B♭ to D♭, via G♭. Bearing Hindemith's conception of musical material in mind, importance must be attached to how the tonal disposition relates to his two series. When judging B♭ to represent the central tonal level, one can see it, in addition to its repetition, in light of *Series 2*, where the perfect fifth B♭-F is considered the harmonically strongest. Meanwhile, *Series 1* is the measure of the progression from B♭ to D♭. Hindemith does not make use of the starting point B♭ as a progenitor, but uses the pitch D♭, which subsequently represents the tonality in the fugue towards which the interlude is heading:

EXAMPLE 17: *Series 1* on D♭, tonal application in Interludium 9 [1-5]

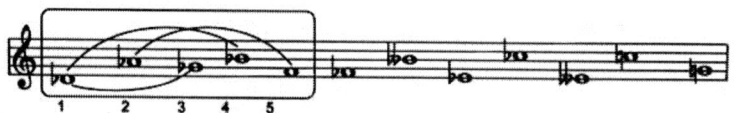

Hindemith applies the first five pitches in *Series 1* as tonal levels in the development of this interlude. He moves from the fourth pitch to the first, and then from the fifth to the second. The third and central pitch in the segment represents the tonal level that then leads to the next fugue. Fuga 10

Hindemith: The Interval as Musical Material

then dwells for a little while in the G♭ tonality by beginning with the interval $D♭_4$-$B♭_4$, which also represents the first two tonal levels in Interludium 9. Hindemith thus establishes an overriding B♭ tonality by using the harmonically strongest interval in a *Series 2* with B♭ as the initial pitch. The function of this piece as a tonal bridge is established through the first five pitches in a *Series 1* with D♭ as progenitor. In this way the tonalities of Fuga 9 and Fuga 10 play together in the interlude.

As mentioned above, the upper voice in Interludium 9 is marked by ornamental figures attached to important melodic points. In addition, Hindemith has created a well-balanced interplay between stepwise motion and leaps, with a slowly progressing rhythmic pulse as the driving force. An analysis of the first ten measures shows the contours of a sophisticated melodic architecture:

EXAMPLE 18: Interludium 9, mm. 1-10, melodic analysis

In the above analysis, the melodic step-progression can be traced in consecutive half-notes (which, in this case, do not indicate note values). The direction of the stems identify a note's belonging to the top or bottom voice respectively. Notes in parentheses are octave transpositions to the level of the preceding melodic motion. Throughout this piece, Hindemith is very consistent in the use of progressions by seconds. This is one of the main reasons why he achieves such a sophisticated melodic balance. The black note-heads without stems show various "breaks" in this stepwise progression. The breaks function as repetitions of crucial preceding notes and are therefore still tied organically into the melody structure. An important facet not shown in the example is the stepwise motion in the lower and middle voices. These progressions also contribute to the overall melodic character of this interlude. From mm. 7 to 10, as later in mm. 16-21, the lower voice in the left hand is particularly significant for the perception of the melodic development. The ornamental figures are part of the two-voice succession in seconds. They constitute a substantial part of the melodic structure, rather than merely functioning as superficial decoration.

One last point to be made about the melody is that it sometimes assumes an important harmonic role, as it builds bridges to new tonal levels. This applies particularly to the latter portions of mm. 12 and 15.

Interludium 9 is an example of how Hindemith uses his insight into the musical material's will to create a piece that is part of a greater cyclical context. The evaluations and considerations made above agree with Hindemith's own views on how a musical analysis should be approached. That there may be more indecisive occurrences on different levels of this music is not least due to the creative possibilities genuine composers always find in their artistic material.

Listeners to this piano piece never lose their tonal foothold, despite the fact that not all the constructional events are easily determined. And yet, it remains questionable whether the ear functions quite so effortlessly as Hindemith claims in *The Craft of Musical Composition*. The aural capacity of perception is not a *tabula rasa*, regardless of whether or not it should be considered "universal." All listeners carry traditions and references, which may render it difficult not to relate a piece such as this to functional harmony. Hindemith would probably disagree with such a conventional orientation, but an unbiased, stylistically uninhibited experience of the interval—the substance of the material—is not easy to come by, even if it appears to be fundamental *per se*. However, the point for Hindemith is not to tone down consciousness of styles and tonal idioms; his analyses aim to show how what he considers universal principles are born out in different styles and epochs. Because of this perspective Hindemith's theories are so central to the understanding of the musical material in the 20th century.

Summary

Hindemith's notion of the *Materialgerechtigkeit* of his art is based on the idea that the musical material has its own will, which limits the degree to which it can be manipulated. The ability to relate to this will requires both knowledge and familiarity with the nature of this particular material. This functionalist perspective is reinforced by the view that any musical movement must be written with the performer and the performing medium in mind. Music must be liberated as much as possible from the external ornament represented by superficial sound. Hindemith agrees that there is a profound connection between numbers and beauty, mathematics and art. He finds in the partial-tone range (or the overtone series, as he calls it) a regularity that can be variously expressed in numbers. Herein lies the key to recognizing musical material as universal and founded in nature. Its regularity even corresponds with the natural, psychophysical capacity of the human ear. Some intervals are easier to determine than others, and when two tones sound simultaneously or consecutively, one of them will usually take priority over the other. Hindemith concludes that the tones of an interval must be linked by different relationships, which can be determined from the overtone series. A set of calculation procedures result in his *Series 1*. The interval with its horizontal and vertical forces thus constitutes the consistency in Hindemith's musical material. In *Series 2* Hindemith presents his calculations of the harmonic and melodic values pertaining to the intervals, where the chords' ability to form roots appears extremely important. These considerations are based on the fundamental importance of combination tones.

The interval is the basis of chord construction. Hindemith develops this insight further through a new method of chord determination. Chords are distinguished essentially through the presence or absence tritones. On the basis of a nature-given regularity one can use a concept such as harmonic value, which, he says, is inversely proportionate to the harmonic tension. The concept of harmonic fluctuation pertains to the undulating movement that is the result of different harmonic values and degrees of tension. Extracting chordal roots and considering them in the light of the supposed intervallic regularities allows for a determination of the tonality of more comprehensive musical progressions. Hindemith's views on melody are also highly significant: Seconds have a particularly strong melodic force, and even the architecturally important tones at the apex and nadir of a melody should make up a progression by seconds. With these considerations, Hindemith provides an important contribution to melodic theory.

To Hindemith, tonality must be considered a universal phenomenon that cannot be avoided. The use of such terms as atonality is therefore absurd; the tonal forces will always be at play. Accordingly, tonal space may be imagined as wide and large: Even the twelve-tone method can be accommodated within it; the question is always which harmonic and melodic possibilities or limitations are inherent in any given compositional procedure.

In his rational outlook, which includes even the results of mathematical calculations, Hindemith agrees with contemporary functionalist views on the artistic material and the process of artistic creation. In a turbulent age he seeks the presumably universal and unchanging phenomena with which modern human beings can identify. The foundations of music are based upon a scientifically recognizable logic that is perpetually true and valid.

Hindemith's perspective therefore reveals even greater dimensions than Schoenberg's "hundred years" perspective. It should, however, be pointed out that Hindemith always regarded real artistic creativity as lying beyond calculation and craftsmanship.

In 1957, Hindemith ordered a number of Schoenberg scores from New York, among others the unfinished opera *Moses und Aron*. In my earlier discussion of Schoenberg's musical material I concluded by suggesting that this work reflects its originator's artistic and moral self-esteem. A similar reflection is also evident in Hindemith's production, particularly in *Die Harmonie der Welt*, an opera whose title refers to the astronomer Johannes Kepler's 1619 treatise *Harmonices Mundi* and whose plot presents the title figure's thoughts and concerns linked to episodes from his life. Hindemith began planning the opera in 1937, just after he had completed the first edition of *The Craft of Musical Composition*. He described *Die Harmonie der Welt* as his *magnum opus*, relegating much of his earlier production to the category of preliminary studies. He did not write the music for the actual opera until 1956-57, but already in 1951 produced a concert version of what he claimed were parts of the operatic music. The three movements of the Symphonie *Die Harmonie der Welt* are entitled "Musica Instrumentalis," "Musica Humana," and "Musica Mundana" respectively, terms derived from Boethius's writings on music. For the program of Paul Sacher's 1952 first performance of the symphony in Basel, Hindemith wrote:

> The symphony's three movements concert pieces derived from an opera presenting Johannes Kepler's life and work, the contemporary events that challenged and limited him, and his search for the harmony undoubtedly reigning in the universe. The movement titles relate to the division of the music into three categories that one often comes across in representations from antiquity, with the aim of referring to all earlier attempts at discerning universal harmony and understanding music as its sounding equivalent.[265]

Hindemith identified with Kepler's cosmological views, not least in his ideas on the musical material. Moreover, the Kepler opera deals with such themes as rationality and superstition, astronomy and fraudulent astrology,

---

[265]Hartmut Lück's comments on the booklet accompanying the CD production *Paul Hindemith Orchestral Works* III (cpo 999 248-2). ["Die drei Sätze der Sinfonie sind konzertmäßig verarbeitete Musikstücke aus einer Oper. Diese handelt vom Leben und Wirken Johannes Keplers, den ihn fördernden oder hindernden Zeitereignissen und dem Suchen nach der Harmonie, die unzweifelhaft das Universum regiert. Die Titel der Sätze beziehen sich auf die bei den Alten oft anzutreffende Einteilung der Musik in drei Klassen und wollen damit auf all die früheren Versuche hinweisen, die Weltharmonie zu erkennen und die Musik als ihr tönendes Gleichnis zu verstehen."]

politics and scientific endeavor. A key component of the work is the question of the astronomer's vocation and his moral duty to society and his fellow human beings. Such questions also touch the core of Hindemith's views on his role, his duties, and his integrity as a composer. If the *Ludus Tonalis* provides an insight into Hindemith's tonal universe, then *Die Harmonie der Welt* may open the door to his larger conceptual universe, with music as its sounding manifestation.

Musical Form

Aspects of Musical Form

Any functional form must be regarded in relation to the inner, constructional principles that support it. Musical form considered in a functionalist context should thus not be seen only as a static construction being realized through clear-cut contours and simple proportions. It should also be associated with the constructive, dynamic processes that constitute a sounding piece of music over a certain period of time. Le Corbusier's belief that the interior of architecture is revealed by its exterior illustrates the complexity of the concept of functionalist form. Complexity also characterizes ideas of form in music.

The introductory chapter of this study included the romantic vision of architecture as frozen music. Hindemith was one of the composers who recognized parallels between these two kinds of artistic expression. He considered intervals as "building stones" and linked musical composition to the art of building in several ways.[1] There is a long tradition in the musical metaphor of connecting what is flexible with sound, the visual impression with the aural. The analogy between musical form and architecture often includes a view of form as the outline, framework, or skeleton of a musical work. The structuring forms of architecture are thus associated with musical forms seen as schemata. This correlation is emphasized through the didactic history of musical form: The practical-theoretical focus on form has its roots in the instruction of composition, whose primary aim has been to teach the technical conditions of the craft of composition. This in turn has encouraged the use of certain directives, initially meant as tools of the craft rather than as a straitjacket constraining the act of composition. The never-ending problem is to reconcile such devices with artistic creativity. Some rules may be deduced from Bach's contrapuntal technique, but this knowledge alone hardly provides one with the ability to create a work of art as Bach did. However obvious this notion may be, this problem has raised its troublesome head with a vengeance as composition directives have also become tools for theoreticians and analysts. Consequently, some may wish to consider and

---

[1]See, for example, *The Craft of Musical Composition,* Chapter III: "The Nature of the Building Stones," 53-108.

evaluate a work of art on the basis of presupposed "laws" and regularities. Many a music teacher has met the challenge of finding a composition that agrees as accurately as possible with a set of generalizing precepts. The fact that compositions worth listening to often breach one or more of these alleged regulations or commands is something we all acknowledge. Hardly any sonata movement penned by Beethoven follows the rules, says Charles Rosen in *The Classical Style*.[2]

We find reflections on what music *is* and even on the foundations of musical composition already among the Pythagoreans and in Plato's dialogues, and textbooks on composition have existed for hundreds of years. Thomas Morley's *A Plain and Easy Introduction to Practical Music*, 1597, is one of the earliest reputed texts on compositional techniques. Johann Joseph Fux's *Gradus ad Parnassum* of 1725 is based on principles still taught to students of counterpoint today.

Versuch einer Anleitung zur Composition, by Heinrich Christoph Koch, was published in three volumes from 1782 to 1793. In these books, Koch discusses what he considers the inner and outer constitutions of a musical work. "The inner" is mainly the area of the genius, but also the region of (personal) taste. "The outer" represents what can be learnt and taught, meaning compositional technique in its narrowest sense: harmony, counterpoint, metrics, rhythmic relations between movements, modulation, and musical form. Koch maintains that "the inner" is the carrier of the so-called aesthetic, while "the outer" refers to the mechanical. Compositional rules thus become mechanical regulations. This view, which also influences the understanding of form, does not contradict the 18th-century author's concern that the primary aim of music is "to please and to move."

Romanticism nurtures the idea of form freeing itself from the control of rigid schemata. Generally, the view of art undergoes fundamental changes during the Romantic period. Christian Friedrich Michaelis and others speak of what is in itself a fulfilled musical work: a piece of music that does not depend on language and imitation, but on the premises of its own being. A work of music exists not to stir certain emotions in the listener's mind, but to realize *itself,* thereby giving access to what is infinite, eternal, and absolute. Michaelis was probably one of the first to use the term "organic form" in connection with music.[3] The constitution of a work is supposed to be organic on all levels, from within and without—musical form and musical content cannot be separated, as Koch would have it. Hegel also sees the

---

[2]See Ch. Rosen, *The Classical Style: Haydn, Beethoven, Mozart* (London etc.: Faber and Faber, 1976), 383-384.

[3]See L. Schmidt, *Organische Form in der Musik. Stationen eines Begriffs 1795-1850* (Kassel: Bärenreiter, 1990), 41.

mechanical aspects as a separate layer in the creation of a work of art, but not in the way that content is separate from form; on the contrary: inadequate design may be due to inadequate content. Koch did not have much of a reputation in the age of Romanticism, nor is Michaelis a well-known writer today. More important for the view on the creation and constitution of a work of art are Karl Philip Moritz and the Schlegel brothers, particularly August Wilhelm Schlegel. They all talk of nature as the model for artistic, organic growth, and of creative talent, which they see as a natural gift. For Hegel, artistic creativity even transcends nature, because the *Geist* of the artist belongs to the noblest of God's creations.

Romantic aesthetics promotes the view that a musical form grows organically out of its own material, and that it is impossible to separate the essence of musical content from musical form.[4] The actual constitution of a musical form depends on the fundamental premises of an individual work. Form and content are seen as relative entities, a view also elucidated by Eduard Hanslick:

> What then is to be called its [music's] subject? The groups of sounds? Undoubtedly; but they have a form already. And what is the form? The groups of sounds again; but here they are a replete form.[5]

A tone is already a form, says Hanslick, implying not only that form and content are one, but also that form and matter must be regarded as relative entities. This view is also found in Aristotle. For Hanslick, the rhythmic-melodic quality of a musical motive and its harmonic foundation is important for a formal development. A work acquires an individual form as a result of a process not based on schemata, but on more general musical procedures, such as motivic transfigurations, the creation of dynamic climaxes, and tension/relaxation. Such principles may apply within various form schemata, which may even be based on them. The individual musical elements as they unfold in a particular work are considered essential premises of formal progression; they may make the traditional framework appear superfluous. This organic-dynamic understanding of form relates in particular to the fact that music proceeds in time. The Romantic view that so-called absolute music is devoid of earth-bound concepts while having the unique character of an ongoing process contributes to Arthur Schopenhauer's idea of music as the immediate and reconciling access to the blind, primal will.

---

[4] Here, content is understood as specifically musical and thus apart from any descriptive, extra-musical inspiration.

[5] E. Hanslick, *The Beautiful in Music,* 122; compare with *Vom Musikalisch-Schönen*, 100: "Was also will man den *Inhalt* nennen? Die Töne selbst? Gewiß; allein sie sind eben schon geformt. Was die *Form*? Wieder die Töne selbst,—sie aber sind schon *erfüllte* Form."

The controversial element in Hanslick's *The Beautiful in Music* is, above all, the view that music does not express emotion but only *itself*. Hanslick rejects the referential aspects of music. He believes that due to its inherent nature, music cannot express anything outside itself. Hanslick's concern is what he regards as the relationship between form and content. His thoughts are in accordance with views central to musical Romanticism: He wants to end the reminiscences of musical *Affektenlehre* (the doctrine of the affects), not the passionate experiencing of music. Despite an unmistakably sober undertone, Hanslick's ideas of musical expression are rooted in his high regard for the essence of music, not in reductionism and formalism. This fundamental attitude is also obvious in his numerous music critiques, but this fact is often forgotten when Hanslick is eagerly quoted today.

"Forms in sounding motion are the sole content and object of music," Hanslick says. He also discusses a number of other aspects of musical form:

> The arabesque, a branch of the art of ornamentation, dimly betokens in what manner music may exhibit forms of beauty though no definite emotion be involved. [...] If, moreover, we conceive this living arabesque as the active emanation of inventive genius, the artistic fullness of whose imagination is incessantly flowing into the heart of these moving forms, the effect, we think, will be not unlike that of music. When young, we have probably all been delighted with the ever-changing tints and forms of a kaleidoscope. Now, music is a kind of kaleidoscope, though its forms can be appreciated only by an infinitely higher ideation. It brings forth a profusion of beautiful tints and forms, now sharply contrasted and now almost imperceptibly graduated; all logically connected with each other, yet all novel in their effect; forming, as it were, a complete and self-subsistent whole, free from any alien mixture. The main difference consists in the fact that the musical kaleidoscope is the direct product of a creative mind, whereas the optic one is but a cleverly constructed mechanical toy.[6]

---

[6]*The Beautiful in Music,* 48-49. Compare with *Vom Musikalisch-Schönen*, 32-33: "In welcher Weise uns die Musik *schöne Formen* ohne den Inhalt eines bestimmten Affectes bringen kann, zeigt uns recht treffend ein Zweig der Ornamentik in der bildende Kunst: die *Arabeske*. [...] Denken wir uns vollends diese lebendige Arabeske als thätige Ausströmung eines künstlerischen Geistes, der die ganze Fülle seiner Phantasie unablässig in die Adern dieser Bewegung ergießt, wird dieser Eindruck dem *musikalischen* nicht sehr nahekommend sein? Jeder von uns hat als Kind sich wohl an dem wechselnden Farben- und Formenspiel eines *Kaleidoskops* ergötzt. Ein solches Kaleidoskop auf incommensurabel höherer Erscheinungsstufe ist Musik. Sie bringt in stets sich entwickelnder Abwechslung schöne Formen und Farben, sanft übergehend, scharf contrastirend, immer symmetrisch und in sich erfüllt. Der Hauptunterschied ist, dass solch unserm Ohr vorgeführtes *Tonalkaleidoskop* sich als unmittelbare Emanation eines künstlerisch schaffenden Geistes giebt, jenes sichtbare aber als ein sinnreich-mechanisches Spielzeug."

Hanslick illustrates the concept of musical form through visual impressions and expressions, not referring to frozen music in architecture but to the "living" arabesque and the ever-changing kaleidoscope. He regards the abstract formation as motion, thus combining the static and dynamic views of form in a way that represents a highly important contribution to this field. Through the arabesque/kaleidoscope metaphor, Hanslick sees both organic growth and construction and the mathematical and geometrical structuring principles as two sides of the same coin. His considerations represent the outlines of an insight that was to become the core of the functionalist concept of form.

Louis Sullivan underscores the organic construction of a form (not its organic growth) in connection with the process of artistic creation. Similar thoughts are found in relation to music, above all in Schoenberg. The aforementioned crisis of tonality also affects the issue of musical form. In early 20th-century music, liberation from traditional and presumably conventional form types is a characteristic feature, partly due to exciting desire, partly to pure necessity. Schoenberg attempted to solve the form problem through motivic construction, a procedure he later found enriched through his twelve-tone method. As a result, writers like Adorno and Dahlhaus attribute functionalist traits to Schoenberg's work. Marked by its construction potential, the motive has fundamental importance as a formal building block.

In the entry "Form" in *The Concise Oxford Dictionary of Music*, Percy A. Scholes discusses views that may also be related to the thoughts of Schoenberg and Hindemith.[7] Scholes states that a satisfactory musical form is found in the balance between two extremes: the continuous stringing together of ever-new musical ideas and the constant repetition of one and the same idea. Giving music material an adequate form means balancing these two extremes in a rational way. The forming principle thus becomes the well-known device of creating unity in diversity and diversity in unity. This presupposes that musical form is something that gradually unfolds for the listener, no matter how much the composer might wish to experiment with the concepts of time. Attention to *time* plays a particular role in Hindemith's views: he regards time as the most important aspect of giving a theoretically justifiable presentation of the nature of form. A second presupposition in Scholes's insight is that the extremes in themselves cannot be subject to what is considered an elevated form of music. Consequently, he does not discuss questions connected to the idea that it may be precisely in the *extremes* that the forming potential of music lies. The question of when the musical idea is really new and when it is in fact repeated is relevant in the study of

---

[7] See P.A. Scholes, "Form," *The Concise Oxford Dictionary of Music* (Oxford etc.: Oxford University Press, 1964), 207-209.

Schoenberg's and Hindemith's music. Bearing Schoenberg's concept of developing variation in mind, one may ask what characterizes a musical idea as *new* in relation to all that has been previously presented. In the same way one can ask whether a musical idea can actually be repeated, or whether it will not always be experienced differently, and thus appear as new.

Musical form remains a multifarious phenomenon. That artistic material assumes a form in keeping with its uniqueness and "will" is an essential characteristic of functionalist thought. However, this view does not entirely cover the organic construction of form. In the introductory lines to this chapter, reference was made to the particular complexity of the functional concept of form. This intricacy also applies to musical functionalism, where the relationship to the fundamental forms, or to the basic or standard forms, is of crucial importance.

The principles underpinning a trained composer's repertoire of forms presuppose that the form of, for example, a sonata movement or a dance tune is perceived as a *gestalt* recognizable in itself. Whether this musical-formal *gestalt* is spatial or temporal is another issue. It can be recognized both visually (through graphic presentation and analysis of the score) and aurally, owing to a formal *gestalt* that will appear standardized at least for those who are familiar with that particular language of music. The degree of recognizability may vary from one form type to the other: it is easier to recognize a waltz, whom meter and rhythm give its unmistakable characteristics, than a complicated sonata movement. A presentiment and clearly defined expectation of the whole is created rather immediately in the interplay between perception and cognition. Dancers recognize the waltz with their bodies, which shows that the waltz can be presented in a quite unambiguous way physically and visually, as a social event or as stage entertainment. Both Schoenberg and Hindemith believe that dance forms represent the most easily recognizable musical forms. Other formal types may be far more difficult to identify, one reason being that the actual representation of the form in the musical work may have distanced itself from its foundation or model, perhaps because its exemplar is not sufficiently unambiguous. A second reason may lie in the tonal language or in the mix of materials from which a musical form is made. The characteristics of musical material vary. Not all materials are suitable for all types of formal design—in that respect music is no different from the other arts.

The use of standard forms in music suggests some sort of agreement on their characteristics as ideal entities or paradigms. The actual form paradigm must be in the composer's mind during the process of creation: there are certain demands that must be met for the work to take form according to the presupposed *gestalt*. This applies to any artistic design. The more clearly the norms are defined, the stronger will be the recognition of the formal pattern, as long as it is based on living tradition or solid convention. Even where an artist feels fully embedded in such traditions and conventions, the standard form *per se* may be external to the composer, reaching beyond his or her delimited contribution.

In the 1920s the use of basic, standard musical forms increased compared to the preceding decades. The timing of this tendency is coincidental with formal norms and standardizing processes in functionalist architecture and design. When composers like Schoenberg, Hindemith, Stravinsky, and Weill employ well-established form types, it is not because of a nostalgic quest for what has gone before, but rather an expression of the desire to realize musical material of the new age in a clear and presumably recognizable form. This procedure presupposes that listeners must also relate actively to the actual form paradigm in order to experience the formal intentions of a musical work. Le Corbusier strongly believes in the identification of human beings with basic forms. Musical functionalism is realized on the formal plane in accordance with such thoughts and the functionalist understanding of material.

Schoenberg: From *Gedanke* to Form

> Und ich weiß, daß
> Architektur, Gliederung, Aufbau,
> mit einem Wort: Kunstvolle Darstellung
> nicht von irgendeinem
> technischen Kunstgriff abhängen,
> sondern, daß sie im Denken selbst liegen.
>
> *Arnold Schönberg*[8]

Introduction

The concept of *Gedanke* is a crucial element in Schoenberg's views on the musical material. *Gedanke* may be interpreted in several ways. For musical form, the concept may embrace the dimensions of a musical work as a whole, a complete artistic totality. Consequently, one might well ask whether it is relevant to categorize *Gedanke* and *Form* as different entities: they might possibly be seen as two sides of the same coin—rather than the one leading on to the other. Yet the from/to heading above signals the notion that certain given conditions must be met for the thought to materialize in a work of art. Schoenberg regards this conviction as imperative.

In the *Festschrift* on the occasion of Schoenberg's 60th birthday, Eduard Steuermann describes music in quite a grand style: "hardly in any other art does the material (the eternally-moving emotional life) strive so restlessly to ever new designs; hardly in any other spiritual area does it so stubbornly defy any acknowledgment of an eternally valid form of the ever-new truth."[9] Hans Mersmann in his book *Die Tonsprache der neuen Musik* (The tonal language of new music) thinks along similar lines but sounds somewhat more concrete and restrained. He points out that there has always been disparity between the progress of the elements of music and its form. By elements, Mersmann means melody, harmony, and rhythm, the components in the concept of music material prevailing at the time. In his opinion, material and form have not developed at the same pace. The historical expansion of musical elements has been marked by spontaneity, while the development of form has always lagged behind: "The elements have always been ahead of the advent of

---

[8][And I know that architecture, structure, lay-out, in other words: artistic creation, do not depend on some technical concept of art, but that they are rooted in thinking itself.]

[9]E. Steuermann, "Zukunftsmusik," *Arnold Schoenberg zum 60. Geburtstag*, 28. ["kaum in einer anderen Kunst drängt das Material [das ewig bewegte Empfindungsleben] so rastlos zu immer neuer Gestaltung; kaum in einem anderen geistigen Bezirk trotzt es so hartnäckig jeder Anerkennung einer ewig-gültigen Form für die immer neue Wahrheit."]

forms; their constitution has been the more progressive and they began to influence the forming process only gradually," he says."[10]

Mersmann's view underscores the challenges of musical form as it was experienced by representatives of the Second Viennese School during the liberation from traditional tonality. He even presents the so-called *Konzentrationsform* ("concentration form") as a formal consequence, as, for instance, in the treatment of musical material exemplified in Schoenberg's piano piece op. 19/1. In a similar vein, Mersmann's *Expansionsform* ("expansion form") can be considered a counterpart of the "concentration form" in the light of a given musical material's constitution. In his article on Schoenberg's *Erwartung* op. 17 included in the *Festschrift* for Schoenberg's 50th birthday, Paul Bekker uses the term "expansive form" for this particular work. The expansion lies in the extension of tonality levels and tonal relationships in a continual process that both expands the experience of time and anchors it.[11] Mersmann regards the contemporary Neo-Classicist trends as an expansion of perspective in the area of a new tonal language. Innovations are combined with the best of what has gone before: "Archaism does not result from need, but from abundance."[12] He presents this fact as being a result of the historical development of the musical material and, subsequently, of the basic elements of music. Such views show that Schoenberg is representative of both formal concentration and expansion, and even of the use of basic forms. Hence, Kurt Westphal's emphasis on Schoenberg as the all-embracing figure in music history, seen in the former discussion on Schoenberg's attitude to the musical material, is strengthened by the way in which the composer relates to the possibilities of creating musical form.

In his article "A Self-Analysis," Schoenberg recalls that the brief, aphoristic works of his earlier production taught him "to link ideas together without the use of formal connectives, merely by juxtaposition." Yet the result would still be *forms*, albeit what he describes as "extremely short forms."[13] What is understood by the concept of musical form will vary at any given time. Yet the view that form is an integrated part of the musical material

---

[10]H. Mersmann, *Die Tonsprache der neuen Musik* (Mainz: Melosbücherei, 1930), 44. ["Immer waren die Elemente dem Werden der Formen voraus; ihre Haltung war die fortschrittlichere und bestimmte erst langsam den Formungsprozess."]

[11]P. Bekker, "Schoenberg: 'Erwartung'," *Arnold Schoenberg zum fünfzigsten Geburtstage*, 280-281.

[12]*Die Tonsprache der neuen Musik*, 57. ["Archaismus entsteht nicht aus Not, sondern aus Fülle."]

[13]"A Self-Analysis," *Style and Idea*, 78.

is ever present in Schoenberg's texts. In this respect Schoenberg is the consummate Aristotelian. He does not regard this insight as an overarching philosophic recognition of art, but works consciously with his musical material, generating its form during the process. The notion is very much part of his practical and technical principles in constructing a piece of music.

Because Schoenberg places emphasis on "the organic," many regard him as a representative of the Romantic tradition. But this can only be upheld with some crucial reservations: First, Schoenberg's ideas of the organic are based on rationality much more than would be typical for the Romantics. Second, his constant focus on the concept of construction makes him—like Louis Sullivan—a figure in the transition towards a new century's understanding of form. Schoenberg's functionalist attitude in particular becomes evident, as his fundamental approach is strongly supported by his constant attention on logic and comprehensibility. The claim that "Schoenberg was really a romantic" is therefore only true in part. By the 1920s, Schoenberg leads the development of musical form in a process that embraces the rise of functionalism. His compositional evolution is vital to establishing an understanding of musical form in the 20th century.

"Formgefühl"

To approach Schoenberg's thoughts on form in a more systematic way, the concept of "feeling for form," or "sense of form" (*Formgefühl*) may be a good place to start. "In my youth a feeling for form was still very much alive; this, without theoretical explanation, told one how a principal subject was to be formed,"[14] Schoenberg recalls. Brahms was not the last of the great ones with this intuitive quality: both Mahler and Richard Strauss drew from the same inheritance, and Schoenberg undoubtedly also includes himself in this distinguished company. Schoenberg links the feeling for form in his recent past to functional harmony and to the established principles of fundamental tone progressions. "This practice had grown into a subconsciously functioning *sense of form*," he says, "which gave the real composer an almost somnambulistic sense of security in creating, with utmost precision, the most delicate distinctions of formal elements."[15] He considers the feeling for form as one of the truly elevated artistic qualities. However, even though he refers to the "real composer" and not to those of mediocre ability, this feeling is not to be considered one of the innate attributes of the genius. A sense of form is developed through learning, and, in the same way as with

---

[14]"Tonality and Form," *Style and Idea*, 256.

[15]"Composition with Twelve Tones (1)," *Style and Idea*, 218.

traditional tonality, such capacity is considered to be rooted in a person's second nature. This does not mean that Schoenberg's formal sense is limited to functional harmony. On the contrary, it is also evident in a dissonant style exclusive of consonance:

> I cannot find a single physical reason justifying the exclusion of consonant chords, but I can give a far more decisive artistic reason. It is in fact *a question of economy*. My formal sense (and I am immodest enough to hand over to this the exclusive rights of distribution when I compose) tells me that to introduce even a single tonal triad would lead to consequences, and would demand space which is not available within my form.[16]

In the article "The Relationship to the Text," Schoenberg states that the "sound" of the initial words of a text may decide the whole compositional development of a song,[17] and finds the same decisive attributes, for example, in a simple triad. Furthermore, he links his sense of form to the experience of a consonant chord's lack of justification in a movement based on dissonance.

At first glance, Schoenberg's formal sense may appear highly intuitive. The reason for his seemingly basic attitude is not that he claims to possess intuition in areas where he might find a failure in logic. Intuition and logic are not competitors in an artistic consciousness—rather they complement each other: logic strives to be a reliable support for the formal sense. "In music there is no form without logic," says Schoenberg.[18] Therefore the form-constituting, realizable intuition must be recognized as being based on logic, at least when the sense of form initiates the directions of a compositional procedure. Schoenberg's concept of logic is complex, and even his formal sense—however intuitive it may seem—is inextricably tied to it:

> For practically any truly new creation the sole criterion is the formal sense possessed by the author, who can say to himself: 'My formal sense, tested in so many cases, trained by the best masters, and the logic of my thinking, which for me is beyond all doubt, and about which I have convinced myself—these guarantee me that whatever I unconsciously write will be correct in form and ideas, even when I renounce the aids given the intellect by theory and convention.'[19]

---

[16]"Opinion or Insight?" *Style and Idea*, 262-263.

[17]See *Style and Idea*, 141-145.

[18]"Composition with Twelve Tones (1)," *Style and Idea*, 244.

[19]"Linear Counterpoint," *Style and Idea*, 292.

Schoenberg goes further in emphasizing the importance of logic for what he considers the unconscious sense of form. It must always be a superordinate objective to make conscious what is unconscious. A skilled composer never sleeps, even when he spreads his wings of intuition:

> Nevertheless, the desire for a conscious control of the new means and forms will arise in every artist's mind; and he will wish to know *consciously* the laws and rules which govern the forms which he has conceived 'as in a dream'. Strongly convincing as this dream may have been, the conviction that these new sounds obey the laws of nature and of our manner of thinking—the conviction that order, logic, comprehensibility and form cannot be present without obedience to such laws—forces the composer along the road of exploration.[20]

In this way Schoenberg makes a point of drawing the gifted artist's intuition of form toward the light of logical consciousness, toning down the Romantic idea of the genius's boundless creativity. *Formgefühl* and *Logik* are mutually productive aspects of the creative process; consequently, Schoenberg gives them both their proper place in his understanding of form. "For I am of course a constructor," he says, somewhat ironically, continuing: "and now I will reveal my true self [...] I must in one way or another confess that I construct while others *'just shake themes out of their sleeves'*; that I think twice, reflect, while true geniuses have no need for neither this nor much else."[21]

Conception and Wholeness, Logic and Form

Schoenberg's concept of construction should be seen in relation to his notion of a musical work as an organic whole. At the beginning of his *Fundamentals of Musical Composition,* he offers a definition of musical form: "form means that a piece is *organized*; i.e. that it consists of elements functioning like those of a living *organism*."[22] Schoenberg's point of departure lies in the Romantic ideal of the artistic organism, where the artwork, with its ontological model in nature, is regarded as an expression of life. Schoenberg's writings are rich in metaphors accenting this view. But his version of the organic whole does not primarily refer to the *form* of a work;

---

[20]"Composition with Twelve Tones (1)," *Style and Idea*, 218.

[21]"Neue und veraltete Musik, oder Stil und Gedanke," *Stil und Gedanke,* 474. ["Denn ich bin ja ein Konstrukteur, und nun werde ich mich selbst entlarven. Werde irgendwie zugeben müssen, dass ich konstruiere, während andere *die Themen nur so aus dem Ärmel schütteln –* , dass ich nachdenke, überlege, während wahrhafte Genies das nicht nötig haben und vieles andere mehr."]

[22]*Fundamentals of Musical Composition*, 1.

it rather involves a kind of complexity that seems to remove the concept from the sphere of Romanticism. Once again, the concept of logic plays a decisive role.

Schoenberg's meticulous motivic work has often been interpreted as organic, in the way that his music develops step by step from a core motive —from a germ cell (*Keimzelle*). This is one of the most persistent myths about Schoenberg's procedures and thoughts. In fact Schoenberg rejects such romantic understandings of artistic growth:

> An attempt to recognize and define the musical idea [*Gedanke*] stands in clear contradiction to the sentimental, poeticizing notion that a composition might arise from the motive as a germ of the whole, as a plant grows from a seed.[23]

Such childish thoughts say nothing about where the alleged seed comes from or what it *is*. "Which comes first, the chicken or the egg?," Schoenberg asks.[24] He has no problem in acknowledging that the presumed poetic view of organic growth originates in how humans experience the reproductive forces of nature. And when a human being is viewed in this perspective, he adds the following subtlety: "But if one understands love as the desire of children to be conceived and born, many things could be shown to be different in this regard."[25] If we dig even deeper, where are, for example, the artistic possibilities of choice supposed to lie? "For if this conception were correct, then only *one single* piece could arise from a motive. But of course, such is not the case. I consider the motive as the *building material* that can assume and realize all forms."[26] The flexibility provided by the vast possibilities of a musical motive makes Schoenberg abandon the growth metaphor.

Schoenberg's point is that whatever is made out of an artistic "seed" is the result of human activity, whether it seems to grow from itself or out of itself, and every human activity—as long as it is not purely instinctive—follows some kind of plan. He thus takes the concept of growth *per se* quite literally and does not find it compatible with the rational foundation of any act of artistic creation. However, he expresses himself in a way that seems indirectly to allow for the notion that in the compositional process, a piece arises according to something like calculated growth. Thereby he approaches Sullivan's ideas of the organic construction that a "master craftsman" may realize. Hence, Schoenberg does not only reject the ideas of Romanticism:

---

[23] *The Musical Idea*, 109.
[24] Ibid.
[25] Ibid.
[26] *The Musical Idea*, note on p. 151.

he even remarks on how far they are from the advantage of a more rational insight that even includes calculation. Those who are familiar with the inscrutable fictional character Rat Krespel created by E.T.A. Hoffmann,[27] a spontaneous and apparently irrational master builder, will recognize a distinct opposition to that curious self-styling in Schoenberg's metaphor of the building process. Schoenberg turns his back on romantically inspired spontaneity in the description of an architect's working procedures:

> Certainly he must first invent his house as a whole, because he cannot possibly begin to lay brick on brick, to join room to room, without a plan. But after inventing the whole he then begins to assemble the necessary particulars that realize his whole.[28]

When a musical analyst takes the notion of organic growth as his point of departure, this does not necessarily imply that the piece was conceived in that way by the composer. It is important to clarify the relationship between artistic conception and compositional construction. "A composer does not, of course, add bit by bit, as a child does in building with wooden bricks," Schoenberg says. "He conceives an entire composition as a spontaneous vision. Then he proceeds, like Michelangelo who chiseled his *Moses* out of the marble without sketches, complete in every detail, thus directly *forming* his material."[29] Hence, the musical piece has already outlined itself in the composer's consciousness before it finds its way to concrete realization. The initial motive that is continuously present in Schoenberg's piano piece from op. 19 is not just the driving force for a controlled process of developing variation; it is also a constant, superordinate entity representing the composer's conception of the whole.

In Schoenberg's view an artistic whole is always conceived before its constituent parts:

> For like any other living thing, the work of art arises as a whole. Just as in the case of a child, where neither an arm nor a leg is first produced. It is not the theme that is the initial idea [*der Einfall*] but rather the entire work."[30]

---

[27]E.T.A. Hoffmann wrote the tale "Rat Krespel," which expresses the longing for *absolute art*, in 1818, and the protagonist is often considered a portrait of Hoffmann's alter ego, Kapellmeister Johannes Kreisler.

[28]*The Musical Idea*, 151.

[29]*Fundamentals of Musical Composition*, 1-2.

[30]"Mahler," *Stil und Gedanke*, 14. ["Denn das Kunstwerk ist, wie jedes Lebewesen, ein als Ganzes Entstandenes. Genauso wie ein Kind, von dem auch nicht zuerst ein Arm oder ein Bein erzeugt wird. Nicht das Thema ist der Einfall, sondern das ganzes Werk."]

Schoenberg even goes so far as to state that the initial conception is perfectly complete: "a real composition is not composed but conceived, and its details need not be added."[31] This notion of a vision supporting a creative process does not imply that Schoenberg regards the composer as a direct mediator of inspiration in the romantic sense. Rather he considers a hard task of construction necessary for realizing the artistic vision. It is a question of committing both heart and mind, and a work of art does not always emerge in a creator's consciousness with the same degree of clarity. In his essay "Heart and Brain in Music," Schoenberg recalls the work on his *First Chamber Symphony*:

> I was certainly no less directed by inspiration when I started my *Kammersymphonie*. I had a perfect vision of the whole work—of course, not in all its details but in its main features. But, while I wrote many of the subordinate themes later in *one* draft, I had to work very hard to shape the beginning.[32]

The view that a conception of an artistic whole is the basis of a creative process pervades Schoenberg's texts on composition. The complexity of his insight is at least in part due to his many different ways of expressing his ideas—so varied in fact that his concept of the musical whole may appear inconsistent. At any rate, the concept contains two primary meanings. First, it can stand for the main traits or design of a piece. In Aristotelian terms one could say that the whole is a representation of the basic features in the determination of a musical work—an image that can be more or less detailed. Schoenberg may have reason to say that no detail is added, as each singularity is part of the realization of the initial conception of the whole. Yet, the composer may well have to struggle with details necessary for getting what was initially conceived down on paper. Second, Schoenberg's concept of the musical whole can mean the main idea or basic principle underlying the music, which may even appear as the essential characteristics of the work. This principle may be described as both the ideal and the structural driving forces particularly significant for the composer's process of creation. Initially such a force can appear to be just as clear or unclear as the idea of the design or shape of the work. The two main aspects of the concept of the artistic whole do not negate each other; they are mutually inclusive.

Schoenberg's complex "whole" can be compared to Sullivan's "function." As previously mentioned, Sullivan's concept of function focuses on the "determination" of a given phenomenon: "the form horse can be compared

---

[31]"Folkloristic Symphonies," *Style and Idea*, 166.

[32]"Heart and Brain in Music," *Style and Idea*, 58.

with and is the logical result of the function horse." But function may also involve "the initiating pressure of a living force," the urging, life-giving principles. In Sullivan's understanding of organism, the compound concept of function becomes the presupposition of a form. For Schoenberg, the conception of the whole—with all its implications—has a similar, fundamental status.

Schoenberg is not blind to the fact that some composers may really feel that they begin with a tiny musical detail. But even if the aim is to develop a work in a conscious way from minute parts, creation cannot come about without the (albeit unconscious) conception of a whole. Subsequently, this totality will, even if perhaps unconsciously, dictate the act of composition. Schoenberg's main point is non-wavering "[t]he conception of the maker, however, proceeds from the whole."[33]

Schoenberg's concept of the whole is thus not identical with musical form in a traditional sense. As in Sullivan's "form follows function," logic is the mediator: it serves as the connective between the conception of a musical whole and the actual creation of a musical form. This leads us back to Schoenberg's fundamental concept of musical logic—a concept that also prevails in his attitude to musical form.

A snapshot of Schoenberg's emphasis on logic can be gleaned from the title of his manuscript *Der musikalische Gedanke und die Logik, Technik und Kunst seiner Darstellung*. His first sketch for a title was *Der musikalische Gedanke und die Kunst, Logik und Technik seiner Darstellung*.[34] While one should not read too much into this, the placement of "logic" in front of "art" offers an interesting summary of the composer's deliberations.

The musician proceeds as does the architect, and "the vision that shows him the whole guides him in every detail to do what makes sense and is meaningful and purposeful, *logical*," says Schoenberg.[35] "The conception does not need logic" and "the presentation requires logic," he writes in the draft to his book project eventually published as *Coherence, Counterpoint, Instrumentation, Instruction in Form*.[36] It can, however, be counterproductive to interpret Schoenberg to mean that the presence of logic in what is conceived is a precondition for its being presented according to logical criteria. His point is that the very act of conception is not dependent on

---

[33] *The Musical Idea*, 125.

[34] See *The Musical Idea*, 94 and 95 (emphasis in the original). The difference is between "The Musical Idea and the Logic, Technique and Art of Its Presentation" and "The Musical Idea and the Art, Logic, and Technique of Its Presentation."

[35] *The Musical Idea*, 151.

[36] *Coherence, Counterpoint* ..., 5.

logical consideration, although what is conceived will reveal its own logic. Schoenberg assumes that there is a type of unconscious—and in a certain sense irrational—comprehension that then materializes by means of rational and logical procedures.[37] But in the same draft Schoenberg also mentions that there are cases where a composer may renounce logic:

> a) if no general intelligibility is aimed at
> b) if the author trusts his intuition
> c) because the presence of external symptoms does not depend on internal logic, and internal logic does not depend on the external.[38]

It is impossible to say whether Schoenberg would have included the list above, written in 1917, in the further work on his book project as it appears to conflict with the more unequivocal emphasis on the importance of logic so pervasive in his later texts. One explanation for this apparent discrepancy may be that at this time Schoenberg had a more rigid view of the concept of musical logic, as his earliest correspondence with Wassily Kandinsky does in fact suggest. In his first letter of 18 January 1911, Kandinsky refers to the importance of construction to the further development of pictorial art. "I just view the *art* of construction differently," he writes. "My view is that the harmony of today is not to be found 'geometrically' but directly in the anti-geometric and anti-logical."[39] Anyone comparing Kandinsky's mature paintings with, for example, his countryman Kasimir Malewitsch's suprematist output will understand what he means. Schoenberg answers Kandinsky enthusiastically less than a week later, to communicate his concurrence with the painter's views. Furthermore, he sees a parallel between what Kandinsky calls "the illogic" and what he himself describes as "leaving the conscious will out of art." Yet he feels compelled to admit that any shape whatsoever that strives for "traditional effects" is not entirely free of acts of consciousness.[40] All conscious shaping is related in some way or another to mathematics, geometry, the golden ratio, and so on. Nevertheless, he seems to believe at this point in his career that the unconscious shaping creates real forms:

---

[37] Hermann Broch also discusses the concept of irrational recognition in "Irrationale Erkenntnis in der Musik," *Arnold Schoenberg zum 60. Geburtstag*, 49-60.

[38] *Coherence, Counterpoint ...*, 7.

[39] J. Hahl-Kohl, ed., *Wassily Kandinsky und Arnold Schönberg: Der Briefwechsel* (Stuttgart: Gerd Hatje, 1993), 15. ["Nur denke ich über die *Art* der Construktion anders" [...] "Ich finde eben, dass unsere heutige Harmonie nicht auf dem 'geometrischen' Wege zu finden ist, sondern auf dem direkt antigeometrischen, antilogischen."]

[40] *Kandinsky/Schoenberg Briefwechsel*, 17-18. ["Ausschaltung des bewußten Willens in der Kunst" [...] "Jede Formung, die traditionelle Wirkungen anstrebt, ist nicht ganz frei von Bewußtseins-Akten."]

> But forming unconsciously, which gives the formula "form = form of representation," this alone creates real forms; this alone provides the models copied by those who are not creative artist, those which, accordingly, become "formulas." But he who is able to listen to himself, to recognize his own need to think profoundly through every challenge, has no use for such crutches.[41]

On returning to Schoenberg's points a), b), and c) above, which allegedly make logic superfluous, later on—in a somewhat wider understanding—he would probably maintain that logic had to be present, even in those particular cases. In the *Gedanke* manuscripts from the 1930s, he addresses this issue again, and is obviously searching for a more open and clearer concept of logic to be used in relation to music. Yet Schoenberg did not embrace what he called the scientific, or mathematico-scientific, logic. In contrast to science, the work of art has no "errors" or incorrect doctrines; art and science differ essentially in this area. Although the human brain is always the same, it does not follow that artistic and scientific logic are necessarily identical:

> It is clear that a *difference in the manner of presentation and in the principles of construction* must also reflect this basic difference and that in art the meaning of what is called *logic* has to be somewhat modified, even though fundamentally the human mind is capable of only *a single manner of thinking*.[42]

Schoenberg rejects the idea that a causal logic of mathematical science should be able to control art. There are areas in art that defy the traditional notion of logic, at least logic as something unequivocal and universal. Herein lies one of the fundamental differences between art and science. In art, changing the relationships between different meanings can even increase the effect.[43] The conclusion is that artistic logic within certain limits is both relative and manipulative. Logic thus becomes in itself a creative tool in the artist's hands. This conviction is important for early functionalist thought: there is a dialectic between the artistic material's will and the artist's will, with an all-embracing concept of logic as a rule of conduct.

---

[41] *Kandinsky/Schoenberg Briefwechsel*, 17-18. ["Das unbewußte Formen aber, das die Gleichung: Form = Erscheinungsform' setzt, das allein schafft wirklich Formen; das allein bringt jene Vorbilder hervor, die von den Unoriginellen nachgeahmt und zu 'Formeln' werden: Aber, wer imstande ist, sich zu hören, seine eigenen Triebe zu erkennen, sich auch denkend selbst in jedes Problem zu vertiefen, hat solche Krücke nicht nötig."

[42] *The Musical Idea*, 117.

[43] See *The Musical Idea*, 115.

Schoenberg wants to connect the artist's visionary conception as closely as possible with logical construction. In his opinion a truly creative intellect has the requisite capacity:

> The fact that the details are realized with the strictest, most conscientious care, that everything is logical, purposeful and organically deft, without the visionary images, thereby losing fullness, number, clarity, beauty, originality or pregnancy—that is merely a question of intellectual energy [...] The inspiration, the vision, the whole, breaks down during its representation into details whose realization reunites them into the whole.[44]

No matter how complex the concepts of the whole and the notion of logic may be, Schoenberg refers to *the* whole—using the definite article—as if it is a "determination" that undergoes a process of realization. The parts realize their functions within this integrated framework, where the vision is broken down before being built up again in concrete form. The interaction between the whole of a work and its constituent components or members is thus vital. Schoenberg's statement, "in music there is no form without logic," concludes the argument.

If, like Schoenberg, one considers a musical work as a living organism or a living body, the parts are to be conceived as limbs or organs, members that execute various functions in the totality of the musical piece. Hence, concepts such as function and functionality become important premises for Schoenberg's understanding of form:

> Above all, a piece of music is (perhaps always) an *articulated organism* whose organs, members, carry out specific functions in regard to both their own external effect and their mutual relations.[45]

Schoenberg's emphasis on "members" or "limbs" (*Glieder*) is significant for his view of the musical work as a living organism. He stresses that these categories must not be confused with "parts," for parts are the result of cutting up the whole. "But I will never obtain members in this way. Members are parts that are equipped, formed, and used for a special function."[46] The members can be both independent of and dependent on each other, as of the whole. In a mechanical structure the various parts do not have the power to function by themselves. The cogs in a chronometer are active, but only when wound up. When the mechanism is dismantled, the parts are ineffectual and dead: only the driving force can be said to be living. In an organic structure,

---

[44]"Constructed Music," *Style and Idea*, 107.

[45]*The Musical Idea*, 119.

[46]*The Musical Idea*, 119.

the members do not function as a result of this kind of driving force but by virtue of their belonging to a "living organism," Schoenberg says. This fact is what creates a unique combination of structural dependence and independence. Consequently, the limbs in a living organism carry out their function even while at rest:

> True members that function, even though they may be at rest, are found only in organisms; here they are activated not by energy resulting from an inner driving power but as a result of their organic membership in a living being, and are independent of both it and of each other.[47]

The principal functionality of a limb is not restricted to its execution of one particular function. The member is per definition "functional" since it already has a position in the organic context through which life flows. Schoenberg explains that the members or limbs of a musical organism can also perform their functions independently, without losing contact with the organic whole. A member can work toward its individual objective while at the same time being part of the body.

An *organism* may survive the loss of some of its members, as it only loses some functionality. Conversely, a *limb* is dependent on the whole: "in the long run, no member is able to live if it is separated from its organism," Schoenberg says, proceeding to an illustration of the construction of musical form:

> To symbolize the construction of a musical form, perhaps one ought to think of a living body that is whole and centrally controlled, that puts forth a certain number of limbs by means of which it is capable of exercising its vital functions.[48]

As a result, the musical limbs or members, however independent they may be, are also adequate representatives of the organic whole. This close and consistent relationship is central to the way in which Schoenberg thinks about an artistic organism, as is evident in the following, which is perhaps one of his most descriptive justifications:

> [...] it became clear to me that a work of art is like every other complete organism. It is so homogeneous in its composition that in every little detail it reveals its truest, inmost essence. When one cuts into any part of the human body, the same thing always comes out—blood. When one hears a verse of a poem, a measure of a composition, one is in position to comprehend the whole. Even so, a word, a glance, a gesture, the gait, even the color of the hair, are sufficient to reveal the personality of a human being.[49]

---

[47] *The Musical Idea*, 119.

[48] *The Musical Idea*, 119 and 121.

[49] "The Relationship to the Text," *Style and Idea*, 144.

It could be argued that Schoenberg is exaggerating when he claims how little is needed for the whole to be comprehended. It should, however, be kept in mind that Schoenberg is not referring to the wholeness of a character with *all aspects* of its concrete appearance. Rather, he is drawing attention to something characteristic that is so fundamental that it *represents* the whole. Therefore, it is not the human appearance that is understood as a whole but something central to it—its "life-giving blood" or its "nature." Schoenberg's metaphors are examples of the way in which he views fundamental features as representative of artistic wholeness.

Schoenberg's use of the term *musikalisches Gebilde* (musical formation) leads to associations with music that is designed, created, and molded. This is connected to his understanding of a living *Zentral- oder Gesamtkörper* (a body that is whole and centrally controlled)[50] which refers to music as a vital body and an organism. The identification between the idea of the centrally controlled musical body and the consummated form of a musical composition may appear obvious, but for Schoenberg, the form rather grows out of the composite of members. When he uses the term *Gesamtkörper* he emphasizes the supreme principle that both keeps the members together and defines their respective functions. A *Grundgestalt*, a motive or theme, may make up the *Gesamtkörper* of a piece. It is possible to consider such entities as representative of the whole, because "in music only the whole itself is this centrally controlled body."[51] A musical motive can thus represent a complete musical work. If a motive is imagined as the smallest building stone or the modest seed, the necessary consequence must be that it bears within itself the whole. The motive represents a principle that in the fulfilled musical work appears in a fully developed form. This insight is also fundamental for Sullivan's focus on what he terms "the germ: the seat of power."

In Schoenberg's opinion, even tonality can be considered a centrally controlled musical body. In this context he points out that a fundamental tone in itself would be relatively lifeless if it did not contain the centrifugal and centripetal forces of its overtones. These endow the tone with life, and subsequently channel functions to the organs. "It lies in its nature to allow the forces that are unified and contained in it to develop and strive away from each other, just as it lies in their nature to do [the same]," he says—reminiscent of Hindemith expressions—and continues:

> Thus they become members, thus they perform functions, thus they independently go their own ways, in which neither another member nor the whole body participates. Yet, thus, they must be also inde-

---

[50]See *The Musical Idea,* 121.

[51]The Musical Idea, 127.

> pendent, able to detach themselves completely from the context and to prove themselves able to breathe and to lead an independent existence.[52]

If music is to be compared to a living being, then the same life principles must also apply, Schoenberg says, and gives the following concise example of his elaborate reasoning:

> [...] a subordinate theme could never have been a principle theme. A G major arising from a C major piece could never stand on its own.[53]

Schoenberg admits to the problematic implications in the above description by characterizing it as a purely logical and ideal conclusion. Practical examples are certainly difficult to find, the main reason being that an entire musical piece cannot be experienced at one and the same time. We encounter it in the form of small sections: while we may perceive a contrasting trio in a minuet as a piece in itself, we are being led into a blind alley when it comes to experiencing the actual musical work. It would be like believing that a hand represents the entire human being in a concrete sense:

> But let us not confuse our ability to infer a man from his hand, for example, or from his handwriting, with the true relationship of members to the whole. For if the hand did in fact express the man completely, why the entire man?[54]

One objection to this statement may be that precisely the representational potential of a limb seems to belong to the essence of Schoenberg's logico-constructive thought: as part of a living entity the member adequately represents the whole. When Schoenberg uses this example, his point is to focus on a hand disconnected from the body, in the same way as the trio is experienced as not attached to the minuet. Such a disassociated member could not represent the organism from which it is separated, since the organism's life does not flow through it. A full comprehension of music must always involve a musical whole. The musical *work* is the focus—as it finally emerges as the concrete manifestation of a totality. This process of musical recognition is certainly not simple for everyone, Schoenberg admits. The musical piece is experienced in time and bit by bit; only a very few are able to comprehend it as a whole. Hindemith's belief is that at any rate, the human ear will orientate itself according to the basic principles of tonality. For Schoenberg, the human experience of a logical construction is given this

---

[52] *The Musical Idea,* 121.

[53] *The Musical Idea,* 123.

[54] *The Musical Idea,* 123.

kind of an elevated status. The preconditions for experiencing totality lie in what he describes as "a very precise knowledge of the whole, and all its parts and their functions."[55] This implies something beyond an intuitive experience of basic features; Schoenberg is talking about an active and conscious logico-musical process of recognition. For a complete experience of the music it is crucial to grasp the principles by which the piece is realized, since the composer's conception of the individual work originates in the whole.

Schoenberg's ideas on the musical organism are indeed complex, as is his concept of the musical whole. At times his way of presentation even seems inconsistent, owing to his attempts to mediate the complexity of his concept in written form. His challenge is thus primarily to find a balance between instantiation and abstraction. In his distinctive use of metaphor Schoenberg expresses himself quite plainly about body and members, organs and blood. Translated into a musical context, however, it is his understanding of the more abstract principles that is important: initially the work is conceived as an organic whole, then the members realize it. The organic body—which gives the members life and holds them together—is made up of the superordinate principles of the piece. In explaining this view Schoenberg's main problem is that the organism metaphor covers both the concrete manifestation of the work in question and the construction principles on which it is based. But when all is said and done, it is precisely this complexity that is at the heart of his ideas.

"Methods of delivering the idea may change in their external form,"[56] says Schoenberg. A key to his more tangible understanding of form lies in his conviction that the musico-logical elaboration of the members of an organism constitutes the connecting link between the *Gedanke*, in the sense of a musical whole, and the musical form. If *das Ganze* and *der Gesamtkörper* are to be recognized with the help of *form*, then form must be comprehensible.

Form, Comprehensibility, and Coherence

"Form, in the arts, and especially in music, aims primarily at comprehensibility," says Schoenberg.[57] This assertion leads back to one of the key concepts in his understanding of music: comprehensibility or *Faßlichkeit*. Schoenberg is convinced that comprehending art is closely related to realizing beauty:

---

[55] *The Musical Idea*, 125.

[56] "On the Question of Modern Composition Teaching," *Style and Idea*, 376.

[57] "Composition with Twelve Tones (1)," *Style and Idea*, 215.

> The relaxation which a satisfied listener experiences when he can follow an idea, its development, and the reasons for such development is closely related, psychologically speaking, to a feeling of beauty.[58]

It should be emphasized that this close relationship between comprehensibility and beauty does not suggest any real identification. Neither is beauty the objective of form. Form in itself, says Schoenberg, has nothing to do with beauty. The objective of form is to promote understanding, but "though the object of form is not beauty, by providing comprehensibility, form produces beauty." In an attempt to further clarify this relationship, he continues: "An apple tree does not exist in order to give us apples, but it produces them nevertheless."[59]

The concept of artistic value depends on comprehensibility, which thus becomes the underpinning of both intellectual and emotional satisfaction. Despite the fruit metaphor for beauty, Schoenberg still does not see the aspects of beauty as an *immediate* result of comprehensibility:

> Evenness, regularity, symmetry, subdivision, repetition, unity, relationship in rhythm and harmony and even logic—none of these elements produces or even contributes to beauty. But all of them contribute to an organization which makes the presentation of the musical idea intelligible.[60]

Does Schoenberg contradict himself with these reservations? His point is that the use of the traditional structural element does not automatically result in beauty, however much they may contribute to comprehensibility. This is reminiscent of Plato's concept of beauty, which includes both what is *truthful* and *good*. The connection between what appears as truthful, functional, and aesthetically fulfilled is a substantial part of the functionalist understanding of art. For Schoenberg, comprehensibility can never guarantee the quality of a musical work. It is never possible to ignore the crucial question of the way in which the different means of composition are being used. Once again one may turn to Hindemith, who rejected the view that the alleged categories "good music" and "bad music" were based on theoretical considerations, regarding them rather as dependent on a number of additional criteria. Schoenberg's refusal to equate rationally based comprehensibility with beauty must be understood in light of his belief that artistic logic differs from scientific logic. This does not prevent him from referring to what he calls the "laws of comprehensibility" (*Gesetze der Faßlichkeit*), which again imply the need for logic to be present in comprehensibility itself.

---

[58]Ibid.

[59]"Eartraining through Composing," *Style and Idea*, 380.

[60]"Brahms the Progressive," *Style and Idea*, 399.

Schoenberg's understanding of form can be compared to that of Loos, and the emphasis on the importance of formal comprehensibility also brings Le Corbusier's purism to mind. What Schoenberg thought about the human ability to associate and identify with what is *formed* makes this connection even clearer. Schoenberg's conviction is particularly striking in his brief and concise comments contained under the title "Theory of Form." The introduction begins as follows:

> A theory of form would have to aim, first and foremost, at showing the significance of all artistic forms—the fact that they try to endow the artistic product (whose shape is conditioned by a material extrinsic to ourselves) with an external and internal constitution permitting us to recognize it as something that corresponds to the quality of our intellect. Through its relationship, analogy with, similarity to other things we think, feel and sense, we are able to grasp it as similar to us, appropriate to us, and related to us. So one must show how the material, against or in accordance with its own aim, is forced by art —by fulfilling the demands of comprehensibility—to adapt itself to such conditions.[61]

The parallel to Le Corbusier lies in the correspondence of the artistic form and the human recognition arising from fundamental experiences such as recognition and identification. Epistemologically, Schoenberg does not move in the same Neo-Platonic direction as Le Corbusier. A deeper identification process is definitely taking place in the course of the perception of a musical form, but this process goes by way of the intellect, which, for Schoenberg, represents human beings' second nature. For Le Corbusier, identification goes through the profound recognition of the universal lawfulness of existence. His certainty presupposes that recognition of the beauty of fundamental forms belongs to human beings' *first* nature.

Schoenberg believes that artistic comprehensibility can be constructed through musical logic. Ratiocinative procedures and compositional craft thus become highly important, leading him out of the romantic sphere into a more rational, functionalist context. The idea that artistic comprehensibility can be presented normatively underscores this position: "The laws of comprehensibility must be understood with especial precision and strictness because of the difficulties inherent in music."[62]

In *The Musical Idea* Schoenberg lists the main points of these "laws."[63] It could be argued that it might be somewhat pretentious, and even unjust, to

---

[61] "Theory of Form," *Style and Idea*, 253.

[62] *The Musical Idea*, 132.

[63] *The Musical Idea*, 132-143.

grant this section from one of Schoenberg's published draft the status of a codex. His presentation is more in the nature of a list of ideas or issues, with each point functioning as a lead-in to further systematization and a later development into a final book version. The presence of overlapping and repetition support such a conjecture. Yet the importance of certain statements that may seem self-evident should not be underestimated. They reveal that Schoenberg's emphasis even stretches to details pertaining to the premises for the human ability to comprehend the art of music. They also reflect his confident anchoring in tradition. Although Schoenberg did not categorize his points into larger groups, a four-group structure is quite evident. The first point is as follows (rendered, as always, with Schoenberg's own emphasis):

> I. What is stated only once cannot be understood as *important*.

Schoenberg begins with an assertion that sounds like an echo from Wittgenstein's *Tractatus*, which is not to imply that Wittgenstein would have endorsed such a proposition about language and repetition. In points I-VI Schoenberg concentrates on the regularity that aims to ensure the understanding of, and division between, "primary" and "secondary" elements, or, as he puts it in his native language, *Hauptsachen* and *Nebensachen*.

The second group opens with:

> VI.[64] The *presentation of the idea* will have to suit the *powers of comprehension* of the intended listener [...]

In points VI-IX, he enumerates some fundamental traits in the human faculty of listening, suggesting how the composer must take these capacities into consideration. Such concerns are to be found throughout the codex. In this segment, they apply to the question of tempo in which the thoughts are presented, to how the listener understands their relevance in relation to the whole, and so on.

Schoenberg subsequently directs the presentation towards the comprehensibility of the various components of a musical form:

> X. This consideration of comprehensibility is even more important in the *smaller components of form* than in the larger [...]

In points X-XVII he refers to comprehensibility of components such as basic motive (*Grundmotiv*), *Gestalten*, phrases, sentences (*Sätze*), and themes. These concepts will be discussed later. In a wide-ranging point XVIII he concentrates on a comprehensibility that is based on components that create coherence. "We call the methods used here *connective technique,* and speak

---

[64]Schoenberg has numbered erroneously by repeating the number VI.

of *linking methods,*" he says. This is the only place where he explains his notions by referring to specific musical compositions, from his own *First Chamber Symphony* to excerpts from the oeuvre of Mozart, Brahms, and Schumann.

In the final group, points XIX–XXII, Schoenberg focuses on the forms most easily comprehended. His last point is:

> XXII. The *dance forms* are among the simplest forms. For example, the waltz of earlier composers repeats the beginning phrase with small, insignificant alterations, usually three or four times, often six or seven times. Hence the popular effect [...].

The conclusion of Schoenberg's draft is thus a focus on the unique comprehensibility of musical standard forms. He places dance forms, with their rhythmic patterns and repetitions, among the most intelligible musical forms. The key terms are memory, cognition, and recognition.

Schoenberg favors using the word *Erkennen*, which denotes cognition, recognition, understanding, and even judgment—a scope of meaning that should be kept in mind when encountering this noun. "The ability to recognize depends very largely upon familiarity with related, similar, or like objects," he writes.[65] Anyone familiar only with a cat will mistake a tiger, leopard, panther, or lynx for an unusually large cat. "Consequently in many ways recognition (*Erkennen*) is re-recognition (*Wiedererkennen*)," he maintains, continuing:

> This is so even where a (relatively) new object is involved whose (old) constituent elements are familiar and can be recognized. To recognize new parts or a new kind of combination is perhaps more difficult; in the former case (new parts) the possibility of comparison is lacking, whereas for the latter purpose familiarity with other types of combinations is necessary.[66]

Schoenberg's occasional use of traditional forms, such as his *Suite für Klavier* (*Suite for Piano*), op. 25, must be understood in this light. The application of standard forms does not imply a return to the past, nor is it like pouring new wine into old caskets, which the Neo-Classical composers have been accused of doing. Nevertheless, Schoenberg's use of basic forms has often been seen as regression. For Schoenberg's pupil Hanns Eisler, his teacher's use of the supposedly "old forms" confirms his thesis that Schoenberg is the so-called true conservative, who even goes so far as to start a

---

[65] *The Musical Idea*, 145.
[66] Ibid.

revolution to become reactionary: Schoenberg's thoughts seem to proceed from tonal liberation and back to formal schemata.[67] Adorno also discusses this phase of the composer's development in an article on Schoenberg's *Bläserquintett* op. 26, which will be discussed later. Adorno regards the sonata form in this quintet as a regression, a return in circular motion from Schoenberg's earlier liberation from traditional form types, or, as he puts it: "Schoenberg's path has returned to the sonata in a spiral."[68] In his essay "Schoenberg est mort," Pierre Boulez stresses that there is a hiatus between the "discovery" of the twelve-tone method and Schoenberg's use of traditional forms:

> Since the pre-classical or classical forms that determine most of his architectures were, historically speaking, in no way connected to the discovery of dodecaphony, there is an inadmissible divide between the infrastructures relating to tonality and a language in which the organizational laws are perceived only summarily.[69]

Schoenberg's plan went awry, maintains Boulez. The twelve-tone method and musical forms transmitted by history are two worlds that have nothing in common.

Schoenberg himself does not share this perspective on the use of traditional form. For him, strengthening the comprehensibility of music is always a crucial challenge. He speaks of so-called old forms without considering them antiquarian. On the contrary, traditional forms are recognizable and may therefore be particularly suitable in new music:

> The old forms in the new music—their employment is so absolutely justified, and accord with my opinion of comprehensibility: When comprehensibility is made more difficult on the one hand, it must be made easier on the other.[70]

---

[67] See H. Eisler, "Arnold Schoenberg, der musikalische Reaktionär," *Arnold Schoenberg zum fünfzigsten Geburtstage*, 312-313.

[68] Th.W. Adorno, "Schönbergs Bläserquintett," *Moments musicaux* [*Musikalische Schriften* IV, *Gesammelte Schriften* 17] (Frankfurt a. M.: Suhrkamp, 1982), 144.

[69] P. Boulez, "Schoenberg est mort," in Paule Thévenin, ed., *Relevés d'apprenti* (Paris : Éditions du Seuil, 1966), 269. ["Les formes préclassiques qui régissent la plupart de ses architectures n'étant, historiquement, aucunement liées à la découverte dodécaphonique, il se produit un hiatus inadmissible entre des infrastructures rattachées au phénomène tonal et un langage dont on perçoit encore sommairement les lois d'organisation."]

[70] Translated from a note from 1927 reproduced in R. Stephan, "Adorno und Hindemith. Zum Verständnis einer schwierigen Beziehung," *Hindemith-Jahrbuch* 1978/VII, 27. ["Die alte Formen in der neuen Musik—ihre Anwendung ist durchaus berechtigt und stimmt zu dem von mir aufgestellten Satz über die Faßlichkeit: Wenn die Faßlichkeit auf der einen Seite erschwert wird, muß sie auf einer anderen erleichtert werden."]

Since standard forms are no longer considered as formulas or crutches, as he suggested in the above-mentioned letter to Kandinsky, Schoenberg sees no reason whatsoever to conceal their direct or indirect use. He even distances himself from the view that he had once been such an innovator of musical form. Much of the supposed renewal was actually connected to traditional forms and well-established principles:

> [...] many of the forms which I was supposedly the first to use in our time will surely be found to have been used by others long before me [...]—if they did not indeed occur in earlier centuries. For example, in my *Pierrot Lunaire*, the dance forms (waltz and polka) and contrapuntal studies (passacaglia, double-fugue with canon and retrograde of the canon, etc.), the pieces for solo instruments (*Der kranke Mond*) and for singing and reciting voice, with accompaniment for various instruments, for which I was cautious enough not to invent the title "chamber-music songs."[71]

In declaring comprehensibility to be the chief objective of form, Schoenberg allies himself with the dominant representatives of the development in architecture and design. Through his use of traditional forms, which is particularly prominent during the 1920s, he tunes in to the general views of structural norms held in his time. His understanding of musical form thus becomes an integral part of the functionalist context. However, geometrical —presumably universal—forms and musical standard forms represent very different phenomena. Musical forms result from the cultivated compositional procedures within a limited cultural context. During this process they have achieved the status of basic forms in the trained composer's repertoire and become second nature for musicians and listeners. Consequently, they contribute to cognition, recognition, and comprehensibility. At this point, Schoenberg's and Le Corbusier's understandings of form are comparable, as they both posit a fundamental recognition of form which requires a deeper human identification. Hindemith also shares this insight.

Nonetheless, Schoenberg's profound sense of artistic sincerity does not give him license to compose music uncritically according to traditional patterns. For example, the principles of the baroque fugue should be treated with caution as they have already had their ultimate accomplishment in earlier times:

> Composing of these [contrapuntal] forms in which the highest achievement has already been reached by composers whose form of expression was that of contrapuntal combinations—composing of these forms should only be undertaken for some special reason.[72]

---

[71]"The Young and I," *Style and Idea*, 93-94.

[72]"Composition with Twelve Tones (2)," *Style and Idea*, 248.

One should only venture into the enterprise of traditional, contrapuntal writing in cases where the aim is a certain temporal reference, and "[t]here are certainly few reasons which might oblige a composer to compete with those *hors-concours* achievements of such great masters, whose native language was counterpoint."[73]

When Schoenberg discusses musical standard forms in a didactic context, as in *Fundamentals of Musical Composition*, he places himself in a conventional mode. He refers to terms signifying the number of sections: binary or ternary form, rondo form, and so on. In the sonata form, proportions and more complex interrelations are in focus, he claims, while in dance forms the main focus is on meter, tempo, and rhythm. However, he constantly points to the variation possibilities within a standard form. He is not content with choosing textbook examples, but rather finds the exceptions to be the interesting facet.

In *The Musical Idea,* Schoenberg also discusses the structural functions of harmony. To introduce a comprehensive chapter on this subject, he writes:

> Harmony is by no means a merely accidental addition to the melody, serving no better purpose than to accompany the melody and to lend a better "coloration" to particular melodic points. On the contrary, harmony fulfills structural purposes; that is to say, it is the framework and, indeed, probably the blueprint of every musical edifice, and everything that happens in a piece through motivic development, variation, elaboration, and thematic work results not only through the participation and the effect of harmony but in particular as a direct consequence of its function.[74]

Musical harmony is a highly important form-structuring element. But more importantly in the functionalist context is the idea of comprehensibility: "[t]he chief requirements for the creation of a comprehensible form are logic and coherence,"[75] Schoenberg maintains. This statement leads back to his fundamental concept of coherence (*Zusammenhang*): If we are to comprehend a work of art, we need to look beyond the work at large and examine both the big and small structural components. Principles that are based on rationality are all important; in *The Musical Idea* Schoenberg states that he can reveal the laws of musical coherence.[76] Like comprehensibility, coherence is also seen from a *logos* perspective. What, then, is the difference between logic and coherence? It could be assumed that Schoenberg's view of musical

---

[73]"Composition with Twelve Tones (2)," *Style and Idea*, 249.

[74]*The Musical Idea*, 309.

[75]*Fundamentals of Musical Composition*, 1.

[76]*The Musical Idea*, 147-161.

Schoenberg: From Gedanke to Form

coherence is based on logic. Initially, this assumption is justified: coherence is really a precondition for musical logic. However, with respect to comprehensibility, there are cases where logic is not sufficient as a cohesive force. Schoenberg's explanation is that a real recognition of musical coherence is something that occurs in the dialectics between the material and the listener's physical and mental disposition. "The limits of comprehensibility are not the limits of coherence, which can be present even where comprehensibility has ceased,"[77] he claims. Perhaps there is coherence beyond human consciousness, in other words: musical connections may be found outside the immediate sphere of human awareness. Consequently, Schoenberg admits that comprehensibility in itself is also a *relative* phenomenon. Aspects of musical time may undermine comprehensibility: a sequence of tones based on logic may be too rapid for genuine coherence to be heard. The possibility of experiencing coherence, and thereby comprehensibility itself, is thus eliminated. The same can occur if the time sequence is too slow, which means that we need certain premises for musical coherence to be established. If just anything were put together to form a musical sequence, the result might be the same as when "a strip of paper is glued to a piece of cork; a chicken feather is glued to this, to which a nail is tied with string,"[78] Schoenberg elucidates. While some might see a hidden polemic towards Dadaist expression here, the description is probably rather an example of the composer's anti-romantic use of metaphors. Schoenberg's main point is that artistic coherence must be based on connective relations between the parts, and these connections and transitions must never invite criticism of superficiality.

"*Related or similar things can be brought into connection with one another* because they have coherence," Schoenberg says, and

> [t]he possibility of connecting tones to one another is based on the fact that they are related to one another. They cohere with one another [...] through common fundamental tones.[79]

Corresponding thoughts are also found in Hindemith's writings. Schoenberg considers the coherence between tones, rhythms, and harmonies so fundamental that it contributes to the constitution of a musical form, since "[t]he formulation of such connections will lead to recognition of *structural principles*."[80] Hence, creating musical coherence is the most important ingredient in Schoenberg's logic-based concept of compositional construction.

---

[77] *Coherence, Counterpoint* ..., 9.

[78] *Coherence, Counterpoint* ..., 61.

[79] *The Musical Idea*, 147.

[80] *Coherence, Counterpoint* ..., 7.

The resulting artistic comprehensibility is based on recognizing similarities, a recognition that is synonymous with understanding:

> *Understanding = recognition of similarity*
> [...]
> 1. *Understanding* is based on the capacity to recognize the similarity among the components to things that are familiar.
> 2. The presupposition for this *recognition of similarity* is the capacity of memory: to remember the new and old components.[81]

The concept of musical understanding is thus a rational phenomenon based on intellectual recognition of the principles that structure musical form. By focusing on constructional coherence he turns away from romantic notions of artistic creation and looks towards the rationality aesthetics of the 20th century.

When Schoenberg speaks of coherence, the concept of *gestalt* is highly significant. Recognizing a musical *gestalt*—a figure, shape, or formation—is fundamentally important for comprehensibility. The experience of a *gestalt* may suffer with too high or too low tempi: "*A succession of tones without regard to duration is in itself hardly conceivable.*"[82] The greatest coherence is between two tones of the same pitch, but tonal repetition alone still does not generate a musical *gestalt*. The same can be said of tones of identical note values. To understand Schoenberg's considerations on this point, his view of *motion* as a fundamental concept must be taken into account. His definition of a motive as "something that gives rise to a motion," and such statements as "one can compare the motive with a driving force," express such a view.[83] Equal note values favor stagnation rather than movement; Schoenberg considers the connection of similar elements as unfruitful.[84]

Schoenberg's understanding of genuine musical coherence is thus dependent on a certain variation of pitch, rhythm, and intensity. A musical motive satisfies these aspects of variation, it is the common denominator of a piece, and therefore becomes the key to creating coherence.[85] Through the motive one even finds the main key to music as an art form:

---

[81] *Coherence, Counterpoint* ..., 11 and 15.

[82] See *The Musical Idea*, 147.

[83] *Coherence, Counterpoint* ..., 27.

[84] In *The Musical Idea,* considerable parts of which were written just after Schoenberg's emigration to the U.S., he comments on this connection with an ironic reminder of his own situation as a Jew in one of history's darkest periods: "*The joining of like kinds is unfruitful* (racial purity). We shall see how far the Germans get with this." [June 11, 1934] *The Musical Idea*, 149.

[85] Ibid.

> Musical art, after all, consists of producing large and small images, which cohere by means of this motive, which in their individual contents likewise cohere with it, and which are assembled so that the *logic* of the total image is as apparent as that of its single parts and of their combination. This logic rests on the meaningful and purposeful exploitation of musical coherences with a view to the total goal.[86]

Schoenberg admits that he has problems defining the "total goal" to which he refers in musical terms, as the aim is not a real and tangible one but rather rooted in the imagination. His thoughts have thus led him to the point where the foundation of his view of a musical creation process based on logic seems to be in doubt. And his considerations are complicated indeed: He seeks an explanation through the metaphor of one beginning a journey with the aim of getting to India and in the worst scenario ending up by discovering America. The aim may be wrong where the way is right, and vice versa. His conclusion is: "[f]or this reason it is impossible to speak of setting a unifying a priori goal in music, and likewise impossible to speak of a conscious logical striving toward such a goal."[87] Schoenberg is pointing out that there may be a dividing line between the vision of the whole and the final, concrete result: The sounding work is the consequence of a logical process whose guiding star was the *vision,* but this insight does not imply that work and vision are identical. Within such a perspective Schoenberg sees the problem of defining the goal, which has been the directive for the creative process, according to the technical terms of the final result. His reservations thus do not conflict with his thoughts on artistic conception and logic, the problem lies in the complexity of artistic mediacy.

Schoenberg attributes to the motive the status and substance as a forming constituent, and motion is one of the motive's main characteristics: "We know that in the *motive* there must be present a certain *unrest* that will give rise to further motion."[88] The innate unrest of a motive sets a movement in motion, and what follows must, according to the laws of coherence, be related to this motive. What proceeds must have in part the same content as what went before. As Schoenberg considers the immediate and plain repetition of music's fundamental components unfruitful, variation becomes a vital compositional device, "that form of repetition in which a number of the constituents are repeated without a change, while a number of others are omitted and possibly replaced by different components."[89] This idea leads to

---

[86]Ibid.

[87]Ibid.

[88]*The Musical Idea*, 153.

[89]*The Musical Idea*, 155.

the principles of *developing variation* and the vast possibilities of a musical motive. The list of potential quoted in the previous discussion on the musical material should thus be supplemented with the principles of *permutation* (*Umlagerung*). Variation procedures generate new elements that must also relate in some way to the initial motive.

Bearing in mind Schoenberg's statement that what is said only once cannot be considered important, the fundamental principles of repetition are significant when creating a musical coherence. In *The Musical Idea* he distinguishes various categories of repetition.[90] His main points are:

1. "The most primitive coherence-producing forms of repetition" are found by means of a repeat sign in traditional forms like sonatas, dances, rondos, and so on. Repetitions with re-instrumentation or octave transpositions belong to the same category.
2. In "slightly varied repetitions," the accompaniment has been changed, the upper voice is partly ornamented, and so on.
3. "Somewhat more richly varied repetitions" are created by means of harmonic alterations, metric changes in the main voice, variations in contrapuntal procedures, and in all other cases where variations affect the structure in a more fundamental way.
4. "Sequences" represent an intermediate form in this context, combining the fundamental idea of unvaried repetition with the displacement to a new tonal level and thus often resulting in modulation.

Through these categories, Schoenberg focuses attention on the potential of repetition as a developmental device. Musical sequencing is a textbook example of such a procedure. There are also cases where there is a reversing effect, as there may be developments where the connection with a starting-point is revealed only gradually:

> A very significant degree of remoteness from the initial *gestalt* is to be found in those variations that introduce a subordinate idea. Often their connection to the *grundgestalt* (frequently an indirect one) becomes clear very late. As a rule these *gestalten* develop forward hardly at all but rather backward: they approach the initial *gestalt*.[91]

Schoenberg also points to the possibility that new musical characteristics (*Eigenschaften*) can be introduced, for instance, when some of the already present traits are definitively discarded. Perhaps the objective is to let these "new" characteristics appear as purely temporary, or the aim could be to develop them, disregarding what has gone before. Such techniques can be particularly useful in transitions, introductions, episodes, or so-called preparations.

---

[90] See *The Musical Idea*, 157-161.
[91] *The Musical Idea*, 159.

Schoenberg: From Gedanke *to* Form

The *logos* on which Schoenberg's laws of musical coherence are based is thus founded on the following construction principles:
1. The starting-point is the motive, which is sufficiently characteristic to initiate a musical motion.
2. The further development procedures are based on the conscious employment of the relationships definable at various levels of the musical structure.
3. The two most important construction principles are found in the dialectics between repetition and variation.

A sounding work emerges in a musical design that agrees with these principles, which all relate to compositional logic and comprehensibility. And musical form is created when the organism's limbs or members are connected in accordance with the basic, life-giving principles of the centrally controlled body.

Elements of Form

"Man's mental limitations prevent him from grasping anything which is too extended," says Schoenberg in *Fundamentals of Musical Composition*. "Thus appropriate subdivision facilitates understanding and determines the *form*."[92] The main reason for the constituting subdivisions of a musical form is, again, that they increase comprehensibility. Human possibilities of identification with a work through its form are still in focus, and here—as with Loos and Le Corbusier—lie the possibilities for deeper aesthetic recognition. In Schoenberg's discussions on form, the view of music as an organism is always present:

> Generally, the larger the piece, the greater the number of parts. But sometimes a short piece may have the same number of parts as a longer one, just as a midget has the same number of limbs, the same form, as a giant.[93]

Though Schoenberg is pointing to the logical and structural unity of a work of music, the contrastive principles are essential for experiencing the constituents of a form—particularly in an extensive composition. Contrasts produce formal components and large forms develop through the generating power of contrasts. The possibilities are numerous, and the need for such devices increases in proportion with the dimensions of a work: "the larger the piece, the more types of contrast should be present to illuminate the main

---
[92] *Fundamentals of Musical Composition*, 1.

[93] *Fundamentals of Musical Composition*, 1.

idea."[94] Schoenberg discusses both the general characteristics of traditional form types and concrete examples from music history in this perspective. Yet he does not see contrast as the counterpart of coherence. On the contrary: he states that contrast *presupposes* coherence. A contrast that breaks coherence can be tolerated in so-called descriptive music, but there is certainly no place for it in a well-organized form. His general conclusion is: "Contrasting sections, therefore, must utilize the same processes by which motive-forms are connected in simpler formulations."[95] In other words, coherence must reach through the contrasts on one level or another; even elements pertaining to contrasts must be related to the motive.

Schoenberg's skepticism to the use of the term "part" for the constituents of a musical work has already been mentioned. His reservation does not, however, prevent him from finding it useful in practice, particularly where larger and relatively integrated elements of a work are concerned. He uses terms like limbs and members when his purpose is to describe the work as an organism, but seldom when he is being analytical in a more traditional sense. Accordingly, in *The Musical Idea* he employs terms such as parts (*Teile*) and components (*Bestandteile*). "Elements of form" (*Formelemente*) is a more general term that includes diverse items that make up form. Otherwise, Schoenberg rarely uses the term "work" or "musical work," seeming to prefer "piece" (*Stück*). "Piece" is already being used in several contexts, he says, but then admits: "if a term other than symphony or sonata were really to become necessary, one would have to use the term *work*."[96]

Schoenberg's presentation of the elements of form immediately reveals what he regards as the logically based components of musical construction.[97] He terms the main divisions of a piece as part (*Teil*) and sentence (*Satz*) respectively; subdivisions are given the collective term "smaller components" (*kleinere Bestandteile*). "Parts" (*Teile*) is used in composite words, above all in connection with main (*Haupt-*), subordinate (*Neben-*), development (*Durchführungs-*), closing (*Schluss-*), and transition (*Überleitung-*). Schoenberg declares that the term *Satz* has several connotations in English, as in first movement (*erster Satz*), choral movement (*Choralsatz*), and so on. However, when speaking of the setting of a choral movement and piano movement, Schoenberg prefers *Setzung* or *Setzweise* (setting or manner of

---

[94] *Fundamentals of Musical Composition*, 178.

[95] *Fundamentals of Musical Composition*, 119.

[96] *The Musical Idea*, 173.

[97] The present section is primarily based on pages 163-175 of *The Musical Idea*, Schoenberg's most systematic examination of this field.

setting) instead of *Satz*, "whereby the first designates the complex, and the latter, the mode."[98] In other words, *Setzung* describes the medium while *Setzweise* represents the way the setting is handled. In a systematic context he also terms the movements in a symphony, for example, as *Stücke* (pieces), as in "*1., 2.*and *3. Stück*." He does so because *Teil*, the term he otherwise would have used, has other connotations, and because he has chosen to employ *Satz* very restrictively in parallel to its linguistic usage:

> I shall use *Satz* to designate only that certain component of form that, through the parallel use in *Vordersatz,* * *Nachsatz,* * *Seitensatz,* * and *Schluss-Satz,* * etc., is characterized as "sentence" in contrast to the period and the *above-mentioned compounds.[99]

Schoenberg's use of the term *Satz* (as sentence) comes close to what is usually understood as "theme," which he agrees may constitute a *Satz*. Yet these terms are not synonymous: *Satz* signals a statement (as suggested above) understood as a relatively self-supporting sentence within a larger whole.

Associated constituents such as motives and phrases are called "smaller components," leading on to the nuances in the diversity of formal elements. According to Aristotelian terminology, a motive would represent both material consistence and a form's *energeia*. As mentioned above, Schoenberg also operates with a concept called the "features of a motive." Such features constitute the smallest structural elements in a musical piece, although they cannot be extricated from the motive itself. The "features" will always be part of the motive's characteristics and will subsequently represent it.

In looking at the motive as a structural element, Schoenberg's descriptions in *The Musical Idea* particularly focus on the fact that a musical motive contains unique form-constituting possibilities. The motive is always the smallest component of a piece or of one of the sections in that piece. Furthermore, it occurs everywhere in a work and is continuously recognizable, despite all changes and variations, and

> [u]pon this alone does the *expansion* of a motive depend, even though one can occasionally assume that the motive will not make use of its full expansion. In reference to its use a motive will be designated as a complex of interconnected features with regard to intervals, rhythm, character, dynamic, stress, metric placement, etc. One must also recognize in the motive indications for its use, for the *manner of its development,* for *variational possibilities,* for "*line,*" etc., etc. The motive is *independent of the phrasing*.[100]

---

[98] *The Musical Idea*, 173.
[99] Ibid.
[100] *The Musical Idea,* 169 and 171.

The *gestalt* represents the next level in a formal construction. A *gestalt* is a unity in which the motive is represented more than once, "in a breath," as Schoenberg expresses it, yet "without possessing the peculiarity of the phrase in performance: in the same breath—caesura."[101] A *gestalt* usually consists of various forms of the motive, but may also consist of nothing but a motivic chain. To live up to its name, a *gestalt* must contain uniquely characteristic features. Intervals and rhythms are the most important structural elements here as well. A *gestalt* does not necessarily need to have more than local significance. If it has more broad-reaching constructive consequences, it is termed *Grundgestalt*.[102]

According to Michael Beiche, the use of the term *Grundgestalt* in musical terminology as an expression of "a formation that is at the foundation of a work" can be traced back to 1922. In reference to Schoenberg, he points to a somewhat later usage in the meaning of "an musical unit situated [with regard to size and impact] between motive and phrase."[103] It is uncertain whether the term was first coined in connection with the twelve-tone method, or whether it was introduced in other, earlier contexts. Neither is it certain if there is any direct relation between the musical term and the emergence of the *gestalt* concept in psychology. Schoenberg's own concise definition in *The Musical Idea* is as follows:

> *Grundgestalten* are such gestalten as (possibly) occur repeatedly within a whole piece and to which derived gestalten can be traced back.[104]

This does not mean that "motive" and "basic *gestalt*" can be taken as synonyms: A *gestalt* will normally be a composite of several motivic forms, and the motive is always the smallest component. In the twelve-tone method the term *Grundgestalt* can be given other meanings, which will be discussed later.

There are also formations that do not have basic constructional consequences, so-called "figures" (*Figuren*).[105] These have much in common with *gestalten*, since the motive can be present in both. The chief difference is that a *gestalt* is experienced as unique even when repeated. The figure, on the

---

[101] *The Musical Idea*, 169.

[102] The German word *Grundgestalt* does not easily translate into English. "A basic *gestalt*/shape" may serve as an explanation.

[103] M. Beiche, "Grundgestalt," *Terminologie der Musik im 20. Jahrhundert*, 175. ["... das einer Komposition zugrunde liegende Gebilde [...] eine zwischen Motiv und Phrase angeordnete musikalische Einheit."]

[104] *The Musical Idea*, 169.

[105] See *The Musical Idea*, 368-369.

other hand, is without structural obligations even when repeated, and any repetitions may be freer than in the other smaller structural components. In this somewhat diffuse delineation, Schoenberg's main point is anchored in part in the element's degree of characteristic features and in part in its structural consequences.

The next levels of construction are "phrase" (*Phrase*) and the various types of "sentences" (*Sätze*).[106] Schoenberg uses phrase purely from a compositional and not from an interpretative perspective. *Phrase* and *Satz* are not identical: "Something called *Satz* will most surely consist of more than two *phrases*."[107] A phrase may appear as a combination of *gestalt* and motivic transformations; Schoenberg even suggests as a simplified definition: "A phrase usually consists of more than one form of the basic motive. Sometimes a phrase is used like a motive."[108] What, then, is the difference between *gestalt* and phrase? According to Schoenberg, a *gestalt*, which is characterized by its distinguishing articulation, becomes a phrase "if it is like a part of speech, perhaps in the raising and lowering of the voice, and so forth."[109] In *Fundamentals of Musical Composition* he treats the phrase as the smallest structural unit, in the sense that it represents a totality of musical occurrences easily combined with other musical events. Even here he admits the close connection to the phrase as a concept of both composition and interpretation: "The term *phrase* means, structurally, a unit approximating to what one could sing in a single breath."[110] Whenever Schoenberg refers to "breath caesura" (*Atem-Cäsur*) in connection with *gestalt*, he is not so much thinking of the concrete presentation of a song but of the more abstract, yet subjective, experience of a limited whole not necessarily marked in such a way in a score.

The points related above are all focused on the small components within musical *themes*. Theme represents the next level in Schoenberg's structural hierarchy. A theme can be made up of periods, sentences (*Sätze*), or chains of sentences (*Satzketten*). In his usage of the term "period," he tends toward the traditional view of the usually eight-measure, non-repeated, caesura-divided unit. The main difference between period (*Periode*) and sentence is in repetition:

---

[106]Schoenberg's *Satz* terms are "Sätzchen—Halbsatz—Satz; Vordersatz—Mittelsatz—Nachsatz." See *The Musical Idea*, 164.

[107]*The Musical Idea*, 173.

[108]*The Musical Idea*,167.

[109]*The Musical Idea*, 171.

[110]*Fundamentals of Musical Composition*, 3.

> The period differs from the sentence in postponement of the repetition. The first phrase is not repeated immediately, but united with more remote (contrasting) motive-forms, to constitute the first half of the period, the *antecedent*. After this contrast, repetition cannot be longer postponed without endangering comprehensibility. Thus the second half, the *consequent*, is constructed as a kind of repetition of the antecedent.[111]

Schoenberg connects construction, not only of the form as a whole but also of its elements, to comprehensibility. In this case the musical period is in focus, and he adds to this the fundamental statement: "The real purpose of musical construction is not beauty, but intelligibility."

Schoenberg's concept of "theme" is extensive. For an overarching definition, he turns once again to the terms motive, phrase, and *Satz*:

> *Theme* is the connection between a number of *motivic transformations* that for their part are usually linked together into *phrases* and often also into *small phrases*, [resulting] in a *unified* form. The *theme* will, so to speak, formulate the problem of unrest present in the basic gestalt.[112]

Schoenberg's musical theme thus involves "the formulation of a problem" on which the work is based, initially represented by a condition of "unrest" at a deeper level of the formal hierarchy. This somewhat philosophical view is, however, rooted in concrete compositional procedures. The musical "problems" implied by the musical *Gedanke* are what is important, and the primary function of the theme is to realize the intellectual, constructive, and motive-related obligations in such a way as to favor the laws of comprehensibility. Schoenberg is again referring to the rational and logically based constructional principles, now in Romanticism's sacred area of the "divinely inspired" musical theme. He argues that "musical theme" as it is used in everyday speech often denotes a *Melodie*, which is a certain type of theme. The lyrical and often emotional *cantilena* is not the hallmark of melody; melody merely represents a certain way of constructing a theme through

> 1. extremely slow and sparing *development*; 2. *concentration* of all events in a single voice, beside which all others become actually stunted; 3. extensive *unification* of all figuration; 4. frequent *repetition* of slightly varied *phrases*.[113]

---

[111] *Fundamentals of Musical Composition*, 25.

[112] *The Musical Idea*, 181.

[113] *The Musical Idea*, 181.

Schoenberg: From Gedanke to Form

In *Fundamentals of Musical Composition* Schoenberg states that a melody is not necessarily rhythmically distinct: it is affected by intervals and harmonies, hence two-dimensional, and on this basis distinguishable from the consummate theme. "Thus a melody can be compared to an 'aperçu', an 'aphorism', in its rapid advance from problem to solution."[114] Consequently, there is a fundamental difference in the way a theme and a melody formulate a musical problem and its resolution. This explains Schoenberg's fundamental ideas on the concepts of theme and melody.

The musical form also makes use of certain supporting elements, the so-called *dienende Elemente*.[115] These are made up of what one would call subordinate parts. For Schoenberg it is relevant to distinguish between "part" and "element," since he regards "elements" primarily as *supports* in a formal progression determined by the musical material. Musical events that may be described by such terms as introduction, stabilization/consolidation, returning and preparation (*Rückführung* and *Vorbereitung*) are regarded as subordinate, or "serving," formal elements.

Schoenberg also considers so-called subsidiary ideas (*Nebengedanken*) as being among the elements of form. He compares the subsidiary second subject (*der Seitensatz*) of a sonata movement to the trio section in a minuet. This comparison does not imply that he considers them to be similar, but merely that they both represent the same *Gedanke* category, or identical levels of ideas, regarding their place in the construction.

The above terms and concepts denote the most important of Schoenberg's structural elements—those limbs or members that have a functional role in the organic and comprehensible construction of a musical form. However, two other concepts need to be examined, namely what Schoenberg calls "stable formation" (*feste Formung*) and "loose (loose-knit) formation" (*lockere [lose] Formung*). These are not regarded as structural elements, rather they represent the two most important principles in his technique of musical construction.

"Stable formations" appear in cases where musical components are organized in relation to a center such as a central tone, or, as the case may be, the harmonic system in itself. This type of formation is characterized by a "concentric tendency."[116] A stable formation then corresponds to a centripetal principle, seen, for instance, in terms of a musical material based on functional harmony. With a motive as the directive, stable formation is given

---

[114] *Fundamentals of Musical Composition*, 102.

[115] See *The Musical Idea*, 164 and 165.

[116] See *The Musical Idea*, 177.

when a form's smaller components are not developed in a way that makes them essentially different from their original (motivic) starting-point.

A "loose formation" implies an "eccentric tendency" that leads a musical development away from a starting-point; as Schoenberg puts it: "if the parts are capable of a certain amount of independent motion [...], which can go so far as to allow individual parts perhaps to escape from the association."[117] Seen in relation to a tonic, this process would be characterized as centrifugal. Schoenberg also includes such terms as "diffuse formation" (*aufgelöste Formung*), dissolution (*Auflösung*), and liquidation (*Liquidation*). Such musical processes only assume a meaning when the purpose is to disconnect individual parts from their context. Yet a looser connection between parts involves some similarities, if ever so superficial: "The most important feature of the loose association is probably the slight or merely external similarity of their connected parts."[118] Thus, even in what might be characterized as a compositional dissolution procedure, Schoenberg emphasizes the importance of coherence for a comprehensible musical progression.

Twelve-tone Method, Basic Form, and Comprehensibility
    Suite for Piano, op. 25, is Schoenberg's first work written in a consistent twelve-tone idiom. He considered this piece to be one of the most important in his entire compositional development. Having begun working on it in 1921, the piece reputedly prompted him to inform his student Josef Rufer that he had found something that, he believed, would "ensure the predominance of German music for the next hundred years."[119] This enthusiastic sense of discovery was palpable also in a letter to Nikolas Slonimsky about fifteen years later: "Here, [in the twelve-tone method] I became suddenly conscious of the true meaning of my goal, for the sake of which I had unconsciously struck this path: order and regularity."[120] This does not mean that order is to be considered any new aspect in his art:

> From the very first I was in possession of a thoroughly developed
> sense of form and a strong aversion to exaggeration. This is no step

---

[117]*The Musical Idea*, 179.

[118]Ibid.

[119]See M. Hansen, *Arnold Schoenberg: Ein Konzept der Moderne*, 169.

[120]Letter to Slonimsky written on 3 June 1937, translated from W. Reich, *Arnold Schoenberg, oder: Der konservative Revolutionär*, 174. ["Hier wurde mir plötzlich die wahre Bedeutung meines Zieles bewusst, dem zuliebe ich unbewußt diesen Weg eingeschlagen hatte: Ordnung und Gesetzmäßigkeit."]

Schoenberg: From Gedanke to Form 235

backwards to order, for disorder has never existed. It is certainly no step backwards at all, but, on the contrary, it is a step upwards to a higher and more perfect order.[121]

Emphasis on "order" is important, not only to the functionalist discourse but also to the reception of Schoenberg's thoughts and music as a whole. His defenders often refer to the logical order in his work. His critics, on the other hand, claim that his music shows lack of order and downright chaos. Characteristic of the latter attitude are the highly subjective metaphors of Walter Dahms, contained in an open letter to the composer in 1912:

> Some days ago the pianist Richard Buhlig played your three piano pieces op. 11. The impression is roughly as follows: first a child thumps aimlessly on the piano, then a drunk bangs insanely on the keys, and, finally, someone sits down on his … on the keyboard. This is how your pieces sound.[122]

In Schoenberg's view, one of the most important innovations connected with the twelve-tone method is the refinement of the ordering principles of music, which are now lifted up to a higher level. This level should not, however, be considered as being beyond the human potential of musical recognition. On the contrary: "Composition with twelve tones has no other aim than comprehensibility."[123]

If contemporary reactions were not always overtly understanding, history would change this state of affairs: Schoenberg's secret hope was that the sounding principles of his method would, in time, gain a place in humans' second nature. A redeeming feature for the skeptical interrogator may be that the method, according to Schoenberg, is as challenging to the composer as to the listener. As seen in the discussion on musical material, he was particularly concerned with the twelve-tone method's form-constituting possibilities: "After many unsuccessful attempts [...] I laid the foundations for a new procedure in musical construction which seemed fitted to replace

---

[121]*Der konservative Revolutionär*, 174. ["Von meinen allerersten Anfängen an besaß ich einen gründlich entwickelten Sinn für Form und eine starke Abneigung gegen Übertreibung. Es ist kein Rückschritt zur Ordnung, denn es hat nie Unordnung gegeben. Es ist überhaupt kein Rückschritt, sondern—im Gegenteil—ein Aufstieg zu einer höheren und besseren Ordnung."]

[122]W. Dahms, "Berlin 1912—Offener Brief an den Komponisten Arnold Schoenberg," *Arnold Schoenberg zum fünfzigsten Geburtstage*, 324. ["Von einigen Tagen spielte der Pianist Richard Buhlig Ihre drei Klavierstücke Op. 11. Der Eindruck ist etwa folgender: erst patscht ein Kind planlos auf dem Klavier herum, dann schlägt ein Betrunkener wie irr auf die Tasten, und zum Schluß setzt sich jemand mit dem ... auf die Klaviatur. So klingen Ihre Klavierstücke."]

[123]"Composition with Twelve Tones (1)," *Style and Idea*, 214.

those structural differentiations provided formerly by tonal harmonies."[124] While he thinks that he has discovered new construction principles that in themselves possess a great potential for comprehensibility, he also considers the possibility of strengthening these principles through the employment of traditional types of musical form. Boulez's assertion of the presumably irreconcilable principles in this combination has already been mentioned. Erwin Stein suggests something similar in his article "Neue Formprinzipien" (New principles of form): "it is debatable whether the old form types correspond to the twelve-tone row's conditions. What was possible in the concise terrain of tonality will not allow to be unconditionally fulfilled with the new means."[125] In addition to the sentiment represented by Boulez and Stein, there is a more general attitude that Schoenberg is letting himself be carried away on the wave of prevailing Neo-Classicism. Another assumption, which does not exclude any of the others, lies in the belief that Schoenberg's real motivation is to demonstrate the applicability of the twelve-tone method also within the concepts of traditional form. In his *Suite for Piano* the supposedly comprehensible, form-constituting twelve-tone principles are combined with recognizable basic forms, traditional forms, or even so-called old forms.

The *Wind Quintet* op. 26, which follows the piano suite, also presents a combination of the twelve-tone method with traditional form schemata. The publisher's introduction to the score opens with a brief note explaining that this opus is the first major work written according to the composer's own twelve-tone method.[126] Then follows a synopsis of the work's form:[127]

1. Movement: Sonata form
2. Movement: Scherzo
3. Movement: Ternary song form
4. Movement: Rondo form

Two contemporary views on the combination of the twelve-tone method with form schemata in this particular piece are worth mentioning. The first is represented by Felix Greissle, Schoenberg's son-in-law, who directed the

---

[124]"Composition with Twelve Tones (1)," *Style and Idea*, 218.

[125]E. Stein, "Neue Formprinzipien," *Arnold Schoenberg zum fünfzigsten Geburtstage*, 289. ["es ist fraglich, ob die alten Formtypen den Bedingungen der Zwölftonreihe entsprechen. Was auf dem übersichtlichen Terrain der Tonalität möglich war, wird mit den neuen Mitteln nicht durchwegs erfüllt werden können."]

[126]However, Schoenberg considered the *Suite for Piano* op. 25 to be his first major work within this method. See "Composition with Twelve Tones (1)," *Style and Idea*, 232.

[127]See Schoenberg, *Bläserquintett* op. 26 (Vienna/London: Universal Edition 7668/Philarmonia 230, 1925/1952).

Schoenberg: From Gedanke to Form 237

first performance on 16 September 1924. Greissle was also the first to write about the work, in *Musikblätter des Anbruch* the following year. The article, entitled "Die formalen Grundlagen des Bläserquintetts von Arnold Schönberg" (The structural foundations of Arnold Schoenberg's Wind Quintet), comes with a brief preface in which the editors of the *Musikblätter* add the proviso that the reader should take the author's background into consideration.[128] Greissle begins by stating that the twelve-tone method represents the discovery of a new structural principle. After giving a brief presentation of the possibilities of the twelve-tone row, he emphasizes that they in themselves ensure recognition, at least to some degree:

> This rests on the understanding that an object does not change, and also remains *relatively recognizable*, if its image is changed by its taking up another position in space.[129]

Greissle attempts to clarify the row's principles by means of graphic illustration, showing them as curves in relation to co-ordinates x and y and inverted axes,[130] a way of showing how fundamental he deemed the formal clarity to be. Yet Greissle had no illusions that the principles were actually perceived by listeners, at least not in his day: "It is clear that such a highly developed technique places great demands on musical perceptivity."[131] The problem is that the ear seeks the form in the area of tonality, he claims, and, generally speaking, the ear will usually seek traces of the old in the new. While we may look for logical connections, we will not recognize them. At this point Schoenberg's use of traditional form types applies: "Probably so as to be understood despite these preconditions, Schoenberg reverts to classical form types."[132] Greissle claims that the purpose of using standard forms is to strengthen the music's comprehensibility by relating it to forms established as part of humans' second nature.

Adorno, in his above-mentioned article "Schönbergs Bläserquintett," also discusses the relationship between twelve-tone method and traditional

---

[128] See F. Greissle, "Die formalen Grundlagen des Bläserquintetts von Arnold Schönberg," *Musikblätter des Anbruch* 7/2 (1925): 63.

[129] F. Greissle, "Die formalen Grundlagen des Bläserquintetts," 66. ["Das beruht auf der Erkenntnis, dass ein Gegenstand sich nicht ändert und auch *relativ erkennbar* bleibt, wenn sich sein Bild ändert, dadurch, dass er eine andere Lage im Raum einnimmt."]

[130] "Die formalen Grundlagen des Bläserquintetts," 65.

[131] "Die formalen Grundlagen des Bläserquintetts," 67. ["Es ist klar, dass eine so hochentwickelte Technik an das musikalische Auffassungsvermögen große Anforderungen stellt."]

[132] "Die formalen Grundlagen des Bläserquintetts," 67. ["Wohl um also trotz dieser Voraussetzungen verständlich zu bleiben, greift Schoenberg auf klassische Formtypen zurück."]

form schemata. His starting-point is the lopsidedness he finds in the quintet if it is regarded in a strict twelve-tone perspective. His question is whether the work can in any way be deduced from the method:

> Does it really fulfill itself in its dodecaphony? What would remain after the subtraction of all twelve-tone events?[133]

Adorno is concerned with the fact that everything, from individual motives to the formal architecture of this work, depends on construction principles quite separate from those determined by the twelve-tone row. He advocates the recognition of truly artistic creative processes of musical composition and argues that this base, at any rate, must be fundamental: To understand the wind quintet on its own terms, one should look at the thematic and formal construction of the work, without taking Schoenberg's application of the twelve-tone method into consideration.

Adorno interprets the quintet as a sonata, yet one extended beyond its limits (*gesprengt*), mainly because it has lost its characteristic harmonic base. Adorno's argument is rooted in the notion that a conventional sonata movement is based on the interaction between delimited harmonic levels. Since in this work , linear construction replaces a traditional harmonic layout, the basic principles of the sonata movement as schemata have been dropped: In Schoenberg's work the sonata has abandoned the schemata and become subject to a neat construction. Thus it has become a kind of "sonata on the sonata," Adorno writes, and from this point the form itself is further developed. Led by this conviction, he characterizes Schoenberg's so-called return to the sonata concept as a "spiral movement" and not a "circular movement." Consequently, the quintet's true formal character emerges:

> It just is not a sonata as such, no later adjustment to an objectively lost ontological postulate; instead it is, if you like, a sonata about the sonata that has become utterly transparent and whose vanishing formal essence has been reconstructed in glassy purity.[134]

In Schoenberg's quintet the sonata has become "conscious of itself," and: "It has ceased to be valid as an isolated, objectively determinative principle for the individual musical event; it has itself been drawn into this

---

[133]"Schönbergs Bläserquintett," 140. ["Erschöpft es sich wirklich in seiner Zwölftönigkeit? Was bliebe etwa, nach Abzug aller Zwölftonereignisse zurück?"]

[134]Adorno, "Schönbergs Bläserquintett," 144. ["Es ist keine Sonate schlechthin, keine nachträgliche Angleichung an ein objektiv verlorenes ontologisches Postulat; es ist statt dessen, wenn man will, eine Sonate über die Sonate, die vollends durchsichtig wurde und deren schwindendes Formwesen in gläserner Reinheit nachkonstruiert ist."]

Schoenberg: From Gedanke *to Form* 239

event."[135] What was general has become a singular occurrence. At the same time the sonata has been torn out of its obscure, emotional foundation, it is illuminated through so-called positive rationality (*gute Rationalität*).

These views relate to one particular composition by Schoenberg. Before proceeding to a closer look at his piano suite, it is worth emphasizing that in their assessment of the relationship between the twelve-tone method and traditional form schemata, neither Greissle nor Adorno reject this combination. Instead, both regard the fusion as constructive. Greissle supports the opinion that the twelve-tone method, in combination with the use of traditional formal types, strengthens comprehensibility; Adorno points out that the formal schemata themselves are purified in this combination. The standard form reaches its final goal through an individualizing process which, historically speaking, has been going on over some time. Adorno perceives the association as a compositional dialectic resulting in a synthesis that is beyond both the twelve-tone method and any formal schemata. He ultimately focuses on the consequences this synthesis represents in the development of music history. This point should always be borne in mind when discussing the use of established standard forms in the context of the expanded musical material of the 20th century.

Construction and Norm: Schoenberg's Gavotte from *Suite for Piano*

Schoenberg's *Suite for Piano*, op. 25, consists of Präludium, Gavotte, Musette, Intermezzo, Menuett, and Gigue. Work on it began already in 1921, but the composition was not completed until 1923. Stuckenschmidt establishes 27 February 1923 as the date on which the Gavotte, the movement that will be examined below, received its finishing touches.[136] The suite may be characterized as a collection of piano pieces whose constituent movements are modeled on Baroque dance forms—the exception being the Intermezzo, which takes the place of the sarabande.

If one combines Schoenberg's statement that the aim of musical form is to attain comprehensibility with his views on the simplicity of dance forms and the general intelligibility of the so-called old forms, one can lift his op. 25 out of the discourse on history and style. In this work Schoenberg connects the twelve-tone method, as a construction principle promoting cohesion, with the normative form canon, thus applying basic compositional principles that

---

[135] Adorno, "Schönbergs Bläserquintett," 144. ["Sie hat aufgehört als objektives Bestimmungsprinzip oberhalb der musikalischen Einzelereignisse isoliert zu gelten; sie ist eingezogen in jene."]

[136] H.H. Stuckenschmidt, *Schoenberg: His Life, World and Work*, 288.

are supposed to echo in the second nature of human beings. The fusion of conscious construction and formal norms makes the work a musical manifestation of functionalist thought. Adorno, who believed that the suite's constructionist features in particular suggest this association, regarded the *Suite for Piano* and the *Wind Quintet* as "a kind of Bauhaus music."[137] Below, the Gavotte movement is analyzed in relation to the concepts of construction and norm. The point of departure is the constructional aspect of this piece—the employment of the twelve-tone method and other components in Schoenberg's thoughts on musical form.

Perceptive music theorists often state that a twelve-tone analysis is not a matter of counting to twelve. But with Schoenberg, this statement is only a partial truth. In his well-known adage emphasizing twelve-tone *composition* over *twelve-tone* composition, his aim is not to discount the method itself, but rather to point out that the real challenge dwells on the creative level. The importance lies in how the method is used, not in its use *per se*. One of the most notable possibilities Schoenberg saw in the twelve-tone method was that of creating unity. He was convinced that the method was especially suited to establishing an inner coherence in the course of extended formal developments. "I believe that when Richard Wagner introduced his *Leitmotiv* —for the same purpose as that for which I introduced my Basic Set—he may have said: 'Let there be unity,'" he writes.[138]

Schoenberg believes that comprehensibility is one of the twelve-tone method's important aims, and he considers the row (the basic set) itself as a separate level of comprehensibility. The row is recognizable; it thus provides both a sense of familiarity and a feeling of unity. Apparently, the basic set was directly supportive in the rehearsals for the opera *Von heute auf morgen* (1930):

> The main advantage of this method of composing with twelve tones is its unifying effect. In a very convincing way, I experienced the satisfaction of having been right about this when I once prepared the singers of my opera *Von Heute auf Morgen* for a performance. The technique, rhythm and intonation of these parts were tremendously difficult for them, though they all possessed absolute pitch. But suddenly one of the singers came and told me that since he had become familiar with the basic set, everything seemed easier for him. At short intervals all the other singers told me the same thing independently.[139]

---

[137]Th.W. Adorno, "Arnold Schoenberg (1874-1951)," *Prismen* [*Kulturkritik und Gesellschaft* 1. *Gesammelte Schiften* 10/1] (Frankfurt a. M.: Suhrkamp, 1977), 176.

[138]"Composition with Twelve Tones (1)," *Style and Idea*, 244.

[139]" Composition with Twelve Tones (1)," *Style and Idea*, 244.

Schoenberg: From Gedanke to Form

In his own discussion on the Gavotte from op. 25, Schoenberg explains some irregularities in the use of the row because it comes as piece no. 2, i.e., at a moment when the basic set should already be familiar after the preceding Präludium.[140] Consequently, knowledge of the basic set itself should also be important to the listener, at least in Schoenberg's opinion.

Michael Beiche points out that the term *Grundgestalt*, used in connection with the twelve-tone method from around 1924, had different meanings. He refers to four main usages. According to these, *Grundgestalt* may denote

> (1) in a general sense a *synonym for (twelve-tone) row*; in a special sense a term (2) exclusively for *the first form in which a twelve-tone row appears*, or (3) all *four row forms*. Furthermore, *Grundgestalt* is used in a diverging meaning (4) by J. Rufer, for whom it is *identical with the category of the musical Einfall*, the *first perceptible form in a composition of the twelve-tone row on which it is based*, whereby *Grundgestalt* is in close *correlation with the term basic row (Grundreihe)*.[141]

In describing the twelve-tone method, Schoenberg himself does not only employ the term *Grundgestalt*; he actually prefers to speak of *Grundreihe* and "basic set."

The entire *Suite for Piano* is based on the basic set, or basic row (the untransposed prime or P_0). The set also appears in retrograde (= R_0), inversion (= I_0), and retrograde inversion (= RI_0). Moreover, the four basic transformations are transposed to the tritone (= P_6, R_6, I_6, RI_6); see Ex. 19 below.

The use of diminished fifths is an important feature of the row: the third and fourth pitches (G-D♭), the seventh and eighth pitches (A♭-D) as well as the row's framing pitches (E-B♭) are all linked by a tritone. Even the main transposition is the one on the diminished fifth; the two row forms on E and B♭ replicate the framing interval of prime, retrograde, inversion, and retrograde inversion. As a result, the transposed row equally contains the diminished-fourth interval D♭-G (between its third and fourth pitches). Like the framing interval E-B♭, this second tritone is present in all forms of the row—occasionally in enharmonic spelling as G-C♯—either in the first or in the last row segment. The third diminished-fifth/augmented-fourth interval

---

[140] "Composition with Twelve Tones (1)," *Style and Idea*, 234.

[141] M. Beiche, "Grundgestalt," *Terminologie der Musik im 20. Jahrhundert*, 175. ["(1) in einer allgemeinen Bedeutung als *Synonym für (Zwölfton-) Reihe*; in einer speziellen als Bezeichnung (2) lediglich der *ersten Erscheinungsform einer Zwölftonreihe* oder (3) aller *vier Reihenformen*; außerdem meint Grundgestalt (4) in einer divergierenden Bedeutung bei J. Rufer, für die sie *identisch mit der Kategorie des musikalischen Einfalls* ist, *die zuerst in einer Komposition wahrnehmbare Form der zugrundeliegenden Zwölftonreihe*, wobei Grundgestalt in *enger Korrelation zum Terminus Grundreihe* steht."]

EXAMPLE 19: Schoenberg, *Suite for Piano,* op. 25, twelve-tone material

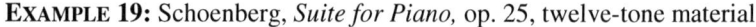

appears comes as either D-A♭/G♯ or C-F♯/G♭. The fact that the diminished fifth between the row's first and last pitches causes the transpositions to fuse so that the transposed prime sets out from where the untransposed prime leaves off, provides Schoenberg with the basis for a unique continuity when linking the rows.

Another interval characterizing the basic set is the minor second, which links the framing pitches to their neighbors both in the row as a whole and in the originally final tetrachord (compare in the prime: pitches 1-2 = E-F, pitches 9-12 = B♮-C-A-B♭. The retrograde of the four above-mentioned pitches corresponds to the letters B-A-C-H, which must have gratified Schoenberg's profound sense of meaningful letters and numbers. Finally, the minor third plays an important role: in the prime it appears as G♭-E♭ and C-A but can also be detected as the frame for the E-F-G progression at the beginning.

In accordance with Schoenberg's conviction that music is an organism, the basic row may be considered the Gavotte's centrally controlled body (*Zentralkörper*). This body harbors the life on which the limbs and members depend. At the same time, the set can be seen as representative of the whole, in the sense that it represents an absolute, basic feature of the entire piece. Since the row continues through all the movements, there is a structural coherence between the Gavotte and the rest of the work. Nevertheless, bearing in mind what we already know about Schoenberg's views, it is not possible to say that this row *is* the Gavotte as it appears as a piano piece. EXAMPLE 20 (on the next page) shows the use of the row in the first seven measures.

Schoenberg's use of row transformations is as follows:

Part I (mm. 1-7): $P_0, I_6, R_6, I_0, I_6, I_0, P_0$
Part II (mm. 8-16): $I_6, R_6, RI_0, P_0, P_0, RI_6, P_0, I_0, R_6, I_6, I_6, P_0$
Part III (mm. 17-24): $I_6, I_0, RI_0, RI_6, P_0, P_6, I_6, P_0, P_0, P_0, I_6$
Coda (mm. 25-28): P_0, I_6, R_0

He applies P_0 in the upbeats to all the main parts, thus strengthening the structure by returning to a familiar point of departure. The coda, however, begins with P_0 on a full beat. The movement opens with the prime of the row and concludes with its retrograde. P_0 is the most frequently used version throughout the piece, with I_6 as a close runner-up. Otherwise, the distribution of row transformations has a statistic rather than analytic interest; the piece as a work of art results from the compositional application of the method.

Schoenberg employs the row transformations in a variety of ways, both horizontally and vertically and not always a regular order from 1 to 12. This is evident from the outset: Already in the first three measures, the pitches 9-12 are played by the left hand before 5-8 sound in the right hand. Corresponding shifts take place throughout the piece; the composer controls the row, not the other way around. In addition to the argument that the basic set should already be familiar to listener's after they have heard the previous movement, Schoenberg points out that each row can be divided into three four-note units. The pitches within these tetrachords always retain their originally given order, but the three units may be treated as (individual) segments that can trade place. The diminished-fifth intervals function as a "relationship" that also makes the rows interchangeable, he says.[142] The conjunction formed by the steps G-D♭/C♯ is particularly important. After this interval connection is presented in the transition to mm. 1 and 3, it appears in every single measure throughout the piece, thus creating a continuous reference to the basic characteristics of the row material and contributing to the experience of musical coherence. The use of row transformations in the first part of the

---

[142] See "Composition with Twelve Tones (1)," *Style and Idea*, 234.

piece is representative also for the remainder, apart from one detail: The first note in measure 5 is $G\flat_4$ although it should be $G\natural$, given its position in P_6. Schoenberg has altered this pitch, possibly to avoid too strong a tie to an E-major/minor tonality through the previous $A\flat$ ($G\sharp$) and the following E, as nowhere else in this piece does he use such tactics.

EXAMPLE 20: Schoenberg, *Suite for Piano*, Gavotte, op.25/2, mm. 1-7, use of the twelve-tone row. © 1925 by Universal Edition, Vienna/Austria; © renewed 1952 and 1973. Reprinted with permission

While Schoenberg employs the twelve-tone row as a force providing unity, the form of the Gavotte is actually created through with the help of its members and limbs, something Adorno noticed in connection with the *Wind Quintet*. It is not suggested that we search in every Schoenberg piece for all the aforementioned elements of form. He presented these in relation to music in general and not necessarily to all his works. Nonetheless, to understand the construction of this piece, it may be useful to demonstrate some of the important formal elements by discussing them in his own terminology.

The Gavotte's motive (M) consists of the upbeat and the first note in measure 1:

EXAMPLE 21: Schoenberg, *Suite for Piano*, the motive in the "Gavotte"

The motive's crucial feature is its interval combination. The opening leap, a major seventh, suggests the possibilities of the minor second, while the remaining two notes build the first of the tritones that are so central to this piece, and the tone pairs are linked by a major second. The two mediated intervals are a major sixth (E_6-G_5) and a major third (F_5-$D\flat_5$). All this is comprised within the first four pitches, or the first tetrachordal segment, of the prime. Owing to the particulars of row construction Schoenberg employs here, the characteristic intervals recur in kind in the other two four-note groups. The central intervals are the diminished fifth, the minor second, and the minor third. Conditions are thus favorable for motivic coherence already when the row is played in its abstract mode, since the motive's characteristics are intimately related to the internal distribution of the twelve tones.

Beyond its pitch outline, the motive contains further distinguishing features. The articulation underlines an elegantly rhythmic profile; the lofty leaps are central to the entire piece. The motive is present throughout this music, and, together with the row, it creates coherence and unity. Schoenberg treats the motive as the basic element of construction in the same way as he does elsewhere in his musical output. In this respect, the twelve-tone method does not involve anything new in his compositional development. The key to the structural aspect of Schoenberg's use of the motive lies in the possibilities the tonal material offers of a rational disposition, one that at the same time liberates it from traditional tonality. Here is a closer look at the structure and its larger units and formations, starting with an overview:

246   *Musical Form*

The Gavotte consists of three parts followed by a coda: Part I = mm. 1-7, Part II = mm. 8-16, Part III = mm. 17-24, and the coda = mm. 25-28. Each part begins with an upbeat following in the wake of a rather strong cadence, or *Kadenz* (K). Further down the structural hierarchy, the first presentation of the motive together with the first left-hand entrance from B♮$_2$ to B♭$_4$ may be considered as the Gavotte's basic *gestalt*. Combining different voices, the motive is presented in several ways that are crucial to the ongoing construction process. Seen in this perspective, the Gavotte's basic *gestalt* would combine the row's first and final tetrachords. In another light, one detects that the right-hand line continued up to the downbeat of m. 2 joins two versions of the motive. The original version, analyzed above, is fused with a more rhythmic variant in which the leaps are elegantly extended. Meanwhile in the left hand, the tetrachord ending with B♭$_4$ in m. 1 is heard in retrograde up to and including the entire first beat in m. 2. Thus a zigzagging shape is emphasized which, encompassing more than two octaves, constitutes another pervasive feature in this piece. There may thus be *two* basic *gestalten*.

Close scrutiny of the development Schoenberg crafts throughout the piece shows that the interaction between these two figurations is significant for the overall construction. It will therefore be most productive to treat the two-hand progression from the upbeat to the third left-hand note in m. 2 as

EXAMPLE 22a: Schoenberg, *Suite for Piano*, Gavotte, overview 1

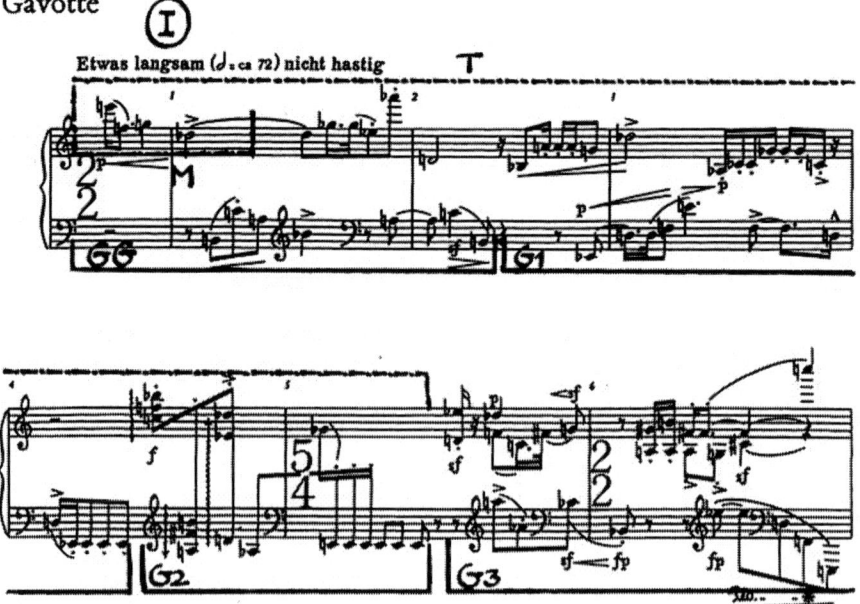

EXAMPLE 22b: *Suite for Piano*, Gavotte, overview 1 (continued)

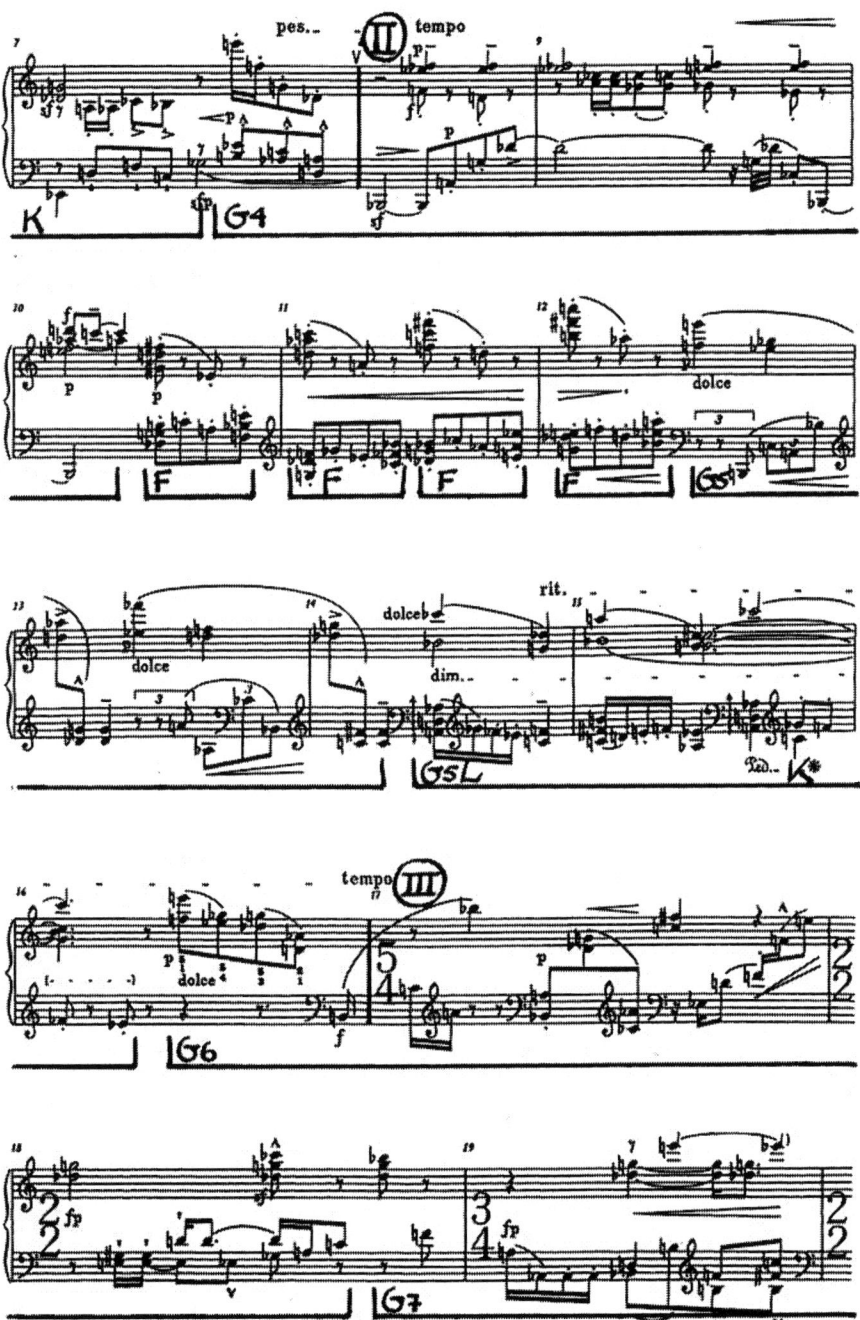

EXAMPLE 22c: *Suite for Piano*, Gavotte, overview 1 (concluded)

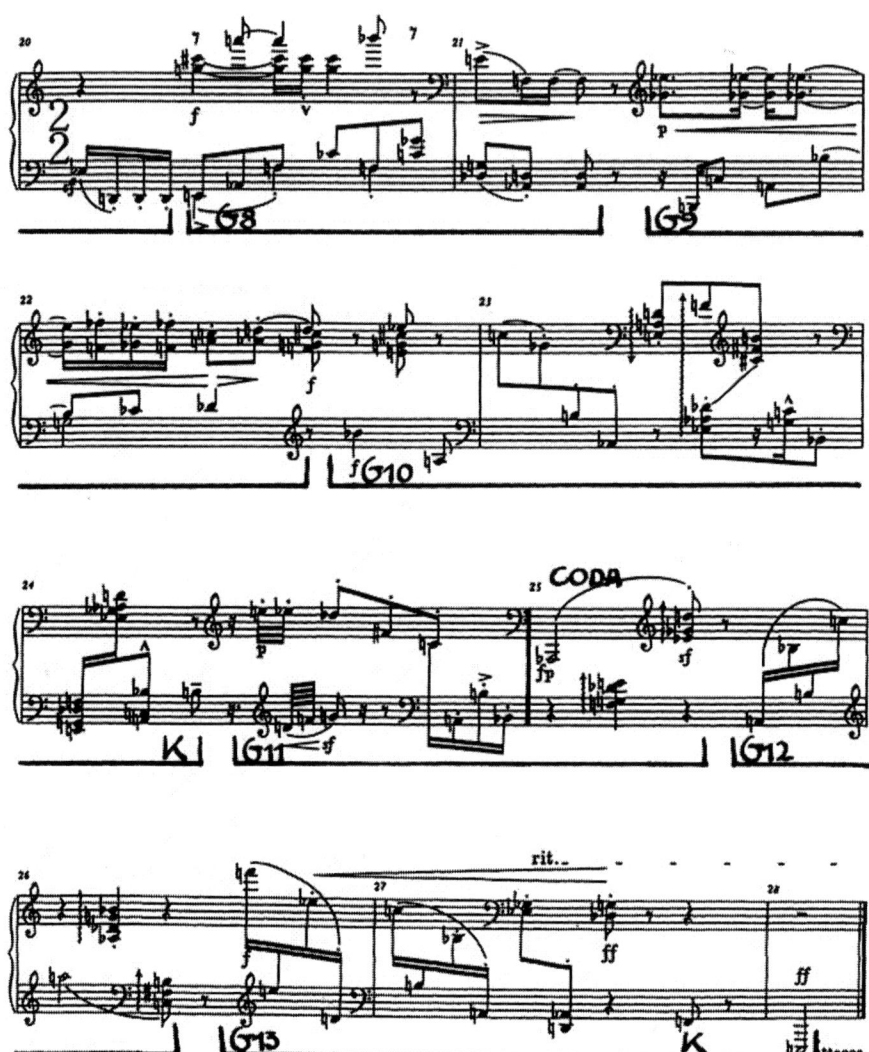

the Gavotte's unifying *Grundgestalt* (GG). That this *gestalt* coincides with the first phrase is no argument against such a view, although Schoenberg principally differentiates the terms *Phrase* and *Grundgestalt*.

This *Grundgestalt* consists of all the twelve pitches in P_0. Accordingly, this is a case of a piece's basic *gestalt* coinciding with the first presentation of a basic set—it appears in accordance with what Michael Beiche refers to as Rufer's view of the concept of musical *gestalt*. In this piece we also see that the use of different versions of the row is usually linked to different members in the construction.

The unit made up of *Grundgestalt* and motive is continuously present throughout the piece, varied again and again and usually either expanded or concentrated. From the upbeat in m. 2 to the first beat in m. 4, one finds the first example of a developing variation of the *gestalt* (labeled G1 in the example). The main principle in this variation is intensification through tonal repetitions in the right hand and the rhythms in the left. The upbeat in m. 4 together with the first three notes of the following measure present a "new" *gestalt* (G2), providing a subtly compressed version of the basic *gestalt* combined with a reference to G1.

Taken together, GG + G1 + G2 constitute what can be perceived as the Gavotte's *theme* (T): GG launches the initial "problem," which is being "discussed" in G1 and supplemented with a "conclusion" in G2. The same thematic development also determines the form of the whole piece: the mild and elegant character of GG is found again in Part II. Part III reveals a more complex development initiated by G1, and the forceful conclusion presented in the coda is prefigured in G2.

The "members" of the piece, to employ the organism metaphor, consist of entities relating to the main elements mentioned above. These help create an integral formal structure that is bound together at all times by the presence of both the row and the motive. In EXAMPLE 22 all the Gs denote developing variations of the basic *gestalt*, the variation principle being decisive for this level of the formal construction.

In Part II, from the upbeat at the end of m. 9 to the first note in m. 12, there is a smooth development of rhythm, articulation, and tonality. The main principle is the employment of sequences: a progression based on repeated formations on ever new levels. The motive is continuously present, and relations to both G2 and the coda are heard. The repetition principle leads to associations to what Schoenberg considers a *Figur*: a continuance that has no structural significance—a succession with no further obligations.[143] This does not mean that the figures are unimportant for the piece as a whole. But as the example shows (where they are marked F), they slide almost unnoticed into G5 and in m. 14 set in motion a "liquidation" of this *gestalt* (G5L).

A particular conceptual problem arises in Part III. From the viewpoint of musical construction, this part has the character of a recapitulation. It might, however, just as well be experienced as a development section because of its inherent complexity and somewhat abrupt nature—an impres-

---

[143] The figure has a certain significance for the sixteenth-note motion in m. 22.

sion that is reinforced by it following on the heels of a Part II that appears quite nicely rounded . In this ambiguity lies one of the debatable aspects of Schoenberg's concept of logic: the question of whether the neat, logical construction can really guarantee unequivocal comprehensibility. One believes to perceive the early contours of the fundamental dilemma vexing the later so-called integrated serialism: the more the composition is based on strict, consistent logic right down to the micro-level, the more difficult it is for the human ear to recognize the music as "logical."

The coda concludes with arpeggios and sixteenth notes, suggesting associations with G2. The formal progression is thus brought to a determined and completely unequivocal conclusion, just as clearly as it was begun by the initial motive.

In his construction of the Gavotte Schoenberg creates coherence and comprehensibility through the possibilities inherent in the twelve-tone method and in the principles of motivic development. He binds larger formal elements—*gestalten*, figures, themes, and parts—into a concrete, formal manifestation of the *Gedanke* on which the conception of the entire piece is based.

Nonetheless, one cannot ignore the fact that Schonberg's op. 25 is one of the least accessible works in his œuvre. This may apply particularly to listeners who hear the work just once or twice. Analysis does bring the work closer—and this is not as banal as it might sound: Schoenberg stressed that he considered analysis an important part of the cognition process. He devoted the greater part of his life to focusing on structures and procedures both in his own music and that of others. That the cognizing subject adopt an analytic attitude is a precondition of the logically based comprehensibility for which he strives. As will be discussed later, he took the initiative to teach not only his students but also the general concert-going public about this view. His attitude reflects his faith in the intellect of modern human beings to seek rationality. There is a utopian element here, certainly no stranger to the understanding of art at the time. How much advantage can be gained from an examination of *Suite for Piano* is necessarily up to the individual, as in all music, whichever way it is treated. The result depends not least on the intention behind the examination of the work. In the functionalist context, the analysis given above reveals a musical expression of the positively loaded idea of *construction*. In a next step, the question of how the concept of *norm* is expressed through this piece will be in focus.

Initially, Schoenberg criticized the tendency of theoreticians to consider standardized forms as a given. "Form" is not something the composer can take hold of *an sich* and then fill with content: form has never existed and will never exist *per se*. Musical form emerges as a new event each time:

Schoenberg: From Gedanke to Form

> the musical form is [...] something that arises, something that each time arises again, and which, apart from the fulfilled work of art, is never anything at hand, transmittable or applicable.[144]

Schoenberg's ideas on the musical organism, at the interface between conception and construction, are expressed in the quotation above. A musical form is unconditionally dependent on the realization through an individual work. But for a form to arise in relation to an established norm, or within a common formal category, it must still exist in the sphere of human recognition. The form is individual, but the principles, and what Schoenberg calls the "eternal laws" (*ewige Gesetze*), are universal:

> Constant here are only the principles, eternal laws, which must just be recognized and formulated in a correct way to be able to produce form and forms in accordance with the prevailing situation at any one time.[145]

Schoenberg's views parallel Le Corbusier's Neo-Platonic attitudes: a listener cannot recognize a musical form through its individual appearance without the constant principles that are a precondition for its representation. To recognize a cat in the leopard, we have to have an idea of the cat, to extend one of Schoenberg's metaphors. To the point that the constant features of music have been deduced from praxis, they have freed themselves from it and found their place on an ideal level. Hence, they have constituted a paradigm, and this is why certain types of form may be recognized irrespective of style and epoch. A musical form exists as a non-sounding idea through the principles on which it is based,[146] but this idea cannot be realized in any other way than through an adequately related singular version. If the term "norm" is used for the idea—understood in relation to Schoenberg's "eternal laws"—and "construction" is its individual realization, then these aspects cannot be separated. Nevertheless, when the following discussion systematically separates the notions of "norm" from those of "construction," the

---

[144]*The Musical Idea*, 424.["die musikalische Form ist [...] etwas Entstehendes, jedesmal neu Entstehendes und niemals außer in dem fertigen Kunstwerk an sich Vorhandenes, Übertragbares und weiter Verwendbares."] (This part of the German draft, which otherwise faces the English rendering in this bilingual edition, is not translated in the publication; hence the English is mine.)

[145]Ibid. ["Konstant sind hiebei nur die Prinzipien, ewige Gesetze, welche nur richtig erkannt und formuliert werden müssen um Form und Formen der jeweilige Sachlage entsprechend zu erzeugen."]

[146]This does not prevent both composer and listener from relating to a sounding model. The point is that the standard form cannot be totally dependent on this exemplar, because then it would lose its presumptive universality.

252   *Musical Form*

purpose is to focus on the essential characteristic of the functionalist orientation toward norm and basic forms. The construction aspect is always the artistic underpinning.

The gavotte, usually described as a rural French dance, became fashionable at the French and English courts in the 17th and 18th centuries. In the Baroque suite we find it as a so-called *galanterie*: a subordinate movement without a fixed place in the suite inventory. Many will be familiar with stylized gavottes from Bach's suites, Grieg's *Holberg Suite,* and Prokofiev's *Symphonie Classique.* Even though they are all labeled "gavotte," these pieces represent quite different musical expressions. On a certain level, however, they do share some important features. In *The Concise Oxford Dictionary of Music* the Gavotte is defined as follows:

> **Gavotte.** A dance form deriving from the Pays de Gap in France, whose inhabitants are known as 'Gavots'. Its music is in simple quadruple time and in steady rhythm; each phrase opens of the 3rd beat of a measure. Often it is found followed by a *musette* after which the Gavotte is repeated.[147]

The description in *Die Musik in Geschichte und Gegenwart* reads:

> Its normal form is that of an air with a binary construction (4+4, 4+8, 4+8+4, 4+12 measures etc.) and a similarly binary meter (2/2); the cadences are strongly emphasized. It starts with two unaccented beats and ends on the downbeat [...]. Its gay movement must not let one forget that it is the most moderate among French dances. [...] The expressive character of the classical gavotte is joyous and lovely, with an original popular and naive color. If it sometimes appears a little more exalted, it seldom renounces its moderate nature. [...] In the music of Bach, the gavotte occasionally loses its dance character in favor of a purely musical habitus.[148]

Whereas *The New Grove Dictionary of Music and Musicians* specifies:

---

[147] *The Concise Oxford Dictionary of Music* (Oxford etc.: Oxford University Press, 1964), 221.

[148] *Die Musik in Geschichte und Gegenwart* 4 (Kassel etc.: Bärenreiter, 1955) 1513. [" Ihre Normalform ist die eines Air mit geradzahligem Aufbau (4+4, 4+8, 4+8+4, 4+12 Takte etc.) und mit ebenfalls geradtaktigem Metrum (2/2); die Kadenzen sind stark betont. Sie beginnt mit zwei leichten Taktzeiten und endet auf einer schweren Taktzeit [...]. Ihre muntere Bewegung sollte nicht vergessen lassen, dass sie doch der gemäßigtste frz. Tanz ist. [...] Der klass. Ausdruckscharakter der Gavotte ist heiter und lieblich, mit einer originellen volkstümlichen und naiven Färbung; wenn sie zuweilen auch etwas gehobener ist, so gibt sie doch nur selten ihr gemäßigtes Wesen auf [...]. Bisweilen verliert die Gavotte bei Bach ihren Tanzcharakter zugunsten eines rein mus. Habitus."]

> Like most Baroque dances, the gavotte was used both as an instrumental and vocal air as well as for dancing. The stylized gavotte, like the dance, had a time signature of 2 or C|, a moderate tempo, phrases built in four-bar units [...] Matteson claimed that the gavotte expressed 'triumphant joy', but most others thought the affect to be one of moderate gaiety, pleasant, tender, avoiding extremes of emotional expression. It was considered a pastoral dance, an association emphasized in J.S. Bach's settings of gavottes in the first two English suites for keyboard, both of which have a drone bass that may be intended to imitate the sound of a musette. [...] Unlike the more serious Baroque dances [...] the gavotte never lost its relative simplicity of texture and clear phrasing. Gavottes were most often written in binary form, or as a set of variations, or as a rondeau [...]. Occasionally two gavottes occurred consequently in a suite, the first then repeated da capo [...].[149]

Supported by these three references, one can arrive at the following characteristics of the gavotte genre:
1. Light but moderate tempo
2. 2/2 meter or *alla breve*
3. Half-measure upbeat
4. Marked cadences
5. Regular beat structure
6. Clear-cut phrase divisions
7. Binary constructions, variations, and *rondeau*
8. Musette or a Gavotte no. 2 as a middle movement
9. Gavotte da capo
10. Mild in expression and usually a certain pastoral character

Although the way in which these individual elements appear may vary from piece to piece, they still represent constituting factors in the gavotte paradigm. This means that there must be a minimum number of components present for it to have the character of the gavotte.

When Schoenberg relates to this specific type of movement, the title in itself is an indicator with important precursors. The crucial question is whether the music delivers what the title promises. Some features are more obvious than others: the piece is followed by a *musette* (not examined here), which appears as a broadly constructed subsidiary idea (*Nebengedanke*) before the *da capo* repetition of the main part. In EXAMPLE 23, direct references to the gavotte norm are marked with unbroken, indirect indications with dotted lines. The heading *Etwas langsam, nicht hastig* (somewhat slow, not hasty), combined with the metronome indication 72 for the half-note, places the piece within the temporal frame of a gavotte. The time signature 2/2 and the half-measure upbeat also belong to the gavotte norm. In the analysis above,

---

[149] *The New Grove Dictionary of Music and Musicians* 7 (London etc.: Macmillan, 1995), 201.

the upbeat was identified as the main constituent of the basic motive. This half-beat therefore embodies both the underlying construction principles and the norm aspects. In the overall form, tempo, meter, and upbeat, Schoenberg has provided frames that agree with the gavotte paradigm, irrespective of their integral positions in the sophisticated musical construction.

The overall form of the gavotte, three parts followed by a coda, has already been acknowledged. The most important reason why the parts are so clearly perceived is because all begin with a characteristic version of the falling, half-measure upbeat. The indication "tempo" in measures 8 and 17 also strengthens the perception of these divisions. Moreover, the cadences at the conclusion of each part are clearly delineated. As seen in the encyclopedia excerpts quoted above, clear-cut divisions are one of the fundamental requirements of a gavotte.

The first two parts consist of a total of 16 measures, in older models a hallmark of regular structuring. However, Schoenberg rejects this option by designing the parts in uneven length: the first part has seven measures while the second has nine. In this way, any symmetry is avoided and the dance connected even on this level to the composer's concept of musical prose. After the first quite clearly delineated measures, there is a break in m. 4, in the middle of the seven-measure unit, through a harshly arpeggiated and partly accented upbeat to the 5/4-time m. 5. Part I then concludes with two measures in the basic meter.

EXAMPLE 23a: Schoenberg, *Suite for Piano*, Gavotte, overview 2

EXAMPLE 23b: *Suite for Piano*, Gavotte, overview 2 (continued)

EXAMPLE 23c: *Suite for Piano*, Gavotte, overview 2 (concluded)

The first three measures are perceived as fairly regular primarily because Schoenberg places half-notes on all three downbeats. This emphasizes the preceding upbeats, which are heard as leading toward something given weight by its duration. With the exception of Part III, all further parts of the piece also open with an upbeat leading to a half note. With this again, Schoenberg is seen maintaining one of the characteristics of a gavotte. In the opening measures, up to the first beat in m. 3, he gives the piece a formal reference frame to which the rest relates. In m. 4-5 it is obviously time to challenge the frame through a break in symmetry, a feature not of the gavotte genre but of his musical prose. The cadence in the first half of m. 7 connects with the opening measures of the piece.

Part II is preceded with an upbeat to m. 8. In an indirect way this part is important to the gavotte paradigm as it refers to structural patterns that are generally associated with stylized instrumental dances. Examples are the sustained seconds in the upper voice in measures 8-9 and the rhythmical figure of two sixteenth-notes followed by two eighth-notes in measure 9.

Other examples are the elegant portato articulations of the right hand in mm. 10-12, the left-hand staccatos, and the pattern of two quarter-notes followed by two eighth-notes and a quarter-note found in mm. 12-14. The rhythm of this figure, anticipated in the transition from m. 9 to 10, is subsequently intensified into a *stretto* structure with a *ritardando* toward m. 16. Schoenberg's use of a so-called *Figure* is therefore very important for the gavotte paradigm: By loosening the intricate structure of the basic construction, he gains in the comprehensibility created by the relation to a formal norm.

Part III consists of eight measures. The symmetry that might have resulted from a binary structure is counteracted here again by four changes of meter (in mm. 17, 18, 19, and 20.)[150] These measures only have a slight reference to the gavotte standard; they seem rather a complex counterweight to the preceding dance part. The few reminders of the genre are so fragmented that they can hardly be perceived as pointers to the norm relations. An obvious exception is the syncopated upbeat in m. 21, followed by elegant sixteenth-notes and eighth-notes.

The four-measure coda returns to the clear profile that characterizes the piece as a whole. Variants of the initial upbeat, combined with the use of half notes, safely reposition the music within the gavotte frame. The measure structure of the movement is 7 + 9 + 8 + 4.

Variation is a key term in the progression of the parts of this piece. Schoenberg uses diverse variation techniques, starting from the very first measures. The upbeat to each of the later parts is a variation of the first upbeat; the notes of the right-hand upbeat to Part II even include those heard preceding the initial downbeat, while the right-hand upbeat to Part III includes those preceding the downbeat in m. 2. Through such structural intensifications each upbeat is perceived as richer than the previous one. The essence of Schoenberg's variation principle is thus perceived in concentrated form in the upbeats, but even beyond them, developing variation is carried through from note to note from beginning to end.

---

[150]In this connection, going back to the basic meter is also considered a change in meter.

Motions by leaps, articulation marks, arpeggios, and the application of clear rhythmical formations give the piece a light and elegant character that is very much in keeping with the characteristics of a gavotte. At the same time, both the dance character and the overall structural expectations are frequently counteracted by camouflaging construction procedures and abrupt insertions exceeding what one expects in the traditional genre. Schoenberg's gavotte thus appears as a play both *with* and *against* the underlying paradigm. In this form of dialectics the piece appears as an individual gavotte defined by its own unique material.

The question of whether listeners actually perceive a norm relationship in this piece is hard to answer. Listeners, particularly in the case of music of this degree of complexity, are not part of an unequivocal mass. One crucial point is their general understanding of Schoenberg's tonal language and the question what kind and degree of comprehensibility may be needed to compensate for what is presumably unfamiliar. Beyond the individual's listening experience it can be established, however, that Schoenberg presents his work in such a way that it does not appear as stylistically distanced: The gavotte's characteristics do not break with his basic style but are rather a part of it. The piece does not refer to anything from the past in a way that would create a distance or a break with its present. Whether it is actually perceived as a gavotte will depend on the individual listener's capacity for such identification. Under no circumstance can this music be associated with another century. The piece is created as an indissoluble unity between construction and norm, and this is the main point when considering it in a functionalist context.

While Schoenberg's aim is to contribute to greater comprehensibility through a formal codex, one should not lose sight of the fact that the point is not really to recognize a gavotte, but rather that this type of identification aids musical recognition in general.

Summary

The starting-point for Schoenberg's ideas on musical form is the notion of a fundamental "feeling for form," or a "sense of form." A sense of form is something that is not inherent but acquired, mainly through the composer's experience with logical procedures. The combination of a feeling for form and logic thus becomes essential for realizing a musical work. Schoenberg generally emphasizes the importance of logic and logical sense. Furthermore, he especially points out that a genuine musical piece is always conceived as a whole. The work does not grow or take form from a motive: it is based on a visionary experience of a musical entirety that subsequently becomes the composer's guiding line in a logical construction. Focusing on the construction aspect is one of the central aspects that associate Schoenberg with the functionalist context. Yet he also uses the concept of "organism" or "body" as a metaphor for a musical work, suggesting that a work can be compared to a living being consisting of joints and members that carry out particular functions in relation to the whole. The idea of a "centrally controlled body," which signals a work's connective driving force, is particularly significant for him. Tonality is an example of such a force.

"Coherence" is another key term in Schoenberg's notion of form. Musical elements with shared features or related characteristics are combined and thereby create coherence. Logic and coherence contribute to a work's comprehensibility, to the ultimate aim of its form. This is the second main point of what gives Schoenberg's ideas functionalist perspectives: A musical design must be clearly comprehended, and in this regard the use of basic forms may provide listeners with a formal identification with what is already familiar. This is where Schoenberg's use of so-called old forms comes in.

Form can be subdivided into self-contained elements, and among these the motive, with all its characteristics, represents the smallest. "Developing variation" is the most important principle for the construction of a musical work. "Liquidation" is the term for the opposite process. The next level in the hierarchy of form is represented by the concept of *gestalt*, a composite of several versions of the motive. If a *gestalt* proves to have significant consequences for the whole work it is called a *Grundgestalt*. A "figure" does not have the same structural importance. Beyond these terms, Schoenberg refers to concepts such as phrase and sentence (*Satz*). A theme (*Thema*) is the formulation of a "problem" that, as an artistically productive "unrest," defines a lower level of the formal hierarchy. By and large Schoenberg applies the terminology known from traditional analysis. Of particular importance for his idiosyncratic solutions in the construction of form are the concepts of "stable formation" and "loose formation," denoting concentric and eccentric forming procedures—toward or away from the respective center.

With the twelve-tone method Schoenberg believes to have discovered new possibilities for the construction of large-scale musical forms. In the use of traditional form types, he foresees that a combination of formal norms and the construction potential of the twelve-tone method will strengthen formal comprehensibility to the maximum. More specifically, he believes that the traditional dance forms represent the musical designs that can be most easily and clearly recognized. Hence, the gavotte from his *Suite for Piano,* op. 25, may be taken as an illustrative example of how Schoenberg's functionalist understanding of form is being realized in his music.

Hindemith: From Vision to Form

> If we cannot, in the flash of a single moment,
> see a composition in its absolute entirety,
> with every pertinent detail in its proper place,
> we are not genuine creators.
>
> *Paul Hindemith*

Introduction

The concept of *vision* is a key component in early-20th-century notions of artistic creativity. Both Schoenberg and Hindemith find this concept vitally important, as a directive in a work's painstaking process of realization. Calling this chapter "From Vision to Form" is intended to emphasize that vision is the underpinning of Hindemith's focus on the importance of compositional craft. When examining Hindemith's thoughts in the light of the anti-romantic attitude of his time, it is crucial to understand that craftsmanship is never an objective but a means. The chosen heading also focuses on the fact that a vision of an artistic whole is a point of departure for Hindemith's views on musical form. There is no disagreement between Schoenberg and Hindemith on this point. Their fundamental consensus does not, however, imply that Schoenberg's concept of *Gedanke* corresponds to Hindemith's *vision*. The two terms cover quite different aspects.

Hindemith concurs with Schoenberg in his conviction that musical form is the realization of an initial vision, but he has a different way of articulating this idea. An intuitive perception of form is so fundamental for Hindemith that he appears reluctant to undertake a comprehensive theoretical examination of structural challenges. The practitioner Hindemith does address this issue, but not the theoretician. Nonetheless, the phenomenologist Hindemith is also present: Musical form, he claims, cannot be understood in terms of theoretical schemata, since music as a developing process is embedded in a reciprocal action of temporal and spatial experiences—much in the manner Schenker and Ernst Kurth see it. "[W]e must entirely abandon the principle of measuring static points alone, no matter how many individually measured items we may collect, and evaluate the actual stream of music,"[151] Hindemith says. This statement is particularly important for his thoughts on form, where the temporal aspect is crucial.

Hindemith's approach to form is characteristically divided into three components. While he appears to be especially interested in the intuitive dimensions of a musical form, he is still a master of "learned" formal

---

[151] *A Composer's World*, 113.

construction. At the same time, he willingly relates his music to standard forms, thus moving between intuition, construction, and tradition.

Hindemith's intuitive sense of form is undoubtedly an important source of his vast output. Peter Cahn refers to the young Hindemith's remarkable progress as an instrumentalist, and also sees parallels to his search for instrumental perfection in his early compositional development:

> At the end of this search he achieves the same confidence as a composer, but this is a confidence marked by his experiences as an instrumentalist. The perfection of the experienced prima vista player who appears to surmount every difficulty at first go finds a counterpart in what one might call Hindemith's prima vista composing.[152]

There are seldom any major differences between Hindemith's drafts and his scores; editing mostly seems to cover the elaboration of details and orthography. "One will not find in Hindemith anything resembling the constant search for the definitive *gestalt* revealed in Beethoven's sketch books," says Cahn. "For Hindemith the draft has primarily a mnemonic function and less that of a stage in the creative process."[153]

Hindemith's intuitive approach nourished by personal experiences may be the reason why he places so little emphasis on the question of form in his texts, not least when compared to his discussions on musical material. Another aspect may be that he does not see the musical form threatened to the same extent as the musical material. "In the formal design of choral movements, now as before, the greatest freedom will be allowed to reign,"[154] he writes. When considering the importance Hindemith places on vocal music as a compositional guideline, this statement has greater impact than may first be apparent.

---

[152] P. Cahn, "Hindemiths Lehrjahre in Frankfurt," S. Schaal and L. Schader, eds., *Über Hindemith: Aufsätze zu Werk, Ästhetik und Interpretation* (Mainz: Schott, 1996), 19-20. ["Am Ende dieses Suchens erreicht er gleiche Sicherheit als Komponist, aber es ist eine Sicherheit, die von seinem Erfahrungen als Instrumentalist geprägt ist. Die Perfektion des routinierten prima-vista-Spielers, der alle Schwierigkeit auf Anhieb zu bewältigen scheint, findet ihre Entsprechung in dem, was man Hindemiths prima-vista-Komponieren nennen könnte."]

[153] Ibid. ["Von dem ständigen Suchen nach der definitiven Gestalt, das Beethovens Skizzenbücher offenbaren, ist bei Hindemith nichts zu finden" [...] "Die Skizze hat bei ihm überwiegend die Funktion einer Gedächtnisstütze, weniger die eines Stadiums innerhalb eines Entstehungsprozesses."]

[154] "Wie soll der ideale Chorsatz der Gegenwart oder besser der nächsten Zukunft beschaffen sein?," *Aufsätze, Vorträge, Reden*, 26. ["In der Formgebung der Chorsätze wird auch nach wie vor größte Freiheit herrschen dürfen."]

Form and Nature

Hindemith's understanding of the musical material is based on the notion that the fundamental principles of tonality are rooted both in our outer and inner natures as human beings. The underpinning of this view lies in his strong, subjective feeling that there is a specific ontology for tonality. As mentioned above, Hans Kayser believed that Hindemith had much to thank him for with respect to *The Craft of Musical Composition*. The two men certainly share many opinions; nonetheless, it is fairly obvious that Hindemith had little sympathy for Kayser's spiritual and speculative deliberations. Kayser confirms this suspicion in a letter written to Gustav Fueter on 9 February 1935:

> At the beginning of the week I was with Hindemith in Olten. H. is a wholly unmetaphysical person, obviously without any particular interest in spiritual and speculative matters. He also told me quite bluntly that his interest, though ardent, was limited to the practical side of my work.[155]

In a commentary on the collection in which this letter is included, Rudolf Haase points out an interesting feature of the encounter between Hindemith and Kayser. It seems that Hindemith was mainly interested in a possible harmonic regularity of thematic construction.

> Kayser must at first have been astonished, since Hindemith sought to know from him—as his most crucial question—whether it would be possible to connect two themes, in a development section for example, with the help of the methods of harmonics*. This was a problem completely unsolvable by harmonic theorems, one that, moreover, really lay quite outside the Kayserian theory of harmonics.[156]

---

[155] R. Haase, *Paul Hindemiths harmonikale Quellen*, 19. ["Anfang der Woche war ich mit Hindemith in Olten zusammen. H. ist ein ganz unmetaphysischer Mensch, sichtlich ohne besonderes Interessen an geistig-spekulativen Dingen. Er sagte mir auch ganz offen, dass ihn nur der praktische Teil meiner Arbeit interessierte, dieser allerdings brennend."]

[156] Ibid. ["Kayser muß zunächst befremdet gewesen sein, da Hindemith—als wichtigste Frage—von ihm wissen wollte, ob mit Hilfe harmonikaler Methoden die Verbindung zweier Themen, etwa in einer Durchführung, möglich sei. Das war ein Problem, dessen Bewältigung mit harmonikalen Theoremen gar nicht möglich war und das eigentlich auch völlig außerhalb der Kayserschen Harmonik lag."]

* Note that Kayser's and Haase's term *harmonikal* relates to Pythagorean and Keplerian notions of ratios and proportions in the universe. What is *harmonisch* in the musical sense, particularly in musical intervals, was certainly included, but the two adjectives are clearly distinguished in German.

Hindemith: From Vision to Form

Hindemith was more interested in whether there is a universal way of understanding the construction of form, or, to put it another way, whether there was a "harmonic" explanation for the sense of form that seemed so deeply rooted in his soul. While Schoenberg would relate such feeling to a sense of logic, Hindemith sees even here the possibility of a natural universality. In his extensive manuscript "Komposition und Kompositionsunterricht," written between 1933 and 1935, he refers not only to the laws of melody, harmony, and rhythm, but also to a presumable regularity of formal design:

> There are eternal laws for melody, harmony, and rhythm, and probably also for formal construction. They are not isolated, but rather most closely connected with extra-musical dynamics of motion, whether these are found in the cosmos or in the plant cell, in the inorganic that takes shape, or in human actions. The artist must follow these truths; they must be the basis for his craft.[157]

Composers draw on the experience of earlier composers, on their own talent, his inspiration, and taste, says Hindemith, but "obviously, even the most independent and most radically inspired talent, irrespective of taste and purpose, must, in the construction of his musical forms, follow a pathway the landmarks of which are immovably fixed by nature."[158] An inherent truth exists as a directive for artistic activity, and within this basic truth form also has its place. Since the nascent days of music, temporal forms have emerged and there has been an instinctive feeling for proportions. This instinctive element is inconceivable unless there is a universal, rationally recognizable logic:

> From the very beginning of music on earth, temporal music forms have been built. Each constructor, moreover, knows instinctively, or by trial and error, or by traditional experience, when structural parts are in good proportion and when they are not. Therefore, some rational, discoverable, and understandable law of construction must exist which could be put into effective operation.[159]

---

[157] "Komposition und Kompositionsunterricht," 53. ["Es gibt für die Melodik, Harmonik und Rhythmik und wahrscheinlich auch für die formalen Bildungen ewige Gesetze. Sie stehen nicht isoliert, sondern sind aufs engste verbunden mit außermusikalischen Bewegungsabläufen, geschehen sie im Kosmos oder in der Pflanzenzelle, in der Gestaltwerdung des Anorganischen oder in der Tätigkeit der Menschen. Diesen Wahrheiten hat der Künstler nachzugehen, sie müssen die Grundlage seines Handwerks bilden."]

[158] *Elementary Training for Musicians* (London/New York/Mainz: Schott, 1974), 159.

[159] *A Composer's World*, 88.

The ideal aim of craftsmanship is to create a connection between the work of art, the cosmos, and human existence: "Those worlds circling above us, all that lives in and around us, the work of art turning in the same circles, this is the unity toward which we will strive."[160] When form is regarded from such a perspective, it is not far removed from Le Corbusier's views on the basic architectonic forms embedded in universal harmony. Hindemith's main challenge seems to be that he has not yet discovered any fundamental proportions on which the formal design of a musical work is based. One knows empirically how a musical form is constructed, and through analytical deductions some directives can be arrived at for the construction of form, "[b]ut the underlying laws upon which such construction is based are still a secret to musicians at least as far as conscious understanding and formulation are concerned."[161] Hindemith does not consider the traditional standard forms as being in themselves basic in any universal or natural sense. He rather suggests that such forms communicate a deeper level of identification that is controlled by a fundamental and integral logos. The composer must relate to this profound level of artistic truth. Hindemith admits that he is not able to prove this fundamental regularity, and, as long as the underlying logos is not revealed, the so-called theory of form can only consist of lifeless schemata. We are impeded by a kind of traditional, historicizing aesthetic that blindfolds us to the advanced, yet basic, principles of formal design. While waiting for a more direct approach to these fundamental principles, the music student must be content with the indirect access that is found in exercises in composition and analyses of form:

> Only then can there be an adequate theory of form, when the laws of sounding forms have been fully discovered. We know the nature of masterpieces, yet up to this day it is unclear what determines their structure. When working we notice straightaway where things appear a bit on the long side, where something is lacking—this feeling can be developed to such a degree that in longer courses of events it can diagnose what is too much or to little even with regard to the smallest note values. However, any fixed, basic facts, developed from natural relationships in the way they given the harmonic and melodic contexts, are completely lacking at present in regard to working with form. I believe that these can only be found when we finally abandon historicizing aesthetics and derive our insights from quite different, probably extra-musical, fields. Until the

---

[160]See "Komposition und Kompositionsunterricht," *Aufsätze, Vorträge, Reden*, 53. ["Die Welten, die über uns kreisen; was in uns und um uns lebt; das in gleichen Kreisen schwingende Kunstwerk; dieser Einheit wollen wir zustreben."]

[161]*Elementary Training for Musicians*, 157.

Hindemith: From Vision to Form

day when such basic facts of structure have been discovered we must therefore help ourselves as best we can. And for this, the ever-renewed combination of compositional exercises and structural analysis is, in my opinion, best suited.[162]

The extensive history of musical performance and music theory has not provided one single provable rule of form, says Hindemith. Artistic logic deduced from individual works is not sufficient for him as it is for Schoenberg: He requires scientific proof. Composers cannot be blamed for concealing their construction rules since they themselves do not know them. Hindemith continues his reasoning by suggesting this enigmatic paradox: "It sounds strange: how could the man who creates a form not know its rules! Nevertheless, it is so."[163] In a combination of experience and rationality something can be said about the proportions of the length (or duration) in music, but that is all. The most pressing problem is that we do not even have a measuring unit for extensions of musical form. Consequently, the rational elements in musical construction are bound to be rather unstable, because

> without solutions to such basic questions, no rational technique is imaginable; as we see in our structural work, it cannot grow beyond the limits of a dexterity supported by simple, empirical insights.[164]

This does not mean that the "good" musical form does not exist. The problem at this point in time is that the basic presuppositions escape rational cognition. The conviction that the essence of a form is based on a natural but at present not systematized regularity is an assumption that should be kept in mind when examining Hindemith's views. Consequently, a major problem when studying Hindemith's ideas on musical form is that he seems to shy

---

[162]"Komposition und Kompositionsunterricht," 101-2. ["Es kann erst dann eine brauchbare Formenlehre geben, wenn die Gesetze tönender Formen ergründet sein werden. Wie die Meisterwerke beschaffen sind, wissen wir. Unklar ist bis heute, was ihren Bau bestimmt. Bei der Arbeit spüren wir sofort, wo Längen sind, wo etwas fehlt, – das Gefühl hierfür läßt sich soweit ausbilden, daß es in größeren Abläufen das Zuviel oder Zuwenig kleinster Notenwerte feststellt. Feste, aus den natürlichen Tonverhältnissen abgeleitete Grundtatsachen, wie sie die Harmonie- und Melodieverbindungen regeln, fehlen aber einstweilen für die formale Arbeit vollständig. Ich glaube, sie können nur gefunden werden, wenn wir endlich einmal von der historisierenden Ästhetik abgehen und uns Aufschlüsse aus ganz anderen, wahrscheinlich außermusikalischen Gebieten holen. Bis zur Auffindung der formalen Urtatsachen müssen wir uns also durchhelfen, und dafür scheint mir die hier empfohlene Art der ständigen Verbindung von Kompositionsübung und Formanalyse die beste zu sein."]

[163]"Betrachtungen zur heutigen Musik," 166. ["Das klingt sonderbar; wie sollte denn der Mann, der eine Form bildet, nicht ihre Formgesetze kennen! Und doch ist es so."]

[164]Ibid. ["Ohne die Lösung solcher Grundfragen ist aber eine rationale Technik gar nicht denkbar, sie kann, wie wir an unserer formalen Arbeit sehen, nicht über eine auf die einfachen empirischen Erkenntnisse sich stützende Handfertigkeit hinauswachsen."]

away from a comprehensive and systematic treatment of this subject until he can accept and give credence to a scientific explanation. He is looking for a methodology that can put the cardinal challenge of musical form into a more concrete perspective. Hindemith's understanding of form thus enters the functionalist context: The art of musical construction and the norms revealed through tradition are connected to human intuition and cognition, which are supposed to be founded on a generally valid, universal logos. Hindemith wishes to grasp this basic logic, but for now he must be content with studying aspects of its singular appearances.

"*Vision, Einfall und Handwerk*"

"But what genius has—and what is far beyond their [the untalented composers'] reach—is vision,"[165] Hindemith says. His definition of vision is the kind of sharp flash of lightening that in the space of a second illuminates the darkness of night so that not only the contours are visible but also the landscape, right down to the minutest detail. In this distinct and tense situation there is a feeling of noticing each little blade of grass, but still not being able to describe every tiny part of the picture. The genuine creator not only has the ability to receive a vision of the complete musical form, he also has the qualities needed to realize it. And, in the construction process, the whole and the details are constantly interacting with each other:

> Not only will he have the gift of seeing—illuminated in his mind's eye as if by a flash of lightening—a complete musical form [...]; he will have the energy, persistence, and skill to bring this envisioned form into existence, so that even after months of work not one of its details will be lost or fail to fit into his photomental picture. This does not mean that any *f sharp* in the six hundred and twelfth measure of the final piece would have been determined in the very first flash of cognition. If the seer should in this first flash concentrate his attention on any particular detail of the whole, he would never conceive the totality; but if the conception of this totality strikes his mind like lightening, this *f sharp* and all the other thousands of notes and other means of expression will fall into the line almost without his knowing it. In working out his material he will always have before his mental eye the entire picture. In writing melodies or harmonic progressions he does not have to select them arbitrarily, he merely has to fulfill what the conceived totality demands.[166]

Hindemith's description of vision, totality, and details strongly resembles Schoenberg's conception of an initial experience of artistic entirety.

---

[165] *A Composer's World*, 70.

[166] *A Composer's World*, 71.

Hindemith: From Vision to Form   267

The concept of *Einfall*, together with that of vision, plays a vital role in Hindemith's views. As stated above, the German term *Einfall* represents an "idea" or "thought" in the sense in which something occurs to a person: something "falls in." However, in this connection idea and thought represent quite different and far more limited phenomena than what Schoenberg understands as *Idee* and *Gedanke*. Hindemith finds *Einfall* so descriptive for characteristic elements in the compositional process that he even includes the German term in the original American edition of *A Composer's World*. The English noun "idea" seems to him far too indistinct when speaking of the composer's creative imagination, but

> *Einfall* from the verb *einfallen*, to drop in, describes beautifully the strange spontaneity that we associate with artistic ideas in general and with musical creation in particular. Something—you know not what—drops into your mind—you know not whence—and there it grows—you know not how—into some form—you know not why.[167]

Der Einfall is the term for an incident that is presumably immediate and inexplicable. Hindemith takes his description further: "When we talk about *Einfälle* we usually mean little motifs, consisting of a few tones—tones often not even felt as tones but felt merely as a vague curve of sound."[168] Hence, Hindemith does not use the term motive in the same way as Schoenberg. He points out that there is no uniform definition of the concept and consequently does not give one.[169]

The *Einfall* is not only a professional composer's privilege. It comes to the layman as well. Consequently, there is room for misunderstanding concerning its real meaning in the creative process: "He [the composer] has had no proper idea," Hindemith reports to have heard often as a mistaken judgement of music that seems not to have sufficient appeal.[170] If the concept of *Einfall* is examined in the light of creativity, what primarily distinguishes the amateur's reception from the professional's is the way it is treated. With the amateur the *Einfall* usually dies away in its early childhood, while the creative musician knows how to grasp it and adequately make use of it. The domains of musical creativeness are not accessible to everyone—"the regions of genuine musical creativity are so far beyond our everyday experiences, that Mr. X will never know what they are and the untalented composer will never enter their inner secrets."[171] The statement, "everybody can have, and

---

[167] *A Composer's World*, 67.

[168] Ibid.

[169] See *Elementary Training for Musicians*, 157.

[170] See "Komposition und Kompositionsunterricht," 47. ["Ihm ist nichts eingefallen."]

[171] *A Composer's World*, 70.

has, scientific ideas, but it takes a scientist to know what to do with them,"[172] also applies to music. In the sketchbooks of the great masters, especially Beethoven's, one can follow the fate of many ideas. This opportunity presupposes that the ideas have already been lifted out of the vague regions of the *Einfall*, "either mentally by addition of the results of constructive conclusions, or even visibly in some jotted-down notes on paper."[173] The construction element thus enters the compositional process at a very early stage. Even the very first instantiation of the *Einfall* depends on construction. Mastery of the compositional craft thus becomes immediately significant, for it is the degree of craft that decides the way from brain to hand. In the original edition of *A Composer's World*, Hindemith uses the following formulation: "Jotted-down notes can be regarded as the first steps away from the source, only if a composer's experience has taught him to reduce the normally very long route from his brain to his writing hand."[174] In the later German version, *Komponist in seiner Welt*, this passage begins with "Only then can the jotted-down notes be considered the first step near the source [...]."[175] Hindemith considers the instantiation itself to be a step *away* from the source, and that it is the composer's skill that decides the length of that step.

A closer look at Hindemith's use of the term *Einfall* shows that he includes two degrees, or levels, where they are divided between the rational and the irrational—or over-rational—dimensions. An *Einfall* may be experienced as seductively mysterious, but it can also be a treacherous friend: If composers rely on it, they must usually walk a long and cumbersome path. For how unique is an *Einfall* really? Miraculously emerging themes often retain traces of other composers' works, which in one way or another have gripped us. "New" motives may frequently prove to contain melodic shapes and structural connections we have already used. Ideas experienced as born irrationally may often be explained rationally. Once we begin to peel off the layers, what is actually "new" may dwindle down to virtually nothing. In an imaginary description of a composition class, Hindemith ends his dissections by saying: "What remains is therefore quite scanty: a couple of notes that are completely impersonal and that could have occurred to any composer any time."[176]

---

[172]*A Composer's World*, 68.

[173]*A Composer's World*, 69.

[174]Ibid.

[175]*Komponist in seiner Welt*, 82-83. ["Niedergekritzelte Notizen können nur dann als nahe der Quelle liegende erste Schritte angesehen werden..."]

[176]"Komposition und Kompositionsunterricht," 50. ["Der bleibende Rest ist recht dürftig: Ein paar Noten, die vollkommen unpersönlich sind und zu allen Zeiten jedem Komponisten einfallen könnten."]

Hindemith: From Vision to Form

In a rationalizing musical analysis of an *Einfall,* as referred to above, we deconstruct it, reverting to what Hindemith considers to be primeval melodic types. He provides no examples, but we can refer in this connection to Ernst Kurth's ideas of *Ursymbole des Volkliedes* (the primeval formulae of the folksong) and *die dynamischen Urformen* (the primordial dynamic forms). The former term refers to certain melodic formulae, while the latter refers to fundamental melodic progressions.[177] In Hindemith's opinion, certain primary melodic types are constant and eternal since they give material to all motivic and thematic formations. Once again he demonstrates a need for a universal, artistic foundation so characteristic of functionalism in the 1920s. Hindemith's thoughts do not imply any parallels between the notion of primeval musical formations and the employment of basic mathematical forms in design and architecture. Musical forms must at any rate be seen as utterly cultivated and refined compared to their primordial roots. These roots rather represent a basic level, a fundamental starting-point for individual, thematic construction, writes Hindemith:

> All themes must be built up from here; we must advance to this point so that we may be able to construct themes that express what we wish to say. We must consciously seek purposive constellations; through practice we must detect the most felicitous among innumerable combinations.[178]

As with Schoenberg, Hindemith sees many possibilities in the use of a musical motive. A personal style is developed depending on the way in which different solutions are given priority. When the composer is so entirely rooted in a style that the principles of evaluation and choice have become subconscious, the unconscious starting-point is no longer a real *Einfall*: the composer has controlled it right from the start. The composer can rely on his or her thought process, which in most cases makes the right choices. This highly developed certainty contributes to the illusion of a genuine *Einfall*. The musical sense, as well as the process of composition, must be controlled so that the peculiarities of the tonal material take over. Hindemith refers once again to the dialectics between the artist's will and the will of the artistic material. This subtle control is rooted in the highest regions of thought, he says, "and since this control leads us to the highest regions of what is notionally perceptible by means of thinking, the *Einfall*

---

[177] See E. Kurth, *Musikpsychologie* (Bern: Krumpholz, 1947), 289ff.

[178] See "Komposition und Kompositionsunterricht," 50. ["Alle Themen müssen von hier aus aufgebaut werden, bis hierher müssen wir vordringen, um Themen so konstruieren zu können, dass sie ausdrücken, was wir sagen vollen. Wir müssen bewusst zweckmäßige Zusammenstellungen suchen, durch Übung müssen wir unter den unzähligen Kombinationen die treffendste herausfinden."]

must dwell in areas that we cannot access through thought."[179] He concludes that a genuine artistic *Einfall* is situated above rational and logical insight. Consequently, an authentic *Einfall* must be found in the mysterious moment that precedes logically based cognition and the rational influence of control:

> *Einfall* can only be the moment, the constellation of forces where, as in the process of fertilization, creation is set in motion; the non-manipulable point from which arises the vision of the future work of art.[180]

An *Einfall* is the spark that ignites that sudden flash of vision. Thus a true *Einfall* is not for everyone: "Few are blessed by nature with this creative moment, they can only be the willing vessel in which the seed will sprout."[181] An *Einfall* liberates a force, and this force pervades in turn upon the rational work of the craftsman, the composer. Such a notion has been connected to Sullivan and Schoenberg earlier in this study. Organic construction is also a key term for Hindemith, and "the seeds," like the motive for Schoenberg, have a wide range of form-constituting possibilities. But the seed, or germ, also has qualities that lay down specific premises for a further creative process: "The composer has many possibilities to give form to the will concealed in the germ, but its inexplicable radiation will always influence the work's nature, *gestalt*, and meaning to the highest degree."[182] Hindemith uses the word *Urzelle*, a term often associated with the Second Viennese School. The composer must work in such a way that preserves reverence for the enigmas of the creative process, he says; "for the rest he will recklessly wish to wish to get to know all the possibilities of the craft so that he can realize the ideas germinating from the *Urzelle* in their purest form."[183]

---

[179]"Komposition und Kompositionsunterricht," 50-51. ["und da uns diese Kontrolle bis in die höchsten Regionen des gedanklich Faßbaren führt, muß der Einfall in Gebieten beheimatet sein, die wir durch Denken nicht erschließen können."]

[180]Ibid. ["Einfall kann nur der Moment, die Kraftkonstellation sein, wo wie in der Befruchtung die Schöpfung beginnt; der nicht beeinflußbare Punkt, aus dem die Vision des künftigen Kunstwerks entspringt."]

[181]Ibid. ["Wenige werden von der Natur mit diesem schöpferischen Augenblick begnadet, sie können nur willig das Gefäß sein, in dem der Samen aufgehen wird."]

[182]"Komposition und Kompositionsunterricht," 51. ["Der Komponist hat viele Möglichkeiten, dem im Keime verborgenen Willen Form zu geben, immer wird aber die von diesem ausgehende unerklärbare Strahlung Art, Gestalt und Sinn des Werkes in höchstem Masse beeinflussen."]

[183]"Komposition und Kompositionsunterricht," 52. ["im Übrigen wird er rücksichtslos alle Möglichkeiten des Handwerks kennen lernen wollen, um die aus der Urzelle entkeimenden Ideen in reinster Formen verwirklichen zu können."]

Hindemith: From Vision to Form

With respect to the development of a musical form, an artistic entirety is the point of departure for both Hindemith and Schoenberg. The work does not grow organically from the *Einfall*, as a more romantic understanding would have had it, but from a specific reconstruction of a conception of a whole according to the qualities of the artistic material:

> Now we work from the large to the small. Contours slowly emerge from the uncertain, almost spatial feeling of the work to be formed, the mass gradually falls into sections, the supporting parts are followed by links and, finally, by the ornamental accessories. It is obvious that here must be formed the harmonic progression, the motions, and thereby also the themes and motives, since we grasp the building components' proportions right up to the last divisions, and invariably add what is lacking in accordance with the material's attributes.[184]

Hindemith's notions of vision, construction, and craftsmanship thus reveals that the origin lies in the enigmatic—and usually unexpected—*Einfall*. This impulse gives the genuinely creative composer a lucid vision of a musical whole. The vision of the whole in turn becomes the real point of departure for the work. For the musical composition to be constructed as closely to the vision as possible, every ounce of compositional craft is required. Nonetheless, craftsmanship will not suffice if all that is at one's disposition is the wondrous *Einfall* and an ephemeral vision. The journey toward the fulfilled musical work is the instantiation of the *Einfall*, the process whereby it is rationalized through the composer's consciousness and brought to the artistic workshop where its multifarious construction potential is realized.

In Time and Space

Careful attention to *time* is essential to Hindemith's notion of musical form. Musical form is primarily temporal, he says, and the aesthetic dimensions of the whole can never be recognized before the music has faded away:

> Thus judgment of the aesthetic effect or technical shape of a temporal form is necessarily retrospective. Nothing can be added or subtracted in the course of the unfolding of such a form (not even single notes) without destroying the form and replacing it by a new one.[185]

---

[184]"Komposition und Kompositionsunterricht," 51. ["Nun arbeiten wir aus dem Großen ins Kleine. Aus dem unbestimmten, fast räumlichen Gefühl des zu bildenden Werkes heben sich langsam die Umrisse, nach und nach gliedert sich die Masse, den tragenden Teilen folgen die Verbindungen und schließlich das schmückende Beiwerk. Es ist offenbar, dass hier der Ablauf der Klänge, die Bewegungen und damit auch die Themen und Motive gebildet werden müssen, indem wir die Proportion der Bauteile bis in die letzten Verästelungen erfassen und den Eigenschaften des Materials entsprechend jeweils das Fehlende einsetzen."]

[185]*Elementary Training for Musicians*, 157.

Hindemith's main point is not that music unfolds over time, but rather that a complete musical form always presupposes the recognition of an entirety. If this view is to have meaning, it must be presupposed that a complete musical design is grasped at one and the same time: were the progression perceived only as something *remembered*, then we would be back at square one. It follows that through retrospection musical time is concentrated in a way that liberates musical form from its temporal premises by drawing it into the perspective of space. Hence, while Hindemith sees music as unfolding in time, he also believes that it must be liberated from the actual temporal process if its form is to be mentally recognized:

> The effect of comprehending as a new superunit what in the course of its development was built up by smaller units is borrowed from our spatial experiences, where this comprehensive judgment is a most commonplace fact—and yet it was a result of a strictly temporal operation.[186]

While Hindemith is speaking here of the recognition of a piece of music as a whole, music's temporal aspects presuppose at the same time a perception of the form as an unfolding process. The structural progression can be understood by means of what he describes as the potential in human consciousness for "mental parallel construction." Contrary to the retrospective, total experience of form, the notion of this kind of parallel construction focuses on the simultaneous experience of a structural progression in time. In Hindemith's notion of form, music's temporal aspects are thus perceived as both a progression and a compression, where the latter applies to the spatial dimensions of the art.

Another important point is that Hindemith understands musical form as always being unique. If one single tone is added or omitted, the form changes. As also for Schoenberg, musical form is always something new that is created. Consequently, the formal progression of two pieces of music can never be the same, no matter whether they have been written by the same composer or relate to the same set of norms. Hindemith's understanding of the relationship between analysis and form is connected to this view. Even though he accepts that analytic procedures may be helpful in the study of musical form, they have but little effect on the creative process that actually constructs these forms. Analysis and practical experience do not provide access to any fundamental regularity:

---

[186]*A Composer's World*, 60.

Hindemith: From Vision to Form

> What is usually taught in schools as "form" is only the analytic process of taking apart pre-constructed forms, and has nothing in common with the creative process of building up such forms—a synthesis based on laws more fundamental than the mere regulations derived from practical experience, or from copying older works.[187]

Moreover, Hindemith accords the spatial perspective a place beyond the compressed temporal dimension that captures the structural totality. The spatial dimensions of music, such as high and low, near and far, right and left, are not the same as what one encounters outside the field of music. Nevertheless, tonal progression undoubtedly gives a spatial feeling, even to inexperienced listeners. Pitch is the decisive element in this instance, as a high tessitura is experienced physically, in the sense that one unconsciously identifies with the energy that creates the very progression. "It is the relative amount of energy that counts for our evaluation of musical space,"[188] says Hindemith. However, this only addresses one of the spatial dimensions, and the spatial experience of music is in fact three-dimensional: The directions right and left correspond to the harmonic and melodic relations between the successive components of a musical progression. The feeling of depth, expressed by a musical back-and-forth motion, can be compared to perspective in painting. An aspect that creates the equivalent in music is the perception that progressions are related to a tonic scale or to other central tones. Hindemith does not identify these imaginary spatial qualities with aspects of the musical form concept. Instead his thinking in analogies, in the manner of Schenker's *Schichten* with "foreground," "middle ground," and "background."

"Rhythmus ist Form"

Hindemith considers the interval to be the basic material of music, and through the interval, the material has form-structuring possibilities:

> Just as in architecture the big supporting and connecting members—piers, columns, girders, and arches—determine the form and size of a building, as well as its interior division into rooms, corridors, and floors, irrespectively of the material of which they are built—so tonal relations introduce order into the tonal mass.[189]

But it is rhythm that contains the forming potential necessary to set a formal progression in motion. "Rhythm is form," Hindemith claims in his

---

[187] *Elementary Training for Musicians*, 157.

[188] *A Composer's World*, 61.

[189] *The Craft of Musical Composition*, 56.

lecture "Über musikalischen Unterricht."[190] Since rhythm decides the temporal aspect of music's proportions, it is through the rhythmical treatment of the tonal material that an actual work of music assumes a form. Hindemith admits that this process is rather complex. Initially, his focus on the combination between interval and rhythm may appear to resemble Schoenberg's concept of the motive. Schoenberg's musical motive is based on the interaction of rhythm and interval, and he believes exactly this combination to lie closest to musical material. Yet, for Hindemith, this combination does not necessarily appear as a compositional seed that would manifest the construction potential in concentrated form. It is true that in *Ludus Tonalis*, particularly in the fugues, Hindemith presents himself as a master builder. Yet he does not regard this type of musical structuring as a precondition for genuine musical recognition. Whereas Schoenberg's compositional guideline is the combination of rhythmic, melodic, and harmonic logic, Hindemith relies on the disposition of interval and tonality and does not consider rhythm as such as inextricably connected to the melodic-harmonic dimension. In his view, a musical development is the interplay of several basic elements, which may have been conceived in separation from one another.

Hindemith regards rhythm as both a living and a life-giving organism. Here lie the form-building principles that transcend what can be captured by traditional analysis: "Restoring rhythm as a living organism in music can not be achieved through analysis but via the recognition of the principles for its formal construction."[191] The essence of Hindemith's belief is that since any musical form develops over time, rhythm must be the element that constitutes its structure. In Western culture it is difficult to find rhythmic forms not bound to meter, he complains. As experiments with Gregorian chant show, its movements become lifeless when meter is forced upon them. Similar examples of unconstrained musical vivacity exist in non-European cultures, in tribes that have avoided being infected by what he calls the "Western 'disease' of organized harmony and its inevitable companion, meter."[192] For Hindemith, metrics functions as the temporal counterpart of organized harmony. The somewhat crass statement quoted above is rooted in the notion that conscious addition of a vertical harmonic element, usually attended by an accompaniment, constrains the free horizontal flow. This does not imply that meter in itself is to be perceived as an artificial addition. Meter is known

---

[190] The lecture was held on 30 October 1948 in Vienna. A summary, first published in 1949, is found in *Aufsätze, Vorträge, Reden*, 207-209.

[191] "Über musikalischen Unterricht," *Aufsätze, Vorträge, Reden*, 208. ["Die Wiedereinführung des Rhythmus als lebendigen Organismus in die Musik kann nicht über die Analyse, sondern muß über die Erkenntnis der Prinzipien seines Formbaus gelingen."]

[192] *A Composer's World*, 86.

Hindemith: From Vision to Form 275

in art and nature, says Hindemith, occurring in poetry and architecture as well as in the regularities of the seasons and the periodicity of organic life.

The interaction of meter and rhythm is what creates a musical form that unfolds in time. Hindemith seeks to approach the temporal aspects of form in a rational way, but then these aspects must be measurable: "The temporal material of music, if it is to be used rationally, must be subjected to measurement, as was the spatial element, harmony."[193] Human beings have a quite reliable ability to undertake metric evaluation. He finds an example in the fact that people tend to group entities into units, even when they hear a long number of completely identical impulses. A psychological interpretation takes place, partitions are inserted into musical meter, Hindemith says, and these are always related to divisions by two or three. Such divisions can be considered basic units of measurement. Metric estimations may be disturbed through frequent changes in meter, not least when both numerator and denominator change in the time signature of a piece. In these cases, metric order may lose ground to free rhythm: "we lose all feeling for metrical order; in our interpretational judgment the metric successions reach a critical point beyond which no meter whatever can be felt, but the feeling of the unrestrained power of free rhythm enters."[194] This means that we end up losing contact with what can be measured. No one has found the basic unit of rhythm, the smallest element that might serve as a measurement for all larger rhythmical organisms. But even the shortest rhythmic motive is complex in its way, and the rhythmic grouping around any accent focuses on meter, not on rhythm. The only common denominator for these two phenomena is the temporal aspect, but, regrettably, rhythm cannot be measured with a stopwatch.

Hindemith concludes that the answer to the inner mysteries of rhythm does not lie in investigations of the physical nature of sound but in the field of music psychology. And while he does not pursue this thought further, it afford him the possibility to broaden his otherwise somewhat rigid view of the universal basis of musical principles: Musical form—both as construction and as fundamental experience—is closely linked with the enigma of rhythm. He believes that what is basic must by definition also be logical, and arrives at the following final conclusion:

> No scientist's research, no musician's intuitive genius, no layman's common sense has ever been able to find ways of measuring rhythm, in an attempt to establish a rational basis for the construction of temporal musical forms.[195]

---

[193] Ibid.

[194] *A Composer's World*, 87.

[195] *A Composer's World*, 88.

With this observation, Hindemith clearly acknowledges his own shortcomings on this point—shortcomings not as composer or artist, but as a theorist. In the text "Komposition und Kompositionsunterricht," he drafts a teaching program for musical form. His methodology does not really present any surprises. He suggests that the starting point should be the *lied* form and its extensions, and that the teaching should progress from there to forms that take their regularity from other sources (as, for example, "small lyrical poems") and to the sonata form."[196] It is characteristic of Hindemith that he emphatically recommend to begin with the *lied* form. He kept Franz Magnus Böhme's *Altdeutsches Liederbuch* in his study—not in his library. Folk songs, and by no means only German ones, served him as a crucial foundation in his teaching and in designing exercises for his composition students. This corroborates that he considered songs as basic for musical experience and as a point of departure in the development of art music.[197]

Hindemith has a special consideration for the diversity of possibilities inherent in the simplest and most fundamental forms of music. He finds numerous examples, not least in the works of the Bach family:

> The basic forms of their [the Bach family's] compositional layouts are simple if not almost primitive, but as if to make up for that, details are inserted into them and added onto them in often conspicuous abundance and diversity. It [the result] is a great miracle of human artistry and organizational capacity[198]

As far as music-teaching methodology is concerned, Hindemith feels obliged to use traditional form schemata. Yet some day in the future it ought to be possible to develop a system of rhythmic construction as the basis for musical form. On its basis, the theory of repetition, variation, and the combination of both would be subsumed under the category of time, and with it the entire theory of form in its traditional outline.[199] The profound certainty of this possibility leaves Hindemith with doubts about the way in which the theory of musical form is usually taught. The shaping forces of meter and rhythm affect the other structural components as well as melody and harmony. All these elements interact with one another, as do our perceptions

---

[196] See "Komposition und Kompositionsunterricht," 84-86.

[197] See W. Salmen, "'Alte Töne' und Volksmusik in Kompositionen Paul Hindemiths," *Musik und Bildung* V1 (1974), 362-369.

[198] "Betrachtungen zur heutigen Musik," 141. ["Die Grundformen ihrer Aufbauten sind einfach, ja fast primitiv, aber dafür sind die Einzelheiten in einer oft unübersehbaren Fülle und Mannigfalt ihnen ein- und angefügt. Es ist ein großes Wunder menschlicher Kunstfertigkeit und Planungskunst]."

[199] See "Über musikalischen Unterricht," 208-209.

of their audible manifestations. At the same time, dynamics, timbre, phrasing, and other parameters may also influence perception without ever disturbing the musical construction.

In *Elementary Training for Musicians,* Hindemith attempts to pinpoint the phenomena that constitute an audible musical form. Structuring is achieved through four main factors. The first two are "(a) Duration, which can be measured by a clock" and "(b) Tempo (uniform and changing), which can be measured by a metronome." At this point, the issue of the proportions within the parts or sections arises. These also develop over time, but more decisive is the relative position they have vis-à-vis each other and with regard to the whole, a relationship that cannot be measured with any certain method. The list continues with "(c) Relative speed of unfolding (proportional inter-relationships of the constituent parts), for which we do not know what means of measurement to use." There is a fourth element that constitutes a musical form but for which Hindemith does not find a measuring unit either, the degree of textural complexity: "(d) Closeness (degree of complexity) of texture, for which, also, we possess no means of measurement."[200]

When sounding material is subjected to temporal construction, this is done by means of the three main principles: repetition, variation, and change. Hindemith's emphasis on the importance of variation in particular invites associations with Schoenberg's concept of developing variation. Hindemith maintains that the possibilities of variation are almost infinite; accordingly, the facility for structuring manifests itself most convincingly in this area. He lists and defines his three foremost construction principles as follows:

(a) Repetition (re-use of one constituent part of the formal entity, on the same pitch level, or in transposition).

(b) Variation (some of the elements of a constituent part are changed while others remain unchanged. For instance, the melodic line may be retained but with different harmonic and rhythmic treatment; or the rhythmic shape of a motive—or melody, etc.—may be retained, but with changed melodic outline and new harmonies). Between the literal repetition of a given material and complete change to new material there are infinite gradations, their complexity increased by the inclusion of the aforementioned subordinate, decorative elements (dynamics, tone-color, phrasing etc.). It is in the application of the principle of variation that a composer's power and intelligence in formal construction manifests itself most obviously.

(c) Change (one constituent part gives place to an entirely different one).[201]

---

[200] *Elementary Training for Musicians,* 158.

[201] *Elementary Training for Musicians,* 158-159.

Whether a musical form is constructed by re-creating a form from the past or by conceiving a new one on a purely theoretical basis, at least one of these factors will be involved. But once again, many possibilities coexist, and not even exclusively in comparison of one form category with another, for

> [t]he same composer, even in two pieces belonging to the same form-category, will never use the constructive factors in exactly the same way. His is an infinite number of possibilities in calculating the dimensions and choosing permutations and combinations for his building stones.[202]

Mental Parallel Construction, Form, and Tradition

If Schoenberg considers comprehensibility the purpose of structure, Hindemith accords what he calls "mental parallel construction" a similar status. He is convinced that a crucial precondition of musical perception is the human capacity for construction. Whereas any experience of music may have a purely emotional aspect, Hindemith believes that the mental parallel construction belongs to the conscious and intellectual domains of that experience.[203] Music appreciation thus also comprises aspects that can be evaluated rationally, since it is founded on rationality to such a substantial degree.

Hindemith's point of departure is the view that music is meaningless until it meets a perceptive mind. And yet, music is not only perceived as a sensual impression in the narrow sense of the word: musical formations and structures can also be *imagined* independent of the momentary sound. The ability to perceive music in separation from its sounding manifestation is essential for both composers and performers, and indeed even for listeners, because this capacity is the foundation of an activity that plays a part in all musical experience: "While listening to the musical structure, as it unfolds before his [the listener's] ears, he is mentally constructing parallel to it and simultaneously with it a mirrored image."[204] The German version of this passage brings this so-called parallel construction closer to the concept of musical form: "While he perceives the musical form as it evolves in front of his attentive ear, he is erecting in his mind, in parallel to this form, its mirror image."[205] The listener is thus assumed to be continuously comparing the

---

[202] *Elementary Training for Musicians*, 159.

[203] See *Komponist in seiner Welt*, 31-40 and *A Composer's World*, 17-53.

[204] *A Composer's World*, 20.

[205] *Komponist in seiner Welt*, 33-34. ["Während er die musikalische Form wahrnimmt wie sie sich vor seinem aufmerksamen Ohr entwickelt, baut er parallel zu dieser Form ihr Spiegelbild in seinem Geiste auf."]

Hindemith: From Vision to Form

components of the actual, sounding composition with its alleged mirror image, trying to make them fit his own mental construction. In other situations the listener may compare them to a construction already stored in his consciousness. The ability to do that is based on experience and training, observes Hindemith: listening always relates to something that has been previously experienced, in one way or another. Here lies the foundation for satisfactory musical recognition:

> Regarded from such a perspective, our ability to perceive music seems to have an important precondition: our memory must hold musical sound pictures or musical imaginations previously stored there. Evaluation of a new musical impression is always related to earlier musical impressions, and, without such an evaluation, no real musical enjoyment is possible. Such an enjoyment can again only emerge when the listener, led by his evaluation, knows at any moment of the musical form penetrating his consciousness in which part of the structural development he currently finds himself and which function this part has in the total form.[206]

In Hindemith's opinion, the very first musical experience in a human life must be based on *motion*, which is fundamental both for human beings and music. Yet

> it is a long way from a primitive participation in music founded on mere associations of motion to a simultaneous and parallel mental construction of a musical form's sounding entity with all its ballast of temporal proportions, harmonic-tonal implications, and melodic lines.[207]

Hindemith postulates the necessity of music evoking a response in listeners through a process of identification. Le Corbusier had similar ideas in connection with the use of geometric forms. He believed that it was this fundamental identification process (for him, based on the relationship of human beings to the cosmos) that made forms *beautiful*. For Hindemith, too, the way to aesthetic experience is through identification through perceptive consciousness, and "the more closely the external musical impression

---

[206] *Komponist in seiner Welt*, 35. ["Von solcher Warte betrachtet erscheint unsere Fähigkeit, Musik zu begreifen, eine wichtige Voraussetzung zu haben: es müssen in unserem Gedächtnis schon vorher gehabte musikalische Klangbilder oder musikalische Imaginationen aufgespeichert worden sein. Das Urteil über einen neuen musikalischen Eindruck bezieht sich stets auf frühere musikalische Eindrücke, und ohne solches Urteil ist kein wirklicher musikalischer Genuss denkbar; solcher Genuss wiederum kann nur eintreten, wenn der durch sein Urteil geleitete Hörer in jedem Moment der auf ihn eindringenden musikalischen Form weiß, in welchem Teil der formalen Entwicklung er sich gerade befindet, welchen Wert und welche Funktion dieser Teil in der Gesamtform hat."]

[207] *A Composer's World*, 22.

approaches a perfect coincidence with his [the listener's] mental expectation of the composition, the greater will be his aesthetic satisfaction."[208]

The gain from any mental parallel construction depends on listeners' individual capacity, says Hindemith. Schoenberg expressed quite similar views when discussing the unfolding of musical logic. The skill must be developed, and the starting-point lies in clear metrics, short and symmetric phrases, and the simplest harmonic-tonal and melodic constructions. "Our present-day composers of marches, dances, and songs see to it that this group of participants in music is not in want of substance for their analytical and reconstructive activity,"[209] Hindemith writes. Again, in a way reminiscent of Schoenberg, he also places dance forms within the category of the most immediately perceptible types of music, while at the same time including a broader range of contemporary entertainment music. For this reason, the following detailed examination will focus on one of his dance movements. Hindemith admits that not even more experienced and ambitious listeners will always be receptive to complicated musical structures. Composers must always plan their work to include points of rest to give listeners breathing space.

Hindemith's main point is that a genuine musical experience depends on the possibility of relating what is newly experienced to something already known. What is perceived as unconditionally new will never give this kind of experience.[210] He concludes that in fact nothing new can be added without undermining the possibilities of listeners' participation. While music's technical level and so-called styles must necessarily change, the essential qualities of art are, and will always be, the same. The intellectual and emotional regions affected by a musical experience remain the same. Thus a modern symphony concert is neither superior nor inferior to the flute tunes of Stone-Age humans; Hindemith again allows for a universal element, one that lies in the eternal possibilities and limitations affecting the human ability to undertake mental parallel construction. His understanding of the musical material—which is so firmly based on regularity in the overtone series and the human ear—has a decisive position in this overall picture.

Where Schoenberg often seems to believe too optimistically in the human competence of comprehension, Hindemith seems too pessimistic. He believes that listeners must be treated with great care. In Hindemith's writings this conviction is underscored by the emphasis he gives to the limitations of a composer's possibilities—in a supposedly chaotic time when

---

[208] *A Composer's World*, 20.

[209] *A Composer's World*, 23.

[210] See *A Composer's World*, 23.

there is considerable willingness to experiment. His considerations may at least in part explain some of the critics' objections to the seemingly moderate challenges listeners encounter in some of Hindemith's works. For both Schoenberg and Hindemith it is important that the musical work must be perceived as clearly and unequivocally as possible, through conscious processes based on rationality. This attitude also has consequences for the way Hindemith constructs musical forms.

Hindemith was a master of construction. His intuitive sense of form was combined with a highly developed feeling for architecture. Ian Kemp was one to highlight this gift: "Hindemith's sense of musical architecture was perhaps the most highly developed of all his musical faculties," continuing in a way relevant to the present discussion: "On rare occasions when his formal structures seem to totter [...] the listener's discomfort is acute because so unexpected."[211]

Hindemith's gift for designing structures are particularly manifest in *Ludus Tonalis*. This opus serves as a comprehensive example of his relation to various types of form-building techniques. As mentioned above, one rarity here is fact that prelude and postlude are retrograde inversions of each other. This particular mirror image has become famous because it is not a case of reversing and turning the music on its head interval by interval. Instead, the notation of the prelude is literally turned around visually, with Hindemith posing himself the nearly impossible task of retaining everything from the positions of notes on the staves and the use of accidentals.[212] For instance, the progression C_4—A_4 in the prelude's soprano clef becomes E_3—C_3 in the postlude's bass clef. The pieces are mirror images of one another in such a concrete way that the postlude could be read from the pages of the prelude by turning the score upside down. The musical architecture is so graphically explicit that it may in itself give pleasure, even to the inexperienced eye studying the notation. As David Neumeyer points out, the sketches for these two parts naturally have a significance very different from Hindemith's ordinary drafts. The notation shows, among other things, that he wrote both pieces simultaneously rather than designing the one from an individual idea and hoping for the best with the other. The subtle use of symmetry on various levels is a characteristic of the work as a whole, and, as such, it has a special place in Hindemith's production.

When it comes to the concept of mental parallel construction there are two main points of importance. First, the work's macro-form is structured according to *Series I* and based on the view of musical material presented in

---

[211] Ian Kemp, *Hindemith* (London: Oxford University Press, 1970), 45.

[212] See D. Neumeyer, "The Genesis and Structure of Hindemith's Ludus Tonalis," 82.

The Craft of Musical Composition. Second, and with respect to the polyphonic base in *Ludus Tonalis*: despite Hindemith's obvious aim to offer a demonstration of the so-called learned counterpoint with a refined use of motivic-thematic material, none of the fugues have more than three voices. This number of voices is the maximum that can be discerned, says Hindemith, as "[i]t is impossible to perceive four or more equal lines clearly."[213] He deems it important that the linearity is also distinguished and felt as consisting of equal voices. The possibilities should be arranged specially for a successful mental parallel construction; it is not enough that the voices run together in a general experience of complex polyphony. The use of linear counterpoint is of great significance for Hindemith's ideas of constructions. Consequently, there is a bridge spanning from *Ludus Tonalis* to his earliest works for the piano. The work of 1917/19, *In einer Nacht... Träume und Erlebnisse*, op. 15 (In a Night... Dreams and Experiences), is a striking example of the young and experimental Hindemith discovering possibilities rather than limitations. In a letter dated 28 November 1917 to his friend Emmy Ronnefeldt, he makes the following wry comment:

> If I work further in this genre, I will one day come to regions beyond good and evil, where one can no longer decide whether what I have written is an elevated kind of music or merely a substitute for music. Yet these things give me giant pleasure. One of the pieces is 9 measures long. I am investing all my ambitions to write as the next one that consists of only 3 measures, theme, development section, coda. The master reveals himself in restraint.[214]

The fourteenth and final movement of *In einer Nacht* is entitled "Finale: Doppelfuge mit Engführungen" (double fugue with strettos). The piece shows that as early as 1917 Hindemith was a master of contrapuntal techniques. By indicating the basic construction principles in the title, he also demonstrates a certain ironic distance to his own procedures. Yet a survey of compositions written in the years shortly before and after 1920 shows that linear counterpoint is not only typical, but that its demands take precedence over those of harmony. The song cycle *Das Marienleben*, op. 27, of 1923 is commonly regarded as a turning point in this direction. In this work the relationships to

---

[213]"Wie soll der ideale Chorsatz ...," 25. ["Es ist unmöglich, vier oder mehr vollkommen gleichwertige Linien klar aufzufassen."]

[214]*Paul Hindemith Briefe*, 70. ["Wenn ich in diesem Genre weiterarbeite, komme ich einmal in eine Gegend jenseits von Gut u. Böse, wo es nicht mehr zu unterscheiden ist, ob das was ich geschrieben habe eine höhere Art Musik oder nur ein Musik-Ersatz ist. Mir machen die Sachen aber eine Riesenfreude. Eines der Stücke ist 9 Takte lang. Ich setze meinen ganzen Ehrgeiz darein, demnächst eines zu schreiben, das nur aus 3 Takten besteht, Thema, Durchführung, Coda. In der Beschränktheit zeiget sich der Meister!"]

the normative form types are particularly interesting: Hindemith's use of *passacaglia, fugato*, and *canon* combines his modernist musical construction with established compositional procedures in a way that results in a unique structural clarity. Even so, the expression is markedly Hindemithian and not Baroque; there is no question either of pastiches or imitations.

The collection of seven *Kammermusiken*, composed in 1924-1927, is perhaps Hindemith's most characteristic contribution to contrapuntal writing. These works stand out for clear-cut contours found on several musical levels. A good example is *Kammermusik No. 7*, op. 46/2, an organ concerto written for Frankfurt Radio and broadcast in January 1928. The head of this experimental radio station, Georg Schünemann, deemed this work particularly accessible because of its clarity of articulation and instrumentation.[215]

Hindemith includes contrapuntal procedures also in his works in sonata form—a form in which he is particularly interested in from the 1930s. His sonata movements are typically not characterized by the dramatic conflict traditionally associated with them but better described with a term coined by Joseph Dorfman, "counterpoint-sonata form," denoting a musical form in which, although it is designed with the structural features of the sonata, the process of composition stems from rules governing counterpoint technique."[216] Dorfman claims that Hindemith must be considered an innovator in this field, thus giving the sonata form a new and refreshing esprit. Dorfman's assessment may be regarded as corresponding with Adorno's aforementioned evaluation of Schoenberg's innovation of the sonata form in the *Wind Quintet*.

In his book *The Music of Paul Hindemith*, David Neumeyer discusses Hindemith's use of certain formal proportions, among them the *golden ratio*, in works written from around 1930 onwards, but particularly after 1950.[217] Given the functionalist context of this study, however, the example to be analyzed here is taken from Hindemith's adaptation of form types. In accordance with his own estimation of the optimal possibilities for mental parallel construction, the following discussion will, as with Schoenberg, concentrate on a dance movement from a suite with formal roots in the Baroque era, a work related, at the same time, to contemporary entertainment music.

---

[215] See H. Kühn, "Vorstellungen über Radiomusik in der zwanziger Jahren," D. Rexroth, ed., *Erprobungen und Erfahrungen. Zu Paul Hindemith's Schaffen in den Zwanziger Jahren* (Mainz: Schott, 1978), 51-52.

[216] J. Dorfmann, "Counterpoint-Sonata Form," *Hindemith-Jahrbuch* 1990/X1X (Mainz etc.: Schott, 1993), 55.

[217] D. Neumeyer, *The Music of Paul Hindemith* (New Haven, CT: Yale University Press, 1986).

Form and Norm: Hindemith's Shimmy from *1922. Suite for Piano*

Hindemith's approach to the construction of a piece has often been compared to that of the Baroque masters. The similarity is, however, restricted to the application of corresponding compositional principles; nowhere does Hindemith make stylistic copies of the past. He always uses his own, modern musical material. His *Rag Time (Well-Tempered)* from 1921 (based on the C-minor Fugue from the first volume of Bach's *The Well-Tempered Clavier*) may sound like an exception, but this orchestral piece is rather indicative of a more general characteristic of Hindemith in the 1920s: his attention both to basic polyphonic principles and to aspects of entertainment music. Tradition is combined with contemporary expressions and the "tempo of the time." Hindemith gives his ragtime composition the following introduction:

> Do you think Bach is turning in his grave? He wouldn't even think of it! If Bach were alive today perhaps he would have invented the shimmy or at least raised it to the level of proper music. Perhaps he too would have selected a theme from the well-tempered clavier of a composer whom for him was a Bach.[218]

These words are typical not only of Hindemith's sense of humor and lack of ceremony, but also of a prevailing view of the 1920s: Since dance types were felt to reflect their time, contemporary suites of foxtrots and shimmies were regarded as corresponding to, for example, Bach's use of allemandes and minuets and Chopin's polonaises and mazurkas. And, indeed, in Hindemith's *In einer Nacht*, the concluding double fugue is preceded by a foxtrot. Neumeyer refers to several unspecified foxtrots, marches, rags, and shimmies from Hindemith's hand early in the 1920s.[219] This output may also be considered in connection with a letter from the composer to his publishers at Schott, dated 22 March 1920: "Do you have any use for foxtrots, bostons, rags, and other kitsch? When I can't think of any decent music I always write such things."[220]

Two years later, in 1922, Hindemith allowed the following self-portrait to be published in *Neue Musikzeitung*: "As a violinist, violist, pianist, or percussionist, I have 'tilled' the following musical soils: all kinds of chamber music, cinema, coffee-house, dance music, operetta, jazz band, military

---

[218] "Glauben Sie, Bach dreht sich im Grabe herum? Er denkt nicht dran! Wenn Bach heute lebte, vielleicht hätte er den Shimmy erfunden oder zum mindestens in die anständige Musik aufgenommen. Vielleicht hätte er dazu auch ein Thema aus dem wohltemperierten Klavier eines für ihn Bach vorstellenden Komponist genommen." A. Werner-Jensen, ed., *Paul Hindemith: Sämtliche Werke* 11,I: *Orchesterwerke 1916-30* (Mainz: Schott, 1987), 286.

[219] D. Neumeyer, *The Music of Paul Hindemith*, 254.

[220] *Paul Hindemith: Briefe*, 92.

music."[221] It is unclear what Hindemith means by "jazz band," as he was definitely no jazz musician by today's standards. He may be referring to his participation in small orchestras that would from time to time add a piece of syncopated dance melodies or a rag. Thus his assumed "jazz experience" may be owed to some confusion of terminology, since in the 1920s and even up to about 1940, the designation "jazz" was closely associated with popular dance tunes and music presented by dance orchestras. Dance music, hit tunes (*Schlager*), and jazz were words commonly used without more definition.

In her book *Opera for a New Republic*, Susan C. Cook discusses the growing popularity of jazz in Europe after World War I, not least in comparison to so-called serious music. The jazz genre made inroads through France, and it was very important for the composers of the time:

> For many Central European composers, jazz was more than an infatuation; it provided a viable alternative to their worn-out nineteenth-century language. Jazz also reflected the modern age, and its widespread popularity with the mass audience made it philosophically attractive.[222]

Jazz was perceived as representing a fresh, exuberant lifestyle, the age of technology and modernity, and the attractive American approach to life. It included artistic and cultural impulses from blacks, something also in evidence in the pictorial arts. The Bauhaus jazz ensemble was active from 1923 to 1933. In 1928, Adorno's and Hindemith's former composition teacher, Bernard Sekles, put together a jazz curriculum at Dr. Hoch's Conservatory in Frankfurt—the first teaching program in jazz ever offered. In Sekles's opinion, jazz was art music, and, hopefully, the courses might lead to what in those days could be enthusiastically described as "a transfusion of fresh Negro blood."[223]

Jazz became very important to composers of concert music, at least for a while, despite growing censure from the right wing of German culture and politics. In a presentation of the period 1920-1932, Hermann Danuser maintains that jazz was the quintessential example of a marked contrast to the old European cultural traditions. Nevertheless, at this time jazz and its influence was highly diverse. The manner in which jazz was received in traditional

---

[221] A. Briner, D. Rexroth, and G. Schubert, *Paul Hindemith: Leben und Werk in Bild und Text* (Zürich/Mainz: Atlantis/Schott, 1988), 78. ["Habe als Geiger, Bratscher, Klavierspieler oder Schlagzeuger folgende musikalische Gebiete 'beackert': Kammermusik aller Art, Kino, Kaffeehaus, Tanzmusik, Operette, Jazz-Band, Militärmusik."]

[222] S.C. Cook, *Opera for a New Republic: The Zeitopern of Krenek, Weill, and Hindemith* (Ann Arbor: UMI Research Press, 1988), 59.

[223] *Opera for a New Republic*, 68-69.

music was more than a protest against the so-called high art; it represented what must be seen as a more comprehensive fact of music history, something that actually put its mark on a whole decade.[224]

This was the time when the young Hindemith was regarded as one of Germany's most promising composers. He showed his interest in elements from contemporary jazz and entertainment music, although to varying degrees. Elements of popular music were significant in both his own and Krenek's and Weill's contributions to a new genre, the *Zeitoper*.[225] Although Hindemith's idiosyncratic composition in this vein, *Neues vom Tage* (1929), succeeded pioneering works by Krenek and Weill, he was still one of the first non-French composers to employ jazz idioms in art music. Susan Cook considers his *Kammermusik* No. 1 as a sophisticated example since it reveals considerable knowledge of jazz in its construction, instrumentation, and texture as well as by means of stylistic references.[226] Hindemith's ability to combine art music with contemporary trends may be one of the reasons why in 1925 Schott turned to Hindemith with a proposal to compose "some sort of a *Beggars Opera*:"[227] "The way in which you have drawn the foxtrot of your *Kammermusik* into the area of serious music would also be the right thing on this occasion" the publisher writes, "a refined version of a popular hit or, its caricature, something that would at the same time serve as a mockery of the modern opera music of a d'Albert."[228] Hindemith never realized this or a similar project; instead it was his colleague, Kurt Weill, whose *Threepenny Opera* (*Die Dreigroschenoper*) gave the musical world one of the 20th century's greatest successes in musical theater.

1922. Suite für Klavier, op. 26 is commonly regarded as a successor to Hindemith's first *Kammermusik*. Susan Cook points out that this piano work proved to become a corresponding success.[229] By and large, Hindemith had a positive attitude to entertainment music. He felt that this kind of music was particularly conducive to the most intelligible manner of musical experience.

---

[224] See H. Danuser, *Die Musik des 20. Jahrhunderts*, 163-164.

[225] The English translation of *Zeitoper* as "topical opera" loses much of the German notion of *Zeit* (time).

[226] *Opera for a New Republic*, 150.

[227] The designation "*Beggars Opera*" refers to Christoph Pepush and John Gay's ballad opera of 1728, the London revival of which in the 1920s was a tremendous success.

[228] G. Schubert, *Paul Hindemith, mit Selbstzeugnissen und Bilddokumenten* (Reinbek bei Hamburg: Rowohlt, 1981), 47. [" Die Art, wie Sie den Foxtrott Ihrer Kammermusik [op. 24 no. 1] in das Gebiet der ernsten Musik gezogen haben, würde auch in diesem Fall das Richtige sein" [...] "eine veredelte Gassenhauermusik bzw., deren Karikatur, zugleich eine Persiflage auf die moderne Opernmusik eines d'Albert."]

[229] *Opera for a New Republic*, 151.

However, he later modified his attitude as his need grew for a more solid ethical base of his artistic vocation. In "Betrachtungen zur heutigen Musik" (Observations on contemporary music) of 1940, he offers the following unprejudiced statement:

> Certainly we all know how fine and pleasurable a well-made piece of entertainment music can be; a fresh swing tune at the right place is better and has greater moral and artistic justification than the protracted and meaningless symphony of one or another third-rate composer at an orchestral concert.[230]

After all, entertainment music has its obvious limitations. Not only is it always commercial, says Hindemith, but even its noblest versions will be controlled by the listeners' need for simple enjoyment. In high art, on the other hand, the composer himself is in control, right through the obstacles of the musical material and without regard for the consumer. "The artistic advantages of entertainment music [...] would have to lie in the art of handling the material,"[231] he argues. Yet with regard to the material preconditions in the traditional sense, he acknowledges that the possibilities in this genre are limited: "I believe that the best thing to do is to consider today's entertainment music as one of several ways of beautifying life and making it pleasant for us, without demanding any return at all."[232]

In the first chapter of *A Composer's World*, entitled "The Philosophical Approach," Hindemith attempts to explain what he believes music is within a concise, philosophical perspective. In this connection he dwells on Boethius and Augustine, with Boethius standing for the regularities of the musical material and Augustine advocating music's spiritual dimensions. These views will be discussed later. Only his statement "music has to be converted into moral power" needs to be mentioned here, as his discussion from a philosophical perspective includes entertainment music.[233] He maintains that it is not right to exclude this musical genre, as long as it conveys a modicum of moral force or a will for spiritual elevation:

---

[230]"Betrachtungen zur heutigen Musik," 156. ["Wir wissen zwar alle, wie schön und erfreulich ein gutgemachtes Stück Unterhaltungsmusik sein kann; ein frisches Swing-Stück am rechten Platz ist besser und hat größere moralische und künstlerische Berechtigung als die langweilige und nichtssagende Symphonie irgendeines drittklassigen Komponisten im Orchesterkonzert."]

[231]*Ibid.* ["Die artistischen Vorzüge der Unterhaltungsmusik [...] müssten demnach in der Kunst der Materialbehandlung beruhen."]

[232]*Ibid.* ["Ich glaube, man tut am besten, unsere heutige Unterhaltungsmusik als eines der vielen Mittel anzusehen, die uns das Leben verschönen und angenehm machen, ohne von uns die geringste Gegenleistung zu fordern."]

[233]*A Composer's World*, 6.

> Even the most cultured mind sometimes feels a desire for distracting entertainment, and, as a principle, music for all possible degrees of entertainment ought to be provided. No music philosophy should overlook this fact. There are many methods of creating, distributing, and receiving music, none of which must be excluded from its theses so long as the slightest effort towards stimulating the receiving mind into moral activity is perceptible. The only musical activities to be condemned are those that do not aim at fulfilling such requirements.[234]

More than anything else Hindemith opposes the commercial aspects of music, along with any musical utterances that invite passive rather than active cognition. At the same time, he demonstrates that he himself begins with quite a broad tolerance for diversities in styles and genres. One reason for looking more closely at the Shimmy from *1922. Suite for Piano* in the context of this study is to corroborate this claim. But the main reason is to give an example of his structural reference to norms that are not limited to "old forms" as those found in Schoenberg's *Suite*. Norms are products of the time in which they are established, and it is to the shimmy, from his own vibrant times, that Hindemith intends to relate the piece investigated below. Including this dance type in an art-music context is more than a youthful flight of fancy; it is representative of a vital trend in the Weimar Republic's new generation of composers. In the following discussion this fact will be taken seriously through an in-depth approach to a Hindemith work that is not often the focus of analysis. The piece will be presented and examined on general, structural premises without appearing completely removed from its historical context.

Hindemith wrote his *Suite* between June 1921 and May 1922, a very productive time of his career. His artistic output over these years was significant with regard to both diversity of genre and experiments in musical expression. The songs from the cycle *Das Marienleben*, begun in June 1922, a mere month after his completion of the piano suite, are as removed as they could possibly be from the urbane, hectic mood of op. 26. In a letter written in May 1922 to his publishers at Schott, Hindemith writes:

> The long-announced piano sonata is now ready. It will reach you within the next days. It consists of March, Shimmy, Night Piece, Boston, and Ragtime. Frontispiece mine. I would deem it a good idea if you could get it printed soon—provided it pleases you—so that it is obtainable at the beginning of the winter season. There are scores of pianists who will play it right away.[235]

---

[234] *A Composer's World*, 7.

[235] *Paul Hindemith: Briefe*, 105-106. ["Die schon lange angekündigte Klaviersonate ist fertig. Sie geht Ihnen in den nächsten Tagen zu. Sie besteht aus Marsch, Shimmy, Nachtstück, Boston und Ragtime. Titelbild von mir. Ich würde es für gut halten, wenn Sie das Stück—

1922. Suite for Piano—here referred to as piano sonata—achieved great popularity: Hindemith was right that many would eagerly take to the work. Yet, in later years he came to view this success with a trifle of embarrassment. To Hugo Strecker, head of Schott Music's London office, he wrote in November 1940:

> However I think it is not necessary to reprint that awful Suite 1922, neither with picture nor without. The piece is really not an honorable ornament in the music history of our time, and it depresses an old man rather seriously to see that the sins of his youth impress people more than his better creations.[236]

Hindemith showed the same reticence when looking back on several other works composed in his youth, particularly the one-act operas from the early 1920s. Other pieces would be subjected to rigorous revision over the years, the best-known case being *Das Marienleben*.

Hindemith's *Suite for Piano* appears as a play on the grotesque, at once as a product of protest and as a garish extension of the bourgeois piano repertoire. Today, the instructions for the last movement, Ragtime, are perhaps more famous that the piece itself:

> *Mode d'emploi—Direction for use!*
> Don't think about what you learnt in piano lessons.
> Don't worry about pressing D sharp with your fourth or sixth finger.
> Play this piece very wildly, but always strictly in rhythm, like a machine.
> Consider the piano as an interesting kind of percussion instrument and act accordingly.[237]

The work is often considered partly in an iconoclastic, partly in a contemporary-craze perspective. It is still situated within a broader pianistic tradition. The somewhat percussive and crassly dissonant movements are familiar not only from contemporaries like Bartók, Stravinsky, and Prokofiev, but also, for example, from Grieg's *Slaatter*, op. 72 (Norwegian peasant dances). In terms of its genre, though, Hindemith's suite belongs to a tradition that can be traced to the Baroque, as does Schoenberg's op. 25, which was

---

sofern es Ihnen zusagt—bald drucken würden, so dass es zum Anfang der Wintersaison schon zu haben ist. Es gibt eine Menge Klavierleute, die es sofort spielen."]

[236]Translated from B. Billeter's introduction in *Paul Hindemith: Klaviermusik I* [*Sämtliche Werke* V,9] (Mainz: Schott, 1990), XI-XII.

[237] "*Mode d'emploi—Direction for Use!!*
Nimm keine Rücksichten auf das, was Du in der Klavierstunde gelernt hast.
Überlege nicht lange, ob Du *Dis* mit dem vierten oder sechsten Finger anschlagen mußt.
Spiele dieses Stück sehr wild, aber stets sehr stramm im Rhythmus, wie eine Maschine.
Betrachte hier das Klavier als eine interessante Art Schlagzeug und handle dementsprechend."

written at about the same time. As a whole, the collection is thus related to a centuries-long concept of a certain constellation or musical genres. The movements of Hindemith's *1922. Suite for Piano* are typical of the entertainment music of the day. And despite the stark contrast in the models that serve as their reference points, Schoenberg's and Hindemith's suites belong formally to the same genre. It is therefore no surprise that they have definite features in common, particularly in their macro-formal construction:

Schoenberg, *Suite for Piano*, op. 25	**Hindemith,** *1922. Suite for Piano*, op. 26
Praeludium	March
Gavotte/Musette	Shimmy
Intermezzo	Nachtstück
Menuett	Boston
Gigue	Ragtime

After the introductory prelude and march respectively, the two suites each continue with a dance movement in moderate *alla breve* tempo. The two center pieces, "Intermezzo" and "Nachtstück," are each conceived to replace the Baroque sarabande but entitled with terms reminiscent of character pieces from the Romantic era. Dance types in a leisurely triple time, a minuet and a slow waltz (the "Boston"), follow in the fourth place. The two suites conclude with a gigue and ragtime, respectively, two energetic pieces in duple meter. Of particular interest in a functionalist context is the fact that both works relate a modernist tonal language to formal norms that are established in the consumers' consciousness. The pieces may be regarded as a musical variant of the functionalist need for form identification.

A corresponding identification of the form in Hindemith's shimmy movement is given in that its roots grow out of early-20th-century African-American culture. By 1920, this "jazz dance" had swept over the dancefloors not only in America but also in Europe. Hindemith seems to have come in contact with it very soon after its arrival in the Old World, and is quick to capture and communicate the impressions of this new dance in his own music. The main thrust of this work and its initial success is undoubtedly due to his great ability to seize the trend of the day, to feel the pulse, rhythm, and tempo of his times. But the fact remains that Hindemith's shimmy is a stylized dance movement, one that will never become part of a popular dance-orchestra's repertoire. It represents a transformation from one genre to another, from entertainment to art music, and in this change of its natural environment for an alien context embodies another trait characteristic of the epoch.

Hindemith: From Vision to Form

One the one hand, Hindemith probably regarded the shimmy fever as purely contemporary. On the other, he also suggested a historical perspective for the use of a dance type belonging to a composer's own times. He did not write much about this particular work after its completion; other sources need to be consulted to gain an impression of the flavor and slant of contemporary German attitudes to this dance. Sheer enthusiasm springs from the pages of *Jazz und Shimmy: Brevier der neuesten Tänze* (Jazz and shimmy: A brief account of the newest dances), published in Berlin in 1922—at the time when Hindemith was writing his piece. In its preface the author reveals that "what the jazz band plays most frequently is the shimmy," before he continues a little later: "If the foxtrot was a disease, jazz and the shimmy are an epidemic that spares neither children nor old people, not even bypassing dignified matrons."[238] The description of the first jazz presentation in Berlin may be of general historical interest:

> Here, jazz made its first appearance in December 1920. It is true that once before, in the summer of 1919, we had a jazz band in Berlin (imported by Fern Andra, one of our best female dancers), but then the time was not yet ripe. The few jazz dancers were marveled and laughed at. Toward the end of 1919, a total of three jazz bands came to Berlin, whose performances "sold like hotcakes" among the great number of foreigners.[239]

Jazz bands at this time performed as dance orchestras, so they invariably introduced new dance forms—not least as an alternative to the commonly popular foxtrot. This was the most important reason why the terms "jazz" and "shimmy" became so closely associated. "Shimmy is certainly no independent dance, but a variety of jazz,"[240] writes C.M. Craig in *Jazz and Shimmy*, an implicit statement that jazz is mostly regarded as a form of dance. This was in fact a prevailing view at the time when Hindemith wrote his piece.

The full name of the dance is "shimmy-shake," which signals how it was danced: with a shaking movement in shoulders and torso. Herein lies the essential difference between jazz and shimmy, says Craig: in jazz, the lower

---

[238] F.W. Koebner, ed., *Jazz und Shimmy: Brevier der neuesten Tänze* (Berlin: Dr. Eysler & Co., 1921), 3. ["War der Foxtrott eine Krankheit, so ist Jazz und Shimmy eine Epidemie, die weder Kinder noch Greise schont, die selbst vor ehrwürdigen Matronen nicht halt macht."]

[239] Ibid. ["Bei uns fand der Jazz erst im Dezember 1920 Eingang. Zwar hatten wir schon einmal (im Sommer 1919) eine Jazz Band in Berlin (eine unserer besten Tänzerinnen, Fern Andra, hatte sie importiert), aber damals war der Boden noch nicht reif. Die wenigen Jazztänzer wurden bestaunt und belacht. Ende 1919 kamen gleich drei Jazz-Bands nach Berlin und fanden bei der großen Zahl der anwesenden Ausländer 'reißenden Absatz'."]

[240] *Jazz und Shimmy*, 58.

part of the body moves; in the shimmy, it is primarily the upper body. The term is also connected to the synonym for *chemise*, French for a nightshirt or loose-fitting garment. The connection between that particular piece of clothing and the dance is evident in the rather detailed instructions:

> Shake your nightshirt. One needs to try the movement with which one would shake the nightshirt off one's shoulders only once to acquire the characteristic shimmy motion.[241]

In this dance, the upper body shakes while the lower body is relatively stable. A number of distinguishing steps were thrown in, but as they have little to do with Hindemith's piece, they do not concern us here. Craig explains:

> All those other extravagant steps that go under the term shimmy [...] are stage tricks. There is only one further step that is justified in the shimmy, one that in America is called the "music box." This is a simple turning on the spot around one's own axis, with tiny, slowly placed steps, in the character of a music-box.[242]

The main characteristic of a shimmy is noticeably the bodily movement, which "is much fun to do and watch."[243] The comic element is an important part of this dance. In the so-called grotesquerie dance, a staple in the variety theater, dance-motions and steps were exaggerated and caricatured, making a particularly lasting impression on the audiences. A rather bombastic R.K. Leonard refers to the futile struggle of serious musicians against jazz. This "madness" is the impact of the time, of the revolution, of Expressionism, and of Bolshevism in the ballroom, he says triumphantly, continuing:

> Then one dances the shimmy. I cannot explain the shimmy either; you must see it at the Scala in order to storm and rage and do nothing the next day except practice incessantly until you succeed with that crossing of the heels. Many laugh, declaring this to be another madness.[244]

---

[241] *Jazz und Shimmy*, 58. ["Schüttle das Nachthemd. Man braucht die Bewegung, mit der man das Nachthemd von den Schultern schüttelt, nur einmal probeweise zu machen, um die charakteristische Shimmy-Bewegung zu haben."]

[242] *Jazz und Shimmy*, 59. ["Alle sonst unter die Bezeichnung Shimmy [...] laufenden extravaganten Schritte sind Bühnentricks. Einzig und allein hat noch ein Schritt im Shimmy Berechtigung, den man in Amerika 'Die Spieluhr' nennt. Es ist dies eine einfache Drehung auf dem Platze um die eigene Achse mit winzig kleinen, dicht nebeneinandergestellten Schritten, die im Charakter in der Tat etwas spieluhrmäßiges haben."]

[243] *Jazz und Shimmy*, 58.

[244] *Jazz und Shimmy*, 121-122. ["Man tanzt darauf Shimmy. Den Shimmy kann ich Ihnen auch nicht erklären, den müssen Sie in der Scala sehen, um darauf zu schimpfen und den nächsten Tag nichts anderes zu tun, als ihn fortgesetzt zu üben, bis das kreuzweise Übereinanderschlagen der Hacken gelingt. Viele lachen, erklären auch dies für Unsinn."]

Some critics found the body movements immoral and objectionable. *Jazz und Shimmy* mentions a notice in the *Berliner Tageblatt* reporting that the dance was forbidden in some American dance halls. "Easy on the shimmy there," was said to be a familiar command in such places.[245]

As far as the music is concerned, jazz—for all its refreshing vitality—was also viewed as boorish, exotic, and primitive at this time, something that was far below the cultural level of Europe. But this particular ambivalence made it so seductive. Hans Siemsen, writing in *Die Weltbühne*, offers the following positive insight:

> It is funny—but beautiful at the same time. Like Picasso's cubistic paintings and Klee's watercolors. Apparently meaningless and without harmony, in reality very meaningful and, precisely through disharmony, harmonious. [...] This music, this rhythm that stamps down every reason, acts like poison, like alcohol, as irresistible as Negro music. Only Negro music makes one blissfully tired and heavy; the music of jazz bands penetrates into the marrow, into the limbs, into the legs. It sets him who understands it properly in motion, like a marionette.[246]

Webster's Encyclopedic Unabridged Dictionary (New York/Avenel 1994) defines the shimmy as "an American ragtime dance marked by shaking of the hips and shoulders" (p. 1315). This explanation is quite appropriate as the dance actually has the moderate tempo of the ragtime, written in either *alla breve* or 4/4 meter. As in most types of dance, there are of course versions in swifter tempi.[247] In *Jazz und Shimmy*, however, the two music examples, both taken from the popular music of the time, are in tempo *moderato*.[248] The melody in the upper voice of a shimmy is usually syncopated and the bass line often has a stride-type style, characteristic of ragtime. A distinctive feature of the shimmy structure is a passage of several measures (a "break") where the music is either quite soft or only performed by percussion. Craig explains: "During these bars the couple stands in one place and carries out

---

[245] *Jazz und Shimmy*, 14.

[246] *Jazz und Shimmy*, 17. ["Es ich komisch—aber es ist auch schön. Wie die kubistischen Bilder Picassos, wie die Aquarelle von Klee. Scheinbar sinnlos und unharmonisch, in Wahrheit sehr sinnvoll und, gerade durch Disharmonie, harmonisch. [...] Diese Musik, dieser jede Vernunft niedertrampelnde Rhythmus wirken wie Gift, wie Alkohol, unwiderstehlich wie Negermusik. Nur macht die Negermusik süß-müde und schwer; die Jazz-Band-Musik geht in die Knochen, in die Glieder, in die Beine. Sie setzt den, der sie richtig versteht, in Bewegung wie eine Marionette."]

[247] Susan C. Cook characterizes the shimmy as a quicker *alla-breve* version of the foxtrot. See *Opera for a New Republic*, 48.

[248] *Jazz und Shimmy* 58 and 59.

in time with the music a trembling movement of the shoulders as mentioned at the beginning; naturally it must never be exaggerated but always just slightly suggested."[249]

Consequently, the norms to which Hindemith related in creating his shimmy were:
1. Moderate tempo
2. Duple meter
3. Ragtime-influenced bass and melody
4. Interval, "break," of several measures with subdued dynamics or solo percussion

Two other characteristic elements were of fundamental importance:
  a) the identification of the concepts of shimmy and jazz invited associations with the motley and "primitive" jazz band;
  b) the shimmy was a dance containing characteristic body movements suggesting humor and grotesquerie, and even erotically unrestrained frivolity.

Hindemith's attitudes to entertainment music extend to the structural attributes of the genre. As layout is concerned, the music is described as never progressing beyond binary or ternary *lied* form. Should transgressions of these simple limitations ever happen, the whole piece would become an individual expression with inherent pretensions that would undermine its entertainment value.[250] With regard to harmony, nothing much has happened in this kind of music since Johann Strauss Jr., Hindemith claims. The emergence of certain chordal expansions has not altered the basic principles controlling the overall harmonic vocabulary. Neither have any great advances been made in melody: "they more or less stayed put where Italian and French operatic music of the previous century had left them."[251] Rhythm is usually carried by the bass voice, with the curiosity that the double bass in a jazz band has little to do compared to what would be demanded of him in the simplest classical piece:

> The bass player in a jazz band plays his continuous beat by hitting the strings with unchanging regularity, and only this or that inserted syncopation occasionally affords some variation in this basic rhythmic pattern, which stretches from beginning to end like a perpetually

---

[249]Ibid. ["Während dieser Takte bleibt das Paar auf dem Fleck stehen und vollführt mit den Schultern im Takte der Musik die eingangs erwähnte leicht schüttelnde Bewegung, die natürlich niemals übertrieben darf und stets nur ganz leicht anzudeuten ist."].

[250]See Hindemith, "Betrachtungen zur heutigen Musik," 156.

[251] "Betrachtungen zur heutigen Musik," 157. ["sie sind etwa dort stehengeblieben, wo sie italienische und französische Opernmusik des letzten Jahrhunderts hingestellt hatte."]

synchronous motor. Consider, by contrast, the diversity shown in the bass voice even in the simplest classical piece of music![252]

In entertainment music the bass voice lacks melodic nuances and variations that in higher forms could become part of a contrapuntal texture. As if to compensate, rhythmic patterns unfold more richly than before. This is due to the tendency toward harmonic and melodic syncopation of rhythmic patterns. Moreover, entertainment music has won genuinely new terrain in tone color and performing style: The keyword is sound effects, a build-up—as well as a swift exchange—of variegated and unexpected tone colors, and an exploitation of the possibilities of technical performance either unknown or formerly unused. Hindemith also admits, "it cannot be denied that serious music, too, was significantly influenced by this [exploitation of possibilities]."[253] Were one to remove these innovative elements, reduce harmony to its basic triads, and adjust the syncopations to the beats, the genre would not have much left to speak for it.

The main point of the present discussion is not, however, Hindemith's evaluation of entertainment music, but rather his general set of norms for the construction of entertainment music, which may be presented in this way:

1. The employment of binary or ternary *lied* form.
2. The use of chord constructions and progressions based on principles of functional harmony.
3. The application of vocal melodic.
4. The use of regular rhythmic patterns with occasional, simple syncopation.
5. A general tendency for syncopation particularly influencing points 2 and 3, to a certain extent even in a constructive manner.
6. Variegated and rapidly alternating timbres and sound colors.
7. The innovative use of instruments and manner of playing.

Using the above-mentioned shimmy norms and Hindemith's views on the characteristics of entertainment music, the following will provide a closer look at his Shimmy from *1922. Suite for Piano,* op. 26. The example on the following five pages shows the layout, with emphasis on three typical elements: Rt = Ragtime trait, Jt = Jazz trait, Dt = Dance trait:

---

[252]Ibid. ["Der Kontrabassist einer Jazzband schlägt in unverändertem Gleichmaß seinen durchgehenden Taktrhythmus auf die Saiten, und nur die eine oder andere gelegentlich eingestreute Synkope bringt manchmal ein wenig Abwechslung in das wie ein ewig gleichlaufender Motor sich von Anfang bis Ende ausdehnende rhythmische Grundmuster. Welche Mannigfalt zeigt dagegen die Baßstimme selbst im einfachsten klassischen Musikstück."]

[253]Ibid. ["Es ist nicht zu leugnen, dass von hier aus auch die ernste Musik wesentlich beeinflußt wurde."]

EXAMPLE 24a: Hindemith, *1922. Suite for Piano*, "Shimmy," overview.
© 1922 by Schott Music, Mainz/Germany; © renewed 1950 and 1990.
Reprinted with permission.

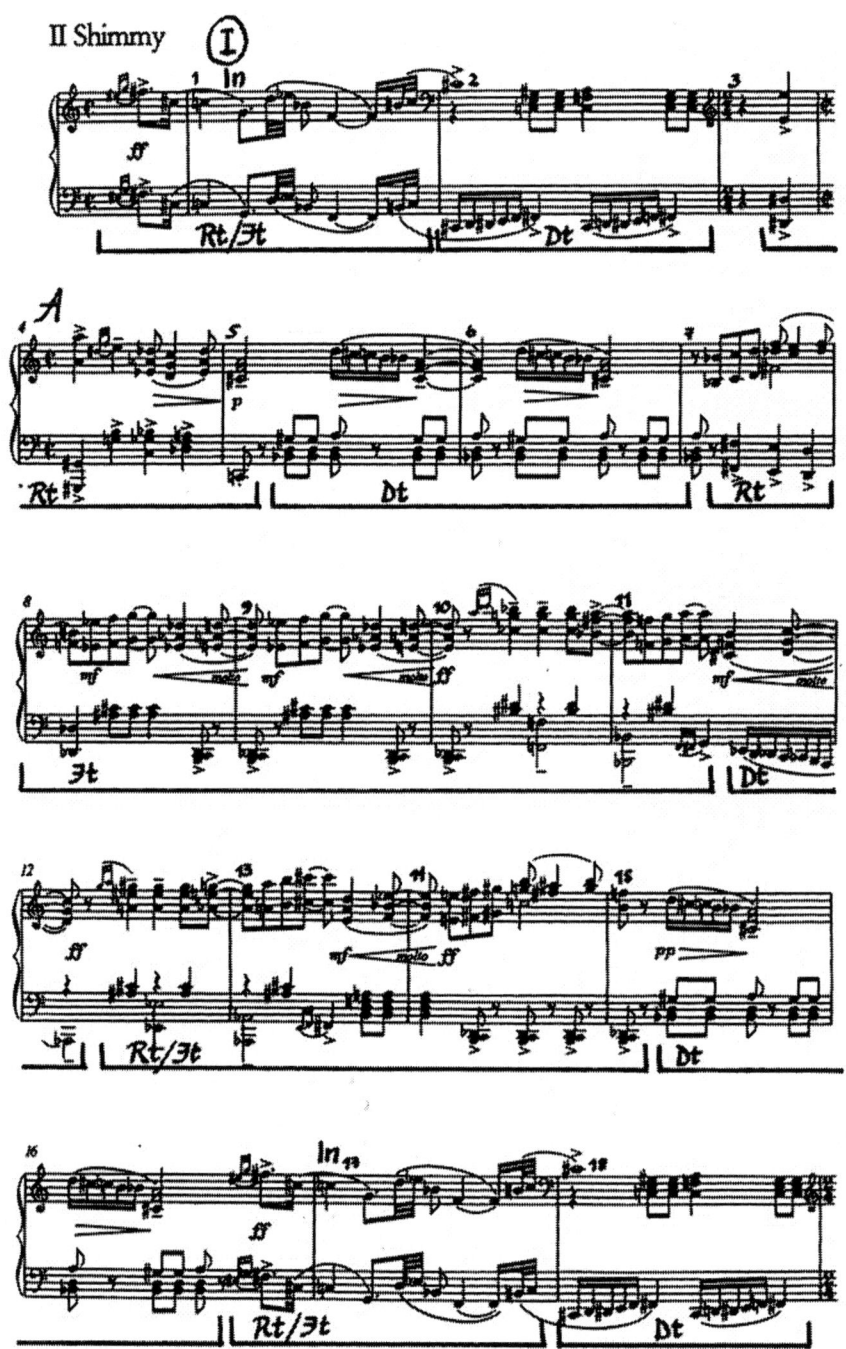

EXAMPLE 24b: *1922. Suite for Piano*, "Shimmy," overview (continued)

EXAMPLE 24c : *1922. Suite for Piano*, "Shimmy," overview (continued)

EXAMPLE 24d : *1922. Suite for Piano*, "Shimmy," overview (continued)

EXAMPLE 24e : *1922. Suite for Piano*, "Shimmy," overview (concluded)

No tempo indication is added to the title "Shimmy"; performers will have to use their own judgment, depending on their notion of this particular dance. While Carl Friedberg was the first to perform the work, Hindemith's friend and frequent chamber-music partner Emma Lübbecke-Job must be regarded as the more reliable source because of her close association with and knowledge of the composer's aesthetics, particularly during his early years. Her scores present a valuable insight into the performance practice of Hindemith's works. In Lübbecke-Job's score the metronome indication 60 on the half-note is written by hand, as is the added comment, "*alles leicht, schlank!*" (everything light, slim!), probably recalling Hindemith's own instructions.[254] The piece is conceived in overall *alle breve*, with a few excursions into other meters. Both the suggested moderate tempo and the duple meter represent features of the shimmy, as discussed above.

The macro-form comprises two main sections, with section II beginning at m. 47. The sections are almost equal in length when the repetition in section II is taken into account. Beyond this first partition, the movement is divided into several individual parts. Main section I consists of an A-B-A'

[254] *Paul Hindemith: Sämtliche Werke* V,9: *Klaviermusik 1*, XIII.

form, while main section II may be regarded as a simple form of developing variation or, perhaps better, as an intensified repetition, marked in the example above as C—C'. This overall form agrees with Hindemith's presentation of the entertainment-music codex.

The upbeat to the piece launches an intro (In) that breaks off abruptly at the end of m. 2. After a rest on the subsequent downbeat, the remainder of m. 3 functions as an upbeat to the first part, A, which ends with the final quarter-note in m. 16. The intro is then repeated, leading up to Part B, which sets out with a corresponding upbeat before m. 20. In m. 31, glissandos of both hands serve at once as a conclusion and as an upbeat to a somewhat modified repetition of the first part, labeled A'. Beginning with the upbeat to m. 44, the original intro is once again repeated, now leading to Part C with an upbeat in m. 46. Thereafter, mm. 60-64[255] function as a transition to a concluding part, C', an intensified variant of Part C. A brief coda in 4/4 time follows with mm. 79-80.

The clear division is a feature both of the shimmy in particular and of dance music in general. Hindemith, however, adds certain irregularities that already on this formal level lift the piece out of the narrow framework of contemporary entertainment music. Beginning with the shift to 2/4 time in mm. 3, 19, 31, and 59, one could argue that the different individual parts start exactly here, in the sense that these measures also become the first of a new part. In practice, these measures function as upbeats to what follows. On the basis of this insight, following layout can be established:

[I]	In:	3 mm.
	A:	13 mm.
	In:	3 mm.
	B:	12 mm.
	A':	12 mm.
	In:	3 mm.
[II]	C:	12 mm. /9 mm. (/repetition)
	Tr :	5 mm.
	C':	14 mm.
	Coda:	2 mm.

The initial overview, which seemed so clear at first glance, thus includes irregularities when it comes to the number of measures and tendencies to asymmetry. By these means Hindemith creates distance to the predictable regularity of entertainment music.

---

[255] In Hindemith's score, the measures in ending 1 are not counted. When reproducing the piece in the example above, I have added numbering for the sake of clarity.

The intro (In) in section I is a natural starting point for a closer examination of each individual part. From the 19th century onward, starting a dance piece in this way has been a familiar custom. Hindemith is true to this tradition in all the movements of his *Suite* except for the third, the "Night Piece." The main purpose of these intros is to signal a specific type of dance. Beyond this structural rationale, the few bars often contain the musical essence of what follows. This is also true for Hindemith's intro. The upbeat and first measure present a unit reminiscent of the unison woodwinds of a jazz band performing a rhythmically pregnant and somewhat edgy melodic movement. The syncopation on the steps B♭-F in the second half-measure is an important allusion to the ragtime genre. Hindemith's shimmy may be best understood when considered as a ragtime dance created with references to the idioms of stylized jazz. The first measure of the intro thus signals two of this shimmy's fundamental musical traits: the relations to ragtime and jazz. In the music examples these are marked "Rt" and "Jt" respectively.

In the second full measure, Hindemith focuses on another aspect of the shimmy genre. Characteristic here is a rolling, chromatic movement in the left hand combined with a simple alternation of eighth- and quarter-notes in the right. More decisive than a renewed suggestion of woodwinds is the rhythmic-melodic motion. It brings to mind the artificial trembling so typical of the shimmy-shake. The suggestive motions toward the accentuated quarter-notes on weak beats contribute to the ambiguity and frivolous undertones in the dance's character. This measure, then, relates to what is emblematic of the dance's physical performance, by means of a musico-choreographic gesture. This trait, marked "Dt," is the second essential feature of the piece:

EXAMPLE 25: *1922. Suite for Piano*, "Shimmy," mm. 0-2

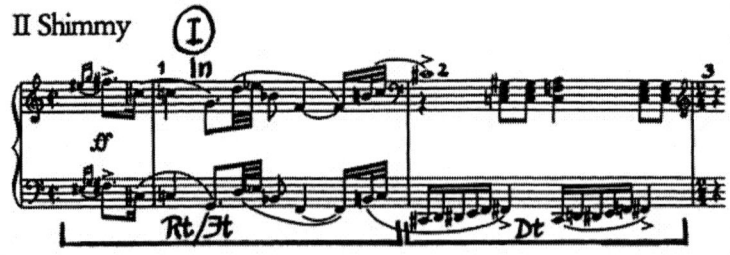

Tonally, the harmonic-melodic aspects of the intro are of great importance. Perfect and augmented fourths combined with minor seconds create an overriding harmonic roughness. Both the tonality and the harmony in this movement are far removed from the realm of entertainment music. The piece is representative of the modern Hindemith of the 1920s, in whose music any bond to traditional tonality is camouflaged rather than revealed.

Part A, beginning in m. 4, opens with a reference to the shimmy as a ragtime dance, through the characteristic syncopated formation in the right hand (eighth-note/quarter-note/eighth-note), already hinted at in the intro's first measure. The octave in the left hand, the leap, and the accentuated quarter-notes all contribute to this impression. The stylistic features relate to the shimmy norm. In m. 5, on the second beat in the right hand, the musical gesture related to dance performance takes center stage. The "spontaneous" and "improvised" physical display is mirrored by the descending sixteenth-note motion, which may be seen in connection with the ascending version in the intro, first on a relatively accentuated beat and then on a weak beat. In m. 7 the ragtime characteristic again predominates. From m. 8 onwards, syncopation is intensified in a way that is reminiscent of the contemporary views of the jazz band as something foreign, primitive, and raw. The impression of musical primitiveness, combined with an intensely suggestive sensation threatening to undermine the feeling of meter, is created with syncopation, accentuation, and *molto cresc.* These features, further emphasized by an abrupt fall by sixteenth-notes towards the transition to m. 12, may also be perceived as indications of the grotesquerie-and-parody aspects of the shimmy. From here on, they continue in an almost threatening, dramatic way, while motions in soft dynamics (mm. 15 and 16) appear as a whimsical yet defensive opposition. Violent and florid contrasts are obviously major elements in Hindemith's understanding of the shimmy and its socio-cultural environments.

The first half of Part B, up to m. 26, has much in common with the jazz-inspired entertainment music of the time: The melody moves mainly by steps; the bass consists of half-notes and forth-note off-beats. There are subtle hints of pieces like Johnny Black's popular shimmy "Cairo Town":[256]

EXAMPLE 26: Johnny Black, "Cairo Town," mm. 1-8

[256]This example is from *Jazz und Shimmy*, 59.

In Hindemith's shimmy the impression of a possible standard pattern is quite mercilessly fragmented through crass dissonances, syncopations, and ties. The accentuation and ties in the bass of mm. 21-22 and 24-25 are particularly striking. A syncopation of long notes disturbs the relatively secure feeling of meter previously established. This "disturbance" becomes a characteristic trait in the second half of Part B, from m. 26 onwards. Here, Hindemith chips off the established meter so drastically that, compared to what has gone before, the passage can be considered a temporary surrender to what he describes as "free rhythm." A complex, contrapuntal texture emerges; various musical gestures are played out against one another through tonal repetitions, broken triads, arabesque-like melodic movements, ornaments, trills, and tremolos. The dynamics and articulation, but even more so the application of polyrhythmics, underscore an impression of the kind of chaotic activities that might be found on the dance-floor in the feverish days of the shimmy.

Glissandi in both hands in contrary motion, extending over most of the keyboard, put an abrupt stop to this rhythmic explosion. At the same time Hindemith introduces a somewhat altered recapitulation of Part A is introduced. This part, which I have labeled A', differs from A in a further progression that, launched in m. 41, leads to a repetition of the intro.

For anyone who has never heard this piece before and is unfamiliar with the shimmy dance, the beginning of section II, Part C, starting in m. 47, may suggest the opening of a contrasting trio: something new is happening here, bringing with it a fundamental change of character. The double bar line in itself signifies a structural division, or at least a transition to a new main part. A regularly rocking, syncopated motion characterizes the accompaniment figure that opens this section. In the alto tessitura of the right hand Hindemith presents a beguiling melody whose descending thirty-second notes are rooted in the more distinct signals of the intro. Further sixteenth-note formations in an improvisatory style shimmer above this alto voice.

A comparison of Part C with the shimmy conventions indicates that this portion must be the equivalent of the "break," the point when the music is toned down while the dancing couples perform their shaking movements on the spot while their feet stay put. Hints at this association with the choreographic gestures characteristic of this dance are found in particular in the varied sixteenth-note figurations of the upper voice and the relative lack of action in the musical development.

With respect to the musical content and form, however, Part C is more than just a brief interrupting break. The thematic material is developed into a transition (m. 60), which has the character of an extended intro. The opening measure and the conclusion in triple meter (mm. 60 and 64) give an intensified feeling of musical motion, creating expectations for the expansion toward a climax.

The last part (C'), starting in m. 65, is the zenith of the piece. The theme is carried on from Part C and the whole progression sounds like a huge, dynamic, textural, and instrumental plateau. No kind of expression is held back: the indications are *breit* (broadly) *con tutta forza* and *rubato*—the latter a term Hindemith seldom uses. From a distance, this "orchestral" piano score, visually divided as it is into three staves, is reminiscent of the texture in, for example, a Rachmaninov piano prelude or an *Etude Tableau*.

Hindemith's Shimmy may seem to end in a parody of the romantic bravura of bygone days. However, Part C' can also be heard as a bombastic exaggeration of the shimmy's passionate intensity. The *rubato* instructions and the changes of meter, the dynamics and the dissonant harmonies, the pompous use of quintuplets and triplets can all be perceived as a caricature of the oversized importance this dance fashion had for the hectic shimmiers of the 1920s. Yet it is not a simple task to explain C' in relation to the shimmy standard. It works as a grand finale that could be used in several contexts. The brief coda, to which the preceding measures in 3/2- and 5/4-time respectively lead up, brings the piece to a close in a manner that combines the frivolity of jazz and the shimmy. It seems as if everything that has come before is being stomped to pieces: the exciting thrill has gone, the shimmy has been used and now it is being discarded.

The ambiguity pertaining to Part C' characterizes not only this second movement, but also *1922. Suite for Piano* as a whole. Hindemith appears to dissociate himself from his music, assuming the role of a remote onlooker. This kind of pretense at authorial detachment is a staple of the so-called *Verfremdungstechnik* (alienation procedure) that will instinctively work both ways; but for this to happen Hindemith must relate to the identity-creating set of norms that belong to the genre.

As far as form in this piece is concerned, Hindemith keeps to the clear divisions that are some of the most definite characteristics of dance music. The use of an intro to state both the type of the dance and its musical singularity is an important signal. Hindemith's music refers to the shimmy as a ragtime dance, as jazz, and entertainment music. Moreover, the musical gestures may be understood as choreographic references to the dance's physical execution; one characteristic being the trio-like Part C, which in this case can be perceived as a "break." The entire piece is based upon the modernist conception of tonality Hindemith favored at the time—hence, the shimmy is clearly lifted out of its reference to trivial tonality. Even the framework of the genre itself is ultimately being challenged: this particular shimmy goes through a process of abstraction whose resulting characteristics resemble those identified in the gavotte of Schoenberg's *Suite for Piano*. The authentic experience of a recognition and identification of the form type will depend, even in Hindemith's piece, on the degree to which the listener is able to follow this unique process. The essential point is that the composer develops the musical layout in a way that makes such an identification possible. This possibility, in turn, links this example from Hindemith's output to the functionalist understanding of form.

Summary

Hindemith's views on musical form are situated within the triangle of intuition, construction, and tradition. The former element is primarily that of the intuitive sense human beings have of proportions. There must be a recognizable regularity in the musical layout on one level or another, but in his own lifetime this kind of logos has not yet been revealed. There is not even any knowledge of a proper measuring unit for form. Until a fundamental level of determination has been defined, traditional structural analyses and compositional exercises will have to be used as before.

Hindemith agrees with Schoenberg that the conception of a work's totality precedes the technical construction of a musical form. "Vision" is the term he uses for the composer's first, inner, and spontaneous perception of a complete piece of music. The *Einfall* is a mysterious flash that triggers this vision. Hindemith believes that more trivial occurrences can also be experienced in such a flash, but they will consist of new constellations of well-known musical phenomena rather than a genuine *Einfall*. The achievement of compositional craft is of supreme importance for realizing a vision by means of a musical form.

Hindemith stresses that musical form develops in time and that it must therefore be evaluated in retrospect. This conviction rests on the notion that the musical progression in time is condensed in space. For both Schoenberg and Hindemith, the musical form is always unique: it is something that is brand new each time it appears.

Musical form originates in rhythm, the vibrant force that sets music in motion and which, besides the interval, is a decisive, basic element of the art. Rhythm and meter constitute a musical form and make it develop in time. In this field the revelation of the enigma of musical form lies in the field of psychology rather than in the physical nature of sound. Certain aspects of formal progressions are measurable by a clock or a metronome, but for the time being, composers and beholders do not have a measuring tool for the inner, formal proportions and textures.

Hindemith regards repetition, variation, and change as basic phenomena in constructing musical form. What is new will always have to be related to something that can be consciously, or subconsciously, identified with something already known, a fact composers should always bear in mind. Schoenberg and Hindemith regard dance forms as the easiest musical forms for the understanding of inexperienced listeners.

Hindemith was a master of formal construction. *Ludus Tonalis* is but one striking example among many of his great gift for musical architecture. In this work Hindemith displays the contrapuntal abilities that are so characteristic of his compositions; skills he applies with his understanding of the listeners' ability to undertake "mental parallel construction." Contrapuntal techniques are an important component even in Hindemith's application of the sonata form, and a subtlety of proportions is an integral part of his formal language.

Hindemith also uses form paradigms, not only those that are regarded as traditional and well established, but also contemporary variants, an example being his *1922. Suite for Piano*. In accordance with functionalist ideals, he combines in this piece his contemporary musical material with trust in his listeners' aptitude for formal identification.

Musical Function

Functional Objectivity

The combination of functionality and objectivity in early 20th-century art is also found in music. The equivalent even applies to the ambiguity mentioned earlier in this book, as the two concepts seem to indicate both the manner in which the musical object relates to its concrete purpose and some essential characteristics of the music itself. This realization leads back to one of the key elements that make the term musical functionalism relevant as a collective designation: "functional" intimates the fundamental ambiguity mentioned above, while at the same time referring to the characteristic features from which the adjective is derived. The connection between *Sachlichkeit* and *Funktionalismus* in architecture and pictorial art inspires Carl Dahlhaus to use *musikalischer Funktionalismus*, "as a label for the attempt to explain the coexistence of tendencies that in themselves pull in different directions."[1] According to Dahlhaus, musical functionalism may be regarded as the successor to musical Expressionism. He admits that functionalism's so-called aesthetization process, whereby the functionalist work seems to move from a realistic purposefulness to Kantian purposefulness without purpose (*Zweckmäßigkeit ohne Zweck*), may seem problematic. However, this aspect can be understood if one draws a parallel to formalist literary theory:

> As a more thorough analysis will show, it [formalist theory] is particularly suited to capture the suggested aesthetization process of functionalism through precise concepts. For by breaking through the smooth surface of an art that has become conventional and by allowing the function a product is to fulfill to turn into form without disguise, functionalism makes us deliberately and drastically aware of the means with which it operates. Thus it converges with formalist theory insofar as it turns the inner mechanisms of the structure outwards. And as soon as the determined, clearly defined purposes of functionalism fade and move to the background, to the extent that what ultimately remains is but a vague impression of functionalism as such, this remainder, tending toward purposefulness without

---

[1] C. Dahlhaus, "Musikalischer Funktionalismus," in *Schönberg und andere*, 57. ["als Etikett für den Versuch, die Koexistenz der an sich auseinanderstrebenden Tendenzen zu erklären."]

purpose, achieves just what the formalist theory expects of artistic means: that it prevent recognition from becoming automatic and instead focus attention on the phenomenon and its structure.[2]

Dahlhaus claims that this focus on the phenomenon itself and its own structure may elucidate Stravinsky's, Hindemith's, and Schoenberg's output in the 1920s. As discussed above, the functionalism concept contains a certain inherent ambivalence. Whether or not this concept in architecture and design seems to have general consensus, it can hardly be denied that artistic autonomy is important even here. When, earlier in his article, Dahlhaus describes characteristic features of musical form and structure and further associates these aspects with a functionalist way of thinking, the idea of artistic autonomy is already present in his argument. To proceed by means of formalist literary theory can therefore seem like a diversion, even though Dahlhaus's procedure affords an interesting parenthetical illustration. However, an important question is how a work's addressee relates, or may relate, to this greater or lesser degree of autonomy.

Neue Sachlichkeit is a term familiar from the musical output in the 1920s. In music as in painting, the term came to represent a reaction to Expressionism and the latter's artistic ideology. Heinrich Strobel was supposedly the first to use the term in print in connection with music. He did so already in 1926, the year following the famous *Neue Sachlichkeit* exhibition in Mannheim. Strobel finds justification for applying *Neue Sachlichkeit* to music above all in the conceptual clarity, the focus on formal aspects, the mastery of the musical craft, and in the supposedly objective design. These musical characterizations also suggest links to the use of the stylistic terms Neo-Baroque and Neo-Classicism, as well as to key elements in the basic understanding of functionalism. Generally, the context *of Neue Sachlichkeit* grants particular acceptance for chamber music, since both the small chamber music ensembles and chamber music's transparent structure are endowed with a new impetus.

[2.]"Musikalischer Funktionalismus," 70. ["Gerade sie [die formalistische Theorie] aber ist, wie eine genauere Analyse zeigt, geeignet, die skizzierte Ästhetisierung des Funktionalismus in präzise Begriffe zu fassen. Denn dadurch, dass der Funktionalismus die glatte Oberfläche konventionell gewordener Kunst durchbricht und die Funktion, die ein Gebilde erfüllen soll, ohne Verkleidung Form werden läßt, macht er die Mittel, mit denen er operiert, demonstrativ und drastisch bewusst. Er konvergiert also insofern mit der formalistischen Theorie, als er den inneren Mechanismus der Struktur nach außen kehrt. Und sobald im Funktionalismus die bestimmten, fest umrissenen Zwecke verblassen und zurücktreten, so dass schließlich nur ein vager Eindruck von Funktionalität schlechthin übrig bleibt, erreicht dieser Rest, der zur Zweckmäßigkeit ohne Zweck tendiert, genau das, was die formalistische Theorie von einem Kunstmittel erwartet: dass es die Automatisierung der Wahrnehmung verhindert und die Aufmerksamkeit auf das Phänomen und dessen Struktur konzentriert."]

Functional Objectivity

What Strobel calls *die spielerische Unbekümmertheit* (the playful unconcern) is particularly important in connection with the musical version of this new objectivity. Herein lies a reference to music's function as an "applied product" through active use. In 1926, writing in *Musikblätter des Anbruch* VIII, Strobel expresses his thoughts on the musical relations to *Neue Sachlichkeit* in pictorial art:

> In its pursuit of absolute clarity and of strengthening the formal, in the joy of accomplished craftsmanship, of playful unconcern and "objective" presentation, the youngest music meets once again with visual art, more particularly, with the newest movement which after the Mannheim exhibition goes under the collective term "Neue Sachlichkeit."[3]

Strobel goes on to describe what he believes is basically a clearly object-related attitude, primarily characterized by a distancing from what is subjectively expressive. On this point Strobel's formulations immediately elicit associations to remarks in Hartlaub's program for the Mannheim exhibition:

> No longer does the musician, in proud awareness of his exalted mission and under strong labor pains, offer more or less honest artistic confessions. Instead he once again composes as a master in his guild, if one may say so. He makes music—beyond individual struggle and strain. Against world-forsakenness and submersion in feelings of old there now stands a new *objective* music-making.[4]

This focus on an attitude of objectivity is key in Strobel's observations. Following a phase in music history based on subjectivity, the composer is now back to mastering his profession, implicitly on this profession's own terms. Also implicit is the belief that the composer thus transcends individual expression and reaches a general level of objectivity, where the work itself is again the autonomous object. From this arises a possible paradox compared to the common understanding of musical history, where *Neue*

---

[3] Quoted in S. Hinton, "Neue Sachlichkeit," *Terminologie der Musik im 20. Jahrhundert*, 314. ["Im Streben nach absoluter Klarheit und Festigung des Formalen, in der Freude an handwerklicher Vollendung, an spielerischer Unbekümmertheit und "objektiver" Gestaltung trifft sich die jüngste Musik wieder mit der bildenden Kunst, und zwar mit der neuesten Bewegung, für die seit der Mannheimer Ausstellung der Sammelbegriff 'Neue Sachlichkeit' gilt."]

[4] Quoted in Hinton, 314-315. ["Der Musiker liefert nicht mehr in stolzer Bewußtheit seiner hohen Mission und unter heftigen Geburtswehen mehr oder minder ehrliche künstlerische Glaubensbekenntnisse. Er komponiert wieder als Meister seiner Zunft, wenn man so zu sagen darf. Er macht Musik – jenseits von individuellen Kämpfen und Krämpfen. Gegen Weltverlorenheit und Gefühlsversenktheit von ehedem steht ein neues *sachliches* Musizieren."]

Sachlichkeit appears rather as a term representing matter-of-factness and anti-metaphysical musical display. But there is in fact no contradiction, since *die Sachlichkeit* becomes manifest precisely in the dialectic between the absolute work and its function.

In Heinz Tiessen's *funktionelle Sachlichkeit* the understanding of music's absolute, universal, and generally valid status-potential turns into the polar opposites of *Ich-Musik* ("*me* music") and objective *Es-Musik* ("*it* music").[5] The restoration of compositional craftsmanship is recognized as being important: The expressionist has been succeeded by a *musicus redivivus*, says Tiessen, and "a newly awakening music-making enterprise creates for itself the foundations for an objective, that is, *specific* new compositional technique that will rest in itself and strives toward its idiosyncratic form as a result of pure and creative music-making."[6] For Tiessen, this aspect of artistic craftsmanship is the quintessence of understanding musical function and objectivity. *Die Sachlichkeit* lies in the pure creative function, in a presumably purified compositional process. Functional objectivity grows organically out of the purity of the material, he says, adding:

> "It" makes music from within me; that is to say that I experience in myself "the organic growth of another subject" [...]. Composition is an unfolding that is pure in itself, the flow of the music-procreating function: Not "I" with my "mood" or expressive aim remain the center of the work of art, rather, the *musical substance around its unfolding from within itself* becomes the center.[7]

It might seem as if Tiessen is drawing recognition of artistic organicism into the 1920s' concept of objectivity in a way that surpasses even the Romantics. However, behind this poetic presentation is a firm understanding of *objectivity* never found in Romanticism: Tiessen intends to demonstrate that knowledge of the musical material and craftsmanlike control, both of which may be considered objective phenomena, can push the composer's intervening subject into the background in favor of the music's own development, of its own supposedly pure substance. Both this musical substance and

---

[5] H. Tiessen, *Zur Geschichte der jüngsten Musik (1913-1928)*, 59.

[6] Tiessen, 59. ["ein neu erwachender Musizierbetrieb schafft sich die Grundlagen einer sachlichen, d.h. *spezifischen, in sich beruhenden* neuen Kompositionstechnik, die zur Eigenform als Ergebnis reinen zeugungsfreudigen Musizierens strebt."]

[7] *Ibid.*, 59-60. [" 'Es' musiziert aus mir – das heißt: ich erlebe in mir das 'organische Wachsen eines anderen Subjekts' [...]; Komponieren ist ein in sich reiner Vorgang des Strömens der musikalischen Zeugungsfunktion: Zentrale des Kunstwerks bleibe nicht 'Ich' mit meiner 'Stimmung' oder Ausdrucksabsicht, sondern zur Zentrale wird *die musikalische Substanz um ihre Entfaltung aus sich selbst.*"]

its development result from the composer's imagination, soul, or spirit. Nevertheless, this new *Lebewesen* (living organism) has its own, independent laws that are determinative for its development, a way of thinking for which Schoenberg's and Hindemith's writings provide good examples. Subsequently, Tiessen's pays increasing attention to the constructivist tendency. He even intensifies his constructivist focus in what he characterizes as the attitude of *applied arts craftsmanship*.

The larger picture of *Sachlichkeit* also includes views of musical interpretation. The interpreter as the subject must make way for a so-called objective musical reproduction—*für eine sachliche Wiedergabe der Musik*. Schoenberg and Hindemith would consider such elements highly significant. Yet this view is far from new. Hegel in his *Ästhetik* already distinguishes between two types of musical delivery:

> One (type) loses itself completely in the given work of art and has no desire to reproduce anything other than what the actual work of art contains; the other, on the contrary, is not just reproducing; he creates sufficient expression and execution not only from the given composition but, more than anything else, from his own means.[8]

When a work demonstrates objectivity and matter-of-factness, its reproduction must also be objective, says Hegel:

> For in all cases when the composition is of quasi objective solidity, such as the composer himself has merely put in tones the thing itself or the sensation filled by it, then the reproduction, too, ought to be of such an objective nature. Not only does the performing artist not need not add anything of his own, he may not even do so, if the effect is not to suffer. He must completely submit to the work's character and wish only to be an obedient agent.[9]

---

[8]G.F.W. Hegel, *Ästhetik B 2*, 323; quoted from H. Danuser, *Musikalische Interpretation* [C. Dahlhaus and H. Danuser, eds., *Neues Handbuch der Musikwissenschaft* 11] (Laaber: Laaber-Verlag, 1996), 276. ["Die eine versenkt sich ganz in das gegebene Kunstwerk, und will nichts weiteres wiedergeben, als was das bereits vorhandene Werk enthält; die andere dagegen ist nicht nur reproduktiv, sondern schöpft Ausdruck, Vortrag, genug, die eigentliche Beseelung nicht nur aus der vorliegenden Komposition sondern vornehmlich aus eigenen Mitteln."]

[9]Hegel, *Ästhetik* quoted from Danuser, 324. ["Ist nämlich die Komposition von gleichsam objektiver Gediegenheit, so dass der Komponist selbst nur die Sache oder die von ihr ganz ausgefüllte Empfindung in Töne gesetzt hat, so wird auch die Reproduktion von so sachlicher Art sein müssen. Der ausübende Künstler braucht nicht nur nichts von dem Seinigen hinzuzutun, sondern er darf es sogar nicht, wenn nicht der Wirkung soll Abbruch geschehen. Er muß sich ganz dem Charakter des Werks unterwerfen und nur ein gehorchendes Organ sein."]

This approach had renewed currency in the 1920s, as the term *Neue Sachlichkeit* was also linked to the focus on the attempted objective performance practice of instrumental and vocal music. The interest in forms of early music and supposedly authentic traditions of performance practice enter here. Moreover, reform movements such as the *Orgelbewegung* or *Orgel-Erneuerungsbewegung* (which strove for a restoration of church organs) and the *Jugendmusikbewegung* (which campaigned to reintroduce lay music-making among the young) played an important role. Hindemith is foremost among composers engaged in one or several of these ventures.

Tiessen associates constructivism with *Neue Sachlichkeit*, not only as a compositional feature but also as a stylistic term. He thereby indirectly refers to two directions in the display of objectivity, as did Hartlaub in his program for the *Neue Sachlichkeit* exhibition. Twelve-tone music represents the manifestation of the constructivist line: "The tendency to '*constructivism,*' closely linked to the 'new objectivity,' has crystallized in the specific form-building principles and working methods of '*twelve-tone music*'," Tiessen writes.[10] In a comparison of this view with Hartlaub's comments on tendencies in contemporary painting, twelve-tone music emerges as corresponding to painting's abstract constructivism, while the more tonally traditional *Neue Sachlichkeit* becomes music's object-related variant. Nonetheless, it is not possible to draw any direct parallel between these categories. It would be misleading to consider, for example, music based on serial principles as having a greater degree of abstraction than corresponding forms built on other systems. Yet it is interesting that art knows a definite division between figurative and non-figurative painting, while music presupposes the opposites of tonal and atonal organizations of pitches. The twelve-tone method is commonly associated with the latter. These concepts, from pictorial arts and music respectively, refer to both irreconcilable and contrary basic principles. The main point for both Hartlaub and Tiessen is that the way in which these opposing attitudes are contemporarily expressed is absorbed into, and even reconciled with, the concept of *Sachlichkeit*. Seen under this angle, Schoenberg and Hindemith adhere to the same *Sachlichkeit* concept.

Heinz Tiessen sees an important tendency in the way functional, immanent *Sachlichkeit* tends towards objective musical presentation, both in expression and through its presumptive capacity of addressing everyone. This view is a main point in the traditional, music-historical understanding of *Neue Sachlichkeit*. Tiessen maintains that what is regarded as music's purpose, the emphasis on musical essentials and formal clarity, must be seen

---

[10]Tiessen, 72. ["Die der *'neuen Sachlichkeit'* nahestehende Tendenz zum *'Konstruktivismus'* hat sich zu besonderen Gestaltungsprinzipien und Arbeitsmethoden kristallisiert in der *'Zwölftonmusik'*."]

in a sociological perspective, as, for example, in similar tendencies in architecture. He defines these features as accommodating the contemporary, general reaction to Romanticism:

> Changed conditions of life, changed ways of feeling, also give the "*neue Sachlichkeit*" a sociological basis, in music no less than, for example, in architecture: Purposefulness, essentiality without ballast, simple clarity of form, which serve the whole and do not originate from egocentric roots or flatter the self-indulgent need for luxury. This coincides with the purely *artistic* position taken against the stylistic attitude of Romanticism.[11]

In the musical variant of the *Neue Sachlichkeit*, the rejection of Romanticism, both as a concept and an epoch, is the key to understanding the apparent need to build an epistemological bridge from pre-Baroque and Baroque to the present era. Admittedly, Schoenberg's views on *Sachlichkeit* did not include these attitudes; here the focus is rather on other central aspects of the objectivity concept. The conviction that the power of renewal lies in reintroducing craftsmanship traditions and enhancing so-called truthful and basic principles of composition. An important justification for this attitude lies in the understanding that earlier epochs combined the leaning toward objectivity with fundamental perspectives of eternity, approaches that are now regarded as valuable contributions to the turbulent 20th-century. Modern man as the subject should enter into dialogue with this supposed kind of objectivity.

What place in this picture should be accorded to the emotional aspects of music, which the immediate past understood so well? Or, as Tiessen worded the question: "Does the culture of objective forms sever the connection between music and emotion?"[12] Of course, emotion can never be conquered, he continues, since emotion is a comprehensive, general category open to a stream of widely differing contents. Consequently, he operates with the concepts *Gefühlsgeste* and *Gefühlskraft*. Rejection of Romantic thought in music means that while the stylistic gestures of emotion are abandoned, its power is most certainly not relinquished. On the contrary, this power is even more concentrated in objectivity, manifested in an operative action as opposed to mere gestures:

---

[11] Tiessen, 73. ["Veränderte Lebensgrundlagen, verändertes Fühlen geben der "*neuen Sachlichkeit*" in der Musik nicht weniger auch eine *soziologische* Basis als etwa in der Architektur: Zweckmäßigkeit, ballastlose Wesentlichkeit, schlichtere Formklarheit, der Gesamtheit dienend und weder egozentrischen Wurzeln entstammend noch genießerischem Luxusbedürfnis schmeichelnd. Dieses trifft zusammen mit ihrer rein *künstlerischen* Stellungnahme gegen die Stilhaltung der Romantik."]

[12] *Ibid.*, 74. ["Bricht sachliche Formkultur die Beziehungen zwischen Musik und Gefühl ab?"]

> Creative activity does not de-soul. Instead, there streams from an autonomous continuity of creative activity an inner power that is more compelling since it is more focused than the thinner, direct emotion. (Just as a deed is a better proof of love than words and gestures of an amorous declaration.) It is the spiritual advantage of absolute, objectively formed music that it can give totality instead of singularity, body instead of plane.[13]

Obviously, Tiessen does not believe that the emotional gestures of Romanticism are rooted in the basic structure of music. According to him, such gestures do not arise from a constructive necessity based on the objective demands of music. Here he strongly deviates from Romantic thought, and neither Schoenberg nor Hindemith would agree with him on this point. Yet, Tiessen's claim of objective, functional composing is invested with a concentrated emotional potential. Anything that is subjective, and hence superfluous, has supposedly been weeded out, and in this way he adheres to music's functionalist perspectives. This does not imply that Tiessen ignores the emotional blind alleys of objectivity. Emotions can never be overcome, and emotions are expressed in typical contemporary musical preferences, "even the 'emotionless' rhythm of a machine or the unrelenting purposefulness of a gigantic building in reinforced concrete are felt."[14] For one who has reached this degree of acceptance of universal feelings, it is but a small step to a point at which objects that are clearly mechanical and devoid of thought become the highly valued, but absolutely anti-artistic, ideal. "The concepts 'objectivity' and 'just music' are frequently abused as false slogans in the beautification of empty artistry,"[15] Tiessen writes. This conviction leads to one of the basic arguments against the *Neue Sachlichkeit* of the 1920s: the tendency toward stagnant music and empty music-making that mocks the essence of art. Tiessen finds it important to show that this inclination does *not* lie in the nature of objectivity but is a trait distinguishing its misunderstood progeny. From a musical-aesthetic viewpoint, the question is where the borders lie, and whether these can be considered constant and eternal.

---

[13]Tiessen, 74. ["Bildnerische Aktivität entseelt nicht; vielmehr entströmt der autonomen bildnerischen Stetigkeit zwingendere weil gesammelte innere Kraft als der dünneren direkten Emotion. (Etwa wie die Tat mehr für die Liebe beweist als Worte und Geste der Liebeserklärung.) Es ist der seelische Vorteil der absoluten, sachlich gestalteten Musik, dass sie statt Vereinzelung Totalität, statt Fläche Körper geben kann."]

[14]*Ibid.* ["sogar der 'fühllose' Maschinenrhythmus oder die unerbittliche Zweckmäßigkeit eines gigantischen Eisenbetonbaues werden erfühlt."]

[15]*Ibid.*, 74-75. ["Die Begriffe 'Sachlichkeit' und 'Nur-Musik' werden oft als falsche Schlagworte dazu mißbraucht, um menschlich leeres Artistentum zu beschönigen."]

Regarded from the perspective of music history, two tendencies in particular describe the musical production in the 1920s. First, there are numerous variants of Neo-Classicism; Stravinsky is usually promoted as their ultimate representative. While several of the elements mentioned above, such as formal clarity and transparent structure are usually linked to this term, it is actually quite difficult to define the concept clearly. Hartlaub's emphasis on the classicist tendencies found in the *Neue Sachlichkeit* movement within pictorial art, as well as parts of Schoenberg's production in this decade, can be perceived from a classicist perspective. Hermann Danuser points out that the *first generation* of new music, appearing around 1910, moves the most in this direction.[16]

According to Danuser, the other main tendency lies in the view of the so-called *mittlere Musik*, a term indicating the middle position between the opposites art music and trivial music, atonality and functional harmony. This concept, for which the non-pejorative "middlebrow music" may be the closest English translation, covers both a general understanding of art and a definite position in an understanding of material:

> firstly, with a view to the demand of being art, through a stylistic level in the middle of the "high" of absolute art music and the "low" of purely trivial music, secondly—to give the spatial metaphor an historico-philosophical turn—with a view to the nature of the musical material through a middle position between the "front" of a strict (free or dodecaphonic) atonality and the "rear" of a traditional, functional-harmonic tonality.[17]

It is particularly the post-war generation of younger composers who are noticeable in this area. The time is marked by a generational shift: in German-speaking regions, the generation of Paul Hindemith and Ernst Krenek, Kurt Weill and Hanns Eisler now sets out to dominate the field of music.

---

[16]See H. Danuser, *Die Musik des 20. Jahrhunderts* [C. Dahlhaus and H. Danuser, eds., *Neues Handbuch der Musikwissenschaft* 7], 114.

[17]*Ibid*. "[zum einen im Hinblick auf den Kunstanspruch durch einen mittleren Stilhöhenbereich zwischen dem 'Oben' der absoluten Kunstmusik und dem 'Unten' schierer Trivialmusik, zum anderen – um die Raummetapher geschichtsphilosophisch zu wenden – im Hinblick auf den Stand des musikalischen Materials durch eine mittlere Position zwischen dem 'Vorn' einer strikten (freier oder dodekaphonen) Atonalität, und dem 'Hinten' einer traditionellen funktionsharmonischen Tonalität."]

Functional Music and Musical Functionalism

Due to the attention paid to the various characteristics of *mittlere Musik* in the 1920s, new genres arose, while the concept of genre itself was seriously questioned. The new ideal, *Funktionsmusik*, led to heated discussion of music's potential for functionality. One of the crucial sentiments informing this ideal was the increasingly negative view on traditional concert activities, which included the belief that public concerts primarily served commercial interests. Leo Kestenberg, a concert pianist and music education reformer, compared giving concerts with retailing music in the same way as selling coffee and lumber.[18] Commercialism had robbed the concert of its original status and spiritual *gehalt*, complained Licco Amar, the first violinist in the Amar Quartet: "Musical culture can no longer be measured by concert activity, whose zenith seems to be past as it has, for the most part, given way to a purely commercial exploitation of music."[19] Views such as these were echoed by critical voices describing concerts as upper-class pursuits reflecting the decadent, capitalist bourgeois society of the period. A significant consequence was a shift in the orientation of composers, who moved away from the center of the concert's traditional arena towards its periphery, to musical activities found beyond the conventional limits. On the one hand, this shift might be toward alternative forms of musical communication, e.g., through festivals and associations that only attracted an audience with a special interest. On the other hand, they might veer toward the new market springing up outside the concert hall, in the movie industry and broadcasting, in music theater and amateur music. At any rate, the point was to activate music's potential through purposeful communication and actual use. For all this, the term most frequently used came to be *Gebrauchsmusik*.

An epistemological view of functional music determined the sentiment that contemporary musical production was too far removed from ordinary people or vice versa. Thinkers rejected the Romantic concept of artistic autonomy; a belief in *l'art pour l'art* was no longer appreciated. Writing *A Composer's World* in 1952, Hindemith comments on composers who, through subtle technique, situated their work high above general human experience: "In doing so they advocate an esoteric *art pour l'art*, the followers of which

---

[18]See L. Kestenberg, *Musikerziehung und Musikpflege,* Leipzig 1921, 8. Here quoted from D. Kolland, *Die Jugendmusikbewegung* (Stuttgart: Metzler, 1979), 56.

[19]L. Amar, "Zur Frage der Gebrauchsmusik," *Die Musik* XXI/6 (1929): 401. ["Gradmesser der musikalischen Kultur ist nicht mehre das Konzertleben, dessen Hochblüte vorbei zu sein scheint und größtenteils einer rein kommerziellen Ausschlachtung von Musik gewichen ist."]

can only be emotional imps, monsters, or snobs."[20] This may at first glance sound like a contradiction to a remark he had made in an enthusiastic letter written in 1922 to his friend Emmy Ronnefeldt: "Here, at last, is music for music's own sake."[21] The reason for this apparent discrepancy of assessment is that for Hindemith, *l'art pour l'art* represents an old-fashioned artistic position far removed from reality, while music for music's own sake describes music that unfolds freshly and purely on its own premises. Essential here is the subjectivity-objectivity relationship, which is typical for how thinkers on art in the 1920s understood the relation of the absolute to the individual.

As discussed above, Adolf Loos questioned the function of art by stating that architecture has nothing to do with the supposedly far-from-everyday-life concept of art. The thought of leading music back to everyday reality became a dominant project after World War I. Karl Gustav Fellerer's words in the *Festschrift* for Hans Mersmann are representative of this attitude:

> Through inhumaneness humanness is awakened, not in the pathos of untruthful emotions but in the reality of life. Here is founded that reaction seeking the comprehensible instead of the incomprehensible, the real instead of the abstract. Recent 19th-century Romanticism cannot satisfy this longing. Human society has changed and with it, thinking and sensation.[22]

This was an age when the concern over the alienation of art affected all its forms of expression, a tendency Fellerer linked to the social upheaval of the times. There was formidable political and economic turmoil; as a result, the place of human worth in modern society was constantly questioned. World War I, with all its grief, brought in its wake the wish for universal peace and brotherhood that transcended all boundaries. Ferdinand Tönnies's antithesis from the late 1880s, *Gemeinschaft* versus *Gesellschaft,* gained relevance in this climate. For Tönnies, the concept of *Gemeinschaft* covers

---

[20] *A Composer's World*, 75.

[21] "Hier ist endlich einmal die Musik um der Musik willen da!" *Paul Hindemith Briefe*, 107.

[22] K.G. Fellerer, "Alte Musik im Musikleben der Gegenwart," in W. Wiora, ed., *Musikerkenntnis und Musikerziehung: Dankesgaben für Hans Mersmann zu seinem 65. Geburtstag* (Kassel etc.: Bärenreiter, 1957), 44. ["Durch das Unmenschliche wird das Menschliche geweckt, aber nicht im Pathos unwahrer Gefühle, sondern in der Wirklichkeit des Lebens. Hier ist die Reaktion begründet, die an Stelle des Unverständlichen das Verständliche, an Stelle des Abstrakten das Wirkliche sucht. Die naheliegende Romantik des 19. Jahrhunderts kann dieses Sehnen nicht erfüllen. Die menschliche Gesellschaft hat sich gewandelt, mit ihr das Denken und Empfinden."] The introduction to the article, from which this quotation stems, is mainly related to the mid-1920s, and thus not to the time when the article was published.

lasting, genuine fellowship, which in turn can be compared to a living organism, while *Gesellschaft* represents a temporary and artificial social construction.[23] In the concept of *Gemeinschaft*, human co-existence is of great significance, a fact that undoubtedly contributed strongly to the concept becoming one of the magical words of the Weimar Republic. The term also appears to reflect both artistic far-sightedness and a general cultural optimism. In his address for the Bauhaus inauguration in 1926, the architect Alfred Arndt echoed the *Zeitgeist*:

> The task is not only to build houses, but above all to build "gemeinschaft"!; for great things are carried only by GEMEINSCHAFT![24]

Arndt includes the idealistic belief that the creative artist had a special task in building a humane *Gemeinschaft*, not only metaphorically speaking but also as an innovative alternative to established society. This idea undoubtedly reinforced the popularity of *Gemeinschaft* in anti-revolutionary, middle-class conservative milieus. However, it is a mistake to believe that a delimited, unilateral concept of *Gemeinschaft*, finally merging into National Socialism, existed in the Weimar Republic. Already in 1917, the art historian Fritz Burger had reservations against using a fellowship or community concept in support of any nationalistic, isolationist view of art:

> The German concept of man and humanity is not based, as that of the French, on the ideal *unity* of *humans*, but on the idea of the *natural community of human beings* as a higher *community founded on life and love*. One can therefore not misunderstand the Germans and German nature to a worse degree than in a nationalistic impulse to demand of the present that it must isolate itself from everything foreign and strange so that a pure German national art may develop. Modern German art and its spirit are fortunately far too strong for such a narrow, doctrinaire school-cleverness to be able to harm it again, as it did in the first half of the 19th century.[25]

---

[23] See F. Tönnies, *Gemeinschaft und Gesellschaft* [1887] (Darmstadt: Wissenschaftliche Buchgesellschaft, 1979).

[24] A. Arndt, "Ansprache zur Bauhaus-Einweihung in Dessau 1926," reprinted in Eckhard Neumann, ed., *Bauhaus und Bauhäusler* (Köln: DuMont, 1985), 8. ["nicht allein häuser bauen, sondern vor allem 'gemeinschaft' bauen ist die aufgabe—denn große dinge trägt immer nur die GEMEINSCHAFT!!"]

[25] F. Burger,: *Einführung in die moderne Kunst* [*Handbuch der Kunstwissenschaft Die Kunst des 19. und 20. Jahrhunderts* I] (Berlin-Neubabelsberg: Athenaion, 1917), 51. ["Der Menschen- und Menschheitsbegriff des Deutschen gründet sich nicht wie der der Franzosen auf die ideale *Einheitsform* des *Menschen*, sondern auf die Idee der *Naturgemeinschaft der Menschen* als einer höheren Lebens- und Liebesgemeinschaft. Man kann daher den Deutschen und deutsches Wesen nicht schlimmer missverstehen, als in nationalistischen Anwandlungen von der Gegenwart zu fordern, sich abzuschließen von allem Welschen und Fremden, um ein national-

Burger is focusing on artistic expression itself from this community perspective. When viewing the *Gemeinschaft* concept in a wider political-cultural perspective, it is important to bear in mind that it was broad and comprehensive. As Heide Hammel maintains in her book on music education in the Weimar Republic, the same ideas also had currency in left-oriented circles:

> All parties in the Weimar Republic defend in their cultural programs the ideal of a *Gemeinschaft*, which can be differentiated with regard to objectives and ethos along lines of party ideology. The ideals of a "community of folk and people" and "the realm of freedom instead of bondage," represented by parties on the left, contain elements of Marxist utopias of the "classless society." This community, identified with the term "society," can ideally be judged as an objective in itself, as a value in itself.[26]

It was in this political and cultural climate that the social democrat Leo Kestenberg could implement his great reform of music education. His vision of reforming musical life was rooted in a preoccupation with the alienation of man in capitalist society, not only in the commercialization of concert life. Such anti-commercial views were also characteristic of Fritz Jöde, the charismatic leader in the extensive *Jugendmusikbewegung*.[27] Nevertheless, Jöde's vision of educating the whole person through music was more conservative, restorative, and nationally oriented. The national element was particularly dominant in the emphasis he and his organization placed on the German folksong heritage. In the ideology of the *Jugendmusikbewegung*, the musical *Gemeinschaft* was both the means and the end, based on the idea that a new age needed both a new culture of music and a new *Volksgemeinschaft*. "Das Musische," a concept referring to the Greek Muses, was recognized as capable of edifying human beings to "completeness" and subsequently providing a community-binding force.[28] *Gemeinschaftsmusik* was used in part as an

---

deutsche Kunst rein zur Entfaltung zu bringen. Die moderne deutsche Kunst und ihr Geist ist glücklicherweise viel zu stark, als daß ihr solche enge, doktrinäre Schulweisheiten nochmals so schaden könnten wie in der ersten Hälfte des 19. Jahrhunderts."]

[26] H. Hammel, *Die Schulmusik in der Weimarer Republik: Politische und gesellschaftliche Aspekte der Reformdiskussion in der 20er Jahren*, (Stuttgart: J.B. Metzler, 1990), 71. ["Alle Parteien der Weimarer Republik vertreten in ihren Kulturprogrammen das Ideal einer *Gemeinschaft*, die je nach Parteiideologie in Zielsetzung und Gesinnung unterschieden werden kann. Die Ideale der 'Volks- und Menschheitsgemeinschaft' und 'das Reich der Freiheit an Stelle der Knechtschaft,' vertreten von den Linksparteien, enthalten Elemente der marxistischen Utopien der 'klassenlosen Gesellschaft.' Diese Gemeinschaft, die mit dem Begriff 'Gesellschaft' identifiziert wird, kann idealtypisch als Selbstzweck, als Wert an sich, beurteilt werden."]

[27] *Jugendmusikbewegung* was an extensive organization containing various branches. Jöde was leader of the main section called *Die Musikantengilde*.

[28] See D. Kolland, *Die Jugendmusikbewegung*, 108-117.

independent category and in part as a sub-category with respect to the so-called *Gebrauchsmusik*. Tiessen's views on the social aspects of contemporary music are particularly relevant in this context. The notions of *Gemeinschaftsmusik* and *Gebrauchsmusik* lead to the most characteristic features of what is characterized as music's shift in function in the post-World War I era.

The term *Gebrauchsmusik* became part of regular musical terminology at the beginning of the 1920s. Linguistically the concept may have been used earlier, but, according to Stephen Hinton who has worked extensively with this concept, Paul Nettl was the first to use it in writing. The claim that Hindemith was the originator, found in music encyclopedias and other music-history texts, is unsubstantiated.

Nettl, writing in 1921/22 about 17th-century dance music, introduced the distinction between *Gebrauchsmusik* and *Vortragsmusik* ("music for use" and "music for performance").[29] Music intended for dancing was thus differentiated from dance suites composed for listeners. Nettl employed the term primarily in a music-historical perspective.

While Adorno referred to *Gebauchsmusik* for the first time in a 1924 contribution to the *Frankfurter Programmheft*,[30] the person credited with having introduced *Gebrauchsmusik* as a relevant term in contemporary music is Heinrich Besseler. In his habilitation lecture of 1925, "Grundfragen des musikalischen Hörens," he discusses what he considers to be a contemporary crisis in the act of listening to music. Since Hugo Riemann's 1873 doctoral dissertation, "Über das musikalische Hören," music has changed considerably, he claims. The narrow musical tradition of Riemann's era no longer exists. What earlier times took for granted has now been questioned, with the result that the present situation of music is multifarious and variegated. According to Besseler, the predominant question is how music can be generally accessible. Certain social conditions must be closely examined: "Every such option of access to music must naturally find expression in definite social formations, and it is there exactly that change will emerge in the most unambiguous manner."[31] Besseler is primarily pointing to the

---

[29] See S. Hinton, *The Idea of Gebrauchsmusik: A Study of Musical Aesthetics in the Weimar Republic (1919-1933) with Particular Reference to the Works of Paul Hindemith* (New York/London: Garland Publishing, 1989), 3-4.

[30] See Th.W. Adorno, "Gebrauchsmusik," *Musikalische Schriften* VI [Gesammelte Schriften 19] (Frankfurt a.M.: Suhrkamp, 1984), 445-447.

[31] H. Besseler, "Grundfragen des musikalischen Hörens," *Jahrbuch der Musikbibliothek Peters* 32/1925 (Leipzig: Peters, 1926), 36. ["Jede derartige Zugangsmöglichkeit muß sich naturgemäß auch in bestimmten gesellschaftlichen Formationen ausprägen, und gerade dort wird ein Wandel am unzweideutigsten hervortreten."]

concert stage, which, he maintains, has acted as the sole measuring rod of performance for generations. The concert has contributed considerably to the crisis of listening: its activity has reached a point where it is spiritually just spinning its wheels:

> That on the face of it, operations carry on as if nothing had happened must not deceive us: it is an idle operation, one that has long lost its earlier experiential weight, problematic for everyone who does not seek to preserve the past from empty piety [...][32]

Besseler believes that the fundamental opposition between performer and listener originates in the act of listening itself. A concert audience is an unconnected mass; there is no musical-spiritual *Gemeinschaft*. Radio broadcasting has completely atomized the audience, and the gramophone has removed the listener from the immediacy of any actual performance.

"This audience lets music come to it in complete passivity,"[33] Besseler writes, thereby introducing his main argument: the act of listening to music is for all intents and purposes a *passive* condition, the concert format favoring the entertainment aspect. A shallow ideal of technical perfection has become the objective in music. Listeners can never achieve this ideal, and it is up to music critics to control performances. Besseler attacks the concert's basic division between the functions of performer and listener, which in keeping with views current at the time could again be perceived as a reflection of the capitalistic *Gesellschaft*. As Besseler notes, any attempt of listeners' identification with performers has disappeared. In such a situation, the accessibility of the event is impeded and, subsequently, music itself undermined.

As Besseler sees it, the concert hall is no longer the place for spiritual growth. Music lovers must be activated through closer participation in the actual unfolding of a musical piece. Besseler thus becomes the dedicated spokesman for *the active listener*. The interaction of playing and singing affords values that are significantly different from what the concert hall can offer, although it must be admitted that the ideal of perfection must then be somewhat mitigated. *Gebrauchsmusik* refers to an active personal approach to music that cannot be part of the concert experience:

> One will initially assume fundamentally different possibilities of access in a music that lacks the characteristic concert attributes established above. The perfection of reproduction is to be considered

---

[32] Besseler, *op. cit.*, 36. ["Dass der Betrieb äußerlich weitergeht, als wäre nichts geschehen, darf nicht darüber hinwegtäuschen: es ist ein leerlaufender Betrieb, dem die frühere Erlebnisschwere längst fehlt, problematisch für jeden, der nicht aus falscher Pietät Vergangenes konservieren möchte."]

[33] *Ibid.* ["Dieses Publikum läßt die Musik in völliger *Passivität* an sich herankommen."]

as inessential, the audience is not to receive the performance as an undistinguished mass rapt in passive devotion but rather as a genuine *Gemeinschaft* of individuals united approaching the music through active reception and joint expectation. Such an art will therefore always accommodate a lasting need, not seeking its audience but rather growing out of it. This is *Gebrauchsmusik*.[34]

For Besseler, the opposite of *Gebrauchsmusik* is *eigenständige Musik* (self-contained music). *Gebrauchsmusik* covers music of a more traditional functional description, such as dance music, work songs, and liturgical music. The person participating in dance, for example, is drawn into a collective activity pervaded by the flow of music: "He does not listen but rather behaves in an actively-outflowing way, without explicitly taking music as something objectively available."[35] Besseler advocates that more of the human senses of recognition should be included in the musical experience. He strives for a sincerity which is sharply opposed to Adorno's view on the *Gebrauchsmusik* concept, for as Adorno says: "*Gebrauchsmusik* skips sincerity, issuing as it does from the empty space of freely posited purposiveness [...]"[36] For Besseler, the key word is *Mitmachen* (participation), a word that indicates action. Consequently, it is also a question of seeing music in an everyday perspective, not as a prosaic occurrence but as a fundamental experience of everyday life. Besseler believes that concert music is meant to lift its audience out of this everyday reality, to set it free to gaze into the spiritual realm, at least for a brief while. The disparaging attitude, with which *Gebrauchsmusik* is considered not a part of high art but rather as something of lesser ambition, must be discarded in favor of a focus on the value of active participation, which is not possible in concert music. Besseler's words seem to echo Loos's writings on architecture's relationship to the concept of art, on the one hand, and to everyday life, on the other. "Everyday reality, out of which exalted art would lead the way, becomes the life element for

---

[34]Besseler, *op. cit.*, 37-38. ["Grundsätzlich andere Zugangsweisen wird man zunächst bei einer Musik vermuten, der die oben aufgestellten wesentlich konzerthaften Eigenschaften fehlen. Die Vollkommenheit der Wiedergabe soll demnach als unwesentlich gelten, die Zuhörerschaft nicht als unbegrenzte Masse in passiver Hingabe das Vorgeführte aufnehmen, sondern als echte Gemeinschaft gleichgestimmter Einzelner der Musik in tätiger Haltung und Erwartung entgegentreten. Eine derartige Kunst wird somit stets einem festen Bedarf entsprechen, sich ihr Publikum nicht suchen, sondern aus ihm herauswachsen. Sie ist *Gebrauchsmusik*."]

[35]Besseler, *op. cit.*, 38. ["Er hört nicht zu, sondern verhält sich aktiv-ausströmend, ohne die Musik ausdrücklich als objektiv vorhanden zu nehmen."]

[36]Adorno, *op. cit.*, 446. ["Gebrauchsmusik überspringt die Innerlichkeit, kommt aus dem Leerraum frei gesetzter Zweckforderung."]

Gebrauchsmusik," Besseler contends.[37] He maintains that music performance relates to the human *Dasein* and its *Alltäglichkeit*, thereby also acknowledging his debt to Heidegger.

When Besseler was studying music in Freiburg, he attended Martin Heidegger's lectures in philosophy. At this time phenomenology pervaded intellectual life, particularly the academic disciplines. In 1927, Heidegger published his thoughts in what was to be his magnum opus, *Sein und Zeit*. Here he introduced the concepts *zuhandenes Zeug* and *vorhandenes Ding*, the former referring to the object for concrete use, the tool for the hand, the latter to the object at hand, without any necessary context of concrete use. In Besseler's writings, *Gebrauchsmusik* becomes *zuhandenes Zeug*, while concert music is understood as a *vorhandenes Ding*. A third fundamental concept, which also can be related to Heidegger and phenomenology, is *die Faktizität*, the factuality, or the foundation in reality. "When Besseler mentions *'das faktische Leben'* as being the essential context or life force of *Gebrauchsmusik*, he necessarily has the phenomenological notion of *Faktizität* in mind," Stephen Hinton explains.[38] Basing his argument on actual life, Besseler mentions a general but at the same time characteristic trend in the contemporary understanding of art. Epistemologically, what he describes is an uncontroversial position as the concept is so comprehensive viewed from the perspective of human existence. The real problem arises when Besseler distinguishes between passive and active musical experiences, between utility music and music outside this concept, or, to use Heideggerian terminology, between *Zeug* and *Ding*. In the example of dance music, what is one to make of the non-participating observer? Besseler suggests that perhaps a more active way of listening does exist: "One could describe refraining from personal dancing activity as 'co-listening'," he says.[39] The next question is, what happens when the same dance music is completely removed from the physical action of dancing? One answer might be that the music is thus removed from its function, just the same as if a hammer were to be hung up as a decorative object. But, in this way, dance music may seem to enter the general category of absolute music. A counter-argument could be that while a hammer can be perceived as a decoration, such a notion does not agree with Heidegger's *Zeug*. A tool may not *in itself* be removed in any genuine way from the premises inherent in its use. Consequently, *Das Zeug* cannot be given a different

---

[37] Besseler, *op. cit.*, 45. ["Die Alltäglichkeit, aus der die hohe Kunst herausführen will, ist für die Gebrauchsmusik das Lebenselement."]

[38] Hinton, *The Idea of Gebrauchsmusik*, 12.

[39] Besseler, *op. cit.*, 38. ["Man könnte das Leitenlassen der eigenen musikalisch-tänzerischen Aktivität allenfalls als *Mithören* bezeichnen."]

function in the way music supposedly can. From Heidegger's standpoint, then, *Gebrauchsmusik* would not be realized without taking its originally determined, concrete purpose into account. Parts of Kurt Weill's musical production, for example, would then seem directly meaningless, not only with respect to his more or less forgotten intentions but also *qua music*. Good *Gebrauchsmusik* both survives and abolishes its own *Gebrauch*. The key question is whether music can be considered a utility object at all.

Gebrauchsmusik developed into a motto of the time, not only in the Weimar Republic but also outside German-speaking countries. The term eventually became quite loaded, particularly from two perspectives. First, it was understood to represent an everyday, dull music without any spiritual value at all; second, it was burdened by its commercial connotations. Adorno's whole-sale rejection was definitively owed to the alleged market orientation connected with the term. Besseler himself was skeptical to the use of the term as a motto, and reacted especially to the commercial overtones which he found exclusionary, not least with respect to forms of church music. The term he ultimately preferred was *Umgangsmusik*, social music, a concept Hinton associates with Heidegger's collocation of *Umgang* and *Zeug*.[40] He also changed the second of the two concepts, earlier termed *eigenständige Musik*, to *Darbietungsmusik*, music for performance. But what happens when *Umgangsmusik* assumes the new function of *Darbietungsmusik*? Problems soon arise that are difficult to solve.

Hanns Eisler's response to the problematic aspects of the term *Gebrauchsmusik* is to try to delineate aspects of the actual terminology. In his *Brief nach Westdeutschland* of 1951 he interprets *Gebrauchsmusik* as a term symptomatic of the materially difficult situation characterizing composers in the 1920s, when they felt compelled to write what they called "music" for quite different practical occasions. This music was to be actively *used*, as opposed to being intended for the concert hall. Eisler suggested *angewandte Musik* (applied music) as a term describing music linked to other forms of art, such as poetry, theater, and dance.[41] However, this delineation also has problems. While it would be going too far to see *Gebrauchsmusik* as synonymous with *Verbrauchsmusik* (music for consumption), there are a number of cases where *Gebrauchsmusik* could also be considered as *applied*. Consequently, one is back at the start. Moreover, some composers of good utility music aimed above all to abolish the qualitative delineation between *Gebrauchsmusik* and *Kunstmusik*. Weill mentions this point in his article "Die Oper—wohin?":

---

[40]Hinton, *The Idea of Gebrauchsmusik*, 20.

[41]See S. Schibli, "Zum Begriff der Neuen Sachlichkeit in der Musik," *Hindemith-Jahrbuch* 1980/IX (Mainz etc.: Schott, 1982), 161.

> We have realized that we must once again provide our production with its natural nutrient medium, that music in its importance as the simplest human need can also be delivered with intensified artistic means of expression, that the boundaries between "art music" and "consumer's music" must draw closer and gradually be abolished.[42]

According to Weill, utility music should have a wider, popular appeal, but not at the expense of the strict demands of serious musicians in some misunderstood form of competition with the lightweights on the market. Critics do not see the force and implications of utility music:

> He [the superficial or hostile observer] far too frequently overlooks that the effect of this music [music for consumption] is not ingratiating but harrowing, that its spiritual attitude is quite serious, bitter, accusing, ironic even in the most benevolent of cases, that neither its texts or its form were possible without the great foundations of an ethical or social nature on which it is built.[43]

Weill is thinking in particular of his own production for the musical theater. As will be seen below, a similar defense of utility music can be found in Hindemith's writings.

Weill is not worried by the prospect of his production being associated with *Gebrauchsmusik*. On the contrary, he presents his point of view with idealism and unconditional enthusiasm. Eisler would rather have understood Weill's works as *angewandte Musik*. This leads us back to the question of terminology, where the term includes both all music meant for concrete, immediate use—everything from dance music to the professionals' *neusachliche* concert performance—and associations with ideology, market interests, and social mechanisms. The intentions of Besseler and others to inject a new vitality into musical life through this concept, however, also threaten to be reversed and to end up representing conservative and capitalist forces. Here *Funktionsmusik* comes in as a concept of more neutral value, as it addresses

---

[42] K. Weill, "Die Oper—wohin?," in S. Hinton and J. Schebera, eds., *Musik und Theater: Gesammelte Schriften* (Berlin: Henschelverlag Kunst und Gesellschaft, 1990), 68. ["Wir haben eingesehen, dass wir unserer Produktion wieder ihren natürlichen Nährboden schaffen müssen, dass Musik in ihrer Bedeutung als einfachstes menschliches Bedürfnis auch mit gesteigerten künstlerischen Ausdrucksmitteln gegeben werden kann, dass die Grenzen zwischen "Kunstmusik" und "Verbrauchsmusik" angenähert und allmählich aufgehoben werden müssen."]

[43] *Ibid.*, 69. ["Er [der oberflächliche oder feindselige Betrachter] übersieht dabei allzu oft, dass die Wirkung dieser Musik [die Verbrauchsmusik] nicht einschmeichelnd ist, sondern aufreizend, dass die geistige Haltung dieser Musik durchaus ernst, bitter, anklagend, im freundlichsten Falle noch ironisch ist, dass weder die Dichtungen dieser Musik noch die Gestalt der Musik selbst denkbar wäre ohne die großen Hintergründe ethischer oder sozialer Natur, auf denen sie aufgebaut ist."]

the diversity while at the same time indicating the essential focus on music's functional aspects. This open-mindedness becomes particularly significant when the concert-like nature of utility music finds its way back to the concert-hall establishments: "*Konzertmusik* [see Hindemith's] is thus *Gebrauchsmusik* for the concert hall," Danuser claims.[44]

The key concept for functional music is *activity*, an activity that is multi-faceted. The term covers both activating the potential use of music in modern society and awakening users, meaning both listeners and performers, to an active musical experience. Functional music in the 1920s expresses often in itself the need for performance energy and artistic self-realization. Usually a certain motion is already embedded in the musical structure, in the score's *funktionelle Sachlichkeit*. According to a so-called *ludus* logic, listeners are meant to be drawn into active, musical recognition. There is also a certain entertainment aspect here—an essential characteristic of *die mittlere Musik*. Linear polyphony is typical of *Neue Sachlichkeit*, and this technique is understood as particularly suited for preparing the way for musical activity. Erich Doflein's statement in his article "Gegenwart, Gebrauch, Kitsch und Stil" is typical of such an understanding:

> The so-called *Neue Sachlichkeit* forced a transition to the utility attitude. Strict, polyphonic forms, for example, demand *execution*, they cannot be *enjoyed*, one must be in their midst, they demand music-making, active use. A strict fugue, for example, an invention, a choral movement based on continuous imitation, are not concert music, but rather *Liebhaberkunst* [amateur art in a positive sense of the word], occupational music.[45]

A significant reason for the amateur movements' preference for polyphonic music was also that this music was found to be particularly formative for the *Gemeinschaft*: the performers themselves felt they were becoming part of a community based on equality in an ideally classless society.

As already suggested, Hindemith contributed substantially to these music-making forms. An interesting question is how Schoenberg and the Second Viennese School relate to the above-mentioned fundamental ideas.

---

[44]Danuser, *Die Musik des 20. Jahrhunderts*, 174. ["Konzertmusik [Hindemith] ist also Gebrauchsmusik für den Konzertsaal."]

[45]E. Doflein, "Gegenwart, Gebrauch, Kitsch und Stil," *Melos* VIII/1929, 294ff. Quoted here from E. Funk-Hennig, "Der Einfluß Jödes und seiner Anhänger auf die Instrumentalpflege der Jugendmusikbewegung," *Musik und Bildung* XI/1987, 857. ["Die sog. Neue Sachlichkeit zwang zum Übergang auf die Gebrauchseinstellung. Strenge, polyphone Formen etwa, fordert den *Vollzug*, sie kann nicht *genossen* werden, man muß darin stehen, sie fordert den musizierenden Gebrauch. Eine strenge Fuge, eine Invention, ein durchimitierter Chor etwa, sind keine Konzertmusik, sondern eigentlich Liebhaberkunst, Beschäftigungsmusik."]

Functionalist thinking is expressed in Schoenberg's understanding of material and form, but what about the third level of the functionalist concept?

Schoenberg's music shows the characteristics of what Tiessen terms *funktionelle Sachlichkeit*. Schoenberg even writes *Funktionsmusik*; perhaps the best-known example is his 1920/30 *Begleitmusik zu einer Lichtspielszene für Orchester*, op. 34. But he would hardly have allowed himself to be associated with the broad company of composers of functional music. Schoenberg opposes most of what could be mistaken for concessions on behalf of his art, and it is meaningless to speak of middlebrow music in connection with his work. In the 1920s his music was often found to be an esoteric expression remote from reality, notwithstanding his fervent hope of wide success with his contribution to the *Zeitoper* genre, *Von heute auf morgen*. Nevertheless, there are aspects in his ideas that also place him quite strongly on the third level of functionalist thought. Once again the key word is *activity*; not in any concrete understanding of functional music, but in the understanding of the decisive importance of *mental activity* for the process of musical recognition. The starting point is not *ludus* logic but the intellectually recognizable logic created by context, *Zusammenhang*. Active recognition of exactly this kind of logic is, for the Schoenberg circle, the opposite of passive musical experience. This is also a point Adorno makes in various ways.

Thus there is a comprehensive understanding of the activity concept; a common denominator for an attitude that may seem multi-sided. This common denominator is the key to the broad attention given to the function of music at the time. As far as Schoenberg is concerned, this focus is rooted in his position in the Viennese milieu at the turn of the century, and it is born as he begins to understand musical material from the functionalist perspective discussed above.

The concept of musical functionalism thus includes a comprehensive functionality level, where *Gebrauchsmusik* only represents one segment of a broad focus on musical activity. Activity is understood as a fundamental precondition for the modern human being's musical apperception: The individual always enters, or should always enter, into some form of active dialogue with music. This activity is considered to be quite different from listeners allowing music to flow over them as a passive way of spending time. In the following deliberations, these aspects of musical functionalism will be discussed through Schoenberg's and Hindemith's ideas on musical activity as a way of obtaining *Erkenntnis*.

330 *Musical Function*

Schoenberg: Active Listening and Musical Recognition

> Ein chinesischer Dichter
> ist doch nicht nur etwas, das chinesisch klingt,
> sondern: er sagt doch auch etwas!
> Was aber sage ich?
> Und abgesehen von diesem Klang:
> *wie* sage ich es?
>
> *Arnold Schönberg*[46]

Introduction

In the *Festschrift* for Schoenberg's 60th birthday, Adorno writes: "After Schoenberg, the history of music will no longer be fate, but be subjected to human consciousness."[47] For Adorno, Hegel's idea of the constant change of human *Bewußtsein* is an important reference point. Consciousness seems to change, as does the reality on which it depends, while at the same time it also plays an active role in forming this reality itself. Adorno's German term *Bewußtsein* describes something that comprises knowledge, certainty, and insight. Undoubtedly, Adorno is right in his description of Schoenberg's significant contribution in attaching importance to these fundamentals in musical recognition[48] in the 20th century. Together they represent Schoenberg's main ideas as expressed explicitly in all his major writings. The focus on the importance of logic for musical development and musical recognition is one of his most significant precepts. Numerous examples of musical logic in connection with Schoenberg's understanding of material and form have already been presented in this book. Schoenberg attaches the greatest intrinsic value also to the act of logical insight: "One thinks for the sake of one's thought."[49] His frequent use of the term *musikalischer Gedanke* is prompted by his view of music's being based on a music-specific notions that can be mediated via logical principles of composition. This logic depends

---

[46] [A Chinese poet is not merely a being that sounds Chinese, he also says something, after all. So what is it I say? And apart from this sound: how am I saying it?]

[47] Th.W. Adorno, "Der dialektische Komponist," in *Arnold Schönberg zum 60. Geburtstag*, 23. ["Nach Schönberg wird die Geschichte von Musik nicht Schicksal mehr sein, sondern menschlichem Bewusstsein unterstehen."]

[48] The German term *Erkenntnis*, which denotes the process of gaining *Kenntnis* (knowledge or understanding) and which Schoenberg, Hindemith and those commenting on their thinking use in this context, has no unambiguous equivalent in English. Anglo-Saxon scholarship commonly renders the word as "recognition" and I will do likewise except in cases where another noun seems more fitting, but the slight discrepancy in meaning should be kept in mind.

[49] Schoenberg, "Neue und veraltete Musik, oder Stil und Gedanke," in *Stil und Gedanke*, 477. ["Man denkt um seines Gedankens willen."]

on the fundamental term *Zusammenhang*. The aim is to create *Faßlichkeit*, comprehensibility based on music's potential for logic. As he remarks on the composer: "the newer his thought, the more he must endeavor to consider the demands of comprehensibility in his presentation."[50] Thematic intentions may vary: the opera *Moses und Aron* imparts a message that is quite different from *Verklärte Nacht*. Nevertheless, Schoenberg considers the communication of the assumed artistic truthfulness as his lodestar, and his concept of logic must also be seen in this perspective. This kind of truthfulness lies in the very structure of music, not in a text or title to which it may relate.

Adorno states that "Schoenberg's music honors the listener by not conceding anything."[51] However, this honorable position is certainly not granted to listeners without reservations. Throughout his life, Schoenberg struggled with the accusation that he did not take his listeners sufficiently into account: an indictment that constitutes what is probably the primary objection to his music. Schoenberg himself considered it of crucial importance that his listeners themselves had an open mind and made an effort, not only toward music that is new but also to music in general. This sentiment is aptly expressed in an ironic remark he made in a discussion with Heinrich Strobel and Eberhard Preussner in Berlin's broadcasting station in March 1931: "No matter how well the sender sends, if the receiver is tuned to a different station, it won't help."[52]

Active listening and an analytic attitude are necessary for recognizing the logic on which music is based. This request, proposed as the all-important precondition for musical understanding, puts Schoenberg's thoughts within the perspective of musical functionalism, as, in this perspective, music must be actively used if it is to have any chance of realizing its epistemological intentions. These views do not, however, develop in any direct connection with the *Funktionsmusik* of the 1920s. Rather they come prior to this remarkable wave of musical production in the Weimar Republic. First, a decisive and comprehensible element of logic is woven into Schoenberg's understanding of music's material and form. Second, Schoenberg represents attitudes characteristic of the conflict that accompanied the emergence of new music, particularly in relation to views on traditional concert activities.

---

[50] "Neue und veraltete Musik," 467. ["je neuer sein Gedanke, desto mehr wird es sein Bestreben sein müssen, die Erfordernisse der Faßlichkeit in der Darstellung zu berücksichtigen."]

[51] Th.W. Adorno, "Arnold Schönberg (1874-1951)," *Prismen, Kulturkritik und Gesellschaft* I [*Gesammelte Schriften* 10/1], 159. ["Schönbergs Musik tut dem Hörer Ehre an, indem sie ihm nichts konzediert."]

[52] "Diskussion im Berliner Rundfunk," *Stil und Gedanke*, 274. ["Der Sender kann noch so gut senden, wenn der Empfänger anders eingestellt ist, nützt es ihm nichts."]

Gebrauchsmusik and l'art pour l'art

When regarding Schoenberg in a functionalist context, it should be clearly pointed out that he did not adhere to a *Gebrauchsmusik* ideology in any way. It is true that he wrote a few less demanding works, especially during his exile in the United States, but they were never meant to be categorized into a utility genre. In this respect, there is a significant difference between Schoenberg and Hindemith.

Schoenberg was quite adamant in rejecting *Gebrauchsmusik*, mainly because he thought it renounced the demands originating from the work of art itself. He viewed this kind of musical output as a vain attempt to give new music to everyone, a fashionable appearance that he claimed was based on hypnotic suggestion and ideological error. The music was neither for everyone nor for some. It was hardly worth listening to once, and the supposed public appeal was nothing but an illusion:

> It has been demonstrated a long time ago [...] that all this *music for the audience*—right to the *impure* objective that lasted only during the compositional process and otherwise went unnoticed—, that this music, then, *is the purest l'art pour l'art. As basically no one liked it*, everyone could content himself with admitting allegiance through applause; yet one made sure not to express the wish of hearing such a shallow piece *a second* time.[53]

According to Schoenberg, composers adhering to the ideology of *Gebrauchsmusik* are forced into a condition of involuntary idealism, where they compose nothing to last and without hope or wishes for the future. First and foremost, Schoenberg denies that there can be any valid attempt at providing quality in this *mittlere Musik* in the way Weill claimed. He even doubts there is any validity in the educational element of certain kinds of utility music. Hindemith, on the other hand, sees possibilities here, and in this disagreement lies further evidence of the fundamental differences between the two composers. Schoenberg fears that the exact opposite will take place in an alleged educational process: that rather than listeners being taught to make an effort with respect to the new music, composers end up feeling forced to persist in making efforts in the wrong direction.

Schoenberg refers to "music for the audience" (*Publikumsmusik*)—music that no one really wants to listen to—as "the purest *l'art pour l'art*." This is

---

[53]"Neue und veraltete Musik," 471. ["Längst aber hat sich [...] gezeigt, dass all diese *Publikumsmusik* – bis auf die *unreine* Absicht, die aber bloß beim Komponieren bestanden und die sonst keiner wahrgenommen hat –, dass diese Publikumsmusik also *reinstes l'art pour l'art ist. Da sie im Grund niemanden gefiel*, konnte jeder sich damit begnügen, sich durch Applaus zu ihr zu bekennen, aber man hütete sich, das Verlangen zu äußern, so ein leichtes Stück ein *zweites* Mal anzuhören."]

an ironic remark, intended as an attack on the popular rejection of the famous doctrine. Yet a closer look reveals that Schoenberg has a more balanced view of this concept. He does not advocate the contemporary view of *l'art pour l'art*, but relates its basic implications to his own artistic and musical understanding in a positive way, regarding notions such as *l'art pour l'art* and *Musik um der Musik willen* as two sides of the same coin. "For there is only 'l'art pour l'art', art for art's sake!,"Schoenberg states.[54] He finds a categorical imperative precisely in this expression. His criticism of Hindemith and Brecht's *Lehrstück* must be understood in light of this essential conviction. In the preface to the *Lehrstück*, Hindemith allows for certain user adjustments. Schoenberg despises the author's attitude, aptly expressed in the following outburst on *Gebrauchsmusik*, which, however, does not reveal his real relationship to Hindemith as a *composer*:

> What, then, is this *Lehrstück* supposed to teach us? How to chatter senselessly, brainlessly, incoherently, unselectively, tastelessly, formlessly? Surely people can do that just as well without him [Hindemith]; surely one should prevent them, not teach them? How does he compose such a piece? How does he himself put it together? How does one make something whose every part can be replaced or omitted? How are such parts made up? Why does he compose it if someone else is allowed to make any and every part? To this mass of questions no serious reply can be given, and really there is nothing more to say.[55]

Schoenberg regrets in particular the lack of pervasive, logical coherence, something that should have been based on the absolute, artistic conception of the *Lehrstück* as a whole. But he also considers the music itself to be too little demanding. If the requirements of intellectual activity are not acknowledged, the music is basically without value. Schoenberg believes that all great art must have novelty value, not in the sense of an avant-garde attitude or sensationalism but in offering listeners a genuine experience: "Music must, however, always be at least new to that extent, insofar as we are dealing with *art*! For only the new, the (as yet) *unsaid*, is worth saying in art."[56] Music that once was new in this sense will never become outdated, he continues. The ability to recognize must be challenged, but this human capacity does not necessarily have to lead to a complete "understanding" of a work of art. Acknowledging the limits of subjective recognition is in itself

---

[54]"Neue und veraltete Musik," 477.

[55]"Glosses on the Theories of Others," *Style and Idea*, 315. The original version, "Glossen zu den Theorien anderer," is not included in the German edition of *Stil und Gedanke*.

[56]"Neue und veraltete Musik," 466. ["So neu muß aber Musik immer sein, sofern es sich um *Kunst* handelt! Denn *nur* das *Neue*, *Ungesagte* ist in der Kunst sagenswert."]

recognition of fundamental importance. Exalted art does not have to be understood by everyone, rather the opposite:

> And I am very glad that I understand Einstein as little as I do Kant, for then I can believe that there is something to it. But I don't what this to be interpreted as insolent modesty on my part. For I am very proud of knowing when I *do not* understand something, knowing well enough what it is like when I do understand. For the same reason one cannot write any higher art music that everyone can understand.[57]

Schoenberg's position on *l'art pour l'art* is based on respect for the innermost nature of art. However, the fundamental question is where the border lies between artistic recognition and disparaging rejection. Schoenberg made two specific efforts at activating musical recognition outside of his select circle of faithful supporters: at the outset of his activities as a public educator and with the founding of the *Verein für musikalische Privataufführungen* toward the end of World War I.

The Public Educator

Arnold Schoenberg's impact as a teacher is highly important. In music history his function as Anton von Webern's and Alban Berg's composition teacher is particularly emphasized. It is difficult to imagine the development of 20th-century music without this brilliant triumvirate. Moreover, the Second Viennese School is not limited to these three men; Hanns Eisler was another composer whom Schoenberg considered to be as talented as his two more famous students.

Critics have maintained that Schoenberg was both authoritarian and demanding and did not always give his students' artistic integrity its due. All documents suggest that Webern and Berg had great respect for their teacher and felt grateful and obliged to him. Yet, this attitude seems to stem from a genuine, deep-felt veneration for the person of their teacher rather than from a negative concession to authority. References from Schoenberg's students tend to express the experience of being near a human being of rare capacity, a man with a captivating personality, rather than having been passively shaped by the master's hand.[58] Another of his better-known students, Erwin

---

[57]"Neue und veraltete Musik," 477. ["Und ich bin sehr froh darüber, dass ich Einstein so wenig verstehe wie Kant, denn darum kann ich glauben, dass etwas daran ist. Aber ich möchte nicht, dass man mir das als unverschämte Bescheidenheit auslegt. Denn ich bin sehr stolz darauf, zu wissen, wann ich etwas *nicht* verstehe; weiß ich doch genau genug, wie es ist, wenn ich etwas verstehe. Ebenso kann man also keine höhere Kunstmusik schreiben, die jeder verstehen kann."]

[58]See, for example, the comments quoted in W. Reich, *Arnold Schönberg, oder der konservative Revolutionär*, 42-46.

Stein, seems especially credible here, as can be gleaned from one of his comments that concurs with the impression Schoenberg himself gives in his writings:

> Schoenberg teaches thinking. He exhorts the student to see with his own, open eyes, as if he were the first to perceive the phenomena. What has otherwise been thought is not to be the norm. Even if our thinking is not better than that of others: what matters is not absolute truth but the search for truth.[59]

Among Schoenberg's writings, *Harmonielehre* and *Fundamentals of Musical Composition* stand out as particularly significant contributions to the field of music theory. *Style and Idea* also demonstrates considerable breadth as well as a determined will to penetrate the phenomena of music. Furthermore, his literary works express a profound need to communicate. The texts collected in *Style and Idea* were written for different occasions; its target readership is correspondingly diverse and varied. Schoenberg's dedicated goal throughout his life was to promote an active and reflective recognition of music as an art. If we look beyond his compositions, his position in the Second Viennese School along with its successors and his extensive literary production are major components of his legacy in 20th-century music.

The pedagogic field in which Schoenberg was active is even broader. In 1901 he moved to Berlin and a year later obtained a teaching position at the Sternsche Konservatorium, aided by Richard Strauss's recommendation. In 1903 he returned to Vienna, where he taught at the Schwarzwald-Schule. In the following year Webern and Berg became his students. As he did not obtain the chair as professor in composition at the Vienna Academy, he worked as a private associate professor outside the ordinary academic program. The next year Schoenberg moved back to Berlin and took over an associate professorship, again at the Sternsche Konservatorium. Then began a more itinerant and uprooted existence, not least due to the outbreak of World War I. In 1918 he moved back to Mödling near Vienna and continued his teaching there. In 1925 he was invited to teach a master class in composition at the Akademie der Künste in Berlin, and so he moved there the following year. As Schoenberg had Jewish roots, he was let go in 1933, at which time he emigrated to the United States by way of Paris. In America he began with teaching assignments at the Malkin Conservatory in Boston. The following year he moved to Los Angeles, where he taught, in part privately

---

[59]*Ibid.*, 42. ["Schönberg lehrt Denken. Er hält den Schüler an, mit eigenen, offenen Augen zu sehen, als wäre er der erste, der die Erscheinungen betrachtet. Was sonst gedacht wurde, soll nicht Norm sein. Ist auch unser Denken nicht besser als das anderer – nicht auf die absolute Wahrheit kommt es an, sondern auf das Suchen nach Wahrheit."]

and in part at the University of Southern California. In 1936 he was called to a chair at the University of California at Los Angeles, leaving him a professor emeritus at this institution in 1944. Even thereafter he still gave private lessons, probably for financial reasons.[60]

To call Schoenberg a public educator may seem like a bit of a stretch. One can hardly claim that he possessed any popular pedagogic attitude, at least not in the Hindemithian sense. As discussed above, he had reservations about the value of music that aims to be accessible to everyone. Nevertheless, it is quite obvious that he hoped that even *his* music would eventually gain a broader support. In the above-mentioned radio program recorded in 1931, he expresses confidence that young people are in fact attracted to *him*, implying not only the new generation of composers but also the popular circles of the *Jugendmusikbewegung*:

> Herr Strobel, don't underestimate the size of the circle forming around me. It will grow owing to the eagerness to learn of an idealistic youth who feels more attracted by the enigmatic than by the mundane.[61]

With respect to his contemporary supporters, it seems that Schoenberg had particularly high hopes for his light opera *Von heute auf morgen*, written in 1928/29. As Mathias Hansen writes: "Schoenberg was allegedly quite convinced that this 'gay, light opera' would win him a success comparable to that of *Cavalleria Rusticana*."[62] History has shown that the reception of this piece did not match Schoenberg's expectations.

Nonetheless, there are also examples of Schoenberg aiming for a further, active recognition of music through listening combined with analytical guidance. Here the public educator enters the stage, which is especially obvious in his open rehearsal of the *First Chamber Symphony* op. 9. This event, described by Willi Reich as a unique pedagogic experiment, took place in Vienna in June 1918.[63] An audience was invited to ten rehearsals with fifteen professional musicians, without any promise of a concert in the traditional sense. In an article entitled "Neue Musik: Meine Musik," written

---

[60] At this time Schoenberg's fellowship application to the Guggenheim Foundation had been rejected.

[61] "Diskussion im Berliner Rundfunk," 281. ["Herr Strobel, unterschätzen Sie nicht die Größe des Kreises, der sich um mich bildet. Er wird wachsen durch die Wißbegierde einer idealistischen Jugend, die sich mehr durch das Geheimnisvolle angezogen fühlt als durchs Alltägliche."]

[62] M. Hansen, *Arnold Schönberg: Ein Konzept der Moderne*, 204. ["Schönberg war angeblich fest davon überzeugt, mit dieser 'heiteren und leichten Oper' einen Erfolg 'à la Cavalleria rusticana' zu erringen."]

[63] Reich, *op. cit.*, 150.

around 1930 and later published as "New Music: My Music," Schoenberg presents what he thinks may be the main listening problem with his music: that he constructs his melodies in such a way that even the expert listeners do not grasp the themes and the whole movements at the first exposure. The primary prerequisite of understanding is memory, he says, and, in music, repetition represents its most important support. "The more graspable a piece of music is to be, the more often all its sections, small or large, will have to be repeated."[64] In his conclusion Schoenberg condenses the problematic inherent in his music into three points which also recapitulate elements already discussed in connection with his understanding of material and form:

> 1. Substantially, I say something only once, i.e. repeat little or nothing.
> 2. With me, variation almost completely takes the place of repetition (there is hardly a single exception to this); by variation I mean a way of altering something given, so as to develop further its component parts as well as the figures built from them, the outcome always being something new, with an apparently low resemblance to its prototype, so that one finds difficulty in identifying the prototypes within the variation.
> 3. Not only are new sections, as so further developed, linked one to another or juxtaposed or lined up—all in the greatest variety of ways—but, particularly, almost the only aid to one's perception of all these types of combination is logic and an acute sense of form.[65]

These points of self-knowledge can be perceived as the backdrop for the public rehearsals.

Schoenberg is not alone in stressing the importance of repetition for experiencing music. Heinrich Schenker also discusses this point, most notably in his article "Das Hören in der Musik," published in an issue of *Neue Revue* in 1894.[66] Schenker is primarily concerned with the importance of the repetition of an unfamiliar work. A certain period of time is needed to become accustomed to such a work, he says, thus admitting that new music needs time to gain a foothold on its own terms. *Angewöhnung* is the key word for a musical recognition that is as complete as possible. This "accustomization" depends on listening to a work more than once:

---

[64]"New Music: My Music," *Style and Idea*, 103. The original version, "Neue Musik: Meine Musik," is not included in *Stil und Gedanke*.

[65]*Ibid.*, 102-103.

[66]See H. Schenker, "Das Hören in der Musik," in H. Federhofer, ed., *Heinrich Schenker als Essayist und Kritiker, Gesammelte Aufsätze, Rezensionen und kleinere Berichte aus den Jahren 1891–1901* (Hildesheim: Olms, 1990), 96-103.

> Admittedly, music presents even at the first listening some elements that enable and facilitate a comprehension of the subject matter, but they are all of them not sufficient to reveal to the passive ear a demanding piece of music, one that is at the top of today's historical development or merely brushes this top.[67]

Schenker, like Schoenberg, assigns the greatest importance to conscious recognition, not only for professional musicians but also for lay listeners or amateurs. An *active* relation to music is an unconditional prerequisite for experiencing it. In this way he anticipates Besseler's criticism of the tendencies toward passivity endemic in the concert business:

> Neither must one underestimate the fact that in advantageous cases, 'habit' is capable of lifting the lay person's naive art appreciatin up to conscious, active enjoyment. And, as expounded above, active enjoyment of music is a postulate, a necessity, since naive enjoyment simply does not quite suffice, cannot suffice for the material mastery of the work of art.[68]

While Schenker's point is active listening, Besseler's is that the listeners are activated by being themselves the performers. On this point Schenker and Besseler both represent Schoenberg's and Hindemith's basic thoughts on the functional level of music.

Schoenberg's public rehearsal in June 1918 demonstrates that his main point was precisely the repetition of the unfamiliar. The audience was given the opportunity to follow the rehearsal of the chamber symphony while also listening to the composer as he elaborated on the process. The music critic Heinrich von Kralik is the most important source for this public performance/lecture. On 4 July 1918 he gives his account in a multi-column feature of the *Neues Wiener Tagblatt* entitled "Ein musikalisches Sommersemester."[69] Von Kralik in non way saw himself as a Schoenberg supporter. Reich describes his treatment of the artist's position in Viennese music life as showing both lightness and benign irony.

---

[67]Schenker, 99. ["Allerdings bringt die Musik auch dem ersten Hören einige Elemente dar, die eine Erfassung des Stoffes möglich machen und erleichtern, aber sie reichen allesamt nicht aus, ein anspruchsvolles Kunstwerk der Musik, das auf der Höhe der heutigen historischen Entwicklung steht oder die Höhe nur streift, einem passiven Ohr aufzudecken."]

[68]*Ibid.*, 101. ["Es ist auch nicht zu unterschätzen, daß die "Gewohnheit" den naiven Kunstgenuß eines Laien in günstigen Fällen zu einem bewußten, activen Genuß zu erheben vermag. Und, wie oben ausgeführt, ist der active Genuß in der Musik ein Postulat, eine Nothwendigkeit, weil der naive einfach nicht voll ausreicht, noch ausreichen kann zur materiellen Bewältigung des Kunstwerkes."]

[69]The quotations from Kralik's account in "A Musical Summer Semester" as well as the overall assessment of the event rely on Reich's account in *Arnold Schönberg ...*, 150-153.

Von Kralik characterizes Schoenberg's initiative as "an experimental teaching with the aim of making the physical and spiritual mechanics of listening receptive for the new acoustic demands, for the sound formations of this uttermost secessionist music."[70] Von Kralik obviously experiences the music as very unfamiliar, something requiring both physical and spiritual accustomization. However, he does not attempt to categorize Schoenberg's teaching as being for beginners but rather, as he puts it, for those who acknowledge that they have more to learn. It is for the diligent, von Kralik continues, those who are not satisfied with any easy enjoyment of art. Thus he is situated somewhere between Schenker and Besseler, indirectly reflecting on the contemporary aversion to the concert form and its drawbacks and harboring misgivings about the contemporary status of listening to music:

> [The event is] for the industrious ones, who are not satisfied with easy, pleasurable enjoyment of art, but who are still not yet properly initiated into the murky secrets of these new phenomena, those who thirst to know how and what is actually to be heard.[71]

Von Kralik then describes in great detail what is unfamiliar in Schoenberg's music, what is new in a treatment of the musical material that seems to reject all traditions, and in what consist the peculiarities that make the intimidated listener ask what the composer might be seeking to express. When commenting on the rehearsals, he finds that the objective must have been to soften up the stubborn sense of hearing—which in itself can be a good description of the process of musical accustomization. "Schoenberg's 'Harmonielehre', a respectable volume, full of wit, very stimulating, cannot remodel the ear with all its investment in clever pronouncements," observes von Kralik astutely; "only methodical invigoration will help here."[72] He also points to the benefit of repetition in any more inaccessible work, advocating not only one but a number of repetitions: "What was still an acoustical horror at the ninth listening may perhaps appear as something familiar and intimate on the tenth occasion, and may perhaps soon be ready to reveal all manner

---

[70]Reich, *op. cit.*, 151. ["Ein Experimentalunterricht mit der Absicht, die körperliche und geistige Mechanik des Hörens empfänglich zu machen für die neuen akustischen Voraussetzungen, für die Klanggebilde der äußersten sezessionistischen Musik."]

[71]*Ibid.* ["Für Strebsame, die mit dem bequemen, genießerischen Behagen an der Kunst sich nicht zufrieden geben, aber in die dunklen Geheimnisse der jüngsten Erscheinungen noch nicht ordnungsgemäß eingeweiht sind, die danach dürsten endlich zu erfahren, wie und was da eigentlich gehört werden soll."]

[72]*Ibid.* ["Schönbergs 'Harmonielehre', ein respektabler Band, sehr geistreich, sehr anregend, kann mit dem ganzen Aufwand kluger Sprüche das Ohr nicht ummodeln" [...] "Da hilft nur methodisches Sichabhärten."]

of secret beauties."[73] Von Kralik's description of Schoenberg's music and its barriers to the listening experience provides an interesting insight into the history of its reception. The critic maintains that Schoenberg's approach to composition represents a rejection of all sentimentality, and avoidance of phrase-based structuring and conventional melodic progressions. Beyond all this there lies the allure of what von Kralik perceives as mature and manly, "*die funkelnde geistige Maschinerie*." Concluding his assessment, he characterizes Schoenberg's music as something approaching a level of perfect fulfillment, and thereby far from any capricious attempt at creating newness at all costs. His use of the expression "the glittering spiritual machinery" also suggests that he is referring to an exalted music experience, representative of a new age in which the machine metaphor is still blessed with positive connotations. However, a monster spitting dissonances and painful noises from its throat is an impediment, von Kralik warns, but:

> [t]ogether with Schoenberg and fifteen determined musicians, a no less hearty, adventurous audience tackled the evil brood. Each and every cacophony was taken on in turn, against its sharpness, hardness, and acuteness the auditive muscles were steeled.[74]

Before the tenth rehearsal the musicians had played their way and the audience had listened their way into the music, and the worst was overcome: "The frightening ghosts seemed more harmless, their appearance milder, their conduct more affable. One could positively begin to feel easy and cozy in their company."[75] After this exciting and complicated process, audience members felt that they could listen to Schoenberg's *Chamber Symphony* as if it was the most familiar of works. Having conquered the Hydra, the development of the work seemed both straightforward and normal. What was earlier regarded as untraditional was now clearly perceived as traditional; attention embraced tradition instead of rejecting it.

Von Kralik's review reveals many details about what Schoenberg must have found important and how his endeavors were received—at least by him, the author. First, the work's formal structure was examined:

---

[73]Reich, *op. cit.*, 151. ["Was beim neunten Male noch akustische Scheußlichkeit war, stellt sich etwa beim zehnten Male bereits als etwas Bekanntes, Vertrautes ein und wird demnächst vielleicht schon allerlei geheimnisvolle Schönheiten zu enthüllen haben."]

[74]*Ibid.*, 152. ["Gemeinsam mit Schönberg und fünfzehn herzhaften Musiker rückte eine nicht weniger herzhafte, abenteuerlustige Zuhörerschar dem üblen Gezücht zu Leibe. Eine jede Kakophonie wurde einzeln angegangen, an ihren Spitzen, Härten und Schärfen wurde die Muskelkraft des Hörapparat gestählt."]

[75]*Ibid.*. ["Die abschreckenden Gespenster erschienen harmloser, ihr Aussehen gemildert, ihre Lebensart umgänglicher. Es konnte einem förmlich wohl und gemütlich werden in ihr Gesellschaft."]

> Structurally: a mixture of single-movement and multiple-movement forms. The content: the typically characterized primary and secondary themes of a sonata allegro movement, the scherzo's mad, fantastic play, lingering song, melancholy, elegy in the 'Quasi adagio,' and a final section relating to the beginning in the manner of a recapitulation. Powerful, development-section storms pile up and go down crackling; pleasant, lovable episodes emerge, with the instruments coalescing in charming, tuneful bliss.[76]

Schoenberg must also have paid close attention to the work's harmonic features, probably focusing on the overtone row. And he seems to have emphasized his characteristic use of fourth chords:

> The natural history of the harmonies, whose wicked appearance causes so much worry and concern, is the theory of fourth chords, a family rich in variants in which absolutely every possible sonic individual is represented. There were many hopeless moments before the final agreement with the agonizing, wild offsprings of the theories on the fourth was achieved.[77]

Willi Reich finds an important methodological aspect in Schoenberg's initiative: the focus on the *inner necessity* of legitimatizing the new music, what can be referred to as "guided accustomization," to use Schenker's term. While Schoenberg never repeated this educational initiative, it must be seen in relation to his better-known *Verein für musikalische Privataufführungen*, the Society for Private Music Performances, instituted the same year.

"Der Verein für musikalische Privataufführungen"
 Der Verein für musikalische Privataufführungen, also called *Der Wiener Schönberg-Verein* or simply *Der Schönberg-Verein,* was founded on 23 November 1918. Paul Amadeus Pisk, the society's first secretary, links its foundation directly to Schoenberg's negative opinion on the public concert

---

[76] Reich, *op. cit.*, 152. ["Formal: eine Verquickung von Einsätzigkeit und Mehrsätzigkeit. Der Inhalt: die typisch charakterisierten Haupt- und Seitenthemen eines erstens Sonatensatzes, das tolle, phantastische Spiel des Scherzos, gesangliches Verweilen, Schwermut, Elegie im 'Quasi Adagio' und ein letzter Teil, repriesenartig Bezug nehmend auf den Anfang. Kräftige Durchführungsgewitter ballen sich zusammen und gehen prasselnd nieder; angenehme liebliche Episoden tauchen auf, die Instrumente finden zueinander in reizvoller Klangseligkeit."]

[77] *Ibid.* ["Die Naturgeschichte der Harmonien, deren böses Aussehen so viel Sorge und Kopfzerbrechen verursacht, ist die Theorie von den Quartakkorden, einem gestaltreichen Geschlecht, in welchem alle überhaupt möglichen Klangindividuen vertreten sind. Es hat manchen schlimmen Augenblick gegeben, bis endlich die Einigung mit den aufreizenden wilden Sprösslingen der Quartentheorie vollzogen war."]

format.[78] Reich takes the thought further, demonstrating a connection between Schoenberg's views and his contribution to Adolf Loos's symposium *Richtlinien für ein Kunstamt*, published in Vienna in the following year. Important points for Schoenberg are, first, the reference to the commercial features of the concert business, second, the idea that the concert seems to invite a negative competition that prevents genuine musical experiences:

> The concert business ought gradually to cease being a business. In a proper organization, which avoids all impresarios, organizers, etc., and addresses the public directly, it would be quite easy to afford what art demands, even without governmental subsidies. The basic mistake of public concert life is: rivalry (*concertare* = to compete or to flight). [...] Thus competition, the need to win, introduces baseness to the artistic endeavor.[79]

These opinions were already shared by others. In his book *Die Welt von gestern*, Stefan Zweig provides revealing glimpses into Viennese cultural life prior to World War I. Schoenberg's aversion to competition should be seen in connection with the uncompromising art market Zweig describes:

> In the Vienna opera, in Vienna's Burgtheater, nothing was overlooked; every wrong note was immediately noticed, every mistaken entry and abridgement censured, and this control was carried out not only by professional critics at first nights but day after day through the alert ears of the whole audience, increasingly sharpened through constant comparison. While everything political, administrative, and moral went on placidly and people were benignly indifferent to any "sloppiness" and indulgent to every offence, there was no pardon in artistic matters; here the town's honor was at stake.[80]

---

[78] See P.A. Pisk, "Der Verein für musikalische Privataufführungen," *Arnold Schönberg zum fünftigsten Geburtstage*, 325.

[79] Quoted from Reich, *op. cit.*, 155-156. ["Das Konzertwesen müsste allmählich aufhören, ein Geschäftsbetrieb zu sein. Bei einer richtigen Organisation, die alle Vermittler, Arrangeure und dergleichen vermeidet und sich direkt an das Publikum wendet, wäre es leicht möglich, auch ohne staatliche Hilfe das zu leisten, was die Kunst fördert. Der grundlegende Fehler des öffentlichen Konzertlebens ist: Der Wetteifer (Konzert = Wetteifer). [...] So bringt also der Wetteifer, die Notwendigkeit zu siegen, die Gemeinheit in den Kunstbetrieb."]

[80] S. Zweig, *Die Welt von gestern: Erinnerungen eines Europäers* (Frankfurt: Fischer, 1992), 33-34. ["In der Wiener Oper, im Wiener Burgtheater wurde nichts übersehen; jede falsche Note wurde sofort bemerkt, jeder unrichtige Einsatz, jede Kürzung gerügt, und diese Kontrolle nicht etwa nur bei den Premieren durch die professionellen Kritiker geübt, sondern Tag für Tag durch das wachsame und durch ständiges Vergleichen geschärfte Ohr des ganzen Publikums. Während im Politischen, im Administrativen, in der Sitten alles ziemlich gemütlich zuging und man gutmütig gleichgültig war gegen jede 'Schlamperei' und nachsichtig gegen jeden Verstoß, gab es in künstlerischen Dingen keinen Pardon; hier war die Ehre der Stadt im Spiel."]

Only when spontaneous contact with the audience has been achieved will it be possible to pay artists as they should be paid and finance a sufficient number of rehearsals, Schoenberg claims. "Audience" refers here to an assembly of sincere music listeners.

The number of rehearsals is important to Schoenberg, not only for the listeners but also for the performers, as can be gleaned from the preparations for the *Chamber Symphony*. Loos's plans for a *Kunstamt* included a reform of the theater emphasizing painstaking rehearsals and a consistent element of renewal. But since new music must be heard several times, Schoenberg could not apply incessant "renewal" to music:

> One is not familiar with music after listening to it just once. The music lover, and particularly the artist who is to reproduce the music, must hear it often. Thus the performances of a small number of works will not suffice, particularly if, according to Loos's proposal, they are to be repeated only after several years.[81]

In the *Schoenberg-Verein*, "rehearsals were careful and thorough, which in public concert life is impossible if for no other than economic reasons," declares Pisk.[82] There were rarely less than ten, he continues, and frequently as many as thirty.

With his *Verein* Schoenberg addresses the issue that prevailed in the 1920s' criticism of the concert. He establishes a coherent enterprise outside the supposedly well-worn concert format. In principle, he shares Besseler's idea that public music life is no longer able to communicate music in any pure, truthful way. For Besseler, commercialism and competitive virtuosity are among the main obstacles to musical listening. Listeners must somehow be brought more actively into the process. However, for Besseler, the main point is providing musical performances with elements that involve the individual as collectively interacting in a broad musical community. It may be this thought that makes Besseler consider Schoenberg's enterprise as the first symptom of a distancing from the traditional concert. He discerned "no initiative toward new community building but to mere exclusivity."[83] But Besseler does not stop there, as he adds that Schoenberg's circle was quite

---

[81] Reich, *op. cit.*, 157 ["Musik kennt man nicht nach einmaligem Hören. Der Musikfreund, insbesondere aber der Künstler, der sie selbst reproduzieren soll, muß sie oft hören. Es werden also die Aufführungen einer kleinen Anzahl von Werken besonders dann nicht genügen, wenn nach dem Vorschlage von Loos diese Werke erst nach Jahren wiederholt werden."]

[82] Pisk, *op. cit.*, 325. ["Die Einstudierung erfolgte mit einer Sorgfalt und Gründlichkeit, die im Konzertleben der Öffentlichkeit schon aus wirtschaftlichen Ursachen unmöglich ist."]

[83] Besseler, "Grundfragen des musikalischen Hörens," 37. ["kein Ansatz zu neuer Gemeinschaftsbildung, sondern zur bloßen Exklusivität."] Besseler mistakenly dates the event to 1910.

closed to outsiders. The truth is that while the *Verein*, in its early stages, consisted of Schoenberg's students and close friends, already three months later a total of 320 members were registered. Anyone considering the circumstances surrounding the foundation of the *Verein* in isolation could feel reminded of the closed Renaissance circles of musical performance and the *salons* of the Romantic period. But Schoenberg's firm objective was to shield the musical experience, not to hide its mysteries. At the same time, the *Verein* facilitated repetitive performances of new music, which were considered decisive for a works' canonization process. Finally, the association also had a pedagogic purpose, as Pisk observes when pointing to its obvious audience orientation. Schoenberg's own music did not have such a central place on the program as one might believe:

> The "Schoenberg-Verein" was not an association for Schoenberg (in the first year he could not be persuaded to program *a single* work of his), neither was it an association for other composers and artists, but exclusively for the audience.[84]

However, Besseler's distinction remains crucial in light of the 1920s' more radical countermeasures against the concert business. It was never Schoenberg's aim to create a broad, playing or singing *Gemeinschaft* through his works or activities. The founding of the *Verein* was no doubt inspired by the thought of creating a *Gemeinschaft*, albeit one with a different nuance. Schoenberg's intention was to form a limited but genuine musical fellowship that had an open mind to the new music of his time. In 1922, Hindemith founded a similar association in Frankfurt am Main, with an outline and aims that were quite analogous, called *Gemeinschaft für Musik*.

Schoenberg places his enterprise in the private sphere. In his book *Die Idee der absoluten Musik*, Carl Dahlhaus refers to Romanticism's view of the symphony as the highest manifestation of absolute music,[85] while referring to the higher status of chamber music, incarnated in the string quartet, as the portal to the so-called inner nature of art. Owing to the public concert activities at the time, however, the symphony came to enjoy the highest position in a wider contemporary understanding:

> That not the string quartet—as the quintessence of chamber music—but the symphony represented the model on which the idea of absolute

---

[84] Pisk, *op. cit.*, 325 ["Der 'Schönberg-Verein' war kein Verein für Schönberg (man konnte Schönberg im ersten Jahre nicht die Erlaubnis abtrotzen, auch nur *ein* eigenes Werk aufs Programm zu setzen), auch kein Verein für die anderen Komponisten und Künstler, sondern ausschließlich für das Publikum."]

[85] Keeping in mind that in Romanticism, the terms *symphony* and *overture* were used interchangeably in reference to absolute music.

music was developed was due less to the nature of the genres than to an aesthetic reflection which in the media sought its orientation in the symphony as a genre in the public concert, while the string quartet, pertaining to a private music culture, remained in the shadow.[86]

Chamber music is understood as originating in a private sphere that can be entered through the will to achieve deeper musical recognition. Schoenberg's enterprise is part of this tradition, or at least of domestic music-making in a wider sense as it is understood in the German concept *Hausmusik*: playing and singing together within the four walls of a home. Accordingly, Schoenberg's term *musikalische Privataufführungen* evokes various forms of musical activity that all challenge the individual, usually within a loosely or more firmly defined fellowship. His efforts thus represents both a renewed and renewing focus on the importance of exactly this element of musical activity.

The first concert of the *Schönberg-Verein*, performed on 29 December 1918, was devoted to works of Scriabin, Debussy, and Mahler, the latter represented by his Symphony no. 7, in a piano duet version performed by the Schoenberg advocates Eduard Steuermann and Ernst Bachrich. Arrangements for one or two pianos, four or eighth hands, were characteristic elements in the association's concerts. The statutes for the *Verein* were first published in February 1919. The prospectus claims that this type of piano arrangement has special advantages as it puts to shame any exaggerated faith in music's dependence on instrumentation, focusing on melody, harmonic richness, polyphony, formal perfection, and musical architecture more than on color. One detects an effort to moderate the importance of music's *sound*, an effort that largely agrees with Hindemith's thoughts on the musical material. The full prospectus, said to have been penned by Alban Berg and dated 16 February,[87] opens in the following way:

> The purpose of this association, founded in November 1918, is to provide Arnold Schoenberg with the opportunity of personally carrying out his aim of offering artists and friends of the arts a real and thorough knowledge of modern music.[88]

---

[86]C. Dahlhaus, *Die Idee der absoluten Musik* (Kassel: Bärenreiter, 1987), 20. ["Dass nicht das Streichquartett – als Inbegriff des Kammermusikalischen – , sondern die Symphonie das Anschauungsmodell darstellte, an dem die Idee der absoluten Musik entwickelt wurde, war weniger in der Natur der Sache als vielmehr im Wesen einer ästhetischen Reflexion begründet, die sich als Publizistik an der Symphonie als Gattung des öffentlichen Konzerts orientierte, während das Streichquartett, das einer privaten Musikkultur angehörte, im Schatten stand."]

[87]The prospectus was later published in abbreviated versions.

[88]Reich, *op. cit.*, 158. ["Der im November 1918 gegründete Verein hat den Zweck, Arnold Schönberg die Möglichkeit zu geben, dass er seine Absicht: Künstlern und Kunstfreunden eine wirkliche und genaue Kenntnis moderner Musik zu verschaffen, persönlich durchführe."]

Modern music is overshadowed by an element of vagueness though, which inhibits the public's immediate experience. This ambiguity strikes listeners, and as a result the acceptance of the work itself, on different levels:

> Vague are for him [the listener] the purpose, direction, intention, area and manner of expression, the value as well as the nature and aim of the works; generally equally vague is the reproduction, and particularly vague is the public's awareness of its own needs and desires. And thus the works are treasured, honored, praised, and acclaimed or disdained, criticized and rejected—all this because of one single effect given by all the parts of the whole: *on account of vagueness*."[89]

These are certainly views with which von Kralik could have agreed. In the case of the *Schönberg-Verein*, creating *clarity* is the express purpose. In order to realize this objective, three things are considered indispensable:

> First: clear, well-rehearsed performances. Second: frequent repetition. Third: The performances must be removed from the corrupting influence of the general public. This means they must not be directed at competition and must be independent of acclaim and displeasure.[90]

The importance of repetition and rehearsal is stated here in plain terms. The third condition, the elimination of competition, indicates a significant convergence with the aim of shielding new music from public concert ritual. In the area of concert halls and public music appreciation, the acclaim or displeasure uttered by an audience and the verdict of music critics granted an exaggerated status marred any unbiased experience. These effects were considered too critical to be allowed to stand in the way of an untarnished and pure musical experience. As the *Verein*'s prospectus claims: "The only success the artist has here is that which should be the most important for him: making the work, and therefore its creator, comprehensible.[91]

Der Verein für musikalische Privataufführungen worked on the basis of public subscription; to attend what began as weekly arrangements, one had

---

[89]Reich, *op. cit.*, 158-159. ["Unklar sind ihm [dem Zuhörer], Zweck, Richtung, Absicht, Ausdrucksgebiet und Ausdrucksweise, Wert, Wesen und Ziel der Werke, unklar ist meist die Wiedergabe, unklar insbesonders des Publikums Bewußtsein von seinen eigenen Bedürfnissen und Wünschen, und so werden also die Werke geschätzt, geachtet, gepriesen und bejubelt oder mißachtet, getadelt und abgelehnt – bloß wegen einer einzigen Wirkung, die von allem gleichmäßig ausgeht: *wegen der Unklarheit*."]

[90]*Ibid.*, 159. ["Erstens: Klare, gut studierte Aufführungen. – Zweitens: Oftmalige Wiederholungen. – Drittens: Die Aufführungen müssen dem korrumpierenden Einfluß der Öffentlichkeit entzogen werden, das heißt; sie dürfen nicht auf Wettbewerb gerichtet sein und müssen unabhängig sein von Beifall und Mißfallen."]

[91]*Ibid.*, 160. ["Der einzige Erfolg, den ein Künstler hier haben soll, ist der, der ihm der wichtigste sein müsste: das Werk und damit den Autor verständlich gemacht zu haben."]

to be a member. Costs were therefore covered by membership fees; these made members co-responsible for the association's activities. This organizational structure shielded the enterprise from spontaneous and superficially curious officialdom. Schoenberg, the president, had at his side a secretary, a treasurer, an archivist, and someone to take care of correspondence, all of whom he himself appointed. Those who led rehearsals, *die Vortragsmeister*, were most important for the musical quality; among these were Webern and Berg, Eduard Steuermann, Erwin Stein, and Benno Sachs.

The *Verein* reported on its activities in a newsletter called *Mitteilungen*. Issue no. 24, distributed in April 1921, may give an impression of the vastness of repertoire covered: it lists 226 performed works.[92] Schoenberg is represented with 15, Webern with 9, and Berg with 5 compositions. Thus the core of the Second Viennese School accounted for only 13% of the repertoire presented at the private performances of the *Schönberg-Verein*. Max Reger tops the list with 34 works, Debussy is not far behind with 26, Stravinsky's 9 equal Webern's, while Zemlinsky and Suk match Berg with 5 works each. Other composers frequently represented include Bartók, Ravel, Scriabin, Mahler, Richard Strauss, Busoni, Szymanowski, and Hauer, as well as a number of younger composers who are less known today.

Many circumstances may influence the repertoire selection of an enterprise such as the *Schönberg-Verein*, among them the number of appropriate works that are actually on hand at a given time. Nevertheless, the breadth of the selection is remarkable, as it embraces both considerable stylistic differences and several generations of composers. Hence the reproach that the enterprise was established to promote Schoenberg's own narrow circle rests on ignorance, as the project had so many other music-mediating dimensions.

Der Verein für musikalische Privataufführungen did not survive more than three years. By the end of 1921 this form of the enterprise had for all intents and purposes passed into history. According to Pisk, it never lacked a faithful public willing to learn. But the association could not avoid the effects of dire economic times: "When the association, despite everything, had to cease operations, the reason lay solely in the devaluation of the currency and in the economic crisis."[93] It is no easy task to spend time on idealistic work that yields no income in times of economic crisis. However, the project was to have a decisive influence on the mediation of new music in the 20th century. It came to be considered as the prototype for organizations that rapidly spread in the first part of the 1920s, such as the *Donaueschinger*

---

[92]See L. Stein, "The Privataufführungen Revisited," in R. Stephan, ed., *Die Wiener Schule*, (Darmstadt: Wissenschaftliche Buchgesellschaft, 1989), 100-101.

[93]Pisk, *op. cit.*, 326. ["Wenn trotzdem der Verein seine Tätigkeit vorübergehend einstellen mußte, so lag die Ursache nur im Verfall der Währung und in der Wirtschaftskrise."]

Kammermusik-Aufführungen zur Förderung zeitgenössischer Tonkunst (founded in 1921), the *Internationale Gesellschaft für Neue Musik* (IGNM, 1922), the New York-based *Composers' Guild* (1922), and others. In Prague, Alexander Zemlinsky created his own *Verein für musikalische Privataufführungen*, with Schoenberg as honorary president.

Summary

Schoenberg's basic requirement that music must be logically comprehensible means that listeners must participate actively in the process of musical recognition. An impediment in his own music is his deliberate avoidance of any recurrence of musical structures. This has to be overcome by repeated performances of whole works. Schoenberg felt that repeated listening to any musical work is also important in a more general sense. This conviction led to the public rehearsals of his first *Chamber Symphony* and the founding of the *Verein für musikalische Privataufführungen*. His insistence that listeners, or "users," be given the opportunity to exchange a passive listening role for an active listening position qualifies Schoenberg as a musical functionalist, even on the concept's third level—that of the focus on the work's intended function.

His initiatives to activate listeners on a broader basis, outside the public concert arena, must not be confused with the more articulated challenges to musical activity facing the new generations of composers in the 1920s. Schoenberg's requirements for the musical work are based on *Faßlichkeit*, not *Gebrauch*. However, the activity he promoted still functions as an important prelude, which places it in a wider context. Schoenberg's commitment coincides with the end of World War I and the beginning of the expansive 1920s. In 1921, Hindemith had his breakthrough at the newly established chamber music festival in Donaueschingen; a year later he contributed to the foundation in Frankfurt am Main of the membership-based association *Gemeinschaft für Musik*. In this way Hindemith follows up and develops ideas first brought forth by Schoenberg. Yet this is also a point where Schoenberg and Hindemith part ways. While Schoenberg considers the work of art in an eternal perspective capable of justifying it at least throughout the near future, Hindemith is more interested in the immediate importance of a composition, its effect on contemporaries. For about a decade Hindemith focused on music-making activity as a counterbalance to public concert traditions. His enthusiastic engagement in this field will be discussed below.

Hindemith: Active Performance and Musical Recognition

> Besser als Musik hören
> ist Musik machen
>
> Paul Hindemith/Bertolt Brecht[94]

Introduction

For all his fame as a composer, Paul Hindemith was also considered one of the greatest viola players of his time. He had started out as a violinist, growing up in a home where the *Hausmusik* tradition was well preserved. As a student, his foundation for a musical career focused on training as a violin performer, and he learned to appreciate his contacts with amateur musicians enough to maintain them throughout his professional life. Already as a child, Hindemith showed practical skills in many fields. Painting and drawing came easy to him and remained beloved hobbies all his life; he was capable of preparing the rolls for his own mechanical music on the basis of drafts, not needing scores.[95] Without venturing into psychological analysis, it may be assumed that the 1920s' focus on practical music must have hit a resonant chord with Hindemith's self-image. The same can be said for the development in Hindemith's views about the composer's role in a new age, for as he declared in 1927: "Today a composer should write only when he knows for which requirement he is writing."[96] A widely defined purpose must always be present, and this fact places him centrally in the musical-functionalist context. Moreover, the attitudes of the 1920s were not a passing fashion that he adopted for a while. At this time he established a lifelong foundation for his ideas—even though the degree of his actual commitment fluctuated. As mentioned above, Hindemith places music mid-way between science and religion, between "the advantages of exactitude in thinking" and "the unlimited world of faith." If his *Unterweisung im Tonsatz* is seen as an attempt to approach the scientifically recognizable aspects of music, *A Composer's World* points much more to the vast horizons of unlimited music recognition. In the latter, Hindemith's emphasis on the importance of active music making plays a decisive role.

---

[94][Better than listening to music is making music.]

[95]This reference is to the realization of the music for *Das triadische Ballett* op. 40/2 for mechanical organ. The suite from this long-disappeared work was published in 1995 on CD Koch-Schwann 3–1202–2 H1.

[96] "Wie soll der ideale Chorsatz der Gegenwart oder besser der nächsten Zukunft beschaffen sein?," 27. ["Ein Komponist sollte heute nur schreiben, wenn er weiß für welchen Bedarf er schreibt."]

As discussed earlier, when considering Hindemith on this third level of musical functionalism, it is obvious that his position differs considerably from that of Schoenberg. Hindemith relates much more to the practical aspects of the specific use to which music can be put, whereas Schoenberg resolutely distances himself from such concerns. At the same time, Hindemith pursued an educator's career that largely paralleled Schoenberg's. Both men treated their vocations as mediators very seriously, but Hindemith was much keener about the role as a public educator, as is especially evidenced in his many efforts to further musical amateurs. In his *Gemeinschaft für Musik* it would appear that Hindemith adopts Schoenberg's commitment to the active vitalization of the listener. Yet, for Hindemith, this initiative is not the culmination of an idealistic commitment, but rather the starting point of an even more determined effort.

"Gemeinschaft für Musik"

In 1922 Hindemith joined forces with the musician Reinhold Merten in founding the *Gemeinschaft für Musik* in Frankfurt am Main. The first event staged by the new association, devoted to the music of Prokofiev, Stravinsky, and Poulenc, took place on 7 July the same year. The membership prospectus opened with the following promise: "We are convinced that the concert in its present form is an institution which must be opposed, and we will try to restore the nearly-lost fellowship between performer and listener."[97] The need to restore the lost *Gemeinschaft* between performer and listener may sound like an echo from Besseler's "Grundfragen des musikalischen Hörens." In fact there is no point in looking for a direct connection— Besseler did not publish his views until a few years later—but both initiatives are representative of concerns prevailing in various segments of music life in the Weimar Republic. Hindemith, like his Viennese counterparts, is convinced that the potential of music life to undergo renewal lies outside the traditional concert establishment. In his 1929 article "Über Musikkritik" he consolidates the idea behind the foundation of the *Gemeinschaft*:

> We must find a way to other forms of music-making and music enjoyment. The earlier the concert in its present form dies off, the faster we have the opportunity to renew music life.[98]

---

[97]"Gemeinschaft für Musik," reprinted in *Aufsätze, Vorträge, Reden*, 8. ["Wir sind überzeugt, dass das Konzert in seiner heutigen Form eine Einrichtung ist, die bekämpft werden muß und wollen versuchen, die fast verloren gegangene Gemeinschaft zwischen Ausführenden und Hörern wieder herzustellen."]

[98]"Über Musikkritik," *Aufsätze, Vorträge, Reden*, 38. ["Wir müssen zu anderen Formen des Musizierens und des Musikgenusses kommen. Je eher das Konzert in seiner heutigen Form abstirbt, desto schneller werden wir die Möglichkeit haben, das Musikleben zu erneuern."]

The prospectus for *Gemeinschaft für Musik* also presents a number of similarities with the idealistic organization model that underpinned Schoenberg's *Verein*. One element is the importance attached to the combination of the so-called most perfect performance possible and the downplaying of the performer's personal status and position: "Any national or personal ambition will remain eliminated. The performers' names will not be made known; nevertheless we strive for the greatest possible perfection."[99] The protected private sphere is also a key element in Hindemith's *Gemeinschaft*, an organization of paying members. The prospectus specifically states that due to the association's intimate nature, its doors are closed to non-members. On the front page of the program for a *Vortragsabend* with music by Honegger and Webern on 24 November 1922, the message is quite clear *Gäste nicht erwünscht* (guests not welcome).[100]

It is also crucial that performances were not reviewed in the news media. Hindemith believed that as critics form part of the contaminated concert business, their assessments devalue both themselves and the system:

> Three-fourths of all concerts are arranged only for the benefit of the reviewers, and they have really nothing better to do than to "evaluate" everything that happens on the podium, without giving a thought to the fact that they have thus long ago devalued both the concert activity and themselves.[101]

This scathing criticism of both the concert business and the critics is again reminiscent of Besseler. The negative focus on reviews expresses an anti-commercial attitude. If music performance really is a commodity to be measured, weighed, and sold, the *Gemeinschaft für Musik* demonstrates resistance to this convention, as most performers are not even to be paid, and any expenses incurred from obtaining scores and renting instruments are to be made up for by membership fees.

The associations founded by Schoenberg and Hindemith respectively differ, however, in two aspects. On the one hand, there is the principle determining program selection in the *Gemeinschaft für Musik*: chamber music is retained, but restricted to unknown new and old music. By focusing

---

[99] "Gemeinschaft für Musik," 8. ["Irgendwelcher nationale oder persönliche Ehrgeiz wird ausgeschaltet bleiben. Die Namen der Ausführenden werden nicht bekanntgegeben, jedoch streben wir die größtmögliche Vollkommenheit an."]

[100] See the facsimile given in A. Briner, D. Rexroth, and G. Schubert, *Paul Hindemith: Leben und Werk in Bild und Text*, 77.

[101] "Über Musikkritik," 38. ["Drei Viertel aller Konzerte werden nur der Kritik wegen veranstaltet und diese hat wirklich nicht Besseres zu tun, als alles, was auf dem Konzertpodium geschieht, zu "werten," ohne daran zu denken, dass sie damit den Konzertbetrieb und sich selbst längst entwertet hat."]

on unknown works there is a novel opportunity for music which for various reasons has not been accepted in the ordinary concert program. Bringing unknown and usually controversial composers into focus was also one of the aims of the *Donaueschingen Festival* founded the previous year. Not only the *Gemeinschaft für Musik* as an association but also its repertoire were thereby outside the concert mainstream. Furthermore, the selection of unfamiliar pieces made it possible to pave the way for the least prejudiced experience and, therefore, for the presumably most objective recognition. The stated aim of combining new and old music within the same frame is also characteristic of the ambition to build a bridge between the old and the new. This is one of the important features of the ideology behind the musical variant of *Neue Sachlichkeit*, a term that was not yet in use. Another essential difference from Schoenberg's *Verein* is that members are invited to influence the program. This invitation allows an even more extensive input from the selective membership, while at the same time showing the beginning of a cognizant focus on the user, a feature that was to become more and more prevalent in contemporary music life.

1922 was the year that Hindemith, due to his definitive breakthrough at the Donaueschingen chamber music festival, was described as "one of those who manages to convince us of his mission as a trail-blazer for the art of the future."[102] This was an especially productive and successful year, even according to Hindemith's own measure. It is telling, therefore, that in a letter to Emmy Ronnefeldt in September that year, after having accounted his various activities, he concludes with the following:

> But my greatest achievement is the foundation of the "Gemeinschaft für Musik" here. We play modern music in front of about 80 invited members at Zingler's in the Kaiserstraße (every two or three weeks); a purely musical event without money matters. The listeners pay nothing, the players get nothing, the very moderate expenses are shared. [...] And the very best of it is: all those Frankfurters don't get to come in!! I have already had lots of trouble because of this since everyone believes they must be part of it. Such is not the case.[103]

---

[102] From a review in *Donau-Bote*, 2 August 1921, quoted in Briner/Rexroth/Schubert, *Paul Hindemith: Leben und Werk*, 66. ["einer von denen, die uns von ihrer Sendung als Wegbereiter der Kunst der Zukunft zu überzeugen vermögen."]

[103] *Paul Hindemith Briefe*, 107. ["Aber das Schönste, was mir gelungen ist, ist die Gründung der 'Gemeinschaft für Musik' hier. Wir spielen vor ungefähr 80 geladenen Mitgliedern bei Zingler auf der Kaiserstraße moderne Musik (alle 2 oder 3 Wochen); eine rein musikalische Angelegenheit ohne Geldgeschichten. Die Zuhörer zahlen nichts, die Spieler bekommen nichts, die ganz geringen Unkosten werden gemeinsam getragen. [...] Und, was das Allerschönste ist: die ganzen Frankfurter dürfen nicht hinein!! Ich habe schon viel Krach deswegen gehabt, weil jeder glaubt, dabei sein zu müssen. Ist aber nicht."]

By downplaying commercialism and the musicians' personal status as well as excluding critics from this membership-based private sphere, Hindemith focuses once again on the main elements of the association's inherent criticism of the concert. His emphasis on the fact that the common Frankfurt public is not admitted reveals his desire to shield the musical experience, which he hopes to be pure and active, from public consumption. This seems to be the way to provide an experience of music on music's own premises. All in all, the letter expresses an enthusiasm and idealism on behalf of music so characteristic of Hindemith, particularly during these hectic years of his early career.

The *Gemeinschaft für Musik* turned out to be a short-lived affair. Its leaders quickly discovered that it was not easy to maintain an idealistic association during those turbulent times. The organization's fragile budget could not survive spiraling inflation. It is ironic that it was precisely the downplaying of the commercial aspects that spelled the association's end, just as with Schoenberg's *Verein*. Idealistic and time-consuming effort that did not generate income can be financially punishing during an economic recession.

It is more than possible that the *Gemeinschaft für Musik* made Hindemith increasingly aware of the composer's ethical and social obligations. The fact that the song cycle *Das Marienleben* was created in the association's founding year is often regarded as a concurrent event, marking a shift in direction in how Hindemith understood himself as a composer.[104]

"Die Verbindung von Volk und Kunst"

The *Gemeinschaft für Musik* and *Das Marienleben* demonstrate two aspects or levels of Hindemith's commitment to music. The first, the association, is the attempt to create new active connections between people and art. The second, represented by the song cycle, aims at a more idealized, but still active, artistic *Gemeinschaft* that promotes spiritual enhancement in a universal sense.

In the preface of the revised edition of *Das Marienleben* from 1948, Hindemith recalls the first performance some twenty-five years earlier:

> The strong impression even the first performance made on the audience—I had not expected anything at all—made me conscious, for the first time in my musical career, of music's ethical necessity and the musician's moral obligations. Though I had given my best with the *Marienleben*, this best was, despite all my good intentions, still not good enough to be laid aside as having been achieved once-and-for-all. I began to glimpse an ideal of a music that would be

---

[104] See Briner/Rexroth/Schubert, *Paul Hindemith: Leben und Werk*, 80.

> noble and as perfect as possible, which I would one day be able to realize, and I knew that from now on *Das Marienleben* would lead me on this path and also serve as a yardstick for approaching this ideal.[105]

Although these words were written retrospectively by a mature and experienced Hindemith in a moment of reflection, there is no doubt that he assigns the *Marienleben* a special role in guiding his compositional development. The essence of his music philosophy may be captured by "awareness of music's ethical necessity" and the "musician's moral obligations," and similar expressions were to appear with increasing frequency in his writings. It is characteristic of Hindemith that he seeks to combine his epistemological ideas with immediate, practical action in the musical life of his time. His emphasis on the concept of musical communication must be understood in this perspective. It affects not only his understanding of the musical material and the identification-creating recognition of form, but also his broader commitment to the function of music as an art.

In the period following the first edition of *Das Marienleben* and the foundation of the *Gemeinschaft für Musik*, Hindemith seems to become increasingly worried about the durability of the new music in modern society. As he writes in 1925 in a letter to his publishers, he anticipates that new music will have to struggle to survive. He even admits that those who oppose modernity may have their plausible reasons:

> *But my main concern is this*: I am firmly convinced that a hard struggle for the new music will break out in the coming years, the omens for this are there. Time will show whether our contemporary music, including my own, will be able to last. I have absolute faith in it, of course, but I am equally sure that the objections to most of the so-called modern music are only too justified.[106]

---

[105]*Das Marienleben*, op. 27 (Neue Fassung), III. ["Der starke Eindruck, den schon die erste Aufführung auf die Zuhörer machte – erwartet hatte ich gar nichts – , brachte mir zum ersten Male in meinem Musikerdasein die ethischen Notwendigkeiten der Musik und die moralischen Verpflichtungen des Musikers zum Bewußtsein: Hatte ich mit dem Marienleben mein Bestes gegeben, so war dieses Beste trotz aller guten Absichten doch nicht gut genug, um ein für allemal als gelungen beiseitegelegt werden zu können. Ich begann ein Ideal edler und möglichst vollkommener Musik zu erschauen, das ich dereinst zu verwirklichen imstande sein würde, und ich wußte, dass von nun an das Marienleben mich auf diesem Wege leiten und mir zugleich als Maßstab für die Annäherung an das Ideal dienen würde."]

[106]*Paul Hindemith Briefe*, 120-121. ["*Mein Hauptbedenken ist aber dieses*: Ich bin der festen Überzeugung, dass in den nächsten Jahren ein schwerer Kampf um die neue Musik anheben wird, die Vorzeichen dazu sind da. Es wird sich erweisen müssen, ob unsere heutige Musik und darunter auch die meinige fähig ist, weiterzubestehen. Ich glaube natürlich sicher daran, weiß aber ebenso gut, dass die Vorwürfe, die man der Mehrzahl der sogenannten modernen Musik, nur allzu berechtigt sind."]

Hindemith is admitting that the permanence of his and others' music is not solely dependent on the composers' honest confidence in their work. Other forces, not necessarily completely negative one, are also involved and cannot be ignored. Hindemith reaches the conclusion that the main problem must lie in the growing gap between music and the people, and here major improvements must be made. The question is *how*. "The most important issue in contemporary music, the relationship between art and the people, can only be solved through purely personal relations,"[107] he claims. When Hindemith refers to "personal relations," he is thinking of connections between various musical interests. In this case he is referring to Fritz Jöde and his comprehensive *Jugendmusikbewegung*. In this youth-music movement he sees great possibilities growing out of contact between new music and an enthusiastic user group.

Hindemith's interest in the *Jugendmusik* connection, firm though temporary, originated in the fall of 1926 when he participated as a guest at the so-called *Erste Hochschulwoche der Musikantengilde* in Brieselang. Here he had the opportunity to study the movement's work and ideas at close range. Hans Mersmann was also active at this convention, and Willibald Gurlitt, Besseler's teacher, was invited as a speaker. Hindemith recognized the potential for establishing a vibrant market for new music—an opportunity for composers to write for a hungry audience. He characterized this idea of coupling users and newly written music as his and Jöde's joint *coup*.[108] However, it is worth noting that he had reservations right from the start about the sectarian tendencies in the *Jugendmusikbewegung*. To Jöde he wrote—not without a hint of irony:

> The constant enthusiasm in which this community dwells strikes the spectator as somewhat peculiar. As I see it, enthusiasm is a rare and big affair; one should not degrade oneself by, for example, extending it even to the meals...[109]

When music is written for a concrete purpose, the purpose itself helps to lay the premises for its design. When written for amateurs, it must accept technical limitations. According to Hindemith, this type of decision does not

---

[107]Letter to Otto Ernst Sutter, dated 5 January 1927, in *Paul Hindemith Briefe*, 131. ["Die wichtigste Frage des heutigen Musiklebens, die Verbindung von Volk und Kunst, ist überhaupt nur durch rein persönliche Beziehungen zu lösen."]

[108]See his letter to Fritz Jöde, dated 12 October 1926, *Paul Hindemith Briefe*, 124.

[109]*Ibid.*, 125-126. ["Ein wenig seltsam berührt den Zuschauer die ständige Begeisterung, in der die Gemeinschaft sich befindet. Ich finde, dass Begeisterung eine seltene und große Angelegenheit ist, man darf sich nicht erniedrigen, indem man sie sich (z.B.) bis aufs Essen erstrecken läßt ..."]

need to devalue the quality of the music: the opposite might well be the case. It is certainly not the degree of complexity that raises music up to the level of a work of art.

"Vorspielen und Selbstspielen"

Hindemith regards contemporary music life as an entirety while firmly believing in maintaining the basic divisions of musical performance. This view distinguishes him from Besseler as well as from other more radical spokesmen for *Gebrauchsmusik*, since his focus is rather on the *proportions* between the traditional functions in the field of music. There are two main types of music performance, he says, *playing for others* and *playing for oneself*: *Vorspielen* is the domain of the professional, while *Selbstspielen* is for the layman. Both tasks are equally important.[110] Most people would agree that these two activities are interrelated. However, Hindemith's point is that their fundamental premises should not be confused. The term *Selbstspielen* lifts the activity out of the concert business. The opening of the preface to *Frau Musica*, a cantata in the series *Sing und Spielmusiken für Liebhaber und Musikfreunde*, op. 45, focuses on this presupposition:

> This music was written neither for the concert hall nor for artists. It wants to provide people who sing and play for their own enjoyment or who perform for or a small circle of like-minded friends with interesting and modern practicing material.[111]

It is characteristic of Hindemith's attitude toward amateur performance that he makes a point of the fact that this music does not belong in the concert hall. The objective is *Selbstspielen* not *Vorspielen*. Moreover, when he mentions that the work is not written for *Künstler*, it is not because he believes it lacks artistic value. The performing artist lives of his profession, therefore his livelihood is based on *Vorspielen*. Hindemith might just as well have used the term *Berufsmusiker*, professional musician, but then he would have missed another point: in the first part of the 20th century the concepts *art* and *artist* tended to be negatively loaded. They were felt to represent what was regarded as a subjective, *l'art pour l'art* principle that was detached from reality. This attitude had gained a foothold in the amateur movement: the noble amateur was the professional artist's direct counterpart. In this preface, Hindemith does not rule out the possibility of amateurs also

---

[110]See "Forderungen an den Laien," *Aufsätze, Vorträge, Reden*, 42.

[111]See the preface to *Frau Musica*, op. 45/1 (Mainz: Schott, 1928). ["Diese Musik ist weder für den Konzertsaal noch für Künstler geschrieben. Sie will Leuten, die zu ihrem eigenen Vergnügen singen und musizieren oder die einem kleinen Kreise Gleichgesinnter vormusizieren wollen, interessanter und neuzeitlicher Übungsstoff sein."]

having the pleasure of playing music for others, but the musicians', not the listeners' wish is to be favored. Hindemith uses the term *vormusizieren*, not *vorspielen*. These words have a slightly different meaning: *Vorspielen* can also mean to perform, in the sense of demonstrating how music should be performed or objectively sound. It was exactly this kind of perfection the amateur movement believed pervaded the public concert and should be shunned. Hindemith underscores that any performance for others belongs in a narrow circle of *like-minded* listeners, that is, on the periphery or in a place completely distanced from the normal concert audience. On the one hand, the preface aims for the type of exclusive *Gemeinschaft* for which the *Jugendmusikbewegung* was known. On the other hand, there is a link between the thinking informing his above-mentioned *Gemeinschaft für Musik* and the conditions for the performance of his own educational works.

Implicit in Hindemith's view is that amateurs are equal to professionals, not with regard to their instrumental skills but owing to their significant place in the whole. They are, moreover, ranked far above the much-chastised passive listeners:

> The music-making layman who is seriously concerned with musical things, is an equally significant member of our music life as the seriously working musician. He is definitely more important than the listener who abandons himself to mere enjoyment, who in his best-known form as concertgoer is fairly limited to an economic factor in today's music business.[112]

Consequently, amateurs should be entirely aware of their position. Hindemith seems to imply that amateurs may be even more significant than professionals: If the term *Vorspielen* is to have any meaning, it must be intended for an addressee or target group that takes on the role of *Zuhörer*, and Hindemith does not appear to overly value this category. Professional musicians and paying concertgoers would then be left to run in circles without purpose and without a musical center. The main point is thus that the quality of the whole can be changed through broader musical activity.

In earlier times, the music life of a society was dominated by amateur activity, with professional musicians and their audiences making up only a relatively small portion. The importance of amateurs peaked in the 17th and 18th centuries: "He [the amateur] played in the orchestras together with the

---

[112]"Forderungen an den Laien," 42. ["Der musizierende Laie, der sich ernsthaft mit musikalischen Dingen befaßt, ist ein ebenso wichtiges Glied unseres Musiklebens wie der ernsthaft arbeitende Musiker. Er ist entschieden wichtiger als der sich bloßem Genusse hingebende Zuhörer, der in seiner bekanntesten Form als Konzertbesucher heute fast nur noch ein wirtschaftlicher Faktor im Musikbetrieb ist."]

professional, he sang in choirs, and for him all chamber music was written."[113] Hindemith may be idealizing earlier times; he clearly does not appreciate the division of musical functions in contemporary music life. In this golden age of amateurs there cannot have been any clear division between *Vorspielen* and *Selbstspielen*: professionals and amateurs must have been engaged in an overarching music-making fellowship. The current division between these two categories must, in earlier times, have been of no importance if not practically non-existent.

Eisler believes the deep divisions in music life to be the result of capitalism and the growth of the modern bourgeois society: "The prevalence of music without words, vulgarly called 'absolute music,' the division between music and work, between heavy and light music, between professionals and amateurs is typical for music in capitalism," he contends.[114] Although Hindemith would probably not have phrased it just that way, his views resemble Eisler's in that he regards the deepening of partitions and the shifting of proportions as part of a negative, capital-controlled societal development. The 20th century is considerably different from earlier centuries, he claims. There has been dramatic growth in the size of music life due to a significant rise in audience numbers. But this expansion has happened at the expense of amateur music performance, thus resulting in a radical shift in the proportion of various functions to the disadvantage of the amateur.[115]

Many people would maintain that the amateur movement never grew as expansively as it did in the 20th century. Hindemith could in fact agree with this opinion. Yet the expected results are not present, one of the reasons being that amateur activities are for the most part concentrated on younger age groups and largely not carried through to adulthood:

> Boys and girls, having played an instrument during their school years, may hardly ever look at it again, once they enter professional life or marry; in exceptional cases only do they join amateur orchestras or choruses; and usually they prefer to increase the army of listener, drown in musical laziness, and lose their function of circulating life blood in the musical body.[116]

---

[113] *A Composer's World*, 250.

[114] H. Eisler, "Geschichte der deutschen Arbeitermusikbewegung von 1848," [*Schriften I: Musik und Politik 1924–1948*] (München: Rogner & Bernhard, 1973), 222. ["Die Vorherrschaft der Musik ohne Worte, auch vulgär 'absolute Musik' genannt, die Trennung zwischen Musik und Arbeit, zwischen schwerer und leichter Musik, zwischen Professionals und Dilettanten, sind typisch für die Musik im Kapitalismus."]

[115] On p. 250 of *A Composer's World*, Hindemith even goes into statistics, claiming that the percentage of amateurs participating in 20th-century music life was reduced from 90% to 1%.

[116] *A Composer's World*, 251.

Hindemith's observations suggest that listening is passive and musically unproductive, linked to a lifestyle that is dictated by consumerism. Still referring to the young amateurs who later drop out of active participation in music-making, he observes:

> They degenerate to unproductive consumers. The goods they consume can be and are easily produced by a small number of musical trusts, consisting of a few leading orchestras, conductors, and soloists and consisting of those concert agents who with their packaged delivery of complete New-Yorkized concert seasons to provincial towns kill all local initiative and paralyze the cities' own endeavors.[117]

Like Adorno, Hindemith is worried about the commodity character of music. But for Hindemith, active *Gebrauchsmusik* is a means that can be used to downplay this aspect and achieve active, non-commercial musical identification.

When Hindemith considers the prevailing trends, he cannot imagine the musician who does not see the shifts in music life as tendencies towards shallowness and superficiality. But perhaps the dramatic rise in public involvement could give both composers and professional musicians greater opportunities, thereby strengthening all music life and allowing it to grow? Hindemith would dispute such a statement, because what musical life has gained in breadth it has lost in depth. Thus his conclusion is that negative rather than positive forces have gained in scope.[118] Composers have lost sight of their moral obligations to society and, as Hindemith constantly reiterates, become addicted to technical perfection and compositional experiments. Symphony orchestras have sunk to the role of distributors of super-refined sound. Professional musicians are recognized for their virtuosity and show a ruthless craving for success and fame. Critics are not attuned to the nobler aims of music. Moreover, the entertainment, radio, and gramophone industries, not to mention *muzak*,[119] strive to line their pockets with the revenue generated by the human need for music. The public is at the mercy of such forces, says Hindemith. And if that were not enough, an army of concert organizers, impresarios, and talent scouts, all basically alien to the art of music, endeavor to extinguish the last light from the yearning for artistic sublimation. In these matters Schoenberg would entirely agree.

---

[117] *A Composer's World*, 251.

[118] *Ibid.*, 242-243.

[119] This term stems from *The Muzak Corporation* founded in Ohio in 1934. Its aim was to build up a music collection to use in practical, everyday situations. Hindemith also employs this umbrella term, which has become widely known and used.

Hindemith does not hesitate to express his view of the imminent decay of contemporary music life. He believes its negative development to be connected with the listeners' decline, observing that "the listener in general has reached an appalling level of degeneration."[120] As citizens of the turbulent 20th century, listeners have lapsed into passive consumerism; subsequently, listening itself has become passive. This resonates with Besseler's views on concert audiences. Besseler was quite categorical and unforgiving in describing listeners' passivity. Hindemith, on the other hand, does not want to be as uncompromising. He feels that the audience is not at fault; the culprits are the unmusical and non-musical forces. In a somewhat patronizing way he says:

> The audiences in this country [the United States] as in any other country with public distribution of music are well-meaning and have the best intentions in respect to music, but they are weak, undetermined, and playful like children. They need, and joyfully accept, understanding leadership.[121]

Hindemith qualifies his view by admitting that all in all, audiences are not a uniform, passive mass. There are degrees of musical awareness, and as long as listeners demonstrate at least some mental effort, they have a moral justification for participation. But benevolent instruction may be necessary, he says, returning to the view that the producers of music must reach an understanding with their market: "the professional can do nothing better than to reach a mutual understanding with the consumers on their inarticulate desires and his ability of wisely and honestly satisfying them."[122] These are indeed thoughts that Schoenberg would not follow, at least not to their ultimate consequences, and there are also limits to how many concessions Hindemith would be willing to make.

The concept of musical activity in its widest sense is the key to the consummate music experience. This activity is something far more than what Hindemith characterizes as "the least mental effort." He refers to musical recognition as being both intellectual and emotional. Common to both aspects is the fact that mental activity is necessary for unimpeded communication between any music and its listeners.[123] Furthermore, musical activity is the tool for preventing the decay of music life, which makes amateur music playing vitally important. Through their musical activity amateurs have the opportunity of entering a fellowship whose aim is to collaborate on building

---

[120] *A Composer's World*, 249.

[121] *Ibid.*, 244.

[122] *Ibid.*

[123] Hindemith discusses this in detail in *A Composer's World*, 17-53.

a work: "once you join an amateur group, you are a member of a great fraternity, whose purpose is the most dignified one you can imagine: to inspire one another and unite in building up a creation that is greater than one individual's deeds."[124] This is an experience that must benefit as many people as possible. Hindemith concludes the preface to *Frau Musica* by saying: "May all who are present, having been instructed in the respective passage with the help of notation written on a board, join in the opening and concluding choruses"[125] In this way the work promotes fellowship and the sense of belonging through creative musical activity that includes everyone. Consequently, the work acquires an even wider perspective: not only is it to be presented by amateur performers, but parts of it must even be rehearsed by members of the audience who are potentially untrained. Both Hindemith's *Lehrstück*, created in 1929 in collaboration with Bertolt Brecht, and his *Cantique de l'espérance*, composed in 1953 on texts provided by Paul Claudel, present this form of shared activity as one of the basic preconditions for performance.

The important outcome of this experience of active participation is that amateurs are thereby trained to listen actively:

> Amateurs of this kind, when listening to music, will not be the stupid receivers, the targets of virtuosity, the idle gourmands of which our audiences predominantly consist. They cannot merely be fed with music of a conductor's or a concert agent's choice. They know what they want, and they intend to get it.[126]

Many would agree that amateur musicians are usually more active listeners than those who do not play a musical instrument. However, it is debatable whether all music amateurs always keep the music itself in the center of the listening experience. Perhaps many amateurs would rather like to change places with professionals. In such cases their aim is rather *Vorspielen* than *Selbstspielen*. Conversely, Hindemith focuses on what he considers ideal amateurs. His objective is to contribute to the development of these amateurs' qualities and position in a positive direction. When following his reasoning, the logical consequence is that if the listeners' decline into passivity is an important cause of the alleged degeneration of music life, a regeneration of the latter will be enabled by an activation of the former.

---

[124] *A Composer's World*, 253.

[125] See the preface to *Frau Musica*. ["Den Eingangs- und Schlußchor mögen die gesamten Anwesenden, denen man vor Beginn der Aufführung mit Hilfe der auf eine Wandtafel geschriebenen Noten die betreffenden Stellen einstudiert hat, mitsingen."]

[126] *A Composer's World*, 253.

When Hindemith speaks of *die Verbindung von Volk und Kunst*, he is not merely referring to the issue of public versus contemporary art, but also to the desirability of closer contact between the people and the phenomenon of music. A step in this direction, as demonstrated in connection with the *Gemeinschaft für Musik*, is that performers and listeners move toward one another by cleansing the public display of the *Vorspielen* of elements likely to overshadow the pure musical experience. *Selbstspielen* achieves a much closer, perhaps the closest possible communication between people and music. Musical recognition does not stop at personal performance. Participatory music-making activates the listening process and thereby becomes the gateway to the contemplative aspects of musical recognition.

"Musik nach Maß"

In order to invite the amateurs' *Selbstspielen*, the music's difficulties must be surmountable. Hindemith demands that modern composers be able to write well also for a purpose, to make music to measure, a claim not limited to the amateur market. While Schoenberg is skeptical of such a concept of measurement, Hindemith never ceases to advocate the importance of craftsmanship in the compositional process. The quotation with which Andres Briner opens his Hindemith biography is typical of the composer's down-to-earth attitude both to the act of creating music and to himself as a person:

> When one goes to a tailor, one does not want his picture or photograph but a well-made suit. If anyone wants to get to know me, let him look at my works.[127]

Schoenberg, though also preoccupied with compositional craftsmanship and musical construction, would never have spoken of himself in such words. This way of thinking shows an objective perspective that would appeal more to someone like Stravinsky. Composers' orientation towards use is not at all new, but Hindemith's emphasis on the importance of being able to write *nach Maß* is particularly characteristic of the enterprising 1920s:

> Just try commissioning composers to write new choral works for specific groups. Pieces made "to measure," so to speak, adapted to the respective chorus's needs and fashioned after a thorough consultation with the choir or its conductor for the specific use.[128]

---

[127] A. Briner, *Paul Hindemith*, 9. ["Wenn man zu einem Schneider geht, will man nicht sein Bild oder seine Photographie, sondern einen gut gemachten Anzug. Wenn sich jemand mit mir beschäftigen will, soll er meine Werke ansehen."]

[128] "Wie soll der ideale Chorsatz...?," 28. ["Man mache doch einmal den Versuch, Komponisten zu beauftragen, für bestimmte Vereine neue Chöre zu schreiben. Stücke, die sozusagen 'nach Maß' den jeweiligen Bedürfnisse des Vereins angepasst wären und die nach gründlicher Rücksprache mit dem Verein bzw. seinem Dirigenten zum speziellen Gebrauch angefertigt würden."]

The preoccupation with so-called objective musical reproduction and the focus on performance practice which in the first decades of the 20th century led to a turn toward Renaissance and Baroque music was accompanied by a renewed interest in older instruments such as the lute, the recorder, and the viola d'amore. Jöde and his large section of the *Jugendmusikbewegung* cultivated this interest, believing that the music and the instruments of past eras were uniquely suited to offering both a satisfactory sound ideal and a starting point for an acceptable, spiritually elevated music. Moreover, this music afforded realistic possibilities for playing on the amateur level. The *Jugendmusikbewegung* provided arrangements and adaptations of masterpieces from the 17th and 18th centuries, and a wide range of amateur composers wrote simple (often rather bad) music. German folksongs constituted the uplifting rallying point, with Hermann Breuer's anthology *Der Zupfgeigenhansl* as common property. Hindemith saw great opportunities for strengthening the connection between people and music particularly through contacts with *Jugendmusikbewegung*.

As a musician, composer, and teacher, Hindemith showed great interest in music of the past, and in folksongs from Germany and other countries. He did not, however, accept an uncritical cultivation of early music; being old did not necessarily mean being good. "There was trash in earlier times, too," he maintains.[129] Similarly, he found among the various arrangements of older music some dreadful mess-ups and described parts of contemporary music written for amateurs as utterly inferior.[130]

According to Hindemith, society has a great need for music; consequently, there is a large, ready market for new music. The amateur movement and amateur potential represent the largest segment of this market. Despite this conviction, Hindemith does not ultimately consider the amateur movement lucrative for himself and his colleagues. Part of the reason is that the finances of amateur movements were dependent on voluntary contributions even more than they are today, and the prevailing attitude was that art and money should not mix. Within the *Jugendmusikbewegung* and similar associations it was not acceptable that a composer should compose for remuneration.[131] Although Hindemith recognizes the contemporary demand for music, he does not believe the composers can simply produce freely and without constraints, expecting unconditional realization. He sees two main components in the musical market: the producer and the consumer, in this case: the composer and the performer. Market dynamics insist on the cooperation of

---

[129]"Forderungen an den Laien," 43-44. ["Früher hat es auch Schund gegeben."]

[130]*Ibid*, 43. "The arranger is always wrong," Hindemith states in *A Composer's World*, 164.

[131]See D. Kolland, *Die Jugendmusikbewegung*, 49.

the two sides, and this interaction offers great opportunities for strengthening *die Verbindung von Volk und Kunst*. The *Gemeinschaft für Musik* was a means of intensifying contact between performers and listeners. An even more important tool could be to open lines of communication between composers and users, as this would increase the amateurs' possibility of achieving beneficial *Selbstspielen*.

Awareness of the market opening for opportunities and perspectives is all very well, but composers are always bound by a number of demands that must be met. Professional composers have a particular moral responsibility to the society in which they live and to their fellow beings, Hindemith says. Professional musicians in general and composers in particular have important educational functions with respect to their consumers. Schoenberg's considerable reservations notwithstanding, this didactic attitude is a distinctive feature of functionalist aesthetics.

On 18 October 1927, Hindemith gave a lecture at a continuing-education course for German choir leaders, most of whom represented the so-called *Chorvereinigungen*, amateur choir organizations. The presentation with the elaborate title "Wie soll der ideale Chorsatz der Gegenwart oder besser der nächsten Zukunft beschaffen sein?"[132] took place at the Hochschule für Musik in Berlin, where he had just been appointed professor of composition. Hindemith talked about the relationship between composers and users. He even went so far as to provide a set of working instructions for composers, including particular proposals that might meet the challenges the music market poses for the music producers. Hindemith's general interest in vocal activities, together with his comments on the characteristics and the nature of choral singing, provide representative insight into his thinking on functionality. "What is true for singing is true for playing too," he writes in the introduction to *Elementary Training for Musicians*.[133] This statement is rooted not only in the idealistic wish that music students should sing more; he was also convinced that the choral song, particularly one that could be sung by an amateur choir, could function as a corrective in the development of contemporary music intended for professional performers.[134] Elaborating on this view he expresses the belief that vocal music is a kind of superordinate directive for instrumental music, a notion also prevalent in the *Jugendmusikbewegung*, where vocal performance was considered both the starting point and the benchmark for instrumental performance.[135] Hence,

---

[132] *Aufsätze, Vorträge, Reden*, 25-28.

[133] *Elementary Training for Musicians*, XI.

[134] See, for example, A. Briner, *op. cit.*, 47-48.

[135] See D. Kolland, *op. cit.*, 78.

from Hindemith's point of view, several opinions expressed in "Wie soll der ideale Chorsatz beschaffen sein?" are equally applicable to instrumental music for amateurs.

Hindemith's most significant conviction in this context is that composers must have a clear purpose for the work they are creating, not only an inner, subjective aim but an objective intention beyond themselves, in the form of a concrete purpose and/or a defined target group. "The time of constantly composing only for oneself is perhaps over for good," he warns.[136] This demand was and remains controversial, as it appears to preclude artistic freedom. At the time when Hindemith held this lecture, his intention was probably to curtail the most extreme negative impulses of artistic freedom, reminiscent of the limits he himself had often considerably stretched in his earlier time as a *Bürgerschreck*. At the same time, he was both troubled and annoyed by the persistent compositional experiments of his contemporaries, which he felt were not based on musical knowledge and had no consideration for the listeners or users. Addressing this danger seemed crucial when speaking to an audience that was basically skeptical to new music and felt threatened by the *avant garde*. Furthermore, all participants could be assumed to have intimate knowledge of the actual situation for amateur performers. Later in life Hindemith came to moderate his view, stating that the real purpose of his statement was to save music from threatening esoteric isolation.[137]

If composers are going to compose for specific users, they must be able to write *nach Maß*. This means that they must execute their work with a craftsmanship that is as perfect as possible, with solid knowledge of the musical medium, their target group, and the purpose. Hindemith's comparison of a composer to the tailor, the craftsman who on the basis of his professional training is able to select the right material for the garment's use, is not just a fancy metaphor: The tailor must know the customer's taste as well as his or her measurements and size. Correspondingly, the composer must communicate with the consumer during the creative process. "Naturally the customers must be allowed the right to be consulted on the nature of the text and the nature and structure of the music; they must also have the right to request alterations and propose improvements," is Hindemith's generous reassurance to the choir leaders.[138]

---

[136]"Wie soll der ideale Chorsatz der Gegenwart oder besser der nächsten Zukunft beschaffen sein?," 27. ["Die Zeiten des steten Für-sich-Komponierens sind vielleicht für immer vorbei."]

[137]See *A Composer's World*, X.

[138]"Wie soll der ideale Chorsatz der Gegenwart oder besser der nächsten Zukunft beschaffen sein?," 28. ["Natürlich müsste den Bestellern ein Mitbestimmungsrecht über Art und Anlage des Textes und der Musik eingeräumt werden, sie müssten auch berechtigt sein, Änderungen zu beantragen und Verbesserungen vorzuschlagen."]

Hindemith begins his description of the ideal choral movement by asking for a rebirth of polyphony, or rather a restoration of the polyphonic principles in a moderately modern tonal language. He puts polyphony first, because this technique expresses what he understands to be the essence of the choral medium in its so-called *Zusammenstellung lebender und gleichwertiger Stimmen*, the collocation of voices that are alive and of equal value. He thus stresses that in their choice of technique, composers must consider not only the audible result but also the ensemble's specific nature. He takes this further by drawing attention to melody and the fashioning of individual voices in polyphonic choral movements. "The melody must be distinguishable from a purely instrumental melodic construction,"[139] he argues; recognition of the nature of the musical medium must be crucial also for the melody. Even though melody has an analyzable architecture, Hindemith still considers it to be on the border between rational recognition and what can be irrationally experienced. In "Wie soll der ideale Chorsatz beschaffen sein?" he also indicates that composers cannot fully master their melodic creation. Rather than merely writing down voices, they must *listen themselves into* the melodic potential to extract the melody. In adding melodies to the polyphonic fabric, every effort must be made to achieve unity. Individual voices should be balanced and mutually support each other. As Hindemith believes that it is impossible to perceive four or more melodic lines of equal value, composers must consider these experiences when creating a polyphonic movement. It is not enough that "the collocation of voices that are alive and of equal value" melts into a higher unit, where, although the listeners can follow individual voices, the overwhelming whole causes both performers and listeners to be lifted up in an experience of polyphonic sound. Polyphony must always be experienced solely on its own distinguishing premises; it must never relinquish the demand of the integrity of individual voices.

The foundation of a well-sounding choral movement is a predominance of consonant intervals. Singers are always dependent on their ear. A predominance of imperfect and perfect consonances will lay a firm ground for musical purity, and therefore Hindemith's recommendation is: "Completely dissonant chords, which we often find employed in instrumental music just for static purposes—in their nature of sound mass representing a weight factor—should be avoided in a choral movement."[140]

---

[139]"Wie soll der ideale Chorsatz ... beschaffen sein?," p. 25. ["Die Melodie hätte sich von der rein instrumentalen Melodik zu trennen."]

[140]*Ibid.*, 25-26. ["Reine dissonante Akkorde, wie wir sie in der Instrumentalmusik oft sozusagen lediglich zu statischen Zwecken – in ihrer Eigenheit als Klangmasse und darum Gewicht – angewendet finden, sollte man im Chorsatz vermeiden."]

Hindemith: Active Performance and Musical Recognition 367

This part of the lecture is most particularly addressed to composers of choral music. In general, however, the starting point for Hindemith's understanding of the musical material, which he believes to be fundamental to all music, is always the human ear and the human potential for a true musical experience. In addition he emphasizes the quality of melodic construction and the logic of linearity. If performers perceive the interaction between different voices in tension and relaxation as logical, the music will come off more easily. This line of reasoning resembles Schoenberg's arguments for musical logic. Yet, Hindemith links users to logic in a much more determined and practical way.

Rhythm must also be considered according to the specific musical medium. Choral movements should avoid "melodic construction taken over from instrumental music, with sharp rhythmic subdivisions and uncommonly strong accents."[141] Instead, Hindemith recommends what might be described as vocally-based melodic rhythm: larger arches, longer lines, and a voice-leading that is not characterized by rhythmic accents.

In *A Composer's World*, Hindemith gives a humorous explanation for the absurdity of the idea that music could give a genuine imitation of something outside itself.[142] With obvious reference to the mechanics-infatuated romanticism of the interwar years he uses a proposed attempt at an imitation of a riveting machine. In "Wie soll der ideale Chorsatz beschaffen sein?" he indicates that neither should different music ensembles attempt to imitate each other's characteristics. "Special sound effects that are not in the nature of the singing voice should be avoided as far as possible," he states.[143] In line with his injunction that composers pay attention to the nature of their target groups, Hindemith demands that they be respectful of the individual instruments'—in this case the voices'—nature. A vocal imitation of purely orchestral effects should be avoided;[144] the same is true for exaggerated dynamic contrasts. The dynamics of choral movements should be balanced rather than contrastive. For the same reason, agogic effects should be used with care. Finally, Hindemith warns against archaic modes of expression: Stylistic imitations of older music are no solution.

---

[141]"Wie soll der ideale Chorsatz ... beschaffen sein?," 26. ["die von der Instrumentalmusik übernommene, rhythmisch sehr scharf gegliederte und außerordentlich stark akzentuierte Melodiebildung."]

[142]See *A Composer's World*, 34-36.

[143]"Wie soll der ideale Chorsatz ... beschaffen sein?," 26. ["Besondere Klangeffekte, die nicht in der Natur der Singstimme liegen, wären nach Möglichkeit zu vermeiden."]

[144]This does not prevent the voices in a vocal movement from being replaced or strengthened with instruments, such as he proposes, for example, in the preface to *Frau Musica*. He is talking of purely instrumental effects.

Hindemith points out the importance of the so-called easy singability of choral pieces. When placing strict functional demands on music capable of being realized through amateurs' *Selbstspielen*, his views harmonize with a wider perspective, where he emphasizes the decisive, general importance of the performing medium's physical possibilities and limitations. This does not mean that the performer should not strive toward what is new. For, as Hindemith writes in the preface to *Frau Musica*: "Just the same, one does not demand of music written today and for today's needs that it must allow to be sight-read by everyone." And he continues: "Here, the music lover is given some nuts to crack."[145] In this cantata for soloists, choir, and string orchestra Hindemith realizes the views expressed in the lecture "Wie soll der ideale Chorsatz beschaffen sein?" A considerable segment of the amateur movement, especially the important *Jugendmusik* branch *Die Musikantengilde*, embraced this work. Eduard Zuckmayer, one of the association's main representatives, thought that *Frau Musica* could be described as nothing less than a model for utility music.[146]

A few years later, in the early 1930s, Hindemith's music begins to show a noticeable stylistic change toward milder expression and more distinctly tonal-harmonic structure. It seems as if some of the views expressed in "Wie soll der ideale Chorsatz beschaffen sein?" become more evident also in his music for professional performers. Experience from his work for and with amateurs appears to color a larger range of his creative artistic activity. Moreover, he seems to consider the aspect of superordinate functionality a reliable servant also for his own and personal musical expression. This corresponds further with Hindemith's view that in the music market, not only the amateur has something to gain through coming to an understanding with the composer. The composer himself gains just as much, if not more, by understanding the amateur:

> Once a writer's technique and style is organized in this direction, so that music which satisfies the amateur's wishes can be granted, his approach to his entire work will inevitably undergo a radical change: the emphasis on moral aspects will now become recognizable also in his works written for the concertizing professional, and now he will talk with a different spirit to the general audience, which, in its basic benevolence, will be ready to accept his leadership towards better goals.[147]

---

[145] See the preface to *Frau Musica*. ["Trotzdem wird man von einer heute und für heutige Bedürfnisse geschriebene Musik verlangen, dass sie von jedermann vom Blatt zu spielen ist.[...] Dem Liebhaber werden hier einige Nüsse zu knacken gegeben."]

[146] See D. Kolland, *op. cit*, 151.

[147] *A Composer's World*, 255-256.

Hindemith steps quite unconditionally into the contemporary field that renews interest in the user potential of art. This is also the reason why he is so closely associated with the term *Gebrauchsmusik*, a term that, as we have seen, Hindemith did not coin and seldom used in his writings. The program for the festival in Baden-Baden in 1927, a continuation of the earlier *Donaueschingen Festival*, contains the following comments from his pen:

> Had our *Gebrauchsmusik* not sunk to today's miserably low level, we would indeed not have needed to concern ourselves with this artistically less important branch of our music life. [...] It would not have occurred to anyone to deny the necessity of utility and consumer music. Public celebrations, balls, ceremonial processions, coffee houses and cinemas are quite unthinkable without music.[148]

The preface of the revised edition of *Das Marienleben* contains a passage that positively describes this genuinely contemplative work as a utility object, a *Gebrauchsgegenstand*:

> In the nature of things they [the songs] were never any sensational success, but they soon formed in music's housekeeping a kind of article for everyday use, something about which one does not make any fuss but the usefulness of which is accepted as a matter of course (perhaps the best a composer can wish for).[149]

That music is not necessarily astounding but rather perceived as *usable* is considered here to be a composer's highest aim. With regard to utility music in general, Hindemith agrees with Kurt Weill that this music actually exists anyway, and that it must be a professional composer's task to enhance its quality. Hindemith also sees utility music as a particularly challenging domain, since it opens possibilities for a purposeful development of music. Concert music in truth only fulfills the composer's demand for technical perfection and economic profit, Hindemith believes. This is the background for his writing music with educational or social propensities in the latter part of the 1920s. In a letter dated 8 May 1930, written to his American patron Elizabeth Sprague Coolidge, he explains this view openly and honestly:

---

[148]"Zur mechanischen Musik," *Aufsätze, Vorträge, Reden*, 23. ["Hätte unsere Gebrauchsmusik nicht den heutigen jämmerlichen Tiefstand erreicht, so brauchten wir uns freilich nicht mit dem künstlerisch weniger bedeutenden Zweige unseres Musiklebens zu beschäftigen. [...] Es wird Keinem einfallen, die Notwendigkeit der Gebrauchs- und Verschleißmusik zu leugnen. Volksfeste, Bälle, Aufzüge, Kaffeehäuser und Kinos sind ohne Musik gar nicht denkbar."]

[149]*Das Marienleben*, III. ["Sie [die Lieder] waren der Natur der Sache nach nie ein Sensationserfolg, bildeten aber im Musikhaushalt bald so etwas wie einen Gebrauchsgegenstand, von dem man kein Aufhebens macht, dessen Nützlichkeit aber als selbstverständlich hingenommen wird [vielleicht das Beste, was sich ein Komponist wünschen kann."]

> In recent years I have largely turned away from concert music and almost exclusively written music with pedagogical or social tendencies: for amateurs, for children, for broadcasting, mechanical instruments, etc. I consider this kind of composition as more important than writing for concert purposes, because the latter is mostly a technical task for the musician, while hardly anything is done for the further development of music. I must therefore view the concert as a purely commercial affair. All the music I have written these last years for concert purposes was written for commercial reasons. I cannot transfer to concert music the idealism I gladly invest in what seems to me extremely necessary for the further development of music. On the contrary, I must balance the one with the other.[150]

Hindemith believes that the way forwards leads through utility music, and eventually transfers the experiences gained with tonally more clearly balanced functional music to his so-called concert music. His most widely played work, the symphony *Mathis der Maler*, is a good example. Advocates of Hindemith compositional diversity in the 1920s admit that in the process, his music loses some of its earlier spontaneity and youthful freshness.

Hindemith's compositional efforts for amateurs culminated in the extensive work *Plöner Musiktag* of 1932. He retained the fundamental insights gained through the following years, even when he began to demonstrate an increasing skepticism to the term *Gebrauchsmusik*. In a lecture in 1940, published as "Betrachtungen zur heutigen Musik," he mentions the historical factors that promoted the term some fifteen years previously, one of them being that, during and after the war, audiences and amateurs emerged who made their mark in concert halls and music schools. Consequently, he sets the term into a time-and-place context of a socio-cultural development, as Eisler did in his way. Hindemith also refers to a way of thinking so poorly concealed in the term itself. "If in Europe today [1940] one wanted to talk about 'Gebrauchsmusik', one would frequently be looked at uncomprehendingly, since no-one can really imagine for what music could be written if not for use," he says, and concludes: "Let us rather strive to write music

---

[150]*Paul Hindemith Briefe*, 147. ["Ich habe mich in den letzten Jahren fast ganz von der Konzertmusik abgewandt und fast durchweg Musik mit pädagogischen oder sozialen Tendenzen geschrieben: für Liebhaber, für Kinder, für Rundfunk, mechanische Instrumente etc. Ich halte diese Art der Komposition für wichtiger, als das Schreiben für Konzertzwecke, weil Letzteres fast nur eine technische Aufgabe für den Musiker ist und für die Weiterentwicklung der Musik kaum etwas getan wird. Ich muß darum das Konzert als eine rein geschäftliche Sache betrachten. Alle Musik, die ich in den letzten Jahren für Konzertzwecke geschrieben habe, ist aus geschäftlichen Gründen angefertigt worden. Den Idealismus, den ich gerne auf Dinge verwende, die mir für die Weiterentwicklung der Musik äußerst notwendig erscheinen, kann ich nicht auf die Konzertmusik übertragen. Im Gegenteil, ich muß das eine durch das andere ausgleichen."]

that is so good as to appear satisfying to the highest degree in manner, purpose, and scoring, and thereby appears as usable in all its appropriate forms of presentation."[151] Despite his functionalist attitude Hindemith suggests that he is somewhat embarrassed by his contribution to the popularity of the term *Gebrauchsmusik*. Later in life, he would have preferred to see the word put to eternal rest. He was surprised that it showed such an incredible ability to survive, not least in America, his home of exile. In *A Composer's World*, he expresses his sentiments as follows:

> Apart from the ugliness of the word [*Gebrauchsmusik*]—in German it is as hideous as its English equivalents, workaday music, music for use, utility music, and similar verbal beauties—nobody found anything remarkable in it, since quite obviously music for which no use can be found, that is to say useless music, is not entitled to public consideration anyway and consequently the *Gebrauch* is taken for granted. [...] when, years after, I first came to this country [the US], I felt like the sorcerer's apprentice who had become victim of his own conjurations: the slogan *Gebrauchsmusik* hit me wherever I went, it had grown to be as abundant, useless, and disturbing as thousands of dandelions in a lawn. [...] Up to this day it has been impossible to kill the silly term and the unscrupulous classification that goes with it.[152]

The basic idea that the artistic demands for quality must be combined with the realization that music is actually to be *performed* came to be Hindemith's guiding principle throughout his life. Thus the principle of musical activity, which then includes concrete *Gebrauch*, were the underpinning of deeper musical recognition.

"Forderungen an den Laien"
Contemporary music life must not only demand contributions from composers, users must also be confronted with their responsibility to participate. Although the market had a great need for music, one should always remain discerning. Just as Hindemith is not willing to equate old music with good music,[153] he doubts that everything new is by necessity good, in the sense that it deserves the amateur's attention without reservation. The notion

---

[151]"Betrachtungen zur heutigen Musik," 161. ["Wenn man heute [1940] in Europa von 'Gebrauchsmusik' reden wollte, man würde häufig verständnislos angesehen werden, da man sich ja im allgemeinen nicht vorstellen kann, für was sonst als für den Gebrauch eine Musik geschrieben sein könnte. [...] Laßt uns lieber danach trachten, eine Musik zu schreiben, die so gut ist, dass sie je nach Art, Zweck und Besetzung in allen ihr angemessenen Darstellungsformen im höchsten Masse befriedigend und damit brauchbar erscheint."]

[152]*A Composer's World*, X-XI.

[153]From "Forderungen an den Laien," 27. ["Nicht alle alte Musik ist gut."]

that one must sing something just because it is new is quite wrong, Hindemith contends.[154] Even worse is singing a new work on the basis of an isolated evaluation of its textual qualities, on account of the text's possible political or ideological content. What are the crucial criteria for the amateurs' choice of repertoire? First, they must look for music demonstrating those features that distinguish a well-written score. It is not enough that the producers seek, to the best of their ability, to satisfy the compositional demands discussed above: If consumers are not able to grasp, recognize, and value a work with this ideal functionality, the music will seldom make it as far as *Gebrauch*. "First it would be desirable," says Hindemith to choirs and conductors, "that everyone embraced the stated requirements."[155]

Most of Hindemith's criteria should be manageable enough for perceptive conductors and skilled amateurs. Yet in the final instance, these criteria are not entirely sufficient, he admits. A work must be functional; it must not be an art product that is difficult to realize. At the same time, a work with functional characteristics need not be worth the time and effort spent on it. The first thing to look for is the work's artistic quality.[156] *Gebrauchsmusik* must not be understood in such a way that it is exempt from artistic evaluation, on the contrary: music's artistic content must always be the decisive criterion for its value and, indeed, also for its utility value.

The discussion about material has shown how Hindemith employs the terms good and bad music. Strangely enough, he never attempts to provide a concise definition of the notion of "artistic quality." This may be because he understands that the conception is so complex that it cannot be delimited. In "Wie soll der ideale Chorsatz beschaffen sein?" he maintains that anyone evaluating musical experience and judging a work's artistic quality does so on the basis of individual musical experience. To evaluate new music, users must simply gain experience and strengthen their discernment through constant involvement in it. Hindemith admits that this requires some effort: "Of course a certain expenditure of energy is involved in taking on something new and therefore strange."[157] Amateurs must be willing to reach for the new and not expect the music to be necessarily easy to play. Users must help to breach the wall built from prejudice and resistance to new music, says Hindemith. They have a responsibility for the quantitative dissemination

---

[154] See "Wie soll der ideale Chorsatz ... beschaffen sein?," 43.

[155] *Ibid.* ["Zunächst wäre es wünschenswert [...] wenn sie alle sich die ausgesprochenen Forderungen zu eigen machen würden."]

[156] *Ibid.*

[157] *Ibid.* "Freilich gehört ein gewisser Energieaufwand dazu, sich mit Neuem und darum Ungewohnten auseinanderzusetzen."

as well as for the qualitative development of contemporary music. Thus Hindemith places great demands on consumers, which may seem just as comprehensive as those he makes on producers. In the course of the creative process, users should communicate with composers, at least where conditions are favorable. They should evaluate both the technical aspects and the artistic quality of the work, be in charge of the performance itself and be aware of their responsibility for the progress of contemporary music. In fact, Hindemith shifts the larger part of the producers' responsibility over to consumers. Representatives of amateur music might claim that in this way Hindemith is laying an overly heavy burden on the user's shoulders. His request, however, must be seen in the light of his idealistic respect for the amateurs' potential: if lay musicians do not yet have broad enough shoulders, they have all the possibilities needed to acquire the necessary strength. Collaboration between the producing musicians and the consuming laymen will help amateurs to develop their taste and improve their knowledge of music.

In April 1930 the journal *Musik und Gesellschaft* published Hindemith's article "Forderungen an den Laien."[158] In the introduction Hindemith claims to be first in publicly expressing the demands to be placed on lay musicians. "Forderungen an den Laien" is clearly focused on phenomena characteristic of the 1920s' *Jugendmusikbewegung*. The article can be understood as a critical glance at the essence of this movement, particularly where it addresses the predilection for old music and historical instruments and the need for a *Gemeinschaft* that often had more sectarian than musical manifestations. The article is clearly a product of its time, although it contains features of general interest. Hindemith stresses that the amateur has a very important role to play in music life, that being called *dilettante* should not be taken negatively: "Der Laie sei sich seines Wertes bewußt" is his terse appeal, "let the layman be aware of his value." Such self-awareness can, of course, also have negative effects, as when it leads amateurs to exaggerated cultivation and glorification of their nature as non-professionals. This would contribute to an artificial opposition between non-professional and professional music performance—in their own favor.[159] Hindemith is convinced that amateurs are, and will be, the part of music life in which *Selbstspielen* and *Vorspielen* both have their natural place; the one neither should nor can preclude the other.

Amateurs should not believe themselves to be so exclusive as to demand that their repertoire solely reflect old music, rarely performed works, or musical curiosities. Neither is playing rare or antiquated instruments the way

---

[158]"Forderungen an den Laien," 42-44.

[159]Hindemith touches on a central point in the ideology of the *Jugendbewegung*. The movement considered itself not only an independent but deemed its activities a superior alternative to the professional concert and its supposed virtuosity.

to go. That type of uniqueness leads nowhere. Amateurs must be aware of their place in the integrated development of music life: "Everyone wants to have something quite special, forgetting that he thus loses the connection to music's development."[160] "He who gathers with others for music-making ought first and foremost to make music," Hindemith continues.[161] In this way he attacks the non-musical activities often connected to the amateur movement. In its efforts to create *Gemeinschaft*, music must be the all-important and not yield that place to other means of promoting fellowship. Although the term *Gemeinschaft* is broad and general, it inevitably suggests the *Gemeinschafts-Ideologie* of the *Jugendbewegung*, where performing music was considered more a means than an end.

It should not be difficult to agree with Hindemith on the importance of the amateur movement for a broad and vital music life. For many people it is a well-known fact that the nonprofessionals can have greater potential than may first be obvious. The question is whether it is possible to share Hindemith's opinion about the active and ideal music user. There is every indication that Hindemith himself believed this type of user really existed, at least as a realizable possibility among amateur musicians of his time. For Hindemith, the path from heart to hand was always short and, as the spontaneous and impatient enthusiast he was, he surely expected immediate results. The most active period in his commitment to inspiring the broad mass of music consumers came to an end in 1932-33. This may be due to several factors, not least to the dark clouds gathering on the political horizon. But it can also have something to do with a certain bitterness and disappointment over the amateur movement itself.

In 1933 Josef Müller-Blattau encouraged Hindemith to write a chapter for the book *Hohe Schule der Musik*. Hindemith worked on this task until 1935. However, political circumstances prevented the publication of his chapter, which was not published in its entirety until its posthumous inclusion, under the title "Komposition und Kompositionsunterricht," in the volume *Aufsätze, Vorträge, Reden*, which Giselher Schubert compiled in 1994.[162] In what was meant to become the second chapter of his contribution, "Die Musik der letzten Jahrzehnte," Hindemith comments on a period that included his own involvement with *Gebrauchsmusik*. In keeping with his views on the position of amateurs in the musical life of the 17th and 18th centuries, he posits that their *mentality* must have changed in a negative direction—a fact

---

[160]"Forderungen an Laien," 43. ["Jeder will etwas ganz Besonderes haben, er vergißt aber, dass er dadurch den Anschluss an die Entwicklung der Musik verliert."]

[161]*Ibid.* ["Wer sich mit anderen musizierend zusammenfindet, sollte vor allem musizieren."]

[162]"Komposition und Kompositionsunterricht," 47-115.

that he regards as a fundamental obstacle for the potential development of both the amateurs themselves and, subsequently, of contemporary music life. "The old [former] dilettante had been modest and mostly made music rather well," he judges, whereas "the new dilettante was arrogant, and in turn could hardly play or sing."[163] Hindemith is not afraid to take the mainly sectarian features he discerns in the amateur movement to task, although he had, hardly a decade earlier, enthusiastically believed just this movement capable of strengthening the link between people and art. What particularly depressed him at this point was that amateurs did not seem willing to submit to instruction, thereby forfeiting the chance to create the foundations for fruitful music development. "Ihm mußte die Musik unterworfen werden," he recalls bitterly; it was *music* that had to submit to the *amateur*. And he continues his description: To find suitable music, the amateur trawled through the whole of music history. Irrespective of whether it was good or bad, he chose music on the sole criterion of his own preference and technical incompetence. Lastly, Hindemith also berates composers who at the time wrote for amateurs:

> Composers who had learnt little found here the acknowledgment otherwise denied them. At a pinch they were able to lead two voices, with three they already wreaked havoc. Their scores were impossible throughout and one wonders that their "settings" satisfied their sectarian brothers, who were not, after all, otherwise undemanding[164]

While Hindemith had often expressed his conviction that producers and consumers must meet in the musical market, here he makes it clear that he fails to see any productive consequences of his efforts. His disappointment over amateurs not following the direction he had imagined, at least not at the speed he had expected, is barely hidden. It appears that Schoenberg's gloomy prophecy of the consequences of involved oneself with amateurs has become his own experience. Yet, however much his text manifests both his bitterness and discontent, he does not lose sight of his vision. Immediate realities in music life cannot shake his firm belief in active performance combined with the genuine potential of amateurs. What does not show concrete results in the present may do so in the future. It would be a mistake to understand Hindemith as only concerned with the respective present. The next level of his thoughts on musical activity concerns his vision of tomorrow.

---

[163]"Komposition und Kompositionsunterricht," 9-60. ["Der alte Dilettant war bescheiden gewesen und hatte meist recht gut musiziert [...], der neue war arrogant, dafür konnte er kaum spielen oder singen."]

[164]*Ibid.*, 60. ["Komponisten, die wenig gelernt hatten, fanden hier die Anerkennung, die ihnen sonst versagt blieb. Zur Not konnten sie zwei Stimmen führen, mit dreien richteten sie schon Unheil an, ihre Partituren waren fast durchweg unmöglich und man wundert sich, dass ihre 'Sätze' den Sektenbrüdern, die doch sonst nicht anspruchslos waren, genügten."]

"Die musikalische Gemeinschaft"

Playing and singing together can promote a strong *Gemeinschaftsgefühl*. Choral singing, often used to strengthen and consolidate a spiritual, ideological, and social fellowship, is a typical example. This kind of activity is employed as a means of inviting general contact between human beings and establishing at least a temporary fellowship among people of often very different backgrounds. For the German *Jugendbewegung* in general, not only for the *Jugendmusikbewegung*, the folk-song was the crucial, edifying foundation. The horrific experiences of World War I, and above all the fact that Germany lost the war, prompted the awareness that political, spiritual, social, and political life needed a new beginning. For Fritz Jöde, this situation meant a radical new approach. Fellowship should extend across national and political borders and a new humanity to be created with, as its foundation, what was called *brüderliches Mit- und Füreinander*, a brotherly feeling of living with and for one another.[165] Jöde considered music performance to be an important tool in this process.

When it comes to Hindemith's view of *die musikalische Gemeinschaft*, it might at first appear that his point of departure is identical with Jöde's views on infinite fellowship. As a soldier in World War I, Hindemith played in a string quartet, inspired and encouraged by the Francophile colonel Graf von Kielmannsegg. The quartet sadly heard of Debussy's death at a private concert for the colonel, just after they had concluded the second movement of the deceased composer's *String Quartet*. In an undated text Hindemith assigns this experience almost visionary importance:

> We did not play to the end. It was as if the vital spirit had been taken from our playing. We felt here for the first time that music is more than style, technique, and expression of personal sentiment. Here, the music transcended political borders, national hatred, and the horrors of war. On no other occasion has it become clearer to me in which direction music must develop.[166]

These words were written in retrospect, probably as late as 1955. The experience of learning about a composer's death while playing one of his works undoubtedly left a strong impression on the 22-year-old Hindemith.

---

[165] See K-H Reinfandt, "Musik als Schöpfung im Menschen," *Musik und Bildung* XI (1987): 853-855.

[166] P. Hindemith, "Über Debussy," *Aufsätze, Vorträge, Reden,* 290. ["Wir spielten nicht zu Ende. Es war, als wäre unserem Spielen der Lebenshauch genommen worden. Wir fühlten aber hier zum ersten Male, dass Musik mehr ist, als Stil, Technik und Ausdruck persönlichen Gefühls. Musik griff hier über politische Grenzen, über nationalen Hass und über die Greuel des Krieges hinweg. Bei keiner anderen Gelegenheit ist mir je mit gleicher Deutlichkeit klar geworden, in welcher Richtung sich die Musik zu entwickeln habe."]

Yet the conclusion concerning the direction music must take, is more typical of the musical thoughts of the mature Hindemith than of the young man's restless need to partake in musical experiments. Hindemith believes that the recognition of everyone having a part in an all-embracing human community must have consequences for music, music performance, and music life. Jöde regarded music as a means; for Hindemith it was both a means and an end. He wished to stimulate an active musical fellowship, one in which the amateur has the key role. If this incident from World War I is considered as a kind of first pronouncement in recognizing the universal character of musical performance, then it can be said that from this point on, the idea of *die musikalische Gemeinschaft* develops into one of the most important directives in Hindemith's musical profession. It is obvious that this progress runs parallel with both his work on theoretical issues and his studies of philosophers of older times. In what follows, these aspects will be examined in more detail.

From "Hören" to "Machen"
 Unterweisung im Tonsatz I (*The Craft of Musical Composition* I) and *A Composer's World* represent projects with rather different aims. *Craft* is a presentation, justification, and rationale for his understanding of the musical material; *A Composer's World* has a much broader aim, as it highlights larger aspects of a composer's world and activities. Roughly fifteen years separate these two books.
 In *A Composer's World* Hindemith once again presents his theories on tonality, but now in a considerably abbreviated form.[167] Anyone wishing to study Hindemith's theories usually considers this book as a summary of his views in this field. Therefore, *Unterweisung im Tonsatz* is justifiably more in focus as far as his thoughts on the musical material are concerned. There is also an interesting difference in the way Hindemith presents his theories in the two books. In *Unterweisung*, Hindemith accords the human ear the status as the ultimate control of intervals. Conversely in *A Composer's World*, he assigns this function to the human voice. He describes the intervals that because of their natural purity are characterized as being received by the human ear with the lowest degree of tolerance for sonic impurity—the octave, fifth, and fourth—as "produced most easily by the singing voice."[168] Initially this may seem self-evident, as vocal performance is always dependent on control by the ear. The hearing and vocal organs are thus indivisible. Hence it should make no difference whether Hindemith chooses to focus on

---

[167] See *A Composer's World*, 77-117.
[168] *Ibid.*, 80.

the ear or the voice as in this connection they represent the same human capacity. Hindemith's difference in emphasis may also be conditioned more by pedagogy than by musical science: *Unterweisung im Tonsatz* addresses the ear-trained teacher, *A Composer's World* the singing and playing amateur. Yet it seems rather implausible that Hindemith, as his later explanation suggests, should base the presentation of something he considers so important and fundamental on such pragmatic premises. Practical educational experiences, among others from teaching theory and composition in the United States, may have influenced his decision. In a general sense singing is, indeed, basically an expression in sound of the person's ability to perceive by ear. The ear is controllable and, to a certain degree, adjustable for the teacher. But the shift from ear to voice may also indicate that Hindemith has actually begun to consider the singing voice as a more reliable controlling device.

The notion that the ear can become accustomed to any number of sounds while the singing voice will always have its limitations is one of the main reasons for Hindemith's 1948 revision of *Das Marienleben*. By all accounts, he began the revision in the late 1930s. He must have been working on *Das Marienleben* and *Unterweisung im Tonsatz* at the same time. In the compositional work he pledges to pay heightened attention to the nature of the singing voice, while in the theoretical work he concentrates mainly on phenomena centered on the human ear. His presentation of tonality theories in *A Composer's World* may suggest that he combines these phenomena in a way that leads to a conscious shift of the perspective itself. This shift, then, results in the active performance, *das Machen*, being presented as an important means of experiencing, recognizing, and clarifying problems which have traditionally been associated more with the theoretical disciplines of music.

The composers' responsibility for a positive and reflective contribution to a musical community is a pervasive idea in *A Composer's World*. While in *Unterweisung* Hindemith emphasizes the importance of relating to the tones' *Verwandtschaft* or relationships, in *A Composer's World* he stresses the composers' moral responsibility for *die Gesellschaft* and above all, *die Gemeinschaft*.[169] The same fundamental ideas resurface in his treatment of Boethius' *De institutione musica* in the latter book. Hindemith's personal understanding causes him to find it necessary to qualify the Boethian *musica* concept through the thoughts on the nature of musical experience that Augustine expresses in *De Musica libri sex*. These considerations will be presented below.

---

[169]The German terms are used here for the sake of comparison. They are taken from the German translation *Komponist in seiner Welt*. In the original text *A Composer's World* Hindemith uses *society* and *community*.

The discussion on Hindemith's understanding of the musical material shows the way in which he abandons the notion of a categorical distinction between good and bad music. In *A Composer's World* he illustrates his view by means of two examples. In the first he focuses on the characteristic features of Gregorian chants, which are sung at religious festivals. While every musician of a certain taste will, he believes, deem these chants the most perfect and convincing unison compositions ever created, complete understanding of their overwhelming linear power is not accomplished through reading or listening; they require active participation: "You must participate in singing these melodic miracles if you want to feel how they weld the singing group into a spiritual unit, independent of the individualistic prompting of a conductor, and guided only by the lofty spirit and the technical excellence of the structure."[170] Hindemith stresses that the optimal experience of these characteristic melodic constructions is gained from an actively performing fellowship or community. Singing these melodies solo would be to draw them out of their real context, he says, adding for those who are tempted: "Don't you feel as if you were expelled from a community of worthy friends? Has the music not lost its savor and assumed a taste of bitterness instead?"[171] Anyone trying to play chant's melody first on a wind instrument, then on a violin, and finally on a piano will experience another strange occurrence: the characteristic qualities of the melody line will fade and in the end appear ridiculous.

The other example he gives comes from Bach's *Well-tempered Clavier.* Admitting that the polyphony would be clear if the fugues were arranged for a string quartet or trio, he warns that they would lose some of their substance and impressive spiritual force. This force must be connected to the degree of *technical resistance* put up by the piano: "In our fugues we have reduced to almost nothing the heavy technical resistance that a player of polyphonic keyboard music has to overcome, since the string players have produced their isolated lines without noticeable effort."[172]

Hindemith concludes that the classification 'good' and 'bad' certainly says nothing about the real technical quality of a composition as long as this evaluation is not based on additional criteria. The distinction presented in *Unterweisung im Tonsatz* I was mainly justified according to compositional technique. The crucial criterion was the question of a composer's sensible or imprudent treatment of the natural and supposedly audible relationships between tones. Hindemith's aim in *A Composer's World* is to give examples

---

[170]*A Composer's World*, 121.
[171]*Ibid.*
[172]*Ibid.*, 122.

of supplementary criteria he believes must play a decisive role in the evaluation process. These take as their starting point the vocal and instrumental performance, i.e., the aspect of *(Musik-) Machen*. Hindemith emphasizes that both examples illustrate important evaluation criteria in the degree of technical resistance experienced by performers. Performance, then, also exercises a decisive influence on our listening experience, on *(Musik-) Hören*.

Musica instrumentalis

The contents of Chapter 1 in *A Composer's World*, "The Philosophical Approach," is symptomatic of Hindemith's increasing need to give his ideas historical depth. His point of departure is the question of what characterizes a composition of *everlasting value*. He attempts to approach an answer by discussing thinkers from antiquity and the Middle Ages. The focus is on fundamental, demanding questions, and key parts of the chapter are affected by Hindemith's very personal interpretations of ancient philosophy. This is not to suggest that the text is superficial or lacks reflection, but rather that Hindemith's lack of a deeper knowledge of the comprehensive ideas that gave rise to these thoughts effects his presentation. Consequently, historians of philosophy may feel doubtful about some of Hindemith's inferences and conclusions. This applies in particular to his presentation of Boethius and Augustine as epistemological opposites. However, the focus in the context of a discussion about musical functionalism is on selected elements of Hindemith's chapter regarded as expressions of his unique understanding of music.

Hindemith frequently gives the impression of basing his ideas on essential features of ancient philosophy. In practice, however, a close look often reveals that his approach is rather the reverse, that he wishes to give his own view greater significance and depth by founding it on thoughts that have endured the passing of time. This attitude is reflected in his assertion, voiced in the same chapter, that he, as a musician and not a philosopher, allows himself considerable freedom when speaking about subjects of philosophy.[173]

With his philosophical approach Hindemith attempts to gain, among other things, factual support for his view that any genuine musical experience implies the subject's active participation. "[W]e must in some way participate, beyond the mere sensual perception of music, in its realization as sound; we must transform our musical impressions into a meaningful possession of our own," he claims.[174] This request applies not only to listeners; composers, performers, and music teachers must equally grow beyond simply registering

---

[173] See *A Composer's World*, 3.

[174] *A Composer's World*, 3.

musical impressions. Hindemith finds support for this view in Augustine's *De musica libri sex*. In this book Augustine describes the genuine musical experience as a complex combination of several factors.[175] Of the five levels into which he divides this process, the first two represent music as physical and physiological phenomena respectively. Our ability to imagine music mentally and the capacity to activate our musical memory are the next two levels. The fifth level—the highest according to Augustine—represents our ability to intellectually evaluate what is heard. Hindemith, takes this to a sixth level, presupposing that through this mental evaluation, we direct our mind toward the order of the cosmos and the unity between our soul and "the divine principle."

Hindemith shares Augustine's notion of the fulfilled musical experience. Hindemith's requirements are, first, that our mental interpretation of musical impressions must be fundamentally important and, second, that music must then be converted, through an active process, to what he calls a *moral power*. In everyday language this mysterious moral power can be paraphrased as a force that effects spiritual enhancement, or as a form of edification. This then places demands not only on ourselves, but also on the music that is the object of our experience. Hindemith admits that this moral imperative, followed to its ultimate effect, may well appear to be too strict. Even the most cultivated listeners will sometimes feel the need for relaxing entertainment. Consequently, various types of entertainment music have their justification. There are many ways of creating, distributing, and receiving music. Nevertheless, a minimum of will to stimulate the receiving individual to moral activity must be an absolute prerequisite.

Defining the border between what Hindemith characterizes as valueless music and light music with a certain moral value is not an easy task. Hindemith never ceases to deplore the fact that in the 20th century, people are bombarded with music from every direction and under the strangest circumstances. The majority of these kinds of musical attacks can hardly be said to be flowing with Augustinian spirit. Like many composers before and after him, Hindemith thought the contemporary music scene to be alarmingly indiscriminate and chaotic. Augustine's view must have gone through extensive liberalization. Hindemith believes he finds an early precursor of this negative process in Boethius's *De institutione musica*. The opening statement in this work, according to Hindemith's own translation, reads: "Music is a part of our human nature; it has the power either to improve or debase our character."[176] This statement implies that music is to be considered

---

[175] The description is based on Hindemith's own interpretations, *ibid.*, 4-5.

[176] *A Composer's World*, 8.

an active factor. Hindemith concludes that this notion of music seeks to reduce us to passive and defenseless receivers of music's force. "No wonder, then, that music abandons its role as a modest aid to moral growth and assumes gubernatorial rights," he says.[177] From this conclusion it is a short step to considering Boethius's ideas as a doubtful defense of any form of musical expression. "Extremes they really are!" exclaims Hindemith in his comparison of Augustine and Boethius: "The Augustinian precept in which our mind absorbs music and transforms it into moral strength; and the Boethian precept in which the power of music, its ethos, is brought into action upon our mind."[178] However, as in *Unterweisung im Tonsatz* I, Hindemith maintains that he favors Boethius's three-part *musica* concept, as he believes that such a division gives music its proper universal dimension. Music's only limitations lie in the possibilities of the musical material and in our intellectual capacity as producers and reproducers. Hindemith gives a correct definition of the *musica* concept's three levels. For *musica instrumentalis* he emphasizes the active aspect of performance: "music as executed by human voices or with the aid of instruments."[179] All the more striking in Hindemith's presentation is the fact that changes the numbering, and with it the order of the levels. Boethius places *musica mundana* on the highest and *musica instrumentalis* on the lowest levels, whereas Hindemith lists the levels as follows:

> 3. *Musica mundana*
> 2. *Musica instrumentalis*
> 1. *Musica humana*

As he does not explain this enigmatic order, Hindemith leaves his readers to wonder whether the implied hierarchy is incidental. However, the paragraph of *A Composer's World* in which this application appears is particularly systematic in both form and content. Although it is possible to question some of his statements and inferences, the chapter does not suggest that it might be based on coincidences. Moreover, Hindemith had been occupied with the Boethian concept for years, and everything in his treatise gives the impression that he was well aware of the original order of its presentation.[180] The three movements in the symphony *Die Harmonie der Welt*, for that matter, reflect the usual apprehension. Avoiding speculation over a plausible reason, Hindemith inevitably adds another dimension to the

---

[177] *Ibid.*
[178] *Ibid.*, 13.
[179] *Ibid.*, 8.
[180] See *Unterweisung im Tonsatz* I, 75.

musica concept. *Musica instrumentalis* does not become just the sounding expression of *musica* that is realized in man and the cosmos. The music created by active vocal and instrumental execution can also be considered the *link* between *musica humana* and *musica mundana*.

Hindemith cannot acknowledge Boethius's *musica* without expressing some reservations. He understands the concept as purely scientific, as a suitable declaration for the high evaluation of music's material aspect that he himself advocates. Yet music must also have a genuine spiritual dimension. Hindemith cannot find this facet in Boethius's writings, but certainly in Augustine's. The ultimate consequence of these venerable thinkers' views is that read in isolation they may both lead astray. Accordingly, the ideal solution must be reconciliation between them in what he describes as "their forceful unification in one single act of will power."[181]

Through his quite personal treatment of Boethius and Augustine, Hindemith reveals the essence of his musical thoughts:
1. Music must maintain its position midway between exact knowledge, i.e., *science*, and limitless faith, i.e., *religion*.
2. Music, represented by active performance, *musica instrumentalis*, is to be considered the central, sounding expression of an all-embracing cosmological whole.

Schematically, Hindemith's ideas can be expressed as follows:

Boethius
Musica mundana
Musica instrumentalis– qualified through **Augustine**
Musica humana

Hindemith's life-long work as a musician, composer, educator, author, and theoretician represents an effort to realize this qualified *musica instrumentalis* through different means. Hence, his high opinion of musical amateurs and the function of amateur performance also apply to the fact that he considers active performance of the highest importance even for musical recognition. In relating these ideas to the above-discussed *musica* model, it is obvious that, both in quality and quantity, active music performance must be of the greatest significance for Hindemith's *musica instrumentalis*. This gives his thoughts on music's function—the third level of the musical functionalism concept—dimensions that reach much further, aim far higher, and are far more profound than a composer's awareness of the musical market in a mechanized century.

---

[181]*A Composer's World*, 14.

"A Singing and Playing Community"

Hindemith believes the deterioration of music life is related to the large extent of passive audiences and the lack of respect given to the flank of active amateurs. His understanding of the musical material is based on what he considers as tonality principles given by nature. He considers music evolving without any tonal basis whatsoever as symptomatic of contemporary degeneration. A particularly alarming effect of this kind of tonal decay is that it excludes the active participation of amateurs.[182] The larger part of the music and musical reality Hindemith meets would thus seem to be affected by degeneration and moral decay; hence his conclusion that the musical objects, their producers, distributors, and consumers do not always reflect Augustine's thoughts. Hindemith is pessimistic of Western culture. From different perspectives he considers the historical development of music during recent centuries to be a story of decline. His attitude runs deep; it also colors his general view of society. The alleged cultural and moral decay seems to be closely associated with a negative social development characterized by the lust for power, pervasive commercialism, and the alienation of the individual. Hindemith feels himself called to turn this development in a positive direction through his versatile musical activity. His vocation endures throughout his life and beyond personal vicissitudes. To Hindemith, the key to a fundamental change lies in a comprehensive realization of his spiritually qualified *musica instrumentalis* in an active musical fellowship transcending the individual. From this vantage point, he lifts his gaze and looks into the illuminated realms of boundless idealism. Lay musicians have a place in Hindemith's "unlimited world of faith," even if they might prove to be a disappointment.

"Amateur music is in essence *Gemeinschaftsmusik*," says Hindemith.[183] In the fellowship of the amateur ensemble, performers participate as equal members, even where some of them lack instrumental or vocal skills. No matter how bad an amateur violinist may be, Hindemith states, there is always room for him in the back row of the strings.[184] But what about the typical solo instrument, the piano, for example? Soloistic piano performance is not really suited to the amateur, Hindemith says. Generally, keyboard instruments have an isolating, psychological effect; because of their solo status they shut the performer off from the blissful fellowship with other players. Amateur pianists must always be alone in achieving their aim—and

---

[182] This matter is given particular attention in his last speech/article "Sterbende Gewässer," 314-336.

[183] *Komponist in seiner Welt*, 259. ["Amateurmusik ist in ihrem Wesen Gemeinschaftsmusik."]

[184] *Ibid.*, 260.

once achieved they are no longer considered amateurs. In Hindemith's opinion the nature of amateur performance is thus more than *Selbstspielen* in a restricted sense. It is not the individual's endeavors to reach his or her personal goal that give the amateur concept its value and weight, but rather the collective effort of a musical community:

> On the contrary he [the amateur], is already from the beginning a member of a fraternity that serves the noblest of all imaginable objectives: mutual encouragement in building a work greater and more important than solitary actions.[185]

Despite Hindemith's own instrumental background, the art of singing, and especially ensemble singing, has a very special place in his musical cosmos. He was most probably stimulated in the vocal direction in 1926, when he encountered the *Jugendmusikbewegung* for just about the first time. A year previously, Hindemith had himself taken the initiative of choosing the ensemble song as the special topic of the *Donaueschinger Kammermusiktage*.[186] For Hindemith, the song is in many ways linked to the ultimate and fundamental recognition of music. His view can be summarized in the following points:

1. The singing voice is closely linked to the human faculty of hearing, and is not easily coerced or manipulated against its own will. The singing voice therefore has a nature given stability,[187] and, consequently, a fundamental constancy against what Hindemith would consider compositional and stylistic offshoots. This view is fundamental to his evaluating singing as the important directive for all music, also instrumental music.
2. An important path to general music recognition and experience thus goes through the singing voice. Concepts such as tonality and musical value/quality can be recognized and experienced through singing, either solo or ensemble.
3. The choir is polyphony's medium. The principles of polyphony stress the choir's essence as a unit of equally balanced voices.

Generally, polyphony is one of the important characteristics of what Hindemith regards as the new, contemporary style. And the roots are deep:

---

[185] *Komponist in seiner Welt*, 260. ["Im Gegenteil, er [der Amateur] ist schon zu Anfang Mitglied einer Brüderschaft, die dem denkbar edelsten alle Zwecke dient: sich gegenseitig zu ermuntern im Errichten eines Werkes, das größer und wichtiger ist als eigenbrödlerisches Tun."]

[186] See A. Briner, *Paul Hindemith*, 48.

[187] See *A Composer's World*, 197.

> In spite of our modern advanced technique of composing, the harmonic and tonal principles underlying this technique are those that were developed partly in the early stages of polyphonic music and partly by the theorists and practicians of the eighteenth century.[188]

Hindemith's high opinion of Gregorian chant has been mentioned above. By and large, he believes vocal music up to 1750 represents the most outstanding achievement of what music history has ever produced. "The isorhythmic motet (thirteenth and fourteenth centuries) reached such a degree of intellectual involution with its interplay of rhythmic and metric patterns, that no later period could boast of such artistry," he writes.[189] In a similar way, he characterizes choral works from 1400 to 1750. But valuable vocal productions are not limited to art music: Hindemith also finds in German *Liederbücher* of the 16th century an incredible concentration of harmonic and melodic material assimilated in the folk-song heritage of a whole nation. He regrets that the music of his time offers neither anything that can match these superior vocal creations nor works suitable for amateurs. In instrumental music, with all its fashionable whims, a certain climax may have been reached. But on behalf of singers Hindemith finds reason to ask:

> Do we have any vocal creations of significance? Have we found a singable but nevertheless original and aesthetically satisfactory choral technique of general validity? Do we know how to provide music with the characteristics of our time for the amateur?[190]

In Hindemith's opinion, the obvious answers to these questions all speak of a deplorable cultural decay. As the quality and breadth of ensemble singing is the best benchmark for an epoch's musical culture, the 16th and 17th centuries represent a kind of cultural zenith, a period when amateurs and professionals together developed the ensemble song both in quality and quantity. Hindemith seems to believe that these features reflect a vanished, ideal society of humility, humanity, caring, and mutual understanding.[191] His gloomy prophecy is that his own time will probably enter the history books as exhibiting the lowest cultural level ever.

Historically, choral singing replaced the singing in smaller ensembles, Hindemith claims. And while a choir can never fully supplant the cultivated, musical communication of the small vocal group, choral singing does have one advantage: The choir is more inclusive as there is room for more singers,

---

[188] *A Composer's World*, 112.

[189] *Ibid.*, 134.

[190] *Ibid.*, 135

[191] *Ibid.*, 199.

and if there is any form of music that can touch and express collective feelings in larger groups of people, it must be the choral song. Therefore, choral song does indeed have a future: "I am convinced that such singing, on a scale completely unknown thus far, will be one of the important forms of musical life in the future."[192] The reason for his faith in this kind of musical activity is the conviction that the choir and choral singing comprise an active musical and social *Gemeinschaft*, which then expresses collective wishes and sentiments. Hindemith suggests that from this activity, developed in both politically and economically turbulent times, a more humane society will evolve, a society characterized by collective virtues and high social morals.[193] His vision is one of a new community based on harmony and mutual understanding.

Consequently, Hindemith advocates both Tönnies's and the Weimar Republic's view of *Gemeinschaft* as an alternative model for the alienating *Gesellschaft*. This agreement ties his vision very tightly to the spirit of the 1920s, a connection that becomes even clearer with his increasing experience of music's decay later in his life. Hindemith's thoughts on renewal assign the key role to amateurs. His desire to revitalize the importance and social position of the ensemble and choral singing unites with his views on the needs and importance of amateurs. The so-called degenerate musical life as well as contemporary cultural life in general can be regenerated through amateurs as choir singers and instrumentalists. Hindemith means this quite literally: he wishes for "a singing and playing community."[194] Amateurs who perform will not only have consequences for national social conditions. Hindemith refers to the German proverb *Böse Menschen haben keine Lieder* as an illustration: "People who make music together cannot be enemies, at least not while the music lasts."[195] This comment on the nature of communal singing leads directly to Hindemith's bold suggestion of the potential global consequences for broad amateur performance: "It is not impossible that out of a tremendous movement of amateur community music a peace movement could spread over the world."[196] While these idealistic statements could be accused of being somewhat naive, it must be remembered that few composers and writers had so vast an experience of musical activity across

---

[192] *A Composer's World*, 200.

[193] *Ibid*.

[194] *Ibid*., 254.

[195] *Ibid*. The full text of the proverb is: *Wo man singt, da lass dich ruhig nieder / Böse Menschen haben keine Lieder*. [Where there is singing, you can safely make your home / Evil people do not have songs.]

[196] *A Composer's World*, 254.

many different cultural and national borders as did Hindemith. At the same time, he had personally experienced the devastating consequences of two world wars and the distressing rigors of emigration. Both factors undoubtedly contributed to the shaping of his ideas.

Most important in the context of musical functionalism is the way in which Hindemith focuses on the significance he feels participatory music-making has and must have, not only in relation to the market and the broad cultural experience. For the modern human being in a new age, the active use of music also contributes to deeper socio-cultural recognition.

Summary

Hindemith's concert enterprise, the *Gemeinschaft für Musik*, may be regarded as an initiative designed in continuation of ideas underpinning Schoenberg's *Verein für musikalische Privataufführungen*. The common starting point on which Schoenberg and Hindemith appear to agree is the wish to facilitate a musical experience based on active recognition rather than only on passive enjoyment. Hindemith's further ideas and efforts may be considered a follow-up of his concrete communication measures from the 1922 *Gemeinschaft*. As he prepares the way for the listener to take the decisive step of becoming an active performer, however, he neither follows on the steps of nor draws conclusions from Schoenberg's thoughts in this particular field. Hindemith rather pursues what he believes to be a navigable, practical path—one upon which Schoenberg would hardly have set out. Schoenberg considers facilitating conditions for personal musical activity nothing other than a misstep. Here, Schoenberg and Hindemith part ways, their different paths reflecting a characteristic feature of functionalism's progress: Schoenberg, 21 years Hindemith's senior, represents an earlier development, still with the ideals of Romanticism as a sounding board, while Hindemith, almost a generation younger, advocates the focus prevalent in the 1920s on concrete user relationships. Yet in all their discrepancies, both composers have the same earnest need to pave the ground for deeper musical recognition in a modern age.

Coda
Schoenberg and Hindemith in the Context of Functionalism

Functionalism has a prominent place in 20th-century aesthetics. The focus on material and form is a main key to the concept's far-reaching importance. A combination of material and form is the precondition for art in general and is thus not in itself unique to the period of time discussed in this book. Functionalism, however, represents a heightened awareness of these two aspects: an artistic concept of truthfulness allows material and form to manifest themselves according to what may be recognized as their idiosyncratic premises. A firm belief in the inevitable "will" of the material and the universal validity of pure, non-ornamental forms is crucial to this understanding. In this study, functionalism has been preferred to potentially competing concepts, because it compiles various characteristics of a conceptual complexity pertaining to important aspects of 20-century art. As a term, functionalism delimits the concept by directly referring to a set of essential features. *Function* becomes a key designation and the common denominator for a profound understanding that also encompasses ideas of the function of art in terms of the individual and society. Applying the concept presupposes that it is freed from the constrictions of a narrow view that only sees a functionalist object's utilitarian value.

Functionalist thinking is directed towards what material and form really *are*. Several important features underpin the functionalist recognition of form and material. These basic traits also shape attitudes to the process of artistic elaboration in a wider sense. Moreover, emphasis is placed on what the components of artistic creation actually are, after they have escaped from the twilight of Romanticism and been brought into the daylight of the 20th century. In the first part of that century, a search for authenticity becomes the driving force in a broad, aesthetic shift from the concept of beauty to the concept of truth. Although these notions originate from the same root, truthfulness becomes a new evaluation criterion and, accordingly, it is given decisive emphasis. The term "beautiful" is regarded as closely related to pleasant, pretty, and lovely, while "truthful" can also comprise what is unfamiliar, unpleasant, and ugly. A distinguishing feature of functionalism is its tendency to treat the true and the beautiful as comparable, in the sense that a truthful expression must also be aesthetically satisfying, or *good*. What at first sight seems to be beautiful but turns out to be untruthful is based on illusory loveliness and therefore cannot be considered beautiful in a deeper sense. This attitude is characteristically found in the rejection of superfluous decoration. The concept of truthfulness thus becomes fundamentally important, not only for understanding art but also for a wider understanding of contemporary culture.

The functionalist understanding of material and form presupposes knowledge and skill, which subsequently strengthens belief in the importance of craft and craftsmanship. Inspiration is often described as a clear but ephemeral flash of light, while craft is the reliable servant of painstaking artistic realization. Such descriptions reflect a conspicuous tendency to demystify artistic creation. Artists do their work and thus do not essentially differ from people in other professions. Like anyone else, they have a function in modern, technological society, hence there is no mystery to the work they perform. Consequently, the acquired craft becomes significant in the process of artistic production, particularly when it materializes in a satisfactory design. Such results increase the status of craft at the cost of the Romantic notion of the importance of inspiration. No longer is inspiration considered an artist's enduring enthusiasm. This is not to say that the concept of inspiration is entirely rejected. It is still as much welcome as before, but it is not considered sufficient as a foundation for creative activity. The term craftsmanship is once again looked upon favorably, being a true witness of the creative process in itself, liberated, as it were, from the gray monotony accorded it by time.

In functionalism, even the use of the concept of creation is toned down. While creating is still conceived as the inherent privilege of genius, the tacit understanding is that genuine artistic activity might not really be within the human domain. Creation belongs to the divine, whereas construction is a far more suitable concept for the mortal variants. What artists do is construct their work in a functional way from the skill and control of their craft—on lucky occasions stimulated by a sharp flash of inspiration. Yet artists are not robbed of their creative abilities. Instead, construction is given increased validity and elevated as essential for the realization of a work of art. Thus the act of construction is also truthful, in the sense that it can be controlled, tested, and analyzed.

The crucial role in this process is played by the rational elements of art. To demonstrate these aspects is imperative as they may both characterize and justify art in the modern age. This is not to deny the over-rational or irrational sides of art; it rather places them within the realm of personal subjectivity and artistic privacy. But over-rational elements are not deemed as important as they were in earlier times. New materials, design concepts, and means of production demand rational innovation. Material must be worked in a purportedly functional way. Rationality is seen to involve a universality potential based on such fundamental concepts as logic and calculation—principles concerned with objective truth.

In the popular understanding of art, emotion or feeling is usually considered a foremost prerequisite. Conversely in the concept of functionalism, feeling is regarded as subjective and irrational, something that eludes the objective grasp of rationality. Consequently, art and the artist do not express feelings but rather thoughts and ideas. Hence, on the premises that can be read in a work's functional construction it is possible to test artistic authenticity and truthfulness. A work does not necessarily contain any hidden subjective feelings; rational thought is just as valid and important. Such views imply a distinct focus on the role of mental recognition in the experience of art.

A principal wish embedded in functionalism is to lead art back to tangible reality and to give it its rightful place in the modern age. This is why architecture and design play such a significant role; application challenges and production premises of a new era move front and center. Questions of the function of art and the growing rejection of the principles of *l'art pour l'art* are important elements. This tendency breaks with the traditional concept of aesthetics, or, rather, with the way in which this concept is understood at the dawn of a new century: "aesthetics" is recognized as being connected to the presumably beautiful expression inherent in art even independently from human reality; at the same time, it may point to the empty, artificial veneer that is eroded constantly by time itself. A focus on function as the embodiment of a new aesthetic understanding develops, implying not just simple utility but also the degree of functionality inherent in the object in terms of material, construction, and form. The three levels of the functionalist concept on which this study is based are:

1. Functional treatment of the chosen material
2. Functional design
3. Focus on the work's intended function

These three levels each embody different aspects of the concept and the terms function and functionality.

However, Romanticism and functionalism are not necessarily opposites on every level. As a category, Romanticism is far more comprehensive than functionalism. Nevertheless, there are certain tendencies in the development of the concept of functionalism that may appear as contrasts to the understanding of art prevalent in Romanticism. These tendencies can be illustrated by means of the following dichotomies:

Romanticism	Functionalism
Beauty	Truth
Inspiration	Craft
Creation	Construction
Irrationality	Rationality
Emotion	Thought
Aesthetics	Function

The juxtaposition above does not imply that functionalism represents a complete break with Romanticism. It rather suggests that fundamental features of Romanticism are toned down, often becoming virtually invisible, while other artistic qualities are given greater emphasis. While extreme interpretations may be found within each pair of categories, these opposites are thus not absolutes. Social-democratic housing may represent a rather grayish example of functionalist architecture. The true reasons for such landmarks do not necessarily lie in the aesthetic concept dominating the era in which they were built, but rather in ideologization, politicization, and economization, i.e., in reasons that are far removed from art. The terrain is thus far more complex than first meets the eye. The most characteristic features of functionalism are its international, universal, and border-transcending elements.

With the growth of functionalism, importance is increasingly attached to aspects that can be discussed and explained in a rational and logical way, while others are disregarded. Wittgenstein's words, "and what we cannot talk about we must pass over in silence," reflect this view. It is true that, in this understanding, the irrational dimensions of art seem to raise suspicion. Yet their existence is not denied. Romanticism, as a phase belonging to the past, thus also serves as a sounding board for functionalist understanding: The search for truthfulness involves a thorough analysis of the concept of beauty, inspiration is the background for praising craft, and construction shows itself to be a form of creation with aesthetic dimensions.

When so much emphasis is placed on truthfulness and rationality, the idea of a functionalist *absolute* may not be very far. Objectivity is a chief characteristic of the functionalist concept; the authoritative educator attitude that marks so many of its pioneers expresses a firm belief in the objectively true and universal. Yet the question is whether this supposed objectivity does not rather represent an illusion belonging to the sphere of irrationality. The search for a given material's idiosyncratic will presupposes the belief that, on one level or another, such a will must exist as an objective entity.

Different solutions are usually proposed. No material is an absolute; the dialectics with the artist's will is bound to reveal new layers of "will." It is, therefore, rather in the *attitude* to the idea of the material's own will that there must be no ambiguity. The assumed will must be uncovered and the artist must be true to it. However, there are different views on what actually constitutes the material's will, and the concrete solutions that follow from them vary accordingly. Hence, functionalism's unequivocality rather lies in the attitude to a set of basic principles. On the basis of this understanding of the interaction between objectivity and individuality it is possible to study two such different composers as Arnold Schoenberg and Paul Hindemith, with the concept of functionalism as the common denominator.

For Schoenberg, progressive views on art and the cultural critique in *fin-de-siècle* Vienna became the point of departure for his lifelong search for artistic truthfulness. Most notably, this search led to his definitive break with traditional tonality in the early 1900s. For Hindemith, a couple of decades his junior, much of the ground had already been gained. Even though Hindemith also began by carrying on from his 19th-century predecessors, his search for musical truthfulness soon began making itself felt in new principles of musical construction and in his growing need for artistic objectivity.

The need to reveal the will of the musical material is the essence of Schoenberg's and Hindemith's ideas at a time when the distinctive features of traditional tonality are considered historical. The point of departure for Schoenberg's understanding of the musical material is the recognition of the Western musical traditions. In his opinion, the material's will is revealed in a characteristic musical motive recognizable in one form or another throughout an entire piece. This motive represents the material's fundamental consistency, which is combined with its own construction potential. Introducing his twelve-tone method Schoenberg adds a number-based rationality to the musical material that is typical for the functionalism of the 1920s. The basic twelve-tone set of a composition represents a pre-forming of the musical material, a new consistency or alloy that contributes both to molding the motive and laying new premises for its construction potential. Schoenberg joins the characteristic search of his time for new materials.

Hindemith could also be called a master at work on musical motives, but, for him, the motive does not represent the basic musical material. He finds the starting point for his material's regularity in natural physics, in the interaction between the partial-tone range and the human psychophysical aural disposition. Hence, his main idea is that the "will" of the musical material is given by nature itself, with the interval as its distinctive feature. In accordance with the need for rationalization exhibited by interwar functionalism, Hindemith bases his work on numeration and sophisticated calculations, finding what he considers to be a universal ranking of intervals according to their relationships and properties. In addition to the principal, rationality-based similarities behind the Schoenbergian and Hindemithian approaches, the two composers agree on the importance of the partial-tone range for functional harmony. Schoenberg does not see any universal perspectives here: the connection to traditional harmony is accidental, and it remains to be seen what scale formations and instrument types are yet to come. Schoenberg does not reject the concept of tonality; rather he is open to a wide range of possibilities. Hindemith, too, regards tonality as one house with many rooms, with space for different systems. The important point for Hindemith is the existence of certain supposedly unalterable regularities of which any composer must be aware. Schoenberg could agree with this. Consequently, there are more similarities in Schoenberg's and Hindemith's understanding of the musical material than are usually assumed, and the functionalist approach provides a key to recognizing this fact.

The functionalist understanding of material has three facets: that any material be accepted as it *is,* that the artist seeks to discover this particular material's will, and that he or she knows how to use it. There is really no conceptual difference between various materials seen *as materials*. Material diversity is respected; differences exist primarily in connection with a relevant material's inherent potential. From a functionalist view, it would be absurd to differentiate between Schoenberg's and Hindemith's understanding of material: Both find their own musical material, are fully conversant with its regularities, and know how to create from it. However, it would be just as absurd to regard their material as identical. To simplify the difference in their approaches, Schoenberg's musical material can be regarded as a modern alloy of cultivated material, while Hindemith's is a basic natural material used in accordance with the idioms of different times and styles. In both cases there is a question of being true to the material's assumed will. Schoenberg and Hindemith work with different types of material, as do other composers. This allows for far broader perspectives: Music based on "extended tonality," the twelve-tone method, or other systems, will always presuppose different materials, each with it unique type of will. Hence, the question is not whether composers are employing this or that material, but in which way they use it. The functionalist understanding of material always rests on an ideally genuine and authentic understanding of an actual material's uniqueness. Composers must thus also know how to differentiate between what really belongs to the material's characteristics and what must be considered suppositions of the past. Furthermore, they should always make use of the relevant traditions of their craft. Perhaps the all-embracing consequence of a functionalist approach to the musical material is that it erases the boundary between tonal and atonal, the supposedly basic premises that have left their mark on a major part of 20th-century music history and debate.

With regard to form, the history of architecture shows the development from, for example, Adolf Loos's anti-ornamental design to Le Corbusier's ideas about the basic form as an objective in itself. Le Corbusier was greatly influenced by purism and Neo-Platonism; he recognized basic forms as expressions of functional norm. The basic form becomes the functionalist ideal, in part because it is considered to invite an identification layer of universal status. Schoenberg's and Hindemith's use of basic musical forms in the 1920s must be assessed with this conviction in mind. The point is to create formal, recognizable identification from new materials. Musical design is to be based not only on traditional forms from the past, although these remain fundamental in the repertoire of both composers and listeners, but also on popular contemporary forms. These forms must have such a strong position in the listeners' consciousness that they are capable of creating identity and accommodating treatment in contemporary types of musical material. The functionalist perspective is vital to an understanding of this tendency. And here, too, Schoenberg and Hindemith are more similar than conventional music history would have it. Consequently, the general significance of such problematic terms as *Neue Sachlichkeit*, Neo-Baroque and Neo-Classicism with respect to form are also toned down. The concept of functionalism in music undermines the idea that the application of fundamental musical forms necessarily leads to a regressive return to the past.

Another important aspect of functionalism is *universality*: while music that could be called functional is particularly associated with the 1920s, its aesthetics is part of a far more comprehensive project. The guiding idea is that the gap between music and the people can be minimized through musical activity. Initially, this activity is not confined to practical performance or to concrete purposes of use; it also embraces active recognition as opposed to passive indulgence. Thus the concept of musical functionalism reveals the fact that Schoenberg's and Hindemith's divergent paths have a common point of departure. To a greater degree than Schoenberg, Hindemith is a product of the 1920s. As he is just embarking on his career at that time, he becomes the representative *par excellence* of functional music. He strongly believes that the new age needs music written for specific purposes. The concept employed to capture this idea, "utility music" (*Gebrauchsmusik*), is well known in the history of Western music. The distinctive feature of the functionalist focus is not, however, the emphasis on utility music as a product in itself, but rather the notion that music must be used, in the sense that the user relates actively to it. Listening is a passive condition, linked to outmoded preferences, to the non-musical mechanisms of the concert business, and to the all-embracing commercialism of the time. The real function of music is to activate a process of recognition. Schoenberg believes that comprehensibility, logic, and coherence are of fundamental importance. Their relevance presupposes conscious human recognition and an active, recognizing subject. His understanding of material and form is based on his belief in mental activity as a presupposition for musical recognition. He also looks for concrete ways of activating the listener or of preparing the ground for active recognition. Examples of implementation include the public rehearsals of his *First Chamber Symphony* in 1918 and the founding of the *Verein für musikalische Privataufführungen*. Hindemith follows Schoenberg's example when he founds his *Gemeinschaft für Musik*, where active recognition and mental engagement are recognized as playing a decisive role for genuine music appreciation. Compared with Schoenberg, he places greater emphasis on relating to the tonality-oriented musical experience than to strict logic. For Hindemith, musical activity is primarily connected to musical performance. In this context, he takes a direction that differs from Schoenberg's. His goal is that listeners become active as performers in a wider musical community. Hindemith believes that active amateur performers will eventually turn into active listeners.

Functionalism focuses more on unity than on the border lines between autonomous and functional forms of expression. For both Schoenberg and Hindemith, the craft aspect of composition is of the greatest importance, although it is Hindemith who appears to be more familiar with the term *craft*. This may, of course, be due to his being more concerned with the craftsmanship of music than Schoenberg. Yet the application of that particular word also needs to be understood in relation to the terminology prevalent at the time when Hindemith started his career. Nonetheless, both composers regard inspiration as a precious but fleeting gift while at the same time emphasizing the toil and grind that is necessary for it to materialize in a musical work. This happens largely through thoughtful construction. While Hindemith occasionally uses the term construction, he often relies on other demystifying expressions, such as the German *Tonsatz*. For Schoenberg, who uses the term more consistently, organic-functional construction represents a 20th-century development of the Romantic understanding of organic growth.

In an extension of compositional rationality, feeling and emotion are terms seldom used by Schoenberg and Hindemith. While neither of them denies the relevance of emotion to art, they judge feeling as something difficult to capture in words, maintaining that a genuine understanding of music cannot be based on individual and subjective experiences. However, Schoenberg consistently employs the term *thought*, or *Gedanke*, both when he speaks of what a composer is artistically trying to achieve and when he considers the real purpose of music.

Hindemith as a spokesman for functional music maintains that it strives toward the same qualitative goal as concert music. His ideal is the well-made composition, whose aesthetic dimensions lie in the construction or fabrication of an individual work—another conviction characteristic of functionalist thought. Schoenberg's wish to "replace bad aesthetics with a good course in handicraft" does not mean that he rejects the aesthetic; rather, he wishes to replace the allegedly poor version of the concept reflecting the faded ideas of the immediate past. Considering his completed and planned textbooks as parts of a greater project in musical aesthetics, he hopes to tie aesthetic dimensions to the principles applied to musical construction. Consequently, for Schoenberg as for Hindemith, good aesthetics is closely linked to craft and to music's immanent, functional aspects.

The concept of musical functionalism is thus relevant for the study of both Schoenberg and Hindemith, for 20th century music in particular and even for music history in general. As pioneers in the understanding of material and form and in the question of the function of art, Schoenberg and Hindemith establish perspectives and approaches that are inconceivable without their common functionalist base. While the primary aim of this book has been focus on their thoughts and ideas, just as vital is its secondary goal: to stimulate the appreciation of Schoenberg's and Hindemith's diverse works on the basis of their intrinsic uniqueness. This implies dimensions impossible to capture in words. At this point, the readers' and listeners' own activity needs to be front and center, to keep to the terminology of musical functionalism. Farther than this an author can never reach.

Bibliography

Adams, Steven. *The Arts & Crafts Movement*. London: Tiger Books International, 1992.
Adorno, Theodor W. "Ad vocem Hindemith: Eine Dokumentation." In: *Impromptus* [*Musikalische Schriften* IV. *Gesammelte Schriften* 17]. Frankfurt a. M.: Suhrkamp, 1982, 210-246.
——. *Alban Berg: Master of the smallest link*. J. Brand and C. Hailey, trans. Cambridge MA: Cambridge University Press, 1994.
——. "Arnold Schönberg (1874-1951)." In: *Prismen* [*Kulturkritik und Gesellschaft* I. *Gesammelte Schriften* 10/1]. Frankfurt a. M.: Suhrkamp, 1977, 152-180.
——. "Der dialektische Komponist." In: *Arnold Schönberg zum 60. Geburtstag 13. September 1934*. Vienna: Universal Edition, 1934, 18-23.
——. "Funktionalismus heute." In: *Ohne Leitbild* [*Kulturkritik und Gesellschaft* I. *Gesammelte Schriften* 10/1] Frankfurt a. M.: Suhrkamp, 1977, 375-395.
——. "Gebrauchsmusik." In: *Musikalische Schriften* VI [*Gesammelte Schriften 19*]. Frankfurt a. M.: Suhrkamp, 1984, 445-447.
——. *Philosophie der neuen Musik* [*Gesammelte Schriften* 12], Frankfurt a. M.: Suhrkamp, 1975.
——. *Philosophy of Modern Music*. A.G. Mitchell and W.V. Blomster, trans. New York: Continuum, 2003.
——. "Schönbergs Bläserquintett. In: *Moments musicaux* [*Musikalische Schriften* IV. *Gesammelte Schriften* 17]. Frankfurt a. M.: Suhrkamp, 1982, 140-144.
Amar, Licco. "Zur Frage der Gebrauchsmusik." In: *Die Musik* XXI/6 (1929): 401-403.
Apostel, Hans Erich. Greetings in *Arnold Schönberg zum 60. Geburtstag 13. September 1934*. Vienna: Universal Edition, 1934, 36.
Arndt, Alfred. "Ansprache zur Bauhaus-Einweihung in Dessau 1926." In: E. Neumann, ed., *Bauhaus und Bauhäusler: Erinnerungen und Bekenntnisse*. Köln: DuMont, 1985, 8.
Babbitt, Irving. *The New Laokoon. An Essay on the Confusion of the Arts*. Boston: Houghton Mifflin, 1910.

Bach, Carl Philipp Emanuel. *Versuch über die wahre Art das Klavier zu spielen.* Wiesbaden: Breitkopf & Härtel, 1986.
Barr, Alfred H. Jr. "Otto Dix."In: *The Arts* 17/4 (1931): 235-251.
Beiche, Michael. "Grundgestalt." In: H.H. Eggebrecht, ed., *Terminologie der Musik im 20. Jahrhundert [HMT-Sonderband I].* Stuttgart: Franz Steiner, 1995, 175-191.
──── . "Zwölftonmusik." In: H.H. Eggebrecht, ed., *Terminologie der Musik im 20. Jahrhundert [HMT-Sonderband I].* Stuttgart: Franz Steiner, 1995, 439-451.
Bekker, Paul. "Schönberg: 'Erwartung'." In: *Arnold Schönberg zum fünfzigsten Geburtstage 13. September 1924. [Sonderheft der Musikblätter des Anbruch* (1924)], 275-282.
Berry, Wallace. *Structural Functions in Music.* New York: Dover, 1987.
Besseler, Heinrich. "Grundfragen des musikalischen Hörens." In: *Jahrbuch der Musikbibliothek Peters* 32/1925 (1926): 35-52.
Blake, Peter. *Frank Lloyd Wright: Architecture and Space.* Harmondsworth UK: Penguin Books, 1963.
Botstein, Leon. "Music and the Critique of Culture: Arnold Schoenberg, Heinrich Schenker, and the Emergence of Modernism in Fin de Siècle Vienna." In: J. Brand and C. Hailey, eds., *Constructive Dissonance: Arnold Schoenberg and the Transformations of Twentieth-century Culture.* Berkely etc.: University of California Press, 1997, 3-22.
Boulez, Pierre. "Schönberg est mort." In: P. Thévenin, ed., *Relevés d'apprenti.* Paris: Éditions du Seuil, 1966, 265-272.
Briner, Andres, Dieter Rexroth, and Giselher Schubert. *Paul Hindemith: Leben und Werk in Bild und Text.* Zurich/Mainz: Atlantis/Schott, 1988.
Briner, Andres. *Paul Hindemith,* Zurich/Mainz: Atlantis/Schott, 1971.
Broch, Hermann. "Irrationale Erkenntnis in der Musik." In: *Arnold Schönberg zum 60. Geburtstag 13. September 1934.* Vienna: Universal Edition, 1934, 49-60.
Burger, Fritz. *Einführung in die moderne Kunst [Handbuch der Kunstwissenschaft. Die Kunst des 19. und 20. Jahrhunderts I].* Berlin-Neubabelsberg: Athenaion, 1917.
Busoni, Ferruccio. *Sketch of a New Esthetic of Music [Entwurf einer neuen Aesthetik der Tonkunst]* In: T. Baker, trans., *Three Classics in the Aesthetic of Music.* New York: Dover, 1962, 73-102.
Carlsen, Jan. "Skyskraperens tyranni." In: *Byggekunst* 3 (1990): 162-165.
Cahn, Peter. "Hindemiths Lehrjahre in Frankfurt." In: S. Schaal and L. Schader, eds., *Über Hindemith. Aufsätze zu Werk, Ästhetik und Interpretation.* Mainz etc.: Schott, 1996, 15-39.

Cook, Susan Carol. *Opera for a New Republic: The Zeitopern of Krenek, Weill, and Hindemith*. Ann Arbor etc.: UMI Research Press, 1988.

Dahlhaus, Carl. *Die Idee der absoluten Musik*. Kassel etc.: Bärenreiter, 1987.

——. *Foundations of Music History*. J.B. Robinson, trans. Cambridge NY: Cambridge University Press, 1983).

——. "Hindemiths Theorie des Sekundgangs und das Problem der Melodielehre." In: S. Schaal and L. Schader, eds., *Über Hindemith. Aufsätze zu Werk, Ästhetik und Interpretation*, Mainz etc.: Schott, 1996, 191-202.

——. "Musikalischer Funktionalismus." In: *Schönberg und andere: Gesammelte Aufsätze zur Neuen Musik*. Mainz etc.: Schott, 1978, 57-71.

Dahms, Walter. "Berlin 1912. Offener Brief an den Komponisten Arnold Schönberg." In: *Arnold Schönberg zum fünfzigsten Geburtstage 13. September 1924*. [*Sonderheft der Musikblätter des Anbruch* (1924)], 323-324.

Danuser, Hermann. *Die Musik des 20. Jahrhunderts* [C. Dahlhaus and H. Danuser, eds., *Neues Handbuch der Musikwissenschaft* 7]. Laaber: Laaber, 1996.

——. *Musikalische Interpretation* [H. Danuser, ed., *Neues Handbuch der Musikwissenschaft* 11] Laaber: Laaber, 1996.

——. "Musikalische Prosa." In: H.H. Eggebrecht, ed., *Terminologie der Musik im 20. Jahrhundert* [*HMT-Sonderband* I]. Stuttgart: Franz Steiner, 1995, 250-269.

Delaere, Mark. *Funktionelle Atonalität: analytische Strategien für die freiatonalen Musik der Wiener Schule*. Wilhelmshaven: Florian Noetzel, 1993.

Dorfman, Joseph. "Counterpoint-Sonata Form." In: *Hindemith-Jahrbuch* 1990/XIX (1993): 55-67.

Droste, Magdalena. *Bauhaus 1919-1933*, L. G. Berthelsen, trans. Cologne: Benedikt Taschen, 1991.

Eckermann, Johann Peter. *Gespräche mit Goethe in den letzten Jahren seines Lebens*. Berlin: Aufbau, 1982.

Eimert, Herbert. *Atonale Musiklehre*. Leipzig: Breitkopf und Härtel, 1924.

Eisler, Hanns. "Arnold Schönberg, der musikalische Reaktionär." In: *Arnold Schönberg zum fünfzigsten Geburtstage 13. September 1924* [*Sonderheft der Musikblätter des Anbruch* (1924)], 312-313.

——. "Geschichte der deutschen Arbeitermusikbewegung von 1848." In: G. Mayer, ed., *Musik und Politik 1924-1948* [*Schriften* I]. Munich: Rogner & Bernhard, 1973.

Fath, Manfred. *Neue Sachlichkeit* [*Mannheimer Museumshefte* I], Speyer: Hermann G. Klein, 1994.

Fellerer, Karl Gustav. "Alte Musik im Musikleben der Gegenwart." In: W. Wiora, ed., *Musikerkenntnis und Musikerziehung: Dankesgaben für Hans Mersmann zu seinem 65. Geburtstag.* Kassel etc.: Bärenreiter, 1957, 44-50.

Findal, Wenche. *Norsk modernistisk arkitektur: om funksjonalismen.* Oslo: Cappelen, 1996.

Fortner, Wolfgang. "Die Wandlung des musikalischen Materials." In: *Melos* 18/6-7 (1951): 164-167.

Frampton, Kenneth. *Modern Architecture: A critical history.* London etc.: Thames & Hudson, 1992.

Freitag, Eberhard. *Arnold Schönberg, mit Selbstzeugnissen und Bilddokumenten.* Reinbeck bei Hamburg: Rowohlt, 1973.

Fuglesang, Signe Horn. "Regionalitet i historisk perspektiv." In: W. Findal, ed., *Nordisk funksjonalisme: Det internasjonale og det nasjonale.* Oslo: Gyldendal, 1995, 18-22.

Funk-Hennig, Erika. "Der Einfluß Jödes und seiner Anhänger auf die Instrumentalpflege der Jugendmusikbewegung." In: *Musik und Bildung* XI (1987): 856-858.

Gassen, Richard W. "Wege der Abstraktion. Auf der Suche nach einer neuen Wirklichkeit." In: R. W. Gassen and B. Holeczek, eds., *Die Neue Wirklichkeit. Abstraktion als Weltentwurf.* Ludwigshafen: Wilhelm-Hack-Museum, 1994, 17-40.

Gill, Anton. *A Dance Between Flames: Berlin Between the Wars.* London: John Murray, 1993.

Goebels, Franzpeter. "Interpretationsaspekte zum 'Ludus Tonalis'." *Hindemith-Jahrbuch* 1972/II (1972): 137-165.

Goethe, Johann Wolfgang. *Maximen und Reflexionen.* Leipzig: Insel, 1988.

Greissle, Felix. "Die formalen Grundlagen des Bläserquintetts von Arnold Schönberg." *Musikblätter des Anbruch* 7/ Teil 2 (1925): 63-68.

Gropius, Walter. *Die neue Architektur und das Bauhaus. Grundzüge und Entwicklung einer Konzeption [Neue Bauhausbücher].* Mainz: Florian Kupferberg, 1965.

Grote, Ludwig. "Das Bauhaus und der Funktionalismus." In: E. Neumann, ed., *Bauhaus und Bauhäusler: Erinnerungen und Bekenntnisse.* Köln: DuMont, 1985, 280-283.

Haas, Robert. *Die Musik des Barocks* [E. Bücken, ed., *Handbuch der Musikwissenschaft* 1], Potsdam: Athenaion, 1934.

Haase, Rudolf: *Paul Hindemiths harmonikale Quellen: sein Briefwechsel mit Hans Kayser.* Vienna: Lafite, 1973.

Hailey, Christopher. "Musical Expressionism: the search for autonomy." In: S. Behr, D. Fanning, and D. Jarman, eds., *Expressionism Reassessed.* Manchester: Manchester University Press, 1993,103-111.

Hammel, Heide. *Die Schulmusik in der Weimarer Republik: Politische und gesellschaftliche Aspekte der Reformdiskussion in den 20er Jahren,* Stuttgart: Metzler, 1990.

Hansen, Mathias. *Arnold Schönberg: Ein Konzept der Moderne.* Kassel: Bärenreiter, 1993.

Hanslick, Eduard. *The Beautiful in Music.* G. Cohen, trans. Indianapolis etc.: Bobbs-Merrill, 1957.

———. *Vom Musikalisch-Schönen: Ein Beirtag zur Revision der Ästhetik der Tonkunst.* Leipzig: R. Weigel, 1854.

Hauer, Josef Matthias. *Vom Wesen des Musikalischen: ein Lehrbuch der atonalen Musik.* Berlin: Schlesinger, 1920.

Hindemith, Paul. *1922. Suite für Klavier* op. 26. In: *Klaviermusik* I. V, 9 [*Sämtliche* Werke]. Mainz: Schott, 1990.

———. *A Composer's World: Horizons and Limitations.* Cambridge MA: Harvard University Press, 1952.

———. *Aufsätze,Vorträge, Reden.* G. Schubert, ed. Zurich etc.: Atlantis, 1994.

———. *Briefe.* D. Rexroth, ed. Frankfurt a. M.: Fischer, 1982.

———. *Das Marienleben* op. 27 (Neue Fassung), Mainz: Schott, 1948.1945.

———. *"Das private Logbuch": Briefe an seine Frau Gertrud.* F. Becker and G. Schubert, eds. Munich/Mainz: Piper/Schott, 1995.

———. *Elementary Training for Musicians*(Second Edition, Revised 1949). Mainz etc.: Schott, 1974.

———. *Frau Musica: Musik zum Singen und Spielen auf Instrumenten nach einem Text von Luther* op. 45/I. Mainz: Schott, 1928.

———. *Komponist in seiner Welt: Weiten und Grenzen.* Zurich: Atlantis, 1959.

———. *Ludus tonalis.* In: *Klaviermusik* II [*Sämtliche Werke* V,10]. Mainz: Schott, 1981.

———. *The Craft of Musical Composition* I: *Theoretical Part.* A. Mendel, trans. London: Schott,

———. *Unterweisung im Tonsatz* I: *Theoretischer Teil* (Neue, erweiterte Auflage). Mainz: Schott 1940.

———. *Unterweisung im Tonsatz* II: *Übungsbuch für den zweistimmigen Satz* (Neue, erweiterte Ausgabe). Mainz: Schott, 1939.

———. *Unterweisung im Tonsatz* III: *Übungsbuch für den dreistimmigen Satz.* Mainz: Schott, 1970.

Hinton, Stephen. "Neue Sachlichkeit." In: H.H. Eggebrecht, ed., *Terminologie der Musik im 20. Jahrhundert* [*HMT-Sonderband* I]. Stuttgart: Franz Steiner, 1995, 312-323.

Hinton, Stephen. *The Idea of Gebrauchsmusik: A Study of Musical Aesthetics in the Weimar Republic (1919-1933) with Particular Reference to the Works of Paul Hindemith.* New York etc.: Garland, 1989.

Hoffmann, E.T.A. *Fantastiske fortellinger.* T. Winje, trans. Oslo: Cappelen, 1972.

Jalowetz, Heinrich. "Schönbergs Werk in der Zeit." In: *Arnold Schönberg zum 60. Geburtstag 13. September 1934.* Vienna: Universal Edition, 1934, 4-9.

Janik, Allan andToulmin, Stephen. *Wittgenstein's Vienna.* New York etc.: Simon & Schuster, 1973.

John, Eckard. *Musik-Bolschewismus. Die Politisierung der Musik in Deutschland 1918-1938.* Stuttgart etc.: Metzler, 1994.

Johns, Donald. "Aimez-vous Brahms?: Ein Hindemith-Schenker-Briefwechsel." In: S. Schaal and L. Schader, eds., *Über Hindemith. Aufsätze zu Werk, Ästhetik und Interpretation*, Mainz etc.: Schott, 1996, 283-293.

Jones, Owen. *The Grammar of Ornament.* London: Bernhard Quatrich, 1868.

Kandinsky, Wassily and Schönberg, Arnold. *Wassily Kandinsky und Arnold Schönberg: Der Briefwechsel.* J. Hahl-Koch, ed. Stuttgart: Hatje, 1993.

Kemp, Ian. *Hindemith,* London: Oxford University Press, 1970.

Koebner, F.W., ed. *Jazz und Shimmy: Brevier der neuesten Tänze.* Berlin: Dr. Eysler & Co., 1921.

Kolland, Dorothea. *Die Jugendmusikbewegung. "Gemeinschaftsmusik": Theorie und Praxis.* Stuttgart: Metzler, 1979.

Kraus, Karl. *The Last Days of Mankind; a tragedy in five acts.* F. Ungar, ed./trans. New York: F. Ungar Pub. Co., 1974.

Kühn, Hellmut. "Vorstellungen über Radiomusik in der zwanziger Jahren." In: D. Rexroth, ed. *Erprobungen und Erfahrungen: Zu Paul Hindemiths Schaffen in den Zwanziger Jahren.* Mainz: Schott, 1978, 47-55.

Kurth, Ernst. *Musikpsychologie.* Bern: Krompholz, 1947.

Laretei, Käbi. "Om och ikring Ludus Tonalis." In: *Musikrevy* 26/1 (1971): 27-30.

Le Corbusier (Charles-Édouard Jeanneret-Gris). *L'Art décoratif d'aujourd'hui.* Paris: Crès, 1925.

——. *The Decorative Art of Today.* J.I. Dunnett, trans. and intr. London: The Architectural Press, 1987.

——. *Towards a New Architecture.* F. Etchells, trans. London/New York: The Architectural Press/Frederick A. Praeger, 1963.

——. *Vers une Architecture.* Paris: Editions Vincent Freal & Co., 1958.

Lessing, Gotthold Ephraim. *Laocoön: An Essay on the Limits of Painting and Poetry.* E.A. McCormick, ed. Baltimore etc.: The Johns Hopkins Press, 1984.

Lester, Joel. *Analytic Approaches to Twentieth-Century Music.* New York etc.: W.W. Norton & Company, 1989.
Loos, Adolf. "Architektur." In: *Trotzdem [Sämtliche Schriften I].* Vienna etc.: Herold, 1962, 302-318.
——. "Karl Kraus." In: *Trotzdem [Sämtliche Schriften* I]. Vienna etc.: Herold,1962, 328.
——. "Kulturentartung." In: *Trotzdem [Sämtliche Schriften* I]. Vienna etc.: Herold, 1962, 271-275.
——. "Ornament and Crime." In: *Ornament and Crime: Selected Essays.* A. Opel, intro., M. Mitchell, trans. Riverside, CA: Ariadne Press, 1998, 167-176.
——. "Ornament und verbrechen." In: *Trotzdem [Sämtliche Schriften* I]. Vienna etc.: Herold, 1962, 276-288.
——. "Zwei aufsätze und eine zuschrift über das haus auf dem Michaelerplatz." In: *Trotzdem [Sämtliche Schriften* I]. Vienna etc.: Herold, 1962, 293-301.
Lück, Hartmut. Cd booklet in *Paul Hindemith Orchestral Works* III: cpo 999 248-2.
Massow, Albrecht von. "Funktionale Musik." In: H.H. Eggebrecht, ed., *Terminologie der Musik im 20. Jahrhundert [HMT-Sonderband* I]. Stuttgart: Franz Steiner, 1995, 157-163.
Mersmann, Hans. *Die Tonsprache der neuen Musik.* Mainz: Schott, 1930.
Mies van der Rohe, Ludwig. "Inaugural address as Director of Architecture at Armour Institute of Technology." In: Johnson, Philip C. *Mies van der Rohe.* New York: The Museum of Modern Art, 1947, 191-195.
——. "The industrialization of building methods." In: Johnson, Philip C. *Mies van der Rohe.* New York: The Museum of Modern Art, 1947, 184-185.
Mitchell, William J. *The Logic of Architecture: Design, Computation, and Cognition.* Cambridge, MA: MIT Press, 1990.
Moos, Stanislaus von. "Le Corbusier and Loos." In: M. Risselda, ed. *Raumplan versus Plan Libre: Adolf Loos and Le Corbusier, 1919-1930.* New York: Rizzoli, 1988, 17-26.
Moritz, Karl Philipp. "Versuch einer Vereinigung aller schönen Künste und Wissenschaften unter dem Begriff des in sich selbst Vollendeten." In: *Berlinische Monatsschrift* V (1785): 225-236.
Moser, Hans Joachim. *Musikgeschichte in hundert Lebensbildern.* Stuttgart etc.: Reclam, 1958.
Neumeyer, David and Schubert, Giselher. "Arnold Schoenberg and Paul Hindemith." In: *Journal of the Arnold Schoenberg Institute,* XIII/1 (1990): 3-46.

Neumeyer, David. "The Genesis and Structure of Hindemith's Ludus Tonalis." In: *Hindemith-Jahrbuch* 1978/VII (1980): 72-103.

——. *The Music of Paul Hindemith*. New Haven, CT etc.: Yale University Press, 1986.

Norberg-Schulz, Christian. "En ny begynnelse." In: W. Findal, ed., *Nordisk funksjonalisme: Det internasjonale og det nasjonale*. Oslo: Gyldendal, 1995, 144-157.

Paddison, Max: *Adorno's Aesthetics of Music*. Cambridge, UK: Cambridge University Press, 1993.

Pisk, Paul A. "Der Verein für musikalische Privataufführungen." In: *Arnold Schönberg zum fünfzigsten Geburtstage 13. September 1924* [*Sonderheft der Musikblätter des Anbruch* (1924)], 325-326.

Pläfflin, Friedrich. "Karl Kraus und Arnold Schönberg: Fragmente einer Beziehung." In: H.L. Arnold, ed., *Karl Kraus* [*Sonderband aus der Reihe text+kritik*]. Munich: Edition text + kritik, 1975, 127-144.

Presler, Gerd. *Glanz und Elend der 20er Jahre: Die Malerei der Neuen Sachlichkeit.* Cologne: DuMont, 1992.

Reich, Willi. *Arnold Schönberg, oder Der konservative Revolutionär*. Vienna etc.: Fritz Molden, 1968.

Rein, Walter. "Musikalische Laienbildung," In: H. Fischer, ed. *Handbuch der Musikerziehung*. Berlin: Rembrandt-Verlag, Konrad Lemmer, 1954, 125-136.

Reinfandt, Karl-Heinz. "Musik als Schöpfung im Menschen." In: *Musik und Bildung* 19/11 (1987): 853-855.

Riegl, Alois. *Problems of Style: Foundations for a history of ornament*. E. Kain, trans. Princeton, NJ.: Princeton University, 1992.

Risselda, Max, ed. *Raumplan versus Plan Libre: Adolf Loos and Le Corbusier, 1919-1930*. New York: Rizzoli, 1988.

Rosen, Charles. *The Classical Style: Haydn, Beethoven, Mozart*. London etc.: Faber and Faber, 1976.

Rukschcio, Burkhardt and Schachel, Roland. *Adolf Loos. Leben und Werk*. Salzburg etc.: Residenz , 1982.

Rössiger, Max. *Der Angestellte um 1930* [Berlin 1930]. In: *Normierung* I [*Tanz auf dem Vulkan*]. Mannheim: Landesmuseum für Technik und Arbeit, 1994, 11.

Salmen, Walter. "'Alte Töne' und Volksmusik in Kompositionen Paul Hindemiths." In: *Musik und Bildung* VI (1974): 362-369.

Schenker, Heinrich. "Das Hören in der Musik." In: H. Federhofer, ed., *Heinrich Schenker als Essayist und Kritiker: gesammelte Aufsätze, Rezensionen und kleinere Berichte aus den Jahren 1891-1901*. Hildesheim etc.: Olms, 1990, 96-103.

Schepers, Wolfgang. "Abstraktion–Funktion–Produktion. Aspekte des Produktdesign 1918-1933." In: R. W. Gassen and B. Holeczek, eds., *Die Neue Wirklichkeit. Abstraktion als Weltentwurf.* Ludwigshafen: Wilhelm-Hack-Museum, 1994, 323-328.

Scherchen, Hermann. "Arnold Schönberg." In: *Melos* 1 (1920): 9-10.

Schibli, Sigfried. "Zum Begriff der Neuen Sachlichkeit in der Musik." In: *Hindemith-Jahrbuch* 1980/IX (1982): 157-178.

Schick, Paul. *Karl Kraus. Mit Selbstzeugnissen und Bilddokumenten.* Reinbek bei Hamburg: Rowohlt, 1989.

Schmalenbach, Fritz. "Jugendstil und Neue Sachlichkeit." In: *Das Werk [Schweizer Monatsschrift für Architektur, freie Kunst, angewandte Kunst]* 24/5 (1937): 129-133.

———. "The term *Neue Sachlichkeit*." In: *The Art Bulletin* 22/3 (1940): 161-165.

Schmidt, Lothar. *Organische Form in der Musik. Stationen eines Begriffs 1795-1850.* Kassel: Bärenreiter, 1990.

Schmied, Wieland. *Neue Sachlichkeit und Magischer Realismus in Deutschland 1918-1933.* Hannover: Fackelträger, 1969.

Schoenberg, Arnold. *Bläserquintett*, op. 26. Vienna/London: Universal Edition 7668/Philharmonia 230.

———. *Briefe.* Erwin Stein, ed. Mainz: Schott, 1958.

———. *Coherence, Counterpoint, Instrumentation, Instruction in Form / ZKIF. Zusammenhang, Kontrapunkt, Instrumentation, Formenlehre.* C. M. Cross and S. Neff, eds./trans. Lincoln, NE etc.: University of Nebraska Press, 1994.

———. *Drei Satiren für gemischten Chor*, op. 28, Vienna: Universal Edition, 1926.

———. *Fundamentals of Musical Composition.* G. Strang and L. Stein, eds. London: Faber and Faber 1967.

———. *Harmonielehre.* Vienna: Universal Edition, 1922/1949.

———. Introduction to *Arnold Schönberg zum fünfzigsten Geburtstage 13. September 1924, Sonderheft der Musikblätter des Anbruch.* Vienna: Universal Edition, 1924, 269-270.

———. *Modelle für Anfänger im Kompositionsunterricht: Lehrgang und Glossar.* R. Stephan, ed./ trans. Vienna: Universal Edition, 1972.

———. *Sechs kleine Klavierstücke*, op. 19. In: *Werke für Klavier zu zwei Händen* [*Werke* A/4,2]. Mainz/Vienna: Schott/Universal Edition, 1968.

Schönberg, Arnold. *Stil und Gedanke. Aufsätze zur Musik* [*Gesammelte Schriften 1*]. I. Vojtech, ed. Frankfurt a. M: Fisher, 1976.

———. *Structural Functions of Harmony*, L. Stein, ed. New York etc.: Norton, 1969.

Schönberg, Arnold. *Style and Idea: Selected writings of Arnold Schoenberg*, L. Stein, ed., L. Black, trans. Berkeley, CA etc.: University of California Press, 1975.

——. *Suite für Klavier* op. 25 In: *Werke für Klavier zu zwei Händen* II/A/4 [*Sämtliche Werke*]. Mainz/Vienna: Schott/Universal Edition, 1968

——. *The Musical Idea and the Logic, Technique, and Art of Its Presentation*, P. Carpenter and S. Neff, eds./trans. New York: Columbia University Press, 1995.

——. *Theory of Harmony*. R.E. Carter, trans. Berkeley, CA etc.: University of California Press, 1978.

Scholes, Percy A. "Form." In: *The Concise Oxford Dictionary of Music*. Oxford etc.: Oxford University Press, 1964, 207-209.

Schopenhauer, Arthur. *Die Welt als Wille und Vorstellung: Ergänzungen* [*Sämtliche Werke II*] W. v. Löhneysen, ed. Stuttgart: Cotta-Insel, 1960.

——. *The World as Will and Representation* II. E.F.J. Payne, trans. New York: Dover, 1966.

Schorske, Carl. E. *Fin-de-siècle Vienna: Politics and Culture*. New York: Vintage Books/Random House, 1981.

Schubert, Giselher: *Paul Hindemith: mit Selbstzeugnissen und Bilddokumenten*. Reinbek bei Hamburg: Rowohlt, 1981.

Selle, Gert. *Design-Geschichte in Deutschland: Produktkultur als Entwurf und Erfahrung*. Cologne: DuMont, 1990.

Semper, Gottfried. *Wissenschaft, Industrie und Kunst, und andere Schriften über Architektur, Kunsthandwerk und Kunstunterricht* [*Neue Bauhausbücher*], H.M. Wingler, ed. Mainz etc.: Florian Kupferberg, 1966.

Simms, Bryan R. "Commentary to Arnold Schoenberg, *Theory of Harmony*." In: *Music Theory Spectrum* 4 (1982): 155-162.

Skelton, Geoffrey. *Paul Hindemith: The man behind the music: a biography*. London: Gollancz, 1975.

Stang, Kaare. *Moderne tider: 1900-tallets stilarter i norsk arkitektur, kunstindustri og design*. Oslo: Cappelen, 1996.

Stefan, Paul. "Zusammenhänge." In: *Arnold Schönberg zum 60. Geburtstag 13. September 1934*. Vienna: Universal Edition, 1934, 38-40.

Stein, Erwin. "Neue Formprinzipien." In: *Arnold Schönberg zum fünfzigsten Geburtstage 13. September 1924. Sonderheft der Musikblätter des Anbruch* (1924), 286-303.

——. "Schönbergs Klang." In: *Arnold Schönberg zum 60. Geburtstag 13. September 1934*. Vienna: Universal Edition, 1934, 25-28.

Stein, Leonard. "The Privataufführungen Revisited." In: R. Stephan, ed., *Die Wiener Schule*. Darmstadt: Wissenchaftliche Buchgesellschaft, 1989, 98-105.

Stephan, Rudolf. "Adorno und Hindemith. Zum Verständnis einer schwierigen Beziehung." In: *Hindemith-Jahrbuch* 1978/VII (1980): 24-53.

——. "Zur Entstehung der Zwölftonmusik." In: G. Schnitzler, ed., *Musik und Zahl: Interdisziplinäre Beiträge zum Grenzbereich zwischen Musik und Mathematik*. Bonn-Bad Godesberg: Verlag für systematische Musikwissenschaft, 1976, 159-170.

Steuermann, Eduard. "Zukunftsmusik." In: *Arnold Schönberg zum 60. Geburtstag 13. September 1934*. Vienna: Universal Edition 1934, 28-30.

Stravinsky, Igor. *An Autobiography*. Unattributed trans. London: Calder & Boyars, 1975 [1936].

——. *Mit livs historie* [*Chroniques de ma vie*], C.J. Elmquist, trans. Copenhagen: Gyldendal, 1969.

Stuckenschmidt, Hans Heinz. "Paul Hindemiths Aufbruch und Heimkehr." In: *Hindemith-Jahrbuch* 1974/75/IV: 12-30.

——. *Musik am Bauhaus*. Berlin: Bauhaus Archiv, 1978/1979.

——. *Schoenberg: His Life, World and Work*. H. Searle, trans. London: John Calder, 1977.

Sullivan, Louis Henry. *A System of Architectural Ornament, According with a Philosophy of Man's Powers*. New York: The Eakins Press, 1967.

——. *Kindergarten Chats* (Revised 1918) *and other writings*. New York: George Wittenborn, 1968.

Tiessen, Heinz. *Zur Geschichte der jüngsten Musik (1913-1928): Probleme und Entwicklungen*. Mainz: Melosverlag/Schott, 1928.

Toch, Ernst. *The Shaping Forces in Music: An Inquery into the Nature of Harmony, Melody, Counterpoint, Form*. New York: Dover, 1977.

Tönnies, Ferdinand. *Gemeinschaft und Gesellschaft*. Darmstadt: Wissenschaftliche Buchgesellschaft, 1979.

Vitruvius. *Om arkitektur: Tio böcker* [*De Architectura Libri X*]. B. Dalgren, trans. Stockholm: Byggförlaget, 1989.

Weill, Kurt. "Die Oper—wohin?" In: S. Hinton and J. Schebera, eds., *Musik und Theater* [*Gesammelte Schriften*]. Berlin: Henschel, 1990, 68-71.

Wellmer, Albrecht. *Zur Dialektik von Moderne und Postmoderne: Vernunftkritik nach Adorno*. Frankfurt a. M.: Suhrkamp, 1993.

Westphal, Kurt. "Arnold Schönbergs Weg zur Zwölftöne-Musik." In: *Die Musik* XXI (1929): 491-499.

Willet, John. *The New Sobriety, 1917-1933: Art and Politics in the Weimar Period*. London: Thames and Hudson, 1978.

Wittgenstein, Ludwig. *Tractatus Logico-Philosophicus*. London/New York: Routledge/The Humanity Press, 1988.

Wölfflin, Heinrich. *Kunstgeschichtliche Grundbegriffe*. Basel etc.: Schwabe & Co., 1970.

Zemlinsky, Alexander. "Jugenderinnerungen." In: *Arnold Schönberg zum 60. Geburtstag 13. September 1934*. Vienna: Universal Edition, 1934, 33-35.

Zweig, Stefan. *Die Welt von gestern: Erinnerungen eines Europäers*. Frankfurt a. M: Fischer, 1992.

List of Illustrations

Music Examples

1	Richard Wagner, *Tristan und Isolde*, opening of Prelude to Act 1 (piano reduction)	76
2	Richard Strauss, *Don Juan*, op. 20, mm. 29–31 (piano reduction)	78
3	Schoenberg, No. 1 from *Sechs kleine Klavierstücke*	120
4	Schoenberg, op. 19/1, the motive in the left-hand upbeat	124
5	Schoenberg, op. 19/1, mm. 0-2	124
5a-h	mm. 0-2 (analysis)	125-126
6	Schoenberg, op. 19/1, mm. 3-5	127
6a-q	mm. 3-5 (analysis)	127-130
7	Schoenberg, op. 19/1, mm. 6-8	130
7a-h	mm. 6-8 (analysis)	130-131
8	Schoenberg, op. 19/1, mm. 9-12	132
8a-b	mm. 9-12 (analysis)	132
9	Schoenberg, op. 19/1, mm. 13-17	132
9a-h	mm. 13-17 (analysis)	133-134
10	The partial-tone row with C as the initial pitch	156
11	Hindemith's *Series I*, based on C	159
12	Hindemith's *Series 2* with C4 as the starting point	162
13	Hindemith's chord series demonstrating fluctuation and value	167
14	Hindemith, *Ludus Tonalis*, Interludium 9	178
15a-b	Interludium 9, tonal analysis	180-181
16	Interludium 9, tonal disposition	186
17	*Series 1* on D♭, tonal application in Interludium 9 [1-5]	186
18	Interludium 9, mm. 1-10, melodic analysis	187
19	Schoenberg, *Suite for Piano,* op. 25, twelve-tone material	242
20	Schoenberg, *Suite for Piano*, Gavotte, op.25/2, mm. 1-7, use of the twelve-tone row	244
21	Schoenberg, *Suite for Piano*, the motive in the "Gavotte"	245
22a-c	Schoenberg, *Suite for Piano*, Gavotte, overview 1	246-248
23a-c	Schoenberg, *Suite for Piano*, Gavotte, overview 2	254-256
24a-e	Hindemith, *1922. Suite for Piano*, Shimmy, overview	296-300
25	*1922. Suite for Piano*, Shimmy, mm. 0-2	302
26	Johnny Black, "Cairo Town," mm. 1-8	303

Figures

1	Koloman Moser, cover page of the periodical *Ver Sacrum* (vol. II/4, 1899)	15
2	Side table, ca. 1903-05, attributed to Josef Hoffmann	33
3	L.H. Sullivan, "Manipulation of the organic," *A System of Architectural Ornament,* from "plate 2"	39
4	L.H. Sullivan, "The Inorganic. Manipulation of forms in plane-geometry," *A System of Architectural Ornament,* "plate 3"	41
5	Peter Behrens, *AEG turbine factory*, Berlin, 1909	45
6	Peter Behrens, cover illustration, 1908	46
7	Kasimir Malewitsch, *Black Rectangle*, 1933	48
8	Kasimir Malewitsch, teacup, 1923	50
9	Marcel Breuer, *Wassily Chair,* 1925-26	55
10	Marcel Breuer, *Picket-back Chair*, 1923	56
11	Gerrit Thomas Rietveld, *Red-blue Chair,* 1918-1923	56
12	Hindemith's classification of chords according to their intervals	164
13	*Series 1* on the title page of Hindemith's *Ludus Tonalis*	175

Index

Aalto, Alvar: 55
Adler, Dankmar: 36
Adler, Guido: *xiii*
Adorno, Theodor Wiesengrund: *xvi, xvii*, 3, 5, 7,16, 69-72, 77, 79-93, 100-102, 104, 112, 137, 142, 197, 220, 237-240, 245, 283, 285, 322, 324, 326, 329, 330-331, 359
d'Albert, Eugen: 286
Amar, Licco: 318
Andra, Fern: 291
Antheil, George: 67
Apostel, Hans Erich: 98
Aristotle: 10, 12, 16, 26, 34, 88, 195, 202, 207, 229
Arndt, Alfred: 320
Augustine of Hippo: 151, 287, 378, 380-384
Babbitt, Irving: *xi*
Bach, Carl Philipp Emanuel: *xv*, 110*n*
Bach, Johann Sebastian: 150, 176-177, 179, 193, 252-253, 276, 284, 379
Bachrich, Ernst: 345
Barr Jr., Alfred Hamilton: 59, 61
Bartók, Bela: 68, 144, 177, 289, 347
Baumgarten, Alexander Gottlieb: 5
Beckmann, Max: 63
Beethoven, Ludwig van: 78, 194, 261, 268
Behrens, Peter: 1, 24, 45-46, 60-61
Beiche, Michael: 230, 241, 248
Bekker, Paul: 201
Berg, Alban: 82, 90, 106, 118, 334-335, 345, 347
Berry, Wallace: 70, 104
Besseler, Heinrich: 322-327, 338-339, 343-344, 350-351, 355-356, 360
Blake, Peter: 4

Boethius, Anicius Manilus Severinius: 159, 190, 287, 378, 380-383
Böhme, Franz Magnus: 277
Botstein, Leon: 17, 113
Boulez, Pierre: 70, 143, 220, 236
Brahms, Johannes: 107-108, 202, 219
Brecht, Bertolt: 63, 333, 349, 361
Breuer, Hermann: 363
Breuer, Marcel: 55-56
Briner, Andres: 362
Buhlig, Richard: 235
Bull, John: 176
Burger, Fritz: 320
Burkhard, Heinrich: 143, 143*n*
Busoni, Ferruccio: 103, 347
Cahn, Peter: 261
Carpenter, Paricia: 100-111
Chirico, Giorgio de: 64
Chopin, Frederic: 76, 176, 284
Claudel, Paul: 361
Cook, Susan C.: 285-286, 288
Coolidge, Elisabeth Sprague: 369
Craig, C.M.: 291-294
Dahlhaus, Carl: *xiii*, 28, 66, 71-72, 87, 197, 309-310, 344
Dahms, Walter: 235
Danuser, Hermann: 107, 285, 317, 328
Darwin, Charles: 42
Debussy, Claude: 345, 347, 376
Delaere, Mark: 70
Dermée, Paul: 50
Dix, Otto: 63, 65
Doesburg, Theo van: 48-49
Doflein, Erich: 328
Dorfman, Joseph: 283
Droste, Magdalena: 67
Dunnett, James: 21, 50

413

Eiffel, Gustave 10
Eimert, Herbert: 104, 136
Eisler, Hanns: 63, 71, 219, 317, 326-327, 334, 358, 370
Erdmann, Eduard: 143*n*
Ernst, Max: 64
Feininger, Lyonel: 65-66
Fellerer, Karl Gustav: 319
Findal, Wenche: 2
Ford, Henry: 46-47
Fortner, Wolfgang: 94
Frampton, Kenneth: 36, 60-61
Franz Joseph, Emperor: 17
Freitag, Eberhard: 97
Freud, Sigmund: 17
Friedberg, Carl: 300
Fueter, Gustav: 262
Fuglesang, Signe Horn: 5
Fux, Johann Joseph: 194
Gay, John: 288*n*
Gesualdo, Carlo, 145
Gluck, Christoph Willibald: *xv*
Goebels, Franzpeter: 176-177, 179
Goethe, Johann Wolfgang von: *xi-xii, xv*
Golishev, Efim, see: Golyscheff, Jefim
Golyscheff, Jefim 104, 136
Greenough, Horatio: 3
Greissle, Felix: 236-237, 239
Grieg, Edvard: 252, 289
Gofferje, Karl: 54
Gropius, Walter: 1, 6, 8, 13, 23, 30, 45-46, 65-66
Grosz, Georg: 63, 65
Grote, Ludvig: 8, 55
Grunow, Gertrud: 66
Gurlitt, Willibald: 355
Haas, Joseph: 143*n*
Haas, Robert: *xiii*
Haase, Rudolf: 262
Hailey, Christopher: *xv-xvi*
Hammel, Heide: 321
Hansen, Mathias: 336
Hanslick, Eduard: 32, 73-75, 85-86, 101, 111, 195-197
Hartlaub, Gustav Friedrich: 61-64, 311, 314, 317

Hauer, Josef Matthias: 101, 104, 136-137, 144, 347
Haydn, Franz Joseph: *xv*
Hegel, Georg Wilhelm Friedrich: 16, 25, 83-86, 88, 194-195, 313, 330
Heidegger, Martin: 54, 325-326
Hertzka, Emil: 27, 143
Herzl, Theodor: 17
Hinton, Stephen: 322, 325-326
Hoffmann, E.T.A (Ernst Theodor Wilhelm Amadeus): 206
Hoffmann, Josef: 33
Honegger, Arthur: 143, 351
Horkheimer, Max: 91
Hubbuch, Karl: 63
Itten, Johannes: 66
Janik, Allan: 18-19
Jeanneret-Gris, Charles-Édouard: 51 (also see Le Corbusier)
Jöde, Fritz: 321, 355, 363, 376-377
Johnson, Philip: 1
Jones, Owen: 36
Kandinsky, Wassily: 66, 97, 209, 221
Kanoldt, Alexander: 63
Kayser, Hans: 159, 262
Kemp, Ian: 281
Kepler, Johannes: 190-191
Kestenberg, Leo: 318, 321
Kielmannsegg, Graf von: 376
Klee, Paul: 66
Klimt, Gustav: 17
Koch, Heinrich Christoph: 194-195
Kokoschka, Oskar: *xiv*
Kralik, Heinrich von: 338-341
Kraus, Karl: 17-20, 42, 71, 97, 109, 113, 149-150
Krenek, Ernst: 82, 144, 286, 317
Kürnberger, Ferdinand: 20
Kurth, Ernst: 260, 269
Lang, Fritz: 52
Laretai, Käbi: 176-177
Le Corbusier: 3, 7, 9-11, 20-22, 26, 31, 33, 45, 50-53, 55, 81, 193, 199, 217, 221, 227, 251, 264, 279, 395
Leonard, R.K.: 292
Lessing, Gotthold Ephraim: *xi, xvi*

Lester, Joel: 75
Lichtwark, Alfred: 60
Lissitzky, El: 10
Liszt, Franz: 76, 176
Loos, Adolf: 1, 5-7, 9, 16-18, 20-21, 33, 42-43, 45, 50-52, 55, 60, 65, 71, 97-98, 108-109, 113, 148-150, 175, 217, 227, 319, 324, 342-343, 395
Lübbecke-Job, Emma: 300
Lukács, Georg: 86
Machaut, Guillaume de: 70
Mahler, Gustav: 78-79, 118, 202, 345, 347
Malewitsch, Kasimir: 47-48, 50, 65, 209
Massow, Albrecht von: 68
Mattheson, Johann: 253
Mersmann, Hans: *xvii,* 200-201, 319, 355
Merten, Reinhold: 350
Meyer, Adolf: 66
Meyer, Hannes: 7
Michaelis, Christian Friedrich: 194-195
Michelangelo Buonarroti: 206
Mies van der Rohe, Ludwig: 11, 22, 45, 55
Milhaud, Darius: 143
Mitchell, William John: 4
Moholy-Nagy, László: 10, 65
Mondrian, Piet: 48, 65
Moos, Stanislaus von: 51
Moritz, Karl Philip: 3, 24, 195
Morley, Thomas: 194
Morris, William: 13
Moser, Hans Joachim: 142, 147
Moser, Koloman: 15
Mozart, Wolfgang Amadeus: *xv*, 108, 219
Müller-Blattau, Josef: 374
Müller, Richard: 62
Muthesius, Hermann: 24, 44, 46, 51, 60-61
Neff, Severine: 111
Nestroy, Johann Nepomuk Eduard Ambrosius: 18
Nettl, Paul: 322

Neumeyer, David: 143, 145, 163, 175-176, 281, 283-284
Nietzsche, Friedrich: 25
Ozenfant, Amédée: 50
Paddison, Max: 86
Paxton, Joseph: 13
Pepush, Christoph: 286*n*
Pythagoras of Samos: *xiii*, 153, 194
Pisk, Paul Amadeus: 341, 343-344, 347
Plato: 9, 20, 26, 53, 194, 216-217, 251, 395
Poulenc, Francis: 350
Presler, Gerd: 60
Preussner, Eberhard: 331
Prez, Josquin des: 70
Prokofiev, Sergei: 143, 252, 289, 350
Rachmaninov, Sergei: 305
Rameau, Jean-Philippe: 69
Ratz, Erwin: 66
Ravel, Maurice: 347
Reger, Max: *xv,* 347
Reich, Willi: 118, 336, 338, 341-342
Rein, Walter: 54
Rexroth, Dieter: 93
Riegl, Alois: 16
Riemann, Hugo: 69, 322
Rietveld, Gerrit Thomas: 48, 56
Ronnefeldt, Emmy: 282, 319, 352
Rosen, Charles. 194
Rössiger, Max: 47
Rufer, Josef: 97, 234, 241, 249
Rukschcio, Burkhardt: 42, 98, 113
Ruskin, John: 13, 23, 30
Russel-Hitchcock, Henry: 1
Sacher, Paul: 190
Sachs, Benno: 347
Schachel, Roland: 42, 98, 113
Schaeffer, Pierre: 73
Schelling, Friedrich Wilhelm Joseph von: *xiii*
Schenker, Heinrich: 169-170, 260, 273, 337-339, 341
Schepers, Wolfgang: 55-56
Scherchen, Hermann: 94-96, 144
Schiffer, Marcellus: 58

Schiller, Johann Christoph Friedrich von: *xv*
Schlegel, August Wilhelm: 24, 40, 195
Schlegel, Friedrich: *xi, xii*, 195
Schlemmer, Oskar: 66-67
Schmidt, Kurt: 67
Schmied, Wieland: 64
Schnitzler, Arthur: 17
Scholes, Percy Alfred: 197
Schopenhauer, Arthur: *xii*, 195
Schorske, Carl Emil: 17
Schreker, Franz: *xv*
Schrimpf, Georg: 63
Schubert, Giselher.: 143, 145, 163, 374
Schumann, Robert: 76, 219
Schünemann, Georg: 283
Schütte-Lihotzky, Margarete: 47
Schmalenbach, Fritz: 58, 60, 62
Scriabin, Alexander: 345, 347
Sekles, Bernhard: 90, 285
Selle, Gert: 14-15, 57
Semper, Gottfried: 12-13, 42
Siemsen, Hans: 293
Simms, Bryan R.: 97
Simonides of Ceos: *xi*
Slonimsky, Nicolas: 135, 234
Spoliansky, Mischa: 58
Stang, Kaare: 2
Stefan, Paul: 77
Stein, Erwin: 79, 121, 157, 236, 334-335, 347
Stephan, Rudi: *xv*
Stephan, Rudolf: 90, 93
Steuermann, Eduard: 118, 200, 345, 347
Strauss, Johann Jr.: 294
Strauss, Richard: 78-79, 114, 202, 335, 347
Stravinsky, Igor: *xii, xvi, xvii*, 68, 71, 83, 87-90, 92, 147, 177, 199, 289, 310, 317, 347, 350, 362
Strecker, Hugo: 289
Strindberg, August: 17*n*
Strobel, Heinrich: *xvii*, 310, 311, 331, 336
Stuckenschmidt, Hans Heinz: 67, 118, 141-142
Suk, Josef: 347
Sullivan, Louis Henry (Henri): 3-4, 6-7, 15, 24-26, 29-30, 33-42, 52-53, 81, 100, 197, 202, 205, 207-208, 213, 270
Sutter, Ernst Otto: 355*n*
Szymanowski, Karol: 347
Taylor, Frederick Winslow: 46-47
Tiessen, Heinz: *xiv*, 26, 69, 94, 312-316, 322, 329
Toch, Ernst: *xii*
Tönnies, Ferdinand: 319-320, 387
Toulmin, Stephan: 19
Twa, Anders: 100
Varèse Edgard: 73
Velde, Henry van de: 46, 51
Vitruvius, Marcus Pollio: *xi*
Wagner, Otto: 38
Wagner, Richard: 76-77, 79, 89, 108, 240
Webern, Anton von: 73, 106, 118, 143-144, 334-335, 347, 351
Weill, Kurt: 63, 71, 143, 199, 286, 317, 326-327, 332, 369
Wellmer, Albrecht: 3, 5, 7-8
Westphal, Kurt: 96, 201
Willet, John: 58-60
Wittgenstein, Ludwig: 18-20, 108, 112-114, 218, 392
Wölfflin, Heinrich: 60-61
Zemlinsky, Alexander: 77, 347-348
Zoroaster: 94
Zuckmayer, Eduard: 368
Zweig, Stefan: 17, 342

About the Author

Magnar Breivik is a professor of musicology at the Norwegian University of Science and Technology (NTNU), Trondheim. His particular field of interest is 20th-century music and aesthetics, with an emphasis on the interrelationship between music and the other arts. In addition to various studies on Schoenberg and Hindemith, he has published articles on such composers as Gustav Mahler, Alban Berg, Ernst Krenek, and Kurt Weill.